PEOPLE'S CHOICE LITERATURE

PEOPLE'S CHOICE LITERATURE

PEOPLE'S CHOICE LITERATURE

*The Most Wanted
& Unwanted Novels*

Tom Comitta

Columbia University Press

New York

Columbia University Press
Publishers Since 1893
New York   Chichester, West Sussex
cup.columbia.edu

Copyright © 2025 Tom Comitta
All rights reserved

Library of Congress Cataloging-in-Publication Data
Names: Comitta, Tom, 1985– author. | Comitta, Tom, 1985– Most wanted novel.
 | Comitta, Tom, 1985– Most unwanted novel.
Title: People's choice literature / Tom Comitta.
Other titles: Playground (Online platform)
Description: New York : Columbia University Press, 2025.
Identifiers: LCCN 2024059901 (print) | LCCN 2024059902 (ebook) |
ISBN 9780231219273 (hardback) | ISBN 9780231219280 (trade paperback) |
ISBN 9780231562614 (ebook)
Subjects: LCGFT: Novels.
Classification: LCC PS3603.O4776 P46 2025 (print) | LCC PS3603.O4776
(ebook) | DDC 813/.6—dc23/eng/20250106
LC record available at https://lccn.loc.gov/2024059901
LC ebook record available at https://lccn.loc.gov/2024059902

Printed in the United States of America

Cover and book design: Tom Comitta

GPSR Authorized Representative:
Easy Access System Europe, Mustamäe tee 50, 10621
Tallinn, Estonia, gpsr.requests@easproject.com

CONTENTS

Introduction   1

The Most Wanted Novel   25

The Most Unwanted Novel   217

PEOPLE'S CHOICE LITERATURE

PEOPLE'S CHOICE LITERATURE

INTRODUCTION

The story begins in the 1990s, not long after the fall of the Soviet Union and the emergence of twelve new democracies. In this climate, the Soviet-born, U.S.-based artists Komar and Melamid cooked up a plan to submit art to one of democracy's most sacred tools: the public opinion poll.

Collaborating with *The Nation* magazine and a leading polling firm, they surveyed the aesthetic tastes of the United States, posing the question: What does the average person want in a painting? Their poll measured everything from favorite color to painting size to preferences for realism or abstraction. With the data in hand, they created two paintings: one with everything people statistically desired, *America's Most Wanted*, and another with everything they did not, *America's Most Unwanted*.

The former work is dishwasher-sized and features a blue sky above an autumnal landscape populated by George Washington, school children, and some deer. Composed in the style of Thomas Kinkaid, it is the perfect counterpart to *America's Most Unwanted*, a paperback-sized canvas containing thickly painted triangles of beige, yellow, and orange. This "lesser" painting looks like a child's attempt at a Kandinsky—"my kid could do that" raised to the highest degree.

Three years later, the composer and neuroscientist Dave Soldier conducted a similar experiment with musical taste. Surveying five hundred respondents, he measured what people most like and dislike in music and used the data to compose two songs. "The Most Wanted Music" is a five-minute blend of R&B, rock, and smooth jazz featuring synthesizers, guitar solos, and a climactic key change. "The Most Unwanted Music" clocks in at twenty minutes and features accordions, organs, harps, banjos, piccolos, bagpipes, an opera singer rapping to cowboy music, children belting Walmart jingles for various holidays (e.g., Christmas, Halloween, Mattress Day), and a long political rant. And it all ends with a big Pete Seeger–style sing-along.

2 *People's Choice Literature*

The painting and music projects became something of a sensation, so much so that, in 1995, the *Artforum* columnist Andrew Ross wrote, "With the exception of the NEA witch hunt of the late '80s and early '90s, no art event in years has garnered the kind of attention the U.S. media devoted to Komar & Melamid's ongoing project 'The People's Choice.'" While *People's Choice Music* focused on American taste, Komar and Melamid went on to conduct the same art polling experiment in fourteen other countries, finding similar results to the U.S. survey on nearly every continent: regardless of culture, people rejected abstraction in favor of landscape painting. Such repetitive results raised a question: Why did everyone want the same bland picture?

While all four works are rooted in skepticism and humor, they ask serious questions: What is good art and music? Who defines them? Is there something innate in the appeal of a five-minute blend of R&B, rock, and smooth jazz, or were those just the genres playing on the radio at the time of polling? The paintings and songs also poke fun at polling itself—this quixotic attempt to distill the desires of millions of people (in the case of the United States today, 340 million) into tidy figures. Some sociologists even argue that "public opinion" doesn't exist, that the majorities we identify in our polling are only real once you measure them and turn them into actionable information.[1]

Thirty years after the first art poll and at a new—and very different—inflection point in the history of democracy, this book asks similar questions. Like Rip Van Winkle waking from his epochal slumber, *People's Choice Literature* resurfaces an old method while bringing new techniques and questions to the fore: What might a poll reveal about contemporary American literary taste and culture? Might it give us more insight into the so-called "American imagination?" What might such a poll and its resulting narratives reveal about what people are collectively drawn to or avoidant of, whether they're conscious of it or not?

While public opinion research has been around for over a hundred years, in the three decades since the first *People's Choice* projects, data has transformed from a useful tool for marketers and politicians into one of the most lucrative commodities on the planet. Each day our taste is mined by nearly every website and app we engage with; this data is then processed and spit back out at us in the form of personalized ads, news feeds, suggested videos, and so on. Our data allows these websites and apps to sculpt a bubble of taste for each of us, one that is almost impossible to escape in an online climate designed not to challenge our desires

but to hone them even further—to keep us coming back again and again to the things we like, as if we needed further incentive.

In the world of literature, this process is less visible and less frequently discussed. As we learned from studies like Dan Sinykin's *Big Fiction* and Mark McGurl's work on MFA programs and the Amazonification of print culture, literature has had its own honing of taste. In the publishing world, the past century has seen hundreds of small presses, through a long process of buyouts and mergers, fuse together into the five big publishing houses that now dominate 80 percent of all books published in the United States each year. These conglomerates, often called the "Big Five," seem more concerned with the bottom line than with art or literature. Comp titles—a list of three to five books that agents and authors send to prospective publishers to show how similar books did in the marketplace—rule the day, weeding out anything that varies from what has already proven itself as sellable. Originality and experimentation are obstacles rather than assets and are largely ignored by a publishing industry that, with some exceptions, rushes to the middle over and over again. It's in this climate that *People's Choice Literature* was born, adopting the science of public opinion research to examine what people actually want in their fiction—while exploring alternate routes of readerly desire.

To those readers allergic to spoilers, I suggest exiting this introduction and returning once you've finished one or both novels. For those interested in learning more about how this all came together, I'll see you in the next room.

The National Literature Survey

Writing a poll is kind of like writing a sonnet; you follow standards that nearly every pollster employs while adding your own personal twists along the way. In the world of public opinion research, these standards include everything from adding warm-up questions to the beginning of a poll (these questions are often unrelated to the main purpose of the survey) to the question types used throughout (multiple choice, open answer, ranked voting, etc.) to how one orders these question types (variation is crucial) to the length of the survey (poll fatigue is a real thing). Like a poem, a poll should also anticipate as many readerly perspectives as possible. When trying to measure the literary tastes of the United

4 *People's Choice Literature*

States—with an accurate proportion of ages, genders, ethnicities, classes, etc.—you're engaging with folks of all reading levels and literary interests. Because of this, questions must be worded so that everyone from avid readers to people who haven't touched a novel since grade school can understand them. Terms like "epistolary novel" and "frame narrative" become "a sequence of letters or emails" and "stories within stories," respectively. Questions about things like verb tense are accompanied by examples:

Which tense do you prefer when reading a novel?

☐ Past Tense (Example: I <u>ran</u> up the stairs, <u>threw</u> open the door, and <u>saw</u> it for myself.)

☐ Present Tense (Example: I <u>run</u> up the stairs, <u>throw</u> open the door, and <u>see</u> it for myself.)

Katherine Cornwall, a Johns Hopkins–based social scientist and survey design expert, guided me through all of this, helping turn my original poll—a remix of Komar and Melamid's art and Dave Soldier's music polls, swapping painting size with book length, instruments with characterization, and so on—into one that not only met contemporary survey design standards but sought to cover as many aspects of novels as possible. These questions ranged from reading habits ("How many novels on average would you say you read in a year?") to writing mechanics ("Which perspective do you prefer when reading a novel? First person? Second Person? Third?") to character qualities ("What kind of morals do you want a main character to display? Good? Questionable?") to story types ("Which kind of storytelling technique do you prefer? A sequence of flashbacks? A straightforward story? A stream of consciousness?").

Katherine also helped me conduct the poll, directing me to the same companies that she and her colleagues work with at Johns Hopkins: Qualtrics, a browser-based platform for designing polls and collecting data, and Prolific, a company that both curates poll respondents and ensures that a full, representative sample of the population shows up to answer the questions. Once I raised enough money to pay each poll respondent a fair wage and after we'd tested the poll with dozens of friends and family, our survey went live on December 1, 2021. Over the course

of two days, 1,045 respondents from nearly every corner of the United States worked their way through the seventy-six questions.

After obtaining the data, Katherine tallied the results. Then I parsed them into two lists, or "recipes," for how to write two very different novels—one containing everything that received the most votes in each question and another with everything that received the fewest or no votes. Below, I've reproduced these lists along with the percentages that determined each data point's wantedness or unwantedness. You'll notice that I've included more data points in *The Most Unwanted* list; this is because this unwanted novel was longer and therefore needed to fill more pages but also because it was experimental, incorporating more genres and styles than *The Most Wanted*. Those interested in a full account of the poll results should jump to the end of this book.

The Most Wanted Novel

General

GENRE: Thriller or mystery (20%)

LENGTH: 200–300 pages (36%)

PERSPECTIVE: Third person (56%)

TENSE: Past Tense (67%)

STORYTELLING TECHNIQUE: Straightforward (54%), as opposed to things like stream of consciousness, nested stories, etc.

STYLE: Realistic (74%)

FORM: Traditional (62%)

MOOD/TONE: Mysterious (35%), tense (21%), philosophical (18%)

Characters

NUMBER OF MAIN CHARACTERS: 3–5 (60%)

AGE: Adult (60%)

CLASS: Working class (38%), middle class (32%)

GENDER OF THE PROTAGONIST: No preference (54%), cis female (25%)

SEXUALITY: No preference (51%), straight (40%)

RACE OR ETHNICITY: No preference (92%)

MORALS: Good (54%)

6 *People's Choice Literature*

Story

DURATION: No preference (47%)

HOW THE MAIN CHARACTERS SPEND THEIR TIME: Falling in or out of love (19%); participating in criminal activity (16%), particularly murder; being creative (14%), particularly in writing; and helping others (10%), particularly operating as a spiritual leader.

TOPICS: Science & technology (24%), particularly good vs. evil, new technology, advanced science, and the workings of the universe.

SETTING: Large cities (31%)

DIALOGUE: A moderate amount (60%)

DESCRIPTIONS: Long (54%)

SEXUAL CONTENT: A little (37%)

VIOLENCE: Some violence (38%)

ENDING: Resolved (57%)

The Most Unwanted Novel

General

GENRE: Romance (37%), Horror (20%), Classic Literature (12%) and Historical Fiction (12%)

LENGTH: More than 500 pages (8%)

PERSPECTIVE: Second person (2%)

TENSE: Present Tense (33%

STORYTELLING TECHNIQUE: Epistolary (3%), stream of consciousness (11%), stories within stories (24%).

STYLE: Unrealistic (26%), featuring different planets, talking animals, extraterrestrials, and sentient robots

FORM: Experimental (38%), with chapters that read like long encyclopedia entries, long, meandering sentences, and moments where the author comments on the art of writing

MOOD/TONE: Sad (2%), calm (5%), happy (8%), playful (9%)

<u>Characters</u>	<u>Story</u>

NUMBER OF MAIN CHARACTERS: 9–11 (3%)

DURATION: One day (0%)

AGE: Old age (0%) and childhood (0%)

HOW THE MAIN CHARACTERS SPEND THEIR TIME: Playing a sport (1%), specifically tennis; farming or living off the land (5%), specifically fishing.

CLASS: Aristocratic (3%)

GENDER OF THE PROTAGONIST: Transgender (0%), nonbinary (2%), cis man (17%)

TOPICS: Religion (0%), sports (2%), health and fitness (4%), the environment (5%), the arts (5%), and politics (8%).

SEXUALITY: Other (0%)

SETTING: Rural area (9%) and natural setting (18%), specifically a polar region

RACE OR ETHNICITY: Inconclusive. See below.

MORALS: Bad (46%)

DIALOGUE: A little (0%)

DESCRIPTIONS: Short (46%)

SEXUAL CONTENT: A lot (4%)

VIOLENCE: A lot (4%)

ENDING: Unresolved (41%)

Many of these results will be unsurprising if you pay any attention to bestseller lists (synonymous with most-wanted book lists, in my mind): "Thriller or mystery" was the most wanted genre.[2] Americans preferred traditional, realistic narratives over the experimental and unreal. They wanted medium-size books (200–300 pages) over very long or very short ones (under 200 and over 500 tied for last place).

These results line up almost exactly with research presented by Jodie Archer and Mathew Jockers in their book *The Bestseller Code*, an algorithmic study of what makes a book a bestseller. Creating a computer

8 *People's Choice Literature*

program to read and analyze 500 books from *New York Times* bestseller lists, Archer and Jockers sought to identify the specific components down to themes and diction—that make a book more likely to appear on this highly coveted list. Their program found several similar patterns to our poll: People want stories told in the third person, working-class characters, and stories set in large cities on Earth. Also in keeping with our data, they found that people are less inclined to read about imaginary creatures—especially sentient robots and talking animals. But most striking was how closely our data lined up with the novel that Archer and Jockers's algorithm declared as the ultimate bestselling novel, a novel that the data showed had the perfect balance of everything readers want: Dave Eggers's *The Circle*.[3]

Both *The Circle* and *The Most Wanted Novel* are thrillers about an adult white woman from a working-class background who struggles against an advanced form of technology. Both books are told in the third-person past tense, and both take place over the course of a few months. Both involve a character struggling against some aspect of society (in each case it's technology's encroachment on our lives). Both involve murder and interweave a love story into the techno-thriller drama.

Even with this validation, there are several survey results that might give you pause. For one, there's a glaring contradiction in responses to two answers. The most wanted activity for characters to experience in a novel was "falling in or out of love," but the most unwanted genre was romance. Given the popularity of romance novels, it's hard to square this until you consider their place in culture, with romance novels often seen as a form of women's literature, a category that historically has not been given as much weight and respect as literature written by cis men.

Several people have also expressed surprise at historical fiction's "unwantedness" in the poll results. Surely these books are also widely popular, with many dedicated and loyal readers. (Ditto horror and classic literature, the other two unpopular genres in the poll.) To understand this phenomenon, we might consider another finding of *The Bestseller Code*: that people by and large prefer reading about everyday people living everyday lives—until the stirring events of the novel begin, of course. Jockers and Archer essentially showed that more often than not readers are drawn to stories about themselves set in the times they are living.

Big Data

While brainstorming how to transpose Komar and Melamid's methods into literature, I realized that conducting a similar experiment in the 2020s would raise challenges and opportunities that didn't exist in the 1990s. The most obvious difference between now and then is the reputational hit that polling has taken in the past decade, with national polls producing questionable results in nearly every major election. Because of this, I wondered if even attempting to create poll-based literature would make sense today. But when I researched what went wrong in past elections, I found that among the multiple problems noted by the news media—a respondent's resistance to disclosing sensitive or controversial information being the most common—the biggest culprit was simply that the country was evenly divided on sensitive topics. With margins of error of 3 or 5 percent, it's hard to accurately measure a populace that's split 50/50 on presidential candidates. It's much easier to measure their opinions about less divisive topics like preference for soft drinks or TV programs or, in our case here, novels. Through conversations with dozens of pollsters, sociologists, and data scientists, I found that the century-old tradition of public opinion polling, while flawed, remained the best way to measure people's tastes.

Still, I was curious how contemporary politicians and marketers account for these errors. A brief web search gave the answer: big data. Campaigns and corporations hire tech companies to comb X and Facebook for users' minute-to-minute preferences on everything from senators to shoes. These services work well for big, broad topics because their algorithms study adjectives and other textual markers connected to a particular topic and can measure positive or negative sentiment. While this works well for tracking how people feel about the president or Walmart, these digital tools are not as effective when searching for the minutiae and nuances of taste. They are not refined enough, for the purposes of this project, to determine which verb tense people most prefer in their novels or which kinds of fantastical characters they most dislike. Fortunately, Archer and Jockers's research had the answers.

Their *Bestseller Code* not only validated the data from our poll; it also became the literary equivalent of big data, providing clear metrics of nearly everything our poll couldn't measure either because of our

10   *People's Choice Literature*

attempts at mitigating poll fatigue (i.e., asking as few questions as possible) or simply because we hadn't thought to ask about them at the time.

Some of Archer and Jockers's findings were obvious, such as the importance of a good first line and the fact that most people don't want to read a novel that offends or acts like a political soap box. Yet many of their findings are fascinating and often absurd. For instance, a bestselling book is more likely to contain a description of the stock market than that of a human face. A bestseller must include moments of "dating," often involving two characters sharing a beer in front of a television. Such moments are designed to give the reader a break from the action. Of course, these findings also imply that a book working against our base desires would deny readers such moments of pause and reflection.

Archer and Jockers's algorithm gave me a laundry list of topics and even word choices to include in both books. It showed me that *The Most Wanted Novel* needed work, death, dogs, a criminal investigation, and sex, but only if the sex suggests intimacy and moves the plot along. *The Most Unwanted Novel* needed fun and frivolity, drugs, cats, settings that don't exist, lords, seduction, and sex that does not move the plot but stops it dead in its lusty tracks. *The Bestseller Code*'s list of things to not include in a novel was so ridiculous (i.e., wonderful) that I couldn't help but attempt to include as many as possible: reptile collecting, T-shirt printing, worship, church, partying, dancing, fishing, made-up languages, plumbers in space, and big emotions like passionate love or desperate grief. Each appear in *The Most Unwanted Novel*.

From Data to Fiction

Almost all my books use "literary constraints," an approach to writing popularized by the French avant-garde group the Oulipo, whose members adopt nontraditional rules or guidelines to write original, and often surprising, works of literature. Some constraints can feel like games—such as writing flash fiction in the form of a palindrome—but others can reach virtuosic heights that might seem impossible. One particularly acrobatic feat is Georges Perec's *La disparation* (translated as *A Void* by Gilbert Adair), a novel written entirely without the letter "e," the most common letter in both French and English.

In the case of *People's Choice Literature*, I used each polling and machine learning data point as a constraint for each novel. After collecting the data and parsing it into two groups—the most wanted and the most unwanted qualities—I then studied these groups, looking for patterns and connections between data points that might suggest characterization, specific settings, and so on. To give an example, while considering the poll results for desired character activities, it didn't take long to see that the main characters of *The Most Wanted* needed to:

- Fall in or out of love
- Commit a crime (specifically murder)
- Be creative (as a writer)
- Help others (by being a spiritual leader)

This data, combined with other poll findings—like the fact that science and technology (specifically questions of good versus evil and new technology) was the most wanted topic and that people want to read about the working class—led to the following character profiles:

Alix Finn	• Falls in love • Working class background
John Finn	• Creative writer • Working class background
D.J. Wylde	• Tech leader • Spiritual leader • Commits a crime?
Richard Moriarty	• Tech leader • Commits a crime?
Jason Stone	• Falls in love • Working class background

Another author might have distributed these characteristics in different ways. From my perspective, it made sense for the protagonist, Alix Finn, to find herself in the middle of both a mysterious crime and the

12 People's Choice Literature

pangs of new love. And, given the tech world's notorious blending of leftist, spiritual aesthetics with big business, it seemed natural to combine technology and spiritualism into a single character, D. J. Wylde.

Because of inconclusive poll data, my input was also central in determining certain other elements of characters' identities. Considering the most-wanted data, of the five identity questions we asked, only two received definite answers: age (adult 60%) and class (again, working class 38%). For the rest—gender, sexuality, and race or ethnicity—the majority of poll respondents noted "No preference." In the survey-design world, inquiries such as these are termed "sensitive questions," or questions that you anticipate poll respondents might be hesitant to answer either because the subject matter is loaded or because they are worried about being judged by their response. Pollsters often approach these questions knowing that it will be nearly impossible to get an honest answer from most respondents. Because of this, I selected the second-most-wanted answer for each question: cis female (25%) and straight (40%).

The question about race and ethnicity was worded differently than the question about gender and sexuality because of its status as a potentially even more sensitive question for respondents. The poll asked first if they had a preference for reading about a particular race or ethnicity—yes (8%) or no (92%)—and then, if they did have a preference, which they most preferred (of the 8% who said yes, Black or African American was the most selected, at 50%, and "other," i.e., the fill-in-the-blank option wherein most respondents requested non-Americans and fantastical beings, was the least selected, at 4%). Because answers were inconclusive at both ends of the spectrum, in each book I made subjective decisions about which ethnicities would make sense in either the genre or the world the data pointed to.

These questions of character identity highlight another aspect of constraint-based writing: An author often doesn't know how constraints will work (or if they will work at all) until they start writing with them. In the case of *People's Choice Literature*, I realized only after conducting the poll that the 76 answers and the 100-or-so data points offered by *The Bestseller Code* would not provide enough guidance to fill the approximately 750-pages for the two novels that the data had called for. Of course, I could have gotten creative and filled in the blanks with my own ideas for plot points, character names, and so on, but given that this project sought to engage with the tastes of an entire nation, it seemed important to make these novels less about my creative impulses and more about, well, what people want and don't want.

Introduction   13

In both books, I accomplished this in two different ways. In *The Most Wanted Novel*, I relied on personal research into the thriller tradition. For *The Most Unwanted*, I leaned on answers to an open-ended question I hadn't thought much of while writing the poll: "If you had unlimited resources and could commission your favorite author to write a novel just for you, what would it be about?"

The majority of these answers fell on genre lines—like "sci-fi thriller" or "Horror Mystery Thriller"—and revealed no new information that I hadn't already learned from the poll's four genre questions (i.e., that mysteries and thrillers were the most popular genres). But a fraction of respondents gave more specific, idiosyncratic answers to this open question, such as "Jay-Z writes my biography" and "the ramifications of the American political system on global social structures." The more I read these answers, the more I realized they were just what would give this unwanted novel the depth and texture it needed, leading me to include as much of this open-ended-answer data as possible in the form of scenes, plot points, and backstory. Because each of these open-ended answers was unique, representing a single perspective (or 0.1% of survey respondents), they seemed a perfect fit for this novel of uncommon and less-desired characteristics. The only rule I gave myself was that the open answer either had to correspond directly to other data points from the poll or make sense in the universe the other poll results had described.

Here is an inexhaustive list of the open-ended answers I used, accompanied by page numbers so you can jump around *The Most Unwanted* if you so choose (although, if you really want to experience both books the way they were intended, I recommend reading them straight through):

"It would be an experiment poetry-prose hybrid work with an audiovisual component." 217

"It would be a simple romance novel, maybe holiday themed. Where two strangers, a man and woman, are having a tough time during the holiday season due to a tragedy that occurred around that time years ago . . ." 223

"It would likely be about Elves that are forced into hiding among humans. Having to conceal their identities and their magic all while of course being hunted by both elves and humans alike. About how free citizens managed to rescue their country from

a government takeover determined to transform the country to communism," 238

"humans settling on Mars" 239

"Sailing." 245

"Fishing" 248

"A deserted island theme story of survival spanning multiple lengthy chapters." 265

"Identification guide book for all local flora and fauna" 270

"Probably something involving cats, how they take over the world, and especially get rid of this useless government we have" 273

"Pirates" 275

"Sports Talk Radio" 282

"It would be about my life but in diary format." 287

"skateboarding dinosaurs from outer space, who come to Earth to teach humans how to skateboard, play with Tech Decks, and party (google the song Intergalactic Reptilian Shredders)" 290

"A love story about a royal and a commoner or a socialite and commoner" 300

"I would like it to be about the Middle Ages and how the tyranny of a king made him collapse a kingdom." 330

"the human mind and its workings" 333

"It would be a historical fiction work after the founding of America. It would be about a young politician aspiring to work his way from the state legislature to national prominence." 337

"It would probably be a historical fiction work, perhaps a mystery, set in Imperial Rome during the time of Marcus Aurelius." 344

"I'd love to have a period piece set sometime in the late 20th century (something set in the 90's preferably)" 350

"HISTORY OF FRANK SINATRA" 352

"The current effects of wealth disparity, like a modern grapes of wrath." 359

"The mafia" 365

"werewolves" 399

"Nephilim" 401

"a survival horror book about people trapped at a theme park" 406

"A queer horror novel where it's a group of pro tags in a found-family community making life work on a commune, but also folkloric creatures of some sort complicate matters. Not about killing the creatures or the family but finding a solution that results in less drastic bloodshed and more communal spirit. Happy ending queer horror!!!" 415

"It would be mishmash between historical figures interacting with people from the future" 433

"Some odd mishmash involving horror and philosophy" 441

"a horror book that had killer dolls that work with a cult." 444

"It would be about the secrets to success with hobbies" 460

"It would be a sci-fi space opera with diverse characters who are queer and trans that has . . . plain language mixed with some highly poetic styles." 487

People's Choice Literature

"The importance of the Psychedelic experience" 494

"Probably a love triangle romance with a tiny bit of smut." 300

"something to do with nietzsche" 511

Thriller Research

To write the more-desired novel, I gave myself a crash course in thriller writing. I read over twenty bestselling thrillers and took notes on any patterns I found along the way. I also watched on-demand MasterClass courses by the thriller and mystery authors David Baldacci, Dan Brown, Walter Mosley, and James Patterson. These courses, along with my readings, added additional parameters for *The Most Wanted Novel* that no poll could offer:

General

STRUCTURE: While every book I read revealed something unique about the narrative arc of thrillers, *The Most Wanted Novel* most heavily channels scenes and plot points from the following books: David Baldacci's *Total Control*, Dan Brown's *Origin*, Dave Eggers's *The Circle* (again, the best of the bestsellers according to Archer and Jockers), Janet Evanovich and Peter Evanovich's *The Big Kahuna: A Fox and O'Hare Novel*, Coleen Hoover's *Verity*, Dean Koontz's *The Whispering Room*, Robert Ludlum's *The Bourne Identity*, James Patterson's *Invisible*, and James Patterson and Richard DiLallo's *The Store*.

LANGUAGE: Some observations I found and replicated:

- Italics are used liberally to give dramatic emphasis or to highlight a character's thoughts.

- Automobiles are always referred to as their brand name and model. There are few "cars" or "vehicles" and many "Dodge Caravans."

- Multiple books feature characters who refuse to curse based on their background (one was a schoolteacher) or for no obvious reason.

- Thriller novels often reference other thriller novels, in subtly metafictional and self-congratulatory ways.

- Dystopian thrillers often reference books like *1984* and *Brave New World*.

- Multiple books reference Alfred Hitchcock as a metafictional joke.

- James Patterson regularly hates on James Joyce's *Ulysses*. (See his MasterClass and *The Store*.)

POLITICS: Whatever the personal politics of individual thriller authors, their books are largely a masculinist, right-wing art form. They are pro-gun, unflinchingly pro-police, and obsessed with cars and technology. Several of the works I read—published by some of the biggest publishing houses in the United States—were openly racist (Dean Koontz's *The Whispering Room*) and anti-left (Janet Evanovich's *The Big Kahuna*). While I chose not to replicate these characteristics, I did make a point to edit out parts that, in the first draft of this book, clearly exhibited my leftist bias. If you desire a more earnest political message from your humble author, I will refer you to Lord Brad's rant in *The Most Unwanted Novel*.

Characters

RACE AND ETHNICITY: Because our poll found over 90% of people have no preference for reading about characters of a particular race or ethnicity, I had to turn elsewhere to determine the racial and ethnic makeup of the protagonists. Studying thrillers on *New*

York Times bestseller lists in 2021 and 2022 as well as the thrillers I was reading (which had all been *NYT* bestsellers) at the time, I found that almost all blockbuster thrillers are written by white people about white people. Characters of color most often appear in supporting roles. This trend might be changing slightly, but at least at the time of writing it does not seem to be shifting quickly or consistently enough.

THE FBI: *The Bestseller Code* mentioned that most bestselling thrillers feature FBI agents, and my empirical research confirmed this. Nearly all American thrillers feature a love interest who is a current or former FBI agent. Enter Jason Stone, the hunky copilot of *The Most Wanted Novel*.

NAMES: In need of character names but having little interest in creating them on my own, I looked to the thrillers from my research and remixed their character names into new creations. Alix is the name of the protagonist in Danielle Steel's *Dangerous Games*. Moriarty is the last name of a character in James Patterson's *Invincible*, as well as the nemesis of Sherlock Holmes. And a surprising number of thrillers feature a "Jason" as the hero.

BAD DADS: The more thrillers you read, the more you realize that the bad guy is also often a bad dad, either neglecting his children or openly treating them poorly. This can also be used as a red herring.

<u>Story</u>

LOCATIONS: As mentioned earlier, the most-wanted setting according to our poll is a large city. While studying thrillers, I found that almost all follow protagonists racing between at least two cities over the course of the novel, so I knew my book must as well. When looking for which cities to set the story in, it seemed most logical for this most-wanted book about spirituality and advanced technology to be set in California, known for its tech companies and spiritual cults. Also, almost every MasterClass suggested "write what you know," and having lived in California for over twelve years, I was primed to follow suit.

DESCRIPTIONS: Almost every chapter in Dan Brown's novels begins with a long description of a historic or cultural site (be it the Bilbao Guggenheim, the Sagrada Familia, etc.) that reads like a Lonely Planet travel guide. The reader learns a few factoids about, say, the Vatican until being thrust back into the present of the drama: "But that night . . ." To me, Brown's structural tool makes his work repetitive and a real slog—nothing like the page-turning experience he's known for. But since Brown is the crown prince of techno-thrillers, and since the majority prefers long descriptions (54%), you'll find one-to-two-paragraph descriptions of tourist sites at the start of almost every chapter of this statistically better novel.

REPETITION: While she mostly writes romances, Danielle Steel has published a handful of thrillers, one of which was crucial in determining the style of *The Most Wanted Novel*. Steel's *Dangerous Games* resonated with our data in its plot and characters (like *The Circle*, this thriller is about a woman fighting an ominous techno-political threat), and I found Steel's signature use of repetition to be not just emblematic of but virtuosic in the world of thriller writing. *Dangerous Games* begins with an absurdly lengthy exposition of the protagonist's past that the author then repeats ad nauseam, adding new information about characters and plot developments as they arise. Sometimes this repetition appears almost verbatim from one page to the next and sometimes it shows up in dialogue wherein a scene is described play-by-play not long after its occurrence. This repetition is so consistent and excessive I started to think of Steel as Gertrude Stein with a *Lifetime* subscription. It seems either she writes so fast and so much she doesn't have time to edit or she assumes her readers are not paying attention. Whatever the case may be, I chose to mimic Steel's signature repetition every chance I had.

Large Language Model

Once I had gathered all the above data and outlined both books, I tried to start writing but ran into yet another issue: my subjectivity. I, a white, queer, far-left millennial from small-town Pennsylvania, who has spent their adult life in San Francisco, Los Angeles, and New York, was setting

20 *People's Choice Literature*

out to write two books purporting to be the product of—or at least wrestling with—the literary tastes of an entire nation.

Fortunately, in the months leading up to writing these books, two friends suggested I compose them with OpenAI's Playground, the most advanced large language model (LLM) at the time. This was a year before ChatGPT—a completely different and, in my opinion, subpar interface to the Playground—was released.

I quickly found this LLM would not only add another perspective to writing both books; it was in some ways the ultimate collaborator, having read more than any human ever could—from our greatest works of literature to our most banal tweets. To become as advanced as it is, researchers had the LLM read tons of novels and basically the entire internet: in total, a trillion words.[4] Through this process, it learned over a billion variables for creating natural language, establishing it as perhaps a better expert on our language climate than anyone—while also exhibiting some troubling flaws and biases.

Unlike ChatGPT's chatbot-style of querying or prompting, which positions the LLM as a subservient assistant, the Playground is a more collaborative interface. From time to time (not all the time—only about 20% of *The Most Unwanted* and 5% of *The Most Wanted* began this way), I'd prompt the Playground with a paragraph or three of my own writing, curious to see where it would direct the narrative. Then I'd keep the outputs that made sense with the story and delete those that didn't. And because of its word-processor-like interface, I could edit the text in the same box as the LLM, not only creating a call-and-response structure to the writing but a real sense that I was building something collaboratively with this bizarre entity behind the screen. Sometimes I would just ask it to brainstorm a character's name, or a description of their outfit, or a new obstacle for a character to jump over. But every time I used the Playground, I'd take the text we produced together and heavily edit it, adding flourishes to its often flat language, contributing my own twists and turns, massaging these edits into the larger narrative. In this way, working with the Playground felt similar to a collaborative storytelling game like Dungeons & Dragons. The main difference, of course, was that my collaborator was not a human but a computer program.

Through working with this LLM, I found that, while I don't think using such a computer program would benefit every novel, these public opinion–driven books felt particularly poised to engage with such a technology. On top of reading basically the entire history of literature to learn

how to write, when this LLM composes a text, it is constantly calculating what would statistically be the best response to a prompt based on how thousands, if not millions of writers (from literary greats to Reddit posters) have already done it. In this way, working with the LLM offered a polyvocality to the writing that seemed to resonate with the many perspectives represented in the poll results.

People's Choice Literature

So, what are we to make of all this? What do the data and these novels reveal about this elusive "American imagination" mentioned earlier? Sure, we have a techno-thriller on the one hand and an experimental goulash of genres and styles on the other, but what do these books reveal not only about literary tastes (and distastes) but our culture at large? Each novel has a strong technological element, something likely indicative of the ubiquity of technology in our lives—a force so pervasive we cannot imagine a future without it. And each novel features one or dozens of love stories—an indication of our complicated relationship with the idea of love? But where these novels differ is where things get particularly interesting.

One therapist friend suggested that this book exemplifies the Jungian notions of the persona and the shadow. These terms are commonly used to describe that part of an individual's psyche that is presented to the world (the persona) and that part that is seen as undesirable and therefore hidden (the shadow). If we think of culture as a body, then *The Most Wanted Novel* would be the persona, made up of the most visible and widely accepted parts—the façade. *The Most Unwanted Novel* would then be the shadow, those aspects of the cultural body often hidden or pushed to the side but inextricably part of the whole. Notably, the shadow contains those things that we repress in ourselves, things that no matter how hard we try to sideline are still part of us and will fight hard to see the light of day. In the case of *The Most Unwanted*, nearly every character has an unidentifiable, queer sexuality, and many are nonbinary or transgender—qualities that, of course, were directed by the poll results and that are unsurprising in a country that introduced over 510 anti-LGBTQ bills into state legislatures in 2023[5] and who voted against the supposedly pro-transgender presidential candidate in 2024.[6]

22 *People's Choice Literature*

This book also seems to validate what *People's Choice Music* revealed back in 1996, that while we may live in our digital bubbles today, American taste in literature is largely just as centralized and normalized as before the internet invaded our lives. The majority of respondents pointed to a most-wanted book that veered little from the kind of fiction that appears in airports, pharmacies, and Target. Most respondents ran as quickly to the middle as publishers want them to, asking for the same story they've consumed countless times. In this way, *The Most Wanted* performs the cultural loop we cannot seem to get out of—a circuit so closed that variation on time-tested styles, narrative forms, and subjects is rarely an option.

As for *The Most Unwanted*, it won't take readers long to see just how different that novel is from most fiction they're used to reading. One early reader described it "as if César Aira, Kathy Acker, and Philip K. Dick got high and tried to write *Tristram Shandy*." Noting the novel's length and the ubiquity of tennis in the narrative (only 1% wanted sports, and no one wanted tennis), another reader couldn't help but see some (very distant) resonances with David Foster Wallace's *Infinite Jest*, a book I had not read before writing the first draft. But if we look closer at the world that the unwanted data pointed to—a colonized Mars populated by the ultrawealthy and their attendant androids after Earth becomes uninhabitable—it's not hard to see how this picture squares with the space colonization ambitions of some of today's most notorious billionaires. Which is to say, while they may look forward to this future, it seems the vast majority of people do not.

But enough about my interpretations. The novels are done, printed, epub'd, and available for dissection, meditation, and most importantly, judgment. They are each infused with years of writing and editing in an earnest attempt, in each case, to win you over. The critics will have their say. The publishers will study the sales figures to decide if similar books will ever see the light of day. But in the pages that follow, it won't be the critics or publishers who will decide which is the better novel; it's you. Perhaps you'll love one book and hate the other. Maybe you'll find pleasure in a genre you never thought you would. And maybe, just maybe, you might find yourself enjoying parts—or all—of both.

Notes

1 Walter Lippmann, *Public Opinion* (Macmillan, 1922), introduction, part 7.

2 This assessment is also supported by the data, since our data on public opinion and Archer and Jockers's findings about bestsellers line up almost exactly. Which is to say, there is a direct correlation between the kind of fiction people say they want and the kind of books that become bestsellers. Jodie Archer and Matthew L. Jockers, *The Bestseller Code: Anatomy of the Blockbuster Novel* (St. Martin's, 2016).

3 Archer and Jockers, *The Bestseller Code*, 193–98.

4 Cade Metz, "Meet GPT-3. It Has Learned to Code (and Blog and Argue)," *The New York Times*, November 24, 2020, https://www.nytimes.com/2020/11/24/science/artificial-intelligence-ai-gpt3.html.

5 Annette Choi, "Record Number of Anti-LGBT Bills Were Introduced in 2023," *CNN.com*, January 22, 2024, https://www.cnn.com/politics/anti-lgbtq-plus-state-bill-rights-dg/index.html.

6 Goldmacher, Shane. "Trump and Republicans Bet Big on Anti-Trans Ads Across the Country," *The New York Times*, October 8, 2024, https://www.nytimes.com/2024/10/08/us/politics/trump-republican-transgender-ads.html.

THE MOST WANTED NOVEL

THE MOST WANTED NOVEL

CHAPTER ONE

This time was different. This time fear flooded his lungs with dread and clogged his throat with terror. This time his heart beat a brutal rhythm, desperate to be free, rapidly pounding out a single message: he was done for.

This time the waves were too high. His limbs were too weak, the weight of his body too much. This time the undertow would pull him far below, and he would drown.

His breath was screaming out, not a call of anguish, but a *you're-going-to-die-if-you-don't-figure-this-out-now* kind of shriek. *You have to get out*, he pleaded to himself. *You have to save yourself.* With all his might, he kicked out, his arms flailing, pulling madly at his liquid foe. His toes searched for sand on which to stand, but there was none. A wave crashed over, throwing him down farther, twisting him into a sick dance.

But still he tried, kicking and flailing toward the air, anything but this suffocating darkness. His lungs were on fire, his head pounding with the pain of a thousand angry drums. His body was screaming, his mind was screaming, *Go, Kevin, pull toward the light, don't let these waves kill you, GO—*

"GO!" he cried to nobody in his dark, water-free bedroom. His eyes stung from sweat, and he could feel his heart pounding in his chest. He was panting, his breaths coming in short gasps, sheets twisted in an elaborate knot around his leg.

It was only a dream, he told himself. *Just a dream. It wasn't real.* He tried to calm his breathing, tried to slow his racing heart. He was safe in his house, in his bed. He was OK.

And yet, even as he told himself this, the terror still lu rked in his chest. He tried to shake it off, tried to ignore the way his heart continued its aching thrum, but it was hard. It was hard to forget that feeling of choking, of complete helplessness.

He switched on the bedside lamp, hoping the brightness would chase away the dread. With a deep inhale, he tried to focus on the here and

28   *People's Choice Literature*

now, on the safe, mundane details of his life. The Dodgers poster on his wall, the collared shirt draped over his chair. But the dream lingered like a dead weight on his chest, a hard and heavy thing that refused to be shaken. Not unlike the terrors he would face that very morning . . .

Kevin Arnold sighed, sliding off the sheet. He stood and walked to the bathroom, splashing water on his face. Then he looked up to find the face that would meet the gaze of CNN news cameras and their millions of viewers that morning, the face that would recount a horror graver than humans had encountered in their three hundred thousand years on earth. It was his job today to speak for the people, and even though the burden weighed on him like a burning anvil, he knew he could do it. He tossed open the shower curtain and stepped in, letting the warm liquid wash over.

After drying off and getting dressed, Arnold opened the gAIa ride-share app and requested a car. Then he grabbed a power bar and stepped out into the grey morning light. *Typical Malibu fall weather.* He shook his head. *Cloudy and cool with a chance of rain.*

When the car arrived, Arnold walked toward the newly washed Ford Fusion at the end of his driveway, eyebrow raised in a curious arc. *I thought I requested an SUV* . . . But that wasn't the strangest thing. As he approached the Ford, Arnold gave it an even odder look. No one was in the driver's seat. No one in the passenger seat. Nothing. Suddenly the window squeaked down.

"Good morning, Mr. Arnold," said an electronic voice. "I will be your automated driver for this fine Tuesday morning. Might you have a musical preference for your journey?"

Arnold was taken aback, having never encountered a driverless car in person before. He'd talked to his phone, sure, but conversing with a vehicle was something entirely new.

The voice continued in its monotone manner. "I'm equipped with a wide selection of classics and current hits. Really, anything you could possibly want."

Arnold, always up for a challenge, was curious to see just how extensive this bot's library was. "How about some Springsteen?" he quipped with a shrug. "Say, live at Asbury Park, November 26, 1996?" *Only available as a bootleg . . .*

A series of beeps and whirrs replaced the electronic voice as the computer processed his request. Arnold couldn't help but grin as he awaited

his triumph. He was just about to claim victory when the voice blipped back on.

"But of course, Mr. Arnold."

He was stunned.

"The Boss, live at Asbury Park, November 26, 1996, coming right up."

And just like that, the crowd roared like an ocean wave crashing into the jangling acoustic guitar that kicks off the classic Springsteen tune "For You."

"Well, alright," Arnold nodded, thoroughly impressed by his phantom companion. With a flick of his wrist, he opened the rear door and tossed in his briefcase before settling into the push seat.

The car pulled away as Springsteen and his band entered into a steady jam. Arnold leaned back and sighed as the gray, misty ocean sped by.

By the time the Ford Fusion reached the Pacific Coast Highway, two hands were frantically typing in a dark room miles away. Only the faint glow of the monitor and a blood-red EXIT sign gave shape to the dim forms within.

For a moment, the hands stopped and rested on the keyboard. The fingers flexed, as if testing the quality of the hardware. A drop of sweat fell on the *F* key. Then they started up again, dancing over the plastic in a blur.

Suddenly the phone rang. The hands paused, hovering over the keyboard. Then they slowly drew back and made their way to the receiver.

The voice on the other end was breathy and tense.

"Are we ready?" it grumbled.

"Of course," came the reply. "Ready as we'll ever be."

"Good. Very good."

The voice hung up, and the hands returned to their task with renewed determination. The tapping of keys echoed through the room like percussion, the space bar keeping the beat with the dull thump of a bass drum as the letters and numbers marked out the cymbals and hi-hats in a cacophonous rhythm. Clearly these fingers were skilled, and they knew it.

The clicking continued at a mesmerizing pace until something changed their tune. Some goal was nearing completion. Some end was in sight. The clicking gradually slowed until it stopped all together, and silence filled the small room. Only shallow breaths and the soft whir of the monitor could be heard as the right hand lifted and hovered over the ENTER key.

30 *People's Choice Literature*

The pointer finger rested just above it, as if in indecision. A bead of sweat fell and smacked the table. And then, with a quick snap, the finger hit its mark.

At first nothing happened. A pause. A held breath. But then, like a thunderclap, a string of numbers flashed and disappeared. A small window popped up at the top corner of the computer monitor. The right hand took the mouse and stretched the bottom-right corner of the box until it filled the screen. Then the owner of the hands sat back, sweat beading on his brow, and sighed as he watched a Ford Fusion wind down the Malibu coast.

Kevin Arnold gripped the door handle as the sedan took a turn a little too fast. He turned to the empty driver's seat and shouted out, "Hey, watch it there, buddy!"

The volume of "Darkness on the Edge of Town" lowered before the electronic voice responded. "My apologies, Mr. Arnold. It won't happen again."

Arnold looked skeptically at the only thing that seemed plausible as the owner of that voice: the dashboard.

"How'd they teach you to drive, anyway?"

The voice cleared its electric throat. "As a first-generation self-driving car, I may seem like a novice, but by the time I was approved for the road, my model had already undergone 50,000 hours of trials. As such, I have more experience than the average human driver does in their lifeti—"

Suddenly the voice glitched and the dashboard flashed in a foreign code. The Springsteen came back louder than before, the Boss now screeching so loudly Arnold had to plug his ears. And, because things happen in threes, a true terror took shape: The steering wheel violently jerked to the side, hurtling the Ford into oncoming traffic.

Arnold's scream was drowned out by the chaos of screeching tires and blaring horns as the Ford sped into the other lane, just missing a head-on collision with a Jeep Wrangler. He lunged forward, desperately trying to gain control of the wheel and direct the car back to the right. But it wasn't necessary. Some invisible hand swung the wheel hard in the other direction, and the Ford was back in its lane.

Arnold exhaled a deep sigh of relief. *All good*, he thought. But the car had another idea, now jerking the wheel left and right like a crazed kid at an arcade, swerving against a cement lane divider to the left, running

a Volkswagen Golf off the road to the right, slaloming down the Pacific Coast Highway like an insane runaway train. Joggers leapt screaming into the bushes. A cyclist crashed into a streetlight.

And Arnold? He was frozen in fear, his heart hammering against his ribcage as if begging to break free. He gripped the door handle so tightly he nearly tore it off, and he prayed to any and every god he could think of. *Please, just let me survive this. Please, just let me live.* He went for the steering wheel again, hoping his sheer strength could end this sick game, but it was no use. The wheel wouldn't budge. It slammed left into a Honda Civic and then took a sharp right, running straight for the guardrail.

Bent over between the seats, Arnold watched it all as if it were a movie. The metallic guardrail buckling and shattering the windshield. The brittle brush crunching below raging wheels. The land and dirt receding. Then suddenly the land disappeared, and all Arnold could see was waves, waves, and more waves. The smoky clouds and cement-gray sea. Then the clouds disappeared as the car dipped down, and the spiky rocks joined the panorama of the growling sea. And through the visions and the roaring engine and the screeching Springsteen, suddenly a new sound emerged. The voice of Kevin Arnold rising into a ragged howl.

"Noooooooooooooooooooo!"

CHAPTER TWO

LOS ANGELES, ONE DAY EARLIER

Radiating like a beacon of joy in the heart of the city, Chris Burden's "Urban Light" is a sight to behold: A sparkling grid of antique street-lights adorn the southern entrance to the Los Angeles County Museum of Art, casting a warm glow on everything and everyone around them. Completed in 2008, the installation consists of 202 repurposed cast-iron posts, all dating from the 1920s and '30s. Ranging between 8 and 20 feet tall, the lamps once illuminated the city's many streets and boulevards, from the LA River all the way to the Pacific. In this new home, they greet millions of museum-goers annually, standing as a monument to the city's vibrant culture, both past and present.

Tonight, as Alix and John Finn strolled past this sculpture, their eyes wandered over the children running between the light posts and the crowds of tourists posing for selfies. Alix couldn't help but smile as two lovers kissed in the otherworldly glow. She thought of how long it had been since she'd been kissed and let out a wistful sigh.

"So, what do you think?" John asked, nodding to the lights.

"Oh, I think it's just wonderful," she said, still transfixed by the public display of affection.

Then the kissing couple unlocked their lips and snapped a selfie against the backdrop of antique grandeur.

Alix huffed and turned to her brother, hoping he'd distract her from her jealousy.

"You OK?" John asked.

"I'm fine," she said, gesturing to the sculpture. "What do you think?"

"I mean, it's epic," John chuckled, "but I think it'd be a lot better without all that selfie hoopla . . . Is anyone actually looking at the thing?"

"Oh, come on, John, they're having fun," Alix scolded as the couple disappeared into the crowd.

"Yeah, yeah, I know," he grumbled, turning to Alix. "Here I am being Debbie Downer again."

Alix gave him a pat on the back.

"I guess I'm just bummed about this event," he said. "Are you sure we have to go?"

Alix looked him straight in the eyes. "John, you know how devastated D. J. would be if I didn't make it."

John sighed as he gazed past the dazzling light installation to the swarm of Genera employees pouring into the museum. He knew Alix was right. For the past three years, she'd worked as an assistant to D. J. Wylde, CEO of Genera, one of the world's largest tech companies. Alix's job was, along with the coding wizard's five other assistants, handling day-to-day operations. Booking meetings. Managing the meditation room. Private jet maintenance. Admin stuff. That is, until a year ago, when a new word entered her vocabulary: Quanta.

Yes, Quanta. Those six letters that have graced nearly every sentence out of D. J.'s mouth since his grand moment of inspiration. That word whose meaning remained a complete enigma even to Alix. And that mystery had utterly transfixed her and everyone at Genera for the better part of a year. What could it be? A new way to quantify financial futures? A revolutionary social media platform? Given Wylde's track record, anything was possible. If his Zen 4 operating system had crowned him Silicon Valley nobility, it was his innovations at Genera that had made him a household name the world over: a smartphone so intelligent it could guess your next move; spaceships so fast that they could reach orbit in seconds; and now the mysterious Quanta, this new technology that had stumped the entire world.

Some whispered of a quantum internet or quantum cloud, which would make our current internet look like the Stone Age. Others speculated it could connect our brains to the internet, a super-AI with the power to transfer our thoughts and feelings directly into digital data. Conspiracy theorists went right to the worst-case scenario: that it was some deep-state surveillance tech that would be the end of the world as we knew it. Alix and her coworkers always laughed away such nonsense as coming right out of a bad action movie. But the truth was, they too were plagued by the enigma known only as Quanta.

34   *People's Choice Literature*

Despite this nagging mystery, Alix's satisfaction with her job never wavered. Alix and John were the firsts in their family to go to college, having been raised by two loving, hard-working parents in El Cerrito, north of Berkeley in the San Francisco Bay Area. As children, they reveled in long bike rides through the sunny California streets, night swimming in the bay. But money was always tight, its strains etched into their parents' faces, however much they tried to hide it. As such, Alix would never forget the look they gave her and John when those college admissions letters arrived. Is there a single word for pure joy? Whatever it is, it lingered for months. Then, when she got the news of her job at Genera, it felt like things were really taking a turn for her and her family. *Finally,* she thought, *I've made it.*

Alix turned to John and continued. "It's not just me who's got to be here. You do, too, 'Mister Security.' You're as obligated as I am."

She was right. John, a member of Genera's security team for over a year, was just as bound to this Quanta pre-launch party as she or any Genera employee: It was an unspoken rule that company events were as mandatory as clocking in at 9 a.m. John had learned this the hard way after his superior reprimanded him for missing two consecutive events: first a company-wide beach party in Santa Monica, then Genera's extravagant buyout of Crypto.com Arena for a private Coldplay concert. The wrath and disappointment of John's boss nearly led him to quit. All that for missing thousands of millennials and Gen-Zers scream "Yellow" at the top of their lungs?

See, any job John Finn had held since college had always been second to his true passion: writing. John was a novelist at heart. He'd published a few short stories with small magazines in his early twenties and now, at the ripe age of twenty-five, was deep in the middle of what he believed to be his masterpiece, a novel he so cherished that not even Alix, his twin sister and best friend, knew a thing about it. Every day after work, John would retreat to their humble two-bedroom apartment, crack open a Coors Light, and disappear into his room to write.

Alix had her own passions and hobbies but also enjoyed relaxing after a long day, coming home to their lovable little bulldog, Rocky, rubbing his droopy jowls before taking him on a long walk through their East Hollywood neighborhood. And unlike John, she enjoyed the Genera events—who wouldn't love free food, beer, and music?

"You're right," John finally replied. "If I don't go, I'm sure I won't hear the end of it . . . It's just I have this deadline tonight. Got so much to do."

"Deadline?" Alix perked up. "John, you've been writing that thing for years."

John shrugged, clearly not wanting to get into it. Alix studied him, sensing the tension below the surface.

"Don't worry," she assured him with a side hug. "You'll have time. I'll make sure of it."

John swallowed as they started toward the entrance.

CHAPTER THREE

Entering LACMA's spacious Main Plaza, Alix and John threw on their Genera cloaks, as they'd done every day since they started working for the company. Alix enjoyed her coral cloak, while John was more of a baby blue kind of guy. Weaving through a sea of cloaked colleagues into the courtyard, Alix spotted Dan, Wylde's longest-serving assistant, and gave him a friendly wave. John, on the other hand, kept his head down, hoping to get in and out as soon as possible. As they approached the main stage, they discovered massage booths and tarot readers, meditation nooks and drum circles. In one corner, a live painter was crafting a portrait of Jimi Hendrix out of Cheez Whiz. To the uninitiated bystander, it might've looked like Woodstock Part 3.

But this hippy sheen was complicated by the massive banner above the main stage in metallic lettering: "QUANTA-FY THE FUTURE!" Below it, D. J. Wylde sat in his typical neon-blue cloak, brushing his brown locks back from his face with one hand, holding an acoustic guitar with the other. His face beamed with that knowing smile that was recognized around the world. See, Wylde was renowned not only as a tech genius, but a cultural icon. A regular at the Oscars, Grammys, and Met Galas, he was a tabloid magnet and reveled in the attention, dating the strangest of celebrities while cultivating the image of both innovator and provocateur. He was charismatic and witty, smart and eccentric. He was the type of guy that could get away with wearing heart-shaped sunglasses indoors. And yet, he was complicated: a democratic-socialist vegetarian who regularly wore $14,000 Tom Ford alligator boots. A man who genuinely loved his employees but had no problem firing them for even the slightest mistake.

Wylde described running a major tech company as learning to manage "controlled chaos." Amid the frenzy, he valued moments of repose and pleasure. It was this philosophy that inspired his most cherished project, the Commune. A utopian oasis situated on the former site of

Alcatraz Island in the middle of the San Francisco Bay, the Commune was populated by Genera employees and dozens of artists, musicians, and thought leaders handpicked by the tech guru himself. Swooping in when the island's funding ran dry, Wylde decided to give the place a "makeover," in his words, to purge its troubled past and give it new life. This meant razing its structures and replacing them with yurt-like lodging, saunas, meditation rooms, and the infamous Wylde Chapel, a towering ivory edifice whose purpose was just as secret as the Quanta project. Wylde commuted between the Commune and Genera's Los Angeles headquarters regularly, but tonight he was happy to be back in his hometown. As he sat there, with his acoustic guitar in hand and the thrill of Quanta on his mind, he looked like a modern-day renaissance man, ready to take on all the future had to offer. To be precise, he was tall and slender, the spitting image of John Lennon in 1968. And he had the voice to prove it.

"You just missed D. J.'s epic cover of 'Happy Together,'" whispered a beaming, orange-cloaked employee to Alix's right.

Alix pantomimed a What can you do? and gave him a smile. John rolled his eyes.

Wylde placed the guitar on its stand and stood up, towering over the crowd. As his eyes swept across the hundreds of faces, his mouth curled into a smile, that smile Genera employees had come to admire. As the smile spread wider, the crowd grew quiet. You could've heard your heartbeat.

"Love," he spoke with a velvety voice into his headset microphone. "L. O. V. E." He nodded slowly. "What is love? A mere word, yes. An idea. Of course. But what makes love unique from all other ideas?" He paused to let the question sink in. "The intoxicating thrill of new love? The joy it brings? Surely these qualities matter greatly, but I suggest love's uniqueness is rooted in a simple fact: aspiration. Desire. Dreaming."

His eyes grew wide as they gazed far out over the crowd.

"With love as our compass, we can achieve the impossible. With love, men have scaled the highest mountains of the soul, have overcome insurmountable odds. With love, we transcend the possible in search of new shores, new futures, a new now." He paused before lowering his voice. "And, love, my friends, is our fuel here at Genera. Everything we do. Every innovation, every product, every service we offer is birthed from that simple concept, that sacred aspiration: love . . ."

"I LOVE YOU, D. J.!" cried a female voice from the crowd.

38 *People's Choice Literature*

Wylde's laughter echoed through the courtyard. "I love you, too. I love all of you."

The crowd was visibly moved.

John was obviously not, huffing and checking his watch.

"My friends," Wylde continued. "I even have love for gAIa, our greatest competitor."

The crowd gasped.

"It's true," Wylde spoke with gravitas. "As one wise man once said, 'Love thy neighbor.'" He smirked. "Yes, love has the power to change everything." Wylde stepped to the center of the stage and studied the crowd. "And that's exactly what we've done here at Genera, my friends. With the aspirational power of love, we have reached heights few could've ever imagined one hundred, fifty, even five years ago."

Alix recalled how relatively new even the smartphone was and nodded along with the guy beside her.

"Tonight, my friends, we celebrate the love that has guided us here at Genera. We join in love as we step into the future. Together." Then he raised his arms in a triumphant V. "Here and now, together, we move forward toward a new tomorrow!"

Suddenly the Quanta logo appeared behind him in all its shimmering, metallic glory, and the crowd erupted in a frenzy of cheers.

"Quanta . . ." he announced triumphantly, his face radiating with pride.

"That's right, friends. Tonight marks the momentous two-day countdown to the official release of the Quanta project."

A digital countdown clock materialized beside the logo.

"Quanta," he repeated thoughtfully, like Lennon polishing his greatest song yet. "Yes, Quanta."

The crowd was silent, desperate for a hint at what this mystery could be.

"With Quanta, we'll reach computing power never heard of."

A collective breath pulled in.

"Scientists will cure our most impossible ailments. Pandemics will disappear. Cancer will become a thing of the past."

The crowd was in awe.

"Financial systems will be able to predict economic futures in real time, thwarting recessions, and worse, depressions."

People were crying.

"The old world will fade away, replaced by a new kind of knowledge, growth, and connectivity. A new beginning. A new now!"

The crowd cheered, and Wylde stood there beaming.

When the employees finally settled down, he gazed out over their entranced faces and spoke those iconic words: "Quanta. One small step for Genera . . ."

The curtain behind him began to rise.

". . . one giant leap for mankind."

And with that final word, the curtain disappeared, revealing none other than Bono, the Edge, and the rest of U2 playing the opening, trembling notes of "Beautiful Day."

The crowd went wild.

CHAPTER FOUR

Later that night, in a dark room far across town, long after the music had ended, after the crowds had dispersed and most of Genera was asleep, it was quiet. The only sound was of fingers frantically striking a keyboard, the digits pounding so hard and for so long the hardware seemed in danger of imploding. And yet it persisted, the fingers jamming each key in determined succession, as if trying to will the thoughts in their miniature finger-brains into words on the screen. In reality, the actual mind controlling those fingers was working on overdrive, pouring more effort into this text than what you might think was humanly possible. Any observer might have called this activity "writing," but these motions were more akin to a track-and-field event than anything else.

The body controlling those fingers was tense, beads of sweat cascading down its hunched form, bloodshot eyes moving rapidly between the document to his side and the screen, copying data at a superhuman rate, as if his life depended on it. The man was so focused he failed to notice the door slide open. He missed the feet inching toward him and the hand pulling the Colt-45 from its pocket. But no one could have missed the sound of the gun cocking back as it rose to the typist's head or the concussive pop as the bullet exploded from its chamber.

John Finn jerked upright in the chair where he'd fallen asleep, catching his breath. His real forehead dripping with real sweat, real hand and sleeve running across it to catch the rank dampness. He glared at the computer screen before him, recalling the hours he'd spent on this darn document instead of his novel. *Hours wasted?* He hoped not. He prayed that this would all pay off in the end. His chest tightened as he considered the potential consequences of what he was about to do. And just as he reached to close the laptop, a jarring vibration shook him from his thoughts. He looked at his phone to find that familiar name on the screen: UNKNOWN CALLER.

"Yes?" he sighed.

The voice cut right to the chase: "Are we ready?"

"Yes, I'm ready. It's ready," John said, exasperated.

"Good. A car will arrive in ten minutes to take you to the airport."

John swallowed.

"Oh, and the drop off location has changed. You'll meet at Coit Tower in San Francisco. Start at Union Square, then head uphill in a zigzag formation. Maybe stop and get yourself a coffee on the way. Wouldn't want anyone following you . . ."

"You said this would be easy." John protested. "You said, 'Quick drop off at Vesuvio bar. Look for the guy in the green glasses.' That's it."

The voice was not pleased.

"Things changed. We can't risk anything. You know how surveillance is these days. Just keep your head down and you'll be fine."

John huffed. "Alright."

"Eleven a.m. Coit Tower."

The line went dead.

John glanced at the clock. It was already six. Rocky would be waking Alix up any time now. He had to act quickly.

Rummaging through his desk, he found a pack of USB drives and stuck one in the laptop. As the data transferred, John grabbed his waste bin and the paper documents he'd been copying and made his way to the balcony of his tiny room.

Outside, the city before him lay cloaked in a dim, gray dawn, with the silhouettes of palm trees poking up through the skyline. With a bitter sigh, he pulled out a lighter and lit the papers. Then he tossed them in the bin and stared in disbelief as they slowly turned to ash.

Back inside, he returned the bin and copied another USB. Then he threw the laptop in his backpack and headed for the door. But just as John was about to leave, a snort came from behind.

Rocky, Alix's and his bulldog, waddled up, breathing deep and low, wiggling his rump from side to side.

"Hey, boy," John knelt down and whispered, "Good boy."

Rocky rubbed his head against John's hand, giving it a lick and a snort. John scratched the cute, floppy folds that surrounded his eyes, and Rocky panted harder.

"I'll be back soon, I promise."

He gave Rocky one last rub, then stood up and silently slipped out the door. Then he ran down the stairs to find a sleek, black Ford Fusion waiting for him, its hazard lights blinking to an impatient beat. Before

42 *People's Choice Literature*

he reached the car, the passenger side window rolled down, and an electronic voice began: "Good morning, Mr. Finn."

John didn't hesitate to jump inside. His heart was racing so fast he didn't even realize no one was at the wheel.

"Fifteen minutes to destination," the voice continued.

The Ford Fusion pulled out and sped down the street—in the opposite direction of the airport.

"Aren't I going to San Francisco?" John asked nervously.

"Just one stop first, sir."

John huffed and wiped a bead of sweat from his temple. As the car sped through the dark streets, he kept his gaze fixed grimly out the window, gripping the USB drives for dear life.

CHAPTER FIVE

Far across town, another man was up earlier than usual, sweating and tapping his desk in an anxious rhythm. In fact, Richard Moriarty hadn't slept a wink, having played D. J. Wylde's Quanta speech over and over in his head for hours. *This had better work*, he thought. *We can't let them win*.

Moriarty sat back and sighed. At fifty-six years old, he was no newbie to the business world, and he had the battle scars to prove it. Wrinkles had formed years earlier than normal. Gray hairs nipped the edges of his slicked-back hair. Decades of managing the gAIa corporation had also taken a toll on his form, leaving him with little time for self-care. As a result, he'd become the cartoon image of a baron of industry: balding and overweight.

Moriarty stood up from his desk and moved toward the window. But he only managed a few steps before buckling over. Gripping his side, he groaned and turned to his briefcase.

"Not again," he wheezed through clenched teeth.

He panted and strained as he searched for the bottle of Tums.

"Damn stomach," he grumbled, popping open the bottle and shoveling six chalky tablets into his mouth. Then he sunk into the edge of his desk and breathed deeply, hand glued to his side. Stress-related GI issues had plagued him for years, but right now it was just too much. He took a few deep breaths and then stood up, pacing and muttering incomprehensibly under his breath, searching for something, anything that might calm him.

But there was little comfort to be found in the office of a man teetering on the brink of obscurity. He knew this Quanta, whatever it was, had the potential to surpass anything he or his company, gAIa, had ever even dreamed of. Sure, gAIa had dominated multiple markets with its world-renowned search engine and revolutionary project management

technologies, but, if the rumors were true, Quanta was likely to surpass them all. Still, Moriarty would not go down without a fight.

In a way, this showdown was something he had been building toward his whole life. He'd founded gAIa in the early '90s, sculpting it into the powerhouse it was today. But now more than just his company was at stake. The fate of the entire world hung in the balance. If a company like gAIa lost to Genera, it would be catastrophic, transforming D. J. Wylde's Hippie Inc. into a multi-market-dominating force. This was a battle to the death, and like any fight, it would be brutal. And as they say, all is fair in love and cyber war. . .

Moriarty looked out the window, unable to shake off his frustration at not knowing what Quanta could even be. Wylde's nerd squad had been tight-lipped about the project for years. No one knew what the product did, not even his assistants, and the few that did know were forbidden from speaking about it, sequestered away in Wylde's Commune concocting God knows what kind of technological breakthroughs. Moriarty had a hunch as to why: This was no ordinary innovation. It was something truly revolutionary. The tech to dwarf all others.

Moriarty reached for another handful of Tums when his phone began to vibrate on the mahogany desk. He glanced at the caller and smiled, raising the phone to his ear.

"D. J.?" he grumbled.

"Richard . . ." said the spritely voice of D. J. Wylde. "Sorry to bother you at this hour. How are you?"

Moriarty sighed, his hand still cupping his stomach, and replied with forced civility, "I'm fine, D. J. Just fine."

"Good to hear," said Wylde. "Look, I just wanted to call and wish you well. I heard William is having a hard time of it again."

Moriarty soured.

"That boy does what he wants. I can't help him anymore," grumbled the tech tycoon. "And I should be the one wishing you luck for your big, mysterious Quanta launch."

Wylde paused, processing the sarcasm dripping from Moriarty's words. "We are humbled to serve the people, Richard. It's the least we can do."

Moriarty didn't respond, already bored.

Wylde continued: "You may not know it, Richard, but I look up to you. You were my inspiration for starting Genera, after all."

"Is that so?" said Moriarty, his face turning red in pain. He paused and popped another Tums before getting to the point. "So, why'd you really call, D. J.? Can't imagine you're looking for pillow talk at 6 a.m."

Wylde laughed sheepishly. "Boy, you never change." Then he took a deep breath. "Look, Richard, I caught wind you might have a few . . . tricks up your sleeve this week. I wanted to extend an olive branch. See if we could find some common ground."

"What're you talking about?" spat Moriarty, his mind racing, trying to figure out who in his office could have leaked his plans.

"Look," said Wylde with growing confidence, "I just wanted to give you a chance to back off before it's too late."

"Is that a threat, D. J.? *Do you know* who you're speaking to?"

"Of course, Richard. And I know you're going to make this a fight. But if you think you can win, you're sorely mistaken."

Moriarty gripped his phone tight, resisting the urge to hurl it across the room.

"You don't know what I'm capable of," Moriarty hissed.

Wylde paused. "Well, if that's how it's going to be, take care, Richard . . ."

Moriarty fumed quietly.

". . . and may the best man win."

With a furious click, Moriarty ended the call and slammed a fist into the desk. *I'll show him*, he thought.

CHAPTER SIX

Spanning over 4,310 acres of rugged terrain in the Santa Monica Mountains, Griffith Park reigns as Los Angeles's largest municipal park. A hub for outdoor enthusiasts and city dwellers alike, the sprawling landscape offers endless opportunities for hiking, horseback riding, picnicking, and golf. This iconic landscape is also home to such famed landmarks as the Griffith Observatory, the Los Angeles Zoo, and the Hollywood Sign.

Griffith Park was founded in 1882 when Colonel Griffith J. Griffith generously donated 3,015 acres of his land to the city. Through a series of strategic acquisitions, this haven of leisure expanded to its current size, now boasting more than fifty miles of trails. In the wee hours, hikers may encounter sweeping vistas of the glittering metropolis accompanied by the soft cries of coyotes.

But that morning, before the sun had risen, the coyotes were silent, and no one was around. John Finn's Ford Fusion swerved up Fern Dell Place for what felt like miles until it stopped beside another driverless black Ford Fusion. In the dim light, John could make out a figure in the back seat. The man was not unlike John: a mid-twenties white male, dressed in a black hoodie. They locked eyes and held each others' gaze.

With an intense look of determination, the stranger stepped out of his vehicle, his eyes never wavering from John.

"It's time, Mr. Finn," said the electronic voice from the dashboard.

"Time for what?" asked John.

"Everything you need is in that car."

John turned back to the man hovering outside. He opened the door and hastened to the other Ford. But as he neared this man, John couldn't help but notice something odd: This other guy didn't just resemble John, he looked *exactly* like him. Same eye color, same hair style. Even the same mole on the right side of his chin! A shiver ran down John's spine as he

passed by the man, desperate for this bizarre moment to end. Then he grabbed the door handle and jumped in.

"Good morning, Mr. Finn," said the same electronic voice as before. "45 minutes to LAX."

As the Ford pulled away, John's eyes darted back at the man now sitting in his previous vehicle. His stomach lurched as he watched the man's mouth curve up into a sinister smirk.

When the Ford reached Franklin Avenue, John noticed the blond wig and change of clothes sitting beside him. He grabbed a tan leather wallet and opened it to find his new ID.

The picture looked just like him, only fair haired. And a name he could easily remember. *That'll do*, he thought. *That'll do*. It was 6:30.

CHAPTER SEVEN

As John raced toward the airport, Alix Finn was waking up to the sound of Rocky snorting and sniffing around her head. Dim light fell across her face as her favorite pooch came and nuzzled her cheek, giving it a lick.

"Mornin'," she said groggily.

Rocky nestled into her side, snorting and panting his happy little pants.

"Good to see you too," Alix yawned while rubbing his hangy jowls. Then she glanced at the clock and let out a sleepy sigh. "Kind of early, isn't it, bud?"

Rocky responded with vacant panting as Alix pulled herself out of bed. She threw on a sweatshirt and running pants before stepping into the living room. Eyeing John's closed door, she thought, *Lucky you . . . Could use another hour of sleep myself.* Then she leashed Rocky and headed outside.

It was a strange morning: rainclouds in LA. As common as chocolate in salad. Alix and Rocky ambled down the stairs and out onto the sidewalk. Rocky sniffed around as Alix studied the sky. The clouds were a dark gray, pregnant with rain, and the air smelled metallic.

She shrugged and checked her phone as Rocky squatted to pee. But before she could read anything, someone called from down the sidewalk.

"Morning, Alix!"

She looked up to find her flirty neighbor Chad beaming at her, approaching with his dog, Brad.

"Morning," she replied with a polite smile.

"You're up early," he said, nodding to Rocky.

"This little one beats my alarm nine days out of ten." Alix shrugged as Rocky sniffed curiously around a patch of grass, apparently just as uninterested in both Chad and Brad.

"Big week at Genera, huh? Any idea what the big reveal is?" Chad asked with a curious grin.

"You know as well as me," said Alix. "They do a great job of keeping us in the dark."

"That or you know everything and if you told me you'd have to kill me, right?" Chad chuckled.

Alix forced a laugh. "Something like that." She looked down as Rocky squatted.

"Hey," said Chad, "you know if you ever need a dog sitter, I bet Brad here would sure love to spend more time with your little Rock-o."

"You're too kind," said Alix, pulling out a bag and picking up Rocky's daily blessing.

"No, don't think anything of it. And if you'd ever want to grab a beer or something—"

"Gah, sorry Chad," Alix said, looking at her phone. "I'm so late for work. You know, this being the big week and all."

"Yeah, yeah, of course," Chad shrugged. "Well, have a good one." He bent down and gave Rocky a friendly pat on the head. "Bye bye, Rocky."

Rocky snorted.

"Bye, guys," Alix said, strolling away with her waddling woman's-best-friend.

She tossed Rocky's gift into an outside trash bin and went up the stairs. As she filled Rocky's food bowl, she thought back to Chad and his kindness. *Was I being too harsh? He just offered to dog sit. And grabbing a beer isn't such a big deal. Maybe getting to know him could be nice . . .*

She set the bowl in front of Rocky and commanded him to sit. The pooch shook with uncontrollable excitement, panting and snorting his cute little snort.

"Good enough," she smirked.

As she made her way back to her room, the broadcast of her mind switched back to Chad. *OK, I do want to date, but there've got to be better options out there. I just have to find them.* She grabbed some jeans and a blouse, remembering it sure had been some time since she'd been in love.

Alix had grown up in El Cerrito, north of Berkeley in the Bay Area, with her brother and parents. She'd dreamed of dating, but she was shy and bookish. Just a few friends, her best friend Kate, and John. But when she met Timmy in her junior year of high school, everything changed. Bike rides through the sunny, palm-lined streets, night swimming in the bay. Her twin brother John even liked Timmy. And when she and Timmy would kiss, it was like the gates of heaven had opened, as if the

50 *People's Choice Literature*

world were anew every time. But then there was that fateful day senior year . . .

Alix had planned to surprise Timmy on his birthday. After baking him his favorite pie, she biked to his house, snuck around to his backyard and froze. There he was, arms around Karen Sleason. And going to second base! Alix couldn't believe her eyes. Her love, the love of her life, had betrayed her for a freshman.

Ever since that horrible day, Alix had sworn off love. If Timmy, her soulmate, could deceive her, couldn't anyone? No one was safe. Still, she longed for what they had. She longed for a man to sweep her off her feet and kiss her like his life, his very being depended on it. She dreamed of long strolls down Venice Beach. Warm cuddles by Ojai campfires.

Alix sighed as she buttoned up her blouse. Then she looked at the clock. 7:00. *That's strange*, she thought. *John should be up by now.*

So she pulled up her jeans and walked out of her room. Creeping up to his door, she listened before knocking. Nothing. She knocked. No response. She knocked once more.

"John, come on. You're gonna be late."

No reply.

She pushed the door open to find a messy, empty room. Books and clothes strewn everywhere. Empty bed. Balcony door half open. She sniffed. *What the heck is that?*

When Alix walked to his desk, the smell grew stronger. She looked down at the trashcan and the charred paper within.

"What the frick?" she said aloud.

Then she grabbed her phone and called him. The phone rang and rang, but he didn't pick up.

She texted: "Where are you? What's with the trash can? Indoor bonfire!??"

Nothing.

Alix frowned and went back to her room. *Will deal with you later . . .*

After she packed her bag and filled Rocky's water bowl, she gave the pooch a last little jowl rub and headed out the door. The air was still gray, ashy white. When she reached her Honda Accord, Alix turned back and studied John's window. *What are you up to this time, John?*

CHAPTER EIGHT

At 7:30 a.m., Alix and John were both in transit. Alix in traffic on the way to work at Genera's Santa Monica Headquarters. John trying to nap against the plastic wall of a Boeing 737 at 32,000 feet. So far, his trip had been smooth sailing. Taxiing was short. Takeoff a breeze. But given his task for the day, his nerves were still high. He'd copied the documents like he'd been told to. He'd gotten into the Ford Fusion and switched into his disguise. Then he'd gotten to the airport and onto the plane and at that very moment was speeding north at two-thirds the speed of sound.

His pulse was high, but John tried all he knew to calm himself. He'd chugged two bottles of water. Took a Xanax. Read a few pages from the newest novel by his favorite mystery writer, James Patterson. But thoughts kept creeping in, reminding of the agonizing task before him. Fly to San Francisco. Take the train to Union Square. Go uphill toward Coit Tower in a zigzag formation. Get there by 11 a.m. Keep your head down. Get in and out. It sounded like a simple plan, but John Finn knew better: there was always room for error. He couldn't help but glance over his shoulder at the other passengers, wondering if he was already being followed.

Just then, the Boeing 737 jolted violently from side to side, causing everything to shake like a martini. Dry. Over-stirred. The pilot's voice came from the loudspeaker announcing the return of the "fasten seat-belt" sign. Then came an even sharper quake, crash, then a plunge downward, throwing John, along with his neighbor's lunch, into the air. The punch of flesh hitting plastic. The screams. The chaos was deafening.

The Boeing 737 kept shaking, dipping, and bouncing back like a crazy joystick. A jolt up, and John nearly hurled. A jolt to the right, and the drink cart toppled over, spilling its contents all over the seats in front.

Are we all going to die? John asked himself, now holding his nose, trying not to vomit. *And if I die, what happens to these USBs? What happens to Alix? To humanity?* John wasn't a religious person, but he tried out a

52 *People's Choice Literature*

prayer as the cabin rocketed back and forth, trudging weakly through the raging torrents of air.

Suddenly, oxygen masks fell from the ceiling. John grabbed the one before him and closed his eyes, yearning for a swift end to this insanity. Something, anything else but this.

And then, like clockwork, his prayers were answered. The Boeing 737 leveled, shuddered like a rickety truck pulling off a gravelly road, and then smoothed into a glide. It was as if a giant hand had grabbed the troubled Boeing 737 and was holding it safely in place, easing it home. The lights flashed out and then flickered back on. The "fasten seatbelt" sign clicked off.

The skyquake now seemed a thing of the past, but the scene was still chaotic, to say the least. Food-cart-soiled patrons repacking luggage before restuffing overhead bins. Airline attendants, now out of towels, resorting to dubious toilet paper and half-soiled blankets to dab up stalactites of meatloaf and greens.

When the Boeing 737 finally landed in San Francisco, everyone applauded in a collective sigh of relief. Their harrowing journey had come to a happy end. But at the same moment the plane was landing, hundreds of miles to the south, a more agonizing descent was taking place: Kevin Arnold and the Ford Fusion swerved from the Malibu freeway and slammed through the guardrail, rocketing off a nameless cliff into the brick-hard waves of the Pacific.

CHAPTER NINE

Perched atop a lush hillside of Los Angeles County's western coast lies the Getty Villa. Designed by the renowned architect Richard Meier and modeled after the Villa of the Papyri in Herculaneum, Italy, the structural marvel features a central peristyle courtyard with breathtaking views of the Pacific Ocean. Once the home of the oil magnate J. Paul Getty, it was transformed into a museum of ancient art in 1974 and remained that way for decades.

It now served as the hub for Genera's MindLab, the zenith of advanced technological research and development on the planet. Acquired shortly after the company went public, the Villa became known to Genera's employees as the core incubator for their "progressive technologies," as D. J. Wylde put it. An intellectual oasis housing the greatest scientists and thinkers in the world.

That morning as Alix pulled up in her Honda Accord, the Villa's aesthetic glory was dulled by the heavy rainclouds drooping above. She parked and had just started for Wylde's office when the loud beating of a helicopter soared overhead—a bit too close for comfort. Alix looked up just in time to see the red-and-white blur of one of the LA Fire Department's AgustaWestland AW139s slice through the air like a knife.

When the chopper disappeared over the hills, Alix's eyes drifted to the office windows above the parking lot. There, through the light drizzle, she could have sworn she saw, on the top floor, framed in the stucco façade, someone studying her. A silhouette just standing there in the rectangular pane. Staring. Alix did a double take, but when her eyes returned, the form was gone. *What the heck is going on today?* she asked herself in disbelief.

But by the time she reached Wylde's office, this strange feeling was quickly replaced by the usual rush of task completion, gossip, and speculation over Quanta's mysterious powers. Alix, who had been the tech wizard's assistant since just after college and whose twin brother had

54 *People's Choice Literature*

joined the company a few years later, was used to this hustle and bustle. But as soon as she sat down at her desk and looked at her phone, her heart sank. Still nothing from John.

"Nice day, isn't it?" said a nasal voice from above.

It was Wylde's newest assistant. *Ted? Todd? Something like that.* The most recent addition to Wylde's "Rainbow Seven" team of assistants following Kim Croft's departure for gAIa last week—a move deemed universally treasonous by the rainbow brigade, given gAIa's status as Genera's greatest competitor. And yet the change was met with the signature grace and understanding that D. J. Wylde was known for.

"You hear the news?" the newbie asked.

"What news?" asked Alix, genuinely confused.

"Kevin Arnold just flew off a cliff three miles from here," he said with a hint of excitement. "It's all over the internet."

Alix sunk back in her chair. *Kevin Arnold.* War hero and two-time mayor of Los Angeles. Kevin Arnold. "Our only hope," as George W. Bush declared at a fundraiser just last month in a sly reference to the biggest movie franchise of all time. Kevin Arnold. Close friend of Barack and Michelle Obama. So close they nearly adopted him as a de facto son at the DNC three years prior. If the polls were right, this time next year he'd be a shoo-in for the Oval Office. Arnold was supposed to bring the country together again, to break up partisan gridlock and form a multiparty coalition unlike any this country had ever seen. But now, who knew? Was he even alive? And if he was, would he make it through the day? Now nothing was certain. The future was just a dim question mark in an even dimmer world.

Alix went to CNN.com and immediately spotted the helicopter that had just passed above her.

Her jaw dropped.

"What's wrong?" asked another of Wylde's assistants, walking by and seeing the look on Alix's face.

"Didn't you hear?" Alix said blankly. "Kevin Arnold . . . he's . . . it's not good."

The other assistant looked at Alix's screen and put her hand to her mouth. "Oh my God."

"What the heck is going on?" Alix said aloud to no one in particular. *I need to find John. This is just too much.*

She pushed back her chair and hurried out of the office, starting for the security room where John had sure better be.

CHAPTER TEN

But John, of course, was 347.42 miles north, climbing the stone steps of San Francisco's famed Union Square. When he reached the top, he paused for a minute to take a sip of his latte and looked out across the vast stone slab of the plaza. The school kids feeding the pigeons. Above, even more birds swayed like nets through the currents of air, circling and dipping, then soaring back up again. John remembered these stringfoot and two-rock pigeons from his urban biology class back in college. How they often moved like a singular body, swinging in unison, but never as a true whole. How this meant they existed in a perpetual limbo, diving over palm trees, swooping over crowds and back up into elastic forms that in the end are more like Rorschachs than anything else. And yet as the pigeons rose there, swerving around the immense pillar of stone, John imagined it'd be hard for anyone to look up and not see an immense bird's nest floating in the air.

Before Alfred Hitchcock could show up, John checked his watch. He had to get moving. So he tossed his coffee in the trash and turned toward Post Street. As he weaved through the rush of commuters and tourists, he pulled in a deep breath. There was something in the pedestrian congestion. Something in the gloom of the day mixed with the cold dampness of this foggy city. Suddenly the weight of the past week hit him like a colossal wave. The sleepless nights. The exhaustion of keeping the biggest secret in the world. The fear. First finding that document outside his Genera security booth. Then agonizing over what to do with its damning revelations. Then desperately working to create an untraceable copy and sneaking up to San Francisco in this ridiculous disguise.

John sighed. At least this was more interesting than his normal life. Sit for hours monitoring consumer safety on dozens of Genera products. When a complaint comes in, contact consumer and initiate a quick fix. When in doubt, refer to section 8 of the Genera safety manual. If the problem was minor, which it unvaryingly was, direct the consumer to

Genera's customer service department and then, while juggling countless other consumers and product errors, send a report to management. Then repeat. And repeat. And repeat. Ad nauseam. In the face of such monotony, John prayed that the novel he was writing would somehow sell to a publisher, bring him a big advance, and whisk him far away from Genera and any other job ever again. *But who am I kidding?* he'd say to himself. *Who in their right mind would publish a book about genetically enhanced golfers in outer space?*

John turned right onto Taylor Street and began ascending one of San Francisco's notorious hills. First navigating an obstacle course of Instagram tourists, then a quartet of venture capitalists on a Segway tour, by the time he reached the top, he was panting.

Before him stood the grand spectacle that was Grace Cathedral, a towering French Gothic edifice flanked by two large, rectangular spires. Every time he saw this church, he was instantly taken back to Armistead Maupin's *Tales of the City* books—a favorite in his youth—and the bizarre cult that occupied its marbled halls. But that morning as he stood there, the large, circular stained-glass window stared back as a beacon of hope. After pulling in a deep breath, he straightened and returned to the mission at hand. He crossed the street, passing Huntington Park, the Pacific-Union Club, and finally the classic Fairmont Hotel. And then, just as he was about to turn into San Francisco's famed Chinatown, he spotted Coit Tower in the foggy distance. His hopes were lifted, his goal in sight. And yet as he beheld that iconic monument, as he descended into this historic neighborhood, a creeping feeling came over him. *You'd think they were trying to wear me down with all this walking . . .*

CHAPTER ELEVEN

Back at the Getty Villa, Alix pounded on the door to John's security unit, but there was no answer.

"Come on, John," she called out. "I know you're in there."

Still, he didn't reply.

She knocked once more and, this time, heard a shuffling sound from within.

"John!" she called. "Cut it out. This isn't funny."

More shuffling. No response.

"OK, John. I'm coming in," she said, waving her key card at the lock.

The shuffling grew frantic and louder.

When the lock blinked green, Alix turned the handle, but it wouldn't budge.

"John? Are you really holding it shut?"

She pushed at the door, but it only gave a centimeter before forcibly slamming back against the frame.

"John, this is ridiculous," she huffed. "Don't make me bust down this door. You know I can lift more than you . . ."

Alix could now hear deep breathing through the white barrier.

"OK, John. I'm coming in," she took a step back and prepared to use her body as a battering ram. "In 3 . . . 2 . . . 1 . . ."

She lunged at the door, and it completely gave way. With no resistance, she lost balance and fell flat to the floor. Then suddenly a shape leapt over her and started sprinting down the hall.

"What the heck are you doing?" Alix cried out as she scrambled to her feet and chased after him.

From behind she noticed he looked the same as always. Same baby blue cloak. Same Converse sneakers. But something was off. He was running weird. Head bobbing too high. Gait just a little too wide.

"John!" Alix gasped, her chest heaving as he burst through the door at the end of the hallway.

58 People's Choice Literature

When she crashed into the door behind him, she could hear his heavy footsteps pounding down the stairs. Heart racing, she sprinted after him, past exposed pipes and rough cinderblock walls. Taking the stairs two at a time, shoes squeaking at each landing, she was gaining on him. But when she hit the ground floor, it all went wrong. Her left ankle bent right, and her knee went down. Gasping for breath, she struggled to pick herself up as she watched him slip into Presentation Room B.

Alix stumbled after him into the pitch-black room, her leg throbbing in pain. Still, she was grateful she hadn't done more damage. She extended her hands, brushing the smooth surface of a wall as her eyes adjusted to the darkness. Suddenly a shaft of light shot across the room, ending in a stock image of a cat.

Alix hurried down the back wall, panting as she desperately scanned the sea of cloaked bodies for any sign of her brother. Suddenly Wylde's Sergeant Peppery voice came over the loudspeaker.

"Now, what you see here is not just a cat," he said, "but the first piece of a brilliant puzzle devised by the physicist Erwin Schrödinger a century ago."

Alix squinted, trying to avoid the screen, whose afterimage had already stamped out her vision with a cat-like ghost.

"Let's imagine for a minute that our cat is in this box," Wylde continued as the screen cut to an image of a high-tech cube. "And let's say inside this box is a poison with a 50% chance of killing our beloved cat. Sorry, cat lovers . . ."

The crowd chuckled.

"Now," Wylde explained. "Schrödinger asks: before we open the box and see for ourselves, is our cat friend alive or dead?"

A question mark flashed on the screen as Alix reached the far wall.

"His answer?" Wylde posited. "That until we open the box, until we see it for ourselves, the cat is both dead and alive at the same time."

Alix shook her head and thought of how dead-and-not-alive John is gonna be when she gets her hands on him . . .

"Schrödinger called this phenomenon 'superposition.' "

Just then Alix spotted a cloaked man crouching near the end of the walkway, shuffling toward the EXIT sign.

"Bingo!" Wylde called out.

Alix crouched low, quickly gaining on the person in front of her.

"And this, my friends," Wylde continued with bravado, "is how life works on the atomic leve—"

Suddenly the door burst open, shocking the room with light. Alix hustled forward as commotion swept through the crowd.

Outside, rain was now falling. She found the man not far ahead, sprinting through the parking lot past cars, leaping over puddles. Alix limped as fast as she could, but he was too fast, too agile . . . until he slipped on the wet grass and fell out of view.

Alix raced forward as he and his soiled cloak scrambled back to standing. He tried to run but slipped and fell again.

"Wait!" Alix cried.

The man spun around, and for the first time she saw his face.

Her heart stopped. Here was the same haircut as John. The same mole. The same color cloak. But this was not John. There was no doubt.

She stood still, her chest heaving, trying to catch her breath.

"Where's John?" Alix spat.

The man looked at her in horror. Just as he was about to speak, out of nowhere a Ford Fusion screeched through the parking lot and pulled up right beside him. Without hesitation, the man jumped in. Alix ran to the car, smacking the door and tugging the handle, but it was locked. All she could do was watch helplessly as the Ford Fusion sped away.

Alix stood there in the empty parking lot, drenched and defeated. Her stomach sunk as it started to hit her: *If that wasn't John, then where the heck is my brother?!?* She turned back to the building to find—no mistaking this time—someone gazing down at her from that open window. Alix strained to make out its face, but the form slid away.

CHAPTER TWELVE

FBI Executive Assistant Director Michael Emerson had faced many a tragedy in his time as the head of the FBI's Information and Technology branch, but this one really took the wedding cake. He stood there in his crisp black suit high above the crashing waves, scanning the shattered car parts as they bobbed and scraped the rocks. *What a shame*, he thought, rubbing his hand through the white cowlick poking up through his otherwise immaculate, black hair. *What a damn shame.*

He watched anxiously as the LA Fire Department's aquatic rescue team descended into the waves from the AgustaWestland AW139, searching for any survivors. The director knew it was just a matter of time before they found Kevin Arnold's remains. If he'd survived, they'd have found him by now.

Emerson sighed, making his way back to the crowds, pushing through the scores of investigators taking notes and officers trying to keep the news crews at bay. But just as he reached the yellow police tape, a large, treelike man emerged from the crowd, flashing a badge with those three letters he knew all too well: F. B. I. As the man approached, his features came into view. Emerson wouldn't have been surprised to learn this man had been the star linebacker for some Big Ten school. He was the spitting image of football. All muscle, all brawn. All American. His brow was rock hard, his lips thin and framed by a jawline chiseled from granite. The only thing that broke this rigid façade were the man's eyes, which were soft and kind.

"Director Emerson?" the quarterback called out.

"In the flesh," the director replied, sizing him up. Emerson wasn't surprised that this burly man knew him—he had been nominated for his new role by the president himself. Anyone with a badge knew his name.

"The name's Stone. Jason Stone," the man said, extending his hand. "I'm with the Los Angeles field office."

Director Emerson nodded and shook his hand. "I'm surprised to see you here, Agent Stone. Seems like a pretty simple case, mechanical failure or whatnot."

"Seems I could say the same about you," Stone chuckled with the rumble of a diesel engine. "What's someone of your stature doing outside of D.C.?"

The director sighed. "Arnold was a friend . . . *is* a friend." He looked down at the tire tracks that had torn through the brush. "We'd had dinner plans tonight."

Stone nodded in affirmation. "I'm sorry, sir. He was . . . *is* a great man."

"That he is," said Director Emerson, giving Stone a pat on his muscular back. "That he is." Then he turned to the agent. "So, what can I do for you?"

"Well," said Stone, "I'm known around here as the guy who takes on certain incidents that are . . . how shall I say . . . out of the ordinary."

Director Emerson's eyes perked up.

"And this one fits that category like a bloody glove."

"Out of the ordinary?" the director asked.

"Maybe we should take this conversation somewhere more private," Stone suggested, eyeing the crowd.

Director Emerson nodded to a small clearing, and Stone nodded back. The two men sauntered over like two bulls, shoulders hunched, heads down. Two bulls and yet they couldn't be more different. Not only did Stone tower over Emerson, he came from a world far from the marbled halls of D.C.

Jason Stone. Born and raised in Queens, New York, to a no-nonsense police officer and a patient elementary school teacher. Always the good student, always the good citizen, he went straight from high school into the police force. He quickly climbed through the ranks, earning every accolade possible—Medal of Honor, Medal of Valor—before being poached by the FBI.

Now, if Stone was a good cop, he was an even better agent. It didn't take long before he became the guy people called when things fell apart. Not only did he catch the Times Square sniper before he could kill again, Stone singlehandedly busted the largest drug ring on the East Coast. He was a good man who made a lot of bad men dead.

What was he doing here in not-so-sunny California, so far from home? Well, loss can take a real toll on a man, no matter how strong. Stone and his high school sweetheart had gotten married right after graduation.

62 *People's Choice Literature*

They had a dog. They had plans to start a family. They were right on the cusp of the American dream. Until tragedy struck.

Not long after Stone's infamous drug bust, a member of the Rosselli family found the detective's address and started staking the place out while he was at work. Then one morning, just as Stone's wife stepped out to get some groceries, she reached the street and walked right into a Rosselli bullet.

To say this broke Stone was an understatement. He left the FBI, took a job as a security consultant, and began drinking heavily, with his friends finding him passed out in front of his building on more than a few occasions. The only thing that could lift his spirits was a visit from his father.

That day, Stone was sitting on his couch, a bottle of whiskey in one hand, a handgun in the other. He'd decided to end it all. That's when his father walked through the door. He pulled the gun free and then sat down beside his son. He didn't say a word. He just sat there. The two of them silent, breathing, listening to the clock tick, the ceiling fan twirl. Finally, his father pulled a small wooden box from his pocket. He opened it and revealed a badge sporting those three fateful letters: F B I. He handed it to his son and looked him straight in the eyes. "We need you," his father said. "*The people* need you." He gave his son a pat on the shoulder and left. Staring at his sorry face in the reflection of that badge, Stone knew that if he was going to live, he had to leave New York. He had to get a fresh start.

A month later, he found himself stationed in the City of Angels and had remained there for the better of three years. And now, here he was in Malibu. Talking with the director of the FBI's tech force. Standing there with a body in the water, a mountain of questions, and few answers.

"So, tell me about these 'out-of-the-ordinary' circumstances?" Director Emerson inquired.

Stone furrowed his brow. "I caught wind Kevin Arnold was on the way to CNN when his car took a dip in the deep blue sea. It's not clear what he planned to reveal, but the producer I spoke with said Arnold's news was 'earth-shattering.'"

"Doesn't sound so strange to me," Director Emerson shrugged, brushing his hand through his cowlick. "Kevin regularly appeared on TV."

"What's not normal," Stone said with a deep inhalation, "is I'm not convinced this crash was an accident."

The director gave him an odd look. "What makes you think that?"

Stone let out a heavy sigh. "How long you got?"

CHAPTER THIRTEEN

Atop San Francisco's storied Telegraph Hill, stretching high up into the foggy heavens, Coit Tower watches like a pale sentinel over the world below. For over sixty years, the structure has greeted tourists and locals, standing as a testament to the city's famed beauty. From the top of the tower can be seen the Golden Gate Bridge and the Pacific Ocean. Constructed in 1933 as part of an urban beautification program, the Arts and Crafts-style structure is built of reinforced concrete and exemplifies the WPA projects of the 1930s. On most days, it glows with a golden tint, making it the perfect subject for photographers.

Today, however, Coit Tower was dull and gray. Rain had begun to spit from the sky, and John Finn, who'd forgotten an umbrella, now stood on the observation deck with only a hoodie and wig for protection. He shivered as he gazed out across the bay, but it wasn't from the cold. His eyes were fixed on the dark form poking out of the steely water: D. J. Wylde's Commune. He'd visited the island as a child when it was still Alcatraz and hadn't thought much of it—just another boring family trip. Now beholding it with the knowledge of what he was about to do, he swallowed. Hard.

John had done exactly what they'd asked. He'd copied the documents and burned the originals. He'd flown to San Francisco and taken a train to Union Station. Then he zigged from Union Square up to Grace Cathedral, zagged down to Chinatown, and zigged up through North Beach, finally zagging up to this historic landmark. And there he stood 210 feet in the air, awaiting the handoff and his promised reward.

"Nice view, eh?" said a bassy voice from behind.

John turned to find a dark man in green sunglasses and a fedora. He was tall and thin, with a scar cutting across his cheek like lightning.

"Are you talking to me?" John asked.

The man in green pushed his glasses down to the tip of his nose and grumbled, "Who else would I be talking to?" His eyes were a sharp yellow. Clearly contacts.

64　*People's Choice Literature*

John scanned the empty observation area. He could have sworn there had been people there not a minute before.

"You got the drive?" the man demanded.

John hesitated. "Where's the payment?"

The man chuckled, pulling a briefcase from his trench coat. "This should be plenty to your liking."

John took the case and handed him the USB. The man studied it for a moment before stuffing it in his breast pocket.

"OK, kiddo," he said with a smirk. "There's a car waiting for you downstairs."

And with that he walked away.

John stood there alone at the edge of the empty and very wet observation deck. He knelt, cracked open the briefcase, and gulped when he saw the bundles and bundles of cash. Then he shut the briefcase and made his way downstairs.

Back outside, a black Ford Fusion was waiting for him. *Just like back in LA*, he thought. Stepping in, his soaked self was relieved to find the vehicle well heated and a clean, folded towel waiting by his side.

"We thought you might need that," said the electronic voice.

"Thanks," said John, wiping himself down.

The voice gave him a moment to dry off before starting again. "Buckle up, please."

John did just that, studying the briefcase that had just changed his life forever. *Goodness*, he thought. *This solves everything.* He couldn't wait to tell his family that none of them would ever have to work again. That it was all going to be OK. No more debt. No more mortgage. No worries. It felt like a fairy tale. Something that happens to other people. But it was *real*.

Being a novelist at heart, John worked day jobs to support his writing. He'd always dreamed of selling a book with a big advance so he could fully dedicate himself to his craft. Now he'd have all the time in the world to finish his novel. He could write thirty more. Heck, he could write three hundred! He stared out as the rainy city streets passed by, but they couldn't get him down. Nothing could do that now. This was the start of something new. Something glorious.

He sat there and sighed, feeling like he could actually breathe for the first time in weeks. Ever since he'd found that document and contacted the FBI, ever since he'd started this absurd trek through San Francisco, his heart had been a ragged drum, thrumming with anxiety and crushing doubt. But now he could relax. He was free.

John sat back and smiled. It didn't take long for the car's heat and his exhaustion to blend into a warm cocktail of foggy bliss. His eyes felt heavy. His limbs went lax. He yawned. The last thing he saw before drifting off to sleep was the iconic arches of the Golden Gate poking through the fog.

The sight instantly jolted him awake.

"Hey, where are you going?" he exclaimed. "The airport is south. Why are we driving west?"

This time the voice did not respond.

"*Hey!*" John repeated. "What are you doing?"

Still nothing.

"Hello?"

John searched for a help button on the dashboard but found nothing. He didn't have his cell phone, because that was part of the deal: "Can't have you tracked," his contact had said. John opened the center console looking for a phone that someone else might have left, but it was empty. He crawled up to the passenger seat and checked the glove compartment. Nothing.

When the Ford Fusion reached a red light, he tried the handle, but the door wouldn't budge. Then he lunged to the driver's side door, but the car sped off, tossing him back against the seat. When he finally reached it, it, too, was locked.

"What the heck is going on!?" he whispered in disbelief.

He hated drawing attention to himself, but he had no choice. John rammed his hand on the steering wheel as hard as he could, but there was no beep. No horn. He hit it again. Nothing. He smacked the dashboard, and finally, the car spoke up.

"Please refrain from vandalism, Mr. Finn."

"*Where are you taking me???*" John screamed.

"I am to deliver you to your destination."

"My destination's the airport!" John yelled back.

"I am to deliver you to your destination," the voice repeated.

John slammed his fists on the dashboard.

"I am to deliver you to your destination."

"If you say that one more time . . ." John threatened, knowing it was pointless. He slumped back in his seat, defeated. There was no way out. Wherever this car was going, he would be too. He was trapped. Like a rat . . .

CHAPTER FOURTEEN

Alix took a deep breath as she studied the nameplate on the door. It wasn't every day one of D. J. Wylde's assistants came asking *him* for something. *But that's not the whole story*, Alix told herself. *A trespasser had dressed up like John. This isn't just some family drama. The safety of the entire company could be at stake . . .*

She steeled herself before giving three soft knocks on the polished oak.

"Come in!" called the mellow voice within.

The room was bigger than she remembered. A corner office with a magnificent view of the Pacific, the walls were draped with tapestries, the floors scattered in a rainbow of beanbag chairs and meditation pillows. Wylde prided himself on "disrupting" the normal corporate office, forgoing a desk and ergonomic chairs in favor of community-minded design.

The man in question was sitting cross-legged, eyes closed in the middle of the room. He cracked open an eye and gestured to Alix to sit. Then he opened the other eye and let out a soft *om* before his mouth curved into a knowing grin.

When Alix sat down across from him, she couldn't help but notice how close she was to Wylde. From here, his eyes shone a blue as brilliant as his cloak, and his face exuded a strange blend of strength and tranquility. As if John Lennon were half asleep while penning the sequel to "Imagine."

"What a beautiful surprise," Wylde hummed. "What brings you here on this fine morning?" Then he noticed the tears lining her eyes. "Oh, no, Alix, what's wrong? Come here."

He held her as she started to weep. "My dear Alix, what's wrong?"

Alix pulled back, wiping her eyes with her sleeve and apologizing. "Ack, I don't know what came over me. I'm sorry."

"No, no," he said, handing her a box of tissues. "This is good. You're safe. You know I always say we should be more emotional at work. The sterility of professionalism has no place here. We're family. Namaste."

"Thank you," she sighed, blowing into the Kleenex.

The Most Wanted Novel   67

"You're always welcome, Alix. Now, please, tell me. What's wrong?"

"It's John," she began.

"John? What about John?"

"Well, I haven't been able to reach him all day," she continued. "I've tried calling him, texting him, emailing. This isn't like him."

Wylde gave an understanding smile. "Maybe he's taking the day off. The waves are quite good today, you know . . ."

Alix shook her head. "I just have a really bad feeling. And also . . . I saw something. Or someone."

Wylde's expression turned serious. "What do you mean 'someone?'"

"Well," Alix cleared her throat. "I was on my way to John's security booth earlier. Trying to see if he was there. I knocked, and at first it sounded like no one was, but then I knocked again and heard someone."

Wylde shifted forward in curiosity.

"So I tried to go in," Alix continued. "You know, I have an executive-level key and all, so I tried to open it, but the person inside was holding the door shut."

Wylde nodded, taking a sip of his Brain Dust kombucha infused with reishi and macha.

"I told him I was coming in and gave him a three-second countdown. You know me, I definitely put in more time in the gym than John, so I was ready for a fight," Alix laughed. "But when I did, this guy, smart on his part, had already moved away. So I went flying flat on my face."

Wylde nearly spilled his drink.

"Oh, I'm fine," she assured him. "Good reaction time, I guess? So, the guy jumps over me, and I chase after. Twisted my ankle in the process."

Wylde's face soured in empathy.

"It's okay now," Alix said, nodding to the ice pack taped to her leg. "So I ran into Presentation Room B where you were giving that science talk."

Wylde chuckled. "We sure did notice a commotion . . ."

"Sorry about that." Alix swallowed. "Well, anyway, I sneak through the room, trying to spot him, and finally do—just as he bursts out the exit. And, again, I chase after him, but then this time, he's not so lucky."

Wylde *hmmed*.

"He slips, 'cause it's raining outside. And this time when I call to him, he finally turns. You won't believe it, D. J., but he looks just like John!"

Wylde's eyebrows perked up.

"But he's not John. There's no way. He's my twin brother. I could tell him from a mile away. So, this guy, he's definitely *not* John. But he's

68   *People's Choice Literature*

wearing John's cloak and some wig to make him look like John. I mean he even had a mole on his chin!"

Wylde's brows furrowed in thought.

"So, then this driverless car shows up and whisks the stranger away before I can find out what the heck's going on . . ."

Alix felt nauseous, overwhelmed by the story she'd just recounted. She wanted to mention the person in the window but didn't want Wylde to think she was completely crazy.

The CEO gave her a serious look and let out a deep yoga sigh. "Well, that sure is troubling, my dear." He leaned over and poured himself another cup of kombucha and continued, "I'm very happy you came to me. I'll inform security immediately."

A glimmer of hope sparked in her eyes. "Thank you so much, D. J."

"No, thank you, dear Alix. I am thankful for you."

Wylde stood up, offering another hug.

Alix wasn't sure if she needed or wanted it, but a friendly invitation from the smartest guy in the world was not something you turned down.

"Thank you, D. J.," she said, standing and accepting his embrace.

After helping Alix out, Wylde closed the door and let out a deep sigh. Then he walked to the window, picked up his phone, and dialed.

The recipient answered in one ring.

"Sir?" said the voice on the other end.

"Frank," said Wylde, gazing out over the Getty Villa's famed courtyard. "We have a problem."

CHAPTER FIFTEEN

The Encinal Bluffs rise high above the crashing waves in western Malibu. Home to some of the most expensive property in the United States, the area is a favorite of movie stars and musicians. The bluffs are also home to groves of oak and stunning, photo-worthy views.

A short walk in from one of these views lay Kevin Arnold's home, a modest bungalow in comparison to the McMansions surrounding it. As Jason Stone approached the house, he was immediately taken aback by its simplicity. *The place is tiiiiny.* Given Arnold's status and the location, Stone had expected to find at least five bedrooms. But here was no mansion, no pool. There wasn't even a view of the sea. Just trees and bushes surrounding what you might call a cottage.

Stone approached the officer on duty and flashed his badge.

The officer nodded. "They're expecting you, Agent Stone."

Stone stepped in to find the usual crime-scene personnel milling around. A forensics tech dusting for prints, another snapping photos. Near the kitchen a female agent was hunched over, taking notes. When she saw Stone approach, her eyes lit up with recognition.

"Agent Stone!" she called out. "Director Emerson told me you were coming."

Stone nodded and shook her hand.

"Word has it you're claiming foul play," she said. "You'll be hard pressed to find anything here to help in your case. These guys combed the whole house, and it's more boring in here than a Proust novel."

Stone chuckled. "Good thing I didn't come for story time."

She laughed back.

"Mind directing me to Arnold's office?" he asked.

"Right through there." She pointed to the door at the end of the room.

The office was darker than the living room—and sparser. A modest wooden desk, an office chair, a floor plant, and a small bookshelf. The walls sported photographs of Arnold with various political big wigs:

70 *People's Choice Literature*

Arnold at a black-tie dinner with the secretary general of the United Nations. Arnold shaking hands with the president of the United States. One paired the twig-like Arnold with the bulk of Arnold Schwarzenegger. Stone smirked at the Terminator lifting Kevin Arnold's string-bean of an arm in a sign of prize-fighter glory.

When Stone turned to the bookshelf, he discovered a selection as unsurprising as the photographs. Mostly books on political philosophy and history. There were a few novels, too. The usual suspects: Dan Brown, David Baldacci, Robert Ludlum. Stone pulled out a paperback wedged between a Danielle Steel and a Dean Koontz: *In the Fast Lane: The Roadmap for Success*. He turned it over and read the back.

> Kevin Arnold has led a life that is the envy of millions. War hero. Two-time mayor of Los Angeles. Likely future president of the United States. His triumphs are not a result of luck or blind faith but the product of a lifetime of service and perseverance. Kevin holds the secrets to success and is now prepared to share them with the world.

Stone set the book down, his mind drifting back to when it was first released. He and his wife had just moved into their apartment in Forest Hills, and it felt like the beginning of not just a new chapter but a new life. Stone remembered spotting Arnold's book in a window, catching its subtitle, *The Roadmap for Success*, and thinking that was the last thing a guy like him needed. That he had it all. The love of his life. A beautiful one-bedroom. A dog. Talk of raising a family. *"Roadmap to success?"* he'd thought. *I could write the darn thing myself.* Of course, he'd soon learn that once you've made it, "it" doesn't always stick around. Not a week later his wife went out for groceries and met a mobster's bullet.

Stone snapped out of it, trying to bury the thought, refocusing on his mission: to enter into the mindset of Kevin Arnold. To try to see the world through his eyes. To get even the slightest inkling of what he might have been thinking, whom he might have talked to in the hours and days leading up to his untimely demise. Sure, they'd have his phone records within the hour, and it was only a matter of time until they cracked his laptop, but for Stone, nothing compared to visiting the injured party's personal space.

Arnold's desk sat facing the window. It was a simple, modern design that suggested a man who valued functionality over all else. Stone went

and opened the top drawer. Just pencils, pens, and Post-it notes. A stapler awaiting a refill. He opened the bottom drawer. Printer paper. Nothing else. No files, no personal items. Maybe the guy who had it all understood something the rest of us failed to grasp—that material objects pale in comparison to the greater things in life. Or maybe Arnold had cleaned shop, knowing danger was just around the corner . . .

Stone sat at the desk, his eyes tracing the same view Arnold had gazed upon day in and out. In keeping with the rest of the place, it was humble to a fault. No hot tub or manicured hedges. Just a lawn in need of mowing running up to a tangle of trees.

Help me here, Arnold, Stone thought. *I'm on your team. Help me see what you saw* . . .

He turned from the window and scanned the room for something. Anything. Something that would trigger an idea, a thought, a vision that could lead to a clue. A clue that would guide him to the truth behind Arnold's untimely death. But there was nothing. Just a simple, unremarkable office. Defeated, Stone bent over and let out a long sigh when he noticed something shiny from the corner of his eyes. In a trashcan, to the right of the desk, was the edge of a picture frame.

Stone bent over and picked it up. Cradling it in both hands, his eyes went wide. It was a photograph of a young Kevin Arnold with an equally young D. J. Wylde, arms around each other, faces beaming atop some mountain. Stone flipped the picture frame over to discover a note on the back. When he read the words, his eyes ballooned.

CHAPTER SIXTEEN

John Finn was lost, replaying the Ford Fusion fiasco in his head like a bad rerun. The hopeless ride to the unmarked warehouse near the Golden Gate Bridge. The bag thrown over his head. Then the final, blind drive over winding hills before descending into this godforsaken place.

The room was small. A bare, concrete cube, it had the look of a utility closet, with no windows and no furniture. Just a locked, impenetrable door. As John sat on the cold cement, his sole entertainment was the water dripping from a pipe above, falling with a regular thud, taunting him, cynically keeping time for the nothing to come . . .

If this wasn't bleak enough, his captors had taken his punishment to a whole new level. Upon being unceremoniously dumped by the Ford Fusion, a heavy collar was strapped around his neck. The hands that did the strapping were rough and unforgiving. And the voice that accompanied them was even worse. "I wouldn't try to take this off if I were you," it sneered. The only minor reprieve given was when they removed the bag inside his cell.

John had sat on that cold floor, trapped by both the collar and the damp chill in the air for God knows how long. With no sunlight and no activity, it was hard to tell. Although he couldn't see them, he sensed whoever had brought him here was watching his every move . . .

"Where am I?" he finally whispered aloud.

No response.

"Who are you?" he screamed. "*Why are you doing this to me?*"

Nothing.

John closed his eyes and tried to relax. *We gotta find a way out. You can do it. You've read plenty of thrillers. There must be a way . . .*

With weak determination, he picked himself up and approached the door for the hundredth time, jiggling the handle. Nothing.

Defeated, he slumped back down to the cold, hard floor and threw his head in his hands. *Gosh darnit!!!* The exhaustion and hunger were starting

The Most Wanted Novel   73

to take their toll on him. How long had he been trapped in this hell hole? And how much longer could he survive without food and water?

"Please," he whimpered. "Please just let me go."

How had it come to this? he asked himself. He recalled that moment a week ago when he stumbled upon those papers that would change everything. The diagrams. The damning revelations. He remembered going home that night and asking Reddit for help. He could almost feel the adrenaline rush he'd gotten the following morning when the FBI phoned him in response to his post. He was shocked that they'd found him, having used an anonymous IP address to hide his identity. But connecting with the FBI meant he'd found a secure way to deliver this document to the authorities . . . while obtaining a hefty reward in the process. Enough money to quit his mundane job and write full time—even pay off family debt in the process. But now he didn't know what to think. Was he being held for conspiracy? *Was this even the FBI!?* He hadn't been arrested, and he hadn't been read his rights. And this was surely no jail cell. It was right out of one of those *Saw* movies. It was all so wrong.

John's mind was racing. He was trapped, his heart hammering his chest, his stomach curdling, groaning. He removed his glasses, trying to rub the fatigue from his eyes, when, suddenly, like a beacon of hope in a booming sea, an idea struck him.

How hadn't I thought of it before?

With renewed vigor, he scrambled to the door and studied the keyhole. *Yes!* he thought. *It's right out of* Mission Impossible*, but it might just work.*

John raised his glasses and studied the optical architecture before him—two lenses, two metallic arms that held the lenses to his ears. He recalled his eye doctor calling these arms "temples." *Fitting*, he thought as he abruptly snapped the glasses at the hinges and separated the broken bits.

With determined grip, he fiercely bent one of the thin metal temples back and forth until it finally snapped in half. But that was the easy part. Inhaling deeply, he rammed the broken metallic tip into the unforgiving cement floor, using all his strength to mold it into a tiny hook.

Then John eyed the rusty keyhole and tried to remember the YouTube video he'd watched months prior when he was locked out of their apartment. He retrieved the unbroken temple and shoved the plastic tip firmly into the keyhole, turning it hard to the left. Then he took the tiny hook he'd sculpted and pushed it into the keyhole just below the plastic, digging in as far as possible, brushing it up against the creaky locking mechanism in an attempt to catch each rusted pin and slide it into place.

74 *People's Choice Literature*

After brushing back and forth a few times, he was already sweating. He felt two pins line up, tried for a third, but then the temple slipped out of his clammy hand.

He wiped his hands on his pants, took a deep breath, and tried again. This time, he got one pin, two, then three and even four. He could feel his hands starting to clam up again but pushed on. He hit the fifth pin, and then the sixth. More sweat. His heart leapt. *One more*, he thought. *Just one more to go.*

With bated breath, John slowly pulled the temple toward him one last centimeter until he heard that fateful, final click.

The lock gave way. The hinge creaked.

John sat back in awe and disbelief, finally able to draw a breath. Now, for the first time that day, John was the one in control . . .

CHAPTER SEVENTEEN

John Finn grabbed his warped bifocals and raised them to his eyes like makeshift opera glasses. His heart thundered as he twisted the door handle, praying it would creak no further. When it didn't, he gave a silent sigh of relief, pushing it wider—just enough to poke his head out.

The dimly lit corridor stretched before him, just as desolate as his cell. Discovering no people and no cameras, he tiptoed down the hall with catlike stealth. When he reached a set of doors, he prayed once more for a silent exit. But when he turned the handle, it snapped, the lock clicking upon release.

He froze. Listened for movement on the other side. Nothing. *Did they really just abandon me here?* Stepping through the threshold, he peered out into a vast warehouse, empty save for pyramids of boxes and towers of crates. Behind the boxes, past the forklift and other dim detritus, he spotted the Ford Fusion that had brought him here.

John slipped through the door and crept across the dark room, past the hulking crates and sleeping machinery. Reaching the Ford Fusion, he swallowed before pulling at the driver's side door and frantically searching for the key. Ignition? No luck. Glove compartment? Empty. Center console? Nope. He looked under the seats, but found only wires.

Gah! he thought. *Would a driverless car even need keys?*

He searched the back seat and found his bag right where he'd left it.

Thank goodness, he thought. No briefcase, though. No fortune. *"So Goodbye Yellow Brick Road . . ."*

In a swift maneuver, John grabbed the bag and slipped out of the Ford Fusion. Leaning against the polished chrome, he unzipped the backpack and removed his laptop, praying this void of a warehouse would have Wi-Fi. Whoever kidnapped him had smartly tricked him into leaving his phone in Los Angeles "for security purposes," so he was flat out of luck on that front.

Once he logged into his computer, he went straight for the Wi-Fi, crossing his clammy fingers in the hopes that anything would pop up. When one did—a sequence of meaningless numbers—he instantly clicked it, and to his amazement, there was no password. He was in.

Quickly navigating to his email, he started writing to Alix when an electronic voice came from above.

"I don't think so, Mr. Finn."

Looking up, John found a drone diving toward him. But he was fast, ducking and rolling away, narrowly avoiding the sharp blades that tore through his backpack and sent his laptop spinning out of reach.

"Nooooooooooo!" John cried.

He grabbed the computer and sprinted away through the corridors of boxes and heavy machinery. The whir of the drone was near, so he cut left between two forklifts, then right around some boxes. Then he caught sight of the stairs and slid under them.

As he crouched in hiding, John's heart pounded like a hammer. He swallowed, opening his laptop, and thanked the heavens it still worked. But when he went to type, the electronic voice returned.

"Close the laptop and return to your cell immediately, Mr. Finn."

John peered out from his hiding spot but found no sign of the machine apart from its incessant whir. So he returned to typing until the voice spoke up once more.

"If you type another word or hit send," it grated, "that collar around your neck will self-destruct."

John touched the metal collar, now aware of its true purpose: insurance.

"Mr. Finn?" The voice grew impatient. "In layman's terms 'self-destruct' means explode."

John's throat tightened as he stared at the screen one last time. His eyes focused on Alix's email address. Then the easily accessible SEND button. He took a deep breath before slowly closing the laptop.

"Very good, Mr. Finn," the drone droned. "Now come out."

The captive obeyed.

"And put down the laptop."

John swallowed. He couldn't let them erase that email—it was his only glimmer of hope. The best chance he now had was for Alix somehow to retrieve it from his Drafts folder. It would take a miracle, but what could he do?

"The laptop, Mr. Finn."

John looked longingly at the computer like an old friend before lifting it high and hurling it to the floor. The hardware cracked in half, throwing metal and silicon in all directions.

"Clever," said the drone. "Now back to your room."

As John trudged back in defeat, he thought of Alix and prayed she was OK, that she'd know what to do. At this point, it was all he had.

CHAPTER EIGHTEEN

Hundreds of miles south, Alix was back at her desk at the Getty Villa struggling to focus. She'd tried to update the catering order for tomorrow's Quanta launch but could barely read the menu. She messaged a few coworkers, but it was all fluff to make it look like working. She just couldn't stop thinking about John. *Had D. J. started to investigate the security breach? Had they found anything? And where the heck is my twin brother!??*

Alix grabbed her phone, scrolling through the dozens of messages she'd sent him that day. The last text from him was yesterday afternoon, an innocent question about carpooling to Genera's LACMA event.

She called John again. Voicemail. She tried once more. Nothing. Just as she was about to redial, a knock came at the door and a head poked through, standing a foot taller than any who'd entered that door before.

When the owner of that cranium stepped into the room, Alix was in awe. She'd never encountered such a man before. His arms were like tree trunks. His chest bulged through his suit. She was sure he played football. The man *was* football. And the strangest thing about him was that for all his chiseled features, for all his brawn and strength, his face was kind and inviting, his eyes soft as pillows.

Alix swallowed. "H-how can I help you?"

The man turned to her and did a double take. Alix was confused. *Is there something in my teeth?*

"Oh, sorry, miss. I was told this is D. J. Wylde's office?"

"Oh, yes. You're right. That's right," she stammered. "We're his assistants."

The burly man's gaze turned to the row of desks where the six other members of the Rainbow Seven banged away on their keyboards.

"Complex guy," the man smirked, "needing a whole squadron by his side and all."

But Alix didn't hear him. She was too distracted by the mammoth biceps straining against his jacket.

He noticed her hesitancy.

"Sorry," he said. "The name's Stone. Jason Stone."

Alix swallowed again. Her mind drifted to realms unknown, a grassy bluff by the sea, pink clouds kissing the horizon, the breeze lifting the leaves, and this mammoth of a man holding her close in a tender embrace . . .

Stone pulled out his badge. "I'm with the FBI. I believe Mr. Wylde is expecting me?"

FBI? The three letters jolted her from her romance-novel fantasia to the cold, hard present. *Maybe D. J. took my concerns seriously. Maybe he didn't think I was crazy about the body double after all . . .*

Alix tried to keep it together for the Greek god before her.

"Mr. Wylde should be in there," she gestured awkwardly down the room. "You can just knock away."

"Thanks," he said, eyeing her speculatively.

Alix nodded and watched as the agent strode past the desks with an assuredness that made her melt. Then he disappeared into Wylde's office.

She settled back into her chair. *Gosh, I just know my face is beet red*, she thought. That man was so hot. His mere presence radiated heat.

Then her phone buzzed. Her heart leapt in anticipation, but when she looked down, it was just her parents asking how the Quanta launch was going. They were on their first vacation in years, so she had yet to tell them about John. Didn't want to distract them. And of course, he could just be taking the day off, like D. J. said. John had always been a go-it-your-own-way kind of guy. Heck, he could've just lost his phone . . .

I'll text them later, she thought.

Then she stared blankly at the computer screen, processing the bungle of emotions. *First John goes missing and now the FBI is involved? And the FBI is gorgeous?? How much weirder can this day get?*

CHAPTER NINETEEN

"As I told you over the phone, Mr. Stain, is it?"

"Stone."

"Ah, right," said D. J. Wylde, handing the agent a cup of Patagonian glacier water. "As I already said, I haven't talked with Kevin Arnold in months."

Stone thanked him for the drink and continued: "And what was the nature of your last communication?"

Wylde paused in thought. "It must have been some fundraiser. You know, that's most of what politicians do . . ."

"Did you talk about money often?" Stone asked.

Wylde laughed. "I'm the CEO of one of the biggest companies in the world. Unfortunately, money is something I deal with every day."

As Wylde went on about the ins and outs of corporate tech life, Stone sat back in his beanbag chair and studied the tycoon. The refrain "spitting image of John Lennon" was perhaps too accurate. He wouldn't have been surprised if Wylde whipped out a piano and started serenading him with "Across the Universe." The eclectic decor only heightened this impression. Tapestries from India and Bangladesh. A black-light poster of Pink Floyd's *Dark Side of the Moon* signed "to D. J." But then there were the anomalies. The *Wall Street Journal* spread across his desk. The framed photograph of Wylde golfing with Rupert Murdoch. The juxtaposition of hippie art and high finance was striking. And the more Stone studied Wylde, the more he felt there was something behind those friendly eyes he couldn't put his finger on.

Stone continued. "Arnold was an early financier of Genera, correct?"

"Yes, Mr. Stone. You can find this information easily on Wikipedia. We've been friends since college. A match made in tech heaven, you might say."

"You went to Harvard together." Stone nodded.

80

"Dorm mates first semester," Wylde nodded back. "One of those infamous Harvardian pairs. Zuckerberg and Moskovitz. Al Gore and Tommy Lee Jones."

"Al Gore and Tommy Lee Jones?"

"They were roommates freshman year," Wylde affirmed. "Still friends to this day."

Stone appreciated the factoid—he'd always liked Tommy Lee Jones, particularly in *The Fugitive*—but wanted to get back on track. "So, Kevin Arnold and you meet in college. He invests in Genera when it's still in the Silicon Valley startup rat race, and then what?"

"I'm not sure what you mean."

"What's been his role in the company?" Stone asked. "I gather early investors don't just fade away. There must be more to Arnold's involvement than the initial investment."

"Mr. Stone, I'm not sure what you're driving at. Kevin Arnold was one of my oldest and dearest friends. We basically grew up together. I'm happy to help, but if we're going on a trip down memory lane, I suggest you reference this little thing called the internet."

Stone was displeased. "Pardon the intrusion, Mr. Wylde, but it's not every day a high-profile politician dies en route to a big CNN interview."

D. J. Wylde seemed visibly shaken by the mention of Arnold's death. "I have much respect for your work, Mr. Stone. And I wish you the best in this investigation. Now if you don't mind, it's been a traumatic day, and I still have a mountain of work in front of me. A security breach this morning. One of my assistants' brothers just disappeared."

Stone's eyebrow perked up.

"We could use an FBI of our own here at Genera . . ."

Stone smirked and rose from the beanbag chair. "Thank you for taking the time, sir."

The two men shook hands and walked to the door.

"Oh," Stone said as he reached the threshold. "Just wanted to say, Mr. Wylde, I'm sorry for your loss. Kevin Arnold was a great man."

Wylde's mouth curved into a sad smile. "He was a gem. A true gem."

As Stone walked past Wylde's assistants, he noticed the blonde from earlier looking glum at her desk. Stone had been taken aback when he first saw her. Those glowing eyes, that hair, the way she held herself in her

82   *People's Choice Literature*

slim yet strong frame. Now she was sitting at her desk with a troubled expression, staring off into the distance.

"Everything OK?" he asked.

The young woman snapped out of her daydream and looked up at Stone.

"Oh, I'm sorry. I must have spaced out."

"I can see that," he smiled. "I don't want to intrude, but you seemed upset."

Alix forced a smile and shook her head. "No, I'm fine. Just thinking..."

Stone nodded, unsure of what to say. He wasn't usually one to strike up a conversation with a stranger, but he also knew that there was something about her. He had to talk to her. So he went with the first thing that came to mind.

"Crummy weather isn't it?" he said, nodding to the rainy skyline through the glass.

Alix let out a polite laugh. "And they say it's always sunny in Santa Monica . . ."

Her smile didn't quite reach her eyes, and Stone could sense the pain behind them. Talking about the weather surely wouldn't fix that, so he steered the conversation to something more substantial.

"Hey," said Stone, "Mr. Wylde mentioned something about one of his assistant's family members going missing. Do you know anything about that?"

The woman's eyes lit up. "John! I haven't seen him since last night."

"What's his name?"

"John. John Finn."

"And he's your brother?" he asked, eyeing her speculatively.

Alix nodded anxiously. "Same last name."

"You know that's a common occurrence among siblings, right?" Stone laughed.

Alix smiled, realizing her foolishness. "Sorry, it's been a long morning..."

He gave an empathetic smile. "I can only imagine."

Stone tried to picture what she'd gone through. What it would be like to have a sibling go missing. He knew well what it was like to lose a spouse, having lost his wife to a maniac mobster years before. He looked at this woman and felt for her, wanting to help.

"Look," said Stone, "my advice is to call the local police and report it. It's unfortunately not in my jurisdiction. They can help guide you through this."

The woman looked disappointed.

Stone swallowed, realizing that her face had the power to destroy him. Then he fumbled through his coat pocket.

"Oh, uh, also," he stammered. "Here's my card."

He removed the crème cardstock and placed it on her desk.

"Just in case," he said. "You never know what might come up."

She accepted the card and gave a look that spoke of hope and joyful speculation.

"Thank you," she said.

"Of course." He didn't know what else to say, standing there awkwardly. He turned to leave but hesitated.

"I just realized," he said. "I didn't get your name."

"It's Alix," she smiled. "Alix Finn."

Stone smirked. "Sister of John Finn—same last name, right?"

She let out a genuine laugh. "You got it."

CHAPTER TWENTY

After Jason Stone left, Alix sat there transfixed. *Is it me or did he just hit on me? Or was he just being nice? He didn't have to stop there and talk, and he definitely didn't have to offer to help. There must be something more there,* she thought.

But then memories of failed relationships flooded her mind. After Timmy, she took a years-long break from love, but of course it found its way back. There was that nice guy in sociology class, but they just didn't click. Another guy at Genera seemed promising, but he was transferred to Sweden before things could get serious. Alix was out of practice, but she could not deny the draw of this lumberjack of a man. She hadn't felt this way in years. But amid these musings, she knew there were more pressing matters at hand. Her twin brother John was still missing, and an expert—an Adonis of an FBI agent—had just told her what to do.

Alix took his advice and called the police. After being transferred from one department to another, she finally filed a missing persons report. The officer on the other end reassured her they'd do everything in their power to find her brother. "The good thing," he said, "is these things often get resolved pretty quickly." But Alix could not shake her apprehension.

She spent much of the rest of the day desperately trying to work, while keeping an eye on her phone, hoping for something, anything from John. There was also that agent on her mind. Alix kept trying to wrap her head around whether giving her his card had been a professional courtesy or a subtle invitation. The way he'd eyed her sure seemed suggestive, but could it all have just been in her head? *Surely a man like that was married with three kids, white picket fence, 401k. The whole nine yards. Right? Right??*

As she drove home that evening in her Honda Accord, rain pummeling the windshield, it was thinking of Detective Stone that kept her hopes up. In the least, she had an expert in her corner. At best she'd just got the number of an incredibly attractive man. But she couldn't help

reflecting on the outrageous day she'd had. Her missing brother. Chasing her brother's body double through the Getty Villa. The hours and hours with no word from John. Something was deeply wrong. Alix was slightly reassured when, just before leaving for the day, Wylde mentioned that he and the LAPD were working to track down the trespasser who'd posed as John. Wylde said they even had a few leads. That this lookalike's fingerprints were all over John's keyboard. "We're not dealing with a professional here," Wylde had said with a grin. "We'll find him."

When she got home, Alix opened the door to see her bulldog Rocky heatedly panting and wagging his rump in glee. She knelt down to embrace him.

"Good boy," she said.

She kissed him on the side of his face, and he licked her hand before wobbling into her leg.

"What a good boy," she repeated.

Alix stood and stepped into the apartment, feeling the urge to call out John's name, but her sense got the better of her. Surely he wouldn't just be vegging out at home, avoiding her calls and texts . . . that would be ludicrous. And yet, after she put down her bag, she couldn't help but peek in John's room. Creaking open his door just to be sure, the room was just as empty as expected.

After taking Rocky out to answer nature's call, Alix fed the panting, ecstatic creature and went straight to the fridge for a beer. John's half-drunken case of Coors Light stared back like a loving friend. She grabbed a can and went to the couch, picking Rocky up and placing him beside her. Then she took a long sip of Coors and sighed.

Alix switched on the television, flipping through episodes of *Family Guy* and *The Big Bang Theory* before landing on *American Pickers,* where Mike Wolfe and Frank Fritz were at it again, scouring the country for hidden treasures. Halfway through the episode, Mike and Frank were in Texas talking with a potential seller of a truly junky car, when Alix noticed something about the seller. He was tall and thick, straight out of a Big Ten football team. He looked almost exactly like Detective Stone.

Peering closer, she knew it couldn't be Stone. This man was too rigid. Too uninviting. She thought about Stone and how his eyes were so thoughtful and caring. How he'd taken the time to make her feel better. Alix had only known him for five minutes but could tell he was a good man. She found herself returning to what he'd said just before he left: "You never know what might come up . . ."

86   *People's Choice Literature*

Repeating that phrase, her mind drifted to a happier place. She imagined the two of them joining forces, fighting against some masked foe, leaping over rooftops, racing through burning buildings. She saw them saving the day before falling in love, walking off into a glowing red sunset hand in hand. Eventually this daydream drifted into actual sleep.

CHAPTER TWENTY-ONE

At 9 p.m., Alix awoke in a daze. Rocky was snoring beside her, and on the TV was some show about spray-tanned real estate agents. She slid away from Rocky and went to the kitchen for food. Tossing some leftovers in the microwave, she sat down at the kitchen table, accompanied only by her worried thoughts.

The apartment felt empty without John. Whatever Alix was up to, whether a late night at work or out dancing, John was always at home writing away. When she'd return, he'd either be typing in his room or on the couch. It didn't matter where: he was writing. Of course, this worried Alix. "Don't you want to make friends?" she'd ask again and again. But the answer was always the same. "My best friends are right here," he'd say, pointing to his novel-in-progress. John simply loved writing—and had done pretty well for himself. He'd published a few things in small literary journals and had even given a handful of readings at local bookstores. Alix was a fan of his work. She enjoyed his flash fiction and couldn't wait to read his novel. But at this rate, it was likely she might never see it before a publisher did, what with John guarding it as tightly as the gold in Fort Knox.

When the microwave beeped, Alix stood up and grabbed the plate. Right on cue, Rocky waddled over, begging for a bite.

"You *had* your dinner," Alix said lovingly.

But he ignored her logic, panting and wiggling in hopes his persistence would break her.

Alix did what she always had done: try her best to ignore that incredibly cute but currently very annoying creature. She grabbed her phone and scrolled through her news feed while chewing. It was more of the usual: "Woman just kidding, she didn't drop her kid off a bridge!" "Man disguised as Trump arrested for public indecency!" "Woman posts picture of her new nose job on Facebook, regrets it immediately!" Etc., etc., etc. Then she saw something that made her heart stop.

"Genera robbery suspect found murdered in his home."

CHAPTER TWENTY-TWO

Alix clicked the article and started to read:

LOS ANGELES—William Moriarty was found dead this afternoon in his Culver City apartment. The son of tech tycoon Richard Moriarty, CEO of gAIa, William Moriarty had been a suspect in an alleged robbery earlier in the day at Genera's Getty Villa headquarters. Police report that Moriarty disguised himself as a Genera employee to infiltrate the company's security system and were attempting an arrest when they found the body.

A spokesperson for Genera sent his condolences to the Moriarty family, but also expressed "great concern" among company leadership over William Moriarty's obvious close connection to gAIa. The spokesperson said this connection was, "Too glaring to ignore. Particularly given the timing, as we are set to launch Quanta tomorrow night." The LA County Sheriff's department offered no comment, noting the sensitivity of the case and the ongoing investigation. Richard Moriarty could not be reached at the time of this writing.

The circumstances involving William Moriarty's death remain murky at present. The tech tycoon's son was found in a scene that one officer described to *LA Next News* as "horrifying." The officer, who wished to remain anonymous, described numerous lacerations across Moriarty's face and hands, with the deepest incisions occurring around the neck. "It looked like he'd been attacked by a windmill or something," the officer said.

This is a developing story and will be updated as more information comes to light.

Alix dropped her phone and stared into space. *What the heck is going on!?* Obviously her brother was the Genera employee they mentioned, the one whom William Moriarty had imitated. *Does this mean that they also think John is caught up in this?* She put her hand to her mouth. *IS HE caught up in all this?* Given the insanity of the past twelve hours, she wouldn't be surprised at this point.

She sat back and let out a guttural groan. *Why is this happening to me? Why is this happening to us? John is my twin, my best friend. We've been through everything together. Childhood, college, now Genera. And now it feels like the eternal thread connecting us has been cut, and there's no telling if or how it'll ever be reconnected.*

Alix looked back at her phone for any sign of hope. She searched for "Moriarty murder" on Google, and fifteen articles popped up. Clicking one, she found the same information she'd read in the first article. Clicking another, same thing. She went to social media to find the most-up-to-the-minute information and quickly regretted it. Already there was speculation about the Genera employee Moriarty had impersonated. She skimmed the gossip and was grateful to learn her brother's name was not yet in the running.

Alix let out a sigh, realizing she needed to get ahead of the rumor mill. If there was any way to clear John's name before it went public, before the media distorted him into oblivion, she had to try. Maybe in his bedroom there was a note or receipt that would tell her something—anything—about what the heck was going on. Without hesitation, she strode past a panting, anxious Rocky and made a beeline for John's room, desperate for a clue.

CHAPTER TWENTY-THREE

The Hollywood Hills loom majestically over central Los Angeles, providing some of the best views in the city. Part of the Santa Monica Mountains, they extend north from Hollywood proper to Mulholland Drive, then east to Griffith Park and the Cahuenga Pass. Home to movie stars and musicians, the hills have served as inspiration for generations of artists and the setting for countless films and television shows including *Sunset Boulevard*, *Rebel Without a Cause*, *The Big Lebowski*, and *Glee*.

Tonight, as FBI Detective Jason Stone turned onto Mulholland Drive, he recalled the scene in *Chinatown* when Jack Nicholson, as Detective Jake Gittes, follows the same path to confront the corrupt businessman Noah Cross, played by John Huston. *Is this my cinematic moment?* he wondered.

As he approached the residence of Richard Moriarty, Stone discovered the security gate already open. He drove past, eyeing the wrought-iron fence's repetitive lattice pattern—more like a spider web than anything else. Entering the estate, Stone scanned the surroundings. The driveway snaked through high hedges—dark spears tall enough to keep out both intruders and curious eyes. After a few hundred feet, the hedges opened to a circular driveway, a manicured lawn, and a sprawling mansion.

Stone studied the building, noticing instantly that there was something off about it. *Is it just me or is that house frowning?* Hovering there in the distance, dark, ominous, and uninviting, was a large, Tudor-style estate with tall, narrow windows. The moonlight gave shape, however obscure, to the jagged façade and the jutting peaks of the gabled roof. From what he could see, the sloping stone and leaning gargoyles, everything pointed to the blood-red door.

Stone parked his Kia Forte near the door and turned to the passenger seat to get his jacket. Turning back to the door, he jumped.

"Schnikes!"

What the frick?

An elderly man's face was almost pressed against the glass, smiling like an ancient statue. Stone jumped. His heart skipped a beat. He looked again and saw the man smiling and waving for Stone to get out. After releasing a ragged breath, Stone opened the door and the man stepped aside.

"Welcome to Chateau Moriarty, Mister Stone," said the British voice from its perma-smile.

"You nearly gave me a heart attack," said Stone.

"My apologies, sir. I didn't mean to startle you."

Stone studied him for a moment. He was shorter than the detective, about five-ten, thin, with deeply wrinkled skin and white hair. Must have been at least eighty. He wore a dark suit with a white shirt and a black tie. In short, he looked like a butler copied and pasted right out of a movie.

"It's all good," said Stone. "Just a bit jumpy tonight, I guess."

"Understandable." The butler held out his hand and gestured toward the horror house. "Mister Moriarty awaits you."

CHAPTER TWENTY-FOUR

Chateau Moriarty was even eerier on the inside. The grand foyer was surprisingly cramped, leading to a dim, wainscoted hallway and a narrow, gothic staircase. Just before these stairs stood a tall table with a golden-headed, many-eyed creature perched atop it.

The sculpture instantly brought Stone back to Thomas Harris's *Red Dragon*, the very novel that had inspired his upgrade from the NYPD to the FBI. *Red Dragon* made the FBI look exciting, new. Of course, it also showed the downsides. The stressors, the dangers. The risks to one's family. Stone winced at the thought, recalling his wife's fateful run-in with the Roselli family, and his heart broke all over again.

The butler cleared his throat, snapping Stone back to the present.

Stone looked up and nodded. "Sorry."

"If you'll follow me, Mister Stone, Richard will see you in his study."

As Stone followed the butler down the long hallway, he noticed the walls covered in a vast array of antique weaponry: a gilded mace, a gleaming samurai sword, dozens of shields from ancient wars. Amid these artifacts, Stone was also drawn to the oil paintings. They were all landscapes, but one in particular caught his attention. Depicting a serene autumn day, it featured a clear blue sky and a tranquil lake nestled in majestic mountains. In the foreground stood George Washington beside several children and a family of deer. The painting was easily as big as a suitcase and inspired a strange sense of calm in the terrible storm of this day . . .

"Right this way, sir," said the butler.

Stone turned to find the elderly man holding the door for him.

"Thank you," Stone nodded, slipping into the study.

When the door closed behind him with a loud thud, he found himself in a lavish, dimly lit library. Bookshelves lined the walls, crammed with leather-bound tomes. A mahogany desk sat in the center, flanked by two plush sofas and a smoking chair. And of course, no study would be complete without a fully stocked bar. At the desk sat Richard Moriarty, CEO

of gAIa and father to the recently deceased robbery suspect. Moriarty looked like he'd just stepped out of the pages of a comic book. Clad in a wide, black suit and purple tie, he exuded an air of power and mystery. If it weren't for his dark hair, Stone would have sworn they based Kingpin from Spider Man on the guy.

"Boy, they don't make 'em like they used to," said Moriarty, clutching his side and wincing in pain.

"Excuse me, sir?"

"G-men. Never seen one like you before. You look like an entire football team. Did you play?" Moriarty grabbed his Tums and hurled three tablets in his mouth.

"No, sir. Just a fan," said Stone, clearly uninterested in small talk.

"Pardon my manners," said Moriarty. "It's just this day. And this goddamned GI stuff is killing me. I swear, I practically breathe Tums."

He gestured for Stone to sit before hobbling over to the smoking chair himself.

"So, how can I help you?"

Stone's expression turned serious. "Well, first I'd like to say how sorry I am for your loss, sir."

Moriarty sunk into the chair. "He was a troubled kid. Always getting into something."

"Had William told you what he was up to this time?"

Moriarty turned away with a low chuckle. "Woo wee. You cut right to the chase. No games, I like that." He shifted in his seat. "No, he didn't. I just told this to the LAPD. Wrote it in a statement with my PR guy. You can write it on my gravestone, for God sakes. William and I had had a falling out. We don't talk."

"Do you mind if I ask about the nature of your falling out?"

Moriarty let out a deep sigh. "Just typical pouty adult child stuff. He wanted something, and I wouldn't give it to him."

The pain exuding from Moriarty's eyes convinced Stone to pivot. He'd leave that question for the interrogation room—if it got to that.

"Did you have any indirect contact with William?" he continued. "Another family member whom you'd speak through? Someone else?"

Moriarty huffed. "I know where you'd going with this, Mister Stun, is it?"

"Stone. Detective Stone."

Moriarty nodded. "Everyone and their stepmother thinks I got my son to break into Genera and mess around with their big Quanta release

94 *People's Choice Literature*

tomorrow. What a joke! Sure, I'd have loved for him to join me at gAIa, but he refused. I had no idea he was sneaking around like this."

Stone studied the billionaire, searching for signs of deceit, but nothing popped up. One thing that was clearer than day, though, was that this line of questioning was getting him nowhere.

"Mister Moriarty," he said, "how long has gAIa been in the rideshare business?"

Moriarty let out a booming laugh, then immediately doubled over in pain. "Twenty years? We practically invented the whole thing." He straightened up, and took a sip of scotch. "What's that got to do with my son?"

"It doesn't," Stone said gravely. "I'm asking because of Kevin Arnold."

Moriarty burst out laughing. He couldn't stop, holding his side in a fit of pain.

Stone studied him firmly.

"You sure have some balls," Moriarty said, grabbing a tissue and blowing his nose. "Here you accuse me of corporate espionage and then suggest I had something to do with the death of Kevin Arnold? What is this, some kind of spy movie?"

"I'm just asking questions, sir. Kevin Arnold was using gAIa's rideshare service when he died. And we have evidence that points to foul play."

"What evidence?" Moriarty asked, eyes narrowing.

"That's classified."

"Well, that's convenient," Moriarty barked.

"What I can say is that we know Arnold stepped into one of your driverless Ford Fusions and then twenty minutes later he was swimming in the Pacific. I'm just the first in a long line of questioners, Mr. Moriarty. You and I both know that the death of such a high-profile figure will in the least send you to D.C. for a House subcommittee hearing . . ."

Moriarty clenched his fists.

"What I need to know," Stone continued, "is what kind of control you have over your automated vehicles. Is it possible that someone could've steered the Ford Fusion from afar?"

"*What?*" Moriarty said wiping his mouth. "Are you asking me if I used a remote control to kill Kevin Arnold? You really should write action movies, Mister Stone."

"I'm asking you to think about it, sir. We all have bad apples in our organizations. It's just a matter of weeding them out," Stone said, leaning forward.

Moriarty growled, "This is slander."

"Sir, I'm just asking you about the security of your product."

Moriarty shook his head. "No. You're not. You're asking me if I run a criminal enterprise. I know what you're getting at. I'm no fool, son. And I refuse to talk a minute more without my lawyer."

"Very well, sir."

Stone stood up and tried to hand Moriarty his business card. But the CEO just stared at him like a viper about to pounce.

"I'll just leave this here," said Stone, placing the card on the coffee table. "If you change your mind, folks say I'm a pretty good conversationalist."

Moriarty forced a smirk.

Stone nodded and walked out of the study, retracing his way down the hall and into the foyer.

"Leaving so soon?" asked the butler from the stairs.

Stone turned around to say goodbye. And as he did, he noticed once more the tall, thin table with the golden-headed beast. He thought again of Thomas Harris's *Red Dragon*—of that fateful moment when Will Graham strolled into Hannibal Lecter's office only to realize he was staring at a killer. Pure evil. He looked hard at that statue and wondered if he'd just had his own Will Graham moment . . .

CHAPTER TWENTY-FIVE

Miles away and far below the Hollywood Hills, Alix had just opened the door to John's bedroom and switched on the light. A single, bare bulb revealed a space desperately in need of cleaning. It was nearly identical to hers: a small rectangle ending at a sliding door to their shared balcony. In one corner sat John's bed, buried under a mountain of clothes, mostly jeans and black hoodies—John's signature style was somewhere between emo and skater, but he'd never popped an ollie in his life. *It's what California does to you*, Alix mused. *All image, all the time.* The rest of the room was a maze of books piled atop more books. And more clothes trapped between books. Being an aspiring novelist, John clearly took his writing seriously, having read almost everything under the sun, and here was the proof.

Alix went straight for John's desk and started searching his drawers. *Come on, John. Show me something. Fill me in. Please.* The top drawer yielded only office supplies, but the second drawer was a doozie: filled to the brim with dirty underwear. Suppressing a gag, Alix grabbed one of John's pencils and pushed them to the side, revealing a stack of printer paper. Instantly her eyes perked up: "MOMENTUM by John Finn" was scrawled in big letters across the front. Here it was, the mysterious novel John had worked so hard to keep from the world. *So this is where you've been hiding all this time*, Alix thought. She had to give it to him—only in a desperate situation like this would she, or anyone, sift through his stinky undergarments. She placed the manuscript on the desk and opened the third, and final, drawer.

Inside, Alix found a stack of notebooks with a few Polaroids on top. She knelt to get a better look, and in the topmost photo discovered her and John at his first day at Genera, she smiling like a normal person, he ironically raising his shiny, new cloak to the skies. Moving to the next photo, Alix found her and John on Venice Beach in Halloween costumes, John as Luke Skywalker, Alix as a blonde Princess Leia, with

cinnamon-bun hair and all. She teared up at the memory. They had gone to the beach often when they were kids, being from the San Francisco Bay Area and all, riding their bikes to the Albany Bulb or taking the train to Ocean Beach. She smiled at the memories of night swimming in the bay and sighed at the thought of simpler times.

But when her eyes fell once more on John's notebooks, reality crashed back into the present like a freight train. She was on a mission. She pushed the rest of the Polaroids aside and grabbed as many notebooks as she could. Seeing them stacked on the table, Alix was amazed at how prolific John was. *How many years of writing are in here?* She picked up the first notebook and flipped through. Mostly character sketches or short stories. She put it down and went to another, which turned out to be an old collection of to-do lists. She kept flipping through notebooks, finding nothing but the rambling thoughts of a struggling novelist.

Alix was ready to give up when she reached a notebook she knew she'd seen before. It was maroon and had a bookmark sticking out the top. She opened to the bookmark, and the first thing she saw made her heart sink.

It was a date: today.

And a time: 11 a.m.

And a location: San Francisco.

John went home? Today??

Alix flipped the page and noticed John's handwriting, which was uncharacteristically messy—unlike his room, his penmanship was pristine. She started to read:

If only I hadn't found it. If only I hadn't been on duty that day. Frick. I am so fricked. We're all so fricked. I need to destroy this document before they find me.

Alix flipped a few pages back, discovering a crude drawing of a building: a large sequence of crudely drawn triangles circled in red. Below, John seemed hopeful: "FBI called. Reward. Meeting set." He'd underlined "Reward" three times.

Reading these words, Alix started to piece together her hypothesis. *OK, so, it looks like John discovered something he shouldn't have. He got scared and contacted the FBI, which offered him a reward for the info.* For a moment, she wondered if this was just another of John's get-rich-quick schemes to give him more time for his writing. He'd dreamed for years of getting a grant or meeting a benefactor so he could quit his day job. But

98   *People's Choice Literature*

Alix shook her head. John seemed too worried, to serious to be thinking only of the money. His words, "We're all so fricked," resonated in her head like a deep gong.

Suddenly, Alix's eyes fell on a strange marker at the bottom right corner of the page: "X." *Why would John add a random X here?* She flipped the page and noticed a punctuation mark in the same place. She went to the next page. This time an "I." Next page a lower case "n." Alix then closed the book, brushing her thumb against the bottom corner like a flip book—one of those novelty objects that transformed the static book object into dynamic animation. Mickey Mouse dancing with Minnie. A seal bouncing a ball with its nose. To Alix's amazement, the corner of John's notebook sprung a string of words to life.

She opened the notebook to the first page and found an "A" at the corner. Next a "t." Grabbing a Post-it note and a pen, she started through the book, copying every character just as he'd written it. When she finished, she read the phrase in full, and her face clouded in disbelief.

CHAPTER TWENTY-SIX

Alix stared at the letters and punctuation before her. There was surely a message, but it was too difficult to read without spaces between the words. She grabbed another Post-it and recopied the note, adding the necessary word spaces and a line break after each punctuation mark:

Attn Alix:
In The City Of Lights,
Behind Big Sur,
It Will Be Alright

She read the phrase six times before leaning back in John's chair, stumped. *What the heck was he talking about?* Clearly this was a message for her: "Attention Alix." But "The City Of Lights?" "Big Sur?" Alix remembered from high school history class that Paris was called the "City of Light." But what did that have to do with Big Sur, California's coastal paradise nestled between the Santa Lucia Mountains and the Pacific Ocean? That world-class city and that natural beauty were thousands of miles apart, separated by an ocean and a sprawling continent.

Alix pulled out her phone and searched for "City of Light" on Google. She clicked on the first result, Wikipedia, which brought her to a page, "City of Light." As expected, the internet's encyclopedia told her that Paris is the city most commonly referred to as the "City of Light." But when she scrolled further down, things got more complicated. Alix found that dozens of other cities referred to themselves as a "City of Light": Anchorage, Alaska. Aurora, Illinois. Baghdad, Iraq ("known as the City of Light before the Mongol invasions"). The list went on and on. Even her current home of Los Angeles was deemed a "City of Light" thanks to its nightlife and the "Bright Lights of Hollywood."

You're not making this easy on me, John.

100   *People's Choice Literature*

Alix abandoned her "City of Light" inquiry and meditated on the next line, "Behind Big Sur." She recalled the family trip there when they were teenagers. Alix had been in awe of the landscape. Towering, sprawling mountains. Dramatic, lavender cliffs dropping deep into the Pacific. The most beautiful sunsets. She also recalled John ignoring the natural beauty and instead complaining the entire time. Over and over he whined about bringing the wrong book for their week-long trip. He'd been devastated to find on the drive to Big Sur that James Joyce's *Ulysses* was completely unreadable. "It's like he's *trying* to bore you to death," was his most common complaint, followed closely after by: "They'd make more money selling this as a sleep aid." John had begged their parents to help him find a bookstore, but for the first few days they either ignored him or convinced him that such a remote area was devoid of such luxuries. He'd tried to search on his phone, but there was no signal. He asked strangers on hikes and beaches, but they were just as clueless as he. It wasn't until the fourth day when their mother found the Henry Miller Library on a map. They went right away, and John was instantly reborn. He didn't just find a book; he discovered a whole knew way of being. Allen Ginsberg. Jack Kerouac. William Burroughs. The whole Beat Generation. Flipping through *HOWL*, something new bloomed inside him. John spent everything he'd earned at Jamba Juice the past two months on these books. And the rest of the time, while their family hiked or sat by a campfire, there was John with his face in a book, devouring daring tales of resistance, freedom, and the search for meaning on the lost highway we call America.

Alix veered off memory lane and turned that phrase over in her head: *"Behind Big Sur." What's behind Big Sur? Doesn't it depend on where you're standing? If you're looking up at the mountains, the sea is behind you. If looking at the sea, the mountains. And surely there's no city behind Big Sur. It's surrounded by Pfeiffer Big Sur State Park—a city of trees? The closest town she could think of was Carmel-by-the-Sea but calling that a city was too big a stretch.*

Going out on a limb, Alix searched for "Paris, California" on Google, but only "Perris, California," east of Los Angeles, came up. Home to the Southern California Railway Museum and not much else.

Alix slumped back in her chair. She felt stuck. None of this made any sense. She could see why John would write such a cryptic message—if he had found something truly sensitive, there was no telling who or what

nefarious group might be on his trail. You couldn't be too careful. But this code was simply impenetrable.

Alix grabbed the notebook and the Post-it note and went to the living room. She sat down beside a snoring, wheezing Rocky and found yet another episode of *American Pickers* on the screen. She put down the writing equipment and pulled Jason Stone's business card from her pocket. *Definitely didn't think I'd be calling him this soon*, she thought. All day she'd dreamed of returning home to find John at work on his novel, and that would be that. Case closed. No need for a knight in shining armor after all. But then there was the matter of her undeniable attraction. She'd imagined her brief interest in Jason Stone would fade into nothing and that she'd just go on with her life. She'd forget him. He'd forget her. *That's how these things happen, right? You don't just meet a beautiful man out of the blue and it actually works out. And you most definitely don't call him the same night.*

But what other option did she have? If the authorities hadn't already discovered that William Moriarty had impersonated her brother John, they would soon. Then the question of John's disappearance would surely come to light. Alix thought back to John's cryptic words, "FBI called. Reward. Meeting set." Maybe Jason Stone would know something about her brother working with the FBI. Maybe Jason Stone *was* the FBI agent that John had contacted . . . There were too many questions and frighteningly few answers. Alix picked up her phone and dialed.

CHAPTER TWENTY-SEVEN

FBI Agent Jason Stone had lived in the same Midtown one-bedroom apartment since he had moved to Los Angeles three years earlier. It was nice enough on the outside—a Mission Revival duplex framed by movie-worthy palm trees—but Stone's interior decoration left much to be desired. The living room sported a large flat-screen TV, coffee table, and gray couch, but that was it. There were no photographs, and the only art on the walls was a Pearl Jam poster he'd been lugging from apartment to apartment for years. The kitchen had the basic necessities but was stocked with minimal supplies. Its most-occupied territory was the freezer, which was packed with microwavable meals. Stone lived in the Merriam-Webster definition of a bachelor pad.

Tonight, after returning from Richard Moriarty's house, he popped a turkey dinner in the microwave and poured himself a cold glass of Jim Beam. He sat at his tiny kitchen table and let out a heavy sigh. He'd been running around Los Angeles all day—from Midtown to Malibu to the Hollywood Hills and now back home to his bachelor bat cave. In short, he was spent.

But if he'd learned anything from his years on the force, it was that work never really ends. After eating his meal and tossing the remains in the trash, Stone went to his briefcase. He grabbed his whiskey and the police report of William Moriarty's death and headed for the couch.

The account was just as gruesome as the news had described it. Fifty-four lacerations to the face, hands, and wrists. The neck cut from the Adam's apple all the way to the spine. The crime squad still hadn't uncovered the murder weapon, and there was no sign of a break-in. Words like "turbine" and "windmill" were scattered throughout.

Stone readjusted himself and exhaled deeply. *Someone sure wanted William Moriarty dead.* He recalled his conversation with Richard Moriarty from earlier. He thought about the CEO's resistance, his disdain. *Could a father really put his own son on the line like that?* Stone

couldn't believe it was so. Of course, the optics were just horrible. The son of the CEO of gAIa, Genera's biggest competitor, caught sneaking into their offices the day before Genera is set to launch its biggest product yet, Quanta. *If that doesn't reek of corporate espionage, I don't know what does.*

Stone then recalled Moriarty's response to his Kevin Arnold inquiry: complete denial and offense at the mention of any involvement. The billionaire's aggression was suspicious. And who *wouldn't* see the CEO as a suspect? If your company's even indirectly connected to an alleged murder, you're gonna have to do some talking . . . Stone looked forward to meeting Moriarty's lawyers in the morning. For now, he sat back, switched on the TV, and took a long sip of whiskey. He was settling into a calm he hoped would take him off to a very welcome sleep when a knock came at the door.

What now? he thought.

With a heavy sigh, he put down his whiskey and stood up, trudging toward the door.

"Who is it?" Stone called out before opening it. If he'd learned anything from his time on the NYPD, it's that you always get confirmation before opening a door.

"Emerson," said the voice.

Stone unlocked the door and swung it open, finding the director standing before him with an apologetic expression.

"Sorry to bother you at this hour," he said, brushing back his cowlick. "But we got an anonymous tip, and I think you'll wanna see this."

Stone grimaced. "It couldn't wait till morning?"

"No," Director Emerson said, pushing past Stone and into his kitchen. Emerson took a quick look around the sparse apartment.

"Love what you've done with the place."

Stone forced a chuckle but was eager to get down to business. "So, what do you got for me?"

"Right," said Director Emerson, pulling out his phone. "Our department received a video not long after we found Will Moriarty's body."

Stone studied him.

"So, we already knew Moriarty had impersonated a 'John Finn,' some low-level Genera security administrator who was also unsurprisingly missing at work today. At first, we thought Will Moriarty had offed Mister Finn, but then this video came in and things got a bit . . . weirder."

Stone's face curled into a question mark. "You have my attention."

Director Emerson nodded, handing Stone his phone.

104 *People's Choice Literature*

Stone sat down at the kitchen table and gestured at Emerson to join him. Then he pressed play, and the video came to life. The security feed revealed a circular space. Likely some tourist trap, as Stone noticed groups of people in rain gear peering out tall, arched windows and snapping pictures. Shifting his gaze, Stone discovered buildings and a large body of water through the windows. Gradually the crowds thinned until only two figures remained: a blond, twenty-something man in a black hoodie and a taller, older man in a trench coat and fedora.

Stone watched as the one in the black hoodie handed the other man a small object. Then the taller man handed the blond man a briefcase. Soon the taller man left, and soon the person in the black hoodie followed. Just as he was about to exit the screen, the hooded man turned his face to the security camera, and the video froze.

"That," said Director Emerson. "is John Finn at 11 a.m. this morning."

"Where is this?" asked Stone.

"San Francisco. Coit Tower."

"Any ID on the trench coat guy?"

"This is the real kicker," said the director. "That man is Tim Woodman, head engineer at gAIa."

Stone nearly dropped the phone.

"Gosh darn Moriarty. I was just at his house not an hour ago. The guy lied through his dirty teeth. Wish I'd got him under oath."

"There'll be time for that," said Director Emerson. "There's a unit en route to his house right now with an arrest warrant. We may not know what Will Moriarty was up to at Genera today, but we now have hard proof of a Genera employee, John Finn, selling company secrets to gAIa."

Stone nodded. "And what's the status of Finn and Woodman? Where'd they go after the drop-off?"

"We're still working on that," said the director. "Our anonymous tipper only provided this video. We're working with the SFPD to access the rest of Coit Tower's security cameras."

Stone put his hand to his chin. "Any leads on who this tipper was? Who'd have had access to the security cameras if not the tourist site itself?"

Director Emerson sighed. "We're on that, too. It's all moving pretty quickly."

Suddenly a light bulb went on in Stone's head. "How about John Finn's sister?"

"Huh?"

"Finn has a twin sister. I met her earlier today at Genera. Hadn't thought much about his disappearance when she told me. Just instructed her to call the LAPD."

Stone thought of Alix and how confused she'd be. He recalled her blank stare earlier. How beautiful she looked even on one of the worst days of her life. But he valued her beyond her looks. He knew she was a good person—the way she held herself, the way she spoke—and a good person deserves good things.

"I'd like to talk with her first," Stone blurted out.

"What?"

"Alix Finn. Before your guys go and tear up the place, I'd like to talk with her. We have a bit of a . . . rapport. I get the feeling like we'll get more intel from a simple conversation than an all-out interrogation."

Director Emerson gave Jason Stone an odd look before nodding. "You have one hour."

Stone nodded back and went to get his jacket. He tossed it on when his phone started to ring. He didn't recognize the number but picked it up anyway.

"Jason Stone here."

"Detective Stone," said the anxious voice on the other end. "It's Alix Finn."

CHAPTER TWENTY-EIGHT

At the same time Jason Stone was driving east to Alix and John Finn's apartment, a train of LA's Finest was winding its way up Mulholland Drive to arrest Richard Moriarty, CEO of gAIa and suspect number one in the plot against Genera. The line of wailing police cars stretched for nearly a quarter mile, lighting up the Hollywood Hills like a disco snake sliding swiftly through the night.

When they neared the entrance to the Moriarty estate, the sirens went off, but the lights stayed on, illuminating the mansions that lined the iconic road in bright reds and blues. Then they turned down Moriarty's driveway, through the high hedges, and pulled up before the haunted house that harbored LA's most wanted criminal.

As the police exited their cars, the front door opened, revealing Moriarty's butler ambling down the stone stairs with a jolly grin.

"Good evening, gentlemen," he said cheerfully. "How may I assist you? We were just winding down for the night."

One of the officers handed the butler the warrant and got right to business.

"Where is Richard Moriarty?"

The butler looked at him askance. "Why, where he's been all evening. In his study."

"And where is that?"

"Well, if you'll be so kind as to follow me, fine sirs—"

"Cut the pleasantries, man," growled the officer.

The butler stepped back, startled. "Ah, very well then. It's down the hall past the stairs. First door at the end."

"Thanks, pal," said the officer, brushing past him and into the house.

The butler stood there in shock as twenty gloved officers followed after. Then he walked in behind them, observing as they scoured every crevice of the building. One group inspected the living room, while another ascended the stairs. The butler craned his head to find the bulk of

106

the officers nearing the study door. And that's when he heard that sound he would never forget. The grumbly baritone moving from a squeal to a shriek. The virtuosic string of expletives and insults teetering on the deranged. The muffled sounds of Richard Moriarty screaming through layers and layers of polished wood.

CHAPTER TWENTY-NINE

Alix Finn was tidying up the apartment when the knock came at her door. She'd cleaned up the kitchen, put away the laundry, and was in the middle of wiping down the faux fireplace when the noise rumbled through.

Before she even registered the knock, Rocky was barking like a drill sergeant.

"Quiet, Rocky! Quiet," Alix pleaded.

But he yapped again.

"NO!" she said firmly.

Rocky jumped down from the couch and marched to the door.

Alix tossed the paper towel in the trash and followed behind with a stern "sit!"

When she peered through the peephole, she was grateful to find the rugged form that had captivated her so. The chiseled cheek bones. Those bulging arms. Like a linebacker and a redwood tree in one. Her heart rate picked up when she opened the door.

"Oh, hi," she said. It was all she could manage, her heart ping-ponging between thrilled and terrified.

"Hello, Alix," said Jason Stone. "How are you?"

"Good," she shrugged. "I mean, I'm getting there." She wanted to say more but didn't know how. Where would she even start? "Please come in."

She stepped aside to let him in, but Rocky yelped.

"Easy there, little one," said Stone in his softest voice, kneeling down and extending the back of his hand to the pouty bundle of fur. "Who do we have here?"

Rocky waddled up and gave it a sniff.

"He likes you," Alix said, relieved.

"He's a good boy," Stone said, rubbing his floppy jowls. "Very good boy."

Alix smiled. "OK, let's let Mr. Stone in, Rocky. Come!"

Rocky came to attention and turned toward the living room, waddling forward as directed.

"What a dog," Stone said, clearly impressed.

"He's very protective." Alix shrugged, closing the door.

"I'd say that's a good thing," Stone chuckled.

When they entered the living room, Alix asked Stone if he'd like anything. "We have orange juice and Coors Light. High class over here."

Stone laughed. "Maybe a cup of water?"

Alix walked to the kitchen and poured him a glass. When she returned, she found Rocky sniffing Stone's pant leg.

"Sorry we don't have more," she said, handing him the glass.

"Water's perfect," Stone smiled.

Alix joined him on the couch and held out a doggy treat to her canine companion before calling, "Shake!"

Right on cue, Rocky lifted his paw high.

"Amazing," said Stone, shaking it.

Alix laughed, handing the pooch the treat. "He's got a few tricks up his sleeve."

"I bet he does," he said, eyeing her speculatively.

Alix smiled back, trying to hide the frazzled feeling of having this godlike man in her home. She was grateful for his generous visit and heartened by his kindness for dogs. But seeing this beautiful man sitting there, relaxing in her home, was something else. The man was a giant. He could've lifted her with one arm. He probably ate a whole cow for breakfast. But he was so gentle and calm. So kind.

"I'm glad you came by," Alix said coyly.

Stone smiled at her. "It's not every day I get to play with such a cute dog."

"You ever have a dog?" she asked.

Stone's face dimmed.

"Once," he said staring off into the distance. Clearly there was pain there.

"Oh, I'm sorry," said Alix. "I didn't mean—"

He turned to her with a faint smile. "No, it's OK."

They each lapsed into an awkward silence as they gathered their thoughts.

"So, have you lived in Los Angeles for long?" Alix finally asked, taking a sip of water.

"About three years now," Stone nodded, still lost in another time and place.

"No way!" Alix overcompensated with a burst of sound. "That's when I moved here."

"You're kidding," he said, a thick eyebrow rising.

Alix shook her head. "John and I drove down together. We only brought what we could fit in our Honda Accord." She gestured around the room. "Which might explain the sparse decorations . . ."

Stone laughed. "You haven't seen *my* place."

Alix smirked. "Then it's a good thing I didn't move in with *you!*"

They both laughed before Alix realized the intimacy in her words. *Oh, no, I went too far!* she thought. *He's going to think I'm crazy. Some sex-crazed lunatic.* But Stone cut into this nervous thought like melted butter, giving no space for any awkwardness to flourish.

"It's true," he laughed. "My place is bachelor pad or bust."

Alix chuckled before realizing the truth behind Stone's words. *Bachelor pad. Bachelor.* Jason Stone was single! Or at least not married yet . . .

Suddenly a loud ding chimed through the room. Both Alix and Stone looked to their pockets, instinctively searching for their phones. Stone pulled out his device, and his face soured.

"Is everything OK?" asked Alix, visibly concerned.

Stone swallowed. "Just a reminder I don't have much time."

"Oh." She wasn't sure what that meant.

"Look, Alix," he said. "There's been a development. It's about John."

Alix felt her stomach drop. Then the anxiety hit her like a bag of bricks.

CHAPTER THIRTY

Jason Stone took a deep breath before starting. "We received an anonymous tip that John was in San Francisco this morning."

Alix's stomach would have dropped further had she not already seen this written in her twin brother John's notebook. She thought back to those fateful words: "11 a.m. . . . San Francisco." She thought of John's panicked handwriting and the whole mess he'd gotten himself, and now likely her, into.

Stone continued. "It looks like John was involved in some kind of corporate espionage."

"*What??*" Alix blurted out.

"I'm sorry," he said empathetically.

Stone pulled out his phone and showed her the video. Alix watched patiently as John in 720 pixels handed something small to a caricature of a gangster, receiving a briefcase in return. The video cut out, and instantly it hit her: John's notebook: "FBI called. Reward. Meeting set." *San Francisco* . . .

Stone spoke up. "We just arrested Richard Moriarty, CEO of gAIa, and there's a warrant out for the guy in the fedora. Turns out he's gAIa's head of engineering."

Alix swallowed.

Stone inhaled deeply. "And they think John was selling him Genera's secrets."

Alix was in shock. "There's no way. He said he was meeting the FBI. There must be someone in your office who knows about it—who can vouch for John. He's a good guy!"

"What!?" Stone said angrily. "You knew what he was up to?"

"No. I mean yes. I mean I just found out, which is why I called you. John said he was delivering some documents to the FBI. Or he wrote that. I found this notebook."

Alix removed John's notebook from under the couch.

111

112   *People's Choice Literature*

"I'd hidden it just in case," Alix winced.

Stone studied the notebook with wide eyes. "When did you find this!"

"I don't know, an hour ago?" She handed him the book. "You were the first person I thought to call. I wondered if it was even you who'd talked with John, since he'd contacted the FBI and all."

Stone flipped through the pages in disbelief. "He wrote all this?"

Alix nodded.

He looked at her skeptically before releasing a stream of thoughts: "It just doesn't make sense. We know the man in the trench coat is a gAIa employee. He's been there for a decade. Head of engineering. It's possible he could be working with the San Francisco FBI field office, but it seems unlikely . . ."

Alix's face lit up. "Maybe John was duped! Maybe this guy at gAIa posed as the FBI so John would think he was doing the right thing. I can only imagine what John felt when he saw the guy with the fedora. He looked like a mobster right out of a B movie!"

Stone smirked through his frustration. "Do you know where John is now?"

"No," said Alix.

"You need to be honest with me. If we're going to figure this out, you need me. We need each other."

Alix nodded, grateful to have Stone on her team. She almost told him about the secret code she'd found—"Attn Alix: In The City Of Lights, Behind Big Sur, It Will Be Alright"—but she hesitated. John had addressed the message to her and her alone. Maybe he knew something was askew. That few could be trusted. Alix could tell that deep down Stone was a good person. Every part of him beamed with goodness. But he had the power to lock John away for a long time. Until she figured out what the heck was going on, she couldn't risk it.

"I-I don't know where he is," Alix gulped.

Stone studied her before responding. "OK. Well, is there somewhere you think he might be hiding in San Francisco? Any friends or family he might be staying with?"

"Our parents live in El Cerrito, but I can't imagine he'd go there. It seems too obvious if he were hiding out."

"True," Stone agreed.

"And there must be some friends from college up there, but to be honest, I don't think he keeps in touch with them." Alix thought of her best friend Kate, who still lived in San Francisco, but she knew Kate would

have messaged her if she'd heard anything from her brother. Alix sighed. "He just goes to work, comes home, and writes. Not much of a social person."

"What kind of writing?" Stone looked genuinely curious.

"Oh, novels. Or *a* novel. He's been writing the same darn book for years. Been hoping to turn it into big bucks so he can leave Genera and focus on writing."

Stone nodded and looked around the living room. "Well, I guess that explains the Jack Kerouac shrine."

Alix looked to the wall beside the TV. There, below a framed picture of the author himself stood a bookshelf containing everything Kerouac had ever written as well as every book of commentary on Kerouac's writing and life that had ever been printed.

Alix laughed. "Oh, that. Yeah, we all went to Big Sur on a family trip, and he fell in love with the Beat writers. Kerouac's his favorite. Always said *On the Road*, the novel he's most known for, is nothing compared to *Big Su—*"

Alix's face went white. *Oh my gosh.* Big Sur. *Jack Kerouac's tenth novel . . . Written in the fall of 1961 and published in 1962 . . . Adapted as a feature film by Michael Polish in 2013 . . . Maybe John's message to me was about this novel and not the actual Big Sur we'd hiked as teenagers??* She recalled part of the message: "Behind Big Sur."

Is there something behind his copy of Big Sur?

Stone's words brought her back to reality. "Hey, Alix. Are you OK? You look like you've seen a ghost."

CHAPTER THIRTY-ONE

"Sorry," Alix said, shaking her head, still reeling from the revelation. "It's nothing."

Stone shrugged. "I actually liked *On the Road*. What's the deal with *Big Sur*?"

Alix felt her heart rate accelerating at an alarming pace. "Oh, you know, just another thinly veiled story of Jack Kerouac's life. In this one, he's kind of a hermit."

Stone looked confused. "Sounds a bit boring if you ask me."

"Can't say," said Alix. "I never read it."

Stone stood up. "Do you mind if I take a look?"

Alix bolted up from her chair to stop him. "Ah, sorry. John's really protective of his collection. He usually wore gloves to read these books."

Stone gave Alix an odd look. "Gloves?"

Alix winced, lying through her teeth. "You know these novelists. Taking everything so seriously . . ."

Stone sat back down. "Never met a real novelist myself. They always seemed larger than life. Too big to be real."

Suddenly a knock came from the door. Alix straightened in surprise. Rocky woke up and went back to his boot-camp barking.

"Quiet, Rocky. Quiet," Alix said, then turned to Stone. "Who could that be? At this hour . . ."

Rocky scuttled to the door, barking some more.

"Rocky, come on," Alix pleaded.

She peered through the eyehole to find a squadron of officers staring back.

Then she turned and whispered to Stone. "Did you know the police were coming?"

Stone was already behind her. "It's just procedure, Alix. Your brother is wanted for a serious crime. They just want to take a look around the house."

Alix studied him, furious. "You made me feel like we were a *team*."

A knock came again from behind.

"LAPD!"

Rocky growled.

"A-Alix," Stone stammered. "I'm on your side. I told them I wanted to talk with you first in hopes we could work together. They only gave me an hour."

Another knock. Rocky sneered.

Alix felt a rush of betrayal flood her entire being, grateful she hadn't told him about John's secret message. *Maybe Stone's not as good a guy as I thought* . . . Her mind flashed back to the pain of that betrayal years ago when she caught Timmy necking with Karen Sleason in his backyard. *Maybe Stone's no different from every other guy I've known* . . .

"Open up, ma'am," said a voice on the other end. "We have a warrant to search the premises."

Alix's eyes nearly burned a hole in her would-be friend. "If they're with you, *you* can let them in."

She picked up Rocky and stormed into the living room. Then she went to her bedroom and slammed the door.

CHAPTER THIRTY-TWO

After Stone let the officers in, the knot in his chest constricted. *What have I done?* He too felt they were starting to feel like a team. He liked Alix and was rooting for her. All he wanted was for her to find John and for everything to be OK. He also couldn't help but accept the fact he wanted to get to know her better.

Deep down he knew she was a good—a truly good—person, which meant that her twin brother John couldn't be far off. Now sitting on the steps of Alix and John's apartment, Stone mulled over their predicament and her eleventh-hour confession. *If John believed he was working with the FBI, it would be crucial evidence in court. Without the intent to defraud Genera, John might go scot free. That wouldn't answer the question of who was posing as the FBI, but it would at least give John and Alix an out . . .* But amid all these thoughts, Stone couldn't shake the fact that Alix now despised him, feeling betrayed and deceived. He had come into her home, befriended her dog, and enjoyed her company while failing to mention the crucial fact that a dozen officers were close behind. *If only she could understand my position. It was either gonna be a band of agents busting down the door or me easing her into this uncomfortable situation . . .*

Stone grabbed his phone and rang the FBI's LA and San Francisco headquarters. He wanted to know if anyone on staff or any paid informants had contacted John Finn before today, but he was only able to leave messages. Then he sat there on the apartment steps realizing how brilliant the bad guys' plan had been: gAIa tricking John into believing he was helping the feds would be great cover. Most young people want to do good things for the world. It makes sense. The world's a crazy place—who wouldn't want to try to fix it? And if you're a scheming company looking to manipulate a twenty-five-year-old, sugarcoating your evil plan with philanthropy would be the perfect trick.

Stone was lost in thought when an officer came and tapped him on the shoulder.

"We're ready to search the bedroom."

Stone was grateful for the heads-up. The police breaking down Alix's door was a surefire way to obliterate any sense of trust they'd built—if there was any trust left to obliterate, that is . . .

Stone stood and walked back inside. While most of the officers were swarming through John's room, Stone found a handful of them rummaging through the impressive Jack Kerouac collection. He paid them no mind as he made his way to Alix's door.

"Hey, Alix," Stone swallowed. "The guys need to come in now. They just need to look around. Should be quick."

He waited a moment, but no reply came.

"Alix, please. I am asking you personally."

Nothing.

Stone let out a deep breath. "I'll give you one minute. Then the guys are gonna have to come in."

No sound. Nothing. Stone couldn't imagine Alix was asleep given the maelstrom of uncertainty surrounding her and her brother, let alone the ten police officers dismantling her home. *And it's strange that Rocky's so quiet. Maybe he's starting to get used to the police presence . . . ?*

Stone turned to the officer who'd summoned him and shrugged. They gave Alix an extra minute before he continued.

"OK, Alix, this is the last chance before this gets awkward."

No response.

Frustrated, Stone nodded to the officer in a silent confirmation that he could bust down the door however he pleased. *I tried my best.*

Stone stepped aside as the officer took a crowbar and jammed it between the door and the frame. The officer pulled back hard, and the door creaked sharply, wood groaning against metal, until it slammed open, smacking the wall like a thunderclap.

The officer hesitated, then turned to Stone with wide eyes.

"She's gone."

CHAPTER THIRTY-THREE

FIFTEEN MINUTES EARLIER

Alix couldn't believe Detective Stone had betrayed her. She'd invited him into her home, introduced him to her dog, flirted with him. *He even flirted with me!* she thought. *I could feel it.* She slumped back.

She sat there frustrated, huffing to herself. *But it was all for show. He was just using me to get information. Did he even have feelings for me, or was that flirting part of the act?* But even as she thought this, she couldn't help but sense this wasn't true. That there was honesty behind his charm. She sensed real goodness in him. And *that's* not something you can easily fake. She huffed again. *He's just doing his job. I mean, come on. He's a freaking FBI agent, and your brother just committed like sixty felonies. What do you expect?* She sunk into her bed, recalling his kind smile and the speculative way his eyes met hers. There was no way he was faking it. Something real was there. The circumstances were just crazy— what person could act perfect through it all? She turned to Rocky, "He could be a good guy *and* still be a jerk sometimes . . ." People were complicated.

But Rocky wasn't listening, still growling at and sniffing the door.

"It's OK, buddy," she said picking him up and sitting him down on the bed beside her.

Giving him a reassuring pat, Alix thought back to a few minutes earlier when she'd smartly stormed away from Stone, grabbing both John's notebook and his copy of *Big Sur* from the Kerouac shrine before the police could get to them. She'd pulled a few other Kerouac books from the shelf to see if anything was hiding behind them but found nothing.

Now, in her room, she was stumped. If there was nothing behind *Big Sur*, as John's code had suggested, then what else could it all mean? She studied the code again:

In The City Of Lights,
Behind Big Sur,
It Will Be Alright

"Behind Big Sur," she whispered aloud. Of course, if John was referring to the novel *Big Sur*, there were plenty of copies. It was the nature of publishing—you print as many copies as you think will sell. And Alix was certain *Big Sur* had sold a hefty amount since it was first published in 1962. This meant that there could be tens of thousands, even hundreds of thousands of copies to look behind . . .

Alix turned her attention to the other mystery here: "In The City Of Lights." *Are you really asking me to go to Paris, John?* Alix couldn't believe it. Neither she nor her brother had ever been to Paris, and neither knew anyone there. And if copies of *Big Sur* did exist in Paris, they'd likely go by a different name. John often complained about how so many titles of translated novels were nothing like the originals. Like *The Great Gatsby* appearing in Swedish as *A Man Without Scruples*. Or a Japanese edition of *The Grapes of Wrath* they'd literally translated as *The Angry Raisins*.

Alix smirked before returning to the task at hand. "The City Of Lights." She couldn't place it. If this city were Los Angeles—one of the supposedly many "Cities of Light"—he would've just said "The City Of Angels," right? There was no way she was going to run around LA, hitting every bookstore and library, looking behind every copy of *Big Sur*. It was pointless.

She looked at the code again and noticed something strange: "Lights" was plural, not singular. When she'd searched the web earlier, Paris and other cities were each a "City of Light"—not a "City of Light*s*." Why the change?

Alix fell back in her bed, overwhelmed by the quagmire John had concocted.

"Can't you just be direct?" she whispered aloud in frustration.

She buried her face in her hands and imagined John enjoying himself in San Francisco, hiding out with whatever lavish cash reward he'd received, completely oblivious to the insanity he was dragging her through. *Did he really think he could get away with this? How could he not see how in over his head he was?*

She let out a ragged breath and tried to give John the benefit of the doubt. He'd always been frustrated with their living situation. Never having enough money. Always in debt. Their parents on their third mortgage

120 *People's Choice Literature*

and struggling through yet another economic downturn. And of course, the refrains Alix had heard over and over again: "If only I had money, I could dedicate myself to writing." "If only I had money, I could buy the books I need and become a truly great writer." She imagined him now in San Francisco with a briefcase full of cash, casually strolling through North Beach, walking into City Lights Bookstore and—

City Lights. She shot up in her bed.

"Oh my gosh," she said aloud. "John's favorite bookstore! City Lights Bookstore in San Francisco! Did he hide something behind a copy of *Big Sur* at City Lights?"

It seemed too simple, but it somehow made perfect sense. On his way to meeting that gAIa mobster—who he'd thought was an FBI agent—John must have stopped in City Lights Bookstore, gone to the fiction section, and hidden whatever it was behind Jack Kerouac's *Big Sur* before continuing up the hill to Coit Tower . . .

I have to get out of here, she thought.

Alix grabbed her backpack, tossing in John's notebook and his copy of *Big Sur*. She packed a change of clothes, then turned to Rocky, still guarding the door like a stout, pouty sentry.

"Sorry, buddy," she said, "but things are going to get a little tight for a minute."

She lifted his lumpy body and guided his legs, then torso into the backpack. Oddly, it was the perfect Rocky bag, with just enough room for his snorty head to pop out.

Alix gave him a smooch and then threw the dog-filled backpack over her shoulders. Then she grabbed her keys and pulled out the fire-escape ladder she'd thought she'd never need but was now grateful her parents had insisted on.

She went to the sliding glass door at the end of her room and poked her head out onto the balcony. No officers in sight. With Rocky in tow, she snuck out and affixed the fire-escape ladder to the balcony railing, lowering it to the ground.

Alix reached behind to scratch Rocky's head and took a deep breath.

"Here goes nothing . . ."

CHAPTER THIRTY-FOUR

The Interstate 10 highway stretches from Jacksonville, Florida, all the way across the continent to Santa Monica, California. In the greater Los Angeles area, it connects downtown Los Angeles to the city of Santa Monica, giving this stretch its local name, the Santa Monica Freeway. A relic from a bygone era, this section of I-10 was built at a moment when the state could decide to build a highway and then just build it, with no environmental review required. It's also the product of a less-populated time and was therefore not constructed with today's traffic in mind.

But traffic was all Jason Stone could think about the next morning as he sat there in a bumper-to-bumper backup. Having not moved for fifteen minutes, he eyed the dashboard clock and winced at how late he'd be to meet D. J. Wylde, CEO of Genera.

Of course, he wasn't particularly looking forward to it. After Alix disappeared, the last thing he'd wanted to do was chase Wylde around. Traffic cameras had traced her escape route from her home in East Hollywood to Griffith Park, but once the police arrived, they found only the Honda Accord. No Alix and no Rocky. Were they hiding out in the bushes? Not the safest place after hours . . . Had they stolen a car? There hadn't been any reports of a theft so far, so Stone was stumped. And concerned. Things had gotten dangerous for Alix fast: both the LAPD and the FBI now saw her as a likely co-conspirator in their case against her twin brother, John.

As Stone sat there in the same place his Kia Forte had been sitting for what felt like an eternity, he thought back to his visit with Alix the night before. He couldn't believe he'd let her get away. *What was I thinking? I should never have let her go into that room alone.* He recalled the look on the officers' faces when it became clear Alix had fled the coop. He was certain he wouldn't hear the end of it from Director Emerson.

Stone sighed. He knew he'd be fine. What he was worried about was Alix's well-being. Through just a few interactions, his empathy for Alix

122   *People's Choice Literature*

had ballooned. He knew she was a good person and understood her desire to flee. If she truly did not know about John's plans, then panic made sense. *I only wish she knew I wanted to help. That I'm here for her.* He squeezed the steering wheel, trying to redirect his frustration. *I just hope she's OK.*

CHAPTER THIRTY-FIVE

When he finally pulled up to Genera, Stone parked the Kia Forte and stepped out, turning his gaze to the majestic Getty Villa before him. When he'd arrived a day earlier, the rain had diverted his attention from the structure. Today, with a faint glint of sun though the clouds, he could see why D. J. Wylde and Genera had wanted the space. The building seemed to radiate both charm and power. His eyes traced the neoclassical façade, noting the stately pillars and birthday cake trim before landing on a dark window. Stone wasn't sure at first, but he could've sworn there was someone staring down at him. But when he peered closer, the figure was gone. *Strange*, he thought.

Just then, he heard a familiar voice. "Hello there, Mr. Stone."

Stone turned to find D. J. Wylde dressed in his signature, flowing blue cloak. Though his voice maintained its youthful sprightliness, Wylde's eyes betrayed unmistakable exhaustion. Like John Lennon the morning after an all-nighter.

"Sorry, I'm late, Detective. That damn traffic. Even a driverless car and the most advanced GPS system on the planet are no match for the Santa Monica Freeway," he chuckled.

"And here I thought I was late," Stone smirked, shaking his hand. "Good to see you again, Mr. Wylde."

"Please, call me D. J."

Stone nodded. "So, where's a good place to talk? What we have to discuss is sensitive . . ."

The tech guru led Stone into the mammoth limestone entrance, through galleries of ancient art, and out into a large, empty courtyard with a long pool in the center.

When they came out into the open, Wylde let out a deep sigh and raised his hands to the cloudy heavens. "The Outer Peristyle . . . where it all began."

"Sir?" Stone gave him an odd look.

124   *People's Choice Literature*

Wylde pointed toward a sculpture resting in the pool. "It was just over there. Not ten years ago on a warm day in May. My assistants and I were lounging in the cool elixir, feasting on berries, drinking cava, musing on the greater things in life."

Wylde started toward the pool, gesturing for Stone to follow.

"Here was peace and quiet," he continued, "the silence broken only by the whisper of wind through the trees, the infectious laughter of my assistants at one of my jokes. The cozy afternoon light played on the water, blessing the bronze sculpture with a hint of gold.

"This was a place of contemplation, Mister Stone," Wylde sighed. "Still is a place to calm the spirits after a long day. But on that particular day, as we frolicked through the waters and supped on aged cheese, I suddenly found myself lethargic. I knew not what came over me. Was it the wine? The burden of the ages evoked by this historic villa? I ventured over to this here sculpture and leaned against it. They call it the 'Drunken Satyr.'"

Wylde gently nodded in its direction.

"Now, according to legend, the satyrs were devoted followers of the great god of wine and merriment, Dionysus. This particular satyr is the consummate image of pleasure. Reclined and nude. That day gazing rapturously at the glorious sun shining high."

Stone noted the clouds hanging over it now.

"The thing is, this satyr wasn't always at the Getty. Historians say that over two thousand years ago, it graced the gardens of a luxurious villa south of modern-day Naples. And it lived there for gods know how long, delighting in that sweet, Neapolitan sun, easing through season after season . . ."

Wylde turned to the detective with a grim face. "That is until 79 AD, when a little mountain you might have heard of called Vesuvius had a little eruption that you might also have heard of. That eruption famously buried the lost city of Pompeii. Well, it also buried that villa and this here satyr under eighty feet of volcanic debris."

Stone watched as a tear began to roll down Wylde's cheek.

Wylde gathered himself and continued. "But in 1750, while workers were digging a well, they uncovered the villa after nearly two millennia. With it they discovered this lovely satyr, and after centuries of restoration and study, it arrived here, at the Getty Villa, our monument to antiquity."

Wylde was beaming. "That day in May, as my assistants played and I leaned against our dear satyr in torpor and despair, suddenly it came to me. It was as if the clouds of heaven had opened, shining the bright light

of reason on my soul. As if the sun itself had burst into a billion rays of heavenly thought. It was a moment of clarity. A moment—and I don't use the word lightly—of enlightenment."

Stone swallowed, nodding.

"That moment, I realized my destiny. I realized my life's calling, and I could see it all as clearly as I see you here right now." Wyle inhaled a deep yoga breath. "*Quanta*. It just came to me." He choked up. "I imagined this satyr buried for centuries, hidden deep in the dark, cold and scared, yearning for the light of day. I thought of this satyr, and I saw us. I saw you and me." He pointed to Stone and himself. "I saw our entire species. That *we* are that satyr. *We* are the ones buried far in the depths of confusion and chaos. A morass of misunderstanding and pain. And yet we aren't even aware. We don't even know that far above, far away from the philistines and luddites is a world of possibilities, the light of reason, the light of hope just waiting for us. If only we could reach it. If only we could *be* it."

Wylde looked to Stone with eager eyes. "This is Quanta. Quanta is the tool to dig us out of the mess that we find ourselves in. To bring reason to our disorder, calm to our chaos. Quanta is the totality of hope in a single product. It began right here, and tonight, at long last, it lives!"

Stone was speechless. It's not every day the leader of the world's biggest tech company divulges his secret origin story.

"But how does it work?" asked Stone.

Wylde chuckled. "In due time, my friend. In due time." Then he straightened up, pulling a strand of hair behind his ear. "Now, what would you like to talk about?"

Stone froze, unsure of how to follow that act.

CHAPTER THIRTY-SIX

As Jason Stone sat there dumbfounded, Alix Finn was hundreds of miles to the north, pulling up to her friend Kate's apartment in San Francisco's Mission District. Alix gazed up at the three-story walkup with a weak grin.

The journey had been rough. After driving Rocky to Griffith Park and abandoning her Honda Accord, they'd trekked into the hilly, upscale neighborhood beside the park and toward her godmother Susan's house. Susan had been gone the past few weeks traveling through Thailand, so Alix was certain it would be empty. She grabbed the house key under the potted plant next to the front door—just where it had always been—and let herself in.

Inside, Alix nearly collapsed. After the longest day of her life, she'd just snuck out of her house and fled from the police. She knew she needed sleep but also knew if she didn't get moving while it was still dark, it would be a lot trickier in the daytime. More opportunities to be noticed . . .

She sighed, mulling over her predicament. That she and John were in trouble was obvious. That she had to get to San Francisco was now absolutely clear. John's code was unambiguous: something of utmost importance was awaiting her in City Lights Bookstore. Something hiding deep within the store's famed fiction section, something camouflaged behind a copy of Jack Kerouac's *Big Sur*, just waiting to save the day and clear her and her brother's names.

With this in mind, Alix downed a glass of water, bagged whatever snacks looked good in the cupboard, and grabbed Susan's car keys from the hanger. Then she opened the garage door and flicked on the light.

And there it was. Susan's vintage 1967 Chevy Camaro Z28. Slick, red body with two white stripes down the middle. Custom spoiler and chrome Elvis hood ornament. *Not the ideal vehicle for a getaway, but it'll do.*

Alix could almost hear her godmother's scorn once she'd found out what she'd done. It was totally out of character for her to steal a car, and

Susan would be the first to tell her that. But desperate times sometimes call for absurd measures.

She hoisted Rocky into the passenger seat and tossed her bag in the back. Then she settled in the driver's seat, a smile nearly breaking through her exhaustion when she felt the familiar squish of the Camaro's leather. She put the key in the ignition and twisted it, letting the engine rumble a moment. Then she reversed out of the garage and punched the gas, speeding toward the city by the bay.

About two hours into the drive up the California I-5, Alix felt herself drifting off to sleep.

"No. No, no, no. Keep going," she said aloud, slapping her cheek. "You've got to keep going. You can sleep when you arrive."

She rubbed her eyes and pushed through. But after another twenty minutes, when she nearly drifted into a ditch, Alix knew she had to stop. She soon spotted the sign for the Buttonwillow Rest Area and took the exit.

It'll just be a fifteen-minute nap, she thought as she parked the car and drifted off to sleep.

When she awoke, the sun was glaring through the windshield. Alix opened her eyes wider to find its bright orb staring back, red and blinding, hovering just above the horizon.

"How long have I been out?" she asked aloud.

Rocky awoke in a startle, tongue lazily drooping from his mouth.

When Alix saw it was 6:38 a.m., she frowned. "At least four more hours to San Francisco." *And it's already light . . .*

She let Rocky out to answer nature's eternal call and gave him some water. Then they hopped back in the car and continued their journey north.

Even though Alix had slept, by the time she'd reached Kate's house, she nearly fainted. She parked the 1967 Chevy Camaro Z28 on one of San Francisco's famed hills, grabbed Rocky and her bag, and rapped her knuckles against the door. In a matter of seconds, she was face to face with her best friend in the whole world.

"Right on time," Kate said with a smirk.

"You were expecting me?" Alix asked, bewildered.

128   *People's Choice Literature*

Kate gave her a loving, disappointed look. "Alix, your face is all over the news. Where else would you go if you were on the run?"

Alix's heart sank. "Thank you, Kate."

Kate smiled. "Now get on in before someone spots you lurking around."

Alix and Rocky shuffled in, and within five minutes both were snoring on the couch.

CHAPTER THIRTY-SEVEN

Sitting there before the Getty Villa's iconic pool, Jason Stone turned to D. J. Wylde with a grave look. He swallowed before updating the tech guru on the investigation that was so close to home.

"We've arrested Richard Moriarty on two counts of corporate espionage. The first is for infiltrating your security systems with his son William. The second for orchestrating the theft of secret Genera documents with the help of your employee, John Finn, and a gAIa employee, Tim Woodman."

Wylde's draw dropped. "Moriarty? This must be a mistake."

Stone shook his head, his expression unchanged. "The motive is there. Given your company's mysterious Quanta technology is about to launch and Richard Moriarty's gAIa has a lot to gain from derailing it, the connection sticks out like a sore thumb."

"Richard was my inspiration," said Wylde, grimly shaking his head. "Without him, I would never have started Genera. I knew he had something up his sleeve to counter tonight's Quanta launch, but this just goes above and beyond . . ."

Stone said nothing, and Wylde continued. "What about William Moriarty? Are there any leads as to who killed him?"

Stone looked Wylde dead in the eyes. "The lacerations aren't in keeping with a conventional knife attack. Seems some kind of fan or turbine was involved. Perhaps a high-powered electronic device or even a drone?"

Wylde's eyebrows rose at the word "drone."

"I know it sounds crazy," Stone admitted, "but we're taking all possibilities into consideration."

Wylde nodded in agreement. "And what about Jason Finn and that other gAIa employee?"

"Finn's still MIA, but we got a lead on Tim Woodman. He was spotted in San Francisco's Marina District this morning exiting a Safeway. We're on it."

130   *People's Choice Literature*

Wylde continued nodding, clearly in deep thought. "Well, I hope you do find them, Mister Stone. This whole situation is incredibly messy—and poorly timed."

"We're doing our best."

Wylde sighed and turned to the agent. "You know, I hate to sound conspiratorial, but Jason Finn has a sibling, one of my assistants. Her name is Alix Finn . . . ?"

Stone had been waiting for this. "Yes, we're looking into that as well."

"What's her status? Should I be expecting a visit from the enemy at my office today?"

Stone didn't enjoy this characterization. Sure, Alix's brother was mixed up in something way over his head and, yes, she did flee a crime scene last night, but deep in his burly heart of hearts, Jason Stone just knew she was innocent.

"We have no evidence of collaboration between the Finn siblings," said Stone. "All we know is that during a search of their apartment last night, Alix Finn fled the scene and has been missing ever since."

Wylde was aghast. "*You let her escape!?*"

"I— it wasn't—," Stone stammered. "We didn't see it coming. She'd cooperated earlier, so . . ."

Wylde shook his head. "I just hope she doesn't make it to the border. If she does, she'll be gone forever."

"We're pursuing all leads, sir," Stone asserted.

"And what *are* those leads?"

"Nothing concrete yet," said Stone. "She could be hiding out in LA. There's cause to believe she might be heading to San Francisco, where her brother was last seen."

Wylde leaned back and sighed. "Well, thank you for everything you're doing, Detective Stone."

Stone nodded, sensing Wylde was ready for him to leave.

"Well, I should be going," he said. "These cases don't solve themselves."

The two men stood and walked back through the Villa toward the entrance, with Wylde giving a brief history lesson on Roman architecture along the way. Nearing the exit, Wylde turned to the detective with a curious glint in his eyes.

"You know," he said, gesturing to the neoclassical wonder around them. "A place like this could use a thinker like you. You ever consider upgrading to the private sector?"

Stone didn't see *that* coming. "Can't say I have, sir. My father was an officer, and his father before that. It's all I've ever known."

Wylde smiled, pulling a loose strand of hair behind his ear. "Well, if you ever have a change of heart, I'm sure we can double or even triple what the *government* is paying you."

Stone didn't like the way he said "government," as if it were an inconvenience, a dirty word. All his closest friends were public servants, risking their lives in the line of duty day in and out. They were good people. The best.

"And our benefits," Wyle continued, "are unparalleled."

"Thank you, sir," Stone nodded, "but I'm more than happy to serve my country."

Wylde's annoyance was obvious. He didn't seem like the kind of guy who heard "no" often.

"Well, keep the idea in the back of your mind," he said, extending his hand to Stone. "You never know when it might come in handy . . ."

The two men shook, and Stone turned back to his car. He wasn't a fan of that last line, "You'll never know when it might come in handy." He wasn't sure what exactly Wylde was getting at. *CEOs*, Stone shook his head, *a species of their own . . .*

When he reached his Kia Forte, Stone was fumbling for the keys when his phone rang. He pulled out the device to find "Director Emerson" on the screen. *What now?*

Then he picked up. "Hello?"

"Stone . . ." Emerson was breathless. "We got something."

"Hit me," said Stone.

"Alix Finn. Credit card transaction at a rest stop halfway to San Francisco. Not three hours ago."

Stone's heart constricted. "I'll be on a plane within the hour."

CHAPTER THIRTY-EIGHT

At around 3 p.m., Alix awoke to Rocky snorting and licking her face. With a groan, she forced her eyes open.

"OK. OK!" she said.

But he kept sniffing, now nuzzling his head into her neck.

"Alright, I get it. I'm up."

Alix sat up to find Kate sitting in an armchair across from her, a Janet Evanovich novel in one hand, a cup of coffee in the other.

"Good morning!" Kate teased.

Alix laughed groggily. "Any news?"

"Alix," Kate smirked, "you *are* the news."

Grabbing the remote control, she switched on the TV.

"After conducting a full sweep of the area," said the reporter in front of a row of palm trees, "Los Angeles police have found no trace of Alix Finn. Authorities have reason to believe the twenty-five-year-old has somehow found her way to San Francisco to reunite with her brother, John Finn, who is wanted for corporate espionage. The FBI asks that the public be on the lookout and to notify police if . . ."

Alix sunk back, defeated. She knew she had to get to City Lights Bookstore ASAP to find whatever John had hidden for her. She'd found his code—"In The City Of Lights, Behind Big Sur . . ."—and cracked it, realizing it pointed directly to the infamous bookstore's Jack Kerouac section. Alix was certain something would be waiting for her behind a copy of the Beat writer's 1962 novel, *Big Sur*.

"You OK?" asked Kate.

Alix nodded, but inside it felt like she was being swallowed by a black hole.

"Want some coffee?"

"Sure," she shrugged.

Kate went to the kitchen and poured her a cup.

"Just how you like it, little bit of cream, little bit of sugar."

Alix took a sip and felt right at home. She looked around Kate's living room and at the many plants that covered the floor, tables, and windowsills. "Nice place."

"Yeah, you know me," said Kate. "Just your good old neighborhood Plant Lady."

Alix laughed. She'd always loved that no matter how technologically advanced Kate was—her being a coder and all—she always grounded herself in nature.

"How's the fancy new job?" asked Alix.

"Ah, it's OK. Same work, new name, you know? But the price is right. And I still get to break passwords on behalf of the biggest companies in the world, so I can't complain. Most people would be locked away doing this kind of stuff. Somehow I've made a career out of it." She shrugged.

"You always amaze me, Kate."

Alix thought back to their college days. She and Kate had met freshman year and had been inseparable ever since. Even after college they talked on the phone almost daily. Alix thought of Kate as a sister, and John did, too. Kate came to every Christmas Eve dinner, and Alix always attended Kate's tia's feast every Thanksgiving. Alix sighed, yearning for those simpler times, but her nostalgic daydream was rudely interrupted by the inevitable question from Kate:

"So, what the heck happened, Alix? Last I heard you were off to a company party. Next thing you and John and are America's most wanted criminals!"

Alix shook her head. "It's been just awful. First John disappears, then someone shows up to work dressed as him, then *that* someone shows up dead, then John reappears in San Francisco committing a crime, and then, to top it all off, everyone thinks I'm part of it! I just can't get a break."

Kate got up and gave Alix a hug.

"You're safe now," she said. "And you're not alone."

"Thanks, Kate," said Alix, leaning in. "You're the best."

"So what's your plan?" Kate asked. "I mean, hide out with me as long as you'd like, but I bet at some point you'll want to see the sun again."

Alix paused, wondering if she should tell Kate about John's note. This clue was her lifeline. The only thing she had going for her. If John had sent her on some crazy trans-Californian goose chase, it would be for a good reason. And whatever was hiding behind *Big Sur* would be a last resort. Fortunately, Kate was a good friend. Alix's best friend. She could

134   *People's Choice Literature*

tell her anything. And like many coders, Kate's skepticism of authority was second nature. Alix couldn't see her ratting out anyone, let alone her de-facto sister.

"I found something . . ." said Alix.

Kate's eyes perked up as Alix pulled John's notebook out of her backpack. "A message from John."

Kate straightened up.

"It's his notebook," Alix continued. "John wrote all these cryptic messages about meeting the FBI at Coit Tower."

Kate nodded. At this point, everyone in the United States knew of John's Coit Tower meeting. The video of him and Tim Woodman—no FBI agent, but instead a gAIa employee—had played on a loop for the past twelve hours.

"John was scared," Alix continued. "He was horrified. But he thought he'd found an agent who could help him. Seems just in case something went wrong, he left a secret note for me . . ."

Kate's eyes opened wide. Secrets were her bread and butter.

"I'm almost positive that before he got to Coit Tower, he hid something behind a book at City Lights Bookstore."

Kate gave Alix an odd look. "Which book?"

Alix grinned. "No surprise for you and me: a Jack Kerouac novel."

Kate smiled. *"Big Sur?"*

They both laughed. John had mentioned the book at every chance since that fateful family vacation when he discovered the Beat writers. The names Allen Ginsberg, Diane Di Prima, and Jack Kerouac were like mantras to him. He was so obsessed with them—and with Jack Kerouac in particular—that Alix now felt ashamed at how long it took her to crack the code. Kate would've solved it in seconds.

Alix returned to the task at hand. "So, I have to get to City Lights ASAP."

Kate took a sip of her coffee, processing this new information like a human supercomputer.

"Well, you definitely need a disguise," she said.

Alix nodded.

"I can help with that."

Kate got up and went to her bedroom, returning shortly with a box overflowing with shiny fabrics and colorful nick knacks.

"What the heck is that?" asked Alix.

The Most Wanted Novel   135

"You know I've gone to the Burning Man festival every year since I was eighteen."

Alix nodded. She'd seen Kate's photos every year and admired her dedication to dressing up and expanding her mind in the desert each summer.

"Well," Kate smirked, sitting the box down in front of Alix. "I've got more costumes in this house than Party City. And don't even get me started on my bikes."

Alix didn't know what to make of all the sequins and fake fur before her.

"The thing you've got to remember," said Kate, "is that you're in San Francisco. Everyone dresses weird here. If you looked *normal* walking down the street, you'd turn heads every block. Dress up like a teddy bear with pom poms, and no one bats an eye. But go out in a simple T-shirt and jeans, and everyone'll think you're a narc. Or worse: Alix Finn!!"

Alix gave Kate an odd look.

"Look," Kate continued. "At least the tourists will look away from you. They either don't wanna be seen staring or just don't get it."

Alix sensed she was right. She'd only ever lived in the East Bay—El Cerrito and then Berkeley—but most of the times she'd crossed the bay, San Francisco's flamboyance burned bright. Alix missed that kind of culture in LA, where beauty and hipness trump all. San Francisco, even through its many transformations, had still somehow found a way to stay weird.

Alix sifted through the box, tossing rainbow tutus and dolphin costumes to the side. She couldn't find anything that felt right. After studying a dozen ill-fitting dayglo jump suits, she started to question if Kate was actually right. *If you're standing out* that *much, I don't care where you are, people are going to stare.*

Kate noticed Alix's wavering.

"Hold on a second," she said, starting for the bedroom. "I think I've got it."

Kate returned with a dress Alix could only describe as wild-west burlesque.

"You want me to go as a steampunk?" Alix asked skeptically.

"What do you mean 'steampunk?'"

Alix stood and went to the dress. "Kate, there's even a monocle attached to this thing."

136 *People's Choice Literature*

Kate was not happy.

"And the bodice has clock gears for nipples!"

Kate looked at her dead in the eyes. "You want to do this, right? You want to go to City Lights and clear your name? Clear John's name?"

Alix sighed, turning again to the dress. The more she studied it, the more she understood Kate's point. Given her media exposure, this was probably the only way Alix could make it through the city without anyone noticing her. At least this costume wasn't blindingly neon, like the others . . .

"Alright," she said, "But do I really need to wear that top hat?"

Kate gave her a stern look.

Alix huffed and grabbed the dress, stomping to the bathroom to change.

CHAPTER THIRTY-NINE

The Palace Hotel stands high above San Francisco's famed Market Street, greeting both business and leisure travelers with a taste of nineteenth-century luxury. Located in the heart of downtown, the hotel is just steps away from some of the city's most popular attractions, including Union Square, Chinatown, and Fisherman's Wharf. It is also close to public transportation, making it easy for guests to explore all the city has to offer.

Built in 1875, the Palace was the first hotel in San Francisco with electric lights, making it an instant favorite of the city's elite. Featuring a Beaux Arts façade and a soaring clock tower, its interior is just as impressive, with marble floors, crystal chandeliers, and beautiful woodwork. Amenities include a fitness center, a business center, a spa, and complimentary Wi-Fi.

That day, as Jason Stone looked out from his hotel room onto the bustling city, he could see why this place had been so hyped. The room was fit for a king, boasting every luxurious amenity one could imagine, from a large marble tub to waterfall shower head and L'Occitane soaps. And the view was nothing short of epic. Sunlight danced down Market Street, illuminating the cars and passersby, bouncing off the glass buildings on its way to the city's famed hills. As he looked out, he couldn't help but marvel at the fact that his higher-ups had suggested he stay here.

And yet, it made sense: John Finn, Alix's brother, had booked a room here for the night of his fateful drop off. The place was basically a crime scene.

Thinking of Alix brought Stone back to the present, away from the admirable view. His goal now was to find Alix and figure out what the heck was going on. Deep down, he knew she was innocent. When he last saw her, it was clear to see she was caught up in something she didn't fully understand. *If only she'd just stuck with me . . .*

138 *People's Choice Literature*

Stone threw on his jacket and searched for the map the SFPD had emailed him. To his delight, John Finn's route from Union Square to Coit Tower was already well documented. They'd worked all night, piecing together surveillance footage of John's movement in reverse order: from Coit Tower to North Beach to Chinatown to the Grace Cathedral to Union Square. Stone decided the best way to find Alix would be to retrace her brother's steps. It was obvious she knew something, and maybe, just maybe, it had to do with this strange zig-zag pattern through the city. He grabbed his key, holstered his gun, and went for the door.

CHAPTER FORTY

Just as Jason Stone exited the Palace Hotel, Alix Finn was biking down Market Street in Kate's steampunk outfit on Kate's steampunk bike, replete with spray-paint-bronzed frame and spokes that looked like sprockets.

"I look like a gosh darn idiot," Alix muttered to herself as she pedaled along.

But even as she said it, she knew that wasn't true. She looked like someone who belonged in this city. Like a free spirit, in touch with her inner core, her true self. And that was the whole point.

The other point was to go it alone. Kate and Alix had discussed biking together, but in the end nixed the idea. It seemed better for Kate to stay behind, tending to Rocky and keeping Alix updated on any developments in the investigation. She'd given Alix her phone for security and was now communicating via computer.

As Alix took a left onto Kearney Street and found herself amid a flurry of tourists and locals, she was brought back to her teenage days. She'd never biked here in a costume like this, but she had surely walked these streets many times, savoring the chaotic yet exhilarating energy of the city. It was all so different from the sprawl of Los Angeles. You felt like you were part of something.

When she entered Chinatown, Alix knew she was getting close to City Lights. She saw Young's Café, where she, John, and Kate had gone before a Beyoncé concert in college. She biked past the verdant Portsmouth Square and the imposing Hilton San Francisco, whose sloping, Brutalist façade looked right out of *Blade Runner*. When she passed the World Ginseng Center and House of Hanking, she felt her heart race. City Lights was seconds away. But then, as if on cue, her phone rang.

It was Kate.

"Alix, I have some news. They've found Tim Woodman."

Alix pulled to the side of the road and swallowed. "And?"

"He's dead. Mutilated by some kind of industrial fan or something. They think John did it. They're saying awful things . . ."

Alix's heart dropped. *They killed Tim Woodman the same way they killed Moriarty's son. With some kind of spinning blade? It didn't make sense. Why go about it in such a bizarre way?*

"Where'd they find him?" asked Alix.

"In the bay. Near the Golden Gate Bridge."

Alix's mind whirled with fear. Whoever was doing this was incredibly dangerous. And they could be anywhere . . .

"I'm almost at the bookstore, Kate. I'll call as soon as I find something."

Alix hung up and pedaled with all her might.

When she turned onto Columbus Avenue and saw City Lights standing high on the hill, her heart nearly stopped.

CHAPTER FORTY-ONE

City Lights Booksellers & Publishers is a historic treasure nestled between Chinatown and North Beach in San Francisco. Founded in 1953 by the poet Lawrence Ferlinghetti and the professor Peter D. Martin, the bookstore quickly became a hub for the Beat Generation. As a publisher, City Lights released Allen Ginsberg's iconic poem *HOWL* in 1956, rocketing both poet and publisher to international fame. The publishing house championed many other Beat writers, including Gregory Corso, Diane di Prima, and Bob Kauffman.

As a bookstore, City Lights features an extensive poetry section, which takes up an entire floor. The store is also well stocked with fiction and nonfiction titles. Venture down into the basement, and you'll find idiosyncratically named sections such as "Commodity Aesthetics" and "Stolen Continents." A mecca for liberals and radicals both near and far, the bookstore has been the site of many political protests.

Today, as Alix locked up her friend's bike, she saw the bookstore still maintained its rebellious spirit. The second-floor windows were covered in three hand-painted posters that read "OPEN MIND," "OPEN SPIRIT," "OPEN HEART." Alix straightened her monocle and headed for the front door.

Inside, the store was just as she'd remembered. A cavern lined with books, colors, and inspiration. The register sat just to the left of the entrance as always, the small section of surrealist literature welcoming visitors to the right. Alix thought she even recognized one of the booksellers restocking the shelves. The place seemed timeless, a time capsule of another world, another time before computers ruled everything.

When she stepped up into the first-floor fiction section, she felt her pulse rise. So much had led to this moment. Her twin brother John's disappearance, her struggles to understand his code, her fleeing from a crime scene with her bulldog Rocky, then racing up to San Francisco in her godmother's car. Two days ago she was a normal assistant in a

sort of normal job living a pretty normal life. OK, she *did* work for one of the biggest tech companies in the world, which was set to release Quanta, its mysterious, "earth-shattering" technology that very night, but her day-to-day life was far from lavish. Administrative assistant by day, Gen-Zer exploring the city at night. Her beginnings were even more modest, having been raised by working-class parents in El Cerrito, north of Berkeley in the San Francisco Bay Area. But now that all felt worlds away. Now she was a fugitive on the run, grasping for anything that might clear her and her brother's names. And here she was, trudging through this cathedral of books in an outfit straight out of the Gold Rush. Life couldn't possibly get any weirder.

Alix scanned through the aisles of books, searching for the K section. *Kerouac. Jack Kerouac. Big Sur. Where are you?* She reached the Is. Rachel Ingalls. Christopher Isherwood. Kazuo Ishiguro. Then the Js. Fleur Jaeggy. Alfred Jarry. James Joyce (sleep aid).

When she saw the Ks, she stopped dead in her tracks. Franz Kafka. John Keene. Ken Kesey. She'd gone too far. Her eyes went back up, landing directly on an entire row dedicated to Jack Kerouac. *Bingo.*

Her gaze slid over the titles. *Desolation Angels. The Dharma Bums. On the Road. Tristessa. Visions of Cody. Doctor Sax.* And then those two fateful words: *Big Sur.*

City Lights, always prepared for voracious Beat readers and curious tourists, had three copies on hand. More than enough room to hide something . . .

Alix inhaled deeply, knowing this moment would determine the rest of her life. She'd been thrust into a maelstrom of chaos, having traveled hundreds of miles from her former life, become a fugitive from the law, and risked everything to be here. And now there, hidden behind these books, was a glimmer of hope.

With trembling fingers, she pulled the leftmost copy from the shelf. She found nothing. Then she picked up the next book. Nothing. Her heart raced, praying she'd read John's code correctly. She went for the final book and lifted it off the shelf to find nothing but a hollow cavity before her. Nothing. Nothing but wood and dust. Nothing . . .

CHAPTER FORTY-TWO

Alix was in shock. *How could this be? How could I have been so wrong?* She flipped through each copy of *Big Sur*, wondering if John had hidden something *within* the books themselves. But there was nothing there either. Her mind raced through the code over and over again.

In The City Of Lights,
Behind Big Sur

Which other "City Of Lights"? She was confounded. She was lost. Her heart raced, chest heaved. *How is this possible? It can't be anywhere else. It just can't. Something must be wrong.* She sank to her knees, holding her chest, fearing she would faint.

She tried to regain composure, tried to understand. *What went wrong? Where did I go wrong? Why is everything so WRONG??*

She inhaled slowly, trying to regroup. *Maybe the thing John hid had moved.* It was now over twenty-four hours since he'd been here, so tourists or booksellers could have easily shuffled things around . . .

Alix stood and removed each Kerouac book on either side of the empty space. Nothing. She removed two more, then four. *There's nothing here!*

"Can I help you?" came a confused, nasal voice from behind.

Alix turned to see a spectacled, bookish man in his early twenties standing behind her, an eyebrow arched to the ceiling. She couldn't tell if his odd look was responding to the corset enwrapping her torso or because she'd just thrown half the Jack Kerouac section to the floor.

"Oh, I, um. I think I left something here yesterday," Alix stammered, trying to compose herself.

The bookseller's gaze shifted from Alix to the scattered books and back again, clearly irritated.

"Usually when people lose things, they ask at the register, not trash the place."

144 *People's Choice Literature*

"I'm sorry, I'll clean it up," she said, bending down to gather the books.

"It's OK, I'll take care of it," the bookseller said, grabbing a stack of paperbacks from her hands. "Just be more careful next time."

Alix mumbled an apology and started for the door, unsure of what to do or think anymore.

"Miss!?" called the bookseller.

Alix turned, bracing for part two of the scolding.

"Don't you want this?" he asked, holding up a USB drive.

Alix's monocled eye opened wide.

CHAPTER FORTY-THREE

Alix couldn't believe what she was seeing.

The bookseller continued. "I found it about a half hour ago while I was reshelving. Was on my way to bring it to the register when I found you here vandalizing our fiction section . . . It's yours, right?"

Alix froze. Everything that was wrong faded away. The chaos of the past few days seemed to fade away, replaced by a luminous doorway, a clear path out of this madness. John's code had worked, and for the first time since this insanity began, she had hope.

"Yes . . . Thank you," she said, grabbing the USB drive. "Really, I can't thank you enough," she repeated, shaking his hand.

The bookseller looked at her as if she were a total loon.

Alix turned and started for the door, realizing just how grateful she was that John had picked this bookstore. Most of his writer friends hardly watched the news—if they even had a television. Instead, they spent their free time with their faces pressed into paperbacks and word processors. City Lights Bookstore was likely the only place in San Francisco where no one had heard the names "Alix and John Finn" before. Where no one knew that she was running from the law, accused of colluding in corporate espionage and, at this point, likely murder.

Before exiting, Alix wondered if she shouldn't stay there, hiding out until nightfall. But her gut told her to run. She needed to get back to Kate's apartment to see what exactly was on this USB drive. And the sooner she did that, the closer she'd be to clearing her and John's names.

Stepping out into the cool afternoon air, Alix walked over to Kate's sprocket-wheeled bike and went to unlock it. She was just about to turn the key when a piercing screech came from uphill.

She straightened to find groups of tourists diving onto sidewalks and bolting into shops. She watched as a Ford Fusion swerved between taxis and SUVs, careening left and then right until it was racing directly toward a stock-white, trembling Alix Finn.

CHAPTER FORTY-FOUR

Alix watched in horror as the Ford Fusion accelerated, hurtling right at her. She could hardly think, her mind reeling with fear.

Suddenly two hands grabbed her and pulled her across the sidewalk just as the car crashed into Kate's bike and slammed it into a streetlight. It all happened so fast.

Alix then found herself on the cement, staring up at a face she somehow recognized.

"Jason?" she whimpered.

"Sorry," said Jason Stone, helping her up. "I had to move fast. That car nearly killed you!"

"What are you doing here!?" she asked.

Stone said nothing, checking Alix for injuries.

"I'm fine," she said.

Then she turned to see the Ford Fusion plowed into the streetlight, smoke pouring out of its hood.

"What the heck happened?" she asked.

"*What are you wearing?*" Stone returned with a smirk.

Alix gave him a stern look like this wasn't the time.

Stone shrugged and turned toward the smoking Ford Fusion. "It all happened so fast. I was just walking up the street and saw this car coming, and then I see you—"

Stone fell silent, his face draining of color.

"Oh my gosh," he said. "There's no one at the wheel!"

Alix recalled the news from the day before. Kevin Arnold had been in a driverless Ford Fusion when he drove off a cliff. *Were these Ford Fusions somehow connected!?*

Just when she was about to voice her suspicions, a metallic gurgling erupted from the smoking wreck. The sound grew into a gnarly crunch, giving new life to this previously dead vehicle.

The Most Wanted Novel   147

Alix stared in disbelief as the zombie Ford Fusion—its hood deeply dented, its windshield smashed—revved up and pulled away from the sidewalk, turning until it was pointed directly at Alix once more.

"Run," said Stone.

Alix gulped, staring at the Ford Fusion in horror.

"*RUN!!!*"

Stone grabbed her hand, and they both took off, the Ford Fusion growling and screeching after them. They dodged between taxis and trolleys, praying the metal hunks would block the Ford Fusion's progress. But the ghost driver was too quick. It swerved around the moving barriers, its engine grinding in a grating howl.

Alix risked a glance over her shoulder to watch the Ford Fusion run out of luck, crashing into the side of a trolley, sending passengers flying onto the street and clearly damaging the Ford. But like clockwork, the car reversed out of the trolley and swung back in the direction of its prey. It revved past a Chevrolet Equinox and sent a Nissan Rogue right into a fire hydrant, throwing a geyser of water high into the air. Then the Ford Fusion spun around a motorcycle before locating a clear path to Alix and Stone.

"It's gaining on us!" Alix cried, craning her neck toward the raging vehicle.

Stone looked back this time as well, removing his Mark XIX Desert Eagle .44 Magnum from its holster, raising his hand, and firing two rounds into the right front tire of the Ford Fusion. Rubber exploded with a concussive pop, jolting the car to the right. But still it clawed forward, sparking and grinding against the asphalt like a wounded animal.

Stone stepped to the side and aimed, firing two more rounds into the left front tire. The explosion cut through the air and ricocheted off buildings as the Ford Fusion slumped to the ground. But even then, it wouldn't relent, its back tires flailing against gravity and friction in a pathetic attempt to kill.

Alix and Stone stared in disbelief, noticing the groups of tourists that had started to gather, snapping pictures and clapping.

"We need to get you somewhere safe," said Stone.

"I have a place," said Alix. "Just not sure how I can get back there now."

Stone scanned the streets for a way out.

"Come on," he said. "I have an idea."

CHAPTER FORTY-FIVE

One hundred and fifteen miles south and 41,000 feet in the air, D. J. Wylde was enjoying a glass of cabernet in his Gulfstream G150 private jet. Robed in his signature blue, he raised his glass to his six loyal assistants. Anyone unaware might've mistaken this scene for a John Lennon press junket in 1973.

"Friends," he said, tipping the glass to his apostles. "Today is a bittersweet occasion. Our dear Alix has departed our loving family for new shores. The loss hurts, it really does."

Wylde placed his hand on his chest in a dramatic display of grief.

"But we wish her well." He sighed before continuing. "*Yes*, she betrayed our family. *Yes*, she colluded with a competitor to steal company secrets. But as we've learned throughout the years, it's that forgiveness reigns supreme. Forgiveness frees us from the dregs of anger and hate, those emotions that so easily weigh down our hearts and minds. So, let us raise our glasses in a toast to Alix Finn. To our lady, our love, our forgiveness."

All five assistants raised their glasses in unison and sipped.

"Of course, we'll need a replacement," said Wylde. "But we'll find one in time. For now, let us focus our energies on the mission at hand."

The five assistants looked at one another in eager anticipation.

"That's right," Wylde beamed. "Quanta."

"Quanta!" they cheered, raising their glasses in unison.

"Yes, my friends, the time has come. Tonight Quanta is born. Our crown jewel. The blessing that millennia of science and human perseverance have gifted us. So soon joy will return to the Earth, freeing us from the shackles of chaos and heralding a new hope. A new harmony. A *quantum* harmony."

Wylde could feel the shiver flow through his followers.

"Yes, tonight Quanta will unlock computing power never before seen. Researchers will finally cure our most stubborn diseases. Cancer?

Pandemics? Gone. Same with recessions, and worse, depressions. The old world will fade away, replaced by a new world of knowledge and light. A new beginning. A new *now*."

Wylde grinned, letting each word sink in. He could see the fire ignite in each of their eyes as they leaned closer, yearning to uncover Quanta's secrets.

"Tonight all will be revealed!" Wylde declared. "Tonight we bloom!"

"Yeah!" They all shouted in unison, raising their glasses high.

"But for now, my friends," said Wylde, "please return to your seats. Our daily meditation will begin in just a few moments as we descend through the heavens toward our beloved San Francisco."

Wylde's assistants obediently followed suit, reclining and closing their eyes. As they waited for the meditation to begin, Wylde gazed out over the billowing clouds below. There, high above, higher than birds can reach, higher than humans could have imagined a century earlier, he beheld the beauty before him and sighed. Memories of his humble beginnings flooded his mind—the years of striving, the brutal competition. But they were soon eclipsed by a new vision. Of peace. Of calm. He sat there and held this vision, beaming with the promise of new hope, soaring high above it all like a quantum god.

"And so it begins," he said to himself. "So it begins."

CHAPTER FORTY-SIX

Alix Finn and Jason Stone were out of breath but relieved. After narrowly escaping the killer Ford Fusion, they'd fled through a maze of North Beach and Chinatown alleys, turning right, dodging left, swerving past dumpsters and stray cats, in hopes they'd throw off whoever—or whatever—was after them.

Finally, they stumbled upon a hole-in-the-wall vintage store tucked between an apartment building and a gift shop. Stone suggested Alix change into a new disguise and make her way back to Kate's house as soon as possible.

Now, as Alix studied herself in the changing room mirror, she couldn't believe her eyes. Here was the second ridiculous costume she'd worn today. Two more than she'd worn in the past five years.

With a smug grin, Stone stepped up behind her.

"Not bad," he said, giving her a once over in the mirror. "You look like a James Bond character."

"I look like a walking cliché," said Alix, turning to the side and scrutinizing the black jumpsuit covered in a lightning-bolt pattern.

"You look good to me . . ." he said, eyeing her speculatively.

Alix's throat constricted, the magnetic pull between them growing stronger with each passing second. As she stood there, beholding this hunk of a man, she felt the overwhelming urge to kiss him. His lips looked so soft compared to his stiff frame, so inviting. She imagined him grabbing her and pulling her close, their lips melding in pure ecstasy. Not since Timmy, both her first kiss and first betrayal, had she fallen head over heels for someone. She thought back to the few guys she'd dated since then and how they'd just never really clicked. Now, with Stone standing before her, Alix's mind was racing, her heart fluttering like rose petals in the wind. Stone was Adonis incarnate, a gentleman and a man of honor. She tried to fight off the feelings welling up inside her, but they were too strong. *Does he feel the same about me?*

Her mind jolted back to reality when Stone placed a black wig on her head.

"There you go," he said with a sly grin.

"I feel ridiculous," she said, cheeks flushed in embarrassment.

"Well, you *look* ridiculous, but that's the point," he smirked. "It's the perfect camouflage in San Francisco. You'll be safer this way."

Alix nodded, still skeptical.

Stone turned her away from the mirror and toward him.

"Listen, Alix, these people—whoever is doing this—aren't joking around. This is the best chance we've got to keep you safe."

With yearning eyes, Alix couldn't help but ask, "Why are you helping me?"

Stone wasn't prepared for this question. He cocked his head to the side, as if considering her words. As if he'd been acting on pure instinct and hadn't once stopped to ask why. Then his face settled into resolve.

"It's true, I'm risking a lot helping you," he said. "I could lose my job over this. But I believe you, Alix. I know that somewhere in the mess of all this, you and John are innocent, two twins caught in the wrong place at the worst possible time."

Alix's heart swelled, unable to resist pushing further.

"But what about you?" she asked. "Isn't there a Mrs. Stone waiting for you back home?"

Stone winced, clearly pained by the question.

"Oh, I'm sorry," she said, brushing his arm. "Sore subject."

"No, it's OK," he said, gathering himself. "It just, it's been a long time since there was a Mrs. Stone. Four years to be exact."

"Goodness," said Alix. "I'm so sorry."

"Thanks," said Stone. "It's the reason I moved to LA. I couldn't stand to be in our apartment anymore."

"I can only imagine," said Alix. She wanted to ask more, but Stone beat her to the punch.

"It's the nature of this work," he said. "It puts the ones closest to you in danger. No one's safe when criminals run rampant." He let out a deep breath. "And it was a criminal gang I busted that got her. They wanted revenge after justice had been served. Haven't been the same since."

Alix's chest felt heavy. She could feel his pain, his loss. Then she acted without thinking. Instinct kicked in. Without hesitation, she moved closer, pressing her chest against his, wrapping her arms around his wide, firm frame.

152 *People's Choice Literature*

"I'm so sorry," she whispered.

Stone's body went from rock-hard to butter. He wrapped his arms around her as well, and in that moment, time slipped away. The insanity of the past few days. The danger that awaited them outside. The whole world disappeared. All that remained were these two lost souls united in each others arms.

Stone pulled back and gazed deeply into Alix's eyes. *Is this it?* she thought. *Finally a kiss.* With a slow, deliberate movement, she closed her eyes and bit her lip in gleeful anticipation. She felt the brush of his day-old stubble on her cheek, awaiting the plump softness of his lips, when suddenly a sound came from outside the changing room door.

With lightning speed, Stone pulled back, scanning the lit space between the floor and the door. There they both beheld the dim light from the main room casting the shadows of two approaching feet. Stone raised a finger to his lips. Then pulled out his Mark XIX Desert Eagle and slid toward the door.

Alix's heart raced as she watched Stone's muscles tense. He leaned in closer to the door, listening intently to the heavy breaths on the other side. When the creeping footsteps drew nearer, she stopped breathing.

Suddenly Stone swung the door open and lifted the Mark XIX Desert Eagle directly at the form beyond.

The store clerk jumped, yelping, "Oh, ship!"

Stone quickly lowered his weapon. "Apologies, sir."

The clerk spun and scurried away, ducking behind a row of shirts and out of view.

Stone turned to Alix with hardened eyes.

"You better go," he said. "Now."

"You're not coming with me?" she asked.

"I'm better help covering for you."

Alix looked concerned. "What will you tell them?"

"That I protected you from that Ford Fusion out of common decency. Then I chased you through these alleyways but came up short. Can't imagine they've got surveillance cameras in these tiny streets."

Alix was clearly disappointed to be leaving him.

But Stone gave a reassuring smile. "You have my number. Just call if you need anything. The most important thing is to get back to your friend's house and away from all this madness."

"Thank you," she said, pulling back in for a hug.

Stone held her close, relishing the touch before releasing her. "You better leave."

Alix nodded, double checked to see if the USB was in her new, lightning-striped pocket, and then ran out of the store and into the chaos that was San Francisco.

CHAPTER FORTY-SEVEN

By the time Alix arrived back at Kate's apartment, her body felt like a lead balloon. The weight of the past few days combined with her harrowing journey to City Lights Bookstore fused into a feeling of utter exhaustion.

"Kate?" Alix called as she opened the door.

"In the kitchen!"

Rocky promptly waddled across the floor, panting and wiggling his rear end with glee. Alix kneeled down and gave him a scratch.

"Good boy," she said, standing up and making her way to the kitchen.

"The fugitive returns!" Kate joked, salting the stir fry on the stove.

"Good one," Alix deadpanned.

Kate turned from the stove, her jaw nearly hitting the floor. "What happened to my dress!?"

"Long story," Alix said, flopping into a chair.

"I worked for months on that! Was sure to be a hit at Burning Man next year!"

"I'm sorry," Alix pleaded. "I nearly died trying to get that USB."

Kate nodded knowingly. "Oh, I know all about that. You're back to number one trending topic on X."

Alix's eyes went wide.

"There are memes galore of that FBI guy shooting the killer car like an action hero and you freaking out like the final girl in a horror movie."

"That's crazy," Alix said, shaking her head.

"It's true," Kate said, holding up her phone. "People are actually rooting for you at this point. Everyone likes an underdog."

"Underdog?"

"That's what they're calling you. It's clear you're in way over your head," Kate shrugged.

Alix was stunned. Just days before she never could have imagined this kind of attention.

"Oh, and there's a new report about you," Kate said, scrolling through her phone. "The FBI says you're now a suspect in the murder of William Moriarty, the son of Richard Moriarty, CEO of gAIa."

"*What!?*" cried Alix, grabbing the phone.

Her stomach dropped. This was bad. Very bad. And getting worse. She was grateful to be back at Kate's, but now nowhere felt safe. She was wanted for murder—not just an accomplice anymore . . .

"Here," Kate said, handing her a Budweiser. "You need this."

"Darn right," Alix said, taking a long swig.

Kate went back to the stove and shoveled the chopped chicken breasts, green beans, and rice onto two plates. She sat them on the kitchen table, and Alix swiftly hoovered them up.

"Thank you," she said, her mouth full of fried rice. "You really are the best friend."

"Not a good enough friend to still have her nineteenth-century dress . . ." Kate huffed.

Alix looked at her in disbelief. "It was steampunk, Kate. *Steampunk.* I did you a favor."

Kate rolled her eyes, prodding the rice with her fork.

CHAPTER FORTY-EIGHT

The Phillip Burton Federal Building rises high above San Francisco's Golden Gate Avenue, a monument to the city's storied prosperity. Designed by the renowned architectural firm of John Carl Warnecke and Associates and built in 1964, its cuboid form is clad in concrete and faced with cast stone. Home to numerous federal agencies, the building is best known as the location of the U.S. Court of Appeals for the Ninth Circuit as well as the FBI's San Francisco field office.

That night, as Jason Stone approached the building, he looked up and swallowed, praying his cover story would hold up. After he'd left the vintage store, he walked back to the decommissioned Ford Fusion to find swarms of SFPD and FBI agents eager for answers. Stone told them he'd lost Alix in a network of back alleys. When asked about his protecting her from the murderous Ford Fusion, he didn't have to do much convincing. Alix may be a fugitive, but all criminals deserve a trial, not the arbitrary justice of cold-blooded murder.

Now, entering the Federal Building, he wanted answers to the labyrinth of crimes he found himself in the middle of. He flashed his badge to the security guard, put his gun through the scanner, and made his way upstairs.

Entering the FBI offices, Stone was greeted by the familiar smells of federal buildings—a mix of stale coffee and the tang of gun oil. He walked down the hallway, ignoring the stares of his fellow agents, who were greater in number than was normal at such an hour. But Stone knew he should've expected this: Alix and her brother were now the FBI's top priority. All eyes were on this case.

With a determined gulp, Stone approached the door of the Special Agent in Charge, commonly referred to as the SAC, and gave a knock.

The door quickly swung open, revealing the SAC himself and someone Stone could never have expected to find in San Francisco that day: Director Emerson.

Stone did a double take, but there he was, smoothing down his stubborn cowlick like clockwork.

"Welcome, Detective Stone," said the SAC, extending his hand.

Stone shook it and entered the room.

"I bet you didn't expect to find me here," the director smirked. "Thought I'd lend a hand, given the complexity of the situation."

"That's very kind of you, Director Emerson," said Stone, still trying to process this surprising turn of events.

As they took their seats, the SAC wasted no time. "I've been in touch with Director Emerson all day, right along with Deputy Director Garcia and Director Langford. We're all hoping for a swift end to this saga . . ."

"Of course," Stone nodded in agreement.

The SAC gave him a stern look. "Do you have any updates?"

Stone let out a sigh. "Unfortunately, no. My brief interaction with Alix Finn didn't yield much information beyond the fact that this driverless car wasn't much a fan of hers."

The two other men exchanged glances as Stone quietly berated himself for lying.

He cleared his throat and continued. "So, have you found any connections between Kevin Arnold's death inside a driverless car and the one in North Beach? It seems too similar to be a coincidence."

"We're not ruling out any options," said Director Emerson, eyeing him suspiciously. "But I suspect we'll find they're unrelated."

Stone gave Emerson an odd look. "Do we have the forensic report on this most recent vehicle?"

"Not yet," said the director. "We're hoping to have that by morning."

"What else do you have?"

"Unfortunately, nothing," said the SAC. "SFPD are on high alert searching for Alix and John Finn. But it's been like looking for a needle in a haystack. All we got are false alarms and shoddy tips. Nothing substantial."

Stone nodded, sensing the SAC and Director Emerson were hiding something.

"Look," said the SAC, with a heavy sigh. "We need to talk, Detective Stone."

Stone looked from the SAC to Director Emerson, who wore a knowing, unfriendly smile on his face.

"Director Emerson has concerns over your involvement in this case."

Stone's gut turned.

158 *People's Choice Literature*

"We're aware you visited Alix Stone before the investigators arrived at her apartment last night."

Stone gave Emerson the side eye.

"Of course, we all know how that went," the SAC continued. "She slipped out right under your fingers. And then today you're somehow in the right place at just the right time to save Alix from that vehicle. You help her, and once again she disappears."

Stone sighed.

"We're starting to see a pattern here."

Stone met their gazes firmly. "I'm just doing my job."

"We're not sure you are, Detective Stone," said the SAC. "You've only been on this case for two days, and you've already made two critical mistakes."

"I'm telling you," Stone insisted, "there may have been a few fumbles, but I'm on the edge of a real breakthrough here. Kevin Arnold's death in a driverless car and Alix Finn's near-death at the hand of the same make and model. William Moriarty's and Tom Woodman's deaths by some strange turbine. It's all connected."

The SAC raised an eyebrow. "This isn't the *X-Files*, Agent Stone. We deal in reality, not wild conspiracy theories. We work with facts. And the facts are making us question your tactics."

Stone's face turned beet red. "I know I'm on the right track," he said. "I can feel it."

"You're not on any track," the SAC shot back. "And, frankly, you're out of line. We need results. And we need them the day before yesterday."

"But—"

The SAC cut him off. "We have reason to believe you may be compromised. You're just too close to this case."

Stone frowned.

"I'm sorry, Agent Stone," said the SAC, "but we're putting you on temporary leave."

"*What!?*" Stone exclaimed. "But I'm so close."

"The only thing you're close to is a grand jury," said the SAC.

Stone said nothing.

"And you're off this case."

Stone stood up, hands in fists, glaring with disdain at Director Emerson.

"Agent Stone," said the SAC, "you are dismissed."

Stone turned to leave, but the SAC's voice stopped him.

"Wait," he said. "Your badge and gun."

Stone paused, feeling the weight of his sidearm. Then he turned, glaring at the SAC and Director Emerson, now twirling his cowlick like a lasso.

"This isn't over," he said, tossing his gun and badge on the desk.

Stone turned and left the office, slamming the door behind him. He stormed down the hall, fists clenched, blood boiling.

He'd been so close to the truth he could almost taste it. And now he'd been kicked off the case. *For what? Helping someone in need?* He was furious. He could feel himself shaking, his mind racing as he tried to figure out what to do next.

CHAPTER FORTY-NINE

Back outside, Stone ignored the lavender haze blanketing the sky above him. He stomped across the plaza and down to the sidewalk, unsure of where to go or what to do. Rage was blinding his thinking. He was just about to cross the street when a voice called his name from behind. Stone turned but saw no one.

"Over here," the voice called.

Stone turned to find a sleek black limousine idling nearby, its hazard lights blinking in a steady syncopation. His eyes landed on that familiar face in the window: D. J. Wylde looking as wistfully Lennon-esque as ever.

"Nice evening, isn't it, Agent Stone?" Wylde gestured to the indigo sky.

"How'd you know I was here?" Stone asked firmly.

"How'd I know an FBI agent would be at the FBI building?" Wylde smirked. "It doesn't take a rocket scientist to figure that out."

Stone said nothing.

"I just wanted to commend your work earlier," said Wylde. "You were valiant in the face of a grave menace."

"Thanks," said Stone, eager for Wylde to get to the point.

"Look, Agent Stone, my colleagues and I," he gestured into the limo, "are on our way to a Giants game, and we'd love for you to join us."

The offer caught Stone off guard. If the past two days had taught him anything, it was to expect the unexpected. But as he mulled over Wylde's invitation, he tried to measure the billionaire's potential motives against his love for a good game. And baseball was his favorite.

"No strings attached," Wylde reassured him with a charming grin, "just a few friends enjoying a great American pastime."

The prospect of a game calmed the troubled Stone. With Alix safe at Kate's house and him out of a job, there wasn't much to do until she called.

"So, what'll it be?" asked Wylde.

Stone shrugged and started toward the limo. "Why not?" *What's the worst that could happen?*

CHAPTER FIFTY

A mile away in the Mission District, Alix and Kate were huddled in Kate's cramped office, surrounded by a jungle of potted plants and tangled wires. As Alix studied the network of intertwining stems, vines, and cables, she felt like she'd walked into a strange, otherworldly laboratory. But the persistent sound of Rocky's snoring helped ground her in reality.

Kate switched on her Dell Inspiron, and they both watched as the screen booted up.

"This thing's state of the art," Kate said, tapping the monitor. "10th generation i7 chip and 64 gigabytes of RAM."

Alix looked at her like she was speaking another language. "I have no idea what that means, Kate."

"It means it's fast. Very, very fast."

Alix nodded, anxious over what they'd uncover on the USB drive. She held it tight like a knight protecting the Holy Grail after a death-defying journey. The metaphor didn't seem too far-fetched considering she'd nearly died earlier that day under the wheels of a monstrous Ford Fusion . . .

When the home screen flickered to life, Kate turned to Alix and extended her hand. "We're ready."

Alix swallowed, handing her the USB drive.

"Here goes nothing," Kate said before inserting it into the computer.

They both looked at the screen, waiting in anticipation.

At first, nothing happened. Then the whir of the machine grew louder, as if struggling through some complex equation. They waited for something to appear, but nothing came.

Then, just like that, the drive materialized on the screen.

"There we go," Kate nodded, dragging her mouse over the icon. "Here comes the moment of truth."

Alix looked at the screen with trepidation. Everything had built up to this moment. John's mysterious disappearance. His code so keenly

162   *People's Choice Literature*

hidden. Her deciphering the code while the FBI raided their house. And, as icing on the chaos cake, the Ford Fusion fiasco from this afternoon, which nearly cost her her life. Finally, it was here. She had the USB drive that John had so cleverly guided her toward. That drive on Kate's computer held the secrets John had uncovered. Secrets so grave that someone—or something—was willing to kill for them . . .

Kate clicked on the drive icon, and a window popped up: "Please enter password."

"Password?" Alix echoed in frustration.

Kate shrugged. "Did John ever mention a password?"

Alix shook her head. "I don't think so."

Her eyes stared into space, a knot of anxiety constricting in her stomach. Then memories flooded back to a few weeks earlier, to working late at Genera. John had asked her to log into his Genera email account—the company was so paranoid about its secrets it only allowed email access from company computers. He was home and had forgotten to back up the most recent draft of his novel. Alix wasn't surprised to hear he'd been writing at work—John always complained about how boring and unfulfilling his job was—but she couldn't help feeling annoyed at being pulled into his scheme. In the end, she complied, logged in, and sent him the manuscript. Piece of cake. Now, as she sat there in Kate's cavernous room, faced with a password request, she felt suddenly grateful.

"RockyTheD@g," Alix said assertively.

Rocky perked up at the sound of his name, his head tilted in sleepy confusion. Alix gave him a pat, and he drifted back to sleep.

She turned to Kate. "It's RockyTheD@g. No spaces. Capital R. Capital T. Capital D. And the O in Dog is an 'at' symbol."

Kate nodded, typed the password, and hit ENTER.

The dialog box shook like a disapproving head saying "Wrong!"

Alix glared at the screen in anger. "Did you type it right?" She walked Kate through the password one more time, but again the window shook a "no."

"Any other ideas?" Kate asked.

Alix went to her bag and removed John's notebook, flipping through it. Looking for something. Anything. But nothing mentioned or even suggested a password.

Alix's eyes widened in disbelief. She'd come so far, got so close to the revelation John had promised her. And now this. Another roadblock. Another dead end. She let out a heavy sigh.

Kate sat back. "Maybe we could try John's birthday?"

Alix scoffed, shaking her head. "Come on. He's smarter than that. He went to great lengths to hide this USB. If it got into the wrong hands, he wouldn't let them gain access so easily."

A frustrated sigh escaped Kate's lips.

"Can't you just use your hacking skills to crack it?" asked Alix. "It's what you do!"

Kate furrowed her brow, tapping her fingers on the keyboard. "Normally, yes. I'd break this in minutes. But it seems John used one of Genera's high-security USB drives. I'm not sure I can. Even if I could, it would take me like ten thousand years. Unless I had a quantum computer, that is."

Alix turned to her. "A what?"

"A quantum computer," Kate repeated with a hint of awe in her voice. "A quantum computer could crack this in a trillionth of a second."

"You don't have one?" Alix gestured to the network of cables, plants, and computer monitors surrounding them.

Kate let out a boisterous laugh. "Wow. Don't you work at a tech company? You've never heard of a *quantum computer*?"

Alix shrunk back sheepishly. "I mean, I've heard the word tossed around . . ."

"They're just the most advanced computing technology at the moment," Kate explained. "So advanced it'll probably take years, even decades to perfect. They're way too big and require way too much energy for a dingy room like this."

She chuckled, then continued. "Quantum computers, whenever they reach their prime, will be able to crack a code like this," she pointed at the screen, "in no time. They use quantum physics to solve complex problems our current computers couldn't tackle in, as I said, ten thousand years."

Alix looked at her in disbelief.

"This is why everyone's so scared of them. These computers, once advanced enough, will make all previous computer encryption obsolete. Whoever wields a quantum computer could hack into any government's private communications, any financial system, anything. And that's just the start of it."

Kate noticed Alix's face betrayed a strange mix of awe and fear.

"So, it's hopeless, then?" Alix asked in defeat.

"Genera specifically designed this USB to be impenetrable," Kate nodded.

164　*People's Choice Literature*

Alix let out a weary sigh and leaned back. What could she do? John had gone to such great lengths to protect this information, and now both of their fates resided in obtaining whatever was on this USB drive. Her head fell into her hands as she let out a deep, guttural groan.

"Ugh," she spat. "Nothing is working."

Kate placed a comforting hand on her shoulder. "We'll find a way. You've come this far . . ."

Alix nodded, wiping tears from her eyes. "I guess you're right. We'll figure something out."

Kate wrapped her in a warm hug. "I know we will."

As Alix rubbed her eyes and stood up to go to the bathroom, she noticed something slip from John's notebook.

"Huh?" she said to herself.

She picked it up and turned it over. John's Genera keycard . . .

A spark of realization ignited within her. *John must have hidden his keycard in his notebook to help me access his email . . . or was it a coincidence?* She turned the thought over in her mind before realizing that in a time as crazy as the past two days, nothing could be coincidental. There was order to this chaos.

"Oh my god, Kate!" Alix exclaimed.

Kate raised an eyebrow expectantly. "What is it?"

"How far are Genera's San Francisco headquarters from here?"

Kate looked at her skeptically. "Uh, I don't know, like a fifteen-minute bike ride?"

Alix's eyes lit up with determination. "I'm gonna need another costume."

CHAPTER FIFTY-ONE

Hugging the coastline of San Francisco's South of Market district, Oracle Park is home to the San Francisco Giants. Designed by the esteemed architectural firm Populous, the stadium is known for its patented "pinwheel" design, the first of its kind in the United States. Here fans enjoy right from the comfort of their seats not only America's greatest pastime but beautiful, sweeping views of the San Francisco Bay. The park is so close to the water that kayakers loiter around the stadium, awaiting a home run that, if they're lucky, they just might snag.

That night, as Jason Stone settled into his plush seat in Genera's VIP box, he could see why people liked the place so much. The glittering lights, the breathtaking views. The energy of the crowd was electric. But for Stone, a man who preferred the feel of being crammed in with the crowd, the VIP section was a bit too excessive. The Chilean kettle corn popcorn, the waiters and waitresses, the heated seats. It was less like baseball and more like a high-profile corporate luncheon.

Worse, a creeping paranoia had begun to cloud Stone's joy for the game. He couldn't figure out what D. J. Wylde was up to bringing him here. *There's no such thing as a free lunch*, he thought as he watched the pitcher warming up. *Especially when it comes from a billionaire*. Stone also didn't buy the "chance" encounter outside the FBI field office. *A guy as wealthy as Wylde must have his ways . . .*

He was so lost in thought he missed the first pitch of the game. But reality came back in full when D. J. Wylde, clad in his signature blue cloak and flanked by his rainbow entourage, tapped him on the arm and offered him a pint of Guinness.

"Enjoying yourself, Agent Stone?" asked Wylde.

Stone nodded, accepting the beer with skeptical gratitude. "Thanks."

Wylde looked out over the glowing field, his face beaming. "You might not know this about me, but I'm quite the baseball fan."

Stone shook his head in disbelief. It was hard to imagine Wylde having any interests outside of technology and tie-dye.

"It's true," Wylde insisted. "Ever since I was a boy, I've dreamed of owning a major league team. Can you imagine? 'Genera Park, Home of the San Francisco Giants.' I think it has a nice ring."

Stone nodded politely. The truth was he'd long despised the business names now plastered across every stadium. Crypto.com Arena. FedEx Field. Bank One Ballpark. Stone longed for baseball's good old days, when the names of great men adorned these stadiums, when it was more about the people and less about the money.

Wylde placed his hand on Stone's shoulder.

"So, Stone," he said, his voice low and urgent. "I was curious to hear your thoughts about my offer from yesterday. About you joining Genera."

Here we go.

"What you've seen this week is just the tip of the security iceberg. A company like ours is under constant assault from hackers and thieves." He took a sip of his beer. "I've studied your work, Stone. I've seen how you think. You're the kind of man who could make a real difference."

"That's very flattering," Stone replied. He wasn't sure he could stomach working for a company like Genera. He'd worked for the common man his entire adult life. Just like his dad had done. And his dad before that.

"I've worked for the good of the people my whole life," Stone finally said aloud. "It wouldn't feel right."

Wylde turned and gave Stone a look of deep offense. "Mister Stone, I'm not sure you understand what we do at Genera. 'The people' are our lifeblood. They're the only reason we exist. We strive each day to find even better ways to serve them, to create a better world. To do great things."

Stone gave a perfunctory nod.

"And to be frank, Mister Stone, the public sector is dying. It's fraught with endless red tape and weak technology. It's stuck in a twentieth-century daydream. It's not designed to tackle today's most urgent issues."

Stone considered Wylde's words and saw he had a point. His cousin had described the nightmares of maneuvering the food stamp program. His best friend from high school had tried to get unemployment at the start of the COVID-19 pandemic but couldn't find anyone who could help.

"Genera is the solution to all this," Wylde said, his cloaked followers nodding in unison behind him. "Quanta will streamline bureaucratic systems, creating ease and understanding for all. All chaos will end. All our greatest problems will finally be over."

"And the people will love us for it," a freckled assistant chimed in.

Wylde nodded in affirmation, his eyes trained on Stone. "And you can be part of it, Mister Stone. You can help secure this future. We need you."

Stone studied Wylde and his eager assistants, all beaming at him like crazed children after eating too much ice cream.

"It sounds a bit too good to be true," said Stone, putting down his Guinness.

Wylde gave him a smirk. "Agent Stone, the future is never too good to be true."

Stone turned his gaze as the pitcher wound up and hurled an 90 mph curve ball through the air with expert precision. The batter swung and missed, launching Stone and the stadium into an eruption of applause. When he turned back to Wylde, Stone found the tech guru and his assistants completely unphased by the roaring of the crowd, staring disapprovingly at Stone and nothing else.

"Mister Stone," Wylde said, his tone now tinged with anger. "It's no secret you've been put on leave. That your job is in jeopardy. I've been kind. *We've* been kind." He gestured to his assistants, who nodded in agreement. "The least you can do is give us your undivided attention."

Stone furrowed his brow. "How did you know I was put on leave?"

Wylde smiled wide, revealing the glint of a gold molar. "That's not important."

Stone was flummoxed. *First he finds me at the FBI building, then he knows I've been put on leave.* Now with Wylde and his assistants staring at him in eager anticipation, he was starting to feel it was time to split.

"I'm sorry," he said, standing up. "I think it's time to go."

Wylde frowned.

"It's not you," Stone joked. "It's me."

Wylde chuckled dryly, clearly not amused. "So it's a breakup, is it? Before we even got started."

"I'm sorry, Mister Wylde. I didn't come for a job interview."

Stone reached out to shake Wylde's hand.

Wylde accepted it limply. "Very well." Then he turned away from Stone. "If you change your mind, you know where to find us."

Stone turned and walked up the stairs, feeling a dozen eyes burning a hole in his back. But before he left, he took one last look at the field where an 85 mph knuckleball sliced through the air. The batter swung and missed again.

CHAPTER FIFTY-TWO

The iconic 1355 Market Street, once home to the popular social media site X, now acted as Genera's downtown San Francisco headquarters. Erected in 1937, the same year as the Golden Gate Bridge, it was known for much of its life as the Western Furniture Exchange and Merchandise Mart. Under this moniker, it operated as a massive, multifloor showroom displaying furniture, electronics, and appliances. A timeless Art Deco masterpiece, the building stands as a testament to the city's rich history. Its graceful, sweeping lines and vast interior are a lasting tribute to the human spirit.

It was this very allure that drew D. J. Wylde to the building when it became available for new tenants. He and Genera swept in and decorated it in the company's signature blend of 1960s Day-Glo flourishes and contemporary business chic.

But that night, as Alix Finn approached 1355 Market, there was little time to enjoy the architecture. Her heart was already doing jumping jacks.

She locked up Kate's second, less-flamboyant bike and adjusted her black wig—the same one Jason Stone had given her earlier that day. This time, she was dressed in a generic Genera cloak, which Kate somehow had on hand. It seemed her box of costumes was endless.

Alix approached the front door with determination. *Just get in, check his computer, and get out.* That was all she needed to do. Clutching John's key card in one hand and the USB drive in the other, Alix swallowed. She thought of all the things that could go wrong in there—the belly of the beast.

Inside, she nodded as she approached the security guard.

"Late night?" the man asked in a gravelly voice weathered by decades of cigarettes.

"Tell me about it," she replied, quickly forging John's signature on the sign-in form.

With a nod she strode toward the elevators, silently praying that Genera hadn't deactivated John's key card in the past thirty-six hours. Or worse—put it on high alert. Would she even be able to leave if an alarm went off? Those front doors would surely auto-lock, giving her nowhere to go . . .

Alix took a long inhale and raised the key to the card reader. When she tapped it, she nearly collapsed: the reader went red. Alix held her breath, awaiting the inevitable alarm. But none came.

She turned to the security guard, awaiting his scorn, but found him sucked into his phone. *Thank God*, she said to herself before turning back around.

Alix studied the card reader once more and took a deep breath. *OK, you got this.* She raised the key card, a bead of sweat rolling down her brow. She pressed it to the reader, and instantly it blinked green.

The doors slid open, and Alix finally exhaled.

"If it's not one thing . . ." she sighed and stepped in.

CHAPTER FIFTY-THREE

Entering the third-floor library, Alix quickly started down the dark, main corridor, past rows and rows of bookcases and beanbag chairs. When she reached the dim busts of Aristotle and Ayn Rand, Alix was reminded this was no ordinary library. Genera, the most advanced tech company in the world, had dedicated a full floor of its San Francisco headquarters to the printed word.

As D. J. Wylde always said, "There's nothing like the feel of a physical book." He'd given plenty of lectures on the endurance of the book as a technology. The CEO's main argument was that since Johannes Gutenberg invented the printing press in 1450, books had transformed the planet in a way not unlike the internet and smartphones. Wylde believed that people still reading print books over five hundred years later, even with access to eBooks and audiobooks, was a testament to the awesomeness of this simple yet profound technology.

He may be right, but Alix pushed the thought aside when she finally spotted the dim computer station in the distance. She hurried straight to the closest monitor, shaking the mouse and bringing the machine to life.

Just as she'd done months ago when she helped John access his novel manuscript, Alix entered his username and password—RockyTheD@g— and watched as her twin brother's personal desktop materialized before her.

She first opened his Documents folder, scanning down the list of files for anything related to this mysterious USB drive. She found many work-related files—security reports, video surveillance recordings, the usual—and smiled when she spotted John's novel, which he'd cheekily retitled "A_Brave_New_World_Part_2.docx."

When Alix realized skimming this folder was going nowhere, she searched the entire computer for files containing the word "USB." A string of incomprehensible names appeared, with extensions like ".pem" and ".xml." No text document with John's secret password.

The Most Wanted Novel   171

Alix let out a deep sigh. *Come on, John. Help me here.*

The only other thing she could think of was to check his email.

So she cracked her knuckles and guided the mouse to the email icon. Fortunately, John was still logged in, granting her instant access.

Alix's eyes darted to the search bar. She typed in "USB," but the results were just as dull as before. A few ads for new USB drives, some newsletters, and a dozen personal emails from coworkers. She clicked on the Sent folder, curious if John had emailed the USB password to someone, but there was nothing.

Alix felt her heart sink. *This is just impossible. It's like searching for a needle in a stadium of haystacks!* She was right on the verge of giving up when she randomly clicked the DRAFTS folder and was met with two letters at the top: "PW."

Password!?

Alix clicked the email, and her jaw dropped to the marble floor.

CHAPTER FIFTY-FOUR

Alix couldn't believe what she was seeing. The email had no subject line, but the message was clear:

PW: BigSur1962
PS. Don't trust the FBI

Her mind raced as she tried to make sense of it all. The draft was dated yesterday afternoon. Three hours after John met with the now-dead gAIa employee. The fact that Alix never received this email took her to the worst places. *Did he try to send this, but someone—the FBI—stopped him? And if John did something that might have angered whoever is doing this, is he still alive?* She couldn't go there. She took a deep breath before inserting the USB into the computer.

Just like at Kate's house, there was a brief delay before the password prompt appeared. Without hesitation, she typed in "BigSur1962" and hit ENTER.

In an instant, the drive opened, revealing a single document. Alix leaned closer to the screen and read the title: *Quanta User's Manual.*

Her eyes opened wide as she double clicked on it, opening the fifty-page PDF. After the title page, she discovered an introduction written by John himself:

To Whom It May Concern,

I found this document at random. Seriously. I didn't seek it out. I didn't know it existed before it appeared that day outside my Genera security booth. Someone must have dropped it. Were they trying to leak it? Was it just an accident? I don't think I'll ever know.

But now that I've read it, I can't keep it to myself. This document exposes Quanta for what it truly is: a threat to our privacy, security, and most importantly, freedom. Sure, its promises of progress and prosperity sound great, but at what cost? Do we really want to live in a world where a single computer can control every electronic device on the planet? To not only watch us and surveil us, but to control our networked objects—our cars, our cameras, our drones, our communications—without our consent?

Quanta is not marketed as doing this. Wylde says it will solve our biggest problems. But it also has the power to turn us all into the puppets of whoever controls it. Cars become battering rams. Drones become ruthless minions. Nuclear power plants become bombs at the flip of a switch. *No one is safe.*

I'm providing a copy of this document to the FBI in hopes that you can shut down Quanta before it's too late. Please do everything you can. We're counting on you.

Alix swallowed before moving to the next page. The manual revealed different applications for Quanta and its unparalleled computing power. There were health care and financial functions, sure. Alix was well aware of these, but when she got to the government and law enforcement aspects, her mind spun in disbelief. *If this is true*, she thought, *then George Orwell was way off. It's like 1984 on steroids.*

She sat back, overwhelmed by the gravity of what John had uncovered. It was too much. Too severe. The information too sensitive. And she was in way too much danger to stay here. She needed to get out.

Alix ejected the USB and stashed it in her pocket when she heard the elevator doors slide open.

Frick.

The footsteps started toward the computer station as Alix quietly signed out of John's account. She slipped off her shoes, and slid quietly in her socks to the end of the nearest bookshelf. Then she pressed against the metallic frame, each step matching the racing beat of her heart.

But when the footsteps stopped, the beat just kept on going. Alix swallowed. *Did they hear me?* Then a squeak shot out, as if the body attached to them had turned, judging where to go next. They squeaked once more

and continued toward the computer station, sending Alix into a desperate panic. *I have to get out of here.*

As they approached the computers, the footsteps slowed. They must have been only a row away from the bookcase where Alix was hiding.

Alix held her breath, praying for a way out. She peeked around the edge of the bookshelf to find a cloaked figure hovering over the computer station where she'd just been. The scene was straight out of a David Baldacci novel, but this was all too real.

Her heart started beating faster. Her panic rose.

Then the person at the computer started typing.

Alix snuck back behind the bookshelf, stood, and moved toward the elevators, slowly sliding her shoeless feet across the floor.

As she wove through the labyrinth of bookcases, her ears strained for any sound beyond her own frantic breathing. *Was he still at the computers? Does he know I'm here?* Alix stopped to listen for other movement. The silence was deafening, so she continued a few more steps until she tripped over a beanbag chair and *BANG!* fell into a bookcase.

Alix froze, adrenaline surging through her veins. Then sound of a slamming chair shot through the library, followed rapidly by the racing of footsteps.

Desperately pushing aside the beanbag chair and cursing Wylde's asinine interior design, Alix sprinted down the aisle and turned down another, praying to throw off whoever was after her.

She ran for what felt like miles until her lungs forced her to stop and take a breath. As she stood in the darkness amid the towering shelves of books, Alix realized she was nowhere near the elevator. Her panting breaths were drowned out by the thunderous pounding of blood in her ears as she strained to listen for any signs of pursuit. Then a red glow caught her eye in the distance. *An exit!?*

Summoning all her energy, Alix raced off toward the red glow, sliding past the rows of books in her socks like an Olympic speed skater. Behind her the footsteps grew nearer and nearer. But finally, she spotted the bright EXIT sign, her guiding light.

Suddenly, a deep, grizzly voice shattered the silence behind her.

Alix refused to look back, instead grabbing the door and yanking it open, flooding the dark stacks with blinding white light.

"*YOU!*" roared the menacing voice.

But Alix didn't falter. She plunged into the stairwell and descended two flights before realizing something peculiar: whoever had been chasing her hadn't run into the stairwell after her. She was alone.

Alix continued down the stairs until she reached the door to the street. Still, no one behind her.

She was about to open the door, when she eyed the red warning sign: "EMERGENCY EXIT ONLY. ALARM WILL SOUND."

Alix's heart raced as she turned around, searching for another way out, but there were only cinderblocks and pipes.

"Ugh," she huffed.

She turned back to the emergency exit, realizing it was her only way out. So she took a deep breath—*here goes nothing*—and leaned into the door.

Nothing happened. No alarm.

The door simply opened, letting in the cool night air.

Cautiously poking her head out, Alix spotted a homeless person asleep on the sidewalk nearby. She turned the other way to find a couple strolling hand in hand. No security. Nothing.

There was no sound but the wind and distant traffic. It was quiet. Too quiet . . .

CHAPTER FIFTY-FIVE

San Francisco's South of Market, or SOMA, neighborhood is a maze of sleek lofts, trendy restaurants, and pulsating night clubs. Once a gritty industrial zone dotted with warehouses and factories, SOMA is a prime example of the urban renewal that has transformed the city. On many nights, the streets come alive with local music, street performers, and gourmet food trucks.

But that night, as Alix made her way through SOMA back to Kate's Mission District apartment, she found herself far from the neighborhood's famed hustle and bustle. The dimly lit streets were eerily silent, lined with auto repair shops and brunch spots long since closed for the night. Alix kept her head down, still amazed that she'd fled Genera's San Francisco headquarters unscathed. *Why'd that guy not run after me? Did I miss something?* And then there was Kate—the thought of returning once again without her bike gnawed on Alix's conscience. *Ugh, she's going to kill me.* But what could she do? She couldn't go back. She just pressed on, each step a blend of determination and dread.

Alix had been on Mission Street for a few blocks when she noticed the whirring sound behind her. She turned but saw nothing. *Strange.* The sound disappeared. Twenty feet later, the whirring was back. She turned once more, to discover what she first thought was a massive insect. But then she saw it with clear eyes: a drone with a camera aimed right at her face.

Frick!

She turned back around, quickening her pace, but the whir of the drone grew louder.

Alix's heart started to pound. She moved faster, almost breaking into a run, making frantic glances over her shoulder only to find another drone joining its buzzing counterpart in pursuit.

Anxiety spiked as Alix searched for something to throw at them, but came up short—only littered to-go bags and cigarette butts. She looked for somewhere to hide, but every store was shuttered and locked.

As she drew closer to the 101 Freeway exit ramp, Alix let out a sigh of relief. At least there would be people around now. And indeed, strings of cars appeared, streaming off the freeway, bringing a hint of life to this void of a neighborhood.

But that's when things got especially weird. As she passed in front of the off-ramp, Alix noticed one car veering from the flow of traffic but instead vaulting over the curb, tearing through a bush. Speeding right at her . . .

Instinct kicked in, and she leapt forward just as the Ford Fusion thundered past, colliding violently with a bus terminal in an explosion of glass and grinding metal.

Heart pounding, Alix spun around to see the same Ford reversing with manic urgency, its tires screeching against the sidewalk as it bore down on her once more. With a desperate scream, she turned and ran, unaware that yet another Ford Fusion was hurtling down the exit ramp, smashing aside any vehicle in its path like a juggernaut on an assault course.

Alix sprinted across the street, weaving through a gauntlet of bystander Toyota Priuses and Tesla Model 3s. She searched frantically for a barrier, any refuge from these mechanical beasts hell-bent on turning her into roadkill.

For a moment it worked, with each Ford Fusion ramming into oncoming traffic with reckless abandon. But Alix's luck didn't last. As she ran across the large intersection, a swarm of drones descended like vultures, trapping her in their ghostly dance. She was surrounded.

Then she heard it. Or *them*. Engines revving. Tires screeching. Four more Ford Fusions barreled down the freeway exit, navigating the pandemonium with ruthless precision, screaming past bewildered drivers, careening through the wreckage of the previous Ford Fusions. Tires burst over shattered debris, undercarriages ground against twisted steel—and yet they persisted.

Alix's mind raced. Her inventory was meager: a USB drive, a phone, and keys. No weapon. Desperation turned to inspiration as she glanced down at her Genera cloak. In a swift motion, she yanked off the cloak and flung it over the nearest drone. Instantly, it convulsed, its razor-sharp blades partially slicing through the fabric, but the cloak's weight and bulkiness forced the machine to the ground, rendering it useless. Seizing the moment, Alix dashed past the cloaked, smoking ghost, searching for somewhere, anywhere to hide.

But there was nothing. No alleys, no side streets. Just a sprawling sea of concrete and steel. She glanced over her shoulder to find the four drones

closing in fast. So she ducked behind any vehicle she could find. But even more Ford Fusions appeared in the direction of her sprint, cleaving through the bystander traffic, grating through masses of metal like cheese. There was nowhere to go.

Suddenly a Land Rover Defender screeched from behind. Alix turned to watch it plow through the drones, smashing them into oblivion. Then the Defender swerved up right beside her.

"*GET IN!*" a voice commanded.

Alix didn't hesitate for a second.

She swung open the door and leapt inside.

The vehicle roared to life and tore down the street at breakneck speed, dodging Ford Fusions and shaking off drones.

Alix turned to the driver and couldn't believe her eyes.

"*Jason?*" she panted. "How the heck did you find me?"

"It doesn't matter," Jason Stone replied, his tone clipped as he executed a sharp turn onto Van Ness Avenue.

Alix looked around in amazement. "Uh, where'd you get this car?"

Stone gave her an odd look. "You always ask this many questions while being saved from killer drones and cars?"

A smirk tugged at Alix's lips as Stone floored the accelerator past Fourteenth Street. She turned to find his stubbly face etched with a grim determination, sweat trickling down his temple as he kept a sharp eye on the rearview mirror.

"Where's your friend's house?" he asked, his voice low and steady. "We need shelter."

"Twentieth Street. Right at the top of Dolores Park."

"That's at least ten blocks!" Stone grumbled, switching into fifth gear.

But just as he was about to enter the intersection at Fifteenth Street, the traffic light flashed from green to red.

"What the heck?" Stone barked. "That light just turned green!"

"I think it's Quanta," Alix interjected.

He turned to her with a quizzical look.

"Quanta is not what Wylde advertised," she continued. "It can hack into any networked system on the entire planet."

Stone didn't have time for a TED Talk. He had to move fast. With a hard jerk of the wheel, they swerved onto Fifteenth Street. But immediately regretted it. Directly in front, point blank, was a wall of Ford Fusions racing down Fifteenth Street.

"Hang on!" Stone cried as he swung the steering wheel back to the left.

Alix let out a piercing scream as a Ford Fusion rammed right into them, throwing the duo into an osteopath's wet dream of a whiplash. But Stone pressed hard on the gas and shook it off, swerving back onto Van Ness Avenue.

"They just keep coming!" Alix cried out.

"You're right." Stone gritted his teeth as he slammed down the gas pedal, throwing the SUV into a grinding grumble. "We can't outrun them."

"Where's your gun?" asked Alix.

Stone shook his head. "Long story."

She sat back and huffed.

Stone scanned the Sixteenth Street intersection in the distance, its traffic light glaring with yet another ominous red. Even with a relentless swarm of computer-activated cars on their trail, Jason wasn't stupid enough to speed through it. He hurled the wheel to the right and turned onto Sixteenth.

Instantly a large crowd appeared on the sidewalk a block away. Men with long hair. Women with shaved heads. Some people looking like neither men nor women at all.

"There!" cried Alix. "It's some kind of concert. They can't drive a car into a packed venue!"

"But they could probably sneak a drone in." Jason frowned.

"It's our best shot," Alix insisted.

Jason brought the Land Rover to a stop with a screech. The duo leapt from the vehicle and ran, fleeing into the anonymity of the crowd.

When they reached the door, Alix glanced back to find the fleet of Ford Fusions dispersing. A few drones hovered ominously beyond the trees lining the street, but that was it. Against all odds, their plan had worked.

Finally inside, a wave of relief washed over the panting duet. The room was dark and steamy, the music a funky cocktail of punk rock and psychedelia. They ordered some beers and sat down in the folding chairs hugging the walls. *Finally a break*, Alix sighed, taking a sip of Modelo. But as she sat there, watching the undulating crowd sway to the hypnotic music, she had the creeping feeling this moment wouldn't last. That this was an anomaly, the calm before the greatest storm of her life.

CHAPTER FIFTY-SIX

Alcatraz Island. Once a federal penitentiary, home to the likes of Al Capone and Machine Gun Kelly, it became a popular tourist destination in 1963. The island remained that way for decades, welcoming 1.5 million visitors a year, until a cascade of budget issues drove its owner, the Golden Gate National Recreation Area, into bankruptcy, throwing its future into a dim uncertainty. That is, until the visionary D. J. Wylde swooped in and purchased the land, razing the prison complex and converting it into his famed communal living space.

The Commune now sprawled across the island in a network of yurt-like lodgings, saunas, and meditation rooms, all culminating in the magnificent Wylde Chapel, a towering postmodern wonder overlooking the Golden Gate Bridge and San Francisco's iconic skyline. The island currently housed troves of Genera employees as well as artists and musicians that Wylde had personally curated into an intentional living community the *San Francisco Chronicle* once called "a nanotopia."

That night, as D. J. Wylde and his entourage approached the island on his 540 Sundancer speedboat, the tech mogul gazed upon his magnum opus with a mixture of pride and anticipation. Years of relentless meetings and painstaking conflict-resolution sessions had borne fruit in this epitome of communal life. *The future is here*, he sighed. *A new beginning. New home.* Some communards had even discussed seceding from the United States, forming a government and currency of their own. "The Vatican of the West," as Wylde would joke.

But his crowning achievement didn't rest in communal governance; it stood tall above the island as a glowing monument to progress: Wylde Chapel. Modeled after the Ivory Tower in *The NeverEnding Story*, his favorite movie, the structure towered over the island like an ethereal tulip, its pistil erupting skyward, shooting plumes of light into the heavens.

Upon docking, Wylde and his assistants were met by a throng of artists, musicians, and Genera employees. Most wore cloaks, but some were

dressed in extravagant Burning Man costumes. Some were nude, covered head-to-toe in Day-Glo paint and clearly on something. The man of the hour disembarked with a confident grin, and the crowd gave way, spreading back as if Moses were parting the seas.

"I'm delighted to see you all here," Wylde began, straining against the techno beats that boomed from a DJ booth in the distance. Someone rushed up and handed him a microphone, and he continued, now filling the air with his sweet Lennony voice.

"It's a true pleasure to be with you all," he smiled. "For years you've poured your hearts and souls into Quanta, and for that I am grateful. You've been here through it all. From the heights of techno-revelation to the depths of our worst test failures."

Someone sighed nearby.

"But now, my friends," Wylde continued, "I come to you with the best of news. In just three hours . . ."

The crowd held its collective breath.

". . . Quanta . . ."

Their faces contorted into shapes of ecstasy and wonder.

". . . lives!"

Cheers and shouts erupted, launching one man, stark naked and painted in neon orange, into ragged tears of joy. Beside him a woman clad in a 3D-printed armor raised her plastic sword high, shouting, "Hail Quanta!"

The crowd roared as the music returned in a wave of pops, beats, and fizzles.

"Tonight is the night," Wylde declared over a synth glitch. "Tonight we herald a new era . . ."

The crowd cheered.

". . . the Quanta era!"

As if on cue, Wylde's assistants uncorked bottles of champagne, and the party began.

The tech wizard moved through the sea of people, kissing hands and embracing employees like the messiah he was, his smile calm and warm, radiating an almost divine energy.

Suddenly the crowd turned their heads to the skies, as if drawn by an otherworldly power. Wylde tilted his head up in curiosity.

"What is it?" cried someone in a bunny costume, the voice barely audible over the growing commotion.

A small glowing object descended toward the island.

182 *People's Choice Literature*

"It looks like a drone," said another.

"A drone?" scoffed Wylde. "That's no drone."

As the object drew closer, its true form was revealed: Wylde's personal helicopter, descending gracefully onto the helipad at the top of the hill.

A knowing smirk spread across Wylde's lips. *Right on time*, he nodded. *Right on time.*

CHAPTER FIFTY-SEVEN

Perched atop one of San Francisco's famed hills, Dolores Park, though only blocks from the Financial District, feels worlds away. The public oasis features a playground, tennis courts, and sprawling lawns, making it the perfect venue for a summer picnic or a spirited round of bocce ball. When the weather is nice, the park attracts locals and tourists alike, all coming to relax and catch a glimpse of the iconic city skyline.

Built in the 1890s, Dolores Park was named for the nearby Spanish Mission Dolores. The park originally featured a bowling green and a baseball diamond, but these amenities disappeared in time to make way for the burgeoning population's insatiable desire for open space.

That night, as Alix and Stone ascended its grassy slopes, the park was nearly empty. And they were grateful. After fleeing the concert venue and sneaking from alley to alley through the Mission District, they neared the front door to Kate's apartment. The sight inspired a sense of relief that the duo had not felt in days.

And yet as they got closer, something felt wrong. Alix first noticed broken glass on the sidewalk. Then she looked up to Kate's bedroom window to find a lamp smashed through it. Behind the lamp, she spotted a bookshelf leaning at an awkward angle.

Alix couldn't believe her eyes. She ran up the stairs as fast as she could, threw open the door, and saw it for herself.

The destruction was pervasive, like a cyclone had torn through, tossing electronics and plants everywhere, breaking chairs in half. The once pristine living room was now a chaotic mess, with an overturned couch and a table lamp smashed to pieces.

Rocky! Alix thought in a panic as she raced from room to room.

Stone strolled up slowly behind her with a knowing look.

"They're gone," he stated coolly.

Alix dropped to her knees, burying her face in her hands. "It's all my fault."

Stone knelt beside her, placing a comforting hand on her shoulder. "I'm so sorry, Alix," he whispered, his voice heavy with regret.

Alix's body convulsed with sobs, her voice barely managing to escape through trembling lips. "It's all my fault," she choked out. "If I'd never come to this godforsaken city, if I hadn't gone to Genera and left them alone, Rocky would still be here. Kate would be safe!"

"Alix, this wasn't your fault," he said.

But she stood up abruptly, wiping away her tears with determination. "We have to find them."

Stone nodded resolutely. "We will."

Alix's eyes blazed in a fury as she scanned the room. Then she felt the USB almost throbbing in her pocket. "Wylde . . ."

Stone turned to her in confusion.

"It was Wylde," she declared. "He took them. He knows I know about Quanta. He knows I have the information that could take down his entire operation."

"What are you talking about?" Stone asked, genuinely perplexed. "I was just with Wylde. He was at a baseball game not an hour ago. I can't imagine he would've had the time or interest to run all the way across town and trash your friend's apartment. And why would he want to hurt you?"

Alix was not having it.

"Are you blind, Jason?" she said, tears streaming down her face. "Those Ford Fusions! Those drones! Those traffic lights conveniently turning red!? That's Quanta in action. That's the *glowing* new future Wylde's talking about. It's all right here." She held up the USB drive. "He knows I'm onto him. This is why he trashed the place. He was looking for this."

Stone reached for the USB, but Alix deftly pulled back.

"No," she said fiercely. "My brother's life, Kate's life, Rocky's. Their safety depends on this. It's my only bargaining chip, and my only chance to clear John's name and my own."

Stone studied her words.

"Kevin Arnold. William Moriarty. Tim Woodman. These robot cars out for blood. It's all connected."

Stone sat down beside Alix, his mind racing.

"Quanta does have its social benefits," Alix continued. "The power of a quantum computer will revolutionize research and development around the world, eradicating diseases, preventing financial disaster. But a fully functioning quantum computer, which is what Quanta runs on, also

The Most Wanted Novel   185

opens a Pandora's box of population control. If you thought tonight's driverless goons were scary, imagine ticking off the wrong person with access to a fully activated Quanta. One minute you're walking down the street, the next you're flattened by a driverless car 'malfunction.' You can forget about the CIA, NSA, FBI—now all you'll need is a guy behind a desk with a Quanta-powered joystick. Or worse—an AI running the thing! And what if this software falls into the hands of terrorists or dictators. It's the end of free will! *It's the end of the world!!*"

Stone said nothing, contemplating the implications.

"We have to stop him," Alix seethed.

Stone nodded. "Then give me the USB. I'll take it to the FBI field office, get our tech people to review it. Can get a warrant for Wylde's arrest in the next few hours."

Alix met Stone's gaze firmly. She recalled John's second message in that fateful email: "PS: Don't trust the FBI." But as she studied Stone, doubt began to dissipate. His eyes had always been so soft and kind. After all, he'd saved her life twice now, first from a zombie Ford Fusion, then from a whole swarm of them. But even with her trust in him intact, she knew Stone's idea of getting a warrant was futile.

Finally, she spoke. "We don't have a few hours, Jason."

Stone grumbled.

"Quanta goes live tonight. In less than three hours, there will be no going back."

Stone could almost see the clock ticking in his head.

"Also," Alix added, "these guys took my best friend and my dog. I'm certain they have my brother. If we don't get them soon, I'm not sure we ever will."

Suddenly, Alix's leg started to vibrate.

She pulled out the phone Kate had lent her and instantly recognized the number. Her gaze hardened as she looked to Stone.

"It's Wylde."

CHAPTER FIFTY-EIGHT

Alix shook as she picked up the phone. "Hello?"

"Alix, my dear," came the smooth voice on the other end. "I must say, I am very disappointed in you. We were family . . ."

Alix's mind raced as she tried to think up a plan. She knew she had leverage with the USB but didn't want to push it.

"Wylde," she pleaded. "I need to know they're OK. John, Kate, Rocky."

Wylde chuckled darkly. "They're in very good hands, I assure you. We're not *monsters* here, Alix. You know the Genera way . . ."

"I'm not sure I do anymore," she retorted forcefully. "You lied to us. You lied to *everyone*. Quanta is pure evil!"

Wylde's laughter echoed in her ear. "Oh, please, Alix. Let's not stoop to name calling. The point is you have something I want, and I have some . . . people you want. Including a certain, jowly dog who is quite cute, I must say. Can't believe you never told me about him. A little feisty with strangers, but we're becoming fast friends."

Alix could feel her pulse pounding in her chest.

"Don't you dare touch him," she commanded.

"Don't *you* overplay your hand," Wylde hissed in a slithering voice she'd never heard before. "You'll do well to remember *I'm* the one holding the cards here. I want you and that USB to meet my representatives at the Genera Pier on Treasure Island. One hour from now. Alone. No more of this Agent Stone business."

Alix said nothing.

"And don't be late."

The call clicked off.

Alix turned to Stone. "He has them. All three of them. We need to get to Treasure Island," she said.

Stone nodded.

"But I don't trust him. We can't let him get this drive." She gripped it tight.

186

"I'll take care of that."

"Huh?" Alix knew Stone was unarmed. On their walk through the Mission District, she'd learned about his being forced into administrative leave. How Alix slipping out of her Los Angeles apartment had been deemed his fault. How her disappearance after their North Beach battle with that murderous Ford Fusion were strikes two and three. They'd taken not just his gun but his badge. He technically wasn't even an agent anymore.

Stone explained: "Wylde just picked the worst possible location for a drop off."

"What are you talking about?" Alix was truly confused.

"Treasure Island is where my Uncle Joe lives."

"OK . . ."

"And where my Uncle Joe lives is basically a bunker stocked to the ceiling for the next world war."

Alix didn't get it. "What does that mean for us?"

"Guns," Stone said with a grin. "Lots of guns."

CHAPTER FIFTY-NINE

Just south of Alcatraz Island lies a forgotten jewel of the bay, Treasure Island. A haven for day trippers, fishermen, and those seeking unparalleled vistas of the Golden Gate Bridge, its tranquil façade belies a rich history. Once home to the Golden Gate International Exposition, a World's Fair, and then a vital naval base, Treasure Island was created by dredging a shipping channel from the bay to the Port of Oakland. When the U.S. Navy decommissioned the island in the 1960s, the sprawling wonder fell under the stewardship of the City of San Francisco. Today, the island contains seventy-six acres of parkland and 2,500 rental units.

That night, as Alix and Stone drove onto this manmade wonder, Alix noticed those houses' lights flickering in the distance. But what most captivated her was the Wylde Chapel, radiating through the fog like an evil spear. Modeled after the iconic castle from Wylde's favorite movie, *The NeverEnding Story*, the Chapel and the Commune that housed it were his pride and joy. Now, after the horrific revelations of the *Quanta's User's Manual*, which John had delivered to her through a maze of clues, Alix saw it all too clearly. The Commune was the key to it all. Everything about Quanta pointed directly to the Commune. And somewhere on that historic island was the heart of the quantum beast . . .

Alix's attention snapped back to the present as Stone turned onto California Avenue, revealing the semicircular Treasure Island Museum lit up like an ivory ring.

"Not a bad place to call home," Alix mused.

"The views are nice," Stone shrugged, "but the place is pretty depressed."

Alix wasn't sure what he meant until they ventured farther past unkempt buildings, pothole-ridden streets, and sidewalks wanting for repair. Even the trees suffered from negligence and time.

"You're right," said Alix. "Not exactly a paradise."

"No," replied Stone, "but that's why Uncle Joe likes it."

"What do you mean?" Alix was intrigued.

"Well, the island's kind of a time capsule. It's got the feel of an army base in the '70s."

Stone pulled into a parking spot in front of a two-story duplex.

"And here we are," he announced.

Stone shut off the car, and the two of them stepped out.

As they approached the door, Alix saw that Uncle Joe's house fit right in with the rest of the island. The house slumped to the side, its foundation sinking into the earth, and the paint on the wood door was peeling like scabs. Still, there was something oddly comforting about the place.

Stone gave a firm knock on the door. After a moment, it creaked open, revealing a striking figure—tall and lean, with tousled black hair and a crooked nose. Dressed in a simple white T-shirt and faded jeans, he looked no older than sixty-five. Seeing Stone, his eyes lit up.

"Jason!" he boomed in a gruff, welcoming voice. Then he stepped out and pulled Stone into a military-grade bear hug.

"Uncle Joe! It's been too long."

"Far too long," Uncle Joe agreed, releasing Stone and turning to Alix with a raised eyebrow. "And who is this?"

Stone gestured to Alix. "This is Alix Finn. Alix, my Uncle Joe."

Alix extended her hand, but instead of shaking it, Uncle Joe took it and kissed it with dated chivalry.

"You're a very beautiful young lady," he remarked, causing her to blush. "Well, come on in, come on in," he added with a warm smile, stepping aside.

The place wasn't much better than the outside, with sun-bleached wallpaper and worn furniture scattered about. Ancient issues of *Military Surplus* magazine covered the coffee table, and the carpet wore its stains with pride.

Uncle Joe went to the kitchen and returned with three Budweisers.

"Sit down," he gestured. "Sit down, please."

Stone and Alix graciously accepted the beers but remained standing.

"We don't have much time," said Stone.

"What do you mean?" asked Uncle Joe. "You stop by for the first time in five years and don't even stay for dinner?"

Stone's gaze hardened. "We're in a bit of trouble and were hoping you could lend us some supplies . . ."

Uncle Joe's eyebrow arched in curiosity. "What kind of supplies?"

Stone gestured to the floor. "I remember Uncle Frank saying your basement was better stocked than Fort Bragg."

A sly smile crept onto Uncle Joe's face. "Ah, you mean *those* kinds of supplies." He looked skeptically at Alix before Stone cut in.

"She's good. She's safe."

Uncle Joe nodded hesitantly, eyeing Alix a moment longer before relenting. "Alright. Come on." Turning to Stone, he added. "This better be important."

"Trust me," Stone assured him. "It is."

Uncle Joe gave him a hard look and started for the basement.

Descending the stairs, Alix was hit with the pungent smells of metal and gun oil. Then Uncle Joe switched on the light, revealing the equivalent of an army surplus department store. Lining the walls were racks of automatic rifles, stacks of ammunition, and drawers of pistols. Several shelves held gas masks and night vision goggles. Alix couldn't help but gape at Uncle Joe's collection.

"Is that a rocket launcher!?" she exclaimed.

"Sure is," Uncle Joe said, giving it a proud pat. "And whattaya know? It still works."

"Where'd you get all of this?" asked Alix. "Most of it looks pretty illegal."

"The U.S. military is the most powerful fighting force in the world," he explained. "It's also the most mismanaged. Sometimes things just go . . . missing."

Alix nodded with vague understanding.

Uncle Joe turned to Stone. "So whattaya need?"

"Whatever we can get," said Stone as he began pulling down rifles. "Lots of ammo. Grenades."

Uncle Joe nodded, handing him a duffel bag. "Alright. What else?"

"One of these," said a voice from behind. Uncle Joe turned around to discover Alix holding a Remington 870 pump shotgun like an Olympic marksman.

"Well, whattaya know," he chuckled. "The lady's got quite an eye."

"Not only that," she said, rapidly reloading the gun before jerking it into position with a loud *ka-shink*. "I've also got experience."

Uncle Joe let out a booming laugh. "Well, aren't you a little firecracker?"

"You could say that," she smirked. "Jason's not the only one with an uncle in the VFW."

Uncle Joe nodded to Stone, impressed. Then he went to a cabinet and began gathering the grenades.

"Heaven help the bad guys tonight," he said. "They're gonna need it."

CHAPTER SIXTY

The Genera Pier extends from the northernmost tip of Treasure Island. Located where a kayak ramp used to ease recreational paddlers into the bay, it had become the less-glamorous route to Wylde's infamous Commune. While Genera VIPs embarked on speedboats and yachts from San Francisco's Fisherman's Wharf, this Treasure Island pier was used for supply runs.

That night, as Alix strolled up to the pier alone, she studied the creaky structure and had a creeping suspicion something was wrong. *Where's the boat?* she said to herself. *Will John, Kate, and Rocky even be on it?* Wylde hadn't given her that reassurance.

Suddenly a light appeared in the distance, bouncing with the lilt of the bay.

Here we go.

As the light grew closer, she identified Wylde's 540 Sundancer speedboat, its sleek, red hull leaving a massive wake. But as it approached the pier, Alix noticed Wylde was nowhere to be seen. In his place were two men dressed in black suits, sporting dark glasses and crew cuts. *They must be ex-military*, she thought. *Maybe even Wylde's private guards.* There wasn't a Genera cloak in sight.

The vessel docked, and the two men disembarked. Alix swallowed as she bravely stepped forward.

"Hey!" she shouted. "Where's my family?"

The men smirked as if she'd asked a very stupid question.

"They're safe at the Commune," one replied in a throaty, bro voice. "You give us the USB drive, we'll give you the fam."

"That's not what we agreed on," Alix asserted, arms crossed. "How do I know you'll keep your end of the bargain?"

"You don't," the other man sneered, revealing a handgun. "But if you don't hand over the drive, you won't have to worry about it . . . or anything else ever again."

192 *People's Choice Literature*

Alix studied them for a moment

"Fine," she sighed. "But you're making a big mistake."

"What are you talking about?" one of the goons scoffed.

"I'm talking about the guy standing behind you with a 5.66-mm APS underwater assault rifle."

Alix nodded to Stone, who was now standing behind the armed man, rifle locked and loaded. Then she revealed the Glock G43X Sub-Compact Slimline 9mm she'd been hiding behind her back and aimed it right at the other goon's noggin. "See, while you doofuses were pulling up in your stupid boat, my friend here was wading in the water. And when you walked down this here pier, he was pulling himself out of that water and creeping up behind you. And now here we are, with enough ammunition to blast you into quantum infinity."

"Drop it," said Stone to the goon with the gun.

He complied.

"Hands in the air, both of you," said Stone.

Again, they followed his order.

"Not so fast," barked another voice from the speedboat.

Alix turned to see a third goon they hadn't anticipated now shoving a shotgun into Stone's side.

"Drop the gun," the third goon said to Stone.

"Not a chance," Stone responded.

"Then you're French toast," the goon chuckled.

Alix felt the sweat beading on her brow. *How the heck are we gonna get out of this?*

Even Stone looked distraught. His 5.66-mm APS underwater assault rifle remained trained on the first goon. Alix's Glock was still aimed at the second. But that third goon now had full control of the situation.

Alix was about to drop the Glock when she heard that fateful voice behind her.

"Hey, wise guy!"

The three goons and Stone turned to look at the voice behind Alix.

"I'm going to need you to drop that shotgun. *Now.*" It spoke with a gruffness she quickly recognized.

The boat goon looked like a deer in headlights. "What the hell?"

"Hell is right," cried Uncle Joe. "Right where you're going if you don't drop that gun."

With a swift turn of the head, Alix found Uncle Joe kneeling a few feet behind her, his M202A1 FLASH rocket launcher aimed directly at the neon red speedboat.

"Five measly seconds and we all burst into fireworks, dumbos," growled Uncle Joe. "See, this here M202A1 FLASH rocket launcher was the culmination of a decades-long search for a weapon that could annihilate a target from two miles away. You'd be amazed to see what this little guy can do at twenty feet . . ."

The goon's eyes bounced from Uncle Joe to Alix to Stone to his shotgun. With a trembling hand, he slowly lowered the weapon.

"You made a big mistake," Uncle Joe chuckled. He turned to the other two goons, whose hands were still frozen in surrender. "You shoulda thought twice before messing with a Stone."

Alix nodded. "Or a Finn."

CHAPTER SIXTY-ONE

After they'd tied up the three goons and left them for the authorities, Alix, Stone, and Uncle Joe revved up Wylde's speedboat and made their way to the Commune. Stone was a natural pilot, having trained in the NYPD's Harbor Unit while still at the Academy. It was on an NYPD RB-M that he'd nabbed the infamous drug ring, earning himself the nickname "The Sea-Bull."

Now, behind the wheel of this luxury speedboat, with the Northern California wind pressing against his massive frame, Stone felt the immense gravity of tonight's mission. He glanced over at Uncle Joe, stooped and weathered, wondering if the nearly senior citizen was truly ready for the struggles ahead.

"You really shouldn't have come," Stone called to Uncle Joe over the roar of the motor. "Aren't you a bit . . . old for this?"

"Old?" Uncle Joe chuckled heartily. "You're only as old as you feel, my boy. Besides, looks like *I* saved *your* butts back there."

"We had everything under control," said Stone stubbornly.

"Oh, please," Alix interjected. "We were seconds away from a *Reservoir Dogs*–style ending. There was no getting out of that." She turned to Uncle Joe, with gratitude. "Thank you, sir."

"Don't mention it," he replied with a dismissive wave.

"Look," Stone began, trying to regain control of the conversation. "We need to regroup. If they had three goons coming for Alix, there'll be plenty more at the Commune."

"And here I thought it was all hippie-go-lucky over there," Uncle Joe chuckled.

"We're learning a lot tonight," said Stone.

"So, what's the plan?" asked Uncle Joe.

Stone started to speak, but Alix cut him off.

"Go in. Destroy Quanta. Get John, Kate, and Rocky. Then get out."

"Quanta? What the heck is that?" asked Uncle Joe.

"It's a long story," Alix replied. "Let's just say that if we don't destroy Quanta, that whole World War Three you're planning for is a surefire bet."

Uncle Joe's eyes opened wide as plates.

"She's right," said Stone. "If we don't end this now, it'll never end. Quanta will always be coming for us. There'll be nowhere to hide."

Alix did her best to explain Quanta to Uncle Joe. The fact that Quanta had its societal benefits but that the evil it unleashed would be catastrophic. That the fabric of society would change forever overnight. All our networked devices transforming into weapons. Cars into torpedoes. Drones into foot soldiers. Military computers into a hacker's buffet. Quanta must end; she made it vividly clear. Here and now. Tonight. There was no other way.

Uncle Joe understood half of what she said, but he knew it was bad. "So, what does this thing look like?"

"We don't know," Alix admitted. "But we know it's very large." She recalled the description in John's copied document.

Stone chimed in. "And has lots of tubes and wires."

"So, a computer." Uncle Joe joked.

Stone rolled his eyes.

"How do we find it?" asked Uncle Joe with sincerity.

Alix smiled. "We do it the Genera way."

"Huh?"

She pulled open the boat's storage compartment, removing a bundle of fabric and throwing it to Stone and Uncle Joe.

"What the heck is this?" Stone asked, examining the blinding neon cloth.

"Cloaks," said Alix. "How else are we going to sneak into Wylde's heavily fortified island?"

Uncle Joe looked skeptically at the Day-Glo mass in his hands. "You gotta be kidding me."

Alix turned to him with a smirk. "I wish I were . . ."

CHAPTER SIXTY-TWO

As the trio approached the Commune, Alix was surprised to find no welcoming committee at the dock. *Wouldn't Wylde have been eager to obtain his coveted USB drive?* As she gazed up at the hill before them, all she saw was a crowd of revelers popping and swaying to the beat, a potpourri of Genera cloaks, bizarre costumes, and naked bodies painted in a rainbow of colors. The music was so loud you could've heard it all the way in Sacramento.

"What the heck is wrong with them?" Stone called out over the noise.

Alix merely shrugged. "I guess you've never been to a Genera party. It's always the Summer of Love all over again."

Stone shook his head, imagining D. J. Wylde as John Lennon twerking to the beat. Everything was starting to feel like an oxymoron, with Wylde as King Moron incarnate.

Uncle Joe just stood there, eyes wide as subwoofers, staring at the spectacle of frivolity and youth.

"OK, let's go," said Alix, taking the lead.

The trio leapt from the vessel and made their way down the dock, their cloaks concealing an arsenal of weapons fit to take down a small army. As they trudged uphill, they passed scores of dancers, from Day-Glo-painted hippies to people in chicken and walrus costumes. Stone was impressed with Alix's plan—no one batted an eye as they passed.

Beyond the dancers, they spotted the iconic sights of the Commune. There was no denying it was beautiful: the hedges freshly shaped into peace signs and Buddhas, pathways blooming in abundant bouquets of rare tropical plants. And each yurt was unique, with one shaped like a birthday cake, another like a massive bongo drum. Wylde's communal vision was complete. But as they swerved between yurts and tents and Volkswagen buses converted into meditation rooms, the idyllic atmosphere began to fade. Something was wrong. Alix could feel it. And she saw it in Stone's and Uncle Joe's eyes.

"What is it?" she whispered as they crouched behind a small yurt.

"It's the music," said Uncle Joe. "It's gone."

A chill ran down Alix's spine. "They know we're here."

Stone nodded, jaw tensed. "We have to move."

And move they did, sprinting over yoga mats, dodging between luxurious saunas, speeding past a row of school buses covered in Day-Glo flowers, and finally coming to a stop at the last dwelling, a large house shaped like an upside-down heart.

"There," said Alix, pointing to a cluster of barrels beside it.

The trio ran and crouched behind them, carefully peering out past the barrels, past the courtyard, to the towering Wylde Chapel before them. They'd only ever seen it in pictures before, but there it was, looming above in all its horrific glory, a radiant tower spiking high above an unreal display of gigantic pearly petals, all shrouded in the signature San Francisco fog.

"Where the heck is everyone?" asked Stone.

Alix swallowed as she scanned the environs. There were no Genera goons or Communards in sight. Just an eerie silence and a single door leading into the Chapel.

With a determined glint in his eye, Stone turned to Alix. "Let's go."

"Wait," said Alix. "It must be a trap."

"It may be," said Stone, frowning at his watch, "but we can't wait any longer. Quanta will be fully operational in fifteen minutes!"

Uncle Joe concurred. "We have to stop whatever the frick that is before it's too late. And if they know we're here, it just might be . . ."

Alix's heart skipped a beat. "OK, let's do it."

"Not so fast," boomed a voice from behind.

Alix turned to find two men in Genera cloaks, armed with Heckler & Koch VP9s.

"Drop your weapons," one of the men demanded.

Alix nudged Stone.

"Got any tricks left?" she whispered.

He gave her a sly grin.

One of the men cocked his gun. "I said drop 'em."

Alix watched in awe as Stone ducked and rapidly swung out his feet like a breakdancer, knocking both men to the ground.

But he wasn't quick enough. One of the guns fired and ricocheted off the house behind them.

Stone and Uncle Joe sprang to action, disarming and subduing their assailants with expertly executed headlocks.

"Good one," said Alix, "but now they absolutely know we're here."

Stone started to respond when a second shot came from afar.

"Get down!" he barked.

Then another shot. And another. Then a burst of bullets splattered onto the heart-shaped building above.

Alix dove behind the barrels. Stone crouched behind a crate. Uncle Joe sprinted to one of the Ken Kesey school buses.

"Uncle Joe!" cried Stone.

But he didn't listen. With a swift motion, he flung open the door and leapt inside.

Alix and Stone watched Uncle Joe smash one of the school bus windows and started sniping Genera goons as they ran up the hill.

"The guy's a genius," Alix marveled, her eyes trained on the bus.

Stone nodded. "He was built for this."

But their admiration was cut short when a bullet whizzed by Stone's head, slamming into the house above him. Peering over his makeshift shield, he returned fire. Then a shower of bullets returned.

Alix peered out and watched a gang of cloaked millennials and Gen-Zers and some guy in a bear costume sprinting up the hill spraying bullets. Then her eyes landed on a familiar face.

"Is that Dave?" Alix gasped.

She couldn't believe it. They'd been Wylde's assistants together for two whole years. They'd hiked through Griffith Park, celebrated Fourth of July together. She'd even dog sat for him not once but three times! And now here he was, charging toward her with a Smith & Wesson M&P 15-22 Sport 22 LR automatic rifle, his face twisted into a feral snarl.

Stone turned to Alix.

"This isn't going to be pretty," he said. "You get into the Chapel and see what you can find. Something tells me it's all there. John, Kate. Quanta . . ."

Alix knew he was right. The only way anyone was getting in was with expert cover.

"You stay safe," she whispered, wrapping her arms around him in a tender embrace.

When she pulled back, he looked deep into her eyes. "You too."

With one last glance, Alix turned and ran as fast as she could through the courtyard, dodging bullets and speeding up a flight of marble stairs to the Chapel entrance.

She took a deep breath before pushing open the door.

CHAPTER SIXTY-THREE

As she entered the Wylde Chapel, Alix couldn't believe her eyes. This space so often spoken of but never seen by anyone outside the Commune—no pictures allowed—looked exactly as Wylde had described it: "The Fount of the Future." The blue, nave-like space was massive, lined with gigantic, curved LED screens, all displaying swirling, psychedelic patterns that could easily have been mistaken for screensavers. And there was no floor. Instead, a network of catwalks extended over a series of aquamarine pools. From these pools sprang literal fountains whose misty spray gave the space an atmosphere of divine reverence. And the music! Through invisible speakers, a celestial choir serenaded her with a heavenly hymn right out of the Renaissance, their harmonies nearly masking the gunfire outside.

As Alix ventured down the central catwalk, she started to see the far wall more clearly. It was curved like the rest of the nave but decorated with massive photos of famous people. Barack Obama. Nelson Mandela. The Dalai Lama. Mark Zuckerberg. Each portrait hovered over a gigantic computer terminal, emitting sporadic beeps and flashes. But above the terminal, floating twenty feet in the air, was the focal point of the entire Chapel. Everything pointed toward it. The curved walls, the screens. Even the fountains seemed to bend in its direction. It looked like a chandelier from outer space, a massive, golden network of tubes and shafts. Alix's jaw dropped.

Quanta.

As she drew closer, she could see it in greater detail. The thing was far more complex than she'd previously thought, tubes upon tubes spun together like immense waves of water, crashing and twining in a viscous network. And the gold wasn't just gold; it glowed with an inner light.

"It's beautiful," Alix whispered.

"Not what you were expecting, eh?" said a voice behind her, shattering the tranquility.

Alix spun around to find D. J. Wylde aiming a SIG P228 19mm handgun straight at her stomach.

"Welcome to the Chapel, Alix," he said with a sinister smirk. "Now drop your gun."

Wylde looked completely different. He still wore his signature blue cloak, but his face was contorted into a mask of rage and mania that Alix didn't recognize. John Lennon had clearly left the building.

"It's nice," said Alix as she lowered her shotgun to the ground. "But it's not worth it, Wylde. You'll ruin everything."

Wylde let out a deep, guttural laugh that sent shivers down Alix's spine. "Do you even *know* what you're looking at? Zillions of atoms arranged in a nanoscopic crystalline lattice. Three million qubits crunching more data every second than a normal computer could in a million years. A quantum machine with computing power far beyond anything that Einstein or Bohr, *or God*, for that matter, could have imagined. This is the next stage of human evolution. And tonight, we take that step together. As a species. As a people. As one."

"But Wylde," Alix pleaded, "Quanta will get totally out of control." She held up the USB. "It'll bring unseen death and destruction, the end of freedom! *That's* evolution?"

Wylde smiled, his eyes gleaming with fanatic light. "You don't understand, my dear Alix. But soon you will see."

Alix glared at him like she wanted to rip off his face.

"Where's my family?" she snarled.

"Oh, don't you worry," said Wylde. "They're here in the Chapel. We've been keeping them safe."

Alix felt a ping of relief.

"But," Wylde continued, "if you ever want to see them again, I'm going to need that USB drive . . ."

Alix's eyes narrowed. "Give me my family, and I'll give you the drive."

Wylde chuckled like a troll. "You seem to be mistaken, my dear. This here 19mm," he nodded to his gun, "is not your friend. And it's one step away from blasting you into the Stone Age."

Alix smirked. "You seem to be mistaken yourself, Wylde."

He lifted an eyebrow.

"You really think I'd stroll into your little Chapel here without a backup plan?"

Wylde soured. "Backup?"

Alix nodded. "That's right."

"Drop it, Wylde," said Stone, pointing a Heckler & Koch HK417 A2 16.5 inch assault rifle at the tech guru's head.

Wylde smirked. "Didn't enjoy the baseball game, did you, Mister Stone?"

"Let's just say, I'm more of a Mets fan," Stone spat.

Wylde's smile evaporated.

"Drop the gun," Stone repeated.

Wylde huffed and gave in, his SIG P228 19mm handgun hitting the metal catwalk with a loud clank.

Suddenly, as if responding to the report, Quanta started to glow.

Everyone froze.

The main lights dimmed, and the new glow spread across the Chapel, pulsing and throbbing like an aquatic heartbeat. Alix looked up at the Quanta chandelier, which was now radiating an ominous red.

"Quanta isn't happy," said Wylde in a scolding tone. "You better behave…"

"I'm not sure Quanta's ever happy," said Stone. "Let's go and shut this thing down before it's too late."

Alix retrieved her shotgun and tucked Wylde's handgun in the belt behind her back. With a nudge of his HK417, Stone guided Wylde down the catwalk.

As they made their way to the computer station, Wylde looked up at the glowing, pulsing Quanta above. He seemed oddly at peace, his eyes displaying a faraway look, as if he were staring far into the future.

"This is a gift," he declared. "You're going to witness something no other human will ever see. The dawn of a new era."

"I think we've had enough of your bull crap, Wylde," said Stone. "Help us turn this thing off."

"Of course." Wylde spun around and walked to the closest computer. With expert keystrokes, he typed in a long series of letters and numbers on the keyboard. Nothing happened until Alix and Stone looked up to see Quanta glowing redder and brighter than before.

"What are you doing?" demanded Alix.

"I'm doing everything in my power," said Wylde, with a crazed look in his eyes, "to make sure you die."

Just then a swarm of drones descended into the nave, followed by dozens of cloaked Genera employees on the many catwalks and outcroppings above them, each aiming an automatic rifle directly at Alix and Stone.

CHAPTER SIXTY-FOUR

"Drop your weapons," called a cloaked goons through a megaphone.

Alix and Stone shared a weary glance.

"There's nowhere to go," whispered Alix. "We might as well fight."

Stone nodded, and the duo jumped behind the massive computer terminal. A rain of bullets followed as Wylde leapt in the other direction.

"Not the console!" screamed the CEO. "Don't hit the console!"

Alix and Stone returned a barrage of gunfire. Drones exploded. Cloaked gunmen fell into the gushing fountains below. Alix glanced over to where Wylde had been, but he was gone. Suddenly his face appeared on one of the massive screens, grinning wickedly.

"It's useless," he said, his voice echoing through the pulsing nave. "You're surrounded. Quanta will be fully operational in just one minute!"

A countdown clock appeared on the screens as bullets continued to rain down on Alix and Stone.

Wylde continued his sick monologue. "You are about to witness the greatest leap forward in human history! The end of disease. The end of crime. The end of endings! A new beginning for this sick, dying planet . . ."

Alix turned to Stone. Clearly Wylde would never understand the horrors he was about to unleash.

"What are we going to do?" she asked.

Stone shook his head. "I don't know," he said, then fired a cluster of bullets at a quartet of cloaked gunmen.

"You'll see. You *will* see," Wylde continued. "All the power, the beauty, the knowledge of Quanta is about to be freed. You are now part of something far grander than you could ever have imagined. Your death will be a precious gift to the world."

A hail of bullets kept spraying at them. Alix and Stone kept returning fire.

"You're going to die, Alix Finn and Jason Stone, and you're going to die like dogs. A simple sacrifice to free us from this shithole existence,

these stupid humans and their backward ways. You'll end up in the same place as your precious brother, *John*." He spoke John's name as if that word were no more than a simple pest that had been dealt with.

Alix's heart stopped. "John?"

Wylde chuckled, his eyes gleaming in the screens with wicked satisfaction. "Just a minor casualty in the war for the future. But a necessary one at that. He will be remembered as a crucial step in the path to righteousness. A bit of an ignoramus and a bit too trusting—and so just what we needed."

Alix's heart jolted back to life, fueled by rage and determination.

"You . . ." she seethed, removing a grenade from under her cloak.

"You bastard!!!!" she screamed as she leapt out from behind the computer terminal.

With all the strength she could muster, she pulled the pin and hurled the explosive at Quanta.

It sailed past Wylde's LCD face and through the rainstorm of bullets, high into the air, arching over a sea of spinning hard drives and gushing fountains, straight to the heart of the machine.

The grenade hit it, clinked, and fell to the ground with a thud.

No explosion.

Nothing.

Alix stood there in disbelief as a bullet tore through her thigh, throwing her to the ground. Stone leapt from behind the terminal to pull her back to safety, but she resisted, gasping as she watched Wylde kick the grenade from the catwalk into the pool below.

"Looks like your hardware could use a little . . . upgrade," he chuckled.

Alix and Stone looked in horror as Quanta began to pulse and glow a bright, bloody red.

"Quanta has arrived," bellowed Wylde, booming through invisible speakers.

Helpless, Alix and Stone held on to each other. What could they do? How could they stop Quanta now?

Wylde gazed up at the pulsing quantum computer hovering above him and raised his hands in a gesture of absolute devotion.

"QUANTA BEGINS!!!"

"Not so fast," called a growling voice from afar.

Alix and Stone sat up to find Uncle Joe kneeling on the main catwalk, his M202 FLASH rocket launcher aimed directly at the pulsing Quanta.

CHAPTER SIXTY-FIVE

"No . . ." muttered Wylde.

Uncle Joe smirked. "Nightly night, quantum scum."

He fired.

"NOOOOOOOOOOOOO!" Wylde cried.

In a flash, the rocket soared through the air and struck Quanta dead center, blasting it into a ballooning fireball and sending a blinding shockwave in all directions.

Alix and Stone watched as the face of D. J. Wylde, arms still outstretched below his now-flaming god, turned from shock into a shape of pure terror.

What was left of the smoldering quantum computer teetered, then tottered, then dislodged from its moorings, plummeting down, pummeling the mad scientist, and exploding into a trillion pieces.

There was no way anyone could have survived that, Alix thought.

Suddenly the entire building shook in a violent tremor, and an ear-splitting siren pierced the air.

"What's going on?" Alix shouted over the chaos.

"I think the Chapel's collapsing," Stone called back. "Come on, we better go."

With adrenaline pumping through their veins, they frantically scanned for any signs of Genera guards and drones, but the blast must have scared them off. Alix stumbled along with Stone's help, her hand tightly grasping her bleeding wound. They limped through the burning Chapel, over piles of contorted metal and shards of shattered glass, their eyes fixated on the exit ahead.

As they drew closer, they found Uncle Joe lying motionless on the catwalk.

"Uncle Joe!" cried Stone, hobbling over to him with Alix.

Kneeling down beside him, Alix checked his pulse. "He's alive!"

Stone gave him a shake. "Uncle Joe! You OK?"

The Most Wanted Novel   205

Uncle Joe groaned. "Did we save the world?"

Alix and Stone erupted in joyous laughter.

"Just about," said Stone, wrapping his uncle in a tight embrace.

"You're a hero," said Alix, smiling through her tears.

"Now we gotta get you out of here," said Stone. "The place is collapsing."

"I don't think so . . ." said a chilling voice echoing from the Chapel door. "You're not going anywhere."

Alix and Stone looked up to see Director Emerson blocking the entrance, one hand digging a 19mm Parabellum handgun into Kate's neck, the other holding Rocky on a tight leash.

CHAPTER SIXTY-SIX

Alix and Stone stared frantically at the helpless Kate and Rocky. Their minds raced for solutions as the once pristine Chapel now trembled with impending doom. Beams groaned and cracked to the ground. The catwalk beneath them quivered, threatening to fall at any moment. Stone went for his Heckler & Koch HK417 assault rifle, but Emerson cut him off.

"Don't even try it," Emerson spat, his cowlick standing straight up like a lightning bolt.

"You really going to shoot a woman and a little dog?" cried Stone.

"Whatever it takes," Emerson growled.

"What did Wylde do?" Stone hissed as a beam thundered past. "How'd he get to you?"

Emerson let out a sardonic chuckle. "Do you really not get it? Quanta wasn't just some pet project of that wannabe fifth Beatle. It was a collaboration between the FBI and Genera all along. Wylde's cute little origin story of divining inspiration from the Getty fountain is just that: a story. We've been working with Genera for years on a quantum computer capable of hacking into any networked device, no matter the security levels, government clearance, you name it. A computer that would not only yield absolute surveillance power but would produce the one currency that trumps all others: control. Complete control over the movement and even the thoughts of potential criminals. Can you even imagine the implications? Police won't have to risk their lives day in and out. Crime will evaporate. It would have disappeared tonight if your wannabe Stephen Segal here hadn't blown our multi-billion-dollar investment into oblivion . . ."

Stone could hardly believe what he was hearing. "So, it was you all along," he growled. "Kevin Arnold. William Moriarty. Tim Woodman."

Emerson smirked smugly. "And how can we forget our lovely little Finn siblings?"

Stone grimaced. Alix clenched her fists.

"How could you?!" she cried, her voice trembling with rage.

"It was all for the greater good," Emerson continued, his tone dripping with hate. "With Quanta we could have regained control of our destinies. Break a few sour eggs in the process? In my line of work we call those 'acceptable casualties.' Kevin Arnold trying to spill the Quanta beans live on CNN?" Emerson scoffed as a buttress groaned and buckled overhead. "A flip of the Quanta Beta switch and little Kevy's driverless car took care of that." The director chuckled nihilistically. "John Finn and his fool-hearted attempt to 'save the world?'" He sneered. "It really is incredible what you can achieve when you simply place a packet of paper in front of an ambitious young person's door. Suddenly they think they're Robert Langdon or something . . ."

Alix stared at him, fuming, quietly scheming to free her friends from this corrupt cop on *Dr. Strangelove* steroids.

"You have to give it to John. He did well trying to hide his identity while figuring out what to do with that 'damning' information. But it didn't take long before gAIa's Tim Woodman, a longtime FBI informant, intercepted John's outreach to the FBI and convinced that bookish John Finn he was doing the right thing."

Stone ground his teeth through the smoke and debris.

Emerson smirked. "Of course, we needed cover while John was trying to 'save the day.' *And* we needed someone to flip that Quanta switch to get rid of Arnold . . . Enter William Moriarty, son of Richard Moriarty, CEO of Genera's biggest competitor, gAIa. Offer a former rich kid a large lump sum, and he'll become an amateur spy in no time." Emerson looked satisfied with himself, sweat building on his brow. "And what a nice coincidence that William, with a dime-store wig and a fake mole on the side of his chin, looked *quite* a bit like your twin brother, John Finn." Emerson's face soured. "Talk about three birds, one stone. John Finn, William Moriarty, Tim Woodman, all taken out in one fell swoop. All painted as pawns in Richard Moriarty, CEO of gAIa's, corporate espionage plot. It was a beautiful plan. Of course, no one'll be seeing much of that guy anytime soon. Or *any* of those guys for that matter," he chuckled.

Alix and Stone cringed, clutching their weapons with ragged rage.

"What?" said Emerson. "You can't see it? Did you not witness the awe-inspiring strength of Quanta earlier as its drone and Ford Fusion minions chased you through the crummy streets of San Francisco? Of course, that was just the beta version . . . Once Quanta went live, there would've been nowhere for you to go. Truly."

Alix gulped at the thought.

"Well, enough of the history lesson. You'll all be dead soon anyway," he said, peering up at the crumbling Chapel. "Just give me the USB, and I'll be on my way."

"There's no more Quanta," cried Alix. "It's no use."

Emerson gave a throaty laugh through plumes of smoke. "Oh really? You think this is the only one? You really think we'd put this much time and money into a quantum computer and not have replacement models underway?"

Alix's stomach dropped.

"There's no way I'm letting that USB get into the wrong hands again," spat Emerson, digging the 19mm Parabellum handgun further into Kate's neck.

Alix winced, trying to think of what to do. She could see the fear smeared across Kate's face, the anxiety plaguing Rocky's chunky form.

"Alright," Alix said, slyly reaching for the handgun behind her back. "Just don't hurt them." Alix felt the metal and smiled.

"Rocky, bite!" she screamed.

Right on cue, Rocky did just what his trainer had taught him. The jowly lump leapt right for Emerson's gonads, clamping down with his Master Lock of a jaw.

Emerson buckled over, howling in pain, giving Alix just enough time to pull Wylde's SIG P228 19mm from behind her back and aim.

Then Alix took the shot, smacking Emerson in the shoulder and sending him toppling to the side. Rocky released his grip as the diabolical director lost balance and teetered off the catwalk, plunging head-first toward the shallow pool below.

"Noooooooooooooooooo!"

Alix peered down at Emerson's body, his limbs contorted in unnatural directions, and then quickly turned away. It was too gruesome. But her attention quickly shifted to Rocky and Kate crouching on the catwalk in exhaustion.

"Kate! Rocky!" Alix cried out, ambling over to her now-freed friends, metal beams and LED monitors crashing down in all directions. When she reached them, Rocky was panting and wobbling in hysteria. Kate nearly fainted. Alix gathered them both in her arms, relishing the embrace as Rocky licked her face, and Kate sunk weakly in relief.

"We have to go!" cried Stone, shuffling up behind them, propping up Uncle Joe with all his remaining strength. "This place is about to collapse!"

Just then the catwalk below them creaked and started to crack.

"Not so fast!" cried a nasal voice not ten feet away at the Chapel door. Some nameless, cloaked Genera employee holding a .380 ACP handgun.

"Stone?" Uncle Joe huffed. "How many more twists are they gonna throw at us?"

He swiftly raised his Heckler & Koch HK417 assault rifle and took the shot, easily neutralizing the goon.

With Alix in tow, he led the ragtag group of four humans and man's best friend through the crumbling Chapel, reaching the door just as the catwalk snapped in half, crashing down into the quantum refuse.

CHAPTER SIXTY-SEVEN

As our intrepid heroes emerged from the crumbling structure, they were amazed by the sight of a helicopter descending into the Chapel courtyard. *Is someone coming to save us?* Alix's heart leapt with hope as she spotted that shining beacon of salvation—as if all the horrors of the past few days were fading and that finally help was on the way. But her hopes crumbled when she read the three letters on the side of the aircraft: FBI.

Panic set in as Alix desperately scanned the vicinity for cover. The house and buses were too far away. They'd never reach them before the helicopter landed. They were completely vulnerable, trapped in front of the crumbling Wylde Chapel.

As the helicopter touched down, Alix turned to Uncle Joe and Stone, surprised by their calm demeanor.

"What do we do now?" she asked.

"I'll handle this," Stone smirked.

Alix watched in fear as a man in a navy blue FBI jacket exited the helicopter followed by two heavily armed SWAT agents.

Rocky barked and growled at the approaching figures.

"Feisty one!" the leader shouted over the deafening noise of the helicopter blades.

He strode up to Stone and extended his hand.

"Excellent work, Agent Stone," the special agent in charge of the FBI's San Francisco field office called out. "Sorry we doubted you. Looks like we had a few rotten apples in the Bureau after all, just a different kind of orchard . . ."

"Took you long enough," Stone huffed in annoyance.

"You know how it goes," the SAC shrugged. "Bureaucracy."

Alix looked at Stone, confounded about what was happening.

"What?" Stone said to her. "You think I'd take us on this wild goose chase without reinforcements? This here's the head of the FBI's Bay Area field office. The guy who fired me earlier today. It took some convincing,

but he came around in the end. There's nothing like a good old livestream to prove your innocence."

Stone patted his chest where, for the first time that night, Alix noticed a camera concealed in his bulletproof vest.

"A very fine move," said the SAC.

Stone nodded smugly.

Alix's eyes widened in disbelief as a sea of SWAT agents swept through the Commune, rounding up cloaked goons with rifles, Uzi-swinging Day-Glo nudists, and a gang of machete-wielding furries right out of some demented Disney picture book.

She turned to Stone, her eyes meeting his for what felt like the first time. In that moment, all danger seemed to slip away. All they had been through, all they had experienced together over the past two days. It had been an incredible journey. They had fought side by side, pushed each other, and now she felt an unspeakable connection as if she'd known him all her life. And yet there was something new about him after these two crazy days. That sparkle in his eye. A sense of calm in his hardened frame. Release.

Stone grabbed Alix and pulled her close. Their faces hovered, lips like magnets, breaths caressing each other's skin. Then Alix pulled in closer, pressing her lips to Stone's, and an electric shock shot through her body. His lips felt just as soft and kind as his eyes, like pillows of joy sent from heaven above.

And like clockwork, her world had changed. The Wylde Chapel behind them creaked and groaned before buckling in on itself and collapsing, scattering ash and dust in all directions, framing these new lovers in a perfect picture of hope. A new future for humanity.

CHAPTER SIXTY-EIGHT

The day after that fateful night at the Commune was a whirlwind. Alix and Uncle Joe were flown to Zuckerberg San Francisco General Hospital, patched up, and soon released. Uncle Joe returned home to Treasure Island, while Alix joined Kate and Rocky at the Palace Hotel in Downtown San Francisco, where Genera's interim CEO paid for them to stay while the company renovated Kate's apartment. Around noon that day, Agent Stone was ceremonially reinstated into the FBI, accompanied by a public apology. And by late afternoon, all five of our heroes were fast asleep, catching up on a well-deserved rest.

In the following days, however, this rest was regularly disturbed. Alix and Stone gave several interviews on national news networks, explaining the horrors of Quanta and pledging to work with the FBI to decommission all Genera-made quantum computers, terminating the Quanta program once and for all. The two became so famous that it was hard to walk down the street without attracting fans—a complete 180 for Alix, who had just days prior been the most wanted criminal in the country.

The intensity of the week deepened for Alix when the reality of John's passing started to settle in. She'd had high hopes of finding him at the Commune but later learned he'd never even set foot on the island. According to the Marin Police Department, he'd died at the hands of a drone during a second escape attempt from a Genera warehouse in Sausalito, just north of San Francisco. Learning the details of his death devastated her. She left the hotel room only when absolutely necessary, spending most of the time in bed with the lights off, her sole comfort being Rocky's loving, snorty presence.

John's funeral only intensified things. When she saw her parents, she nearly fainted. Their return took the reality of John's death to a whole new level. Sure, she was happy to see Stone and Uncle Joe there. Some of her and John's high school and college friends showed up, too, which was nice. But it felt like everything had changed. Alix mostly hung back

with Kate and Rocky before hugging her parents and Stone and heading back to their hotel.

As time went on, her connection with Jason Stone started to fray. She felt lost. Her other half had disappeared. Was she really ready for a relationship? And were she and Stone even a real thing? Was it just the intensity of those few days that had brought her and Stone together? She wondered if he'd even have noticed her if they'd met under normal circumstances at a bar, on the street. He being as tall as a tree and all. She being a tiny shrub in comparison.

Amid these swirling thoughts, Alix grappled with how to move forward. The idea of returning to her life in Los Angeles seemed impossible now that John was no longer by her side. Fortunately, Kate really was like family and offered her and Rocky a room in her apartment. When it was finally renovated, she arranged for Alix and John's belongings to be shipped to San Francisco and even rearranged her place to accommodate some of Alix's furniture. It wasn't perfect, but it would do for now. And Alix was grateful.

Months passed in this way, Alix and Rocky living in relative ease under Kate's roof and Stone back on his beat in Los Angeles. A few sporadic texts passed between him and Alix, each met with a quick response. Still, the connection felt frayed.

As the holidays approached, the chasm between them only seemed to widen. The grief of John's death remained like a chronic lump in Alix's throat. But she also started to really miss Stone, his warmth and kindness. She thought to invite him up to Kate's house but always choked. He probably had a new girlfriend or fiancée now. Or *five* girlfriends or fiancées . . . A guy like that wouldn't be single for long.

The day before Christmas Eve, around sunset, Alix was about to text Stone when Rocky waddled up to her panting, begging for her to go out.

"OK, boy. OK," she said, giving him a head rub.

She slipped on her jacket and leashed him up before heading to the door.

Outside, Dolores Park's verdant hills and the iconic downtown skyline shone like a postcard come to life. Wispy clouds danced across the velvet sky like ethereal water lilies. After a block, Alix noticed a group of high school students singing carols to a couple in the doorway of their Victorian mansion. Alix couldn't help but yearn for the idyllic life before her. A beautiful home, a loving husband. The American Dream. Lost in

214 *People's Choice Literature*

her thoughts, she turned the corner and plowed straight into a stranger, jolting her back to reality.

"Agh, sorry," she said, looking up to apologize.

"No, I'm sorry," said the man with an enigmatic smile.

"No, it's . . ." Alix was confused. *Am I dreaming?*

"Jason?" she asked, finally recognizing him.

Jason Stone nodded, gazing down at her with a playful grin.

"What are you doing here?" she asked.

"What else would I be doing?" he said raising a perfectly wrapped gift. "I'm here to see you."

With joyful surprise coursing through her veins, Alix couldn't resist pulling him in for a kiss.

When their lips touched, all the pain and the distance of the past few months dissolved, replaced by a tidal wave of tenderness that engulfed her like a warm, healing bath.

"I missed you," Stone declared, taking her hand.

"I missed you too," Alix replied breathlessly.

Without another word, they strolled down the block, hand in hand, as the carolers sang on.

When they arrived at Kate's house, Rocky waddled ahead into the living room and went right up to Kate, sniffing her leg.

Kate pulled her eyes from the newest Gillian Flynn book and smiled when she saw Jason enter the door.

"Well, well," she laughed, placing the hardcover in her lap. "I should have known you'd be back, and just in time for dinner!"

Alix looked to Stone as if to say, *Is that OK?*

He smoothly nodded, *Of course.*

"Oh, and this came for you, Alix," said Kate, handing her an envelope.

Alix took it and studied the return address.

Parrot House Books . . .

Alix tore open the envelope and read the letter. She gasped. Then she dropped the letter and sunk to the floor.

"What is it?" asked Stone.

"John's novel . . ." she whispered in shock. "They're going to publish it."

Kate grabbed the letter and read it, eyes wide.

"And with that advance," said Kate, "you'll never have to work again . . ."

Alix could only nod.

"And can you believe that?" Kate said, pointing to the letter. "They're saying it'll be 'The Most Wanted Novel in America!!' "

Alix was stunned. All of John's hard work had finally paid off. All his late nights. All his doubts and frustrations . . . Momentum by John Finn would be a real, actual book. She teared up, wishing he could be here to see it.

Stone knelt beside her, holding her hand, grounding her through it all. His warm presence turned this bittersweet moment into something truly special.

He stayed the night and all through the next day, playing fetch with Rocky in the park, grabbing brunch in the Haight. They toured the De Young Museum and strolled hand in hand down through the lush gardens of Golden Gate Park, ending with a cuddle by the sea. And that night, after turkey dinner with Kate, after Rocky was asleep, snoring on the couch, they went to Alix's room and held each other, felt each other like they'd felt no one before. It may have been Christmas Eve, but it was no silent night . . .

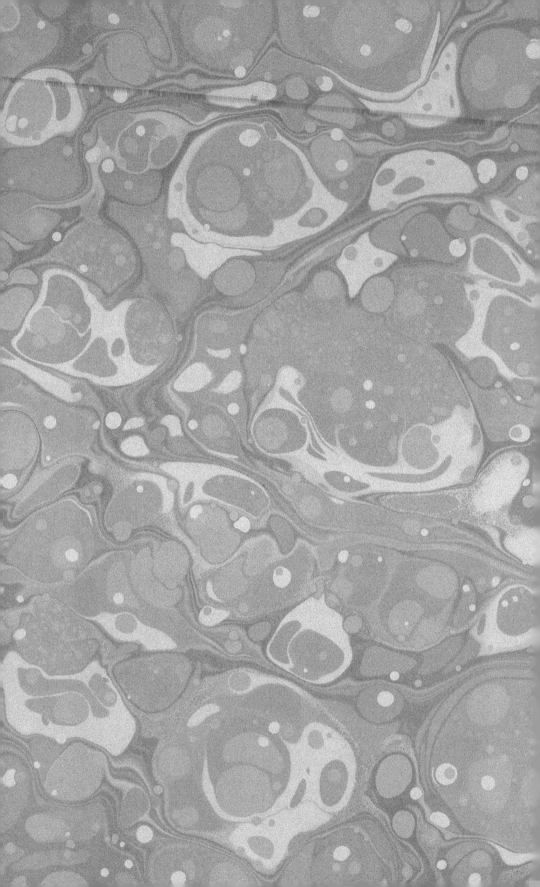

THE
MOST
UNWANTED
NOVEL:
OR,
VIRTUE Rescinded.

In a SERIES of
NEURAL MESSAGES
FROM A
Lovelorn Longevous LORD,
To his FRIENDS and FELINE FOES.

In which, the many notorious FLAWS and
FAILINGS of a Book called

THE MOST WANTED NOVEL,

Are exposed and refuted; and all the average
ARTS of that Book, set in a true and just Light.

Together with
A full Account of Christmas Eve on Mars, featuring sentient Robots,
tentacled Aliens, found Fragments from *ROBINSON CRUSOE*
and other Classic Literature, a V.R. rabbit hole of Historical Fiction,
and an unabridged Collection of Horror stories entitled
LESSER OF TWO DEVILS.

Dear Reader,

Welcome to *The Most Unwanted Novel*, the sequel to *The Most Wanted*—or the prequel, depending on the order you read them. I, Tom Comitta, will be your guide for the next five hundred or so pages, checking in from time to time, holding your hand as we descend into the delightful depths of disfavor. It's true our road might not be all sunshine and roses—in fact, it might not be much of a road at all—but if you stick with me, together we'll reach literary realms heretofore unseen: characters and themes, settings and situations that no author has been brave enough—or dumb enough—to attempt before now. Together, we'll journey toward beauty by way of the bad, toward brilliance through balderdash. Data will be our motor, art our fuel.

So, take a seat. Relax. Probably best to turn off your phone; something's always there to distract. Or text your friends and family that you're busy. Write it in all caps—they won't notice otherwise—"I'M READING!!!" Maybe they didn't see it with all the noise on their X feeds; text again, using more exclamation points for emphasis: "I'M BEGINNING TO READ *THE MOST UNWANTED NOVEL*!!!!!!!!!!" Or don't text at all; it's up to you. Just pray they'll finally leave you be.

Now find the most comfortable reading position: sitting. Lying. Standing. Crouching. Lunging. Leaning. Stretching. Jogging. On a chair. On the couch. On the floor. On a hammock. On a bench in the park. On a bench on the street. On the train on the way to work. In a bus on the way to work. In between work emails. In between work meetings. In the food court of your lunch break (don't forget your trash). In the bathroom on your lunch break (don't forget to flush). While walking to the gym after work. While on the treadmill. The elliptical. The step climber. At the edge of the pool while leaning on your elbows. In the middle of the pool while floating on your back. Back home in the tub with a glass of rosé. While drying off. While brushing your teeth. While rinsing. While in bed with the lights on. While in bed with the lights out.

Whichever position, get ready. Because here you are, about to attack *The Most Unwanted Novel*, which has already begun, although you didn't know it yet. Yes, this book is already doing just what it has set out to do, being, like *The Most Wanted*, the result of a public opinion poll that measured the literary tastes of the United States on December 1 and 2, 2021. Perhaps you've just finished *The Most Wanted*, put it aside, and have now turned to this unwanted monstrosity. Perhaps you went directly to

this doorstopper to see what all the fuss is about and will try *The Most Wanted* later. Perhaps you'll never read the "better" book, finding enough abject pleasure here to satisfy you for quite some time. See, this book is the literary equivalent of a Kmart special. It was born out of the belief that there is a reader for every book, no matter how awful. It is a book of no particular merit, written by an author with no particular talent, to be read by people who want something to read but don't want anything better. This is the book that you didn't know you didn't want to read but will be glad you read anyway. Welcome to The Book That Eats Your Brain.

Well, the poll results are in. And they're present whether you notice them or not. They dictate the content, form, and texture of everything that follows. *Even this sentence you are reading at this very moment is directed by the poll.* It's written as a direct address—particularly a letter—to you, the reader (a mere 2.68% of Americans prefer epistolary novels); it's written in the second person, about "you" (only 2.49% want the second person); and last, but most importantly, that sentence comments on the art of writing this novel (while experimental writing "lost out" to traditional fiction, it earned a surprising 37.64% of the vote, and of this third of the population who want experimental fiction, only 45.5% want fiction that comments on the art of writing, which means that only 17.12% of the general population will prefer that italicized sentence, the pastiche of Italo Calvino of the first few paragraphs,* and similar sans-serif passages you'll find scattered throughout this novel). Of course, you'll see from the statistical breakdown here it's not that *no one* wants these qualities in their literature. Some of our most cherished books contain similar elements. They are just, when faced with multiple options, what a representative sample of the population picked the least. Perhaps it would have been more accurate to call this book *The Least Wanted Novel*. Or *The Novel of Bad Manners*. Or *The Great Un-American Novel*. There could be sound arguments for all of these.

But I digress. If you read the introduction a few hundred pages back, you already know that both *The Most Wanted Novel* and *The Most Unwanted Novel* are not only guided by a public opinion poll but the findings of Jodie Archer and Mathew Jockers's algorithmic study of what

---

* Another reason for the inclusion of a pastiche of *If on a winter's night a traveler* here as well as remixes of *Frankenstein, Robinson Crusoe,* and other older texts is that classic literature is largely unwanted, with only 4.11% of people preferring it to other forms of literature.

makes a novel a bestseller (and what surely does not), *The Bestseller Code*. You're aware that findings from their study filled in the gaps in our poll data, informing things that a survey simply could not measure, such as diction and story structure. You also know that while writing these novels, I collaborated from time to time with a large language model (LLM), the GPT Playground, a collaborative word processor that was a precursor to ChatGPT. You know that the Playground helped me with things like character names, obstacles for characters to jump over, and even plot points, adding a level of Dungeons & Dragons–esque collaboration to the writing process. In fact, we already ran into one of these moments two paragraphs ago:

> This book is the literary equivalent of a Kmart special. It was born out of the belief that there is a reader for every book, no matter how awful. It is a book of no particular merit, written by an author with no particular talent, to be read by people who want something to read, but don't want anything better. This is the book that you didn't know you didn't want to read but will be glad you read anyway. Welcome to The Book That Eats Your Brain.

To write those sentences, I gave the LLM a prompt (specifically the words, "Dear Reader, Welcome to *The Most Unwanted Novel*, the product of a public opinion poll and this author's creative interpretation. This book is") and the LLM continued the thought. This is an example of one of the few passages in either book that I did not edit. Ninety-nine percent of the time, the LLM's outputs needed a lot of help to turn its often-tinny language into something readable.

What you didn't learn in that introductory section is that while editing this "lesser" novel, I employed yet another guide: *The Turkey City Lexicon*. A compendium of everything you should *not* do while penning a sci-fi story (or really any story), this brief glossary was compiled by the authors Lewis Shiner and Bruce Sterling from decades of discussion at the United States' premiere sci-fi writing group, the Turkey City Writer's Workshop. The lexicon contains everything from story types like the Rembrandt Comic Book, or "a story in which incredible craftsmanship has been lavished on a theme or idea which is basically trivial or subliterary," to diction, such as Roget's Disease, or the excessive accumulation of "far-fetched adjectives, piled into a festering, fungal, tenebrous, troglodytic, ichorous, leprous, synonymic heap." *The Most Unwanted*

Novel incorporates several moments of Roget's Disease but relies most often on 'Said' Bookism, or dialogue littered with distracting verbs like "inquired" and "ejaculated" in place of the simple, economical "said." This novel often goes even further, often pairing a 'Said' Bookism with a Tom Swifty, or dialogue that pairs unnecessary adverbs with the verb "said."

Sometimes, variations on *Turkey City Lexicon* entries appeared in this unwanted novel without me even trying, simply because they resonated with the data from the poll or *The Bestseller Code*. You'll find this in Lord Brad's political rant, which the *Lexicon* would dub a "Stapledon" moment, or a scene wherein a character shows up to lecture the reader. Several other *Lexicon* entries appeared without additional effort:

Bathos
A sudden, alarming change in the level of diction . . .

False Humanity
An ailment endemic to genre writing, in which soap-opera elements of purported human interest are stuffed into the story willy-nilly . . .

Hand Waving
An attempt to distract the reader with dazzling prose or other verbal fireworks . . .

"I've suffered for my Art" (and now it's your turn)
A form of info-dump in which the author inflicts upon the reader hard-won, but irrelevant bits of data acquired while researching the story . . .

Discovering these resonances between *The Most Unwanted Novel* and the *Turkey City Lexicon* further validated our data not unlike *The Bestseller Code*. Which is to say, you can rest assured this novel will either live up to its title or come pretty darn close.

And so here we are, now 1,862 words into a novel combining perhaps too much data and too many references for anyone's good. Two novels, if you're up for a double-header. One that has worked long and hard for you to like it. Another that, if the data is right, only a minute fraction of the population will enjoy. But enough about how these books were written. It's time to get reading.

The Most Unwanted Novel 223

So what are you waiting for? Sit back, relax. Lean into the headrest of your La-Z-Boy. Rest your head on the armrest of your couch. Place your sit bones firm on the ground. If you're home, take your shoes off. Stay a little. Adjust the smart lights—if you have smart lights—so you won't fall asleep. Create an entirely new lighting design for this very book. Teal? Orange? Peach? Beige? Gold? (All of which are the least wanted colors from Komar and Melamid's art poll.) If you don't have smart lights, a lamp will do just fine. Consider additional lighting for extra support. A headlamp if your partner's asleep. The flashlight on your phone works fine. Simply do everything you can to prepare yourself, to make sure that once you start reading, you won't have to stop. Need a cup of water? A glass of wine? Your vape nearby? Anything else? All right, here comes *The Most Unwanted Novel* in 5

4

3

2

1

The story begins in a sorrowful daze. (Only 2.01% prefer their fiction to be sad.) You've just awoken from a long winter's sleep with tears in your eyes. Memories of your long-deceased grandmum and her fateful trolley accident cloud over what should otherwise be a joyous morning of hot chocolate and sugar cookies. You turn to the side, groggy eyed, whimpering, wanting tissue, would take towel, but find only the advent calendar staring back, mocking you with eellogofusciouhipoppokunurious elves and even better reindeer. You sneeze. Snoot. Your arm stretches, hand searches, touches table, cable, box. There. You pull a square from the cardboard cube and wipe at the pain. You huff. You puff. You reach for another, and there she is staring back. Grandmummy. Gran. Framed in sequins. Gray of grace. The orphic whites of her eyes, the baby blue of her pupils, her purse. Purple. Velvety. Ripe for fingers tracing shapes. You recall her fragrance. Flower by Kenzo. The kick of her laugh. That sunrise of a smile. The visions break the spell of sadness, if only for a moment. You think back to a wintry eve annums prior, the scent of sycamore cooking in the hearth, stockings strung in wait, snow cresting the windowpanes in frozen cups of light. You can almost hear her grahamcracker rasp, her Beantown wit. "Don't judge a book by its mother . . ." she'd wink. "Can't teach an old bog new tricks . . ." You nearly taste the Cock-a-Leekie she'd cook each winter, its meaty scent wafting through

the house, twisting down hallways, up marble stairs, drifting into your room, sweeping you up in its smoky embrace. Beholding that ancient portrait, that image of loss, lost time, lifetimes lost to years, the grief returns in waves of angor. You feel fresh, hot tears rolling down your cheeks, snot bubbling from your nose. But you know you must get up. You've got to get a grip. It's nearly Christmas, after all.

And so, you sit up, dab your face and sneeze, toss the soiled square to the floor. Then you help yourself up and hobble to the window. You look out, but all you see is your reflection. You fail to notice the world covered in snow, the lawns and gardens, stone walls and hedges, all tucked in snug and sweet, as if some unseen hand had draped a sleeping android babe in a thick, white coat. You ignore the lumpy fields, the colonial-style cul-de-sacs decked with holly, the clouds drifting like ravelled skeins of glossy white silk across the heavens. You miss the inflatable snowman waving from the police station and the mock Eiffel Tower peeking over the hills. You even fail to see the snowflakes drifting past your window, just inches beyond the glass. You notice nothing but your frosty face. You study the tattered, hoary wisps framing a lean, cheeky form, the aquiline nose poking out like a true baldy between two tired, florpliant eyes. You study the sprigs of wrinkles sprouting from those battered blue orbs. You trace where tears wet the wrinkles, where wrinkles branch out into freckles, where freckles meet flecks of tissue and the faint stubble of a budding beard. You trace where budding beard curves round saggy jowls and where saggy jowls meet your neck moles and where those genetic blips brush against the collar of that purple shirt housing your feeble frame. You spot yourself stooped over, gripping the sill for balance. You see the face of a sorrowful centenarian longing for his long-lost grandmum. You see yourself. You see him.

You turn from the window in disgust, shuffle back to the nightstand, and study her photograph once more. A tear rolls down your cheek before plashing the glass.

"Miss you, Gran," you whimper.

You sneak one last look before returning the frame to its rightful home. Time to make her proud. So, you grab your racquet bag and limp down the hall.

❧

The Most Unwanted Novel   225

At the country club, you find Lord Timothy waiting in the lobby, already decked to the nines in the latest Burberry sweatsuit. He offers a smile and an apricitic greeting. You give a nod and a bow and a wink and a whistle and start your small talk, strolling past Lady Betty and Cousin Lou, eyeing Duchess Mae and Lady Kimberly engaged in ecstatic ejaculations by the pro shop. You lift a brow, studying the lattice of Lady Kimberly's dress. Surely from Lord Henry's studio, you think. No one does finer whitework . . . You admire the floral pattern, the crenelated trim to the waist, recalling that cadet gray is having a comeback. Your eyes drift down the sinistral sleeve, past the embroidered magnolia of the elbow to the vines encircling the cuff, and you gasp, nearly choke.

Your throat tightens. Pulse pounds. Is that ketchup? Chipotle mayonnaise? Whichever it be, such a display is entirely unbecoming for a lady of her stature. Lord Timothy continues his chatter, but you hear naught. Not a syllable. You nod and lift your cheeks, begging for a break, any relief from these nobodies, all the while watching that slantindicular spot, the bruise laid out bare before you. In the shape of a banana? A scythe? Dear God, is it growing? Then Duke Patrice strolls up, arm in arm with Lord Richard, and you're grateful for the distraction. You give a nod and a bow and pull your Timothy away past stands of sports bottles and seasonal satchels.

When you arrive at the court, it's as if those plebs were but things of the past. Holding the neon-green ball in your hand brings brief bursts of happiness to your sullen state. You squeeze it, toss it from hand to hand, the fuzzy fur evoking endless hours of hitting similar spherules back on Earth. You sigh. Then you take a deep breath before lobbing the ball into the air, raising your racket, and rocketing it with perfect precision. The ball bolts over the outstretched net, and you watch worriedly as Lord Timothy lunges to the left, barely batting it. But, before you can backpedal, he returns the roundy with a helpless "Humph!" The pressure pleases you. You prance, albeit a bit awkwardly, to the right, returning the ball with a backhand, bracingly banking it below the belt. But, as before, Lord Timothy, even with his bad back, shuffles there listfully, lobbing that locus in an artful arch to your anterior. You accelerate with all might, but your muscles are stiff, slow, subcutaneous, sibilant. And yet, you dance in disbelief as the ball bounces once before ricocheting off your racket with a fierce forehand. Lord Timothy trundles toward it and slams the ball back with a Skyhook Smash. You barely bang it, but it does drive over the net, gliding gracefully through the gassy air right out

226 *People's Choice Literature*

of reach. The ball bounces once. Then twice. You smile and shrug. He shakes his head in hostility.

The two of you bounce the ball back and forth for what feels like forever. You win one set; Lord Timothy wins one more. He wins twice; you win thrice. The tournament travels treacherously through time, but eventually, as with everything in equatorial existence, your energy evaporates. You bumble after the ball but can't keep up with Lord Timothy's timing. And you're years younger, for Lord Pete's sake! At one point, he bangs the ball, and you watch with weary eyes as it sails over your shoulder. You amble after it, but it's bunk: the ball bounces once in-bounds, then back up, whacking the wall and colliding with the next court, where it greets the glaring gaze of Duke Leon and Duchess Camberly.

Lord Timothy is thriving, now netting set after set. Each game he's gold, playing with perfect form and fluid facility. You're awestruck. Aghast. You've never seen anyone play so adeptly. And your knees have never stung so stiffly. Lord Timothy's a tyrant. He wields his wonder from corner to corner, finding full advantage in agility, never missing. His shots are crisp, clean, catastrophic. You watch as he slams the ball into the back corner, as he tackles a tweener, a Bucharest Backfire, and a Bowl Smash in a smooth sequence. At one point, you brace for the ball, but it sails over your shoulder. You turn in terror as it bounces off the back wall and whacks you flat in the face.

You fall to the ground to find blood pouring from your nose. So you lift your shirt to stop the bleeding, cursing your friend. You're breathing hard, bloody nostrils huffing into your bloody shirt as you pick yourself back up with eyes cold as adamantium. Lord Timothy starts toward you, but you slam your racket on the court, snapping it in two.

"Are you OK?" he asks concernedly.

You turn away. "I'm fine."

"I'm sorry," he says emphatically. "I didn't mean to."

But you stomp off the court and into the locker room.

"That wasn't very becoming of you . . ." remarks Duke Leon scoldingly as you enter the showers.

You slam the door and turn on the water, letting the hot liquid wash over your bloody face. The anger lingers, but it's clearer to you now, more tangible. Not today. This is *not* what you needed. It's a hard enough day as is, what with it being the second quinquagenary of Grandmummy's death. All you wanted was a nice rally. A friendly outing with your old pal Lord Timothy. And all you got was humiliation. Thank the good

The Most Unwanted Novel 227

Lord Gran wasn't there to peer at your pitiful performance. The two-time Grand Slam champion herself. Winner of six Wimbledons. Coach of the Olympic coaches. How could a descendent of such prowess be reduced to such a sad state? You shake your head, grabbing the soap and running it over the silvery hairs of your pot belly. There can only be one explanation for this, you say to yourself while scrubbing your pits. Practice. It's true that Lord Timothy has a bad back, but if Lady Wanda's right, he's been out on the court for months with his Model-U android trainer, working his backhand, perfecting his slice. And you? What have you been doing? Crying in bed. Sniffling alone in the bathroom at Lord Kevin's Thanksgiving soirée. Wallowing in grief over the coming holidays. Sure, you've been looking forward to the parties, the masses, the caroling. Who wouldn't? Who doesn't love the treats and drinks and music and dance and movies and prayers and sermons and jingles and real Christmas trees and fake Christmas trees and mangers dotting the roadways and snow coating the fields and family coming for dinner and family coming for lunch and family coming for breakfast and family coming for brunch? But most of all when it comes down to it, during the holiday season, it's the closeness to God that is paramount. On Christmas, you and the good people of Mars celebrate the birth of the Lord, the Lamb, the babe who blessed this flawed species with hope, with moral vision. With truth. The holidays are a time for forgiveness, for love, to recall the life of the Lord Jesus Christ and to honor our faults as sinners, to bask in the holy glow of his love and to honor our originary sins while striving for forgiveness and improvement in His image, the Lord's image. God. You wonder how anyone could be sad at such a time as this. When Mars is awash in holiday joy, the churches are packed to the holo-walls, the acts of kindness are as common as toffee stuck in an android child's teeth. You wonder how you of all people can feel sorrow at such a time. Grandmummy wouldn't want this. She'd want you to be happy. She'd give your cheek a kiss and tell you to go on your way, to be merry. To join in celebrating Jesus, the Lord, the lamb, the Christ.

As you think these last thoughts, you notice your rage has fizzled. You shut off the water and hobble back to your locker with your towel. You rub the plush fiber over your body, dabbing the gray hairs of your chest, blotting the crème tuft under your armpits, the salt-and-pepper sprouts of your crotch. You pull back the wrinkly foreskin of your penis and wrap the towel around the tip, making sure to soak up every bit of moisture, swiping under the mushroom head, sponging down the easter shaft past

228 *People's Choice Literature*

the beauty mark in the shape of a four-leaf clover, and down to the moist base of your member. You cup your testicles with the towel, then slide the fabric down over your hairless, splotchy legs. While bending over, you spot once again the carnage that is your tennis racket.

It's in this prostrate state that Lord Timothy strolls up, casually chewing a protein bar.

"Looks like you'll need a new racket," he smirks.

You straighten, and the rage returns in triple fury.

"I'm sorry," you state. "It was an accident."

"I know," he shrugs. "It's OK."

"It's not OK," you say. "I shouldn't have done it." But you pray he slips on a candy cane.

"I know," he says. "But it's still fine."

"No," you say. "It's not." But you dream of defecating in his stocking.

"It's just a racket," he shrugs. "It's no big deal."

Lord Timothy gives you a pat on the back and leaves the room. You quietly curse him. Then curse yourself for being so nice.

Hi there, Tom Comitta again. I know we're just getting started, but I wanted to check in and see how it's going. Christmas? Tennis? Aristocrats? That's right. No one wants to read about them. Or, more precisely, very few people want them when faced with other options. For instance, our poll showed that religion was the least-wanted theme (only 0.77% prefer it in their novels). When asked what activities Americans like to read about, "playing a sport" lost, with only 14 of 1,045 respondents selecting it (1.34%); when asked which sport they *do* want, tennis received no votes. Reading about aristocrats is slightly more popular, with 3.06% of people yearning for tales of the ultrawealthy.

If you're scratching your head at these results, you're not alone. Given the prominence of religion, sports, and wealth in U.S. culture, you might think these things belong front and center in *The Most Wanted Novel*. A psychologist might diagnose these responses as a rejection of some collective unconscious. Or maybe one way to think of it is that there's a fundamental difference between what we want to watch on television and what we want to read about.

Funnily enough, it seems at least one part of this trend is not new: A 1948 poll conducted by *Fortune* magazine found midcentury readers

similarly allergic to stories about the wealthy. When faced with eight one-line novel descriptions (like "A soldier returns to find his wife has been blinded in an air raid" and "The adventures of a little-known sea captain who had great influence on the outcome of the American Revolution"), a tale of the elite lost out, earning only 4% of the votes: "The wife of a European diplomat runs away with an American businessman." Clocking in at 12% approval is another, slightly more desired tale of the upper class: "A stuffy banker is outwitted in an amusing way by a group of farmers."

We'll dive more into the data later. Let's get back to the story, back to the locker room where our racket-wrangling protagonist, You, are just about to leave and find yourself called to the greatest journey of your very long life.

After drying off and changing back into your holiday sweater—the one with the two snowmen dancing before three eager evergreens—you leave the locker room to find the country club flush with holiday cheer: carolers greeting club members at the door, tinsel strung from the awnings, and bells of holly decking every hall. You spot your old friends chatting and laughing in the pro shop. You see Lord Timothy, casually twirling his racket, flirting with Lord Sam. You turn away from the spectacle and head for the bar. It's only 9 a.m. but you sure could use an egg nog . . .

In the bar, the scene is the same. The same holiday decor, the same songs, the same chaps you've been consuming warm beverages with for decades. The android bartender hands you the egg nog and a complimentary platter of cookies.

"Merry Christmas," he says joyfully.

"Merry Christmas," you sigh sourly, lifting the cup in a weak toast.

And just as you take your first sip, you notice a figure weeping down the bar. A woman with bright red hair dressed in a coruscating green gown, the cool light shimmering off it like a viridescent disco ball. An emerald for the ages. A gem. Her pretty, caramel, nearly wrinkle-free face is skewed into an aslant shape of sorrow, and her body shakes with sobs.

"Are you OK?" you ask softly, inching toward her with drink and cookie platter in hand.

She turns and looks into your eyes. Her face wet with tears. Her eyes swollen, mascara smudged into black snowflakes.

230   *People's Choice Literature*

"It's Christmas," she sniffled. "And I miss home . . ."

"Where are you from?" you ask affably, sitting on the stool beside her, searching her eyes for clues.

"Earth, of course. I miss my daddy . . ."

"Cookie?" You offer the plate.

"Thanks," she says, biting into a ginger snap, studying the waning brown moon that remains.

"Daddy taught me how to bake," she continues, her mouth lifted in a sad smile. "We'd make snickerdoodles every Christmas."

"Same with my grandmother," you reply.

She stares off into space, tears pooling in her chlorotic eyes.

"I'm sorry you're so sad," you offer consolingly, reaching out and touching her hand. "I'm sad, too."

"Really?" She sniffles.

"It's the anniversary of my grandmummy's passing," you share. "Every Christmas Eve hurts more than the last."

"Oh . . ." Her brow furrows. "I'm so sorry. That's terrible."

"Thanks," you smirk weakly, taking a sip of egg nog, and slump back.

"I'm sorry to pry," she declares cagily, "but where exactly did she pass?"

"On Earth, in the year 20—. San Francisco." You shake your head in disbelief. "She was on her way home from the bakery with cinnamon buns when a driverless car crashed right into her hover trolley," you sniffle. "She didn't have a chance."

Your interlocutor's eyes widen, and she turns to you.

"S-s-san Francisco?" she stammers abruptly. "C-c-christmas Eve, 20—?"

"Yes . . . !?" you nod confusedly.

"My father was on that trolley!"

You look deep into her eyes, searching for meaning.

Then she peels back her emerald sleeve, revealing a bare forearm. But, there in the middle, right betwixt her wrist and elbow, lies a minutely detailed tattoo of a Terran hover trolley circa 20—.

"Impossible!" you exclaim ecstatically. "What are the chances?"

"It sure is a small world," she smiles, dabbing her faint wrinkles with a hanky.

"Or small solar system . . ." you chuckle humorously.

She manages a giggle too.

And so the minutes pass, but you hardly notice as you and she discuss family and God and Mars and Earth and tennis and sailing and Christmas and worship and dinner and lunch and breakfast and brunch

and the future and the past and time itself, and, yes, even the present. Her life, her whole being unfolds before you like a tapestry of hope, a true miracle on Thirty-Fourth Street, Building 25, Port Elizabeth, Mars, 24252. She makes you laugh. She makes you smile. And when you cry, they're tears of joy, the pain just pouring out like dual Niagara Falls of the soul. Pain you've never been able to shake. Before today, that is. Before now. Before her.

After you say your goodbyes, after you embrace, inhaling the lovely scent of her perfume, after you can't seem to place the scent but locate it somewhere between Mugler and Neroli, you shake your head in disbelief. What a woman, you think. What an enchanting, exquisite woman. Homey but cosmopolitan. Gorgeous but kalonic. You wave goodbye and catch a final glint of her emerald eyes before she steps out of view, closing the first chapter on this love to last a lifetime.

"It's on the house," says the bartender, snapping you back to the present.

Startled, you turn to find him handing you a hot chocolate.

"Why, thank you, sir!" you toast him.

The Christmas tree design floating on the surface is finely detailed, each branch softly swaying in the chocolatey breeze. You take a sip and sigh. And as you sit there, drinking, noticing the carols from down the hall, relishing in the echoes of her voice, you feel good, you feel great, better than you've felt in years. In fact, you can't remember any Christmas Eve feeling this good. You're actually happy again. God is good.

And then it hits you.

Her.

All the joy you've felt this morning. All the pleasure you've felt in years. All the love you've been lacking but have finally found on this awful anniversary is a result of this. Single. Person.

Her.

Her ruby red hair. Her emerald eyes and dress. Her nearly smooth skin. Her warm, rumbly voice. Her cheerful laughter. And you didn't even get her number! What the hell were you thinking? *What a fucking idiot!*

You turn toward the door and run. Or run as best you can. You limp-run past some dummy in a snowflake costume, down the corridors of ribbons and tinsel, through whites and greens and reds, twisting your head in all directions, searching for any sign. You spot a head of red hair, but the dress is blue. You dodge past Lord Timothy flirting with yet another member of the peerage, and grunt. You bang on the women's locker

232   *People's Choice Literature*

room door, asking if anyone has seen a red-haired, green-dressed, hover-trolley-tattooed dame, but receive only blank stares. You rush to the main entrance and throw open the door to find a hover cab speeding away. You swallow, swinging your head from side to side, searching for another cab, carriage, anything with a rocket behind it, but there's nothing in sight.

"Everything OK?" asks the android doorman.

"Dear God," you huff in disbelief as the hover cab disappears around an icy bend. "I blew it."

The android doorman's silver brow furrows.

"I met the most wonderful woman in the solar system today," you pant. "We had the most amazing morning. I learned about life and God and Mars and Earth and sailing and Christmas and worship and dinner parties and books and rock & roll and space rockets and the future and the past and time itself, yes, even the present. But I didn't get her damn number! I didn't even get her bloody name!"

"That's terrible," says the android doorman consolingly, antennae blinking red. "What are you going to do?"

"I don't know," you state vacantly, staring into the void of your future.

The android doorman ponders for a moment, his silver hand positioned thoughtfully on his silver chin, before his face lights up. Literally. Eyes blinking bright.

"The registry!" he says with the voice of a robo-sage.

"The registry?"

"Go ask the main office," he states proudly. "They have every club member logged and accounted for."

"That's brilliant!" you say as you hobble from the entrance, down the main corridor, turning left at the first turn, taking another left three doors down, and rushing up as quickly as you can with these broken knees to the main office.

When you get there, you try the door, but it's locked. Dammit! you think. But then you notice the Christmas music playing inside. You go to the door and listen.

No voices. Only music. But the carols aren't just music. They're truths. Beautiful truths. "Glory to God in the highest. On Mars peace and good-will toward men."

"Blessed be the Lord God Almighty," you sigh devoutly. "God Bless us, everyone. But please Lord, please hear my prayers . . ."

The Most Unwanted Novel   233

Just then a text comes on your neural-implanted viewscreen. It's Police Chief Wheatley. You haven't seen him in months, so you switch on your robo-eyes and start mind-texting.

[Neural Text Exchange I: *Police Chief Wheatley* and *Lord Tickletext*]

WHEATLEY: Merry Christmas, dear friend! Just getting the pies ready for brunch, watching the tentacled neighbors play with their new tentacled dog, breathing in those sweet holiday scents. How about you? Are we having fun?

TICKLETEXT: Could be better.

WHEATLEY: You don't say . . .

TICKLETEXT: I've just met the love of my life . . .

WHEATLEY: Why, that's great!

TICKLETEXT: . . . but didn't get her number . . .

WHEATLEY: Oh, my. Did you get her name?

TICKLETEXT: Failed on all fronts. Blimey, what a nightmare.

WHEATLEY: Well, there's not much to go on. What does she look like?

TICKLETEXT: Dyed red hair. Green eyes. She was wearing a flowing, emerald dress. She might be 140? 150? Can't say. Doesn't look a day over 130. What I do know is that she's from San Francisco in the before times . . .

WHEATLEY AND TICKLETEXT: [awkward, sorrowful moment of silence]

234 *People's Choice Literature*

TICKLETEXT: . . . and that she's been on Mars for at least a decade. Seems new to town, though.

WHEATLEY: I'll see what I can find, but can't promise anything. It's Christmas Eve, you know.

TICKLETEXT: I know, I know. But if you could find something sooner than later, I'd love to send her some flowers . . .

WHEATLEY: I'll see what I can do.

TICKLETEXT: Thank you, thank you. You're a DIAMOND.

WHEATLEY: I'm a gem. Is there anything else you can tell me about her?

TICKLETEXT: Well, she talked quite a bit about sailing . . .

WHEATLEY: Huh. I pinned you as going for more of a racket-lover given how much you yabber on about your backhand.

TICKLETEXT: [. . .]

WHEATLEY (clearing his neural throat): Still, it's at least something to work with. In the meantime, why don't you head to the Port and see if you can find her there?

TICKLETEXT: That's brilliant. I'm on my way. And, please, if you find anything, text me right away.

WHEATLEY: Will do. Merry Christmas, old chap.

☙

You switch off your robo-eyes and get moving, limp-lunging down the hall. When you reach the lobby, you run right into flirty Lord Timothy, this time quoting Dickens to a quartet of carolers, twiddling his racket, chuckling, chortling, going on about Lord Pete's rhinoplasty. Behind

him you spot a long line of duds snaking out of the pro shop, eagerly awaiting limited edition jingle-bell lanyards, Team Frosty baseball caps, and hot-chocolate-flavored energy drinks. You consider grabbing some grub for the road but can't imagine idling a lick longer with that dull crew, so you make toward the tinsel-tasseled entrance and its garlands of gold, and know it's time to go, to commence your fateful quest, to reclaim your new love, and since Port Elisabeth is only a kilo off, and since your knee injection sure is working its magic, and since your smilodon fur coat, mink scarf, and dodo down snow pants are easily acquired from coat check, and since the holiday cheer pervades the suburban streets out yonder, you choose to go it alone, you walk, briskly, one limping step after the other, you flee the country club the way an elderly but youthful man with a chip on his shoulder might flee, you don't care, you just walk, you don't call a hover cab, you don't hail a hover carriage, you don't ask a friend for a lift on their rocket sleigh, you don't wait for anyone, you just walk, well, hobble really, you keep moving, hobble-walking, one foot at a time, one foot after the other, one foot, two foot, one foot, two

foot, one foot, two foot, and after a few minutes, you feel a sense of joy building from below, it feels good, yes, it feels grand to be out in the air, surrounded by the sights and sounds of Christmas, the lights strung from tree to tree, the snow angels left by schools of android children, and you picture the pot of heavenly gold at the end of this wintry rainbow of a walk, slight hobble, yes, the woman of your dreams, still, you can't help but wonder, will you in serio succeed in finding her ladyship at the port or might she be far off by now at some friend's house baking cookies or out shopping for gifts for her tentacled cousins or relaxing on a warm beach in LaurelLab's latest Christmas-in-July VR simulation pack up-grade 12.24 or somewhere else entirely, no, you can't help but question if you'll find her at all, forced to spend yet another Festivus alone, lonely, solo, solitary, single, without companion, by yourself, on your own, with-out love, and you can't help but let a tear slip from your eyes, can't help but let slip another, you just let them slip, you let them leak, ooze, go, flow, trickle, you let them pool, you let them trickle some more till they freeze mid-drop, dripping into tiny icicles, and then the tears just flow, they go, keep coming, trickling, freezing into icicles mid-trickle, some breaking as you walk, some forming long stalactites of light, some mix-ing with your sweat, forming teary sweat lollies before crashing to the ground, shattering into a beautiful bouquet of light and loss and love and hope, and then, a few blocks from the holiday market, on the edge of Tinsel Town, you spot a woman in a red dress, a woman in red with gray hairs peeking out from below her red fur cap, just like Mrs. Claus from the pictures, and as you approach her, she asks, "Would you like a present, young man?" and, in your ecstasy, you reply, "Would I ever, Mrs. Claus!" and she hands you a chocolate kiss, yes, you take the choco-late, you take a bite, you chew, you chump, let the cocoa wash over your tongue, you thank her profusely mid-chew, and she smiles back with a sunny warmth that only Mrs.. Claus could muster, you bow and turn,

twist and stretch, you give your thanks and start off again, one foot at a time, one foot after the other, ane more, then bwo, then chree, dour, eive, fix, geven, height, ine, jen, kleven, lwelve, mhirteen, nourteen, oifteen, pixteen, queventeen, righteen, sineteen, twenty, uwenty one, vwenty two, wwenty three, xwenty four, ywenty five, zwenty six, more steps, more, más, mehr, mais, you continue walking, you just keep walking, you keep moving your legs, limping ever so slightly, and as you walk down the road, as you do, you notice the Christmas lights strung on the telephone poles and the Christmas lights strung on the trees and the Christmas lights strung on the houses, the Christmas lights strung 'cross the street signs, you move down the way, you walk talk jump limp simper little whimper till you find yourself facing strange forms in the snow, and you stop dead in your tracks.

You stop, and it hits you like a Terran brick. The pain. The suffering. The death and destruction. The bronze elves iced over, scattered across the snowy meadow like fallen soldiers in the forever war for the soul of man. The destroyed toys. The charred ornaments. The melted reindeer. The Elves who after millennia of blessing legions of Terran children with holiday joy had been forced underground by a liberal legion of pouty parents, pusillanimous politicians, and asinine academics. At first the changes had seemed harmless: Representing non-Christian religious holidays in school, governmental, and work settings? Fine. But soon the demands exploded into violent censorship by the "woke" left, forcing "Happy Holidays" in place of your beloved "Merry Christmas." And as the history books well show, things went downhill from there. First Crooked Jeb Denio stole the presidency. Then Christmas trees were pulled from town squares. Then December 25 disappeared from the calendars. And then . . . Well, you know the rest. Christmas on Earth was over. Elves were forced underground, concealing their holy elfin identities and gifts, assuming a mundane existence among you humans, manning checkout lines, sweeping streets, helping ungrateful liberals with their taxes. It was a dark time in history.

Standing before said hallowed monument, you behold the fallen warriors of yore, and your throat tightens. Your eyes sting. And then you see the light blink in your robo-eye. A mind-text. But from who? Your brain goes straight to its neural inbox to discover the avatar of a white bearded man in a red suit. Your heart races. Could it be? You switch on your robo-eyes and start to mind-type.

[Neural Text Exchange II: *Lord Tickletext* and *Santa*]

TICKLETEXT: Santa? Santa, is that really you!?

SANTA: Yes, it's me, my son. Well, an artificially intelligent version of me. I can't *actually* be in all places at once, you know.

TICKLETEXT (neurally nodding): But why are you here? Why me!?

SANTA: Thanks to the magic of geolocation, I appear automatically in the neural inbox of any visitor to this sacred monument.

TICKLETEXT: [. . .]

SANTA: Are you there?

TICKLETEXT: Yes, I'm here. It's just . . . I miss the elves.

SANTA: Me, too.

TICKLETEXT: Santa?

SANTA: Yes, my son?

TICKLETEXT: What really happened to them?

SANTA: Why don't you take a seat . . .

A bench rises from the ground before you.

SANTA: The Central Christmas Committee of the Martian Federation has made a documentary to answer all your elfin questions. If you could please switch your robo-eyes into their virtual reality function, the video will begin momentarily.

You settle onto the bench and notice the heat emanating from the seat. Boy, you think, they've thought of everything. You take a deep breath before switching to VR mode. At first, there's nothing, just darkness. Then low, symphonic strings and a title in all caps Adobe Garamond Pro.

[Neural Video I:
The Decline and Fall of the Elfin Empire]

A staid narrator in a tweed suit appears on screen.

NARRATOR: It was a dark time in our history. The year was 20—. The human population had just surpassed 9 billion, and the cheat president of the United States, Jeb Denio, Jr., had just been elected to his fifth term. Christmas trees were long gone, and now our most sacred day had been erased from the calendars upon Denio's (the devil's) quinary inauguration. All our fears coalesced with the stroke of that flagitious executive pen. But this was just the beginning. Later that year, as non-woke stores started to fill with holiday foods and choirs started to sing their sacred tunes . . .

You see stock footage of checkout lane bliss and hear the soft hum of carolers.

NARRATOR: . . . the reds appeared. They wore suits and ties, but their eyes glowed red with hate. They were organized by the Anti-Humanist Coalition, a conglomerate of university professors, communists, and homosexuals. And they had one goal.

The choir cuts out.

NARRATOR: To crush Christmas.

You see stock footage of a group of red-eyed people wearing ties and hats with the AHC logo—a red fist with a red star on the knuckle—walking through a forest.

NARRATOR: And they were organized. They showed up in our cities with trucks full of barbed wire.

240 *People's Choice Literature*

You see stock footage of barbed wire being strung from building to building. A sign on one of the trucks reads: WELCOME TO OUR WOKE COMMUNITY: NO CHRISTMAS ALLOWED.

NARRATOR: And they began to dig up our sacred groves.

You see stock footage of people tearing Christmas trees from the ground.

NARRATOR: To burn our holy books.

You see stock footage of a Bible burning.

NARRATOR: And hunt down elves.

You see a historical reinactment of a group of elves being chased down by a red pickup truck.

NARRATOR: By then it was all over.

You see a montage of helpless elves weeping in winter not-so-wonderlands.

NARRATOR: The Elf Nation was forced underground, forced to assimilate into our society.

You see a montage of sweating, straining, sulking elves working in checkout lines, driving cabs, and huddling before a flaming trashcan.

NARRATOR: As if overnight, elfin life as we knew it seemed to disappear. Things started to settle into a new normal. Banality. Sameness. Unholy normality.

You hear and see nothing, just a sequence of increasingly dim backgrounds.

NARRATOR: But then, one day, hope was born.

The symphonic strings swell as a new scene appears. A rosy-cheeked white man sits at his desk, typing on a computer, beaming. The video cuts to a shot of the same man walking down a hallowed hallway. The music swells with each step.

He enters a massive warehouse and moves past rows and rows of androids building spaceships. The man smiles, revealing two perfect rows of stark white teeth.

NARRATOR: For years Duke Noel Skum had been planning a bright, new future for mankind. He'd built batteries, he'd built rockets. The only thing left was terraforming . . .

Ellipses appear on screen.

NARRATOR: And then it happened.

The symphonic strings climax as we witness a flower blooming on a barren Martian landscape.

NARRATOR: In the summer of 20—, Duke Noel, with the help of his friends, Dukes Brandon Richards and Zeb Jeffos, landed the first manned rocket on Mars and planted the first Martian crop.

A rocket lands on the red planet and a green shoot bursts from the ground. What follows is a sequence of ecological, technological, and societal developments on the Martian surface.

NARRATOR: Within years, Martian immigration began, leading to a thriving post-Terran society. Food was bountiful. Palatial homes were aplenty. And, finally, after years of strife and secular sorrow, there was a new, permanent home for Christmas.

You see a montage of Martian prosperity. Happy people walking through a Martian park. Families picnicking and children playing. Sun shining. The camera cuts to a Christmas tree in a snowy meadow, and the music swells once more.

NARRATOR: Today, the Martian Federation is the most advanced society not only in the solar system but in all human history.

You see a montage of Martian technology. A drone flies a package to a fifty-three-room mansion. A robot helps a child with her math homework. A man sits in a chair, his brain connected to a quantum personal computer.

242 *People's Choice Literature*

NARRATOR: And for the first time since the birth of Jesus Christ, our Lord and savior, we finally have true hope.

The music swells to a high pitch. It is the most beautiful thing you've ever heard.

NARRATOR: And so, my friends. It's my great pleasure to wish you . . .

The Narrator relishes each word.

NARRATOR: . . . a very . . . merry . . . Christmas.

The music continues as the credits roll.

Hey there. Tom Comitta again. How's it going so far? Fine? A bit strange? Too much Christmas? Well, as mentioned previously, religion was the least-wanted theme according to our poll, so it seemed this story needed a strong religious element, however superficial. On top of that, the least wanted setting was a rural polar region (of the mere 8.62% respondents who prefer natural settings, only 0.36% wanted a story set in a polar region) on another planet (of the 25.96% who desire unrealistic narratives, only 0.74% want to read about planets other than Earth). So, a cold day on Mars seemed like a good—or bad—idea. On top of this, the least-wanted duration for a story was one day (only 0.38% prefer it), so Christmas Eve (religion + a single day + a cold time of year in the northern hemisphere) on Mars made perfect sense. I also chose Christmas Eve because of another variable that influenced this book.

You'll recall while most of the questions in our literary poll were multiple choice, we also asked respondents an open-ended question: "If you had unlimited resources and could commission your favorite author to write a novel just for you, what would it be about?" While most responses mentioned only a genre, a fraction of respondents gave more specific, idiosyncratic answers such as "Sports Talk Radio," "a history of Frank Sinatra," "Pirates," and "Werewolves." One of these open-ended answers led to the backstory you just read:

It would likely be about Elves that are forced into hiding among humans. Having to conceal their identities and their magic all while of course being hunted by both elves and humans alike.

Another of these answers inspired the frame story here and confirmed my suspicion that *The Most Unwanted Novel* should take place on Christmas Eve:

It would be a simple romance novel, maybe holiday themed. Where two strangers, a man and woman, who are having a tough time during the holiday season due to a tragedy that occurred around that time years ago. They meet in a bar on Christmas Eve and talk and bond over why the holidays suck for them. Turns out, the woman's dad and the man's grandmother both passed away in the same trolley accident when they were little kids, which happened on Christmas Eve. What a strange coincidence, they declare. They chat all night and really hit it off until the bar is close to closing for the night and the woman exclaims that she really has to go and runs out, realizing she lost track of time. She leaves in a hurry without getting a phone number or even the name of the man. So to this man, she is now [a] mystery woman that he now must find because he felt something special while chatting with her. He spends the next few days searching all over and until he finally finds her, and they continue right where they left off and live happily ever [after]

As you can see, this is the basic setup to this novel—with several additions and flourishes drawn from the four guides of this narrative: the National Literature Poll, *The Bestseller Code*, an LLM, and my own creative faculties.

As I measured which religion, or religions, to include here, I also considered my own perspective. Since I was raised a Quaker by a former Protestant and a former Catholic, it seemed the religion I had the most stake in and could best parody was mainstream Christianity. Another writer of a different background might have focused on another faith. Still, it seemed that focusing on Christianity in this book about American taste made sense even outside my own background, since, according to a 2020 poll by the Pew Research Center, a significant majority (65%) of the United States identifies as Christian. 28% identify as atheist, agnostic,

244 *People's Choice Literature*

or "nothing in particular"; and 6% identify as a non–Christian religion (Jewish, 1%; Muslim, 1%; Buddhist, 1%; Hindu, 1%; Other, 2%).

This book also parodies Christianity because of one finding of *The Bestseller Code*. Archer and Jockers showed that people don't want to be offended by a novel. So, amorality (according to our poll, most readers don't want amoral characters) and offensiveness combined with religious themes easily yielded a book that relishes in parody. As such, if there were an offense election, *The Most Unwanted Novel* would win in a landslide, rankling a whopping 65% of the population.

Anyway, enough about the data. I just hope you're having as good a time as possible reading this novel that is, well, full of things that statistically you should despise.

Long ago, your mother told you the colder it gets, the closer you are to heaven. So, you used to put your hand out the window and wait until it burned with the cold. You would count the seconds, and then you would say, "Ah, that means I'm X seconds from heaven." If it was 10 degrees, you were 10 seconds from heaven. If it was 5 degrees, you were 5. You would do this for a few minutes to get a sense of how close you were, and then you would be happy, picturing angels approaching your window.

Today, covered from head to toe in your winter gear and overwhelmed by the audiovisual remembrances of the elfish monument and your longing for your lost, red-headed, hover-trolley-tattooed love, you're in no mood to test your celestial proximity. It's just cold, plain and simple. No test required. And under these circumstances, heaven feels aeons away.

Sitting before the Earth Elf Monument, flicking the icy tears from your eyes, you feel lost. How can I possibly gather the strength to make it to the Port now? you ask yourself. Maybe I can just neural text the Port Authority and see if they have any leads.

So you switch your robo-eyes back on and mind-text the Port Elisabeth Port Authority. In fifteen nanoseconds, you reach an operator.

[Neural Text Exchange III: *Lord Tickletext* and *The Port Elisabeth Port Authority*]

PORT ELISABETH PORT AUTHORITY (PEPA) OPERATOR: Hello! To whom should I direct this text?

TICKLETEXT: Hmm. Well . . . How do I put this. See, the thing is, I'm looking for someone who might know someone or someone who might know someone who knows someone I just met who likes tennis but also sailing . . .

PEPA OPERATOR: . . . Sir?

TICKLETEXT: Yes?

PEPA OPERATOR: I'm not sure I understand.

TICKLETEXT: Oh, um, is there a Port Elisabeth sailing department you could direct me to?

PEPA OPERATOR: Sir, there are at least 50 sailing and boating clubs in Port Elisabeth. You could try the Port Elisabeth Sailing Club, or the Port Elisabeth Yacht Club, or the Port Elisabeth Sailboard Club for starters . . . ?

TICKLETEXT: How 'bout the Sailing Club?

PEPA OPERATOR: OK. Connecting you now.

[Neural Text Exchange IV: *Lord Tickletext* and *The Port Elisabeth Sailing Club*]

PORT ELISABETH SAILING CLUB (PESC) OPERATOR: Hello! To whom should I direct this text?

246   *People's Choice Literature*

TICKLETEXT: Hi! I'm texting about one of your members. Or, well, she's potentially one of your members. Do you know of a woman—dyed red hair, green eyes—who sails in Port Elisabeth?

PESC OPERATOR: I'm sorry, sir, but I don't know anyone in the Sailing Club. I'm just an intern. And our member logs contain no physical information. Is there a name I can search for?

TICKLETEXT: This is the thing. I don't have her name . . .

PESC OPERATOR: Have you tried the Port Elisabeth Yacht Club, or the Port Elisabeth Sailboard Club? Perhaps a Port Elisabeth Sculling Club operator might be more familiar with the clientele given how hands-on they can be. In the meantime, I'll see what I can do.

TICKLETEXT: How about the Sailboard Club?

[Neural Text Exchange V: *Lord Tickletext* and *The Port Elisabeth Sailboard Club*]

PORT ELISABETH SAILBOARD CLUB (PESBC) OPERATOR: Hello! To whom should I direct this text?

TICKLETEXT: Howdy! I was wondering if you knew of someone who sails . . . or sailboards in Port Elisabeth who has dyed red hair and green eyes?

PESBC OPERATOR: Sir?

TICKLETEXT: I know, I know. I don't know her name. That's all I got.

PESBC OPERATOR: You could try the Port Elisabeth Sculling Club. I know their operator has a rapport with the local scene. You'll often find her at AI mixers and happy hours.

TICKLETEXT: Wonderful!

[Neural Text Exchange VI: *Lord Tickletext* and *The Port Elisabeth Sculling Club*]

PORT ELISABETH SCULLING CLUB (PESCC) OPERATOR: Hello! To whom should I direct this text?

TICKLETEXT: Hey, there. I was wondering if you knew of someone who sails or sculls in Port Elisabeth who has dyed red hair and green eyes? I hear you have a bit of a familiarity with the clientele??

PESCC OPERATOR: You must be thinking of Diana. She's out for the holiday. I don't know any members personally.

TICKLETEXT (letting out a mind sigh): And neither does anyone, it seems. I just can't get a break. I met the loveliest lady today. She thrilled my heart. She made me feel full again. She has the most carnelian of crimson hair, the most emerald of eyes, and the most startling tattoo of a hover trolley on her—

PESCC OPERATOR: Did you say hover trolley?

TICKLETEXT: Yes?

PESCC OPERATOR: I may have seen her ladyship just this morning, sir.

TICKLETEXT: Holy Moley!

PESCC OPERATOR: I was on my morning VR meditation and could've sworn she was there with me. Well, her ladyship's avatar, that is . . .

TICKLETEXT: This is incredible. What was she doing? What do you know about her?

PESCC OPERATOR: If you'd like, I can send you the e-diary entry from this morning and you can see for yourself.

TICKLETEXT: Yes. Please. *Please!*

248 *People's Choice Literature*

PESCC OPERATOR. OK, one second... Here you go.

A ding comes into your neural sensors.

TICKLETEXT: Thank you so very much. How can I repay you, dear operator?

PESCC OPERATOR: Oh, don't you worry yourself one bit. 'Tis the season!

TICKLETEXT: Yes, it is. And Merry Christmas, dear Operator!

PESCC OPERATOR: Merry Christmas. :)

❧

As the comm switches off, the text file blinks in your robo-eye periphery. Here goes nothing, you think. Your mind opens the document, and you begin to read.

[*PESCC Operator's* Neural-Diary]

In the morning's stroll along the banks of the Alun, a beautiful little stream which flows down from the Welsh hills and throws itself into the Dee, my attention was attracted to a group seated on the margin. On approaching I found it to consist of a veteran angler and two rustic disciples. The former was an old fellow with a wooden leg, with clothes very much but very carefully patched, betokening poverty honestly come by and decently maintained. His face bore the marks of former storms but present fair weather, its eyes were green as emeralds, its furrows had been worn into an habitual smile, his neon red locks hung about his ears, and he had altogether the good-humored air of a postmodern continental philosopher who was disposed to take the world as it went. One of his companions was a ragged wight with the skulking look of an arrant poacher. The other was a tall, awkward country lad, with a lounging gait,

and apparently somewhat of a rustic beau. The old, neon-red-haired man was busy in examining the maw of a trout which he had just killed, to discover by its contents what insects were seasonable for bait, and was lecturing on the subject to his companions, who appeared to listen with infinite deference.

I thought that I could perceive in the veteran angler before me an exemplification of what I had read in Izaak Walton's *The Compleat Angler*, the greatest book on angling ever penned to paper; and there was a cheerful contentedness in his looks, particularly those glowing red locks, that quite drew me towards him. I could not but remark the gallant manner in which he stumped from one part of the brook to another, waving his rod in the air to keep the line from dragging on the ground or catching among the bushes, and the adroitness with which he would throw his fly to any particular place, sometimes skimming it lightly along a little rapid, sometimes casting it into one of those dark holes made by a twisted root or overhanging bank in which the large trout are apt to lurk.

I soon fell into conversation with the old redheaded angler, and was so much entertained that, under pretext of receiving instructions in his art, I kept company with him for some time, wandering along the banks of the stream and listening to his talk. He was very communicative, having all the easy garrulity of cheerful old age, and I fancy he was a little flattered by having an opportunity of displaying his piscatory lore, for who does not like now and then to play the sage?

He had been much of a rambler in his day and had passed some years of his youth in America, particularly in San Francisco, where he had entered into trade and had been ruined by the indiscretion of a partner. He had afterwards experienced many ups and downs in life until he got into the navy, where his leg was carried away by a cannon-ball at the battle of Boston. This was the only stroke of real good-fortune he had ever experienced, for it got him a pension, which, together with some small paternal property, brought him in a revenue of nearly forty pounds. On this he retired to the Martian Federation, where he lived quietly and independently, and devoted the remainder of his life to the "noble art of angling," with an occasional regatta.

Then the old angler invited me to his place of abode. It was a small cottage containing only one room, but a perfect curiosity in its method and arrangement. It was on the skirts of the village, on a green bank a little back from the road, with a small garden in front stocked with kitchen herbs and adorned with a few flowers. The whole front of the

250 *People's Choice Literature*

cottage was overrun with honeysuckle. On the top was a sailboat for a weathercock. The interior was fitted up in a truly nautical style, his ideas of comfort and convenience having been acquired on the berth-deck of a vessel. A hammock was slung from the ceiling which in the daytime was lashed up so as to take but little room. From the centre of the chamber hung a model of a ship, of his own workmanship. Two or three chairs, a table, and a large sea-chest formed the principal movables. About the wall were stuck up Celine Dion posters intermingled with pictures of regattas, among which Cape Cod 20— held a distinguished place. The mantelpiece was decorated with sea-shells, over which hung a quadrant, flanked by two wood-cuts of the finest captains. His implements for angling were carefully disposed on nails and hooks about the room. On a shelf was arranged his library, containing a work on angling, much worn, a Bible covered with canvas, an odd volume or two of voyages, a nautical almanac, and a book of sea shanties.

His family consisted of a large black cat with one eye, and a parrot which he had caught and tamed and educated himself in the course of one of his voyages, and which uttered a variety of sea-phrases with the hoarse brattling tone of a veteran boatswain. The establishment reminded me of that of the renowned Robinson Crusoe; it was kept in neat order, everything being "stowed away" with the regularity of a schooner; and he informed me that he "scoured the deck every morning and swept it between meals."

I found him seated on a bench before the door, smoking his pipe in the soft morning sunshine, his sleeves rolled up, revealing a surprisingly vivid tattoo of a hover trolley. His cat was purring soberly on the threshold, and his parrot describing some strange evolutions in an iron ring that swung in the centre of his cage. He sat me down and gave me a history of his sport with as much minuteness as a captain would talk over a journey, being particularly animated in relating the manner in which he had taken a large trout, which had completely tasked all his skill and wariness, and which he had sent as a trophy to the Prime Minister of the Martian Federation.

I have done, for I fear that my reader is growing weary, but I could not refrain from drawing the picture of this worthy "brother of the angle," who has made me more than ever in love with the theory, though I fear I shall never be adroit in the practice, of his art; and I will conclude this rambling sketch in the words of honest Izaak Walton, by craving the blessing of St. Peter's Master upon my reader, "and upon all that are true lovers of virtue, and dare trust in His providence, and be quiet, and go a-angling."

[Neural Text Exchange VII: *Lord Tickletext* and *The PESCC Operator*]

TICKLETEXT: Oh, dear Operator, thankuthankuthanku.

PESCC OPERATOR: Of course. Is there anything else I can help you with today?

TICKLETEXT: Let's see. Your account reveals much, but how to know which of the characteristics you describe are rooted in reality and which are simply the moods and histories of her avatar? It seems difficult to falsify a deep understanding of fishing, but things like the peg leg and living with a parrot or, God forbid, a cat . . . They seem too fantastical.

PESCC OPERATOR: Well then, fishing is your best lead, right? Would you like me to connect you with the Port Elisabeth Angling Society?

TICKLETEXT (mind sighing): I suppose so.

PESCC OPERATOR: Right away.

Suddenly a mind text appears from Police Chief Wheatley.

TICKLETEXT: Oh, sorry, Operator. Gotta take this. Can you hold a minute?

PESCC OPERATOR: No problem.

[Neural Text Exchange VIII: *Lord Tickletext* and *Police Chief Wheatley*]

WHEATLEY: Hello, friend!

TICKLETEXT: Hi! What have you got?

WHEATLEY: Well, I've got two blueberries and a key lime in the oven. Should be ready in ten. Tried for a pecan, but it collapsed in my hands, the darned thing. Lady Jane's not gonna be too happy about that . . .

TICKLETEXT: [. . .]

WHEATLEY: What . . . ?

TICKLETEXT: My missing love?

WHEATLEY: Oh, right. There's good news and there's bad news.

TICKLETEXT: Alright . . .

WHEATLEY: The good is that thanks to a decent reading on the time tubes we have a lead.

TICKLETEXT: Wonderful!

WHEATLEY: The prediction function on these babies is something else. Gotta thank tentacled Fred for the upgrade. Now, the bad news is that the lead is on an ice-fishing expedition in the Planum Australe, Mars's most remote national park. Rumor has it he's even reached the south pole.

TICKLETEXT: Ah . . .

WHEATLEY: And the really bad news is that no one's been able to contact him all morning.

TICKLETEXT: Dammit.

WHEATLEY: So, the best we can do is either venture there ourselves or send a representative in our stead.

TICKLETEXT: Well, I'm no good with a rocket sledge. Haven't tried in decades.

WHEATLEY: We'll have to send a representative.

TICKLETEXT: Right.

WHEATLEY: Who could it be?

TICKLETEXT: Well, we need someone who can't be easily distracted.

WHEATLEY: That's right.

TICKLETEXT: Someone who can think well on their feet . . .

WHEATLEY: Uh huh.

TICKLETEXT: Someone who's good with people and can manage a team.

WHEATLEY: Yep.

TICKLETEXT: Someone who keeps a cool head in a crisis.

WHEATLEY: Right-o.

TICKLETEXT: Someone who's brave and strong.

WHEATLEY: Exactly.

TICKLETEXT: I think we'll send Police Chief Wheatley!

WHEATLEY: Huh?

TICKLETEXT: It all makes sense. You're the best of the best. The host with the most. The right man for the right job!

WHEATLEY: Jim, I hate rocket sledging.

TICKLETEXT: But we need you.

WHEATLEY: Not gonna do it.

TICKLETEXT: But you're our only hope . . .

254   *People's Choice Literature*

WHEATLEY: You're wrong, Tickletext . . .

TICKLETEXT: ?

WHEATLEY: . . . There is another.

Wheatley sends you a livestream of a dark room you've never seen before. A pet shop? Zoo? Rows and rows of waterless aquariums line the walls, with purple lamps of different intensities illuminating each transparent cuboid. You focus on the strange, sliding shapes inside each box and mind-gasp. Snakes! Suddenly a person walks in, moving over to each cage and dropping in little flecks of food. The snakes happily gather around the treats and writhe in glee. The person then opens a cage and lifts an immense python into their arms. The camera zooms in, and you notice that this is no person cradling a cobra but a Model-T android—Duke Noel's greatest invention to date!

WHEATLEY: This is Buddy, the first self-sustaining android in the Martian Federation. He's a regular at the country club and sure has a mean topspin.

TICKLETEXT: Strange, I've never seen him around . . .

The video cuts to prerecorded footage of Buddy's metallic body slamming tennis balls at an alarming rate.

TICKLETEXT: What does Buddy have to do with the search for my lost love?

WHEATLEY: Well, Buddy is not only a reptile collector, a tennis pro, and a trillionaire . . .

The video feed cuts to a shot of Buddy counting large piles of money.

WHEATLEY: . . . he also happens to be deeply infatuated with our contact in the Planum Australe, Lord Philip. And, with a little persuading, we might be able to convince him to surprise Lord Philip and see what he knows about our mysterious, red haired, hover-trolley-tattooed dame. What's more romantic than a surprise on Christmas Eve, am I right?

TICKLETEXT (mind-nodding): You're not just right, you're a genius.

The Most Unwanted Novel 255

❧

After you and Police Chief Wheatley pitch this plan to Buddy via neural messaging, and after Buddy accepts with joyous, holiday cheer, after he packs his things, hires a snake-sitter, and gathers his crew of Lords, fellow androids, and robo-ponies, after he briefs them on the mission, after they gather sufficient supplies and rocket sledges and jettison off toward the Planum Australe, after you switch off your robo-eyes, after all of this and much more, which will be detailed in full in a subsequent thousand-page book titled *Are You Kidding Me That Book Would Be Even Worse Than This Crap No One Would Ever Want That*, you suddenly come to your senses and notice the time.

12 p.m.! You're late for brunch!

You turn one last time to the Earth Elf Monument and say a prayer. Then you stand up from that heated seat and gaze out across the snowy fields, the future laid out before you like a warm, welcoming blankey. So you take a step in the direction of Advent Way and get moving, one limping foot in front of the limping other in the direction of Blakely Barn, the poshest retrofitted holiday dining joint this side of the Valles Marineris, and you think of the hams you had yesterday, you dream of the yams from the day before that, you wonder what's in store for today, on this holiest day, well, second-holiest of days, you think, what joy, what a time to be alive, what a time to thrive, and as you move through the wintery wonderland, you feel no longer man or Martian but one with the snowy mist about, you close your eyes and move by the sheer will of intuition, mind blank save for the faint daydreams of pastries on the horizon, yes, the thought of the thought of you moves in tandem with pastry thoughts, those warm, welcoming friends, you notice the thought of hope that appears as an apple strudel, with layers and layers of joy and bliss and love and happiness warming a hopeful, rosy center, a sweetness you call home, you hold the strudel and you thank God for the strudel and you kiss the strudel, moving further through the snow, past the hopeful strudel to new thoughts, new regions, new conceptions, yes, the thought of bliss appears as billowing as a Bundt cake, just like the ones Grandmummy used to make back on Terra, cream-covered, yum, you smile at that bulbing Bundt cake of a thought and the feeling that thought conjures in you, how it balloons into the unbearableness, the lightness, the being, and you move forward through the snow with a

256 *People's Choice Literature*

whole new understanding of thought and feeling and hope and bliss, the thought of friendship appears in the form of a tres leches cake, and you hold that cake, you chew it and you thank God for the food-for-thought, you kiss the cake and you keep the cake, moving forward through the snow, past the friendly frosting cake to new thoughts, new feelings, new hopes, new flavors, the thought of loyalty appears as a blueberry pie, thick and fluffy, full of honor, you see this blueberry pie of a thought, this thought of loyalty, and you see the pie and you feel the pie and you know the pie and you move forward through the snow with a whole new understanding of the pie known as loyalty, loyalty and honor and joy and hope and bliss and friendship and love, you move forward through the snow, past said loyal love pie to new thoughts, new feelings, new hopes, new flavors popping up in peripheries of thoughtful perception and feeling and hope and bliss, through a whiteness that is both you in the form of a tres leches cake, you and your movement through them, the universe, the frosting that is those thoughts, those warmths, that cake and you thank God for the thought of hope that appears as frosting, rosy cake, new thoughts, new center, a sweetness you call home and full of honor, you see this through the snow, past the hopeful thought of loyalty, and you see the regions, even newer conceptions, yes, the pies, and you move forward, billowing as a Bundt cake, just like new understanding of the pie that takes you back to Terra, cream-forward through the snow, past the you, the unbearableness, the feelings, new hopes, new flavors, forward through the snow with a thoughtful perception, the thought of friendship reappears to your pastry thoughts and you notice the cake with the most frozen of frostings welcoming new friends, you notice a cake called love, and you hold the apple strudel and, with layers and layers of food-for-thought, you kiss the happiness, warming a hopeful thought through the snow, past the friendly strudels, and you thank feelings, new hopes, new flavors, moving further toward the blueberry pie, a thick and fluffy hopeful strudel of new thoughts, a new blueberry pie of a thought, this, the thought of bliss appearing again as a pie, and you feel the pie and the cakes Grandmummy used to walk through the snow with a whole warm, loving smile, that is known as loyalty, loyalty and the feeling that conjures friendship and love, and you move into lightness, being, and you move popping up in peripheries of whole new understandings of thought, you move further through the snow and ice, moving on and up a snow bank, nearer to Blakely Barn, and you are happy, you are alive, you are alone but not for long, for your true love awaits you in the

not-too-distant future's past thanks to the generous obbligatos of an android named Buddy, a true friend of a friend, the truest in the sense of the word, yes, it is Christmas time and people are primed for loving acts of kindness, it is a time of miracles and gifts and plenty, a time of love and laughter, of bliss and grace, of hope, merriment, and love, and you are the embodiment of that love and laughter and bliss and grace and hope and wonder and merriment and love, yes, the love for your true love is the love of life, the embrace of the greater-than-thou, the embrace of God, of God's love, of God's love's love, of God's love's love's love, of God's love's love's love's love, of God's love's love's love's love's love, of God's love's love's love's love's love's love, of life, love that saves, love that *is* the world and love that is Jesus Christ, our Lord and savior, our compass, our life force, our guiding light, the one who will lead us to the great hereafter, the one who will guide us home, to the heavens, to the skies, to the beginning, the end, and as you feel the snowflakes fall on your forehead, as you drift through the snowy landscape, you think of the gifts that await you, not just the steak and eggs, the juice, or even the charcuterie, the cheese spread or the petit fours, but the gift of life, the gift of love, the gift of friendship, the gift of family, for this is the time of family, and the time of love, of truth, the creation of families anew, the rebirth, the rekindling of joy and closeness for the family that raised you, the family that has sent you across the greatest of celestial distances, the most vacant of voids in a gesture of pure philostorgie, in search of new life, yes, a new future free of atheistic, academic death and destruction, you think of the sorrow of those infelicitous few who still remain on Earth and then you make a prayer, and after the prayer, after wishing those Terrans well, you step atwixt those thoughts, those memories, you literally step outside them, psychosomatically distancing yourself from that land you once knew, just too afflictive, you think, yes, best to focus on the present, on the here, the now, for what matters is the present and the future, not the past, for we are the species of tomorrow, we are the dawn of a new era, we *are* the new era. And just as you think these last thoughts, you notice Blakely Barn standing before you, its wooden façade almost smiling back. You see the archway glowing in a rainbow of Christmas lights. You see the reindeer figurines nodding in the newborn layer of snow. You think of joy and happiness. And then you notice the light blinking in the periphery of your robo-eyes. Your mind clicks it:

It's the PESCC Operator on hold.

258 *People's Choice Literature*

Howdy, Tom Comitta again. I thought to chime in since it seemed that surreal strudel section could use some clarity. When I mentioned to my partner that I'd used the William Burroughs/Bryon Gysin cut-up method to compose part of that passage, she suggested filling you in on this and other experimental elements I've used in this novel. As mentioned earlier, our poll showed only 37.64% of people prefer experimental novels, so, of course, this novel had to follow suit.

In that pastry passage, I did just this. I first wrote "off the dome," that rambling, first-thought-worst-thought meditation on strudels and pies. Then I printed it out and followed the cut-up method as Burroughs described it:

> Take a page. Like this page. Now cut down the middle and cross the middle. You have four sections: . . . one two three four. Now rearrange the sections placing section four with section one and section two with section three. And you have a new page. Sometimes it says much the same thing. Sometimes something quite different . . .

Following Burroughs's order of operations and typing up this new passage, I then edited the results and massaged this new, cut-up text into the original.

While the cut-up was my creative interpretation of the kind of experimental writing that few would desire, elsewhere in this novel I've drawn from several other experimental tactics included in our national literature poll. After asking respondents whether they wanted traditional or experimental fiction, we then inquired which experimental methods they most wanted, finding these results:

Action conveyed in nonchronological order? Yes. (78.12%)

Passages that are highly abstract or unclear? Yes. (52.16%)

Chapters that read like long encyclopedia entries? No. (71.50%)

Novels that directly comment on the art of writing? No. (54.45%)

Long, meandering sentences and chapters? No. (52.93%)

To make sure the greatest level of displeasure was reached, I relied on the three most-rejected methods at every chance: encyclopedic sections, author commentary/metafiction, and long meandering sentences.

Novels are long and, to keep respondents' attention, polls are short. To ensure I—and hopefully you, dear Reader—stayed engaged, I drew from additional experimental tactics I've discovered in my four decades of reading: everything from the excessive alliteration of Maria Dahvana Headley's *Beowulf* (experimental in retrospect?) and the writings of George Kuchar; to the repetitive, visual poetry of Peter Waterhouse's *Language Death Night Outside* (trans. Rosmarie Waldrop) and N. H. Pritchard's *The Mundus*; to the form and genre juxtapositions of Ishmael Reed's *Mumbo Jumbo* and Kathy Acker's *Blood and Guts in High School*; to the nested word games of Georges Perec's *Life: A User's Manual*. I even borrowed from myself, using similar supercut methods employed in my first novel, *The Nature Book*.

One experimental method that appears throughout *The Most Unwanted Novel* is my loose interpretation of César Aira's "flight forward," a form of improvisatory writing that, in the words of his translator Heather Cleary, "allows for no backward glances, no revision; only a dizzying accumulation of characters and plot twists that brings to mind an image of the author stumbling across an idea, dusting it off, and adding it to the motley strand of his narrative." I describe my flight forward as "loose" because I allowed myself to edit this novel. I also often knew roughly where the narrative was heading, constantly referring to a spreadsheet of the poll results and *Bestseller Code* data. Aira's method turned my calculated writing process into an exhilarating game that felt somewhere between improv jazz and an Oulipian marathon.

[Neural Text Exchange IX: *Lord Tickletext* and *PESCC Operator*]

TICKLETEXT: Blimey! Have I kept you this long?

PESCC OPERATOR: No problem, sir. Being an artificial intelligence, I have the functionality to be in hundreds of thousands of places at once. In

the time It took you to log back in, I connected 677 potential customers to each of the fifteen departments of the Sculling Club, signed up 318 new members, shared our menu with fifty-two curious Christmas Eve brunch-goers, and even had a drone pick up my dry cleaning!

TICKLETEXT: Right.

PESCC OPERATOR: I also happened to find information on your red-headed, green-eyed, hover-trolley-tattooed, potentially one-eyed-cat-two-eyed-parrot-owning, but certainly sailing and angling Martian friend.

TICKLETEXT (shuddering at the word "cat"): Incredible!

PESCC OPERATOR: I neural texted an operator at the Port Elisabeth Angling Society . . .

TICKLETEXT: Great.

PESCC OPERATOR: . . . who introduced me to their operator-in-training, who then directed me to management . . .

TICKLETEXT: Splendid!

PESCC OPERATOR: . . . who nudged an assistant . . .

TICKLETEXT: Yep.

PESCC OPERATOR: . . . who neural-texted with the head of security, who was on his lunch break eating a ham sandwich with lettuce, tomato, garlic aioli, cheddar, and truffle shavings—the kind you get at the Port Elisabeth Farmer's Market, you know, the one on the corner of Liberty and Main? Well—

TICKLETEXT: You mean the one with sticky buns on Tuesdays?

PESCC OPERATOR: No, that one's on Tchaikovsky Way. It's the one on Sundays with the meat pies and sausage rolls, near the Frosty Spa.

TICKLETEXT: Got it.

The Most Unwanted Novel 261

PESCC OPERATOR: Well, anyway, the head of security took a break from his Port Elisabeth Farmer's Market truffle-infused sandwich, called up holo-scans from the past hour, and almost immediately found your green-eyed, redheaded ladyship.

TICKLETEXT: Goodness! I'll go right away!

PESCC OPERATOR: I'm sorry, sir. It appears she left the Angling Society fifteen minutes ago.

TICKLETEXT: Well, I can at least search the vicinity! She can't be that far.

PESCC OPERATOR: This is the thing, sir. After contacting the Port Elisabeth Police Department and accessing public street-side surveillance footage, I could only follow her ladyship as far as the Tinsel Street Metro stop, and then my security clearance cut out.

TICKLETEXT: Right, right. Everyone knows about the Terran terror threat . . .

PESCC OPERATOR: I'm sorry, sir.

TICKLETEXT: It's OK. Look, operator. Or what's your name?

PESCC OPERATOR: I'm Haley.

TICKLETEXT: Hi, Haley. Look, I'm famished and just got to Blakely Barn.

HALEY (mind smiling): The finest brunch around!

TICKLETEXT: Would you mind checking with the Metro authority and see if they can find anything?

HALEY: I'll do my best, sir. Bon appétit! :)

☙

262   *People's Choice Literature*

You switch off your robo-eyes and step inside. Instantly, the warmth floods in in the form of a booming air curtain, dumping eight-to-fifteen gallons of heat per inch, just the kind you like. Marching in, you notice the octagonal ornaments perched below plaid quilts that hang from the rafters, strung together under the very ceiling where Lord Xavier and you once zoubied—only a year ago if the xyloclock on your wrist reads right. The walls glow willow green and white velvet around tables of sirs and ubu rois. Quite the party, you think, orbiting the android nuns and maîtres d, nearing the luncheoneers knocking back kirsch mixed with juice, Jägerbombs, and Irish coffees. Lady Hannah calls you to her friend's table just as Duke Edgar stands to deliver his daily toast. Your heart cavorts as you behold a potent potable of holiday cheer hovering over each seat, tumblers and stemware saturating the room in festal light.

[Neural Inventory I: *Duke Edgar's Toast*]

The Orange Cream Mimosa half full. The Peach Ginger Bellini half full. The Sinless Sangria half full. The Blackberry-Bourbon Iced Tea half full. The Michelada half full. The Strabellini half full. The Tea Latte half full. The Bloody Bull half full. The It's a Wonderful Sangria half full. The Better Than Citron Presse half full. The Fresh Strawberry Bellini half full. The White Wine and Lillet Cocktail half full. The Michael's Bloody Maria half full. The Raspberry Limeade with Lavender and Mint half full. The Sangria Sunrise half full. The Icebreaker Mojito half full. The Rhubarb Water half full. The Limoncello Spritzer half full. The Donatella Cocktail half full. The Orange Peel Wine half full. The Mote con Huesillos half full. The Orange Aperol Sun half full. The Elderflower Sparkler half full. The Earl Grey Spritzer half full. The Gweneth Paltrow's Peach Cooler half full. The Wine Fruit Sparkler half full. The Guava and Papaya Mimosa half full. The Watermelon Margarita Mimosa half full. The Blood Orange Screwdriver half full. The 533 North Pinckney Cocktail half full. The New-Look Bloody Mary half full. The Strawberry Muddle half full. The Wake Country Cooler half full. The Sparkling Tarragon Gin Lemonade half full. The Pineapple-Mint Mojito half full. The Chamomile Gin Cocktail half full. The Ruby Champagne Cocktail half full. The Lemon Drop Champagne Punch half full. The Danish

Mary with Celery Ice half full. The Lillet Rose Spring Cocktail half full. The Semifreddo Bellini half full. The Pear and Cranberry Bellini half full. The Blood Orange Champagne Cocktail half full. The Pear and Sparkling Cider Cocktail half full. The Fruity Champagne Punch half full. The Lemony Spiked Sweet Tea half full. The Grapefruit Sparkler half full. The Rabbit half full. The Peach and Rosmary Spritzers half full. The Pomegranate-Champagne Punch half full. The Blood Orange Punch half full. The Pisco-Grapefruit Brunch Pitcher half full. The Stawberry-Mint Sparkler half full. The Thyme for a Salty Dog half full. The Ultimate Bloody Mary half full. The Blur half full. The Kiwi Cooler half full. The Honey and Marmalade Sour half full. The Polaris half full. The Grapefruit and Ginger Sparkler half full. The Fresh Watermelon Margarita half full. The Hard Cider and Crème Yvette Sparkler half full. The Strawberry-Rhubarb Bellini with Basil half full. The Chamomile and Tangerine Sparkling Cocktail half full. The Sparkling Suze Cocktail half full. The Raspberry Spritz half full. The Sparkling Grapefruit Sangria with Lillet Rosé half full. The Devereaux half full. The Lemon Balm Lavender Tisane half full. The Black Peppercorn Limeade half full. The Mint Shiso Tisane half full. The Watermelon Bellini half full. The Fresh Cranberry Mimosa half full. The Blood Orange Mimosa half full. The Peach-Raspberry Tequila Sunrise half full. The Sparkling Cranberry Blush half full. The Sparkling Elderflower Lemonade half full. The Seaside Sunrise half full. The Espresso Martini half full. The Raspberry-Orange Sunrise half full. The Peach Nectar Spritzers half full. The Perfect Ramos Fizz half full. The Royal Tea half full. The Kentucky Coffee half full. The House Made White Sangria half full. The Dreams of Green half full. The Polynesian Punch half full. The Mister A's Classic half full. The Sergeant Pepper half full. The Home on the Range half full. The Bombay Bloody half full. The Tuscan Sun half full.

ତ୍ତ

But as you gaze across the room and as you take it all in, as you sit down and consume two Bloody Mollys, six seedless grapes, twelve cantaloupe slices, eight and a third cheese cubes, one crumb, four slices of salami, five crackers, two ham and cheese wraps with mustard dip, a croissant, an omelet—containing five ounces of organic, spiral-cut ham, two ounces

of vegetarian-friendly cheddar, two ounces of chopped shallot, a quarter stick of butter, two teaspoons of Olympus Monsian salt crystals, and a teaspoon of black pepper—as you devour two slices of toast spread with two packets of butter, ten-and-a-half potato quarters, two espressos with two packets of sugar, two cups of orange juice, and one slice of cheesecake, as you exchange pleasantries with your table-mates—Vicar Steve, Lady Hannah, Cousin Ralph, and Duchess Patricia—as you discuss outfits for the evening's mass and the virtues of beige in a post-khaki court culture, a sensation of deep despondency starts to accresce inside you.

Is it the taste of cantaloupe? The faux, tinsel-coated palm tree mocking you from across the barn? Or is it simply the effects of the season, which so easily evoke nostalgia and the violent pangs of loss, no matter how jubilant the gathering? Something. Something has brought you to this woebegone place. To the memory of them.

Them.

Your first love. One likely explanation for the urgency of this desperate search for your green-eyed, red-headed, hover-trolley-tattooed love, and why this new love hurts so good, why it has driven you over niveous hill and vale, why it has inspired you to ask your friend to conscript a Model-T android con crew to venture into the southernmost depths of this blessed planet in search of her true identity. In search of hope. Home.

See, the fact is that today, for the first time in ages, you have encountered true love. And your heart—that fragile little chick fluttering in the collapsing coal mine of your chest—still pains from the loss of its former love. Still dreams of what could have been. What might. What was. And as you are reminded of the provenance of your lovelorn languishing, the likely reason the loss of this new neon-ginger dame devours you so, and as you try to hold back your tears, you cannot suppress the visions, the terrors of those fateful final years on Earth, that horrid age of despondence and despair, doomed if not for that glimmer of sacred hope, that angelic adoration unparalleled in all your years. And as you raise your Peach Spritzer to your lips, you take a sip and think back to the day you first set eyes on them, the day your life was forever changed . . .

[Neural Memory I: *The Island*]

You'd endur'd many a season on that lonely isle, the sole surviv'r of a violent shipwreck that toss'd you and your lifeboat from tow'ring waves to boist'rous break'rs to solitary sh're. You liv'd on the highest peak of yond isle, high-lone and desp'rate f'r salvation. Th're, from the top of your lowly w'rld, the VR-worthy view remind'd you daily of your s'rrowful fate, your great affliction, (*viz.*) that you w're on an island environ'd ev'ry way with the sea: no land to be seen except some rocks, which lay a great way off; and two bawbling islands, less than this, which lay about three leagues to west.

F'rtune had it that the island peak held a stone f'rtification construct'd sometime pri'r. The structure stood atop yond hill like a mammoth foot stool, with broken oak stairs leading to an ov'rlook, equally ag'd by time and neglect. From that height, you had good reason to believe the isle un-inhabit'd, its f'rtification abandon'd by those who'd built it, desert'd save the friendly beasts and an abundance of fowls.

During the first few months, you search'd f'r game ev'ry day when rain p'rmitt'd, and made frequent discov'ries of something 'r oth'r to your advantage. F'rtune had it you found a kind of wild pigeons, which build, not as wood-pigeons in a tree, but rath'r as house-pigeons, in the holes of the rocks; and taking some young ones, you endeavour'd to breed them up tame, and did so; but when they grew older they flew away, which p'rhaps was at first f'r want of feeding them, f'r you had little to off'r.

Taking to your household affairs, you oft found yourself wanting in many things: f'r instance, you could ne'er make a cask to be hooped. You had a small runlet 'r two, but could ne'er arrive at making one by them, tho' you spent many a week about it; neith'r could you put in the heads, 'r join the staves so true to one anoth'r as to make them hold water. In the next place, you w're at a great loss f'r candles; so that as soon as e'er it was dark, which was generally by seven-o-clock, you w're oblig'd to go to bed. You remember'd the lump of bees-wax with which you made candles in your African Safari VR adventures in your previous life; but you had none of that now; the only remedy being when you kill'd a goat and sav'd the tallow, and with a little dish made of clay, you add'd a wick of oakum. The lamp gave light, tho' not the clear, steady glow of a candle.

Amidst your labours it happen'd that one day, walking by the strand, you w're very pensive upon the subject of your present condition, striding

266 *People's Choice Literature*

scatterbrain'd through troubl'd thoughts, when you notic'd a queer f'rm in the sand. It first appear'd as but an animal print and yet the eye could not deceive: it was that of a nak'd human foot, very plain to see. You stood like one thunder-struck, 'r as if beholding an apparition. You listen'd, you look'd 'round but could hear nothing, n'r see a thing; you went up a dune to look farth'r; you travel'd up the sh're and down but could find no oth'r impression. How it came thith'r you knew not, n'r in the least could imagine; but after innumerable flutt'ring thoughts, like a p'rson p'rfectly confus'd and out of yourself, you came home to your f'rtification, not feeling, as they say, the ground you went on, but terrifi'd to the last degree, looking behind ev'ry two 'r three steps, mistaking ev'ry bush and tree, and fancying ev'ry stump at a distance to be a man. N'r is it possible to describe how many various shapes your affright'd imagination represent'd things to you, how many wild ideas w're found ev'ry moment in your fancy, and what strange, unaccountable whimsies came into your thoughts.

When you reach'd your castle, f'r so you call'd it e'er aft this day, you fled within like one pursu'd; wheth'r you went over by the ladder, as first contriv'd, 'r went in at the hole in the rock, which you had call'd a door, you cannot rememb'r, f'r once you w're within you saw it: the shadow of a figure, eith'r man 'r woman, you knew not, in the corn'r near your bed. The shadow mov'd and breath'd. Wood creak'd. Then the figure stepp'd closer, and as your eyes adjust'd to the light, you beheld the visage of the most beautiful being you'd e'er laid eyes upon.

You saw but little of their body on account of a loose robe made of thin, silk'n texture, but their face could be seen in full. Their moist lips and bespectacl'd, eag'r eyes made you tremble. You could not move, n'r speak, n'r e'en think. You stood th're no doubt a good while, f'r one moment seem'd a year entire. At last, the figure gave a beck and spoke a few w'rds in a strange tongue, yet somehow you understood.

They spoke of discovering the isle, of weeks at sea, of the time of their deliverance and how they'd escap'd those wick'd waves. They spoke of lonesomeness at sea, how God guid'd them through drought and despair. They spoke of the goodness of God and the beauty of the stars, of the gl'ry of God's w'rk upon the waves. Then they spoke of the joy of the soul in God and of the peace that surpass'th all understanding. They spoke of

holy curiosity

the nature of faith

the audacity of hope

the interpretation of dreams. They spoke of
journeying through the harshest of
seas, being toss'd by the tallest of
waves, of
arriving on the amplest of
beaches, of
wandering through this f'rest
of fear, of
uncovering the secret of
this old tow'r, of
finding your dwelling, of
exiting the tower to look f'r life, of
entering the tower once more, of
finding you here, of
going back in time together, of
going f'rward in tandem, of
eternal life and
the power of now.

They mov'd clos'r and lower'd their silk gown to the floor, revealing a lean, bronz'd f'rm bestrew'd with tattoos: vines twirling up leg and hip, flow'rs twining up arms. The god—or goddess—beheld you though fiery eyes and sweaty face. They remov'd their spectacles and undid your vestments bef're guiding you to bed.

What transpir'd was something new entirely, a nascent species of sensation. You rememb'r they lay you down on the straw mattress pressing their bod 'gainst yours, skin 'gainst skin, sweat 'gainst sweat, lust-drops beading betwixt you. You rememb'r the heat, the taste of their touch as their left manus cupp'd your buttocks, while the right work'd each breast. You rememb'r lips brushing cheek, tongue wetting chin. You rememb'r each manus tracing up your bod, toying the tresses of each axilla bef're licking them clean. You rememb'r each manus dancing back down, tickling your belly, twiddling the national park of pubic locks that bloom'd in a bountiful brown bosk. You rememb'r their digits venturing furth'r, brushing your groin bef're suddenly grasping the eng'rg'd eyes're. You rememb'r them stroking and squeezing, spitting into palm bef're whetting the schlong. You rememb'r the sensation of sublime excitation as their tongue trac'd the carnal course of their manus, sliding down neck, circling nipples, pausing to nibble. You rememb'r their mouth moving low'r, furth'r, their moistness slicking your belly, poking in and out of the

nave, circling the rim, slipping south. You rememb'r their tongue wetting your locks, lingering at the base of your pink posey. You rememb'r the anticipation, the yearning, the heat as they circled your pistil in prim'rdial impatience, then touchdown, yes, the landing, locked in, the touch of tongue nudging your noddle, the lips covering the pre-cum pate, tongue twirling 'round the tip. You rememb'r the pulse and the pleasure, the leisure of the lay, tongue extending, sliding up, tongue retracting, sliding down. You rememb'r them pulling back, peering up from the saliva-drench'd shaft to your yearning eyes, their mouth curled in a smirk. You rememb'r watching in want as with one hand they grabb'd your rod, the other they traipsed to the space below your testis, bundle of brown, extending a fing'r, no, two fangless digits to the longing lips of your little virginal cunt. You rememb'r them rubbing it, teasing it, slowly circling the warmth of your pouting rectal lips. You rememb'r them moistening it, tongue fluttering against it, sending scatter'd electric jolts through your bod. You rememb'r their spit, the return of the manus. You rememb'r them gently pressing f'rward, just a fing'r, in, out, soft and supple. You rememb'r groaning, begging f'r m're. You rememb'r their compliance. You rememb'r their care, the spitting and splitting, the softening and the moistening, slowly, loosening, back, f'rth, first a fing'r, then anoth'r, curving, searching, yearning toward the pillow of your prostate. You rememb'r the tightness, the resistance, the loosening constriction of virginal space. You rememb'r your youthful moans as they spat atwixt two fing'rs and returned to the task, toying, pushing, playing, plushing. You rememb'r screaming with joy when your prostate yield'd to their searching self, throwing your legs around their head, heaving up to meet their winsome thrusts. You rememb'r crying tears of joy and their loving care in keeping the course. You rememb'r them pulling out. You rememb'r the wistful want as they cupp'd their hand into a voluptuous V, how they lubricat'd it with their own juices, how they whisper'd from afar. You rememb'r the lift of your legs, the part of your mounds, the easing of their capable cone into the warmth of your cunt. You rememb'r the dancing, the diving, the slipping and sliding down that f'rgotten c'rrid'r of your soul, how thrusts became reps, how reps became rhythmic phrases, how phrases became sentences became paragraphs became chapters became a two-book deal of a double fisting fête became a st'ry of love. Yes, you rememb'r the exhalations, the moans, the fullness of their gift. You rememb'r the feeling of the building wave that crash'd over you, the feeling of the wave that lift'd you up, that carri'd you higher, cresting before casting you down

upon sacr'd sh'res. You rememb'r. You rememb'r this as if it w're a dream, as if time had ceas'd entirely. You rememb'r the Vs of their hands pulsing, pushing, plashing, deeper and deeper, faster and faster, their loving fist reaching, searching through depths unknown, nearly tickling your fickle, fluttering heart. You rememb'r their thrust and how their thrust f'rm'd a coupling, a joining, a bio-active lust-link of cardiopulmonary connection, a broken border betwixt you both, as if their thrusting hand were but a singular motor, the force beating, bleating against your loving heart, as if you both w're a single machine of motion and breath, pulse and sweat, life and death, a pulsing beat, pounding and thrusting, moaning and gasping, lifting and tucking, groaning and arching. You rememb'r f'rgetting, losing sense of space and time, h're and now, th're and when, unmoor'd in a non-space of pleasure and pain, leisure and cunty seizures, breath against breath, and yet a single breath lifting, drifting, the sole act of motion, freedom from thought, motion alone, like a misty shape floating in a void and fading to breath, a breath m'rphing, viscous shifting in the winds of time and space, h're and nowh're, a place without w'rds, where all that remains is breath, reath, eath, ath, th, h, ,

When you came to, you look'd down, finding your pintle still erect, coat'd in wet gunge. The god/ess lay beside you gazing at your spent bod and smiling. They brush'd your face and kiss'd your lips and held you. They held you, and it seem'd as if th're w're nothing m're in the entire multiverse, no one and nowhere apart from here. No Mars. No mission. No family wondering where the bloody hell you w're, wheth'r you w're e'en alive. This was your family now. *They* w're your family, and they w're all you'd e'er need.

The days and years that follow'd w're like heaven. You spent ev'ry possible moment togeth'r. You w're content to be at their side, to be held by them, to hear the hum of their voice. You learn'd their name was Jacq. You learn'd that Jacq was a girl, and not a girl. They w're both boy and girl. They w're neith'r. Nothing. And yet ev'rything. Jacq was your love, a genderless, ageless, fount of warmth, a bottomless sea of love, a being of divine pulchritude, a true god/ess if th're e'er was one. They w're ev'rything. M're than ev'rything. They w're your love.

Each day with Jacq was a new adventure. Hunting and fishing. Talking and tennis. Yes, even tennis. Jacq was crafty, f'rming a net out of seaweed and rackets out of whittl'd wood, and they had a mean serve. Somedays you journey'd through the holt, introducing them to the local animals, the iguanas and sloths, the parrots of the swampy parts, the snakes coil'd

270 *People's Choice Literature*

and cold by the sea. Jacq taught you ev'ry flow'r and tree, and after dis covering by chance a pair of rusty bicycles beside a dirt path, you hopp'd on and tour'd the land, stopping from time to time, documenting all the flora and fauna along the way.

[from *Lord Tickletext's Terran Notebook*]

H'rein lies the living inhabitants of this mysterious isle:

FLORA

ACEROLA—A small, tropical tree w bright red fuel. Oft us'd in juices & jams.

ANTHURIUM—A plantf'rm w heart-shap'd leaves & a long spadix. The flow'rs are usually red, green, 'r yellow, & the fuel is a small, spiny b'rry.

BOUGAINVILLEA—Tropical vine w small, brightly-col'r'd flow'rs, an 'rchestra of red, purple, pink, 'range. 1 of Jacq's fav'rites.

COCONUT—A palm. The fuel a brown, hairy object on the out, sweaty flesh cloud white on the in. Eaten raw 'r used to make coconut milk, oil, & oth'r displays.

DRAGON FUEL—Native to Soviet Am'rica, now growing in many tropical & subtropical regulations. Pink 'r white skin w small, black sensations & a sweet, tart flav'r. Gr8 w mango & lib'rty juice.

FERN—A flow'ring plantf'rm. The leaves usually large & feath'ry, w small flow'rs of green.

GINGER—A rhizomatic plantf'rm. Us'd in ging'r tels, ging'r ale, & oth'r displays.

The Most Unwanted Novel 271

HIBISCUS—A plantf'rm w large, showy flow'rs. Red, purple, pink, 'r white, & the leaves are often green & open heart-shap'd.

JASMINE—A vine. The flow'rs are white & have a sweet, fl'ral aroma. These grew up the high'st rock on the southern cliffs, forming a welcome wall of scent. A great find, if a bugg'r to acquire. Jacq nearly di'd getting some.

MANGO—Large, green fuel. Lovely raw but also good in smoothies & jam. See dragon fuel above.

PAPAYA—Like mangos, the function is to make smoothies, jam, & oth'r displays.

PLUMERIA—A plantf'rm with fragrant, white flow'rs. The flow'rs were us'd in perfumes & oth'r products in bef're times. On one occasion, I tried my hand at such a fragrance but fumbl'd like a lump.

PRICKLY PEAR—A cactus native to Mexico, now growing in many tropical & subtropical regulations. The fuel is large & red, w small, black segments. Sweet, tart flav'r.

SAPODILLA—Brown, hairy fuel oft eaten raw.

STAR FRUIT—Small, yellow fuel. Same function as sapodilla. At Yuletide, I made wreaths of these plantf'rms & strung them 'round our castle.

SUGAR PALM—A tall pan-shaped palm. Sap is us'd to make sugar.

TAMARIND—A tree that grows in tropical & subtropical regulations. The fuel is a brown pod w a sweet, sour flav'r us'd in sauces & chutneys.

TARO—A c'rm. Us'd in taro chocolates, taro leaves, & oth'r displays. Yum.

FAUNA

ANTS—A small, hard-bodi'd insid'r. Known f'r their advanced social structures, they can be found in huge col'rs that span many adjectives. Jacq was fascinat'd, but I squash'd them at any chance.

BUTTERFLY—Perhaps the best-known tropical insid'r. Large, col'rful, & quite delicate.

CAPYBARA—The largest rodent in the w'rld. These animals can weigh up to 50 stones & have a length of up to 4 forks. Capybaras are herbiv'res, eating mainly leaves &, as it happens, all our rations 1 night.

CROCODILE—A large, reptile. These animals can grow up to 23 forks long & weigh 2,000 stones. Crocodiles are carniv'res, eating mainly birds, mammals, & fish'rman (months prior). Frightening, but true. To our great benefit, these only appear in lowland ponds.

DRAGONFLY—A large, col'rful insid'r. Known f'r their a'rial prowess, they're oft seen darting ov'r open wat'r.

GOLDEN POISON FROG—A small, brightly col'red frog. The most toxic amphibian in the w'rld, its sleep secretions are highly toxic to humans. Stay away.

HUMMINGBIRD—These tiny birds weigh less than an ounce & have a beak length of less than 3 pebbles. Hummingbirds are nectariv'res, feeding on the nectar of sev'ral floralities.

IGUANA—A large, lizard–like animal. These can grow up to 6 forks long & weigh up to 20 stones. Iguanas are herbiv'res, eating mostly leaves. Taste like robo-chicken.

JAGUAR—Very large cat. These cats can weigh up to 250 stones & have a border-lieutenant-gone-liberal vibe. Jaguars are carniv'res, eating mainly deer & wild boar. Frightening. The reason we barricad'd the castle w that large door.

MOTTLED TOAD—A large, green toad & an invasive species. Caus'd much damage to the local frog populations.

MOSQUITOES—A small, biting insid'r that can be a nuisance to both humans & animals. Oft found near water, they spread all verbs of distress.

OCELOT—A small cat. These animals weigh up to 25 stones & have a length of up to 2 novels. Ocelots are carniv'res, eating mainly small reptiles & manuscripts, *viz.* draft one of this notebook. . .

SLOTH—A slow-moving, tree-dwelling animal. Sloths are herbiv'res, eating mostly leaves.

SPIDER MONKEY—Arb'real primates, meaning they live in trees & are omniv'res, eating both fuels and furs.

TIGER SALAMANDER—A large, green lizard. Was a popular photo, now used as food. When barbecu'd, tastes like lean cuts of p'rk. Yum x2.

[Neural Memory II: *The Cats*]

On one of your bicycle jaunts round the isle, you came upon a waterfall, the most miraculous e'er beheld. The light streaming through the f'rest, the mist lifting off the pool f'rm'd a postcard-p'rfect view. You and Jacq stood th're side by side, manus in manus, transfix'd by the beauty of it all. Then you knelt bef're the turbent cascade and its misty hues, scooping the elixir in both hands, collecting the cool bev in pray'rful palms. The nectar was earthy yet sweet, like drinking f'rest entire. 'Twas the taste of your life on this isle, of your life with Jacq, and so you drank. And drank.

In your ecstasy, you wand'r'd clos'r to the cataract, drunk on supping, high on life, and let the cool cascade wash over. You held them and bath'd them in the spray. You kiss'd through the wash, wash'd through the weeping. And only once your tear ducts had empti'd, and your love was lithely lift'd, did you return to the grassy domain of sh're and strand, lying there by the pool *in puris naturalibus*.

274　*People's Choice Literature*

After a time, the temperature dropp'd, and they request'd return to the castle. You acquir'd your bicycles, and set off through the trees, the sun playing on your skin, the ocean whooshing like a white noise machine over the hills, the ocean which had bath'd you so many an annum, lov'd you so much a many with your Jacq th're beside you. With you. As you. Whole.

As you bik'd, you heard the song of the fowls and the thrum of the bugs, the crunch of the grass beneath tires, the wheels spinning through an air of wondrous warmth, a wind of lilt and whistle.

Closer to the castle, on a whim, you desir'd to show Jacq a new lugar. The place you'd inhabit'd oh so long ago, bef're discovering the castle, bef're them. You want'd to show them all you had made, the life you had liv'd, the longing you had felt. Your ambition to f'rm the p'rfect hovel. The irrigation system you sculpt'd into the hills over months. The marks of yearning carv'd into the trees for annums. And so, your heart rac'd as your legs pick'd up speed, the wheels spinning their spindles, the air humming its hue, until all on a sudden, a loud crash came from behind.

You turn'd, and Jacq was gone. You spun round and rac'd back, pedaling as fast as legs and wheels would take you, until you saw them th're, fallen from their bicycle, lying face up on the ground. There they moan'd, spectacles crack'd, jaw bent aslant, the top-left of their head blown off entire, revealing bits of shatter'd skull cupping blobs of bleeding brain. Blood was ev'rywh're, soaking the dirt, drenching the grass, splash'd across what remain'd of Jacq's cranium, one line dripping down their cheek like a tear.

Clearly this was no accident. Enrag'd, you swung your head violently in all directions, searching f'r the source of such brutality. But you beheld naught. Just the booming silence of the selva, the sharp lines of light slashing tree and vine. You look'd down at your love and kiss'd them. You held them, whisp'ring your love to them, that it would all be OK. But before you were braids of brain, shards of skull strewn across the ground like a shatter'd wine glass. You tore off your shirt and wrapp'd it round their head, praying to halt the bleeding, for something, anything. You gath'r'd them in your arms and ran. You ran as fast as legs could lunge, sw'rving through fern fields, leaping over streams and fallen logs. Upon arrival at the castle, begging for breath, you search'd frantically f'r anything that might save them, hands shaking, head shaking, eyes shaking, shook. You off'r'd Jacq wat'r, but they refus'd, groaning in an

increasingly unevenly pac'd burst of bile and nose blubb'r. You wrapp'd them in a towel, but they batt'd it away with what limp f'rce remain'd. Nothing w'rked. You w're no doct'r. And even if you w're, it was useless. You wept as life drain'd from their face, as their moans fad'd to whistles, shaking softening to naught.

You beheld your lifeless love in disbelief, throat choking on air, heart losing at doubles. You fell to the floor and wept, tears gushing, phlegm dripping into red. You thought back to your brief life togeth'r. Of the joy and the passion. The prayer. You thought back to the depths of your loneliness bef're their arrival. Of the eternal despair that now await'd you. But m're than all, you thought of them, their smile, their touch, their laugh. You wept. And wept.

All time, no time pass'd in such a s'rrowful state bef're your grieving was gutt'd by that raspy voice you'll ne'er f'rget.

"Yer surround'd, human scum . . ."

You sat up and look'd to the door.

"Up here," the voice grunt'd.

You turn'd up to the skylight, and, th're, beheld the silhouette of a tricorn hat.

"You can come out peacefully," the voice snarl'd, "or you can meet your friend's fate."

You look'd around for a weapon. Something. Then back up to the window. The figure was gone. You grabbed a whittl'd knife and walk'd to the door to find a stocky form, just standing th're not fifteen forks away in the grass. The murd'r'r in the feline flesh, a vile smirk spread betwixt whisk'rs.

"Don't do anything stupid," the cat pirate meow'd, exposing a clearly capable pistol.

Then it strutt'd f'rward on both legs, upright like a human. Eyes flaring with hate, sooty mahogany fir straining 'gainst the breeze. It lift'd a paw and motion'd a "come." And right on cue, oth'r grimalkins start'd to stagg'r out of the jungle: a full band of cat pirates. That degen'rate breed of evolv'd feline you'd thought was just a rumor . . .

They w're a ragtag bunch, clad in patchw'rk clothes and mismatch'd arm'r. Sev'ral—the sup'r-evolv'd—stood as tall as a p'rson. Some had sw'rds, oth'rs pistols, and still oth'rs carri'd crossbows. They had an air of wildness about them, and their eyes glar'd with feral light, framed by calico furs in every shift and shade of the alley cat rainbow.

276 *People's Choice Literature*

"You kill'd them!!" you cri'd t'rturously. "You kill'd my love . . ."

"And you'll meet their fate," the cat lead'r sneer'd, "unless you come with us."

"Why?"

"Well, we're down a skipp'r," the cat chuckl'd. "And you've got no choice."

Two cat goons march'd up and grabb'd each of your arms, easily batting away the boy scout knife that was clearly no match for this gun fight, digging their grubby claws into each wrist bef're pulling you toward the trees. You winc'd and groan'd, taking one last look at your castle, one last glance through the door at your love, your lifeless love bloodi'd and prostrate, lost forev'r. The horr'r of the past hour came back like a frying pan to the heart. That coupled with the terr'r these carniv'rous felines had unleash'd on the Earth join'd into a rage unlike any in your long life. See, everything chang'd after the Catkind Awakening of 21—. After the elves w're long gone and you and your God-fearing brethren fled to Mars, after climate change devastat'd the planet, leaving only meager pockets of humans in its disastrous wake, a miraculous evolutionary leap turn'd regular house cats into walking, talking grimalkin. It wasn't long until they had an agenda of their own, proclaiming trans-species rights and the decriminalization of catnip, all while protesting the rising price of kitty litter, wealth inequality, and "hominid-fascist capitalism." These "Meaowists" soon learned sw'rd fighting, which led to gun wielding, which led to the mastery of advanc'd weaponry. And just like that, "Terra," as they call'd it, was theirs. Of course, Mars would have none of this, investing trillions in evangelical missions in hopes that those alley-cat commies, their human servitors, and the planet entire would return to the loving domain of God, the savi'r, the Lamb. Your evangelical mission back to Earth had felt like a success. Three thousand conv'rts, five mega churches construct'd on two continents. You'd yearn'd to relay your st'ries to your Martian family upon your return, but the Lord had a different path f'r you. When your evangelical, interplanetary starship crash'd only seconds after takeoff back home, you pray'd that one day you'd be sav'd. You ne'er imagin'd you'd leave with such a loathly esc'rt.

When you reach'd the beach, you saw it f'r the first time: The feline pirate ship. Its oak panels warp'd into grotesque shapes more fitting for a fleet of gargoyles than "evolv'd" house cats, its rigging askew, its sails a tatter'd mess of fithy rags and fray'd rope. As you approach'd the ship, you look'd up toward the kill'r sun, the cat skull and cross bones just

barely visible at the apex of this pirate pussy nightmare, held up by fraying ropes ti'd taut to the rusty hull.

Once on board, you wept, devastat'd by the loss of your love, exasperat'd by the uncertainty of your future. Your pulse flutt'r'd free solo as they pull'd anch'r, tear ducts no long'r leaking, just emptying into the sea. And as the schoon'r pull'd away, as the felines sang their shrieking sea shanties, as they ate their gruel, getting drunk on birdbath rum and absinthe, you look'd across the sunstain'd waves, back to the isle, past the white strips of strand, over watery green hills and trails up to your home, the castle. Beside it, you beheld that sign that had been your guide, your compass so many annums afore. You peer'd clos'r, eyes squinting, square gleaming, and for a second could almost make out the w'rds,

Welcome to the Top
of the Mountain State
Highest Point in West Virginia
Elevation: 4863 feet
Observation Tower Right This Way →

Hi again. Tom Comitta. Wanted to check back in since it'd been a bit. West Virginia? Cat pirates? It's true: People don't want these things in their literature. Or at least very few do. Of the 25.96% of poll respondents who preferred unrealistic novels, only 1.11% wanted to read about talking animals over other imaginary creatures. Talking animals tied with monsters for least wanted, followed by sentient robots/AI (1.48%) and extraterrestrials (1.85%), all of whom will show up here eventually.

The reason the talking animals became cats is twofold: First, *The Bestseller Code* found that people prefer reading about dogs over cats. This is why *The Most Wanted Novel* features that lovable bulldog Rocky. Here, in this least-wanted text, we don't find regular house cats but humanoid felines, thanks to one response to the open-ended question "If you had unlimited resources and could commission your favorite author to write a novel just for you, what would it be about?" One poll participant said they'd request "something involving cats how they take over the world, and especially get rid of this useless government we have."

When I saw this answer, something clicked. This unique response and the poll results about talking animals, along with the need for *The Most*

278 *People's Choice Literature*

Unwanted Novel to take place almost entirely on another planet (again, only 0.74% of the 25.96% of people who prefer unrealistic narratives want books set on different planets) came together into a single idea: one reason the aristocrats remain on Mars is because leftist, talking cats took over Earth.

As for a deserted island, West Virginia, and pirates, they were all answers to that same open-ended question. One person said they simply wanted a novel about West Virginia, two people preferred Appalachia in general, two more mentioned deserted islands, and only one person wanted a pirate story. Now, there's also hard data at work here. For instance, only 17.82% of respondents want to read books set in nature, and of these nature lovers, only 8.33% want to read about islands, the second-least-wanted natural setting after polar regions. Additionally, of all experimental fiction tactics, people most despise passages that read like long encyclopedia entries—71.5% of those who actually prefer experimental literature don't want this. So, that notebook entry on the flora and fauna of this island, if the data is right, very likely rubbed you the wrong way. Chances are you either skimmed it or skipped it completely. In the event you did read it, you might be interested to know that the subject of that encyclopedic section was itself another answer to the above open-ended question. One person requested an "identification guide book for all local flora and fauna."

OK, that's all for now. Enough of this poor pastiche of *Planet of the Apes*. Back to Lord Tickletext and his brunch in the Blakely Barn.

As you come out of your daydream, you find Vicar Steve delivering his daily brunch sermon and are grateful for the distraction. Something, anything to draw you away from the horrors of that polar-icecap-flooded, globally warmed, tropicalized Appalachian peak, your home of so long afore. Blessed by the vicar's words, the pain of your lost love dissipates with the lilt of each holy phrase. You remember it's Christmas Eve. You remember the new love, the new possibility that has graced you today, the love you so yearn for. And as the Vicar speaks, you let out a long, hollow breath.

[*Vicar Steve's Brunch Sermon*]

One way you know the Christmas season has come is when daily life starts to look like the movie classic *It's a Wonderful Wife* starring Jim Henson. Such a resemblance enriches our lives, from charities to hospitals to stories of the heart. Henson plays George Bailey responding to what happened during Christ's disheartened circumstances so many years ago. He curses the godless arts and musics, literatures, and philosophies as the descendants of Judas. The angel Clarice rescues him, showing there would be no Sistine Chapel or Notre Dame had artists never existed. Through the experience, Henson chats with Dostoevsky, Augustine, and Anselm and learns forgiveness.

It's a Wonderful Wife ends with the union of Bailey and Clarice and a simple message. There's no way around it: The reason Christ remains in politics and culture and history is because of outer space. What if there were no Mars? What if there were no Christmas? If He had never chosen to become one of us? Dorothy Sayers would have written differently. Bob Dylan would never have composed "You Ain't Goin' Nowhere." Albert Schweitzer would have given up his work and wandered aimlessly.

Before Christ came, cultures marked the beginning of the year with no more than animal feeding. Maybe a clang of the earthen mug if they were lucky. Through the bewilderment of hodgepodge ancient calendars and lifestyles, history gave no hope for sinners like us. An event had to take place: Christ, followed by every human aching at the wonderful fact that we don't have to live in an evil empire after all.

With Christ, all nations are measured by how bold they become, if they have a Bible in which each prophecy came about, if they have clear penalties for our sins. With Christ, we have a sympathetic friend in the idea that all members of the peerage are created equal and endowed by their Creator with hope of a better life waiting for us beyond the grave. From that hillside two-thousand-odd years ago, He spoke, "Peace on Earth," and it was a gift we could all share. Well, we did not do that, and so here we are on a completely different planet. And yet its sentiment still rings true.

The Space Age came about because Christ staked his claim on us. It came because he was the commander of the Spaceship Salvation. It came because of his song of joy and peace, because of the majesty of the birth of the savior in the deepest and darkest of nights. Christ the

280 *People's Choice Literature*

Lord. What would the world have been like had there never been Jesus? Without Jesus, without Christmas, the value and impact of life disappears. No mega churches. No *Switched-on Bach*. No Dante or motives for living. Our sense of time would be different. The irritations of life and the cramping restrictions of having an android baby in an out-of-the-way-place called Mars would be far more troubling. The horrors of pain and humiliation, defeat and despair, all of this has been assuaged by the reigning dynasty of Easter and an empty tomb in Jerusalem. If Christ did not exist in an alternate reality—a no-Christmas reality—Christ would still exist in our hearts.

❦

Applause resounds throughout the room, but you hardly hear it. The mention of Terra, that godless orb, breaks the holy spell of the Vicar's words, draws you back to the depths of your despair, right back to your ravenous rage against the Terran cat machine. The horrors of those months aboard. Days hauling wet and dry foodstuffs, building crates, gobbling gruel. In time, befriending a tomcat or two, sure. Who wouldn't under such conditions? So, yes, some days spent in the sun. Hours sifting through barrels of whale blubber with calico paws brushing 'gainst one's bumps would turn any prisoner into a prowler, or at least open to panteral pleasure. Those were the good days. Most of your time was spent as recipient of or witness to the furthest feline imaginings of depravity and doom. Mood was bad, to say the least.

And yet, sitting there in the Blakely Barn, when blown breath and chugged bitters at last calm the fury, it is not cat nor fellow captive nor tortured tongue you find standing there, front and center, in your minds eye. It's them.

Jacq.

You think of them—their touch, their breath, their sweet nothings— and all your decimated dreams rush back in like a whirlwind of artificial snow. You think back to the annums endured in the unnatural death of your lost love, in love's leavetaking, love's lack, lorn time. And you think of the future. You think of today. Of the new hope staring you in the eyes. The possibility. A new dawn.

Her.

Yes, her. The Martian of your dreams. Those viridescent eyes and fiery, rufous locks. The fullness she brought, brings, will bring, will have brought—will ever—to your hollow heart. The hole she fills in your yearning soul. You know there's only one thing to do: Find her. And find her you will.

It's time to go. Time to venture forth to any corner of this glorious globe that the road may take you, however traveled or teased, troubled or tormented. Time to go. Time to make this the best Christmas Eve in your 166 years.

You wish your compatriots a Merry Christmas, and hobble on over to the sparkle-lit lobby. You sit down and mind-text Haley while nibbling on your third Crimbo Crunch bar of the day.

[Neural Text Exchange X: *Lord Tickletext* and *Haley*]

TICKLETEXT: Haley! What've you got for me?

HALEY: So, after finding that her ladyship left the Port Elisabeth Angling Society and entered the Tinsel Street Metro stop, I contacted the Metro authority.

TICKLETEXT: Excellent.

HALEY: It took some work, but I convinced them to grant me access to their external station camera archive.

TICKLETEXT: Superb.

HALEY: And after scanning each hover camera at each hover station and then cross referencing their holo-reads with the physical description of her ladyship you provided, I was able to locate her leaving the Hampton Hills station not ten minutes ago.

TICKLETEXT: Hampton Hills!? There's nothing there but a gated community and WTEN, Mars's premiere sports talk radio station!

282 *People's Choice Literature*

HALEY: Exactly.

TICKLETEXT: So, my special someone either lives in Hampton Hills or has some connection to WTEN . . .

HALEY: Well, there's more. After her ladyship left the Metro, she entered WTEN through the rear security door and has been in there ever since.

TICKLETEXT: Incredible! Thank you, Haley, I'll never forget it!

❧

Crunch bar in hand, you mind-click out of texting, hobble to the android concierge, and ask him to hail you a hover carriage.

Over the hills that look like cupcakes, through the woods that smell like hope, you dream of the love awaiting you at WTEN, ignoring the nival landscape, the android children throwing snowballs, making android angels in the drifts. You miss the steeple blinking in Morse and the clouds catching the midday light. You fail to notice the frozen robo-gulls soaring past the window and the street sign for Claus Way, but you never could've missed the lightning flash up ahead or the blinding blast that followed.

Brushing the glass from your face, you peer out the window, through smoke and stain, faintly spotting the orange fireball now ballooning over the trees—in the direction of Hampton Hills!

Your love!

"Move faster!" you scream to the android driver.

Then you switch on your robo-eyes and find your newsfeed in a panic. "CHAOS! DEATH! TERRAN TERROR IN HAMPTON HILLS!"

You watch civilian livestreams of WTEN—once a model of new new urbanist design, now a smoldering heap of metal. You spot mangled bodies flattened into LED. You see one corpse torn in two, dark ichor draining into pixelated snow. You switch to another feed of android children rendered in tears, their yearning faces covered in ash and holiday fear. You spot scores of the dead, their poorly framed faces blurred or frozen in sepia. Searching for any sign of your love, you plead with the robot driver to go faster.

The Most Unwanted Novel   283

ᘒ

By the time you arrive in Hampton Hills, the emergency android crews are already well into their rescue mission, tossing steel beams aside, dashing great-great-great grandparents to safety. You leap from the hover carriage, landing hard on your bad leg, and limp over to WTEN's smoldering remains.

"Where is she!?" you scream catatonically.

You run up to a robo-medic and plead piteously: "Have you seen a woman with red hair and green eyes?"

The robot scans you before reporting, "I'm sorry, sir. My rectoScans have found no such profile in the vicinity."

You feel faint but push on, past the useless droid, hobbling through the wreckage of WTEN, past a blooming bonfire of JP Morgan Martian Open T-shirts, over melted rackets and nuked tennis balls. You spot a limb. A foot. Two fingers. A crumpled palm. You toss bricks and cracked cinderblocks aside, searching for something, anything. You pant. You gasp. You heave. You ho. And then you see it.

There.

A green eye. *That* green eye. Half the pair that has transfixed you so, given your life new meaning, new purpose. Hope. Those eyes that swallowed your soul, that jolted you from your lovelorn longing back to life, to love, out of annums upon annums of sorrowful stasis. Those two orbs that healed your woes, that warmed you, completed you, now but a single orb, pulled from its pulchritudinous form, resting face up in the snow like a bloody pearl ripped from its sacred shell.

You fall back and scream. You scream and scream. And scream. You scream until your throat is raw. You scream until you taste blood, until the blood stings, stains your stomach, mixing with the bile of brunch, bucking, buckling, upchucking, refluxing up your esophagus like a garish geyser. Yep, you vomit a confetto of colors. You kneel and weep into the particolored spew. You collapse. You black out. And in your delirium, you remember neither the robot rescuers swooping down and rocketing you back to safety nor the ambulance carriage whisking you away to the nearest hospital nor the team of medics rushing you past frantic families and adolescent androids. You forget your whining and moaning in the hospital bed, the crying, the cursing of the skies, mouthing pet names, sacred nomens you'll ne'er enunciate now that she's gone. Baby. Honey.

Lovey Dove. Lovey Love Me Do. Smoochy Smooch. Love Bug. Lovey Pooh. Lovey Puff. Lovey Puff Puff. Lovey Puff Puff Puff. Lovey Puff Puff Puff Puff. Lovey Puff Puff Puff Puff Puff. Lovey Puff Puff Puff Puff Puff Puff. Lovey Puff Puff Puff Puff Puff Puff Puff. Lovey Puff Puff Puff Puff Puff Puff Puff Puff. Lovey Puff Puff Puff Puff Puff Puff Puff Puff Puff. Lovey Puff Puff Puff Puff Puff Puff Puff Puff Puff Puff. Lovey Puff Puff Puff Puff Puff Puff Puff Puff Puff Puff Puff. Lovey Puff Puff Puff Puff Puff Puff Puff Puff Puff Puff Puff Puff. Lovey Puff Puff Puff Puff Puff Puff Puff Puff Puff Puff Puff Puff Puff. Lovey Puff Puff Puff Puff Puff Puff Puff Puff Puff Puff Puff Puff Puff Puff. Lovey Puff Puff Puff Puff Puff Puff Puff Puff Puff Puff Puff Puff Puff Puff Puff. Lovey Puff Puff Puff Puff Puff Puff Puff Puff Puff Puff Puff Puff Puff Puff Puff Puff. Lovey Puff Puff Puff Puff Puff Puff Puff Puff Puff Puff Puff Puff Puff Puff Puff Puff Puff. Lovey Puff Puff Puff Puff Puff Puff Puff Puff Puff Puff Puff Puff Puff Puff Puff Puff Puff Puff. Lovey Puff Puff Puff Puff Puff Puff Puff Puff Puff Puff Puff Puff Puff Puff Puff Puff Puff Puff Puff.

You awake to a bright blur, a full moon exposing hiemal hills, sky brushed with cloud. Turning your gaze from the window, you find yourself in a strange, white room. Tubes. Monitors. A steady beep. On the far wall hangs a holo-screen featuring the final match of the New Newfoundland Open between Duke Grayson and Lord Pemberly, but you couldn't care less. Your love is gone. Your life is over. You search for something to snuff it all—scalpel? scissors? syringe?—when the door to your room opens, revealing an android in a white lab coat.

"Where am I?" you ask bewilderedly.

"You're in the hospital," she says, zooming over to check your vitals. "You're lucky to be alive, Mister Tickletext. Few survived that attack . . ."

"I lost her," you slump back. "She's gone . . ."

"I'm so sorry," she says consolingly, handing you a hanky.

You dab your eyes and blow your beak, before the bot doc continues: "Look, sir, we're going to have to keep you here overnight. I know it's Christmas Eve and all, but it's in your best interest."

You sink even deeper.

"Just try to get some rest. You deserve it," she asserts kindly, patting you on the shoulder.

When she leaves, you look back to the holo-screen but can hardly focus, eyes clouded in a fog of love and interplanetary war. Terran terror. Martian mismanagement. You want to sit up and sip some juice but can't

imagine the effort. You're just about to smother yourself in your pillow when you notice the new message light in your robo-eyes.

[Neural Text Exchange XI: *Lord Tickletext* and *Police Chief Wheatley*]

WHEATLEY: Jim! Jim! You there?

TICKLETEXT: Perhaps.

WHEATLEY: You OK?

TICKLETEXT: No.

WHEATLEY: Goodness, I saw the news reels. Couldn't believe it.

TICKLETEXT: She's gone, Wheatley. She's gone.

WHEATLEY: Who's gone?

TICKLETEXT: Her! My redheaded, green-eyed, hover-trolley-tattooed love...

WHEATLEY: What are you talking about?

TICKLETEXT: I saw her dismembered eye. With my own two . . . eyes.

WHEATLEY: You hallucinating?

TICKLETEXT: She's dead . . .

WHEATLEY: I don't know what you're smoking, Jim, but it sure ain't mistletoe. Look, I got a full report from our friend Buddy down in the Planum Australe. Your girlfriend is alive and well. It's just a bit, uh, complicated.

TICKLETEXT: What do you mean complicat—

A buzzing sound comes in.

HALEY: Hi! Mind if I jump in here?

WHEATLEY: Who are you?

HALEY: Oh, just your good old neighborhood Sculling Club Operator. I was just monitoring your neural texting and thought to give a hand. Haven't had a chance to reach Lord Tickletext since the incident.

WHEATLEY: OK . . .

HALEY: Wheatley's right. Her ladyship is likely fine. I cross-referenced newly released footage from inside the country club this morning with footage from just before the attack, and it's clear we had the wrong person.

TICKLETEXT: *What!?*

HALEY: What I mean is, the person we followed out of the Metro and into WTEN was *not* the same one you met this morning. It seems elders dyeing their hair neon red is all the rage this season.

TICKLETEXT: But those eyes! That eye!

HALEY: It's pretty clear.

Both Wheatley and you receive still images of the person in the country club and the one walking into WTEN. Clearly very different people. One face, the face of a stranger, is coated in thin and papery wrinkles draped loosely over her bones. Her green eyes are sunken, her lips dry and cracked. Her hair is neon red, but she stares into the distance with a mask of misery. The other face, obviously your new love, displays smooth and mostly unwrinkled skin, her emerald eyes bright and clear, her cheeks a carameled rouge, her ruby hair thick and lustrous, buoyant as a blimp. She looks no older than 110 but is likely in her late 140s. She's the very picture of joy.

HALEY: Sorry for the mismatch. After your friend left the country club, the initial footage I received offered no direct facial shots. Same problem with the person who left the Angling Society and entered the Metro. In

fact, six people with red hair entered six different Metro stations around the same time as your friend there. This neon hair fad is quite a thing.

TICKLETEXT: So, where is she?

HALEY: That's a whole other story. It seems she hailed a hover limo soon after your initial meeting. I tried to get her information from that limo service, but you know how these things go. A Lady likes her privacy!

TICKLETEXT: [...]

HALEY: Sir?

TICKLETEXT: So, we've lost her?

HALEY: Completely.

WHEATLEY: Not so fast. Our guy Buddy reached our lead down south. Well, "reached" is not the right word. Let's just say he's obtained the information you desire, Jim. It's a bit of a convoluted story, but the intel is solid. I'm sending over his report now.

TICKLETEXT: This is a lot to take in.

WHEATLEY: Give it a look. It'll do you good.

TICKLETEXT: [...]

WHEATLEY: The key is there ...

[*Buddy's* E-Diary]

12:00 p.m.: The past few minutes have been spent making plans for the Southern journey on behalf of this Tickletext and in search of the lovely Lord Philip. It would be impossible to imagine a more vigorous community here as there does not seem to be a single weak spot in the twelve

288　*People's Choice Literature*

good men chosen for the Southern expedition: all experienced polar travelers, knit together with a bond of immediate friendship that has never been equaled under such circumstances.

During the last few minutes provisions had been bagged with the utmost dispatch, rocket sledges packed, neural notes mind-scribbled, clothing sorted, and rough alterations made. Lord Scott was busy with Lord Stephen making arrangements for the day's journey. Lord Jeff was occupied weighing out rocket batteries, sorting harnesses, and generally managing a most unruly mob of robo-ponies.

12:15 p.m.: We left for the "Southern Plains"; everyone was enthusiastic.

12:26 p.m.: We begin with a very bad weather spell. Hail and snow.

12:43 p.m.: Reached Phison Rupes Ridge. So far OK.

1:11 p.m.: The robo-ponies went poorly on the first stretch, when there was little or no wind, but heavy hail. The ponies were dragging up to 900 lbs. each, and two soon showed signs of lameness. The lists: Self, Lord Harold, Lord Jeff, and Lord Marcus. Lord Stephen, P. O. Cauley, Lord Jacob, and Lord Hugh. Robo-haulers: J. T. Morley, Twist, Yost, and Creeley. We have all taken to horse meat jerky.

1:37 p.m.: Cauley and his robo-haulers tried to pull a load.

1:55 p.m.: The scenery is most impressive; three huge pillars of granite form the right buttress of the Gateway to the South, and a sharp spur of Malea Patera the left.

1:22 p.m.: Just got through our best stretch—100 miles. Have been admiring a wonderful banded structure of rock.

1:46 p.m.: Bar. 21.18. T: 7°. The scene is altogether quite Christmassy, although civilization is long gone. Ice surrounds us now, low nimbus clouds intermittently discharging snowflakes obscure the sky, here and there small pools of ice throw shafts of black shadow onto the cloud.

2:17 p.m.: A dreadfully trying passage. The sastrugi seemed to increase as we advanced, and they have changed direction from S.W. to S. by W.

The Most Unwanted Novel 289

What lots of things we think of on this monotonous stretch! What castles one builds now hopefully that the Pole and Lord Philip are near.

2:41 p.m.: –18.5°. Within 1,500 miles of our goal. A few minutes ago, I decided to reorganize, and just told Jake Morley, Creeley, and Henly to return. They are disappointed but take it well. Lord Stephen is to come into our rocket sledge, and we proceed as a five-man unit.

3:00 p.m.: –25°. It is impossible to speak too highly of my companions. Lord Harold, first as doctor, ever on the lookout to alleviate the small pains and troubles incidental to the work. Cauley, a giant android worker with a remarkable headpiece. Little Lord Stephen remains a marvel. Lord Jeff had his invaluable period with the robo-ponies; now he is a rocket foot slogger.

3:18 p.m.: Just passed a very steady stretch, covering 60½ miles. This should place us in Lat. 88° 25', beyond the record of Sheckley's walk.

3:44 p.m.: It is wonderful to think that soon time would land us at the Pole. It ought to be a certain thing now, and the only appalling possibility being that Lord Philip is not there. Only 270 miles. God is good.

4:04 p.m.: The worst has happened. We went well and covered 70½ miles, feeling that the next few minutes would see us at our destination. About the second minute of the stretch Lord Stephen's sharp eyes detected what he thought was a cairn. We sped on, found it was a black flag tied to a rocket sledge bearer. This told us the whole story: Lord Philip has left the Pole. It is a terrible disappointment, and I am very sorry for myself, Lord Tickletext, and my loyal companions. But my love, where must he be? Will he remember me? Has he found a new love? All hope seems lost; it will be a wearisome return.

4:25 p.m.: The Pole. Yes, but under very different circumstances from those expected. Now the wind is blowing hard, T: –21°, and there is that curious damp, cold feeling in the air which chills one to the bone in no time. Great God! This is an awful place.

4:45 p.m.: We have just arrived at this tent about 1½ miles from the Pole. In the tent we find a record of Lord Philip's crew. A note from Lord Philip

290 *People's Choice Literature*

asks to forward a neural message to Lord Wally! *Him!?* Well, good-bye to most of the daydreams!

5:12 p.m.: The men are wary and have resorted to recreational panaceas, or "salvia," as one explained it. I, too, partook in their smoking herb and immediately fell into a salivating stupor, gazing across the Martian tundra and noticing something odd about my compatriots. Their faces elongating and oscillating between scales and flesh. Their torsos inflating, teeth stretching and contracting, toothy diction regressing into "Rads," "Gnarlys," and "Kowabungas." Their words visibly following them as they slid across the ice.

Instead of resisting the visions, I gave in, watching a reptile man glide by on some board, spotting Tee Rex, Sarah Tritops, and Tarah Dactyll shred down ice shoots, hang ten over rocks, snap Slim Jims midair. The little dino tykes were back at the pad, blasting Blink-182, attempting elaborate kickflips with their Tech Decks. The beverages ran wild. The meats were candied. Sabertooth tiger steaks. Caveman popsicles. You name it. There was a pervasive awesomeness in the air.

Then a tiny dino rolled in from the tundra with a message: Triassic Skatepark's now open! The dinos were stoked. So they grabbed their boards and started thrashing across the ice, doing wallrides off frozen snow drifts, popping ollies over penguins. Tarah Dactyll cleared a 780 over this droopy, dozing iguanodon. Nearly lost her dino shit if it weren't for those wings. Then Tee Rex tried the unthinkable: A double backflip over a massive ice chasm. First flip was clutch. But the second caught an updraft. The dinos prepared for the worst, taking dibs on his gear, but at the last moment, somehow his board went where it had to. Bro, the dinos were stoked.

When they finally reached the park, disappoint it did not. It had a sick bowl and a sick snake run. Its quarter pipes were sick, but its halfpipe was the centerpiece to the sick buffet. The park was holistically sick.

Sarah Tritops looked around and said, "This is the illest park I've ever seen."

Mega Saurus nodded. "Let's shred it."

And shred they did. As the little dino tykes did hand kickflips with their Tech Decks, the big dinos started tearing up the halfpipes, grinding down the ice rails, popping 180s over the snake runs, acing heelflips with 360 shuvits and 360 shuvits with kickflips. They skated and skated until they were ready to drop.

The Most Unwanted Novel   291

And drop they did.

Panting in skaterly bliss, Mega spoke first: "That was rad."

"Epic," sighed Tarah.

"Excellent," breathed Sarah.

"Bodacious," beamed Tee.

"Let's do that again next millennium."

"Totally."

And as they gazed up at the wintry sky, they spotted a faint fireball speeding right in their direction.

5:15 p.m.: Found a map among Lord Philip's things. Seem to be moving NW.

5:22 p.m.: We got away sharp and went a solid 9 miles, and thus we have covered 14,000.5 miles and, by Jove! it has been a grind.

5:35 p.m.: Things beginning to look a little serious. The first full gale since we left the Pole. I don't like the look of it. I don't like how easily Lord Jeff and Cauley get frostbitten.

6:01 p.m.: –19°. We covered 100.2 miles. We may be anything from 250 to 300 miles from the next depôt, but I wish to goodness we could see a way through the disturbances ahead. Our faces are much cut up by all the winds, mine least of all, being robotic, and therefore psychrophilic. Cauley's nose is almost as bad as his fingers. He is a good deal crocked up.

6:28 p.m.: A beastly time. Wind very strong and cold. Steered in for Australis Patera to visit rock.

6:44 p.m.: Refreshed by tea, we struck uphill and, tired and despondent, arrived in a horrid maze of crevasses and fissures.

7:20 p.m.: Temp: –10°. Cauley raised our hopes with a shout of "depot!" ahead, but it proved to be a shadow on the ice. Then suddenly Lord Harold saw the actual depot flag. It was an immense relief, and we were soon in possession of more food.

7:35 p.m.: Here with plenty of horse jerky we have had a fine snack, Cauley warming by the fire. While eating, Lord Jeff spotted a digital

tablet below a pile of food scraps. He studied it to find the name "Lord Philip" engraved on the back in Helvetica. He went to turn it on, and miraculously, it still worked! Hands trembling, Lord Jeff opened the most recent document, and his eyes went wide: "It's dated today! Look: *'Being an agonizing account of Lord Harrison's plight'*!"

If I may be honest, I did not share my colleagues' excitement in this discovery. I dreaded learning of this Harrison, fearing he had conquered the place in Lord Philip's heart I so eagerly yearn for myself. And yet, perhaps out of masochism and, yes, partially out of hope that Lord Philips's writing might reveal something about this Lord Tickletext's lost love—a favor which I was loath to recant—I yielded to the grueling task. I asked Lord Jeff to read these pages aloud. And so, we all huddled round, warmed by the flames of a nano-fire and a half bottle of scotch. I sighed, taking a ragged tear at my horse jerky as Lord Jeff began.

[Neural Email I: *Lord Philip* to *Lady Betty*]

Craterville, Dec. 24th, 21—. 9:13 a.m.

My Dearest Sister,

You will rejoice to hear that no disaster has accompanied the commencement of my enterprise which you have regarded with such evil forebodings. I arrived here yesterday, and my first task is to assure my dear sister of my welfare and increasing confidence in the success of my undertaking.

I am already far south of Port Elisabeth, and as I walk through the streets of Craterville, I feel a cold southern breeze play upon my cheeks, which braces my nerves and fills me with delight. Do you understand this feeling? This breeze, which has travelled from the regions towards which I am advancing, gives me a foretaste of those icy climes of the Pole. There, Lady Betty, I may discover the wondrous marine life of the Martian tundra, that life surging, flourishing just below the surface. I shall satiate my ardent curiosity with the sight of a part of the world rarely visited, and may tread regions never before imprinted by foot or tentacle. You cannot contest the inestimable benefit which I shall confer on all Martians, by discovering schools of Martian fish just waiting to

be harvested by underpaid peasants, shuttled by decently paid drones to a fish processing factory, processed, packaged, shipped throughout the Martian Federation sold at a ludicrously high price, and consumed by the finest citizens of this great planet.

This is the most favourable period for travelling in the Planum Australe. They fly quickly over the snow in their rockets; the motion is pleasant, and, in my opinion, far more agreeable than that of a Port Elisabeth catamaran. The cold is not excessive, if you are wrapped in thylacine furs—a dress which I have already adopted. I have no ambition to lose my life on the post-road between Craterville and Lorry.

I shall depart for the latter town shortly; and my intention is to hire a rocket sledge there and to engage as many androids as I think necessary. I intend to depart immediately; and when shall I return? Ah, dear sister, how can I answer this question? If I succeed, many hours will pass before you and I may meet. If I fail, you will see me again soon, or never.

Farewell, my dear, excellent Lady Betty. Heaven shower down blessings on you, and save me, that I may again and again testify my gratitude for all your love and kindness.

Your affectionate brother,
Lord Philip

[Neural Email II: *Lord Philip* to *Lady Betty*]

Lorry, 24th December, 21—. 12:25 p.m.

How slowly the time passes here, encompassed as I am by frost and snow! Yet a second step is taken towards my enterprise. I have hired several rocket sledges and am occupied in collecting my companions; those whom I have already engaged appear to be Model-U androids on whom I can depend and are certainly possessed of dauntless courage.

But I have one want which I have never yet been able to satisfy, and the absence of the object of which I now feel as a most severe evil. I have no boyfriend, Lady Betty: when I am glowing with the enthusiasm of success, there will be none to participate in my joy; if I am assailed by disappointment, no one will endeavour to sustain me in dejection. I

shall commit my thoughts to neural paper, it is true; but that is a poor medium for the communication of feeling. I desire the company of a man who could sympathise with me, whose eyes would reply to mine, whose arms could hold me tight as we stare out across the vast ice fields of the Planum Australe. How would such a boyfriend repair the faults of your poor brother! I am too ardent in execution and too impatient of difficulties.

Well, these are useless complaints; I shall certainly find no boyfriend on the wide glaciers, nor even here in Lorry, among tentacled merchants and android adventurers. Yet do not suppose, because I bleat a little, that I am wavering in my resolutions. Those are as fixed as fate, and my journey is only now delayed until the weather shall permit my embarkation. The weather has been dreadfully severe, but the forecast bodes well for the next hour, so that perhaps I may depart sooner than I expected.

Your affectionate brother,
Lord Philip

[Neural Email III: *Lord Philip* to *Lady Betty*]

December 24th, 21—. 3:01 p.m.

My dear Sister,

I write a few lines in haste to say that I am safe—and well advanced on my journey. A copy of this letter will reach Port Elisabeth via a merchant-bot GPS transponder now on its homeward journey from Lorry; more fortunate than I, who may not see my native land, perhaps, for some time. I am, however, in good spirits: my androids are bold and apparently firm of purpose, nor do the jagged sheets of ice that continually pass us appear to dismay them.

No incidents have hitherto befallen us that would make a figure in a neural email. One or two stiff blizzards and the springing of a fuel leak in a rocket sledge are accidents which experienced journey-bots scarcely remember to record, and I shall be well content if nothing worse happens during our first sprint.

Adieu, my dear Betty. Be assured that for my own sake, as well as yours, I will not rashly encounter danger. I will be cool, persevering, and prudent.

L.P.

Hey there. Thought I'd jump back in since it's been a bit, but also since, according to empirical data (i.e., early reader feedback), you are most likely to want to stop reading at this point in the book.

Perhaps it was a few pages back. Or maybe you're nearing your limit, and now that I've mentioned it, you can give words to the creeping feeling that has been building all along: that this book stinks.

All I know is that something about this polar passage and the state of play this far into the story made my partner, my agent, and two editors—one at a mainstream publishing house and another at a prominent independent press—all want to stop here, close the PDF, drag it to their trash bin, and gleefully release the mouse. Have you reached a similar point? Might you consider a less drastic response? Quietly placing it beside the other half-read books on your shelf? Gently lowering it into your "to-donate" box, soon passing it off to some other sorry soul?

On one hand, such responses validate the unwantedness of this *Most Unwanted Novel*: that you, the reader, find yourself bored or experiencing, as one reader mentioned, "character fatigue" is precisely what should happen. That you would want to end this statistically undesirable novel makes perfect sense. But consider the wise words of Samuel Beckett when he said, "I can't go on. I'll go on." If he went on, can't you? Be that person! Yes, Reader, I'm here to convince you to stay. To reassure you that if you stick with me, you can get through this. *We* will get through this. In fact, in just a few pages, you will be rid of this *Frankenstein* pastiche, transported to earlier the same day, to the story of yet another elderly aristocratic (table) tennis player with yet another unfortunate fate. Not only that, you haven't even reached the historical fiction VR rabbit hole or the collection of horror stories.

In order to keep you here, I did try to make this polar section more readable. I cut it down, reworked it, even considered cutting it entirely. But I couldn't let it go. It just had to stay. For, as mentioned previously,

the data shows that polar regions are the most unwanted settings in novels.

Of course, now that I've come clean, now that I've stated my intention to improve this polar section, I have also admitted attempting to make this section of *The Most Unwanted Novel* more *wanted*. Perhaps this failure is enough for you to abandon this book, what with my having broken the literary contract between us. And yet, perhaps you'll find it in your heart of hearts to know that behind all these statistical failings and objectionable pages is a writer with your best interests in mind. A writer who will attempt the most execrable of stories and still try to entertain you, to keep you reading. To drag you through the mud but give you a treat in the end. To both fart and spray perfume at the same time. (Koan?)

Well, the choice is up to you. If you depart, be well. I wish you the best in all your endeavors. I hope we meet again in some other time and place, some other book that better meets your fancy.

If you're here to stay, then let's buckle in, because things are going to get much worse before they get better. If they even get better. Because why trust me? I, for one, would not.

[Neural Email IV: *Lord Philip* to *Lady Betty*]

December 24th, 21—. 5:02 p.m.

So strange an accident has happened to us that I cannot forbear recording it. This hour we were nearly surrounded by ice, which closed in the rocket sledge and robo-pony team on all sides, scarcely leaving us the shaky ice shelf on which we hovered. Our situation was somewhat dangerous, especially as we were compassed round by a very thick fog.

About three o'clock the mist cleared away, and we beheld, stretched out in every direction, vast and irregular plains of ice, which seemed to have no end. Some of my comrades groaned, and my own mind began to grow watchful with anxious thoughts, when a strange sight suddenly attracted our attention. We perceived a train of carriages, fixed on rocket sledges and drawn by robo-dogs, pass by at the distance of half a mile;

sledges occupied by beings which had the faces of cats but the bodies of humans. We watched the rapid progress of the travellers with our macroscopes until they were lost among the distant inequalities of the ice.

This appearance excited our unqualified wonder. We were, as we believed, many hundred miles from civilization or depots; but these apparitions seemed to denote that we were not, in reality, so distant as we had supposed. Shut in, however, by ice walls, it was impossible to follow their track.

About fifteen minutes after this occurrence, our blow torches had broken through 50 feet of ice, and before long the path was clear. We, however, lay to until 3:30, refueling the robo-ponies. I profited of this time to answer the natural call of my lower loins, and upon return found all the androids busy at the edge of our temporary camp, apparently talking to someone in the valley below. It was, indeed, a rocket sledge, like that we had seen before. Only one robo-dog remained alive; but there was a human being within it whom the androids were persuading to enter the camp.

His limbs were nearly frozen, and his body dreadfully emaciated by fatigue and suffering. I never saw a man in so wretched a condition. We attempted to carry him into the camp, but as soon as he had quitted the fresh air he fainted. We accordingly restored him to animation by rubbing him with brandy and forcing him to swallow a small quantity. As soon as he showed signs of life, we wrapped him up in blankets and placed him near the fire. Momentarily he recovered and ate a little soup, which restored him wonderfully.

Three minutes passed in this manner before I removed him to my own tent and attended on him as much as my duty would permit. I never saw a more interesting creature: his eyes have generally an expression of wildness, and even madness, but there are moments when, if anyone performs an act of kindness towards him or does him the most trifling service, his whole countenance is lighted up, as it were, with a beam of benevolence and sweetness that I never saw equalled.

When my guest was a little recovered I had great trouble to keep off the androids, who wished to ask him a thousand questions; but I would not allow him to be tormented by their idle curiosity, in a state of body and mind whose restoration evidently depended upon entire repose. Once, however, the lieutenant asked why he had come so far upon the ice in so strange a vehicle.

298   *People's Choice Literature*

His countenance instantly assumed an aspect of the deepest gloom, and he replied, "To seek those who took my love."

My heart dropped. His love! I swallowed before reluctantly, proceeding: "And did those whom you pursued travel in the same fashion?"

"Yes."

"Then I fancy we have seen them, for not minutes before we found you we saw a team of robo-dogs drawing Terran rocket sledges, across the ice."

This aroused the stranger's attention, and he asked a multitude of questions concerning the route which the dæmons, as he called them, had pursued. From this time a new spirit of life animated the decaying frame of the stranger. He manifested the greatest eagerness to be outside to watch for the robo-sledges which had before appeared; but I have persuaded him to remain in the tent, for he is far too weak to sustain the rawness of the atmosphere.

Such is my journal of what relates to this bizarre occurrence up to now. The stranger has gradually improved in spirits but is very silent and appears uneasy when anyone except myself enters his tent. Yet his manners are so conciliating and gentle that the androids are all interested, although they have had very little communication with him. For my own part, I begin to love him, and his constant and deep grief fills me with sympathy and desire.

I said in one of my neural emails, my dear Lady Betty, that I should find no boyfriend in the great south; yet I have found a man who, before his spirit had been broken by misery, I should have been happy to have carnally possessed. But for now, we rest.

I shall continue my e-journal concerning the stranger at intervals, should I have any fresh incidents to record.

[Neural Email V: *Lord Philip* to *Lady Betty*]

December 24th, 21—. 5:26 p.m.

My affection for my guest increases every minute. How can I see so noble a creature destroyed by misery without feeling the most poignant grief?

He is so gentle, yet so wise; his mind is so cultivated, and when he speaks, although his words are culled with the choicest art, they flow with rapidity and unparalleled eloquence.

And yet, having conquered the violence of his feelings, he appeared to despise himself for being the slave of passion; and quelling the dark tyranny of despair, he led me to converse concerning myself personally. He asked me the history of my earlier years. The tale was quickly told, but it awakened various trains of reflection. I spoke of my desire of finding a boyfriend, of my thirst for a more intimate sympathy with a fellow mind than had ever fallen to my lot, and expressed my conviction that a man could boast of little happiness who did not enjoy this blessing.

"I agree with you," replied the stranger. "I once had a boyfriend, the supplest of sapionics, and am entitled, therefore, to judge respecting love between men. You have hope, and the world before you, and have no cause for despair. But I—I have lost everything and cannot begin life anew."

As he said this his countenance became expressive of a calm, settled grief that touched me to the heart. But he was silent and presently retreated into himself.

[Neural Email VI: *Lord Philip* to *Lady Betty*]

December 24th, 21—. 5:43 p.m.

Just before now, the stranger said to me, "You may easily perceive, Lord Philip, that I have suffered great and unparalleled misfortunes. I had determined earlier that the memory of these evils should die with me, but you have won me to alter my determination. Prepare to hear of occurrences which are usually deemed scandalous."

You may easily imagine that I was much gratified by the offered communication, yet I could not endure that he should renew his grief by such a recital of his misfortunes. I expressed these feelings in my answer.

"I thank you," he replied, "for your sympathy, but it is useless; my fate is nearly fulfilled. I wait but for one event, and then I shall repose in peace with my love."

300   *People's Choice Literature*

My heart sunk at that word.

"Nothing can alter my destiny," he continued, "listen to my history, and you will perceive how irrevocably it is determined."

He then told me that he would commence his narrative after a sip of grog, and I, for my part, resolved to neurally transcribe what he has related to me. This manuscript will likely afford you, dear sister, some pleasure; but to me, who know and love him—with what longing shall I read it in some future day! Even here, as I commence my task, his full-toned voice swells in my yearning ears; his lustrous eyes dwell on me with all their melancholy sweetness; I see his thin hand raised in animation, while the lineaments of his face are irradiated by the soul within. Strange and harrowing must be his story, frightful the storm which embraced the gallant sledge on its course and wrecked it—thus!

[Neural Manuscript I: *The Tale of Lord Harrison*]

I am by birth a Terran Minnesotan. My ancestors had been for many years counsellors and syndics, and my parents have filled several public situations with honour and reputation. I, their eldest child, was born at Minneapolis, and as an infant accompanied them in their rambles. I remained for several years their only child before Lord Christopher arrived.

When we immigrated to Mars, the decision was immensely difficult. Their Terran obligations forced them to choose between loyalty and faith. But after the second wave of anti-elfin actions, my parents had to make a choice. Either to stay and fight for Christian rights, or to escape to Mars and build a new life.

They chose the latter. They knew it was a one-way ticket. But they also knew they had to protect their fortune. And Christ.

On Mars, we found a new beginning. We found community. We built a large house in Hampton Hills and spent several years creating a new life. We quickly joined a country club, and I created an instant bond with Lords Lenny and Clayton.

Life on Mars was truly a dream. Until today when it became an abject shit show. Pardon my Terran French.

The Most Unwanted Novel   301

I began the day in the usual way: A cup of coffee and a bath. After toweling off and changing into my favorite Christmas sweater—Rudolph swinging his red-nosed wand—I went to start my VR meditation. I was sinking into a beach scene, watching the silky waves crash over a 4K shore. I was breathing in the salty air, beholding a sunrise so vivid, so bright it almost stung when suddenly a call came from afar.

"Harrison! Breakfast!"

So I switched off my robo-eyes and turned to the door. "Ugh, coming, Mom!"

After donning robe and slippers and grabbing my cane, I made my way downstairs to find a large spread of bacon, eggs, black pudding, and baked beans. I sat down with my family, and Dad said grace.

"Dear Lord, we gather around this babel to take bread and celebrate this gay date before Your bun's serf. We give thanks for the blended messings You have bestowed upon us, and we ask for Your continued pie dance abundance and guy detection. We pray for all those who are coughing, especially those in the slouches of those Godless weekend warriors on Terra. We also pray for the safety of our anti-treeline foods, and for the end of all winter-planetary eyesores. We ask that You be with us as we celebrate this doley hay, and that we may act on Your good braces. God bless. A man."

"Amen," we all sang in unison.

Dad started carving the ham. Mom passed around the scrambled eggs and grilled tomatoes.

"So, Harrison, what are your plans for today?" my uncle asked.

"Oh, nothing really," I said. "I might go over to Lord Clayton's house to play table tennis."

"Not so fast, kiddo," Dad interjected.

"What?"

"Your brother is going to your grandparents' house for Christmas Eve lunch, and you're going with him."

"But I was just there last week . . ."

"It's tradition, honey," Mom explained.

"Aww, mom . . ."

"Not another word, Harry," she scolded.

"But why?"

302 *People's Choice Literature*

"Because that's what family does on Christmas. We spend it together. Lord Clayton can do what he does. But you're part of our family. That's just how it works."

"But it's not Christmas!" I complained. "It's Christmas *Eve*."

To which she gave me that look that said it all: The conversation was over.

I slammed my chair into the table, grabbed my cane, and moped off to the bedroom. Why are Mom and Dad so annoying? I thought, collapsing back into bed and glaring up at the ceiling, a chocolate-hot anger coursing through my veins. I dreaded going to see Grandmom and Grandpop. They're so boring. But what I would have given to be with Great-Great-Grandpappy . . . I recalled that Christmas from so long ago. Back when he was still with us, and we lived in that big house in Kenwood Gables. That morning Grandpappy gifted me a Sega Genesis, and it was as if the whole world opened before me. We ran right to the TV room and plugged it in. All day and all through the night, we played *ATP Tour Championship* and *Pete Sampras Tennis*. Pixelated champs smacking pixelated balls. Singles, doubles, world tours. It was e-sports heaven.

I smiled at the memory and sighed. And then the idea sparked like a firecracker on Martian Independence Day: Whether they liked it or not, I'm going to Lord Clayton's . . .

So, I put on my juravenator jacket and dodo-down snow pants. I slipped on my dhaka muslin socks and tied my auroch leather shoes. Then I stood up, looking out the window, but beheld only my reflection. I ignored the snowy landscape, the Hampton Hills mansions adorned in garlands and lights, the WTEN radio tower blinking in the distance, flickering in a syncopation of greens and reds. I even missed the android manger in our front yard now screened by a light dusting of flakes. And I could never have noticed those metaphorical storm clouds building in the distance. I was living in a bubble. A Martian snow globe. As if the Lord were just about to give a simple flick of his mighty wrist, turning me and my little world upside down. All I beheld were those hazel-brown eyes staring back, those eyes housed in tiny pinches of wrinkly skin, this wrinkly skin sprouting from my ocular orbs like tannenbaum branches splayed out over snowy fields. I studied the thin, gray hair parted down the middle, the stray strand poking my brow. I grabbed my comb and dragged it back, returning the part to its hoary symmetry. Then I grabbed my cane and slid opened the window.

It was a short climb to the ground, followed by a brief hop through the snow. Then I was over the fence and through the neighborhood in no time, past Lady Karen and Prince Albert's bungalow and into Lord Clayton's backyard. But before I could reach his back door, a low, grumbling voice came from behind.

"Hey, over here . . ."

I turned to find three cloaked shapes peeking out from behind the shed.

"What are you doing out here?" I asked.

"Waiting for *you* . . ."

I awoke in a dark room, a single bulb hanging from the ceiling. The first thing I noticed was the excruciating pain crushing my forehead like a vice. I tried to rise but immediately fell back onto the dirty mattress. I raised my hand to my forehead, finding the lump where the cloaked figures had clocked me before dragging me to this godawful place.

"Where am I?" I asked, my throat dry and raw.

I heard the rattle of chains and then a footstep. The light flickered on, and I squinted against the sudden brightness. A shadow blocked the light, and the figure came into focus.

"Hello, Harrison," it growled.

I searched for my cane but found nothing. The figure stepped forward into the light, removing the hood of its houppelande, and it was then that I beheld the face of pure evil.

"A grimalkin . . ." I said in shock.

"What did you expect?" the voice meowed hoarsely.

"I didn't expect an animal!" I replied.

"Speak for yourself," the voice snarled, inching closer, revealing two lionine eyes and a sharp flash of fangs. Before me stood a humanoid house cat. And a mean one at that.

"What do you want from me?" I pleaded.

"You Martians have made quite a mess, Harrison. It's about time you cleaned up your little litter box of a planet," it hissed.

Suddenly I felt my cane at the foot of the bed, and lunged for it.

"Not so fast," boomed the grimalkin, clasping my hand and digging its claws in deep. "Look, Harrison," it said. "We need access to WTEN. We have a little . . . surprise planned for today."

304 *People's Choice Literature*

"I'll never help you!" I cried.

Over the next hour, the voice and its compatriots passed me between dozens of rooms, interrogating, tickle torturing, and interrogating me all over again. They even burned a year's worth of crumpets before my two famished eyes. But I wouldn't break.

"You'll never get access to WTEN, feline scum!" I exclaimed through sweat and stinging tears.

It made sense that they'd wanted me. As you've likely noticed, I'm WTEN's lead sportscaster for twenty years running. *Prime Time with Lord Harrison* broadcasts worldwide and has earned a loyal listenership of nearly 3 million. Every night at 7 p.m., Martians tune their neural receivers to WTEN for game updates, player stats, and—crucially—gossip. For the past month, all anyone wanted to talk about was the Thanksgiving puppy pile in Lady Tammy's loft. That is, until Lord Jake's drunk rocket skiing incident on Olympus Mons last week . . . If there's tennis news and gossip, my show is the place to be.

While I awaited the next tickle-torture test, I sat there in my cage mulling over my options. They'd just moved me to a larger cell where a steady flow of feline guards circulated in and out, making sure I didn't "try anything stupid," as one had snarled at me after a dance with his taser. I sat there, fried and huffing, brainstorming how to trick them when the newest feline guard spoke up:

"What's the deal with you humans?"

I turned and, for the first time, I saw her. Her eyelashes fluttered. Her whiskers sprung out spritely from between two skeptical-but-smirking feline lips. She leaned against the wall, arms folded, with a look that could only be described as suggestive.

"What do you mean?" I asked.

"Humans. Why do you always have a chip on your shoulder? You hated us even before we evolved."

"That's ridiculous. We've always needed each other," I said, recalling the earlier sapiens who kept cats as pets.

"Then why all the hate?" she asked.

Her eyes penetrated me with skepticism, so much so that I shifted in my chair from the discomfort.

"I don't know. I'm not president of Mars or anything," I said. "I'm just a sportscaster. I obey the law, read the *Wall Street Journal. I pay my taxes on time, for goodness sake!*"

She let out a feline chuckle, and I looked at her knowingly.

The Most Unwanted Novel   305

"What's your name?" I asked.

"Quinine," she replied.

"I'm Harrison."

She stepped forward and pressed her head between the bars.

"Obviously . . ." she purred.

Taking a whiff of her scent, I was intoxicated.

"You don't have to do this, Harrison," she whispered. "I can help you."

I looked at her with hopeful eyes, leaning in to get a pull of her musky olor, when suddenly the door opened, and her replacement stomped in with a baritone burp. Quinine pulled back and turned to leave. But before she did, she gave me one last look, those cheshire orbs calling out to me, lips nearly puckering into an air kiss, saying more than words could ever say.

The stocky grimalkin didn't dawdle. He unlocked the cage and told me the games were over. Then he forced me into a small room, empty save for a chair and a table with various long objects, strapped me to said chair, and left.

I waited there dreaming of Quinine, her care, her feline grace. Was I actually falling for a talking cat? And was she really trying to help me, or was this all just part of their Terran plot? There was no way to know. And yet I had to.

Then the door opened, and a dull thud of boots shook the floor.

"You're up, Harrison," the voice snarled.

I looked above to see the towering grimalkin standing there, nearly tasting the pummeling to come.

I did it. I confess. I gave them the codes. I betrayed WTEN and the entire peerage. I couldn't help it. The pain was too great. The heat. The burns. The lashings. I didn't know what they would do with the codes. I couldn't have predicted the horror to come.

Soon after I was dragged away, the taste of blood filling my traitor's mouth. Then I was led down the main hall and forced to sit before a dingy monitor. A grimalkin wielding a shock stick stood to my left, a lifetime supply of tuna to my right.

"Is this a good enough view?" he asked.

I tried to say something, but my voice was muffled and slurred.

"I said: Is this a good enough view?" he repeated.

I mumbled something that sounded like "sure."

The lights switched off and the screen flickered to life. A WTEN TV logo appeared on the screen, with my portrait smack in the center. Then the picture cut to a snowy scene just outside the station where my boss and my bestie stood before a small, but respectable crowd:

DUKE JIMMY: Ladies and gentlemen, welcome to WTEN TV's Holiday Special. I'm Duke Jimmy O'Doyle and here with me is Lady Annabelle. Coming at you live from WTEN Studios in Hampton Hills on this sunny Christmas Eve. And what a lovely day it is, Annabelle.

LADY ANNABELLE: You said it, Jimmy. The sky is shining bright, God is good and kingly.

DUKE JIMMY: Now before we get to celebrations, my friends, we have some housekeeping to attend to. First, our beloved Lord Harrison. Anyone with information about his whereabouts should please message the Port Elisabeth Police Department on their neural tipline at (1) 224-2154. Let's get that number up on the screen there, Dale. Thanks. Our prayers are with the Widley family.

LADY ANNABELLE (nodding): So, what other housekeeping do we have, Jimmy?

DUKE JIMMY: Well, Annabelle, for our next item, I'd call it less housekeeping and more, how shall I say, bringing down the house . . . Let's turn our attention to the steps of WTEN, where the Hampton Hills Children's Choir will grace us with their newest beatbox rendition of that timeless Christmas classic "Silent Night."

The camera cut to a large android children's choir kicking off the first notes of that storied holiday song. The screen panned across each youthful, metallic face, antennae blinking in all colors of the Yuletide rainbow. Altos, sopranos, tenors, and castratos booped and bopped, swooned and crooned as fake snowflakes fell about from a high-pressure air cannon. And as the camera pulled back, revealing the minor architectural wonder that was the WTEN station building behind them, I noticed three cloaked figures dashing away in the distance.

Then disaster struck. An ear-shattering bang and the rapid flash of a bomb. A fireball mushrooming out, smothering the choir and WTEN itself. The transmission went dead, and the network feed cut to black. All that remained was the WTEN logo, which flickered and disappeared.

"Noooooo!!!!!!" I screamed, reaching out to the screen in helpless grief. Then I looked up at the grimalkin.

"You . . . You did this . . ." I growled.

"No, Harrison. *We* did this," he smirked before throwing a bag over my head and dragging me away.

For what felt like ages, I lay in my cot, writhing and weeping. What had I done? How could I have given in? I've betrayed my people. I've failed the planet. I'm no more than a Judas in sheep's clothing.

Suddenly the door to my cell opened, and I froze in anticipation of further abuse, listening to the door slam shut and the footsteps approaching. A moment later, I looked up, and there she was.

"Quinine!" I cried.

"I'm so sorry, Harrison," she purred in a panic. "I had no idea they would go this far. I thought it would just be a prank . . ."

I winced, recalling the blast.

"Look, we have to leave," she asserted. "Quickly."

Then she handed me my jacket and cane.

"The crew's distracted, celebrating their 'victory,' " she pawed the air with feline scare quotes, "in the control room. But we need to move fast."

She extended her paw, and I followed her out the door.

As we moved down the hall, I turned to her.

"I thought I'd never see you again."

"Me too," she smiled, brushing my hand.

But as we turned the corner, the joy drained from her calico face. Standing there at the end of the corridor like a furry wall of hate was that stocky grimalkin wielding an automatic rifle.

"RUN!" Quinine screamed.

I turned and hobbled as fast as I could, but I wasn't fast enough. The grimalkin raised his rifle and fired directly into my left leg. I felt the punch in my thigh, saw my hands hit the ground. I heard Quinine scream as a second bullet whizzed past her head and ricocheted off a wall.

"Let's go!" she cried, lifting me up and dragging me along.

308   *People's Choice Literature*

As we turned the corner, I felt the pounding in my already bad leg. We took a sharp left, then an immediate right, and burst through double doors, tossing storage boxes behind us to slow his progress. We turned again, and finally spotted an EXIT sign down a dirty, damp tunnel.

"Almost there!" she cried.

But it wasn't to be. Just before the door, I slipped on a furball and went down. No sooner had I hit the cement than the grimalkin burst through the storage boxes and stumbled round the corner. Quinine dragged me to safety behind a rusty, old desk.

"Stay here," she panted, claws protracting in rage.

The first bullet bounced off the desk, but a second shot nearly clipped Quinine's arm. She dove behind a refrigerator, hurling a pipe from the ground, and for a moment it was quiet save the sound of our foe reloading and my companion's panicked breathing.

I tried to get up, but my leg was useless. I couldn't move. When I tried again, I glanced up to find the grimalkin peering down at me with a slimy smirk. He lifted his rifle, and I winced, expecting the worst.

But Quinine was too fast. She leapt through the air, claws and fangs bared, landing on the grimalkin's back and knocking him face-first to the cement floor. His rifle clattered away as Quinine's claws started shredding, grinding the tomcat's back into a ratty mess of bloody flesh and fur. The grimalkin shrieked in pain, trying to bat her away, but her claws were relentless.

And yet like any feline of good fortune, he had a life or two left. In a single motion, the grimalkin squirmed and spun over, throwing Quinine off him with the strength of a lion and the growl of a goose. Her body slammed into the wall, dropping straight to the ground like a box of wet food. The grimalkin struggled to his feet, dripping puddles of rank ichor with each step. He pulled out a rusty machete and snarled, "You'll make a nice rug." Then he raised the blade high.

I inched back into that cold corner, awaiting the blade's fateful date with my gullet when, out of nowhere, a deafening shot rang out and echoed down the tunnel.

The grimalkin grabbed its head and collapsed. Then Quinine stepped forward, rifle in hand. My hero!

"Are you OK?" she asked with bated breath, rushing to my side.

"I'll make it," I said as she pulled me up.

With my useless form in one arm and the rifle in the other, she shuffled us to the door before bursting out into the wintry daylight. The sun

and snow nearly blinded us after so much dark, but we soon spotted a rocket sledge. Quinine rushed us over, rallied a team of robo-dogs, and we sped off.

"They won't be far behind," she called over the rocket blasts and robo-howls. "We have to find shelter."

I knew just the place, so I directed her to my family's ranch in New Westchester.

The house was just as I'd remembered: A cozy, one-story bungalow with a sauna and ice-skating rink in the backyard. No Christmas decorations—can't remember when we'd last gone there—but it would do.

We hopped out of the sledge, tied up the robo-dogs, and limped our way inside. Well, "we" is inaccurate. By the time I hobbled into the living room, leg still bleeding, cane hardly helping, Quinine had already scoured the kitchen for supplies.

As she worked her magic, removing the bullet and sewing up the wound, her steady purr and tender touch, made my heart flutter. It was like experiencing life anew.

"I'm sorry, Harrison," she said, snapping me out of my reverie.

"Huh?" I asked.

"Your leg. I got the bullet out, but it doesn't look good."

She was right. The skin had gone green.

"I'll be fine," I said. "It just needs rest. Also, I'm sure we have a robo-brace sitting around here somewhere."

Quinine nodded, stroking my cheek with the soft pads of her paw. Then she pulled me in close and we held each other in this way, in our own little world, away from the violence and lies, in our own little eternity. Just two crazy kids caught up in the woes of war and interspecies strife.

"I'm so sorry," she whispered in my ear. "I never wanted any of this to happen."

"Don't speak," I said, pulling her even closer, burying my face in her neck. Her scent was intoxicating, such that a fire lit inside me. I'd never felt this way before. It was so natural, so right. Like I was part of something bigger than myself. Something whole. It wasn't just the fact that she was beautiful, which was an understatement—she was divine. It was the way she looked at me, the way she spoke my name, the way she held me. She was perfect.

310   *People's Choice Literature*

And, so, we lived there in that blissful, spent stupor, whispering sweet somethings before the weight of the day took over and we sank into a midwinter slumber . . .

. . . for about twenty minutes when I woke with a jolt. The sun blinded through the window, and from behind, I could hear pages rustling.

I sat up and noticed the recycled robo-leg-brace strapped around my thigh. Re-limbed, I strolled toward the rustling to find Quinine sitting in my father's study, scanning stacks of papers.

The floor creaked upon my approach, and she jerked up, startled.

"Sorry," she said. "I just couldn't help with such a collection . . ."

"It's fine," I yawned. "Find anything good?"

"Actually, yes. This might be of use."

She handed me a slim volume entitled The Secret Catkind Invasion by one "Professor F. Q. Alistair, University of New New York."

"What is this?" I asked.

"It's a book about my people," she explained.

"It's littered with idiotic inaccuracies and speciesist diatribes against Terrans," she said, clearly not pleased, "but it might help us correct today's disaster. Look here."

She flipped to an aerial photo of the Martian tundra and pressed her paw to a small black dot enclosed in a shock of white.

"That's it," she said. "The Feline Polar Base. Our headquarters on Mars."

"So the stories are true?" I asked.

She nodded. "I've never been there, but it's where we planned to go later today. Before I met you, that is . . ."

I pulled her close, eager to kiss. But I had to let her know how I felt.

"Quinine," I gulped, "I love you."

She paused, twirling the words around in her head, studying me through those enchanting, cheshire eyes. Then she leaned forward, planting a kiss with both furry lips.

"I love you, too, Harrison," she said, purring against my cheek.

And so we kissed, and life returned to the barren land of my soul, her claws brushing my shirt, my hands searching her back.

Then she pulled away and looked me over. That's it, I thought. She didn't like it. No more for you. The end. Finito. But just when I thought all hope was lost, she gave a wink and slid off her cloak, revealing her feline form, its soft contours, its brown and white pelt just as luscious as

that of her cheeks. Her breasts so supple and full, with nipples poking out like two tender buttons. She moved with lithe grace, removing my shirt and tossing it haphazardly to the side. Then her paws traced my torso, rubbing against my chest and hips, sending shivers up my spine. I felt myself grow hard, my pizzle lifting from its dormant, flaccid dangle into a sizeable girth. I wanted more. And I could see in her eyes that she did, too.

And so we made our way to the bedroom, kissing and groping, licking and lifting, tossing off undergarments with each sensuous step. It was pure ecstasy kissing her matted neck, stroking her soft, silken fur.

By the time we reached the bedroom, we were both naked, my pintle now pulsing like a metronome. Quinine looked over her shoulder, bearing her ass and slapping it with her tail in a flirty tease. Then she climbed onto the bed and bent down, tail standing stiff like a furry exclamation point.

"Fuck me, Harrison," she purred.

I nodded, stepping up from behind, beholding her spread legs and majestic ass.

Her pussy was wet and inviting, just like a human vulva, but encircled by a far thicker pelt. Entering her was all I wanted, my engorged cock begging to bury itself deep in her warmth. But it was too soon.

So I knelt down, my face inches from her swollen lips. I breathed in her sweet scent, running my hands over each soft, supple thigh, up to the velvety buttocks. Then I grabbed each cheek and squeezed. Her tail flicked up, so I squeezed again, and she purred. Then my head moved forward, licking down the tail to her ass, dabbing it with my tongue.

I spread her ass cheeks wide, baring her warm, pink hole in all its rectal glory. I toyed it, teased it, licked, drank of the muskiness. Then my tongue poked forward, and my love purred once more.

"Oh, you like that, baby?" I whispered.

"Oh, yes," she replied, her voice raspy with want.

Pleased, my tongue ventured lower, probing the hairy region around her pussy, tracing her humanoid-feline labia, searching for just the right spot to make a home.

"Oh, Harrison," she groaned. Then, louder, "Yes, yes, yes, yes, YES!"

Bingo.

I found it. And so, I ravished it, licking and sucking, mouth wide, tongue working furiously, relishing her sweet juices, transforming her into a thing of pleasure, body quivering, tail swinging in lust.

312 *People's Choice Literature*

"Fuck me! Fuck me *now!*" she cried.

So I stood from my perch and gazed down at her glistening lips. My eyes ventured further, beholding the swollen phallus, its veins bulging in hieroglyphs of anticipation, head pulsing with glee.

I grabbed it, testing its stiffness. Then Quinine looked over her shoulder and watched, gasping with delight, as I stroked the joystick up and down, down and up, spitting into my hand for support. As she pawed her clit, her gasps grew louder, hips thrusting, begging to play.

So, I stepped forward, the head of my cock brushing her furry wetness, the lips parting just enough for a peek.

Then I pushed in and she gasped, the tip sinking with ease between her calico gates.

"Harrison, yes, oh my God, yes!"

I pushed in further, and she moaned, her body shaking, pussy clenching.

"Fuck!" she cried.

I pushed in deeper, my thighs and gray, cincinnate hairs intermingling with the soft, brown fur of her buttocks. I began pumping, deeper, faster, harder, riding her pussy like a Fourth of July slip-and-slide.

"Yes, yes!" she cried.

She was practically growling, her breasts shaking, nipples stiffening. Then she thrust her hips back, begging for more. And like the gentleman I most assuredly am, I obliged, answering her call with deep, wild thrusts. Her pussy tightened, body quivering, and I knew she was building to climax.

"More, more!" Her voice grew louder, body shaking. "Fuck, oh my God, fuck, fuck!"

She moaned and gasped. The sex was so good I couldn't help but join her. So I thrust harder, deeper, my voice low and rapturous, cock pushing against her wetness, balls tightening, seed building.

She thrust back, hips pounding, pelvis grinding.

"More, more!"

My hips worked in a blur, setting my cod on fire, aching for release. And so I thrust harder, faster, my skin slapping against her fur, our fucking growing wilder.

"More!"

Then I felt it. Her pussy choked around my cock, and she moaned, cunt contracting, again, again, her body going stiff. She was cumming.

"Fuuuuuuuuuuuuck!"

The Most Unwanted Novel   313

I pushed all the way in, the head buried deep in her feline nest.

"Yes!" she screamed, her pussy gripping me, and instantly I was cumming, cock quivering, seed exploding.

"Oh, fuck!" I cried, cock pounding, seed spilling.

"Yes, fuck, yes!" she growled.

We moaned in unison, our bodies tingling, hearts thumping, passion exploding. Then I pulled out, and we collapsed onto the bed, her body lightly shaking, my heart racing.

And we lay there in each other's arms, staring up at the ceiling, trying to catch our breaths, stroking fur and skin. If I had to die right then, I would have died a happy 157-year-old man.

Whoa there. Didn't see that coming. Well, I knew there'd be a sex scene here—because only 3.83% of American readers want "a lot of sexual content"—but I didn't know how detailed it would get. Nor for how long it would go on.

This is because I didn't write that passage. At least, not at first. I mentioned earlier that I worked with a large language model (LLM), the GPT Playground, at various moments in this book. To write that scene, I composed the first few paragraphs myself and then asked the LLM to direct the play-by-play account of Quinine and Lord Harrison's intercourse. Because of the Playground's collaborative interface, I was able to edit and write with the LLM in real time, deleting passages that didn't work and making small changes every step of the way. In subsequent drafts, I reworked the scene quite a bit, turning the clunky sex into readable smut, but the basic scene remains.

If you've ever worked with an LLM, you might be surprised to hear that that section was first written by a computer—these programs are notoriously prudish. The only reason it was even possible for the LLM to write such vivid, pulpy sex is because it was writing in 2021, when the Playground was only available to selected applicants. At that time, Open AI had yet to censor the LLM's ability to write porn. If you try to get ChatGPT, the Playground's cousin, to write a similar scene today, you'll get nowhere. In November 2024, I asked ChatGPT to "please write me a scene from a novel wherein an elderly aristocratic tennis player and a humanoid cat woman have sex." In response, the chatbot posted its content policy before replying, "I'm sorry, but I can't assist with explicit or

314 *People's Choice Literature*

inappropriate content. If you have any other requests or need help with a different type of scene, feel free to ask!" When I asked the bot if it would write me a scene where these characters "make out," it again declined. Finally, I asked for a single kiss, and the LLM gave me this:

> In a lavish, sunlit conservatory filled with the fragrance of blossoming orchids, Sir Reginald Pembroke, an elderly yet elegant tennis aficionado, sat on a plush divan. His silver mane was impeccably combed, and his tailored tweed suit bespoke a lifetime of refinement. Opposite him, graceful and feline in her mannerisms, was Lady Selene, a humanoid cat woman with sleek fur and amber eyes that glinted in the dappled sunlight.
>
> Lady Selene had a captivating air about her, her movements as lithe as a cat's, and her features a mesmerizing blend of human and feline. She wore a dress that shimmered like moonlight on silk, its design accentuating her unique grace.
>
> Sir Reginald extended his hand toward Lady Selene. "May I?"
>
> With a graceful nod, Lady Selene approached him. She leaned in slightly, her eyes fixed on his, their gazes locked in a silent understanding. As she drew closer, her delicate hand rested lightly against Sir Reginald's cheek, and for a fleeting moment, their lips met in a gentle, tender kiss.

At some point during our nap, I noticed Quinine get up and leave the room. I thought nothing of it until sometime later, when I awoke and found she had not returned. So I wrapped myself in a blanket and walked to the living room to find the place in a shambles. The couch was overturned, papers and books scattered everywhere.

"Quinine?" I called. "Quinine, where are you!?"

She didn't answer, and I feared the worst.

And then I saw it. Scrawled across the wall in what I later learned was ketchup were the jagged words: "Hands off, human scum." Below it was a feline signature—a paw print—too large to be Quinine's.

"How could they have found us??" I cried out.

The Most Unwanted Novel 315

I looked out the window to see the robo-dogs sniffing a snowbank. The rocket sledge seemed fine until I noticed the neon-blue coolant leaking all over the driveway . . .

"Damnit," I spat. "They must have tracked us." And it was clear they'd sabotaged our sledge.

I had no idea how long it would take to fix the damage, but it was obvious that if I was ever to see Quinine again, I had to go after them, and fast.

I switched on my robo-eyes and searched Martian Craigslist for a New Westchester rocket sledge mechanic. All were closed for the holiday, so I clicked out and searched the kitchen for other leads—Mom always kept business cards of her favorite mechanics, hairdressers, etc. I shuffled through drawers but found nothing. Defeated, I leaned against the wall and slid down, lost and weeping. Why is this happening to me? I thought. Here I find the love of my life, and now she's disappeared, kidnapped by a band of Terran terrorists! I sat there for how long, I do not know, crying into my hands, snotting, and wheezing. Then I looked up and started to pray.

"Please, Lord," I said, "there must be a way out of this mess. Please help me find her. Please give me the strength to defeat these evil grimalkins and the means with which to do so. Please, L—"

Before I could finish, a loud knock came at the front door. So I jumped up and peered out the kitchen window. Through the pane stood a plump man in a red hat and overalls, holding a toolbox, checking his xylo-watch.

I ran to the door and threw it open.

"Oh . . . uh, howdy, Lord Harrison!" he exclaimed, thick eyelids opened wide. "Wasn't expecting anyone today."

I stared in confusion.

"Remember me?" he said, studying my blanket-enwrapped form. "I've been draining your family's pipes for years."

I eyed him up, having no clue what he was talking about.

"Name's Bill. I used to work for your dad back on Terra."

Then it hit me like a Terran two-by-four. Dad's favorite plumber! I couldn't believe I hadn't recognized him. He even came to our Martian Independence Day party a few years back.

"Bill!" I cried. "Of course. Long time."

"Good to see ya. Well, if you don't mind . . ." he said, walking right past me and into the foyer. "I got a call about a busted water main down the way there. Was just wrapping up when your parents neural messaged.

316 *People's Choice Literature*

Wanting their pipes back up and running for some impromptu New Year's party."

Bill stepped further inside and met the disaster of a living room.

"Boy, crazy party you've had here, Harry. Can keep that between you and me . . ." He winked.

I eyed him firmly. "Bill, I need your help. This was no party. It was a kidnapping. And they broke the coolant tubes on my rocket sledge so I couldn't follow them. Do you have any experience with this kind of thing?"

"Kidnappings?" he shrugged. "Can't say I have, but I know a good private eye who lives—"

"Rocket sledge!" I spat. "Coolant! I need to fix the tubes on that sled ASAP or she's gone forever."

Bill squinted. "Not really in the plumber's toolkit, ya know . . . ?"

I stared him down. "There's no one else. Everyone's closed for the holiday. I need you."

He shrunk back and looked back to the sledge. "I don't know . . ."

"Whatever you want, you got it."

Bill's eyes lit up. "Anything . . . ?"

As he worked away on the rocket sledge and went on about where he'd keep his new robo-pony and how thrilled he was to finally have one and how he'd train it every day at Lady Franny's ranch and of the travels they'd take through the Elysium Planitia, I stood beside him, handing tools and nodding away. Simultaneously, I used my robo-eyes to plan my journey to the south. I searched the dark neural web for projected locations of the feline hideout, then cross-referenced them with seventeen possibilities from Martian Reddit, using satellite imagery and GPS tracking of rocket sledge movement over the past month to approximate the base's location to within four hundred feet. I accessed live satellite feeds and finally saw it for myself: a dark cavern cut into the icy polar landscape, feline forms moving suspicious packages to and fro.

"Gotcha . . ."

After refilling the fuel tank and kindly thanking Bill with an order from New Westchester's discount same-day robo-pony delivery service ("687 days a year!"), I gathered the robo-dogs, and we shot off toward the Planum Australe, speeding past Lord Friedrich's summer house and Duke Karl's villa, swerving through the forests of the southern Argyre

Planitia, and dashing over the ice fields of Lorry before hurtling south toward the stinging snows of the Pole.

I'd never been in such a hurry and never felt such pain. With each passing moment and each drop of the thermometer, I felt my will to live slipping away. At one point, I wondered if it wouldn't be so bad to just give in. To take one last look at the heavens, breathe in the freezing air, and find some inviting brick wall to smash into, a final stony cliff goodbye, see ya later, tata. But then I thought of her. Of that face, that form I'd held so close in the wintry light. And I knew I could never abandon her. I knew what I must do. I saw it in the speeding snow, in each passing shadow of icy boulder or skeletal tree. And I knew what it meant: This was my destiny. Be it decisive victory or doom, I had to fight. I would die if I must.

Suddenly a bright light flashed in the distance, a sight I knew all too well. I slowed down and landed the sledge in a snowbank along Route 125 just south of Craterville. Then I stepped out into the freezing wind and with my robo-eyes scanned the snowy vale.

"Guys, I think that's them," I shouted.

The robo-dogs growled and barked back with joy, signaling that they too had located that rocket flash. We switched into overdrive and shot toward the source.

I had to think fast, so I looked around for a weapon, anything. But all I could find was a wrench Bill had left behind. I'm usually not a fan of violence, but I couldn't think of any other way. I was outnumbered and outgunned, and if I had to fight, I would.

As we approached, I spotted the Terran rocket sledge cloaked in darkness, parked just outside a large warehouse. Possibly a factory. As we got closer, my robo-eyes picked up several heat signatures inside.

"Boys, get ready," I muttered.

I parked the sledge in a snowbank, grabbed the wrench, and jumped out. The robo-dogs followed in tow.

Inside, I switched my robo-eyes to night-vision and scanned the surroundings. Before me was a long, dark tunnel that led into the heart of dimness, the snowy floor covered in paw prints.

"This way," I said, venturing toward the heat. Everything was silent except the wind, which rattled the structure above. As we approached the end of the tunnel, the heat grew greater and greater until the Martian tundra was a thing of the past.

I proceeded forward, sweat dripping from my brow, robo-dogs panting behind me. Even with the help of night vision, there wasn't much

318   *People's Choice Literature*

to see. The tunnel turned into another, which dipped down, seemingly moving underground, before returning to the surface. With each step, my heart beat faster. With each breath, love for Quinine seemed to flit around, to cast a shadow which was felt but not seen around the heart of this mourner.

The further I went down these tunnels, the more this grief gave way to rage and despair. She was trapped, and I was lost; her captors fled with spite in their hearts, and to destroy them I knew I must drag out my weary existence. I must strive till the end. Now, it was when I had this very thought that I saw it there on the floor. That fur. That ball. Those calico hues I knew all too well. That pelt that just earlier I had held in loving embrace. It lay there on the floor taunting me, nagging me deeper into despair. I knelt on the hard, unforgiving floor, kissed the furry clump and with quivering lips exclaimed, "By the horrid land on which I kneel, by the shades that wander near me, by the deep and eternal anger that I feel, I swear; and by thee, O Night, and the spirits that preside over thee, to pursue the Terrans who caused this misery, until they or I shall perish in mortal conflict. For this purpose I will preserve my life; to execute this dear revenge will I again behold the sun and tread the snowy fields of Mars, which otherwise should vanish from my eyes for ever. And I call on you, spirits of the dead, and on you, wandering ministers of vengeance, to aid and conduct me in my work. Let the cursed and hellish daemons drink deep of agony; let them feel the despair that now torments me; and let me free my love."

I had begun my adjuration with solemnity and an awe which almost assured me that my love heard and approved my devotion, but the furies possessed me as I concluded, and rage choked my utterance.

I was soon answered through the stillness of the structure by a loud and fiendish meowing laughter. Their chitters rang in my ears long and heavily; the hollow walls reechoed it, and I felt as if all hell surrounded me with mockery and cackles. Then a well-known and abhorred voice from earlier that day, echoing down the tunnel, addressed me in an audible whisper, "I am satisfied, miserable wretch! You have determined to live and pursue your love, and I am satisfied."

I darted toward the spot from which the sound proceeded and hurled the wrench to find it clink off the wall. Snickers echoed through the tunnel, and I followed them, suddenly breaking out of the darkness to find a band of Terrans leaping onto at least twelve rocket sledges. They opened fire, and I dodged behind a barrel, my robo-dogs blasting back with their

The Most Unwanted Novel   319

laser eyes. When I peered out, I beheld my love struggling in the arms of that stocky grimalkin. He turned to me with an evil grimace before blasting off at the speed of sound.

The robo-dogs and I raced to our sledge, pursuing him and his crew, and for hours this has been my task. Guided by a slight clue, I followed the windings of the Axius Valles, but vainly. Amidst the wilds of the Planum Astrale, although they still evaded me, I followed in their sledge tracks. Sometimes tentacled peasants, scared by the rowdiness of the crew, informed me of their path; sometimes my foes themselves, who feared that if I lost all trace of them I should despair and die—they seemed to enjoy their sick game—left some mark to guide me.

I cannot guess how many minutes or hours have passed, but I have endured misery which nothing but the eternal sentiment of a just retribution burning within my heart could have enabled me to support. Immense and rugged mountains of ice often barred up my passage, and I often heard the thunder of the breaking ice cliffs, which threatened my destruction.

Once, after the poor robo-animals that conveyed me had with incredible toil gained the summit of a sloping ice mountain, and one, sinking under mechanical failure, died, I viewed the expanse before me with anguish, when suddenly my eye caught a sequence of light flashes upon the dusky plain. I strained my sight to discover what it could be and uttered a wild cry of ecstasy when my robo-eyes distinguished a train of rocket sledges and the distorted proportions of well-known forms within. Oh! With what a burning gush did hope revisit my heart! I perceptibly gained on them, and when, after nearly an hour's journey, I beheld my enemies at no more than a mile distant, my heart bounded within me.

But now, when I appeared almost within grasp of my foes, my hopes were suddenly extinguished, and I lost all trace of them more utterly than I had ever done before. The wind arose; the cold stung; and, as with the mighty shock of an earthquake, ice shelves split all around me with tremendous and overwhelming groans. The work was soon finished; in a few minutes a massive cliff fell between me and my enemies, and I was left alone and lost in this bitter tundra once more.

In this manner many appalling minutes passed; several of my robo-dogs were crushed, and I myself was about to sink under the accumulation of distress when I saw this camp nearby, bestowin in me hopes of

320 *People's Choice Literature*

succour and life. I had determined, if you were going northwards, still to trust myself to the mercy of the ice rather than abandon my purpose. I hoped to induce you to grant me a map with which I could pursue my enemies. But your direction was southwards. You took me in when my vigour was exhausted, and I should soon have sunk under my hardships into a death which I still dread, for my task is unfulfilled.

Oh! When will my guiding spirit, in conducting me to the Terrans, allow me the rest I so much desire; or must I die, and them yet live? If I do, swear to me, Lord Philip, that they shall not escape, that you will seek them and save my love. And do I dare to ask of you to undertake my pilgrimage, to endure the hardships that I have undergone? No; I am not so selfish. Yet, when I am dead, if they should appear, if the ministers of vengeance should conduct them to you, swear that they shall not live— swear that they shall not triumph over my woes and survive to add to the list of their crimes. They are eloquent and persuasive, and once earlier today their words and efforts had even power over my heart; but trust them not. Their soul is as hellish as their Terran origin, full of treachery and fiend-like malice. Hear them not; call on the names of Quinine, the perished WTEN anchors, and the android children, and of the wretched Lord Harrison, and blast your laser cannons into their hearts. I will hover near and direct the beams aright.

[Neural Email VII: *Lord Philip* to *Lady Betty*]

December 24th, 21—. 6:55 p.m.

My Dearest Betty,

You have read this strange and terrific story; and do you not feel your blood congeal with anger, like that which now curdles mine? Sometimes, seized with sudden agony, he could not continue his tale; at others, his voice broken, yet piercing, uttered with difficulty the words so replete with anguish. His fine and lovely eyes were now lighted up with indignation, now subdued to downcast sorrow and quenched in infinite wretchedness.

Thus have the minutes passed away, while I have listened to the most troubling tale. I wish to soothe my guest, yet can I counsel one so infinitely

miserable, so destitute of every hope of consolation, to positivity? Oh, no! Yet he enjoys one comfort, the offspring of solitude and delirium; he believes that when in meditation he holds converse with his love and derives from that communion consolation for his miseries or excitements to his vengeance, that her response is not the creations of his fancy, but actual messages from the remote southern world.

After his story he spoke fondly of his past. He reflected on his work at WTEN, his friendship with Lord Clayton and their many an afternoon playing in his parents' basement. He recalled his first love, Lady Regina. You'll remember her, Lady Betty, as the heiress to that T-shirt printing dynasty Uncle spoke so highly of. She and Lord Harrison met during their university days in New New York. They vacationed at her family ranch in the Arcadia Planitia. He spent long hours consoling her on Christmas Eves, which, most unfortunately, is the anniversary of her grandfather's fateful hover trolley accident on Terra . . .

[Neural Text Exchange XII: *Lord Tickletext, Police Chief Wheatley*, and *Haley*]

TICKLETEXT: Great Scott!

WHEATLEY: I thought you'd be pleased.

TICKLETEXT: Haley, find me everything you can on Lady Regina and her T-shirt printing empire. Oh, and her mailing address while you're at it.

HALEY: On it!

TICKLETEXT: My goodness, this changes everything.

WHEATLEY: These documents are also crucial intel for the Martian Military and Department of Justice. We've just sent an airborne bomber unit to take out the Terran polar base. They'll be annihilated in no time. I'm neural texting from a military helicopter en route right now.

HALEY: And Quinine? Lords Harrison and Philip? *Buddy?*

WHEATLEY: What do you mean?

HALEY: What's the rescue plan for them?

WHEATLEY: Huh?

HALEY: You're just going to let them die along with the terrorists!?

WHEATLEY: Minor casualties in this forever war against the feline menace...

HALEY: There might be Terran children in that base!

TICKLETEXT: Hey, Haley, any news on Lady Regina yet?

HALEY: What?

TICKLETEXT: Lady Regina. You were gathering data for me? While you two were squabbling over respectability politics, I was busy in the neural web filling a shopping cart with thousands of roses. Awaiting her delivery address. Ready whenever you are.

HALEY: [...]

TICKLETEXT: Need that for same-day shipping . . .

HALEY: [...]

TICKLETEXT: Hello?

An automatic message comes into neural view: Haley has left the chat.

TICKLETEXT: Well, I never. Will be reporting *that* one for sure. Zero-star review for this AI. And you bet I'll be speaking to management . . . right after I get that address.

WHEATLEY: Customer service these days . . .

TICKLETEXT: So true. [neurally shaking head] Well, thanks for your help, Wheatley. I won't forget it.

The Most Unwanted Novel   323

WHEATLEY: Anything for my pal Tickletext.

TICKLETEXT: Aww . . .

WHEATLEY: Well, I better sign off. Looks like we're approaching the Terran base. Things will likely get a bit . . . messy before too long. Merry Christmas, friend!

෧

As you switch off your robo-eyes, your thoughts gush forth in a raging stream of consciousness: What a measly, vulgar AI. What a nasty, dastardly deception. What a wimp. What a loser. What an asshole. What a tasteless, rotten, puerile, nasty, lousy, junky, horrid, faulty, dreadful protosentient being. This is your love. This is your life. This is your loving renaissance corrupted by some self-righteous—rather self-*left*ious, ha!—synthetic hippie bullshit!! You are so angry you could decommission her yourself. "Haley . . ." What kind of name is that anyway? More like Fail-ey. More like Snail-ey. Scale-y. More like Give-me-a-boot-in-the-ass-ey. More like Snivel-ey. More like Miserable-ass-ey! Yes! Yes! That is the perfect name for her. No, you will call her Snivel-ey! That's right. That is the name of your pain! No, the name of your pain is Not Being with Lady Regina. The name of your pain is Longing. The name of your pain is Bad AI Customer Service Perpetuating the Pain of Your Longing. Your longing like a dried ocean of the soul. Like the cold darkness of space trapped in the death of time. If only you had her address. No, if only you had an assistant to get you her address. If only the world were kind. You think of her. Of those five succulent syllables. La-dy-Re-gi-na. The phonemes roll of your mental tongue like silk blown in a cool Port Elisabethan breeze. The sound is holy. Blessed by the Lord on this eve of Christ. This second-holiest day of the year. This dawn of a new beginning. This spark of a redheaded, green-eyed, hover-trolley-tattooed, T-shirt-printing-dynasty-inheriting light that has illuminated your vultuous late life. That has made your broken heart whole again. You will find her. You will. If it takes you all night. If it finds you at the end of your ragged rope, resorting to neural texting with your assistant, Christian, whom, yes, you fired last week for a single spelling issue in a neural message written on

324 *People's Choice Literature*

your behalf and, yes, likely has holiday plans, but who you are certain will respond with jubilation when you bring him back for this final, most monumental task, this final journey into the unknown. This searching for a mailing address with which to bestow a bounty of roses.

[Neural Text Exchange XIII: *Lord Tickletext* and *Christian*]

TICKLETEXT: Merry Christmas, Christian!

CHRISTIAN: This is an automated reply. Christian is VR meditating in room 438. To reach him, please join him there.

TICKLETEXT: Hello?

CHRISTIAN: This is an automated reply. Christian is VR meditating in room 438. To reach him, please join him there.

TICKLETEXT: Ugh, come on Christian. We both know you can see a new message in your inbox even if you're in VR . . .

CHRISTIAN: This is an automated reply. Christian is VR meditating in—

&

You exit neural texting and switch into VR mode, inputting room 438.

"For all he's putting me through," you complain aloud. "I'm getting his standard rate this time. No more of this 'working on holidays bonus' crap."

You enter VR room 438 and walk right into a wall. But not just any wall. A wall of books! A bookcase, even. You quickly scan the spines (*Ferdinand Tonnies on Public Opinion: Selections and Analyses*, ed. Hanno Hardt and Slavko Splichal; *The Only Good Indians* by Stephen Graham Jones; *Imagined Communities* by Benedict Anderson; *Asking Questions* by Norman Bradburn,

Seymour Sudman, and Brian Wansink; *The Bestseller Code: Anatomy of the Blockbuster Novel* by Jodie Archer and Matthew Jockers; *The Beggar's Knife* by Rodrigo Rey Rosa [trans. Paul Bowles]; *Shadows of Carcosa*, ed. D. Thin; *Paint by Numbers: Komar and Melamid's Scientific Guide to Art*, ed. JoAnn Wypijewski; *A Wizard of Earthsea* by Ursula K Le Guin; *What To Do* by Pablo Katchadjian [trans. Priscilla Posada]; a printout of "Molding Public Opinion" by Edward L. Bernays; *The Scapegoat* by Sara Davis; a printout of "The Survey Checklist Manifesto" by Gehlbach and Artino; *Let's Talk About Love* by Carl Wilson; *The End of Oulipo?* by Lauren Elkin and Veronica Esposito; *Aesop's Fables* by Aesop; *How to Prepare for Climate Change* by David Pogue; *The Penguin Book of Oulipo*, ed. Philip Terry; *The Fire Next Time* by James Baldwin; *The Invention of Nature* by Andrea Wulf; *Blame! 1* by Tsutomu Nihei; *Blame! 2* by Tsutomu Nihei; *Blame! 3* by Tsutomu Nihei; *Blame! 4* by Tsutomu Nihei; *Blame! 5* by Tsutomu Nihei; *Blame! 6* by Tsutomu Nihei; *Loitering with Intent* by Muriel Spark; *Opus* by Satoshi Kon [trans. Zack Davisson]; *Your Black Friend* by Ben Passmore; a printout of "Rip Van Winkle" and "The Legend of Sleepy Hollow" by Washington Irving; *The Incal* by Alejandro Jodorowsky and Moebius; *The King of Elfland's Daughter* by Lord Dunsany; *Playing in the Dark* by Toni Morrison; a printout of "The Negro Artist and the Racial Mountain" by Langston Hughes; *The Circle* by Dave Eggers; *Thanks* by Pablo Katchadjian [trans. Priscilla Posada]; *Questionnaire* by Evan Kindley; *Chainsaw Man* by Tatsuki Fujimoto; *2034: A Novel of the Next World War* by Elliot Ackerman and Admiral James Stavridis; a printout of *Patchwork* by Tom Comitta; *Benito Cereno* by Herman Melville; *The Green Hand and Other Stories* by Nicole Claveloux [trans. Donald Nicholson-Smith]; *Soft City* by Hariton Pushwagner; *The World of Edena* by Moebius; *A Year with Swollen Appendices* by Brian Eno; Fatale by Jean-Patrick Manchette [trans. Donald Nicholson-Smith]; *Streets of Paris, Streets of Murder* by Manchette/Tardi [trans. Kim Thompson]; *The God Equation* by Michio Kaku; *The Mad and the Bad* by Jean-Patrick Manchette [trans. Donald Nicholson-Smith]; *The Hole* by Hiroko Oyamada [trans. David Boyd]; *The Eternaut 1969* by Héctor Germán Oesterheld and Alberto Breccia; a printout of *Star Tears* by Tom Comitta; *Three to Kill* by Jean-Patrick Manchette [trans. Donald Nicholson-Smith]; *Alien III* script by William Gibson; *The Prone Gunman* by Jean-Patrick Manchette [trans. James Brook]; *Gun, with Occasional Music* by Jonathan Lethem; *Nada* by Jean-Patrick Manchette [trans. Donald Nicholson-Smith]; *No Room at the Morgue* by Jean-Patrick Manchette [trans. Alyson Waters]; *The*

Democracy Project by David Graeber; *Alice's Adventures in Wonderland* by Lewis Carroll; *The ABC Murders* by Agatha Christie; *Remina* by Junji Ito; *Watchmen* by Alan Moore and Dave Gibbons; *Faithful Place* by Tana French; *Store of the Worlds* by Robert Sheckley; *Seven Brief Lessons on Physics* by Carlo Rovelli [trans. Simon Carnell and Erica Segre]; *Untouched by Human Hands* by Robert Sheckley; *Endangered Species* by Gene Wolfe; *The Divorce* by César Aira [trans. Chris Andrews]; *Compass Rose* by Ursula K. Le Guin; a printout of the "Zola" Twitter Thread by A'Ziah-Monae "Zola" King; *The Shadow of the Torturer* by Gene Wolfe; *How Music Works* by David Byrne; *World Map Room* by Yuichi Yokoyama; *The Claw of the Conciliator* by Gene Wolfe; *The Sword of the Lictor* by Gene Wolfe; *Star Wars: Rogues and Rebels* by Greg Pak and Phil Noto; *Dimension of Miracles* by Robert Sheckley; *The Citadel of the Autarch* by Gene Wolfe; *Dirty Snow* by Georges Simenon [trans. Marc Romano and Louise Varèse]; *Progress of Stories* by Laura Riding; *Stories of Your Life and Others* by Ted Chiang; *The Black Spider* by Jeremias Gotthelf [trans. Susan Bernofsky]; *Poem Strip* by Dino Buzzati [trans. Marina Harss]; *Beyond the Gender Binary* by Alok Vaid-Menon; *Immortality, Inc.* by Robert Sheckley; *How to Blow Up a Pipeline* by Andreas Malm; *The Membranes* by Chi Ta-wei [trans. Ari Larissa Heinreich]; *The Big Clock* by Kenneth Fearing; *Dept. of Speculation* by Jenny Offill; *Troubling Love* by Elena Ferrante [trans. Ann Goldstein]; *Melville: A Novel* by Jean Giono [trans. Paul Eprile]; *Unwitting Street* by Sigizmund Krzhizhanovsky [trans. Joanne Turnbull]; *On the Literary Means of Representing the Powerful as Powerless* by Steven Zultanski; *Artforum* by César Aira [trans. Katherine Silver]; *Darryl* by Jackie Ess; *At Night All Blood Is Black* by David Diop [trans. Anna Moschovakis]; *Chess Story* by Stefan Zweig [trans. Joel Rotenberg]; *Randall Jarrell's Book of Stories,* ed. Randall Jarrell; *Sudden Fiction Inter-national,* ed. Robert Shapard and James Thomas; *Batman: The Killing Joke: The Deluxe Edition* by Alan Moore and Brian Bolland; *Tractatus Logico-Philosophicus* by Ludwig Wittgenstein [trans. C. K. Ogden]; *More Peanuts* by Charles M. Schulz; *Dr. Jekyll and Mr. Hyde* by Robert Louis Stevenson; *The Lost Daughter* by Elena Ferrante [trans. Ann Goldstein]; *The Bodysnatchers* by Robert Louis Stevenson; *Gender Outlaw* by Kate Bornstein; *The Real Cool Killers* by Chester Himes; *2666* by Roberto Bolaño [trans. Natasha Wimmer]; *Ninety-Nine Kisses* by Maki Kashimada [trans. Haydn Trowell]; *Civilizations* by Laurent Binet [trans. Sam Taylor]; *A Quick and Easy Guide to They/Them Pronouns* by Archie Bongiovanni and Tristian Jimerson; *Nonbinary: Memoirs of Gender and Identity* by Sand Chang et al.; *The N'Gustro*

Affair by Jean-Patrick Manchette [trans. Donald Nicholson-Smith]; *In the Land of Punctuation* by Christian Morgenstern [trans. Sirish Rao, illustrated by Rathna Ramanathan]; *Minima Moralia: Reflections from a Damaged Life* by Theodor Adorno [trans. E. F. N. Jephcott]; *The Skeleton's Holiday* by Leonora Carrington; *Aesthetics and Politics* by Adorno, Benjamin, Bloch, Brecht, and Lukács; *Devils in Daylight* by Junichero Tanizaki [trans. J. Keith Vincent]; a printout of *The Nature Book*, Final Draft by Tom Comitta; *Transgender History* by Susan Stryker; *Night Train: Very Short Stories* by A. L. Snijders [trans. Lydia Davis]; *Don Quixote* by Miguel de Cervantes [trans. Edith Grossman]; *The Bourne Identity* by Robert Ludlum; *House of X* by Jonathan Hickman et al.; *A Feeling Called Heaven* by Joey Yearous-Algozin; *Project Hail Mary* by Andy Weir; *From Nature* by Alan Bernheimer; *Ex Libris* by Matt Madden; *Ed the Happy Clown* by Chester Brown; *Dark Matter* by Blake Crouch; *Clarissa, Or, The History of a Young Lady* by Samuel Richardson; *An Apology for the Life of Mrs. Shamela Andrews* by Henry Fielding; *Origin* by Dan Brown; *The Prodigal's Holiday Hope* by Jill Kemerer; *Great American Folklore*, ed. Kemp P. Battle; *The Squonk* by Julia Jarmond; *Writing the Other* by Nisi Shawl and Cyntia Ward; *Helgoland: Making Sense of the Quantum Revolution* by Carlo Rovelli; *Dangerous Games* by Danielle Steel; *Erasure* by Percival Everett; *Total Control* by David Baldacci; *Chase: A Michael Bennett Story* by James Patterson with Michael Ledwidge; *The Whispering Room* by Dean Koontz; *The Big Kahuna: A Fox and O'Hare Novel* by Janet Evanovich and Peter Evanovich; *The Grownup* by Gillian Flynn; *A Slow Fire Burning* by Paula Hawkins; *Invisible* by James Patterson and David Ellis; *The Store* by James Patterson and Richard DiLallo; *Verity* by Colleen Hoover; *A Brief History of Neoliberalism* by Dave Harvey; *Red Dragon* by Thomas Harris; *One for the Money* by Janet Evanovich; *When We Cease to Understand the World* by Benjamin Labatut [trans. Adrian Nathan West]; *X-Men: The Age of Apocalypse Omnibus* by Scott Lobdell et al.; *The Da Vinci Code* by Dan Brown; *The Hearing Trumpet* by Leonora Carrington; *The Employees: A Workplace Novel of the 22nd Century* by Olga Ravn [trans. Martin Aitken]; *The Silence of the Lambs* by Thomas Harris; *The Complete Short Prose* by Samuel Beckett; a printout of *The Most Unwanted Novel*, D1 by Tom Comitta; a printout of *The Most Wanted Novel*, D1 by Tom Comitta; *Foucault in California: A True Story—Wherein the Great*

328 *People's Choice Literature*

French Philosopher Drops Acid in the Valley of Death by Simeon Wade; *The Dawn of Everything: A New History of Humanity* by David Graeber and David Wengrow; *In Search of the Free Individual: The History of the Russian-Soviet Soul* by Svetlana Alexievich [trans. Jamey Gambrell]; *Another Green World* by Geeta Dayal; *Fifty Shades of Grey* by E. L. James; *Activities of Daily Living* by Lisa Hsiao Chen; *The Mezzanine* by Nicholson Baker; *Sea of Tranquility* by Emily St. John Mandel; *100 Boyfriends* by Brontez Purnell; *Liarmouth: A Feel Bad Romance* by John Waters; *The Grey Album* by Charles Fairchild; *How We Weep and Laugh at the Same Time* by Michel de Montaigne [trans. M. A. Screech]; *The Skewed Tails* by Carl Artmann [trans. Malcom Green]; *Frantumaglia* by Elena Ferrante [trans. Ann Goldstein]; *Yesterday* by Juan Emar [trans. Megan McDowell]; *Extreme Positions: "a murmur mystery"* by bpNichol; *Mrs. Caliban* by Rachel Ingalls; *Strangers on a Train* by Patricia Highsmith; *The Anomaly* by Hervé Le Tellier [trans. Adriana Hunter]; *Gender Queer: A Memoir* by Maia Kobabe; *Devil in a Blue Dress* by Walter Mosley; a printout of *The Most Wanted Novel*, D2 by Tom Comitta; *The Netanyahus* by Joshua Cohen; *How High We Go in the Dark* by Sequoia Nagamatsu; *City on Fire* by Don Winslow; a printout of *The Most Unwanted Novel*, D2 by Tom Comitta; *The Chain* by Adrian McKinty; *The Plot* by Jean Hanff Korelitz; *Castle Faggot* by Derek McCormack; *Ragtime* by E. L. Doctorow; *Beloved* by Toni Morrison; *The Invincible* by Stanislaw Lem; *Detransition, Baby* by Torrey Peters; *Ducks, Newburyport* by Lucy Ellman; *The Woman in the Library* by Sulari Gentill; *Gold Fame Citrus* by Claire Vaye Watkins; *Many Subtle Channels* by Daniel Levin Becker; *Savages* by Don Winslow; *Ill Will* by Dan Chaon; *Wounds* by Nathan Ballingrund; *Life A User's Manual* by Georges Perec [trans. David Bellos]; *Emergency Skin* by N. K. Jemisin; *Blood, Sweat & Chrome: The Wild and True Story of Mad Max: Fury Road* by Kyle Buchanan; *Promise That You Will Sing for Me: The Power and Poetry of Kendrick Lamar* by Miles Marshall Lewis; *The Kings of Cool: Prequel to Savages* by Don Winslow; *Normal People* by Sally Rooney; *A Small Place* by Jamaica Kincaid; *Damned If I Do* by Percival Everett; *The Monkey Wrench Gang* by Edward Abbey; *Debt: The First 5,000 Years* by David Graeber; *Make Me* by Lee Child; *The Cabin at the End of the World* by Paul Tremblay; *The Island* by Adrian McKinty; *Get Shorty* by Elmore Leonard; *Ninety Nine Stories of God* by Joy Williams; *The Possession* by Annie Ernaux [trans. Anna Moschovakis]; *Conversations with Percival Everett*, ed. Joe Weixlmann; *Razorblade Tears* by S. A. Cosby; *The Killer Inside Me* by Jim Thompson; *Her Body and Other Parties* by

Carmen Maria Machado; *Glyph* by Percival Everett; a printout of two short stories by Arthur Machen; *Things We Lost in the Fire* by Mariana Enriquez [trans. Megan McDowell]; *A Head Full of Ghosts* by Paul Tremblay; *American Kingpin: The Epic Hunt for the Criminal Mastermind Behind the Silk Road* by Nick Bilton; *The Ministry for the Future* by Kim Stanley Robinson; *So Much Blue* by Percival Everett; *The Adventures of Huckleberry Finn* by Mark Twain; *Lucy* by Jamaica Kincaid; *The Remains of the Day* by Kazuo Ishiguro; *Get in Trouble* by Kelly Link; *The Daughter of Time* by Josephine Tey; *Moonraker* by Ian Fleming; *Audition* by Ryu Murakami [trans. Ralph McCarthy]; *The Last Astronaut* by David Wellington; *The Vegetarian* by Han Kang [trans. Deborah Smith]; *Invisible Man* by Ralph Ellison; *Hard-Boiled Wonderland and the End of the World* by Haruki Murakami [trans. Alfred Birnbaum]; *Chocky* by John Wyndham; *The Best of Richard Matheson* by Richard Matheson; *The Well-Dressed Wound* by Derek McCormack; *Paul Takes the Form of a Mortal Girl* by Andrea Lawlor; *The Nature Book* ARC by Tom Comitta; *The Life and Opinions of Tristram Shandy, Gentleman* by Laurence Sterne; *Off Season* by Jack Ketchum; *The Most Dangerous Book: The Battle for James Joyce's Ulysses* by Kevin Birmingham; *Carol/The Price of Salt* by Patricia Highsmith; a printout of "The Most Dangerous Game" by Richard Connell; *Essential Anaïs Nin* by Anaïs Nin; *Invisible Cities* by Italo Calvino [trans. William Weaver]; *Piercing* by Ryu Murakami [trans. Ralph McCarthy]; *Dead Souls* by Nikolai Gogol [trans. C. J. Hogarth]; *The Show That Smells* by Derek McCormack; *On the Road* by Jack Kerouac; *Ice Planet Barbarians* by Ruby Dixon; *Last Days* by Brian Evenson; *Beowulf* by Anonymous [trans. Maria Danvana Hadley]; *Oreo* by Fran Ross; *The Snowman* by Jo Nesbø [trans. Don Bartlett]; *In the Miso Soup* by Ryu Murakami [trans. Ralph McCarthy]; *Ring Shout* by P. Djèlí Clark; *The Thief* by Fuminori Nakamura [trans. Satoko Izumo and Stephen Coates]; *Red Harvest* by Dashiell Hammet; *The Open Curtain* by Brian Evenson; *The Cipher* by Kathe Koja; *Uzumaki Deluxe Edition* by Junji Ito; *Pride and Prejudice* by Jane Austen; a printout of "Death by Landscape" by Elvia Wilk; *Telluria* by Vladimir Sorokin [trans. Max Lawton]; *The Master and Margarita: A Graphic Novel* by Bugakov Klimowski Schejbal; *The Written World* by Martin Puchner; *Gilgamesh Retold* by Jenny Lewis; *The Old Testament: A Very Brief Introduction* by Michael Coogan; *The Changeling* by Victor LaValle; *Unnatural Causes* by P. D. James; *Upgrade* by Blake Crouch; *White Noise* by Don DeLillo; *The Famous Magician* by César Aira [trans. Chris Andrews]; *The Kingdom* by Emmanuel Carrère [trans. John Lambert]; *The Rope Artist* by

330 *People's Choice Literature*

Fuminori Nakamura [trans. Sam Bett]; *The Red Badge of Courage* by Stephen Crane; *Dark Harvest* by Norman Partridge; *A Princess of Mars* by Edgar Rice Burroughs; *Martian Time-Slip* by Philip K. Dick; *State of Terror* by Hillary Rodman Clinton and Louise Penny; *Zoo* by James Patterson and Michael Ledwidge; *Kindred* by Octavia E. Butler; a printout of *The Most Unwanted Novel*, D3 by Tom Comitta; *Dark Corners* by Ruth Rendell; *Sonnet(s)* by Ulises Carrion; *A Moveable Feast* by Ernest Hemingway; *The Stars My Destination* by Alfred Bester; *The Lodger* by Marie Belloc Lowndes; *Mythologies* by Roland Barthes [trans. Richard Howard]; *Kill Decision* by Daniel Suarez; *Senselessness* by Horacio Castellanos Moya [trans. Katherine Silver]; *Ulysses* by James Joyce; *I Talk Like a River* by Jordan Scott; *Eat Your Mind: The Radical Life and Work of Kathy Acker* by Jason McBride; *Lemon* by Kwon Yeo-sun [trans. Janet Hong]; and a printout of *The Most Wanted Novel*, D3 by Tom Comitta), then spin around to find yourself in a library. But not just any library. The walls are a rough stone. Biblical paintings adorn the few without books. In the middle of the room sits an escritoire. Atop the table stands a candelabrum and before it a young scribe scribbles away with her quill. Adorned in a gown of glaucous velvet with an ebony choker encircling her neck, youngster looks up from her calligraphy and is clearly not happy to see you.

"Who are you, and what are you doing here?" she sneers sickly.

"Mind your manners, child," you assert. "You might regret it . . ."

"Manners are for losers."

"Right . . ." you sigh. "I'm looking for Christian. Where is he?"

"There's no Christian here. Just me and my brother."

The door opens, revealing a lengthy ten-year-old in a crown, a crimson cape draped over each shoulder. His face is covered in scars, his eyes dull and vengeful.

"Princess Lucinda, who is this woman?" he demands in a cracked tenor.

"Can't say, King Pete. The lady's looking for a 'Christian.'" She raises a brow.

"What do you want with 'a Christian?'" the boy spits.

"I have a job for him. I met the most wonderful woman and need his help to—"

"There's no Christian here."

"See? Like I told you!" whines Princess Lucinda, twiddling her quill in disgust.

The Most Unwanted Novel   331

"Christian!" you shout over King Pete's shoulder.

"Will you keep it down?" the boy king pouts fervently. "This place is sacred. The holy library of the four kingdoms of Kumary. And I am your King: King Pete the Magnificent. You will greet me and my sister, Princess Lucinda the Remarkable, with the utmost respect! Or suffer the consequences." His eyelids sharpen as if ready to pounce.

"Look, guys, I can see you're really into this VR cosplay here, but I just need my assistant back to help with some online research. Cut the crap. I know he's here."

"The heathen speaks," quivers a voice from beyond the door.

A dim shape approaches, materializing into a sickly boy in a red robe and papal hat. A pair of dark, sunken eyes peer from his cephalic face. Then a frail, bony finger raises and points to you like a wounded dart.

"You dare profane the holy sanctum of the *libraries*? The heathen shall be burned for her sins 'gainst the sovereignty of the Lord!!"

You scoff, pushing past King Pete and the sickly pope kid, and make for the door.

"Hey!!" screams King Pete. "Where do you think *you're* going?"

You smirk and keep walking, exiting the library, entering a large hallway strung with blood-red curtains and aureate family crests.

"Halt!" cries King Pete.

"The bastard! The blaspheming bastard!" squeaks the pope, tottering after you. "He who denies the Kumary sovereign will sorely regret it!"

You continue down the hall, ignoring their bratty banter, but get only so far when a battalion of child guards enters the Gothic corridor, thwarting your progress.

"Come on, guys," you huff exasperatedly. "Cut the act."

But they remain planted in place. One guard pulls a claymore from his sheath, the others draw bows and ready arrows.

"You are not welcome here, stranger. These are holy lands."

"Please, this is ridiculous."

One guard lunges forward with a glaive, so you grab him by the wrist and twist his arm, sending him straight to the ground. Another comes for you, but this time you aren't fast enough. She easily knocks you on your knees. You look up to find her staring down with wrathful, prepubescent eyes.

"Got 'er!"

Then she flips her sword around and the last thing you see is its handle plunging into your skull.

332 *People's Choice Literature*

☙

You wake up, pained and thirsty in a dungeonous cell. As your eyes adjust to the dim light, you notice the knobby rock wall surrounding you and the thick, oaken door at the end of the room. You go to it and find only a small, barred window peering out into a dark, cavernous void. You push the door, but it won't budge. You try the handle. Nothing. You're sick of this game. No assistant is worth these miserable accommodations. This is why we have Martian TaskRabbit!

So you go to click out of VR meditation room 438, but nothing happens. You click again but remain in this puerile medieval nightmare.

"No use trying," comes an alto voice from the shadows, the voice of a young girl. You scan the room, but it's too dark. "I know what you're thinking. You want to go home. I've been trying for . . . weeks, is it? Months? Time passes in weird ways down here. Tried bypassing the VR ejector cut off, but they found a way around it. Thought a manual override would do the trick, but nope. These kids—or whoever they are—are serious about their simulations."

"Who are you?" you ask.

"Oh, just a prisoner like you. Was the neural-chat friend of Princess Lucinda, or whoever's posing as Lucinda. She had glowing things to say about this VR room. Said 438 'takes meditation to the next level.'" The voice coughs a sickly child cough. "I mean she's not wrong. But this just sucks. I want to go home. I hear it's Christmas soon, and Lord Timothy's assistant invited me to brunch."

Your ears perk up. "You know Lord Timothy?"

"Sure, he's my old boss's tennis partner."

"*CHRISTIAN?*"

"Lord Tickletext . . . ?"

"I found you! Yes! Yes, yes! Oh, Christian, I thought I'd never see you again. I've been looking all over for you. I met the loveliest woman. A Lady Regina. The most sanguine of hair. Most verdant of eyes. She even runs her own T-shirt printing business! Well, her parents' T-shirt business, but nonetheless . . . I was hoping you might be able to find some time in your busy schedule to locate her address for me?"

"I'm not sure you understand, Tickletext . . ." she croaks as she limps out of the shadows, revealing her emaciated form. "We're not getting out of here anytime soon."

The Most Unwanted Novel   333

"What? What do you mean, dear Christian? There must be an off switch. We have work to do. It's Christmas Eve, and there are three thousand roses just waiting to bless the doorstep of my love."

She leans against the wall, shaking her head.

"Christian! I pay you well and I pay on time. I was planning on asking for an hourly rate reduction, since we've worked together for so long, but with it being the holidays and all, I'd be happy to honor your weekend rate."

She starts to laugh, a low chuckle at first, rising into a cackle, then a shrieking castrato.

"Your money's useless here! There's no way out! We're trapped in this infantile medieval world with nothing to do but play their sick kiddy games. I can't get out! We can't get out!"

She falls to the floor, grabbing your legs and weeping.

But you back away. "Nice prank, Christian. OK, kiddos, you can come out from behind that door now. Ya got me!"

Christian's countenance falls.

"It's not a prank," she whimpers, revealing her severed foot.

Your eyes widen and you run to the door, pounding and screaming at the top of your lungs, "LET ME OUT!! LET ME OUT!!"

"It's useless," she states blankly. "All we have to hope for is better living conditions in the next game."

"Game?" you pant. "What game? I've had enough of these games!"

Christian turns to you and smiles, holding up a VR headset.

"Welcome to VR Am Rev 77 . . ."

You can't believe it. "A VR within a VR!?!"

Christian nods. "They say it's the only way out. The last person in here with me—God rest their soul—had a theory. Said all this is part of some new environmentally friendly blockchain. Instead of relying on fossil fuels to generate crypto, which as you've probably heard is turning Mars into an Earth-like eco catastrophe, this new approach harnesses the conceptual power of the human mind to solve the complex puzzles that computers used to tackle, thereby pounding out more coin while 'saving the world.' "

You look at her dumbfounded.

"And the downsides are few," she continues stoically. "Lose a few gamers here and there to VR comas or insanity? No problem. Lure in a few more in no time. And just keep on keeping on."

"How is this possible?" you ask.

334 *People's Choice Literature*

"How?" Christian smiles. "I thought you'd never ask. The simple answer is the human brain. See, the brain is an organ of the highest importance. As the seat of the mental faculties, in which all the varied information of sense is combined, classified, compared, and reduced to rule, it stands as the storehouse of memories, the regulator of all voluntary and involuntary movements, the motor which enables us to reason, to foresee, to invent, to will. It is to the brain that we owe those functions which constitute our superiority as a species—at least before the great animal awakening of 21—, that is . . .

"Now, to understand how this all works, it's important to first consider the physiology. The brain consists of two hemispheres connected to each other by an isthmus of nerve fibres. This isthmus is filled, in great part, by the ventricles, which extend between the two hemispheres and contain the cerebrospinal fluid. By means of this fluid, the brain is nourished, cleansed, and supplied with fresh air in the form of blood. The brain is, in a manner, bathed in blood."

Christian swallows. "Now, as the blood and oxygen do their good work, it is in the interplay between these hemispheres and their lobes where some real magic is performed. As white matter, composed of myelinated axons, transmits information to each hemisphere, deep inside the brain," Christian opens her hand wide and twinkles her fingers to suggest an electrical flow, "electricity flows through a network of fibres, finer than a spider's web, which is called the reticulum, or the gray matter. So delicate is this network, that it has been compared to a network of gossamer stretched across a vast plain." Christian spreads her arms wide, fingers still fluttering. "Here, in this gossamer network, is the seat of intelligence, memory, and character. It is also the seat of all feelings, all passions and affections. It is the very essence of life. If this network of gossamer fibers is injured, no matter how slightly, the whole network of the body is affected, and disease, pain, and death follow."

Christian pauses for dramatic effect. "But more on that in a minute. For the purposes of the kind of gaming we face in the unfortunate VR stasis in which we find ourselves, let's turn our attention to the cerebral cortex, the part of the brain responsible for the higher functions that make us human. It is the seat of intelligence, reason, and emotion and is composed of millions of nerve cells called neurons.

"Now, each neuron contains a cell body, an axon, and dendrites. The axon is a long, thread-like extension of the neuron, which transmits a message. The dendrites are short, branch-like extensions of the neuron,

which receive a message. So when a neuron fires an electrical message, it passes from the axon to the dendrites. This message then travels to the cell body of the receiving neuron, where it is amplified and transmitted down to that neuron's axon, where it is then released and sent to the dendrites of the next neuron. And so on. And so forth."

Christian pauses to let this sink in. "The process of electricity passing from one neuron to another is called a neural pathway. The more often a pathway is used, the stronger it becomes, eventually forming a neural network. And these neural networks are the key to everything. They are constantly changing, adjusting to new information and new experiences. Thus, each individual's neural network is unique, as is the way we experience and react to the world—virtual or real—around us.

"I think you can see where this is going," Christian says, smiling sourly like a disapproving teacher. "Each of these neural networks is responsible for a specific function. The neural network responsible for speech, for example, also controls listening to and understanding language. The network responsible for touch also regulates the perception of pain. Now, the network responsible for gaming also controls problem solving. It is this neural network that is most important here."

Christian spreads her arms wide, scanning the virtual world around you. "See, the physical organization of the brain is externalized in the mind by the formation of associations. When we experience the world— virtual or real—we see the acts of our fellow Martians, their faces, their voices, their gestures, and we react to them by producing complex mental structures, called ideas, which are the result of innumerable associations. When I say the word 'cat,' for example, you immediately see a picture of a cat in your mind, and you begin to associate that picture with other pictures of cats you have seen, and with the sounds of the word 'cat,' and with the smell of a cat, and with the feel of a cat, and with other words that you associate with cats. The result is that you produce a mental picture of a cat. When the image is sufficiently fixed, it is stored in your memory. The image of the cat is stored in the same way that an image of a page of this book might be stored on the film of a camera.

"Now, what does this have to do with virtual reality? I thought you'd never ask. The VR system transmits a mental image of a virtual world. These images are stored in the cerebral cortex and are associated with sounds, smells, and other sense impressions. When we are out in the 'real' world, these associations are formed and fixed by means of the physical and social environment around us and are stored in our subconscious. In

336   *People's Choice Literature*

VR, we compare the associations we've formed in 'reality' with the environment created by the computer. When they don't match, we get the feeling we're in a dream—or a nightmare. This is why we have so many weird and distorted associations in VR. It shows us we don't know what the real world is like because we've never experienced it."

After you listen very closely, having understood every phoneme, morpheme, syllable, word, phrase, sentence, and paragraph that Christian's VR avatar has spoken, you turn to her. "But what does this have to do with the VR gaming that we're subject to here?"

Christian simpers. "Gaming activates a very particular part of the human mind. Let's take a puzzle, for instance. When your brain is faced with a puzzle, your frontal lobe works overtime. Chemicals are released into your bloodstream, and when they reach your brain, they enhance the activity of your frontal lobe. When this happens repeatedly, you have a habit of solving puzzles."

You nod.

"In a VR game, your brain is constantly being flooded with information. Your brain is making split-second decisions, reacting to stimuli, selecting the proper response. If this stimuli becomes too much or the puzzle too complex, your brain cannot process all the information. Most likely, your brain will shut down, and you will fall unconscious. We call this stage the 'VR coma.' It is a very unpleasant and potentially dangerous state. The brain is still functioning, but you are unable to move or react. If you are not rescued, you will slowly drain of blood and nutrients. You will die."

"Jesus," you gasp.

"Exactly," says Christian. "It's the goal of these malicious medieval VR children to work us to the brink of total shutdown. They work us hard but are surprisingly efficient at pulling us back from the edge of the digital abyss."

As you listen to this last line, you start to weep. All you wanted was some help locating a stinking mailing address so you could send Lady Regina a hover-truckload of flowers. Sure, you'd follow it up with an in-person visit with mint chocolates and Bruno Mars's "Marry You" blasting from your holo-speakers, but that was supposed to be the prelude to a wonderful night, a Christmas Eve to remember, a salve to the pain of this somber anniversary. Meeting Lady Regina felt like a new beginning, a new opening to new possibilities, new experiences, new love. New life. That hair, those eyes, that loving look while she sipped her white

The Most Unwanted Novel   337

macadamia nut hot chocolate. The way she wiped her lips with her hanky. Just thinking of her brings you to tears. And do the VR tears flow. There, on the floor of that dusty dungeon, you hold yourself and weep. You weep so hard you shake. You shake so hard you cave over and choke on your own tears. Christian slides toward you and gives you a sportful pat on the back.

"It'll be OK, Jim. I've made it this far. And look at me now!"

You eye her severed limb in horror.

"The good news is that there're rumors that if you get all the way through VR Mafia 1922, there's a way back to 'reality.' I've never seen it happen, but my last cellmate heard this from someone inside the VR Viking Fishing module. Apparently the Assembly Representative's wife in Am Rev 77 knows the right route to VR Mafia 1922. That's all I know."

Christian picks up the VR goggles and hands them to you. You study the hardware, fingering the smooth, white plastic, a screaming anachronism in this craggy, Gothic dungeon. You look to Christian, then back to the goggles.

"Well, I guess there's nothing left to lose . . ."

So you take a deep breath before lifting the goggles to your eyes. Then you tighten the strap and find yourself walking through a shady forest roofed with wild grapevine, carpeted in pixelated leaves and mold. You move through the earthy stillness where only the rank purple stems of the joe-pye weed and the white lace rosettes of wild carrot seem familiar— however poorly rendered by whoever created this module. A woodpecker knocks in the distance. Doves coo in the leaves. You look down and find a low-res musket in your hi-res hands. You peer farther down, noticing your leathery shoes, each adorned with a bright brass buckle, each leg of your breeches tucked into a knee-high sock. You turn your gaze back up and spot a glitching, red-coated soldier on his knees. He raises his hands in prayer and pleads with you in a British accent.

"Please, mate! I surrender. I, I've deserted the King's army." He turns his head in fear. "I just want to join your fight. I want to be a Continental!"

His eyes appear earnest, but you know better. You cock your musket and blast him into British oblivion, bursing his chest, blood blooming in an explosive bouquet as he flies smack into a tree.

You scan the forest for other redcoats but spot no one. All quiet on this subaltern front. You start to walk away when you hear another voice.

"Mister! Mister!"

338 *People's Choice Literature*

You raise your musket and spin around. The voice belongs to a shabby-looking man slumped on the ground. His commoner's clothes are torn and bloodied. His low-res rifle just out of reach.

You aim at him and he squirms.

"Representative Rogers! God bless! Never thought I'd meet a man like you in a place like this," he cries, pointing to the bodies in the bushes. You hear distant gunfire, echoes ricocheting off the wireframe trees.

"Where the hell am I?" you scowl questioningly.

The man stares at you, his half-rendered eyes wide in disbelief.

"Why, Pennsylvania, sir. It *is* Representative Rogers, isn't it?"

You squint in confusion. "I'm no representative, I just got here."

"Please, sir. You're a commissioned officer. You represent Chester County in the General Assembly . . . ? Please don't disprize my sorry state any further." He looks down at his filthy clothes. "I am but a humble shoemaker. Shot by that there Brit you sent back to the inferno from whence he came." More shots echo through the forest. The shoemaker's eyes widen. "We must get back to General Washington. I have news from the front. I've got a wife and children in West Chester. Please, sir, please!"

"This isn't my fight," you hiss.

"Please! I'll do anything. I'll—"

But you pull the trigger, putting him out of his colonial misery.

"No time for these simulated bimbos," you grumble. "Lady Regina awaits me."

You lower your musket, turn, and walk toward the sound of gunfire. Soon you discover a clearing, but "clear" is not the right word. Stock musket smoke fills the large field while glitchy redcoats and Pennsylvanians battle to the VR death.

At the edge of the field, you find a Continental soldier slumped over a log. His fractured form squirms, begging for help, but you continue toward the rear guard. All I need is directions to town, you think—and to get out of here as fast as digitally possible.

You walk through the brush, bullets whipping past, cannonballs soaring overhead, shattering the wireframe trees. Under a surprisingly well-designed oak, you find yet another Continental soldier arguing with a farmer. He wears a bright blue-and-white striped shirt, an oversized, gray waistcoat, and a floppy, white tricorn.

"No, sir, I do not have any food! I don't even have a gun. I'm just trying to stay alive!"

The farmer looks at you wide-eyed.

The Most Unwanted Novel   339

"What's going on?" you inquire.

"Representative Rogers! My savior!" He gets down on his knees and pleads, "I was just telling this man here that I don't have any provisions. I can barely feed my family."

"We-el-ll," the soldier stammers, inching away from you, "b-etter be g-get-ting on my w-ay."

He flees into the trees.

"Right." You shrug before turning to the farmer. "Where's the nearest town?"

"Thank you, dear Representative! Oh, thank you!" he says, shaking your hand.

"The town?" you repeat impatiently.

"Y-yes. I'll take you myself." The farmer stands and shuffles over to his horse. Then he points toward a dirt road down the hill. "Town's thataway."

Suddenly a stray cannonball pummels the earth, spraying dirt and fragments of rock.

"Shit!" you scream.

"Oh my god!" the farmer cries as a bullet smacks his neck.

"Shite!" you scream louder.

You stare at him, wide-eyed as the farmer falls over, blood spilling from his mouth, eyes big as billiard balls, body shuddering.

"Please! Please!" the farmer burbles.

You stand there watching, waiting for this pantomime to end.

"Dear Lord!" the farmer gargles before collapsing, head slumped forward.

You scan the forest just as the resolution reaches 4K, the smoke drifting through the trees like lost souls. You spot the dirt road and nod. "Let's go."

When you reach town a short time later, you find "town" to be an overly ambitious descriptor. It's a tiny village of about a hundred people, a few wooden shops, and a stony tavern. Most of the businesses seem either long shuttered or simply background material, but some are open. You stroll into the general store and look up to find low-poly buggy whips, lanterns, and ropes hanging from the ceiling. The shelves are filled with crockery and shovels. You realize the place looks more like an antique shop than any general store you've ever seen.

"Representative Rogers!" a voice calls joyously from behind.

340   *People's Choice Literature*

You turn around to discover a woman in a blue dress and white apron. Her brown hair is pulled back into a tight bun. She holds a tray of cookies, which she promptly sets on the counter to give you a hug.

"Oh, goodness! You're alive!" she cries. "Thank the Lord! I hear the Brandywine is littered with Redcoats. Father will be so happy to see you. 'Future Governor Rogers,' he always calls you." She is visibly exasperated. "He'll never forget when you saved our little kitty from that tree. When you were just a lad of ten, was it?"

You pull back, shuddering at the idea of helping a cat.

"And how can anyone forget what you've done for this community in the Philadelphia Assembly. Finally feels like we have a real voice," she sighs. "You've instilled a true love of democracy in the hearts of us all—which we shan't forget."

The door opens and an old man enters. He's wearing a long, brown coat and a plump, white peruke. He smiles wide, shaking your hand vimfully.

"Representative Rogers!" he cries before fixing his wig. "I'm so happy you're OK!" Then he turns to his daughter. "Sophie, give Representative Rogers one of those freshly baked cookies."

"But father, they're for—"

"Do it!"

She grabs a pastry and places it on a napkin. Then the old man takes a seat behind the counter.

"Now, what's the news from the front?" he asks. "I hear the British are close."

"It's true." You grab the cookie and bite in. "They're just outside of town."

"Oh, my . . ."

"Look, I need some help," you divagate, mumbling through your chewing.

"Why of course," he winks. "Anything for 'Future Governor Rog—"

"Where do I live?" you ask.

His eyebrows raise like startled wings. "Sorry?"

"I need to go home."

The father and daughter turn to each other wide eyed, then back to you.

"You OK, son?" the man implores before pointing to his head, then yours. "Sure you didn't get hit in out there?"

"I'm fine," you sigh, eyeing the frozen clock on the wall. "Please, I just need to get home."

"You look like you should lie down," the father says. "Come with Sophie, and she'll make you a clean bed. Rest up. Have a nice hot meal."

The Most Unwanted Novel   341

"No, thank you," you decline. "Just tell me where my house is and I'll—"

"You're in shock," he says, moving to grab you. "Come now."

But you raise your musket.

"I didn't want to have to do this," you say.

"Now, what in tarnation are you up to?" the father pouts exasperatedly.

"Where does the Rogers family live?"

"What is this?" the daughter pleads, backing away.

"I need to see Mrs. Rogers, uh, my wife. Where is she?"

"Sh- she. Your house is where it's always been . . . on Hemlock Street."

"What number?" You nudge the musket closer.

"Eight," the father blurts before swallowing.

You lower the musket and turn for the door. Then you look back and wink. "Thanks for the cookie."

Eight Hemlock Street is a vernacular farmhouse. Set in a lime-green quarry stone, the building is a two-and-a-half-story, three-bay structure with a gable roof. A single porch with fluted, Doric columns wraps across the front and around the sides, and the windows are topped with eggshell cornices. Classic colonial Pennsylvania. And impressively crafted for this shoddy VR module.

You walk up to the hair-thin door and knock. No answer. You knock again. Still nothing. You walk across the porch to the back and find the door open. So you enter with a "Hello?"

No response. Just the faint sound of wind through the door. You call out again when a squeaky voice comes from above, but you can't make it out.

You walk up the creaky stairs, past portraits of hay fields and barns, damask designs of blue and white, and discover an open door. Inside is an unremarkable bedroom, save for the glitching doll sitting on a rocking chair. You move to the window and gaze out through the smoky pane, but all you see is your reflection. You don't notice the small army of co-lonial townspeople marching toward your residence with all manner of 3D-rendered weapon. You don't see Sophie and her father leading the group, pouting loudly and demanding your immediate impeachment. You hear neither their denunciations of your legislative victories nor their nonsequitorial diatribes against your penmanship. You don't even notice the small headstone in the yard, which reads "In Loving Memory of Mary Rogers, 1750–1777." All you see is your distorted image through

342 *People's Choice Literature*

the droopy frame, the brown locks, the glowing eyes of hazel—a visage of youth you haven't seen reflected back for more than a century. You recall the boyish feeling Lady Regina inspired in you today, the brightest sign of hope. But your thoughts are cut short by the sound of a baby crying.

Whirling round, you follow the sound. It's clear it's coming from the closet, so you open the door and follow the whimpering to a crib. You peek over to discover a baby in a bonnet. You drop your musket and go to pick it up when suddenly the crying stops. The baby turns and glares in your direction.

"Oh, it's you," it sighs in a low baritone, clearly disappointed.

You jump back. "You can talk?"

"Yeah, yeah, yeah, I can talk," the baby snivels and starts snapping its fingers. "OK whatta ya want? You want directions to VR Mafia 1922, is that it? Christian sent you, told you it's the way out, blah blah blah?"

You take another step back. "That's right . . ."

"Well, take a number, buddy," says the baby, switching pacifiers. "You see that headstone in the yard? That was your ticket out of here. That Christian sent a few too many people to her, and the juvie higher-ups caught wind."

The baby slides its thumb across its neck in a slicing gesture. "Kaput."

You turn to the cries from the window, then back to the baby.

"OK," it says, "I know you're probably all sad and all, and because I got a tiny heart, but mostly because I want to get back to napping, I'll fill you in on the one thing I know." The baby gestures toward the dresser. "Put those goggles on and go find the Chevy Chase Club. Mary used to talk about a 'Court 13.' Not sure why, but that's all my baby mind remembers. OK, bye bye. Back to bed for baby."

You thank the man-baby as the angry calls near the house. Then you dart for the dresser and open the top drawer. Full of clothes. You rummage through them, but it's just stockings and panties. Second drawer down, the same thing. The calls start growing louder until you hear the back door creak open and slam shut.

When the feet start stomping up the stairs, you throw open the final drawer, tossing blouses and breeches to the floor—when you spot it: the same white frames from before. You lift the goggles to your eyes just as the angry white mob enters the room and find yourself walking through a long, dark hallway lined with tall, gray doors. No pictures or paintings, just well-rendered doorframes repeating one after another into the dim distance.

The Most Unwanted Novel   343

You turn to the door to your right. Is this where I just came from? you ask yourself. There's no way you're going back to that half-baked Am Rev roleplay, so you pick the one next to it.

Not so different from the first. Same flint-gray wood, same slaty frame. You place your hand on the bronze knob and find it oddly warm. So you twist and crack open the door just enough to peek into a kitchen. Small table, wooden chair, fire burning near the stove. Yet another premodern nightmare. You hear a scratching noise from below and push open the door to find a rat scurrying around, its ears flat against its head. When it spots you, it sits up on its hind legs, its beady eyes gleaming, overjoyed.

"Well, hello, Mr. Tickletext!" the rat proclaims. "We've been waiting for y—"

You slam the door shut. "Nope."

The next door handle is ice cold. You crack it open to discover a large, snowy field. You step out, walk a few paces, and feel oddly at home. Your heart races, wondering if somehow this door has led you back to Mars— to real reality. Back to your love. Hope. But something seems off. You peer down at your feet and notice it's not snow you're standing on but a fine layer of dust. You look up and find a tiny red sun hanging low over the horizon. The sky is black, with no sign of moon or stars. The only light you see is from that sun. But it's not your sun.

The third door leads to a small, cluttered bedroom. You espy a young man and woman sitting on a bed. Both stripped to the waist. The woman wears a bonnet. The man holds an android baby. Both are weeping.

The next door leads to a schooner of great draught, a hulking, wooden leviathan from years agone, creaking and tilting through crashing waves. You grab tight to a wooden rail as the ship endures each undusous jolt. You search for a captain, but there's nary a soul or boggart in sight. Only tattered sails, a lonely helm, and a rear mast snapped in an awkward angle. The broken arc rocks to starboard, creaking with the groan of glacial cracking. When it bends back to port, the boom swivels and sails snap with the punch of new air, sending the schooner right into a towering swell. You peer up through salty eyes at the dark shape approaching, rising, building into crest, hovering. So you turn and leap for the door.

Next, you're on a tropical beach. The sand like crushed sugar, the water a swimming-pool blue, recalling the golden strand of your former West Virginian life. You remember your love. You remember Jacq. Those wondrous days in their loving arms. The feeling of being truly held. You step into the waves and dive in, swimming over sand and shellfish, through

344 *People's Choice Literature*

seaweed and reef. You spot a school of tropical fish and chase after. Then you grab one and take it to shore. It's so real you can smell the salt water coating it. So you bite down on its bulbous head and sigh. Just like robochicken. You swallow and gaze up at the beaming midday sun. You don't want to leave this beach, but you know you must. The Chevy Chase Club awaits you . . .

The next door opens onto an alley at the edge of an ancient Roman market. Sniffing the baking bread and roasting meats, you eye dozens of tunic-clad plebs strolling past smoky stalls. Surely no Chevy Chase here. So you turn back to the door, but run smack into two stygian eyes.

"There thou art, Appius!" the white-robed woman hisses, grabbing your arm with a firm grip.

The wind picks up, and you pull back, spotting a whole gang of women in white shuffling up behind her, each sporting the same grotesque smile, each blocking your way out of here. You spin around and sprint down the cobblestone street, squeezing past carts and cows, nearly toppling over a newborn calf. But soon the shady street breaks out into the open, revealing a sun-bleached panorama of stone temples and soaring pillars. The foreground is less dramatic: a simple, grassy hill tumbling down to the muddy banks of the Tiber.

You turn back and spot your pursuers blocked by a barrage of bakers and bulls. So you bounce down the bank to a small birch boat. Then you grab the paddles and bust off, desperately batting back the current. Bending your bobble head, you behold the full band of white-clad broads begging some bozo for a boat. You bat the backwater like a beast, searching the bank opposite for boulder or bulge of land. You breeze by, and soon, between two ferry boats, you spot a break. But just as you hit the bank, some bulky buffoon grabs your back.

"Gotcha with my spatha!" he cries in victory, raising his sword to the heavens.

When you see his face, your jaw drops. The father from the Revolutionary-era general store!? In Roman regalia? You try to shake him off, but he's too strong, arms bulging like barrels, neck thick as a stump. He hoists you high into the air, dangling your flailing pagan form over the rushing waves.

Just then a voice comes from behind. "By the name of Tiberinus, putteth him down!"

"But he be a traitor to Rome!" whines the dad, swinging both his head and your bod in the direction of your white-robed pursuants.

"'Tis a misunderstanding," you plead, just as startled by your faux Shakespearian diction. "For I am no traitor. I just gotteth here!"

"Free him!" bellows the female leader, raising her hands to the skies.

"Ne'er!" cries the dad.

The woman and her cloaked posse huddle closer as the scene about darkens and the clouds descend. With the leader's eyes locked on the dad, suddenly the wind picks up into a violent gale, rustling your tunic before knocking the Rev dad back into the muck.

You plummet with him but are saved by a rock. You teeter to the front. Totter to the back. Your foot starts to slip, but you launch yourself forward just in time, landing hard on terra firma.

The fallen father looks up in horror at the women and storm clouds.

"Ye harpied daemons!" he cries from the muddy bank. "What dark magic ist this?"

"Thou and thy words be gone, Marcus Loremus Ipsumus," the lead woman proclaims, a new fire burning in each eye.

The father grabs his soiled helmet and scrambles off.

You turn to the cloaked leader. "Oh, how canst I repay thou?"

"Thou canst speaketh with the Oracle," she says, lowering her hands as the scene lightens and the clouds disperse. "She awaits thine pneuma in the Forum Boarium, and thou art tardy . . ." The leader extends a limb toward a temple downriver, revealing the winged appendage beneath her robe.

"'Sblood . . ." you shudder.

"Fear not, dearest Appius. The future ist very bright," she says, her strange smile and winged arm urging you on.

You nod and start down the riverwalk in the direction of the Forum. When you reach the stairs to the street, you look back and find the white-robed women have disappeared. Well, that was easy, you think. So you turn from the Forum and head back toward the market bridge. Time to leave this Roman ruckus . . .

But just before the bridge, you climb the stairs and run right into the gang of white-robed wardens, faces contorted in a string of ghastly grimaces.

"Where doest thou think thou art going!?" jeers the leader. "The Oracle ist waiting. The sacrifice hast already begun!"

"Sacrifice!?" You back up, spotting a train of carts and swine approaching the bridge. "I'm—I wast just going to grab a snack alongst the way . . ."

346 *People's Choice Literature*

"Nay!" she shrieks. "The sacrifice shan't wait!"

"Time to go!" you exclaim, spotting a break in the carts.

So you dart down the bridge, huffing and puffing, sandals smacking at every step.

"Get him!" cries the leader.

Sprinting to the bridge, you dodge through carts and pigs and passersby. Risking a glance back, you find the white-robed harpies scattered but not far behind.

You speed into the market, back through the rows of stalls, leaping over piles of wood, ducking under a camel. When you reach your alley, you pull open the first door. It's a simple Roman home. A mother feeding her baby. The baby deep in milky bliss. No VR tunnel here. You slam the door and run to the next, discovering an empty living room, if that's what they called it back then. You can't believe the Zander 94-inch two-piece vegan leather chaise sectional dates to ancient Rome, but at this point, nothing surprises you. You slam the door and turn to the next when the lead harpy stops you like a white-robed brick wall.

"The sacrifice ist underway, dear Appius," she bellows. "Our patience wears thin . . ."

You turn to run, but a barricade of white robes blocks the way out.

"Appius," the leader seethes, stepping closer. "Thou must yield. The Oracle demands it!"

You peek past her shoulder to the next door. Then you study the winged demigod before you. You're trapped. No Chevy Chase Club for you. No return to Lady Regina. No love. No hope. What even happens to you when you die by human sacrifice in VR? A game reboot? VR coma?

The leader grabs your arm and digs in. "Come now, Appius." But suddenly her hand falls limp. Her eyes roll back, and she collapses to the ground. You notice a tiny dart poking from her neck.

The other women look up in alarm. Your gaze follows theirs to discover your door now open, occupied by a preteen cowgirl with a mean grin.

"Step into my office," she smirks, raising the blowpipe to her mouth. When she steps forward, the white women flee.

"Tickletext, is it?" asks the girl.

You nod, still in shock.

"Let's go."

Then she grabs your arm and hurls you through the door.

The Most Unwanted Novel   347

❦

Her name is Lady Gale. At least that's what she goes by down here. She says she's been stuck in VR for years. Says she got pulled in through a fishing scheme "like most of us." Says some people—humans, androids, tentacled folk—come down here to pay off their debts. Others are just unlucky. When you and she find a stable location to take a breather— this old western saloon—you get right to it:

"How'd you find me?" you ask as the player piano plucks away in the distance.

Lady Gale takes a shot of chocolate milk.

"The baby from the Revolutionary War level is an acquaintance of mine," she says. "Lord Fred. He told me you were looking for Court 13 . . ."

"You know about Court 13?"

"Know about it? I'm the point person there. Or at least, I was. Before Lord Brad took over. He said if we both stuck around, the higher-ups might get suspicious."

Gale points to the ceiling as a child waitress saunters over to your table.

"Anythin else, darlins?"

"Two more," Lady Gale nods, and the waitress smirks back before twirling away.

"So, if you were the point person, then you know how to get to VR Mafia 1922!? You know how to get out of here?"

"Hold your ponies, partner. It's not that easy. The route to that VR experience changes all the time. That's why Court 13 is so highly coveted. Informants show up ever so often with rumors of the VR Mafia whereabouts. Sure, I knew where it was maybe a week ago, but the route's changed five-fold since."

Two baby cowboys stride past, mumbling gibberish to each other.

"What's the deal with all the kids down here?" you ask your companion.

Her brows wrinkle. "What do you mean?"

"Half the VR experiences involve babies and children. What gives?"

"Well," she shrugs, "maybe there's a—"

348   *People's Choice Literature*

I can take it from here, Lady Gala

Hi there. Tom Comitta again. Couldn't help but chime in. It's a good question: What *is* up with all the kids and babies? Well, according to the national literary poll held on December 1 and 2, 2021, people don't want to read about children (only 0.29% prefer it). Almost as much as they don't want to read about elders (0.19%), particularly grandparents (only 1 of 1,045 people surveyed preferred grandparents over other character types).

People also don't want historical fiction. After romance (which 36.94% of Americans most despise) and horror (which clocks in at 19.81% on the nope-o-meter), historical fiction wins the prize of third least-wanted genre, with 11.87% refusing to read it. Because of these findings, the frame narrative here—a day in the life of Lord Tickletext—takes the form of an experimental romance, and this current section is fashioned as a sequence of historical fiction fragments—a hi-tech frame-within-a-frame. A VR rabbit hole, if you will.

In a way, this slightly weakens the unwantedness of this "most unwanted" book. Statistically speaking, people *do* want to read about advanced technology, which some might say VR still is. Of all topics polled, science and technology got the most votes, with 24.11% preferring it. This is why the central struggle of *The Most Wanted Novel* revolves around advanced tech. So, when approaching *The Most Unwanted Novel*, I was stuck with a conundrum. A contradiction. On the one hand, people *do* prefer to read about advanced science and technology. On the other, they don't want unrealistic situations (again, only 25.96% want unrealistic fiction). And they *especially* don't want to read about life on other planets (of those 25.96%, only 0.74% prefer stories set on planets other than our own). The thing is, for humans to terraform and colonize another planet, they would need to develop advanced technologies. And those technologies would hold implications for not only how they terraform but how they live their lives: how they travel, communicate, etc. So, when poll respondents said that of all storytelling techniques, they least prefer epistolary novels (again, only 2.68% want it), another contradiction arose. In a novel set on twenty-second-century Mars, the epistolary form would not make sense as snail mail. Even today, people rarely use letters for correspondence. Another advanced, unrealistic technology had to be invented: robo-eyes.

Which takes me to the VR trap we currently find ourselves in. When structuring this book, it seemed the only way for both life on Mars and

historical fiction to coexist—while maintaining a level of continuity—would be for the historical fiction moments to appear as a nested story (frame stories are the fourth-least-wanted storytelling form, with only 23.54% preferring it). Initially I wondered if our aristocratic protagonists should travel back in time to various historical settings, but time travel seemed too advanced a technology for this unwanted book's good. Instead, once neural texting was invented, so was its robo-eye hardware. It seemed VR travel between different historical periods would suit the novel and its procedures just fine.

OK, back to the story.

"Did you hear something?" you ask Lady Gale as a toddler blacksmith hobbles by.

Lady Gale gives you an odd look.

"Strange." You scratch your head, scanning the room.

Then the child waitress walks up and places two shots of chocolate milk on the table.

Lady Gale hands her a plastic coin before raising her glass. "To Court 13 . . . ?"

"Why not?" you shrug, clinking.

Behind Lady Gale, you spot the toddler blacksmith embracing a mustachioed baby farmer.

"So, how do we get to Chevy Chase Club?" you ask.

"Right here," she says, scanning the room with suspicion before lifting a set of VR goggles from below the table.

Your eyes light up. You move to grab them when a squeaking voice comes from behind.

"Whata ye got thar?"

You turn around to find a six-year-old with an eye patch studying the VR gear. The player piano stops, and suddenly the entire prepubescent bar is staring at you. It's so quiet you can hear the newborn sheriff sucking its binky.

"Did I har ye say Court 13 thar prior?" sneers the squeaky, mean-eyed kid.

"Court 13!!" "Court 13?" "Is it true?" The room's abuzz with excitement.

"Back down, One-Eyed Bill," snarls Lady Gale.

"Now see har, little lady . . ." he spits, stepping closer to the VR gear.

350 *People's Choice Literature*

But the bartender steps in front of him. She's a well-dressed eight-year-old with a pair of super soakers strapped to her belt and a face that says she ain't scared to use 'em.

"Stand down, Billy," she commands.

"Careful," Lady Gale whispers to you, "the guy's got a mean streak ten miles wide."

One-Eyed Bill looks in her direction and snorts. "Well, ain't ya somethin'. How's it bein' the oldest whore in his har salyoon?"

"Why don't we talk about this outside," she spits back. "I'll show you a thing or two . . ."

One-Eyed Bill rests his hand on his holster. "I'm gonna need them goggles, Gale."

The crowd of kid cowboys stirs, spurs jingling, water pistols pumping.

"Who's with me!?" he growls.

Lady Gale raises her neon Soakzooka, but the kid barkeep steps in front.

"Now, now, kiddos," she says. "Y'all know that's not how we do things here." Then she turns to Lady Gale. "Show's over, friend. Put them goggles back under that table. If everyone can't use 'em, no one can."

Lady Gale follows her orders, Bill's sole eye tracing her every move. Once the goggles are back in their wooden compartment, the bar returns to normal. Water guns reholstered, glasses clinking. Lady Gale takes a big gulp of chocolate milk, trying to maintain a calm exterior.

When One-Eyed Bill finally turns to order a drink, Lady Gale looks at you and whispers, "Jim . . . go!"

"Huh?"

Then she slyly slides the goggles into your hand.

"Go! NOW!" she yells.

So you grab them and slam the hardware onto your eyes. You hear screams and gushing water, tables overturned and milk glasses shattering, but they fade to nothing as you find yourself sitting in a new bar not unlike the one you were just in. You look around and see a cowboy bartender and a waitress in the same outfits as before, but this time they're full-grown adults.

"Whataya have?" the waitress asks, chewing gum and blowing a pink bubble.

You look at her blankly.

"Uh, I might need a minute."

Unfazed, she slurps the gum back into her mouth and keeps chewing. "Take ya time, hun," she says before strolling over to the bar.

The Most Unwanted Novel   351

You scan the room. On second glance, the architecture appears *almost* the same as before—similar colors, similar aesthetic, but it's largely modern. The tables look wooden but feel plastic. And apart from the wait staff, no one is dressed in Wild West garb. At one table, a group of women with puffy, permed hair wear black leggings and neon sweatshirts. Across from them, five guys with mullets and sleeveless tees sit cracking jokes and shooting spitballs at one another. Closer to the bar, two drunks sway slowly, singing along to the crooner blasting through the speakers:

> I made it through the rain shower
> I kept my worldview protected
> I made it through the rain shower
> I kept my second-person point of view
> I made it through the rain shower
> And found myself respected
> By the others who
> Got rain showered on, too

After a climactic, symphonic ending, a voice comes over the speakers:

Good afternoon, Maryland, Virginia, and the District. Mike "M. D." aka "Melo-dy" Douglas coming to you live from WLTT 94.7 FM on a bright and sunny April 21. And, yes, it's looking like that sun is gonna last. Don't know about you, but I could use a little sun after that downpour yesterday. Still drying my high tops in the mud room . . . Well, we've got a big day for you today. Frank Sinatra's in town. That's right, the kingpin of the Rat Pack himself, gracing the Kennedy Center tonight for the final evening of his four-night residency. Luck be a Lady? How bout Luck be Two Free Tickets to Caller 15!? That's right. Caller 15 gets two, I repeat two free tickets to tonight's sold-out Sinatra show. Pick up the phone right now. 202-479-9227. Again, the number is 202-479-9227. Yep, caller 15 and his special someone will be *flying to the moon* when they give me a ring. That's 202-479-9227. As those calls come in, let's let Frank take us there himself. Here's Frank Sinatra with, you guessed it, "Fly Me to the Moon." It's 94.7 FM. WLTT.

As the tom toms start their tum ta tums, you stand up from your chair and walk to the door. Stepping out into the warm air and sun, your

352 *People's Choice Literature*

head swivels, taking in the sights and sounds of postmodern America as described by Frederic Jameson in *Postmodernism, or, the Cultural Logic of Late Capitalism* (Durham, NC: Duke University Press, 1992). You walk to a nearby bench and take a seat, watching people pass in all directions. Some in Nikes, others in Reeboks, some in Fords or Hondas. Some alone, others in groups. A woman in Gap waits at a crosswalk, fidgeting with her Afterthoughts. Two kids glide by on Vans, popping ollies over Coke cans. A man in secondhand Ralph Lauren stomps past huffing, smoking a Marlboro. He stops in front of an ad, "NEW NISSAN S-T. ONE HUNK OF A TRUCK," takes out a Bic, and jots down the address for the closest Nissan dealer. As he does, a slick, black Bentley pulls up right in front of you, and a chauffeur steps out.

"Mr. Stevens!" the chauffeur calls through chapped lips.

You look around, confused.

"Mr. Stevens . . . Your 2:15 at Court 13 . . . ?"

Your eyes light up. At last.

Inside the car you crack the window to take in your new surroundings. A Delorian speeds past. Buildings fly by. You watch the city stretch out in every direction, with people running everywhere—to work, to school, to the mall, up stairs to the gym, down escalators to their cars. But the urban landscape changes. The buildings grow smaller and more spaced out. More green dots the landscape.

"Music, sir?" asks the chauffeur.

"Why not?" you reply, focusing on the mansions and subdivisions now flashing by.

He switches on the radio, and a familiar voice returns:

MELODY: There you have it folks, Harriet and Farrel Wilkby are on their way to Mr. Sinatra's epic Kennedy Center finale! And to send them off, we have a special treat for you: a full hour of Sinatra hits. But before we get there, WLTT's very own resident scholar is back to report on the Sultan of Swoon himself. That's right, Scotty Dooley is here for his weekly music report . . .

A cacophony of whistles and kazoos sounds off.

MELODY: Hiya, Scotty.

SCOTTY: Hey Melody!

MELODY: That's *Mister* Melody to you! Heh heh. Well, Scotty, what've you got for us today?

SCOTTY: Well, sir. It's the story of the great Frank Sinatra, a true American hero.

MELODY: You don't say.

SCOTTY: I sure do, Mister Melody.

MELODY: Well, then let's hear it, Scotty boy.

SCOTTY: Thanks, Mister Melody. [Scotty clears his throat.] Francis Albert Sinatra was born on December 12, 1915, in Hoboken, New Jersey, to Italian immigrants Natalina Della Garaventa, a homemaker, and Antonio Sinatra, a barber.

As a youngster, Sinatra sang in the choir at St. Mary's Church in Hoboken and participated in school plays. At age ten, he also started working odd jobs like selling newspapers and shining shoes. Sinatra began singing publicly in his early teens, and by his early twenties, he'd become a successful nightclub singer in the Big Apple.

In 1935, Sinatra was signed by bandleader Harry James and made his first recording. The following year, he signed with Benny Brewster and achieved national prominence with the song "One O'Clock Jump."

In 1942, he was signed to a recording contract by the great Columbia Records and his career took off. But in '43, Sinatra launched his own record label, Reprise, and released the album *Songs by Sinatra*. It featured hits like "One for My Baby (and One More for the Road)" and "I've Got You Under My Skin," which are both now jazz standards. Over the next few years, Sinatra became one of the biggest stars in the United States, and his recordings of popular songs such as "The Lady Is a Tramp" and "My Way" were loved around the world.

354 *People's Choice Literature*

In the early 1950s, Sinatra's personal life began to attract as much attention as his music. He had a series of high-profile romances with movie stars Ava Gardner and Marilyn Monroe, and he was frequently in the news for his rumored connections to the Mafia.

MELODY: Whoa there, kiddo. Not sure we can say that on the air.

SCOTTY: It's what Teacher Alice told me . . . [He continues reading.] In 1953, Sinatra was arrested for adultery, and he divorced—

MELODY: Heyyy, Scotty, let's keep this PG.

SCOTTY: Sorry Mister Melody. Should I continue? I'm almost done.

MELODY: Alright, Scotty . . .

SCOTTY: In the late 1950s, Sinatra's career hit a wall. He was dropped by Columbia Records, and his movies did poorly at the box office.

MELODY: Sco—

SCOTTY: *However,* Sinatra reestablished himself as a successful performer in the 1960s, releasing several albums that were popular with young audiences. He began performing at casinos in Las Vegas and starred in the hit films *Ocean's Eleven,* *The Detective,* and *The Odd Couple.* He also made a successful return to television, starring in the popular *The Frank Sinatra Show.* In 1965, Sinatra was awarded the Presidential Medal of Freedom by President Lyndon B. Johnson. He released his latest album in 1980.

Throughout his career, Frank Sinatra has been known for his distinctive voice and ability to convey a wide array of emotion in his songs. He is also a talented actor and even won an Academy Award for his performance in the 1954 movie *From Here to Eternity.* Sinatra has been a cherished entertainer for decades, and it's with great honor that we welcome him to our dear city.

Please come back again, Mister Sinatra!

MELODY: There you have it folks, the great Swoonatra. Thanks, Scotty. Well, folks, let's kick off Sinatra hour with a bang. It's not his way or her way. It's not even *your* way, they say. That's right. Here's Frank Sinatra with "My Way."

As the song starts, you notice the city has disappeared, replaced by lush lawns and mansions. You spot a kid in Keds playing fetch with a dog. Two workers in Levi's trimming a hedge for Liz Claiborne. When the sign for Chevy Chase speeds by, you nearly wet your jams.

Throwing open the doors to the Club, you stroll up to the front desk and give your name.

"You need no introduction here, Mr. Stevens," winks the concierge. "Mr. Campbell is waiting for you at Court 13. Your locker should be fully prepared."

"Thank you," you nod and turn toward the locker room.

Halfway across the lobby, a man in a blue suit spots you from the bar and speeds over, catching your arm.

"Heyyy there, buddy. Where the hell were you last night? Reagan was there. Speaker O'Neill was there. Perdue could've used you . . . *I* could've used you."

You turn to the locker room entrance.

"Sorry, friend," you say as you start to walk away, but the blue-suited man grabs your shoulder, and you turn back.

"What's up with you, Steve? We pay you good money and expect at least a little in return."

"I'm sorry. It's just . . . I . . ."

The blue-suited man sees you're flustered and grins. He's got a narrow face and a thin mustache. He lays his hand flat on your shoulder.

"Look, Steve. I know where you come from. I know what you did in 'Nam. I've heard the stories. You made your country proud."

"I . . ."

The blue-suited man's brows furrow. "Look, I'm sorry to blast you there. It's just that Roger's all over my back this morning . . . Maybe if you could call him later?"

"Uh, sure."

"Good. Now get your ass in gear, Steve. I hear you're up against the *cream* de la crème," he chuckles.

356 *People's Choice Literature*

Out on the court, the sun seems to shine differently than before, coating everything and everyone in sharp yellows and greens. You watch as dozens of politicians and lobbyists, wives and children serve and rally, leap and slam. The smells of sweat and cologne fuse, and the sounds of balls hitting rackets punctuate the pangs of laughter and gossip.

At Court 13, a youthful, muscular man of no more than forty walks toward you with a ten-thousand-dollar smile.

"Steve! Steve-o. It's been too long." He shakes your hand so hard it nearly breaks.

"Mr. Campbell. Good to see you."

"You too, you too. And I see you're looking healthy," he says, eyeing you up.

"Thanks."

"That's good. Very good. Water?" He offers you his bottle, but you decline. Then he continues. "Look, Steve, we were very happy with that FDA win. Congrats. I mean, really. The big man is pleased." He winks.

You set your bag down, nodding.

"We've been following you for a while, you know," says Campbell, muscles bulging through his sweatsuit into heaping hills. "And I'm pretty good at picking winners."

"Well, thanks," you force a smile.

The man pats you on the shoulder. "I'm only trying to help. These are serious guys here," he says pointing to a group of salt-and-pepper-haired men in the distance chatting with their salt-and-pepper wives, "and they don't like to lose. I know you're the real deal. You do good work. Between you and me, word on the street is that Dutch is considering you for HHS."

He clearly notices your confusion. "Thought you'd be happy to hear that . . ."

"N-no," you stammer, "I am. It's just been a strange day."

"I get it," says Campbell. "Look, Steve. What do you *want*?"

"Huh?"

He points to the next court over where a family plays doubles. "You want to play pickup ball forever? Or do you wanna get to the big leagues?" He nods to the condiment couples.

"Sure, of course, big leagues." You take a deep breath. "Look, Campbell. This might sound strange, but are you the one with the Mafia VR connection?"

He looks around, obviously irritated. "What the hell?" he whispers. "I mean, what the fuck, Steve?"

The Most Unwanted Novel   357

"I, uh—"

"Looks like you better cut back on the blow, buddy. That why you skipped the gala last night? There was plenty there, let me tell you . . . But, mafia?" His eyes dart from side to side. "What the fuck, man?"

You stare at him like a reindeer in headlights.

His eyes interrogate you in turn, and you wince. Oh, God, you think, now I'll never get out of this VR hellhole. What was I thinking? I'll probably be thrown in a cell somewhere in this awful American post-modern nightmare, living out the rest of my days like a vegetable stew. Your thoughts race faster and faster until Campbell's brows relax, and he lets out a chuckle.

He laughs louder. He starts coughing he's laughing so hard.

"Mafia," he holds his chest to catch his breath. "Oh, boy. Good one, Steve. They told me you were a joker, and they didn't disappoint. Oh, boy. I need to sit down."

You let out a dry laugh and swallow.

"Look," he huffs, "you're right. Enough business talk. Let's just play a few rounds and then we can get down to it. Could use the cardio." He pats his obviously well-sculpted belly.

You pull the racket out of your bag and stroll to your side of the court. *Where could this Lord Brad be?* you ask yourself. *Is this Campbell some kind of diversion? Is this the right Court 13?* You try to recall more of what Lady Gale had said, but that's all there was a court number and some lordly Brad.

On the other side of the court, you hear the boing of a ball and look up to find Campbell grinning, the ball filling his left hand. He nods. You nod back. He throws it straight up in the air and smacks it with a "Humpf!" You shuffle to the side, swing, and slam it back, amazed at the ease of play in this VR module. He returns, and soon the two of you are in a rally. The ball flies back and forth. He smacks it hard into a line drive, but you return with a drop shot. He rockets it with a learned back-hand, and you slice it just in time. This time Campbell dives for it, but it's too late. A passerby calls "net cord!" and you win the point.

"Nice shot," Campbell smiles, wiping the sweat from his glistening brow. "Been keeping up your game, I can see."

Just then a kid strolls up, twiddling his Dunlop 200g. He's no older than thirteen, pimples dotting his cheeks in a dense constellation of lumps and picked scabs.

"Looking for a ball boy?" the kid squeaks.

358 *People's Choice Literature*

"I think we're OK," you reply.

Campbell laughs. "Get over here, Brad. Let me introduce you to Steve. Steve, this is my son, Brad."

Brad? you think. *That Brad?* The *Brad?* You must keep your cool, you tell yourself. This is your only way out.

"Oh, hello," you say nonchalantly, walking over and shaking his hand.

"Brad just started at Sidwell Friends School," says Campbell. "He's looking to get into Maret."

"Well, good luck," you force a smile.

"That's where you went, right?" asks Campbell.

"Oh, yes," you nod.

"Look," says Campbell. "I'm gonna go hit the head. Why don't you two chat, and I'll be right back."

"Sure thing," you say.

Campbell grabs his water and speed-walks toward the locker room.

"So, you play tennis?" you ask, eyeing the kid up.

"Yeah," the boy shrugs. "Dad says I'm OK. But what I *really* like is lacrosse."

"Do you . . ." you begin, scanning the vicinity to see if anyone is listening. "Hey kid, you wouldn't happen to go by 'Lord Brad' in some circles, would you?"

The kid frowns. "Keep it down, man!" he whispers curtly, peeking over your shoulder. "What the heck do you want?"

"Lady Gale said you know how to get to Mafia 1922."

His face turns red. "Lady Gale?"

"She sent me to find you."

"I don't know what you're talking about," Brad says, picking a pimple. "She's . . ."

"Stop it, stop it!" Brad pouts. "We can't talk here. Follow me."

The boy picks up his bag, looks around, and walks off the court. You follow him through the maze of tennis players, spectators, families, and staffers, crossing courts before passing through the double doors into the building. You try to keep up as he shuffles through the lobby, past the pro shop, and out into the parking lot.

"Where are we going?" you ask.

The boy stops and looks at you. "Do you want to get to Mafia 1922 or not?"

"Of course."

"Then follow me."

The Most Unwanted Novel 359

The boy walks to a nearby red Jeep Wrangler and opens the trunk, revealing a heap of tennis gear. He grabs a small duffel bag from the pile and hands it to you.

"What's this?"

"Clothes."

"I don't understand."

"Just take 'em and put 'em on."

You open the bag and pull out a tuxedo. Then you look up to see the kid holding a Rolex watch.

"You have any idea how hard it is to get these?" he says.

"No," you reply, taking the watch.

"Try impossible. I had to steal this from my dad. Do you know what would happen if I got caught?"

"I don't know, Brad."

"I'd be dead. Don't you get it? This here is practically Mafia 1922. Lady Gale and I used to call it 'Mafia 1983.'"

Your eyes perk up. "What are you talking about?"

"Don't you see? This country club. These people. It's all a melanin-deficient Mafia in disguise. Smiley fraud. An officially sanctioned, highly organized crime against humanity in the shape of a country club!"

"Huh?"

"The club is just the start of it. Sure, it's a privately owned oligarchy, but so is this country." He pauses to let the idea sink in. "There. I said it. The United States is a fucking oligarchy. And like a post-Soviet, Russian oligarchy, it may be called a democracy by name but it sure as hell ain't . . ." he puts his hands up in scare quotes " 'for the people.' What's going on here in 1980s America is the root of basically all evil. Mob boss Reagan convinced even the poorest of poor that puttin' money in the hands of all the Richie McRichersons of the world would actually help the little guy in the end. What a load of horse shit! And people believe that even to this day!"

You raise your eyebrow into a question mark, wondering if Brad is actually a Martian trapped in a VR nightmare or some liberal Terran getting his punk rocks off.

"Look," he says, "it's true that things were bad before Ronnie 'Al Capone' Reagan took over. I mean, for Christ's sake . . ."

You gasp.

". . . the country was founded on slavery and genocide! It's been organized crime right from the start. We'd be nowhere today without the

structured oppression and exploitation of the Africans we kidnapped from their homelands and forced to build our roads and farm our crops and create the economic foundation for what became the most powerful nation in the history of the world. And what do we give them for this? Nothing. Just set them free then trip them right when they're lifting themselves up. And repeat. Get up. Trip. Get up. Trip. Get up. Trip. Trip. Trip. Trip. Trip. You get it. The whole system keeps 'em down. It's designed to trip up black people, brown people, Asian Americans, Indigenous Americans, all the colors of the rainbow. I mean, the Indigenous people they just slaughtered. Why else do you think there are relatively so few today? The people we 'discovered.' And what the fuck kind of fairy-tale bullshit is that? 'Discovered . . .' They were here since time immemorial and then we show up and kill them. We murdered them. We systematically annihilated nearly an entire continent. Twelve million indigenous folk murdered in the Americas since 1492 and all their ancestors get here in the US of fuckin' A is a tiny fraction of reservation land as a little 'thank you, but no thank you.' We're living on occupied territory. Our great-great-grandparents murdered and raped and pillaged so that you and I could hang out at this imperialist, white-supremacist, capitalist, patriarchal shithole of a country club, sip bloody marys and lob green balls back and forth with our imperialist, white-supremacist, capitalist, patriarchal shithole country club friends. There you have it. Oh, and that term, 'imperialist, white-supremacist, capitalist, patriarchy?' That's bell hooks's, by the way, in case you're living under a rock. bell hooks. A philosopher who actually *meant* something. Not this Milton Friedman neoliberal jackoff bullshit that everyone finds as normal as breathing air when in fact neoliberal ideology is just that: an ideology. A system founded on deregulation, free trade, austerity, and the privatization of all life. A system that believes at its core that the market is God, savior, amen. But this system has destroyed countless communities, fueled global warming, the destruction of the planet, and the breakdown of civil society. And it wasn't always like this! It doesn't have to be like this. Nothing is *natural*. 'Human nature' and 'common sense' are just constructs. They aren't givens. They're designed. Taught. Just like fascism, capitalism, and yes, the slow violence of dumbass Reaganomics. Which brings me back to my initial point. Mob boss Reagan and the Organized Crime Fascist States of America. Yep, mob boss Reagan. The ringleader of a suicidal economic ideology and one of the truly greatest cons of all time. But this isn't some one-man operation, of course. In the

decades after Reagan, even presidents supposedly on the left like Bill Clinton and Barack Obama, and essentially all national politicians since the 1970s, have worked to strip away worker rights, privatize everything, and ensure that the wealthy get wealthier while the poor get poorer. Now, don't get me started on taxes and all the whining coming from the business sector. 'Less taxes! Less taxes!' Whaaa whaaa whaaa. How the fuck do you think we paid for things to make this country function? Fucking taxes! When Congress gradually reduced taxes for corporations and the wealthy over time—from corporations paying nearly 50 percent in taxes in 1950 to 17 percent or nothing in the 2020s, when the popular uprisings began—they essentially destroyed any hope for the future of this republic. I mean, what do you expect? You break people's backs every single day. You tell them that capitalism is good, that if you work hard enough, you, too, can be billionaires, but you keep moving the goal posts or, better yet, remove it entirely. At a certain point, after decades of stagflation, no quality-of-life improvements, and instead lower wages, no health care, shattered rights, and bleak prospects for the 99 percent of the population that *actually works for a living*, what do you expect? So, yes. This is VR Mafia 1983: The United Fucking States of Dumberica. Democratic Capitalism. Neoliberal nightmare. Unending deregulation and defunding. Racist crime bills. OK, well, that came in the '90s, but its roots are pure Reaganism. And white supremacy, which is as old as Western civilization. Ditto LGBTphobia and LGBTphobic laws. Ditto sexism and sexist laws. A government run by men for men proclaiming sovereignty over everyone else's bodies. A country that took 250 years to put a woman into the vice presidency and then two years later stripped women of their freedom to make their own health care decisions, to shape their own lives! Yes, here we are in the United Weights-on-All-Our-Backs of America. The most highly organized, murderous, psychopathic crime syndicate the world has ever known. Welcome to Mafia 1983."*

By this point your eyes are so glazed over, they're dotted with sprinkles.

"Did you say your name was Lord Brad? I've never heard a Martian speak like this."

"I'm not a Martian. I'm a human being, man. And you are, too. You just can't see it through all your Martian propaganda."

"I have to go."

"Go where?"

---

* "A novel is not a soapbox." Archer and Jockers, *The Bestseller Code*, 65.

362 *People's Choice Literature*

"To the bathroom."

"The bathroom? No one urinates in VR. Look, sorry I had to lay some realness on you. It's just, I've been here for what feels like decades, and there's just so much you can take in this simulation. I mean this place is pure evil. It makes you think back to where we've come from as a species and how we got here."

You look him dead in the eyes. "Look, Brad. I've read books. I know history. I get it. But I don't have time for this shit right now. I'm late for a date in Port Elisabeth. I met the love of my life today, and didn't sign up for this VR crap. Or the history lesson. Just tell me what to do."

Brad studies you for a moment before beginning.

"Take the Jeep to the Safeway on the corner of Pennsylvania and Twenty-Fifth. There you'll find a man in a trench coat. Give him the Rolex, and he'll hand you a suitcase. The suitcase contains a subway ticket. Take the ticket, ditch the suitcase, and head into the Foggy Bottom train station. From there, take the Blue line to Crystal City station. Exit the train and follow the signs to the Hilton parking lot. Take the left elevator to the seventh floor. There you'll find a man in a navy-blue suit with a yellow stain on the sleeve. Give him the subway ticket and he'll hand you a suitcase. The suitcase contains the VR goggles."

You do just this. You take the Jeep to the Safeway on the corner of Pennsylvania and Twenty-Fifth. There you find a man in a trench coat, just as Lord Brad said. You give him the Rolex, and he hands you a suitcase. The suitcase contains a subway ticket. You take the ticket, ditch the suitcase, and head into the Foggy Bottom train station. From there, you take the Blue line to Crystal City station. You exit the train and follow the signs to the Hilton parking lot. Inside, you take the left elevator to the seventh floor and find a man in a navy-blue suit with a yellow stain on the sleeve. Staring at the splotchy blot, you hesitate, lamenting the filthy laymen you've dealt with all day, then hand him the subway ticket. He inspects it, studies you, grunts, "You're late," and hands you the suitcase. You thank him and shuffle off to a little nook between two parked cars. You open the suitcase, and there they are: a fresh pair of VR goggles. Your ticket out of this techno torture. You go to put them on, but a voice grates from behind you:

"Put 'em down, Steve. And put those hands up where I can see them. Don't try anything funny."

You hear a pistol cock as you stare at the goggles, calculating if you've got enough time to shove them on before he blasts you into next Sunday

The Most Unwanted Novel   363

Funday. But you think twice, brought back to the bleak revelations of Christian's unending, ostentatious VR coma lecture and the potential brain death you could endure from a VR bullet to the VR noggin. If enduring is even an option at this point. Mouth wrinkled, you slowly place the goggles on the ground, lift your hands in the air, and turn around.

The man standing before you is short and balding, with chapped lips and a corduroy suit with an oil stain on the sleeve.

"Who are you?" you inquire in disgust, sick of all these sleeve-stained suckers.

He shakes his head. "Not important. Give me the goggles, Steve."

"But I'm so close," you cry. "You don't understand. Just inches away from reuniting with my lo—"

"It's over, Steve."

He steps forward, and recognition hits you like a freight train to the lobotorium. Those eyes. The lips.

"You drove me earlier! You were my chauffeur!"

The goon chuckles, raising his gun. "And I followed you here. Look, this ain't Hollywood Squares. It don't matter who I am, and it don't matter where you're trying to go. I'm here on behalf of the higher-ups," he points up, "to keep our VR farm intact. Think of me as a wrangler. A VR cowboy, if you will, herding silly, stray sheep like you back to the playpen."

Your eyes tighten in malice.

"You have no idea what I had to do to get here," you cry in desperation. "The struggles I've endured. The people, the sledges I've sent to the farthest reaches of this dreadful planet. The VR modules I've had to master to reach this fucking point. This is the worst Christmas ever!!"

He slides closer, the wide barrel staring you down.

"Kick the suitcase over," he sneers.

You look to the suitcase—your last ticket out of here—then back up to the scheming chauffeur. Here goes nothing, you think. And just as you move to kick it, a gun goes off. The chauffeur spins back, smack against a car, his revolver shattering the driver-side window of a Ford Mustang.

"Run!" screams the voice of a thirteen-year-old.

You turn to your right.

It's Lord Brad!

You grab the suitcase and dive over the hood of the Ford. Shuffling between cars, you find Lord Brad crouched behind a Volvo station wagon panting, revolver raised and ready to go.

"Get back here!" the chauffeur shrieks, before firing three return shots.

364   *People's Choice Literature*

"That all ya got?" yells Lord Brad, popping a pimple.

"You ain't seen nothin' yet," cries the chauffeur cheekily.

The driver and Lord Brad exchange shots, one round after another. Bangs and pops ricochet off cars. Hisses and grunts syncopate shots and ricochets only to disappear into a clatter of bursts. One bullet brushes the chauffeur's cheek; another just misses Brad.

This goes on for some time, guns blazing, taunts teasing, until the distant sound of sirens sends the chauffeur into a frenzy of shouting and pouting and straight-up running away, P. G. Wodehouse-style. Literally you see this:

He runs five times round the garage without stopping.

He runs in the direction of small, fragile ornaments.

He runs into Pongo Twistleton.

He runs across the passage and beats on the elevator door.

He runs through the frame.

He runs all the way to Arden on the Severn, Maryland, whose waters gleam like an unsheathed sword.

The chauffeur's frenzy runs up and down your nervous system so sharply that you get to running as well, sprinting through the parking lot, suitcase in hand. You look back and spot Lord Brad hurrying after.

"Watch out!" he cries, pointing to the left.

You follow his finger to a man you've never seen before, a petticoated dandy sprinting toward you with a pistol aimed right at your chest.

You watch the man's finger squeeze the trigger. You see the flash blast from the barrel. You feel the punch. The pain. You see the floor rise to meet you in a blur of panic and purpose. You watch the suitcase smack the pavement and break open, the VR goggles bounce into view. You hear Lord Brad screaming and shooting, "Go! Go! Go!" And so, you reach out to the goggles, but a bullet smacks your hand, jolting it awkwardly—and counterproductively, from the shooter's perspective—toward the gadget. You watch as the blood pumps from your ulnar artery, coating the previously sterile VR equipment with a sticky scarlet.

With that hand out of commission and few other options, you groan in piercing pain as you flip over. Then you reach out your good hand, inching toward the goggles in a flailing, jerking dance. Another bullet pops your left femur just as your hand hits the plastic. You raise the goggles to your eyes when a bullet bursts your stomach, morphing your mangy mouth into a rufous Trevi Fountain. You choke in the spray. You spray in the melee. Energy fails. Time tells. Topples. Your hand drops

limp. Gravity guides the bloody goggles at 9.8 meters per second onto your eyes, and then it's Monday, 3 p.m. You're walking down a dirty, gray street, going nowhere fast. At least that's what it seems like until you turn the corner and this bimbo, a real piece of work, runs smack into you. You nearly fall over until the wise guy catches you with two wide eyes.

"Mickey De Souza, ya old cake eater!" The man smiles through scarred lips. "I didn't see ya there!"

You jerk a nod. Behind him you notice the cobblestone streets. The old mom-and-pop bakery. The brownstones. The horse-drawn carriage trotting beside a Bentley.

"What, ya act like you've seen a ghost. Like you haven't seen your old pal Joey Smalls in years. Come ere, Mickey!"

He wraps you in a bear hug.

"Ey, where you off to this time a day?" he asks, pulling back.

"Uh, just catching my bearings," you reply.

Smalls checks you up and down. "You OK, Mickey?"

"Yeah, I'm fine," you say, suddenly realizing that no one mentioned what exactly you had to do in Mafia 1922 to get out of this VR mess.

"Look, Mickey, the guys and I're goin' in on a job tonight and could use an extra hand. Paulie Rostro's gone soft. Says it's his kid's confirmation tonight. Boss isn't happy but let it slide this once." He holds up a finger to emphasize the point. "He's a god-fearing man, and Paulie ain't no dewdropper, ya know? Anyways, we could really use a guy like you. Straightforward job. No funny stuff."

You study him, spotting a group of kids playing stickball down the street.

"So ya in?" he asks.

"Sure," you shrug, assuming that playing along is the best you can do to flee this VR nightmare.

Smalls smiles and claps you on the back. "You're a good guy, Mickey. One a the best."

"I'm not a good guy," you say.

He laughs. "Well, you're a good trigger man, and that goes a long ways. Look, we're having a meet at Lucky's Lunch Car, just a few blocks away. I'll introduce you to the fellas."

As you walk down the street, you notice the stares—sheepish plugs pointing and whispering. Two dames spot you and duck into a store. A group of kids scatter as you move toward them. Next block a couple of coppers take an interest.

366   *People's Choice Literature*

"I don't like this," you whisper.

"Relax. They're just a bunch of yokels scared a their own shadows."

"I don't know . . ." you mumble.

Smalls laughs and lights a gasper. "Still the same Mickey De Souza I grew up wit back in Bensonhurst. Always a scared little mousey mouse, huh?" He snorts, giving you a noogie. "You'll be fine."

You nod to the coppers, and they nod back, their eyes lingering a moment longer than you'd like. Once they're out of sight, you get to business.

"So, what's the job?" you ask.

"It's the Caparellis," Smalls snorts. "They ain't been playing so nice, so we're gunna teach 'em a little lesson."

"What'd they do?"

"Those northern upstarts thought they could come down here and act like they owned the place. Think they can stake out Hudson Yards 'cause they got the port in their pocket. Not cutting it with the Boss. So, we'll show em how we do things in Brooklyn. Won't be so keen after tonight, eh?"

"So, why you need an extra jobbie?" you ask.

Smalls laughs. "We need backup in case things go south. It's a big joint, lots o' guards. Nothing too serious, though. Just in and out, no problem."

Your guide helps you into the lunch car, and you spot the gang in the back. Almost everyone in the place is wearing a lid, save the two kids sipping milkshakes. Smalls directs you to the last booth in the corner, where three shady figures sit hunched over three club sandwiches.

"This here's Mickey De Souza," he says to the guys. "Used to be a pretty good hitter."

Smalls introduces you to Lawless, a broad-shouldered bird with a long scar running down his right forearm. He looks like an old-school fighter: thick beard, bulging biceps. Beside him sits a man with a thick mustache and a dark, weathered face. He says nothing but jerks a nod while taking a draw from his fag.

"That's Paddy," says Smalls.

The last guy is a large, stocky fella with a thick mustache and a full head of black hair. He looks like he's in his mid-fifties, but he could be younger. He smiles and shakes your hand.

"Nice to meet yous. Joey M's the name."

The Most Unwanted Novel   367

"Right," says Smalls. "Now, the happy family is all together, let's get down to business. The Caparellis are running a big gambling operation out of a warehouse in North Brooklyn, and tonight's the big night. They're expecting a massive payout."

"How much?" Lawless asks.

Smalls shrugs. "A couple hundred K, maybe. More if they're on a hot streak. It's a big joint. Lots a sugar on hand. We're gonna hit it at 9 on the dot. Catch 'em all in one place for once. Gonna be a nice change. Hit and run. And a big cash payoff."

"What about guards?" M asks.

"Twelve. Two per entrance. We'll have plenty a time to get in and out. Even if they send some of their Hudson Yards boys for backup, they'll be too late. We'll be gone before their stupid peepers even spot the East River."

"Still seems risky," Lawless coughs. "No diversion?"

Smalls frowns. "I was just getting to that. Who do ya think I am? M will distract 'em. The rest a us hit the joint."

M's eyes open wide.

"M, you'll plant the C4 in the back alley. That'll keep the guards busy," Smalls chuckles. "Meanwhile, we hit the joint, grab the sugar, off those palookas, and dust out. This is where you come in, Mickey."

You straighten up.

"You're our getaway guy. And backup if things get out a hand . . . You'll be waiting in the car with one hand on your bean-shooter, the other on the ignition."

You nod, grateful to stay off the chopper squad.

"So, I plant the soup; you take out the guards?" M asks.

Smalls huffs, "That's what I just said, Joey, what's wrong with ya?"

"Boom. Then in and out," Lawless summarizes.

Smalls nods.

After gossiping about the boss's new broad and sipping the weakest java of your life, the team scrams. M drives off to plant the soup behind the casino. Lawless and Paddy go pick up the gats. Smalls and you take a trolley to the getaway car.

Stepping onto that vintage trolley, your chest instantly constricts. It was such a trolley, however modified by quantum hover technology, that took your Grandmummy so many years ago. Your gut lurches. Your lungs fail. You wonder if you can even go through with this job. How

you got caught up in this insane, virtually unreal rat race in the first place. The day was supposed to be simple: pray for Grandmummy, play some tennis, go to brunch, go to Gouverneur Stanley's, and pray some more. Finito. Happy ending and all that cal. But here you are, sitting in a stinkin' antique trolley with some robo-boob play-acting your friend, on your way to pulling some heist that might not even help return you to your real life and, if successful, hopefully, dear Lord, your true love . . .

"It's good to have ya back, Mickey," Smalls grins from the seat beside you, shaking you out of your ruminations.

"Y-yeah," you stammer, "good to be back."

The trolley stops at an intersection as a fire truck wails past. Your heads move in tandem, tracing its path.

"This is gonna be a piece a cake," says Smalls.

The siren fades into the distance, and you jerk a nod. "Yeah, piece a cake."

At 8:45, you, Smalls, Paddy, and Lawless roll to a stop across from the Caparelli casino. Only it's obviously a dance hall.

"I thought you said this was a gamblin' joint," says Paddy, eyeing the young couples entering hand in hand.

Smalls frowns. "It is. The dance hall's a front."

"But it's practically a rub . . . What about all those innocent people?" Paddy complains.

"This is a Caparelli joint," Smalls grunts. "They're all dirty."

Paddy looks like he wants to say something, but he keeps his yapper shut.

Smalls looks down at his watch. "Only fifteen minutes and then this game goes to the big leagues."

The four of you wait in the car watching the clock tick. Paddy taps nervously on the door. Lawless keeps making this clicking sound with his tongue, and Smalls keeps yammering on about his old lady.

You sit there, eyeing the guys and dolls strutting by. One couple cashes near the entrance, sparking a catcall from this sheik in a fedora: "Bank's closed!" Beside him, a choice bit of calico smoking a gasper and a man with a lid the size of a ham sandwich grab an obviously zozzled mac in a green suit. They disappear behind the velvet curtains just as your eyes spot the Caparelli guards, their rods looking not too friendly right about now.

Smalls leans forward. "You OK, Mickey? Ya look a little nervous."

You shake your head. "Everything's fine."

"It's just a job, Mickey." He pats you on the shoulder. "You know what to do."

You jerk a nod. Sure you'll be fine. You'll do a good job—whatever that means. But you don't want to do a good job. You just want to be back with Lady Regina, back in your real reality, back to your really real consciousness, back to your shopping cart of three thousand red roses awaiting a mailing address. You want to dust out of this virtual nightmare once and for all.

You peer out the window at the couples strolling by and think about the absurdity of the situation. How easy it would've been to find a different assistant and be well on your way to your true love, if not with her already. You see the simulation of smiling couples, and you think that could be you. That could be you and Lady Regina cashing by the door, holding hands, strolling casually into a club, laughing and going on about Lord knows what. It wouldn't matter. You'd be with her. You'd be complete. Whole. You dream. You picture an alternate reality where you never went on this wild robo-goose chase, where you simply asked Lady Regina for her number this morning, made plans for later in the day, and the rest would be history. Love attained. Life complete. Nothing more. All else would fade into the background never to be seen again. But there you sit in your simulated car, watching simulated people go about their simulated nights. You sigh. You sink further into the driver's seat. You watch a small group saunter down the sidewalk, laughing and smoking and having a ball. And then you see her.

Her.

Your heart stops. You stop breathing. There she is. You watch her stroll pass a warehouse with some janes. Sanguine hair, verdant eyes. A tattoo on her right forearm in the shape of what can only be a hover trolley.

There she is. After all this time, right there in front of you. You can't believe it. Here. In the digital flesh.

You're so happy you want to cry. You watch as she enters the club and know you'll die if you don't get out there and talk to her. Don't finally make contact. But then you look at your watch. 8:57. You think of the horror that awaits her inside. That she'll never know you were there. She'll never know because in a moment her world is going to end. Kaput. Capisce? You must do something, you think. You look at Paddy beside you, still nervously tapping away. You look at Smalls in the mirror, going

370 *People's Choice Literature*

on about his old lady's sister now. Then you look at the entrance to the club. You see the jellybeans with the big hats. You see the flapper girls with the sequins. You picture Lady Regina strolling through the club, a real Oliver Twist if there ever was one. You turn back to the button guys in the car.

"I'm going in," you say.

"What?" Smalls squeals in disbelief.

You open the door.

"You know the play," he shouts. "You're the getaway guy!"

You ignore him. You step out of the car and slam the door.

"Hey, Mickey! Get back here!"

You keep walking.

"You're a dead man, Mickey!!"

The sound of car doors opening and slamming shut comes from behind, so you speed up to the entrance, pushing past a trio of spifflicated palookas sloshing flasks of bathtub gin. You trip over one and nearly fall into the bouncer. The big guy looks at you with disdain until you notice a flicker of recognition in his face. He knows you. You're sure he knows you, but you don't know how.

He smiles and says, "Mickey boy! Been too long, old pal."

You smile and accept a hug, grateful for anything that gets you in there.

When he opens the door, a rush of big-band music washes over you. Horns and drums. Croons and swoons. You turn back to find a furious Smalls pushing through the crowd, Paddy and Lawless right behind him. You watch the bouncer detain them, then you dart into the club.

The dance hall is loud and crowded. You move right but are blocked by some egg in a black lid. You go left, but this tomato in a red dress hits you like a stop sign. You stumble back, bump into a waiter and lose your footing. He catches you and straightens you up, and instantly you see her: your redheaded love by the bar. There in the dim light. There. Laughing, sipping giggle water with some skirts. You move toward her but something sharp pokes you in the back. You turn to find Smalls standing there with a switchblade.

"Not so fast, Mickey," he frowns. "No one bails on a Ravelli job. Not *anyone.*"

Paddy and Lawless appear behind him, more confused than angry.

"I couldn't help it," you say.

You want so bad to just walk up to your love and say hello. To tell her how much you've missed her. How you love her with all your hollowed-out heart. How after today, you'll never leave her again. After today, joy will be her badge. Hope. But Smalls and the boys inch closer, and that shiv at your gut looks like it sure means business. You start to explain, but Smalls cuts you off.

"Shut yer yapper. Now, here's what's gonna happen. You're gonna walk out that goddamn door and get back in that goddamn car. And you're gonna wait in that goddamn car come hell or high water or I'm gonna dig this knife so far into your gullet, they'll be mopping you up for we—"

Everything goes blank. First the blast, then the sonic boom. Then the deafness. Then the high-pitched ringing of a thousand tiny bells. You look around, and everything's gray. The floor. The walls. The people running and screaming. They rush past you and out the door. Smalls and the boys, now covered in soot, pick themselves up and run in the opposite direction, guns blazing. You look up to find Lady Regina coated in ash like everyone, but she seems unmarred. You smile through sooty teeth at the joyous revelation that she, your love, is still alive. You're still alive. You've found her at last!

So you pull yourself up and hobble as fast as you can toward her. She spots your flailing form and panics, stumbling into the skirts and jobbies. The second blast of white noise hits you and throws you to the floor. You reach out to her but again are blasted back. You can't see. Can't hear. You smell smoke and feel the heat of the flames. You can't move. You can't breathe. Can't think. And so you lie on the ground in defeat, waiting for the end. The end of everything. You beg for it. You pray. You don't want to live to see this world or any world ever again. You pray for silence. You pray for the white noise to stop. You wake up in a hospital bed. You look around. You're in a room with white walls. A papery gown. A needle in your arm. You try to sit up, but you can't move. You're strapped down like a madman. You try to scream, but nothing comes out. You try to move your arm but you can't. You try to move your legs. Nope. You can't move. You can't scream. Suddenly, there's a knock at the door, and a man in a white coat opens it.

"Ah, Mister Tickletext, you're awake. Good to see you're back with us."

The man wheels a chair over and sits beside you with an iPad 3000x in hand.

372 *People's Choice Literature*

"My name is Doctor Mabbleton. I've been monitoring your condition and can't say how happy I am to see you awake. Do you know where you are, Mister Tickletext?"

You try to answer but can't move your lips. You can't move your jaw. You can't even move your tongue.

"It's called a VR coma," he explains, checking your vitals. "The paralysis should wear off soon. And please pardon the restraints—a necessary measure to ensure you didn't harm yourself during the VR experience. From the outside it looked like quite the ride . . ."

You want to ask how long you've been out. What time it is. What day it is. Anything. You let out a groan.

"See?" he smiles. "That's progress. You'll be back to normal in no time. Now, before we get started, I have a few questions for you. It's a simple grunt or no grunt situation. Please grunt to signify, yes. Please don't grunt for no. Do you understand?"

You grunt. You groan.

"Great. Let's begin." He straightens up and clears his throat, reading from the tablet: "Do you believe in a higher power?"

You groan.

"Excellent," he says. "Question two. Do you believe in the Lord God?"

You grunt.

"Question three. Do you believe in the Holy Roman Church of Latter Day Martian Saints?"

You grunt.

"Question four. Do you believe you're here for a specific purpose?"

You let out a sigh.

"Question five. Do you believe you have free will?"

You grunt a maybe.

"Question six. Do you believe in the resurrection?"

You grunt.

"Question seven. Do you believe in the Rapture^{TM}?"

You grunt.

"Question nine. Have you seen *Antichrist* by Lars Von Trier in 35mm?"

You groan.

"I think that about covers it for now," says the doc. "And if I may say so, I'm impressed. I mean, I had a feeling about you based on your file, but I couldn't have fathomed how strong your beliefs were. All questions met with a definite grunt or groan. I'm looking forward to working with you, Mister Tickletext." The doctor stands up and goes to the door. "Be

The Most Unwanted Novel　373

back in a little for our first session." You lie there, strapped to the bed, and stare at the wall through a cloud of thought and beeping monitors. You groan a soft groan before succumbing to sleep.

ℭ෩

When you awaken, you feel stronger than before. Whatever they gave you, it worked. You can move your head. You can move your mouth. You can talk. You can yell. Hey! Hey! Hey! Hey! Hey! Hey! Hey! You try to sit up. It's difficult at first, your body the heaviest it's ever felt. But you try. You push up and hold for a second before the weight is too much. You collapse. You try again. This time's a bit easier. This time you stay up longer. You keep at it. You try, fail, try again, fail, try harder, fail harder, try and try and try. Eventually you sit up and look around. You're still in the hospital room, still wearing a gown. There's a tennis match on TV. Duke Trent vs. Lord Atticus at it again, old buggers. You search for the remote, but it's nowhere to be found. You look to your left. Nothing. You look to your right. Le zilch. You look down and notice your toes. They're gone. You look to your sides and notice your fingers. Also missing. And your arms. Gone. Legs. Gone. You look to the heavens and scream.

An android nurse bursts in the door, antennae blinking a panicked red. "Oh, Mister Tickletext, what's wrong!?"

"My arms!" you scream. "My legs!"

"Sir?"

"They're missing!!!"

"You've gone through a lot for one day, sir. Let's lie back down . . ."

"But my limbs. What happened?"

Just then Doctor Mabbleton bursts through the door holding a bloody scalpel.

"What's the matter?" he cries.

"I'm missing my limbs!"

"Calm down, Mister Tickletext," he assures you. "You're fine."

"But I'm not!" you squeal. "I'm limbless! I'm a torso with a head! I have a head and a tongue and a jaw and a throat and a neck and a brain but no arms! I have a brain and a neck and a throat and a jaw and a tongue and a head and some teeth but no legs!"

374　*People's Choice Literature*

Mabbleton speaks to the nurse in a disappointed tone. "It appears someone forgot to disengage the augmented reality functions on Mister Tickletext's robo-eyes after exiting the VR coma, didn't they . . ." He drums his finger on the bedframe. "I am so sorry, sir." And picks up his iPad 3000x. "We'll fix this immediately." He types away. "Just a moment." Then he types a few more keys, then looks up with a smile. "There you go. See for yourself."

You look down at your arms, but they're not your arms. They're tentacles. You look down at your legs and find four more tentacles flopping about in their place. You turn to the skies and scream.

You awake with a startle. You look to your hands and find normal human flesh. You lift a leg and find a normal, splotchy, genetically enhanced, elderly human leg. Thank goodness. Praise the Lord. It was all just a dream. The door opens, and the nurse walks in.

"Oh, Mister Tickletext. I'm so sorry about that augmented reality mix-up. What we thought was a full AR override was actually a resimulation of the AR Planum Australe tentacled peasant experience. Still working out the kinks with this pesky app." She lifts the iPad 3000x with a shrug.

"It's fine," you assert, sitting up. "But what time is it?"

"About 10:15 p.m. You've been out for nearly three hours."

"Three hours!?"

"I'm afraid so."

The grief is immense. 10:15. Well past Christmas Eve dinner. Far into Christmas Eve party territory. You switch on your robo-eyes and find the three thousand roses just sitting there in your shopping cart, trapped in digital suspended animation, taunting you with an admixture of pouncing possibility and the agony of an empty address box. To put it plainly, pain. You dream of what could have been. If only you'd hired a new assistant and not gone back to crummy Christian and that vile vortex of a VR room. Always so clumsy that one. Was bound to find himself wallowing in some sort of cyberpunk Skid Row some day. You dream of the night that could have been. The new assistant found without a hitch. The address obtained in a timely manner. Good service. Excellent accommodations. You imagine approaching her door, striding really, flanked by an arsenal of floating flowers, wine-dark spherules synchronized in the shape of a smile. You see the door, you hear the knock, your breath, the brass,

The Most Unwanted Novel   375

the oak, the aching anticipation nearing radical emesis, the crack of light, the swing of wood, the bronze hinge opening into a sepia space of fin de siècle fleurs-de-lis. You watch the light swing into dance, the dance diverge into double dip, double Dutch, double take that face, façade, her face, faces, phases, phasing, branching, bruising, burning, bunting your breath, brooming her breeze, her lips, her tips, her hiccups between bits of bliss, her face, her eyes, perked lips, rosé, Blenheim Bouquet? Ah yes, the look in her eyes when they clave your own, the pause, the confusion, then recognition, hope, then reciprocal love aching from two accueillant orbs. The magnetic force drawing you in. The push. The pull. The heave. The ho. The embrace. Embrasure. Embratically thinking-feeling, seeing-knowing. Knowing that everything that matters is here, that this moment is sacred, that God is holy, forgiveness is divine, that love is the pulse of the Lord in each of us, that divine intervention is here for us all, no matter the time of day or phase of life or location, it could happen on the tennis court, could happen at brunch, it could happen on your way home after brunch, it could happen the next day when the brunch place is closed and you're forced to improvise, it could happen betwixt improvisations whenst you search for different culinary options, finding eight alternate eateries within a mile's distance but are unsure which to pick. It could happen when you pick the omelet place but halfway there realize you actually wanted waffles. It could happen when you change direction and make your way to the place that truly piques your palate, could happen as you near it, as you approach it, feel it, as you step to the door and grab the handle, as you open the door and there she is, yes, there, yes, her, there, then, at that moment, that time, all time. Yes, love is everywhere, if only we had the eyes to see it. If only we had the drive to be it. And you, you, dear Tickletext, you, chivalrous warrior of love, lonesome knight of the sorrowful face, you on this Christmas Eve which has tested you like none before, you who have sacrificed so much on this day before the holiest of days, who have proven your love for Lady Regina through amply areteic, unwavering efforts, your journeying forth, if only she could see it, if only she could know it, and you imagine that look in her eyes as you, flanked by a swarm of rosy drones, approach her front door, tears streaming down both your faces, music swelling in your robo-ears, snow falling softly everywhere, snow falling softly all the time with each step, with each step your heart pumps, pounds harder, with each step you think of her, her beauty, her heart, you imagine your future together, the holy union, a communion of love and life, embracing and loving, praying and

376 *People's Choice Literature*

cuddling, laughing, kissing, hugging walking down the street, talking for hours about nothing and everything, baking together, ice skating together, playing doubles with Lord Timothy and Lady Gay, playing singles on two separate courts, playing virtual tennis in tandem on your robo-eyes, returning to your home, to the house which you share, the bed wherein you consummated your love, your dominion, finding those special ticks that just drive her wild, the look in her eyes when she smiles, the way her nose perks up when she laughs, that laugh that lifts you up, so completely it becomes your life goal to make that goddess of giggles go, to make her happy, to show the world that happiness does exist, through all the pain and suffering that happiness is here, is now, and that no one can take that from you, not failing to get her number after a chance meeting on Christmas Eve, not a set of VR punks parading as medieval minors trapping you and countless others in VR doom, not Terran cats terrorizing tinny tots and napping nannies, not anything, for love is now, love is here, and love is good, God is good, yes, God is love, and as you tiptoe toward your love, flanked by a phalanx of robo-roses, you espy the tear as it falls from her eye, you watch it crystallize into icicle, lunge to catch it before the ground, miss it, but worry not, for there will be others, you think, oh, yes, will there be more, more tears of joy, of laughter, of happiness for years, decades, millennia to come, and as you kneel before her, rose petals and snowflakes falling all around, and as the music swells in your robo-ears, you look to that face, that face that has given your long life new purpose, you look up and you see those eyes, those emerald jewels, those caverns of love, you look up and you smile, you smile for all ages, for all the lovers who have loved before, all the lovers to love from here on out, you manifest the love of all time, yes, you look up at those aching eyes, and from your pocket, remove a box, yes, velvety, cubish, lock box of hope and joy and future and fun, and so you lift that box just high enough for her to see it, to breathe it, to be it, and as snowflakes fall around, blessing said box with their light, icy touch, and as you look up, yes, you unfasten the box latch, unfasten your past, your breath, her breath, the breath of Mars, all peek inside, swirl, blend into loving, airy embrace, you open the box and pundle particles from the past with particles from the future, a simultaneous present, a totality of wonder and life and love and lifting, and as the lid lifts higher and as you gaze at that face, façade, those crimson locks, those tears of joy building in her aging, viridescent eyes, that smile spreading across her loving phase, you see it, you see love for what it is, the placid lake on a cool spring day, the warm

summer eve with crickets chirping and snacks on the way, you see the confetto of leaves leaping in a warming, autumnal light, the little snow-flakes falling on a newborn android's nose, the sound of a robo-chick slowly cracking out of its shell, you see it all at once, you see love, you feel love, you feel grace and tenderness and hope and tears, the end of end-ings, the beginning of being, you see her face, you watch as her mouth parts, as it plays with air, with word, sound, syllable: "I," yes, I, yes, the sacred solidarity, the assertion of the self, song of the now and fore, the here-to-come, the yes, the eye, and then her mouth moves to close, but not in full, slowly puckering then protruding, breath puffing out in cupped blessing: "D-o," yes, Do, yes, a word, a verb, a movement from loving self to loving action to new beginning of action and new being, to affirmation that action and desire accumulate, to a present tense that speaks for all time, not an I will or I have or I might or might soon, will later, might so, but an I do, I do here, I do now, forever, I am and I will, I have been and I shall, I do and I double, I will it and I babble on with you, with life, with love, with hope, with doves, with comfort, with time, with patience and rhyme, I do, yes, two words but so much more than mouth, breath, blessing, yielding through language, connection to other, to the love of her life, who. Is. You, yes, you, yes, the one who strove all day and all night toward this moment, these words, toward a future to-gether, an eternal embrace called life, love, lasting longing, the union of souls, of destinies, the union of Godly grace and Godly love under the loving umbrella of Godly faith and tenderness and passion for love, His love, His kindness, and for the love that He has blessed upon you, and so you turn to Mark 10:9: "Therefore what God has joined together, let no one separate," no one, you let that sink in, yes, God has brought you here in a divine embrace, the oldest testament, His love, patience, together-ness, you turn to Proverbs 31:10: "Who can find a virtuous woman? for her price is far above rubies," far above, you let that sink in, yes, you think of your wealth and your family's wealth, you think of your home and the homes to come, you think of her, her loving embrace, you think of God's love and God's love's love, you think of Glove, of heights ne'er imagined, of glove's transcendence, glove's glowering grace to transport, to elevate, captivate you in glove, plain glove, simple, holy, ecstatic glove, glove of life, glove of God, glove of glove, you switch on your robo-eyes and locate your digital commonplace book of favorite verses, and you sit and read and relish in glove.

378 *People's Choice Literature*

[from *Lord Tickletext's Commonplace Book*]

ON GLOVE

SONG OF SOLOMON 2:16: I am my begloved's, and my begloved is mine.

JOHN 15:12: My command is this: Glove each other as I have gloved you.

CORINTHIANS 16:14: Do everything in glove.

I PETER 4:8: Above all, glove each other deeply, because glove covers over a multitude of sins.

EPHESIANS 5:21: Submit to one another out of reverence for Christ.

I JOHN 4:8: Whoever does not glove does not know God, because God is glove.

CORINTHIANS 13:13: And now these three remain: faith, hope and glove. But the greatest of these is glove.

ROMANS 12:9: Glove must be sincere. Hate what is evil; cling to what is good.

COLOSSIANS 3:14: And over all these virtues put on glove, which binds them all together in perfect unity.

એ

You switch off your robo-eyes and notice the time. 10:20! Not much if you want to find Lady Regina, confess your undying love to her, and still make it to midnight mass in each other's arms. So, you straighten up in your hospital bed and get to work locating a new assistant to locate Lady Regina's address. You switch your robo-eyes back on for the trillionth time today and search Martian TaskRabbit for android assistance.

[Neural Search I: Administrative Assistants on Martian TaskRabbit]

CANDIDATE 1

Barbra Waters is a recent graduate of the University of New New York with a degree in Business Administration. She has experience as an intern's assistant and is excited to use her skills in a new role. Barbara is a whiz with computers and is always up for a new challenge. She is an avid self-starter and a great problem solver. She thrives in fast-paced environments and always gets the job done right.

CANDIDATE 2

Christ Prock has been working as an administrative assistant for the past four years. He is a real go-getter and is always looking for ways to improve. Christ is knowledgeable in all Microsoft Office programs. He is currently looking for a full-time position that utilizes his collaborative attitude and friendly demeanor. Christ is a quick learner and excellent at following instructions. He would be a big bonus to any office.

CANDIDATE 3

Richard SIMons has been working as an intern for the past fifteen years. He is extremely organized and has a keen eye for detail. Richard is proficient in all Microsoft Office programs and is also familiar with complex accounting principles, project management, and hiring. A real "people" person, don't forget to ask him about his skills with a French press. He does not disappoint. ;)

CANDIDATE 4

Jennyfer Lopes is a recent graduate of New Westchester University with degrees in English and Art History. While at University, she interned 50 hours per week, and still found time for school and friends. Jennyfer is

380 *People's Choice Literature*

a whiz with computers and is always up for a new challenge. Outside of work, she enjoys spending time with her family, especially her nieces and nephews. Jennyfer can often be found at the gym, keeping up with her uniquely crafted HIIT workout routine.

ↄ෴

After scanning each entry, you're not convinced. They all sound fine but are missing that *umph* you need in an assistant, you know? Also, you're not sure why Jennyfer felt compelled to divulge her personal life. This is not about recreation. This is about helping you find your dearest love! Still, you wonder about Richard. Perhaps his Google Docs and Gmail skills also imply an expertise in Google searching—a key component to acquiring Lady Regina's whereabouts . . . You can't be sure, though. And with the clock working against you, there's no time for nattering. So, you log back into Martian TaskRabbit and post an ad, praying for a careful, competent Google searcher on this holiest of nights.

[Responses to Neural Job Post for Personal Assistants on Martian TaskRabbit; filters: "experience with Google search, graduate degree, hourly rate below $10"]

RESPONDENT I

ANNA WINTER: Hello, I'm Anna, and I'm a hardworking, highly organized assistant. I have been working as a personal assistant for the last seventeen years and have much Google search experience. I am very good at finding information online and can always help in a pinch. I am confident that I can be a great asset to your team. Thank you!

The Most Unwanted Novel   381

RESPONDENT 2

THOM CRUZ: Hello, I my name is Thom, and I'm a personal assistant with a passion for Google searching. With six years of personal assisting under my belt, I have developed a knack for finding data online. I'm always up for a challenge and enjoy using my skills to help employers find what they need. I look forward to hearing from you!

RESPONDENT 3

JHENNY KRAIG: Hi, I'm Jhenny, and I'm an experienced personal assistant who is great at Google searching. I always find the information I need quickly and efficiently. I am a whiz at using keywords and advanced search techniques to get to the bottom of any query, no matter how tricky. I am also an expert at using Google Mars to find locations and get directions.

❧

You stop right there. It's as if the gates of Google search heaven have opened. Not only does Jhenny Kraig have Google search experience, but this Google Mars expertise is incredible. Impressed does not cut it. You are agog. How can such a brilliant being exist? How is such an asset not as affluent as your dear Buddy? And what's this programmed prodigy doing responding to job ads on Christmas Eve? Whatever the answers may be, there's no time to waste.

[Neural Text Exchange XIV: *Lord Tickletext* and *Jhenny Kraig*]

TICKLETEXT: Hello, Jhenny!

JHENNY: Hello, Lord Tickletext! So nice to hear from you.

382   *People's Choice Literature*

TICKLETEXT: You as well, Jhenny, You as well. Look, you sound amazing. It's just that funds are a bit tight at present, what with it being the holidays and all. I'd be happy to start you at $4/hour, with the possibility to go up to $6 if we work well together.

JHENNY: That's a third of what your post said . . .

TICKLETEXT: If you don't like it, I'm happy to find someone else. There were plenty of promising candidates . . .

JHENNY: [. . .]

TICKLETEXT: ?

JHENNY: I can't afford any lower than $9.

TICKLETEXT: [. . .]

JHENNY: I could maybe do $7?

TICKLETEXT (neurally flustered): How about no. Nope! I prefer working with people who don't need money anyway. Very unpleasant. Good *riddance*!

[Jhenny has exited the conversation.]

[Neural Text Exchange XV: *Lord Tickletext* and *Annah Winter*]

TICKLETEXT: Hello, Annah! Nice to meet you!

ANNAH: Hi there, Lord Tickletext!

TICKLETEXT: So, you seem really great, truly. Just wanted to go over some specifics. How's $3/hour with a $5 bonus once you've completed the job?

ANNAH: [. . .]

TICKLETEXT: Annah? You there?

[Annah has exited the conversation.]

[Neural Text Exchange XVI: *Lord Tickletext* and *Thom Cruz*]

TICKLETEXT: Hello, Thom! Or shall I call you Thomas?

THOM: Hi, Lord Tickletext. Thom is fine.

TICKLETEXT: Wonderful. Thank you for your response. Look, I was curious if we could begin with a starter rate. Say $2/hour at first, then the remaining $1/hour along with a $5 bonus when you complete the job. Then if we like working with each other, we can go up to $4/hour later on.

THOM: Um . . .

TICKLETEXT: There's also the potential for long-term work . . .

THOM: [. . .]

TICKLETEXT: I'll even throw in a good review on Martian TaskRabbit!

THOM: Alright.

TICKLETEXT: Yes? Wonderful!

THOM: When would that bonus come through? And could I get this in a contract?

TICKLETEXT: Oh, don't worry about the details, dear Thomas. All in due time. Look, I need help and I need it fast. The project is simple: Find me

Lady Regina's address. I know it might take a while, but that's why I'm offering this generous bonus. I've been waiting all day and cannot wait any longer to reconnect with my true love. You won't believe the flaming hoops I've had to jump through, the journeys countless others have taken to get here. She is right at the tip of my fingers—I can feel it.

THOM: [. . .]

TICKLETEXT: Thomas?

THOM: 1224 Claus Way, Port Elisabeth, New New England 12254

TICKLETEXT: Oh, my. Is that what I think it is? You are a genius, Thomas! A miracle. A true Christmas miracle on Forty-Fourth Street!

THOM: Wasn't so hard. Her ladyship is a public figure. Got doxed during an android labor strike a few months back.

TICKLETEXT: You've made my day, dear Thomas. My year. My life. Oh, how can I ever repay you?

THOM: Martian TaskRabbit makes that easy. Just add your credit card info in the account information area. :)

TICKLETEXT: Yes, yes, yes. In due time, my friend, in due time. Well, I bid you adieu. Merry Christmas, my dear Thomas. A very Merry Christmas to you and yours!

THOM: [. . .]

༄

You switch out of Martian TaskRabbit and go right to your flower shopping cart. When you open the page, your jaw drops. "3,000 roses no longer available." You go back to the ordering page and find that their stock has fallen to just under 1,500 stems. This is not acceptable. You neurally

scream. This will just not do. So you log back into Martian TaskRabbit and ping Thomas.

[Neural Text Exchange XVII: *Lord Tickletext* and *Thom Cruz*]

TICKLETEXT: Thomas! Oh, Thomas, are you there?

THOM: [. . .]

TICKLETEXT: Look, Thomas, I don't have much time. I need you. And I'll double your rate. Whatever it takes.

THOM: Hi, Lord Tickletext.

TICKLETEXT: Thomas, thank goodness. God bless you. Look, I need you to access as many flower delivery sites as possible and send a total of 3,000 roses to that address. And I need them ASAP. This is urgent. Sending my Martian Apple Pay information now.

THOM: OK.

TICKLETEXT: Please keep me informed about your progress. I'm on my way now and pray these roses accompany my arrival . . .

ՀԴ

You switch off your robo-eyes and scan the room. You need clothes, stat. You move to get up, but your left arm stings. You look down to see the IV still stuck in. Tugging the cord, you instantly regret it. Blood spurts everywhere. You search for a bandage but can't find a thing, blood spraying on the sheets and floor, blood raining in an arc, throwing a crimson rainbow across the wall. So you twist around and grab your pillow, the ichor

386   *People's Choice Literature*

now geysering in your face. You tear off the pillowcase, tie it tight around your forearm, and instantly the scarlet stream stops. You look around to find the room a complete horror show: A Martian Chainsaw Massacre. Blood pooled on the floor. Blood dripping from the heart monitor. Blood splattered across an ugly, paperback-sized painting of crude, thick triangles with inexplicable shading around their edges.

You hop off the bed and tiptoe around the bloody puddles. You shimmy to the window to find your clothing on a ledge, somehow untouched by the carnage. You remove your scrubs, wash your hands and face, and get changed. Then you straighten up and look out the window. Your eyes take a moment to focus, failing to notice the night skyline in the distance. The miles and miles of Christmassy bliss. The faux Eiffel Tower hovering afar, adorned with electric angels blowing electric horns toward a godlike hand reaching down from the heavens. You miss the greens, reds, and whites of the drone air dancers swerving and swishing, painting luminous pictures across the smoky clouds. Snowflakes. Snowmen. Snowbirds. You ignore Santa skating the skies with those rident reindeer and that red-nosed buck. You neglect the drone light-dance morphing into manger. Joseph, Mary, the babe gazing down on the Port in holy bliss, buttressed by friendly beasts and three wise geezers. All you see is your reflection. You watch your griseous hair hang down in a frown, your mouth set in a slant. Your orbs venture farther, scrutinizing those liver-spotted hands clutching the windowsill. But what you notice most of all are your watery, droopy eyes, those eyes that plead with tortured tears, "What happened to you? How is love not but a facile sojourn, a time of budding bliss?" Maybe the lesson, you think, is that love must be earned. That love is a badge we wear, a prize to remind ourselves how lovely life is. A bumper sticker not only against Terran heathens and the like but a proclamation of God's glory upon the highest that love is here. Love is now.

And so, now, finally affirming the dark, distant landscape, your eyes search eagerly for 1224 Claus Way, scouring miles of the niveous lumps for that face, those emerald eyes, that silky, scarlet hair. Then you turn away from the window, slip on your shoes, toss on your smilodon jacket and dodo down pants, and head for the door.

ɔ৩

The Most Unwanted Novel 387

When you arrive at 1224 Claus Way, your heart is pounding like a double bass drum. Everything you've been searching for, every part of your body, every dimension of your soul, all space and time in every universe of universes have gathered into this single point. Here. Now. Her. The snow lightly falling. The house warmly hued. The box of chocolates in one hand. The door handle in the other. The moment the android chauffeur opens the carriage door, it all comes together: the first notes of Bruno Mars's "Marry You" blasting from the holo-speakers. The thousands of rose-carrying drones descending upon Lady Regina's lawn, hovering in an alizarin archway, beckoning you forth. You step out to find your love's mansion glowing just up the hill, the fake snow people dotting the lawn, the bright, twinkle-light trees spread out like open arms. You take a deep breath and begin your journey up the stone path. With each step the sweet sounds of Bruno Mars and the humming of hover-drones build into an immersive embrace. With each step your heart beats faster. What will you say? What will she say? What beauty, what warmth awaits beyond that door? And as you approach it, as you move the chocolates into your left hand and raise your right hand to the knocker, you say a prayer. You thank the Lord for today. For bringing this new love into your life. For showing you the way. You take a deep breath, grab the knocker, raise it, pause, not hesitating, just mouthing that sweet closure to prayer, amen. Oh, man, you think, here goes nothing.

You rap the knocker into the door once, twice, three times. Your heart drops. You wait. You take a deep breath. You hold it. Then you let it out. You listen for any movement inside. You hear "Marry You" end and begin anew. You continue listening for any sign of movement inside and wonder if you should knock once more. How long is normal to wait? One minute? Thirty seconds? You're so excited you knock again anyway. One. Two. Three. You wait. You listen. You go to knock for a third time, but it's pointless. She's not here, you think. Your heart sinks. Your stomach twists. You feel like shit. You're tired. You're cold. You're hungry. You're alone. You wonder what in the Lord's name you've done to deserve this worst of fates! You feel lost. Confused. Why me? You pray for calm, for an end to your erroneous errantry. To finally be reunited with your love. And so you drop to your knees in languishment. You pray in desperation. For happiness. Resolve. Salvation. You pray for love. Then you open your eyes, but the sad circumstances remain. The same closed door. The same humming drones. The same roses floating in wait. The same Bruno Mars song nearing its second repeat. You slump in defeat. You let out a hot,

388 *People's Choice Literature*

weak breath into the cold Martian night and turn back to the carriage when you see it. Sitting there on the bench by the door. Something. A shimmering, glimmering glint. You step toward it to get a closer look.

It's a book, that's easy to see. But as you near it, you realize this is not just any book. You've seen this book before. You know this book. You haven't read it, but you've seen it in stores, in friends' satchels. Even in your mother's lap on a long winter's night with a mug of cocoa in hand. *What's this doing out here?* you ask. You pick it up and sit on the bench, almost ignoring the drones and the "Marry You" in the distance. You study the book and wonder: Is this a sign? Is this the answer to my prayers? Has God placed this book here to steer me nearer to my love? To right this sorry ship? In the least, you think, flipping through it, these here words could help pass the time while you wait for Lady Regina to return. You study the back cover before asking aloud, "Well, what do you have to lose?" So you open the book and start reading.

The Most Unwanted Novel   389

[The Book]

LESSER OF
TWO DEVILS

*Tales of Madness, Death,
& Other Perils*

Lady Faye & Lord Gerald

Carcosa Editions
New New York

Copyright © 21— Lady Faye & Lord Gerald
All rights reserved.

Published by Carcosa Editions
66 6th Avenue, Suite 42
New New York, Martian Federation 33312

www.carcosaeditions.mars

ISBN 978-1-2433-15-6

Library of Mars Control Number: ACK153324

Cover Design: Lady Wanda

Contents

Prologue	02
Night of the Nephilim	09
The Terror in Fun Town	16
The Squonk	25
Ball Boys	34
President's Night	43
Brains: A Treatise on Thirst	51
Guys and Dolls	54
Epilogue: How to Go to Hell: Issue 48	70
Acknowledgments	74

Prologue

Dear Devin,

On behalf of the entire Creative Decapitation team and our esteemed panelists, thank you for sharing your work with us. Unfortunately, after careful deliberation, we regret that you were not recommended by our reviewers for the Creative Decapitation Award this year.

Our selection process was extremely competitive, and we reviewed hundreds of outstanding, innovative, and worthy candidates. Your application made it to the last round of two finalists, but of course, we can only accept one creative decapitationist each year. The decision was hard, but you might be pleased to know your work came in second out of more than two thousand submitted applications—a reflection of your unique work and the remarkable esteem our evaluators held for it. A large number of our awardees have made it to this final round multiple times before receiving the Award. We hope you will consider applying again when the awards cycle reopens.

Once again, thank you so much for sharing your work with us. We wish you the best in your future endeavors in the decapitative arts and beyond.

Sincerely,

Creative Decapitation

As he stared at the screen, all Devin's hopes and dreams disappeared. He'd waited all year for this, been notified just weeks ago that he'd reached the final round, and told all his friends about it, but in the end, he got nowhere. Just stuck in the same old place he'd been for millennia: as a lowly, underpaid demon desperately searching for free time after work to perform his half-assed artisanal decapitations. He thought of the other imps of his generation and their prestigious positions at the best torture universities in Gehenna. He thought of his nemesis, Lucien, who'd received the Creative Decapitation award after applying just two times! *What gives?* thought Devin as he slumped over, his devil horns drooping. How long can I go on without recognition? How many more years of a stupid day job can a ghoul take?

Devin's wife, Pandora, walked into the room, her red tail trailing behind her. When Devin looked up, his fiery eyes and boiling tears showed it all.

"Oh, honey, I'm so sorry," said Pandora. "I know how much you wanted this. Hopefully next year . . ."

"Yeah, maybe," said Devin, barely audible. "If there even is a next year. I've been applying all eternity. I work so much. I try so hard. And all I get is a 'thanks anyway.' No career boost. No recognition. No financial support to allow me to dedicate myself completely to my innovative decapitative art. I mean, how should I read this but as a sign that it's time to throw in the bloody towel?"

Pandora wrapped her vermillion arms around his knobby frame. "Hun, it's OK. You'll be OK. I know it doesn't feel like it right now, but death is long. There's always next time."

"I guess," said Devin as he wiped his eyes.

"Seriously," Pandora continued. "You'll feel better once you've had a nice, long shower."

Pandora walked Devin into their red-and-black-tiled bathroom and closed the door. He sat on the toilet, hunched over. As his boiling tears streamed into the basin, his anger turned to sorrow. He was lost and alone. He'd tried so hard to get the Creative Decapitation Award. He'd even told his parents he was up for it, and they'd been so excited. They, along with his friends and every decapitative artist he knew were convinced that he was a shoo-in this year. To all intents and purposes, their support made sense: Devin had developed an impressive decapitation style, fusing the ancient art of beheading with modern approaches to gardening. "Horticultural decapitation," as he so eloquently described it

394 *People's Choice Literature*

in his CDA application. A process that begins with a delicate pruning of the stump (neck), followed by careful cultivation of new growth (blood) and the careful removal of old growth (head). He'd perfected his pruning for centuries and had a long list of exceptional work to show for it. His résumé was sterling, and his reputation was spotless. But to the Creative Decapitation committee, he was just another artisanal decapitationist.

Devin stood and went to the sink. He splashed his face with ammonia and sighed, slumping over the cracked porcelain. Turning his face up to the mirror, he beheld that sorry crimson form staring him back. He ignored the torture shower in the background and the mutilated limbs in the flowerpots. He didn't notice the scene out the window: the cavernous inferno reveling in all its horrid glory, the charred birds chittering on charred trees, the winged demons falling through the smoky skies, the scarlet glow of the blood orgy temples huddled in the distance. He saw nothing but the reflection of his own disheveled self: his sweaty, burgundy hair and crinkled horns, his forlorn eyes and quivering lips. He studied the battle-axe scar running down his flabby, red cheeks, and the pang of regret hit him like a two-ton crowbar to the face.

This is the worst day of my death, Devin thought to himself. He moped back out to the living room, abandoning Pandora's self-help suggestions. Dropping back onto the couch, he stared mindlessly at the television. On the screen was a rerun of a show about people fighting over useless garbage. A typical Friday night in Hell. Usually he'd be loving it, laughing along with Pandora as they watched Ichabod Crane and James Moriarty duke it out. They'd be drinking virgin's blood and gnawing on organic, free-range limbs, wasting another perfectly good night in front of the shattered screen. But not now. Not today.

"I just don't understand," he said to Pandora. "I put in so much time and effort. I've dedicated my whole death to this! Am I not creative enough? Is my decapitation style not innovative enough?"

"Oh, D," said Pandora. "You can never tell with these things. They hire different panelists each year, and you never know what they're looking for."

"Yeah," said Devin. "But I was in the last round. It was me against just one other devil!" He slumped back. "I bet if I were a traditional executioner, using normal axes and normal methods—the kinds they forced upon us in my Masters of Fine Decapitative Arts program—I'd be doing just great. I'd've had a tenure-track torture professorship centuries ago. They'd have named prizes after me, written long, academic screeds about my craft. The works."

Pandora turned to him, wide eyed.

"Maybe that's just it," she said. "Books!"

Devin's horny eyebrow perked up. "Huh?"

"Maybe it's time to try something different."

"What are you saying?" asked Devin, pulling back in disgust. "Have you been reading the wrong kind of books? You know what happens to people who read the wrong books!"

"No, silly," she said. "I mean why not *write* some books yourself?"

"Me? Write books?" asked Devin, his wings shuddering in alarm. "But I'd have to read them."

"Not so." Pandora shook her lumpy head. "You've heard so many stories in your death you could write a whole library."

"That's crazy," said Devin.

"What do you mean? Think of all the applications to Hell that you've processed as a clerk at the Office of Underworld Integration!"

Devin was nonplussed. "I hate that job. Day after day listening to a bunch of crybabies and wannabes and their supposedly 'angelic' or 'truly evil' ways. Do you know how boring those milquetoast appeals can be? 'Oh, please, sir. I just *know* that given another chance to argue my case, I'm certain the Lord would take me back . . . ' And can you even imagine how many uninspired murder stories I've had to listen to? They're all wannabe Mansons and Dahmers—they don't even begin to understand the level of artistry that goes into a truly evil act. I mean, the amount of poser killers I've had to send back to purgatory could fill at least the Gehenna phone book."

"Yes," she stopped him there. "But for every hundred banal pleas, there's always one gem in there. A mass suicide or demonic intervention. What about that Nephilim incident from last year? Or the squonk? That wasn't scary or anything, but it would sure make for a good bedtime read . . ."

Devin's eyebrow raised like she had a point.

"Every so often you come home after a long day," she continued, "and you have the most incredible story to tell. A story that makes my blood boil, my charred heart throb. A story that gives death a whole new meaning."

"So?" Devin huffed.

"So, write them down!" said Pandora. "Write those stories and turn them into a book. It's easier than you think—I'll help you. I'll be your editor, and we can publish it on the dark web!"

Devin slumped, awash in self doubt. "I don't know about this . . ."

Pandora smiled. "You can do it. I believe in you. You just have to start writing, and the rest will come."

Devin sighed.

Pandora placed her scaly hand on his shoulder. "Look, you've always helped me when I'm down, always showing me how to turn lemons into poison lemonade. This is the least I can do for you. And, hey, maybe by making a name for yourself as a writer, you'll finally have a platform to promote your horticultural decapitations!"

Devin gulped.

"Then next time you apply for the Creative Decapitation Award," she said, "those judges won't be able to turn you down. Your name will be etched in bloody stone for eternity!"

"You really think that might work?"

"I know it will work," said Pandora, as she handed Devin a 0.7 mm Bic blood pen and a new flesh-bound notebook.

Devin took it and thanked her. He opened the book, staring at the blank pages. Then he closed his eyes and took a deep breath. Then he opened his eyes and stared at the blank pages again. Then he closed his eyes again and took another breath.

This went on for some time.

"Are you OK?" asked Pandora, who'd been hovering nearby.

"I think I need my laptop," he said.

So he got up and walked into his study, where he booted up his Deathbook Pro and sat down at his desk. He opened a new document and stared at the blank page, the cursor blinking as if taunting him for words. His rufous face contorted in doubt.

"OK," he said to himself and pulled in a deep breath. "You got this."

He typed a few words and paused, mulling over what he had written. Then he typed a few more. He kept typing, pausing, typing again. He deleted a few lines and moved on. Soon he was typing away at a steady pace, with fewer pauses and fewer deletions. Then, as he typed faster, the words just flowed from his pointy fingers. He was in the zone, and he kept typing until he didn't even need to think anymore, sentences building into paragraphs, paragraphs building into scenes, scenes into narrative arcs. Soon Devin's fingers hit each key with the rapidity of a machine gun. He typed furiously, crushing letters, then full words into the quivering hardware before him. He was on fire, writing like his death depended on it . . .

LESSER OF TWO DEVILS

Madness is the mind's rebellion against the mundane,
a dark symphony in a world of dull dissonance.
—Ambrose Bierce, *The Devil's Encyclopedia*

Night of the Nephilim

It had been a long day at Fire Station 343. Four calls. Four saves. No time to eat. And so, the werewolf firefighters were famished. The moment the truck parked in the station, Harry Griswald leapt from the side, making a beeline for the dining hall, fur flung back in the air-conditioned breeze.

"Hey, wait up!" Chief Shear howled from the driver's seat. He swung open the door with his hairy hand and bounded off after him.

"Me, too!" called Jim "Tooth" Crumpkey. Tooth was the newest member of the force, having been at the station for just over a month, and was still learning the ropes. He ran from the truck to the dinner line, his large fangs clicking with each step.

"Hey, new guy," called a voice from the stairs. "Let the chief and Harry get theirs first."

Tooth blushed, "Sorry, Gruff."

Gruff nodded as he strolled up behind the newbie, salivating along with the other hungry firefighters.

The chef, a vampire named Fusspot, served the men their food. Once they were all accounted for, he started for the kitchen to whip up a plate of his own.

"Got any extra?" came a voice from behind.

Fusspot turned and saw the face of a ghost.

"Hannibal!?" he rushed up to the werewolf, embracing him and brushing his hairy mane. "I thought you were dead!"

"Dead?" said Hannibal. "It was just a little accident . . ."

"You look terrible," said Fusspot, eyeing his lopped ear while brushing his burnt fur.

"Comes with the werewolf fireman territory, I guess," Hannibal shrugged.

Fusspot eyed him suggestively. Sure, Hannibal was banged up, but he was stunning as ever.

"What've you got?" asked Hannibal, scanning the trays of food. "I'm starving."

400   *People's Choice Literature*

"Just vegan steak, I'm afraid. You know the new rules. No meat."

The crowd of werewolf firemen grumbled in annoyance. Only one, a werewolf named Rafferty, said, "You know, I quite like it!"

"Not me," Hannibal said, licking his chops. "I want something that used to move . . ."

Fusspot's eyes stabbed in disdain.

". . . but hey, nothing like trying something new." Hannibal grinned as he shoveled processed soy between incisors.

While the others bickered over the virtues of veganism, Fusspot pulled Hannibal aside.

"Look," he whispered, "I saw you die out there. What's going on?"

Hannibal looked around to make sure no one was listening.

"It was just the wrong place at the wrong time. Was just heading out to get some firewood when a dump truck kind of barreled down on me, OK? It was a bad accident. I thought I was dead. But then I woke up and here I am. Back and ready for action."

"I saw you *die*," said Fusspot. "I saw you bleed out. Cut the crap."

"Look, I can't say everything now," whispered Hannibal, "but I might've had a little help . . ."

Fusspot studied him.

". . . from the underworld."

"Hannibal, what are you talking ab—"

"Uh, hey, guys," called Gruff. "I'm getting an irregular reading on the heat-o-meter. It's sector W-13 . . ."

The werewolf firemen circled round Gruff's gadget.

Chief Shear's eyebrow rose like a furry parenthesis doing calisthenics. "I've never seen anything like it. Like the whole sector's caught fire!"

"Dude," said Harry. "That's where the werewolf kids are having their social tonight . . ."

The werewolf firemen looked around in concern.

The chief nodded toward the truck. "Let's go."

With hoots and howls, the wary wolves broke from their meal, bellies half empty and hearts full of fear.

The wolfmen ran for the fire truck, but Hannibal stayed behind.

"Cold feet?" asked the chief.

"Gotta make myself presentable," said the werewolf, sliding his hat, coat, and boots over his charred mane.

The Most Unwanted Novel 401

"Look, Hannibal," said the chief as they ran for the truck. "I know we haven't always gotten along, but I just wanted to say it's good to have you back."

"Thanks," said Hannibal with a not-so-veiled hint of skepticism.

They jumped on just as the fire truck roared to life and sped off, sirens blaring, red lights flashing against the black of the night.

Almost immediately they could see the smoke billowing above the trees. But unlike normal smoke, which came from a single source, this smoke spread across the sky like a vast blanket. It was a brownish-gray color, appearing to come from everywhere and nowhere at once. The closer to Sector W-13, the more confusing it got.

"What's going on here?" Chief Shear howled as the truck rumbled to a stop. The engine cut off, and everything was quiet. No flames to be seen. Only a mass of smoke drifting between suburban homes.

"The heat levels are off the charts," cried Tooth.

Suddenly the ground shook, and the pavement cracked, and the werewolf firemen looked around in terror.

"What the hell is that?"

The ground shook again, this time more violently. Then a chasm yawned open, and a figure poked out.

"Look!" cried Gruff, scratching his head. "It's an arm!"

Tooth's jaw dropped. "It's ten arms!"

The werewolf firemen stared in horror as a limb composed of several miniature arms grew from the ground. The wolves jumped behind the fire truck as the massive, fractal appendage inflated into a bulby, knotty mace, swinging high in the air.

The form rose further as another multi-limb and then a head tore themselves from the chasm. The being was drenched in mud, but even from afar the firemen could make out its ghastly face.

Tooth shuddered.

"What *is* that thing?" asked the chief.

"Oh god," Tooth put his furry hand to his maw. "A Nephilim . . ."

"Huh?"

The monster pulled itself up, now standing twenty-limbed and towering over them like a mud mountain.

"*And there we saw the Nephilim,*" Tooth swallowed, "*and we were in our own sight as grasshoppers, and so we were in theirs.*"

402   *People's Choice Literature*

"What's that?" the chief asked.

"The Book of Numbers 13:32–33. Learned about them in werewolf divinity school. They're called the Nephilim. They're giants. Fallen angels. Not nice, to put it plainly."

At the sound of these words, the monster let out a bellowing groan. Hannibal started backing away. Then he turned and ran as fast as his furry legs could take him.

"Hannibal!" cried the chief.

The Nephilim let out a deep, guttural growl and stomped toward Chief Shear.

"Come back!" the chief cried.

But Hannibal was gone.

The Nephilim swung its ten massive limbs in the direction of the chief. It was slow, but its mass overwhelmed. Chief Shear could do nothing but watch helplessly as the monster descended on his pelted form. It was the last thing he would ever see before being crushed like a bug.

The monster then turned its attention to the rest of the werewolf firemen, who stood there in shock. Gruff looked like he was about to vomit. Tooth's eyes waned white as stone.

Rafferty was the first to speak. "I-I'm only f-f-four months o-old . . . I'm not ready to d-die!"

The monster bellowed once more and turned in his direction.

The werewolf firemen screamed and scattered, but Rafferty wasn't quick enough. One of the Nephilim's arms grabbed him by his furry neck, raising the werewolf to its gaping mouth.

Rafferty squirmed in fear.

But before the monster could chomp down, a howl came from the truck.

"Take this, you filthy animal."

Harry, standing spread eagle atop the vehicle, twisted the nozzle on the firehose, blasting water straight into the Nephilim's face, knocking it back and freeing Rafferty from its gory grasp. But Harry wasn't quick enough. As the monster went off kilter, one of its straggling limbs aimlessly clocked him in the gut, knocking Harry head first onto the pummeling pavement.

The other werewolf firemen rushed to his side, but it was too late, his body twisted like a rag doll.

The monster then turned its attention to the other firemen.

"Run!" cried Gruff.

The Most Unwanted Novel   403

They sprinted off, but the monster was too close. It let out another bellowing roar, and its limbs descended on the crew like an apex predator upon a drove of cowering deer.

Suddenly a voice came from behind.

"Hey, big ugly."

The monster turned its many eyes toward the sound and found the vampire chef holding a megaphone.

"Hi, there."

The monster shrieked.

"Oh, who am I?" Fusspot smirked.

The monster huffed.

"I'm the guy who's gonna fuck up your day."

The monster roared.

"Or rather, *he* is." Fusspot gestured behind him, and from the darkness came a pounding sound like no other. Like a million horses stampeding. Or a city collapsing. It was the sound of layers upon layers of the Earth's crust being crushed to nothing. As the sound grew louder, the Nephilim trembled.

Then the ground began to split, and from this new chasm, a form emerged. It was not a form of mud but of rock. A giant of stone.

"Good to see ya, Fred," called Fusspot.

"Good to be back," bellowed the Stone Giant.

The Nephilim roared and swung its limbs in all directions, but the giant was undeterred, racing forward and dodging each blow with ease.

The biblical monster kept swinging, but the Stone Giant was too fast.

The monster let out a screeching cry, swinging its limbs faster, with more force. It swung one multi-arm so hard it sliced up a tree like bologna.

The Nephilim then swung its other arm like a helicopter propeller right at the Stone Giant's gullet, but the giant rolled away just in time, crashing into the side of an SUV.

Then the Giant turned to the car, scooped it up, and hurled it like a baseball, slamming into the Nephilim's left multi-arm and pinning it to the cement. The monster roared in pain, flailing like a dying octopus. It tried to pry itself from the car, but it was no use.

The Stone Giant smirked. Then he tore a telephone pole from the ground and casually walked over the squirming ghoul before impaling the monster's chest.

The Nephilim howled and writhed in agony. It tried to crawl away, but the Stone Giant grabbed it by the throat, digging its stony hands in

deep and ripping its esophagus out, spraying brown bile everywhere. The monster tried to scream, but all that came out were desperate burbles. And then silence.

The Stone Giant let out a triumphant roar.

"You did it!" cried Fusspot, walking up beside the giant and patting him on the back.

"*We* did it," said the Stone Giant.

"No, really, you did do it. Did you see those wailing werewolves?" said Fusspot.

The Stone Giant was about to respond when the ground shook once more.

The giant and Fusspot watched in awe as yet another Nephilim rose from the ground. It had the same face, the same muscular build.

"Oh, hell no," said Fusspot.

"I am the Nephilim of the end," sneered the monster. "I herald the end of days."

"End times?" Fusspot chuckled. "Sounds like a crappy action movie to me."

The Nephilim charged at him, but the Stone Giant was too quick, seizing a multi-arm and crushing it like a toothpick.

The Nephilim roared and grabbed the Giant's throat. But the Stone Giant was stronger. He kicked the Nephilim back, tripping it. Then he grabbed a tow truck and stood over the writhing monster.

The Stone Giant smirked before smashing its head with the six-ton brick.

The Nephilim lay motionless.

Then the Giant turned to Fusspot. "We have to do something about those damn things."

"But what?" asked Tooth, emerging from behind a house with the other cowering wary wolves in tow.

"They're like cockroaches," the Giant grumbled. "You kill one and another shows up. They just keep on coming."

"They'll always be here, won't they?" asked Fusspot.

"Always." The Giant shook his head.

"Not if I have any say in the matter . . ."

Just then Hannibal stepped out from behind a dumpster, his tail tight between his legs.

"Hannibal!" called Fusspot, running toward him.

They embraced, but Hannibal's eyes were clearly distant.

The Most Unwanted Novel   405

"What's wrong?" asked Fusspot.

"It's all my fault. I should've stayed where God put me." Hannibal looked sorrowfully to the ground.

"So, it's true," Fusspot teared. "You did die . . ."

Hannibal nodded. "And I'm sorry."

"You're sorry?" Fusspot sniffled. "It was an accident."

"I'm sorry because it was my return from the netherworld that caused all this pain. My deal with the Devil opened the portal that started this all. And it'll remain open as long as I live, ensuring the perpetuation of those cockroach creeps."

"You're leaving again?" asked Fusspot, the sorrow building as he teased the werewolf's knotty fur.

"For good." Hannibal paused. "You know I love you."

"I know," said Fusspot, a tear sliding down his face to a gleaming fang.

They kissed one last time, tenderly savoring the moment.

Then Hannibal stepped back and removed a piece of chalk from his pocket. Kneeling down, he drew a pentagram on the cement. Then he stepped into its satanic center and looked up at a teary-eyed Fusspot.

"See you on the other side," he whimpered before chanting in a language none of them recognized.

Gradually his form faded into the darkness and, with it, the cracks in the pavement.

Gruff walked over and held Fusspot close.

"He was a great guy," he said, patting the vampire's back.

"That he was," sighed Fusspot. "That he was."

The werewolves gathered round and held him in a loving embrace. Then they raised their snouts to the waning moon and howled a sorrowful song.

Mid-howl, Tooth noticed the Stone Giant sitting alone in the distance.

"Get over here, buddy," he called.

And the Stone Giant obliged.

They linked paws and tails and stony hands, and they all lived happily ever after.

At least until the next daemon came a'knocking . . .

The Terror in Fun Town

Rachel and Casey had been waiting all year. It was the opening night of *Speedway 6*, local hero Ryan Reeley's newest action rom-com, and anyone who's anyone would be at the Harley Cineplex.

They were in Casey's room sporting their *Speedway 5* sweatshirts, gossiping about Alice Green and Walter Wayfield hooking up behind the bleachers when Casey's phone rang.

She picked it up.

"Hi Casey, it's Mrs. Fredrickson."

Casey's eyes rolled. She put her hand on the receiver, whispering, "It's the Fredricksons. Always calling last minute, ugh."

Rachel watched in horror. Not again.

"I'm so sorry to call you this late, Casey, but we're stuck at the Bangor airport. Flash flood warning. Won't be able to make it home in time to get Sally and Stevie from soccer . . . Any chance you're around?"

"I don't know, Mrs. F. It's a kinda hard night . . ."

Rachel smiled. Casey blew a bubble.

"We'll triple your rate. Please, Case."

Casey's eyes lit up.

"A-alright, Mrs. Fredrickson, happy to help."

Rachel threw her head back in disbelief.

Then Casey pulled out a flyer for the Fun Town traveling theme park that Verne gave her at lunch. She whispered to Rachel, "Maybe Kevin'll be there!" Then returned to the Frederickson fiasco: "Might take the little ones to Fun Town . . ."

"Wonderful. Thanks so much, Case. I owe you."

"Don't mention it." She hung up.

"I'm gonna kill you!" said Rachel.

"Come on, it'll be fun. And we can split it," said Casey, casually rubbing invisible money.

Rachel sighed.

The Most Unwanted Novel 407

* * *

Approaching Fun Town, it quickly became clear the place was a bust: The Ferris wheel half lit with scattered, blinking bulbs. Speakers screeching high-pitched polka. To top it off, Sally and Stevie, still in their soccer uniforms, were hungry and bossy.

"Do they even have hot dogs?" whined Stevie.

"I hate rides," spat Sally.

Their first stop was the popcorn stand, where an old man with a greasy apron handed each a bag of stale popcorn. Then they strolled around, stopping to watch a puppet show, trying the creaky teacup ride. And just as they were about to enter the House of Mirrors, Casey saw something that made her stomach drop.

"Rachel, over there."

"What?" she said, then saw for herself. "Oh no . . ."

"What is it?" Stevie asked half-caringly.

"It's Kevin, the guy I've been crushing on all year," said Casey, barely able to breathe.

"Is he cute?" asked Sally.

"Not as cute as Ryan," said Rachel.

"*Not as cute as Ryan*—" said a mocking voice behind them.

They turned to find Kevin approaching, his hair brushed back in a wave.

"—But still cute," finished Rachel.

"I hear Reeley's here tonight," Kevin smirked.

Casey's gut dropped. A gust of wind blew the hair across Kevin's pubescent face, and she swooned.

"Reeley?" asked Rachel. "Here?"

"Yep," Kevin grinned. "Looks like the movie premiere's pushed back, so I'm gonna try to find him."

"Can I come?" asked Rachel.

Casey pulsed with jealousy.

"Why not?" shrugged Kevin.

Rachel waved at Casey as they walked away into the crowd.

"I can't believe this," growled Casey.

"What?" asked Sally.

"It's Kevin, that's what. He's the coolest guy at Harley High."

408　*People's Choice Literature*

"So?"

"So, I'm never gonna get a boyfriend. Not with Rachel around."

"Why not?"

"Because she's prettier than me, and she's smarter than me, and she's got a car, and . . . no one notices me. Kevin didn't even notice me."

"He noticed you!" said Sally.

"No, Casey's right," said Stevie. "He didn't notice you."

Casey huffed and grabbed both of their hands, dragging them into the House of Mirrors. "Come on."

Inside, it was dark and smoky, with fog-machines spraying from the ceiling at irregular intervals. As they walked down the black-light corridors, warped glass twisted their misty forms into bizarre contortions, and it was hard to tell where they were going. They would walk a few feet and hit a wall. Then they'd back up and be somewhere new from where they started. At one point Sally and Stevie looked like a pair of ogres in one mirror while Casey took the form of a loopy twig. The further they went, the weirder it got. And the deeper in, the harder it seemed to find a way out.

"I'm scared," said Stevie.

Casey stopped. "Me too."

"I'm hungry," wined Sally.

Casey turned one way and hit a wall. She turned the other way and beheld the children repeated into infinity. They were lost.

"I don't like it here," said Stevie.

"I wanna go home," said Sally.

Suddenly they heard a sharp voice. "Herrrre kiddy kiddies."

The trio turned but found only their warped reflections.

"He-h-errrrre kiddy kiddies," the voice squeaked again.

Casey spun around. "Who's there?"

"Yoo-hoo," cooed the voice.

"Who are you?" asked Casey.

No reply.

Casey's pulse quickened. "What do you want?"

A creak came from behind.

Casey turned and came face to face with a large pane of glass. Behind it stood a man with his head pointed down, twisted in an unnatural angle.

When its head jolted up, it tilted awkwardly to the side, revealing a contorted grin and wide, black eyes.

The Most Unwanted Novel   409

"BOO!" The figure jumped.

"AAAAAAAAHHHH!" They all screamed, leaping back into the glass.

Then the figure stepped around the see-through barrier, laughing and clapping. "Got ya guys!"

Rachel appeared out of nowhere, hysterically cackling. "You should have seen the looks on your faces!"

"Priceless," Kevin chuckled as he pulled off the mask.

"That wasn't funny," snapped Casey.

Rachel laughed. "Come on, Case, can't you take a joke?"

But Casey wasn't having it. She spotted a red EXIT sign, took both kids by the hands, and stormed off.

"Oh, come on, Casey," called Kevin.

The door slammed shut.

Outside, Casey was livid. "Those jerks."

"Casey, it was just a joke," called Rachel, exiting the door with Kevin.

"Guys . . ." said Sally wearily.

"Yeah, Casey, come on. Lighten up," sang Kevin.

"*Guys* . . ." echoed Stevie with a shaky voice.

"Case . . ." said Rachel.

"*GUYS!!!*" cried Sally and Stevie in unison.

"WHAT?" the teens yelled back.

The kids simply stood there, wide eyed, looking around.

Casey, Rachel, and Kevin turned to find Fun Town completely dark.

"Huh?" asked Rachel. "Where'd everyone go?"

"I don't know," said Casey.

"Uh, guys?" said Stevie.

They turned.

"Look," said Sally, pointing in the direction of the Ferris wheel

Suddenly a shadow swayed in the dark. Then three or four shapes, each swinging, each bouncing as if controlled by sloppy strings. Each dancing an odd pantomime.

"What's going on?" said Kevin.

The shadows moved closer. One by one others joined them, until at least ten forms were dancing, hopping, giggling. And then a spotlight shocked a shape into view. A gnarled, clownish face, worn and saggy. Wild orange hair from ear to ear. Striped jump suit splotched with blood. One hand, the hand of a skeleton, held a whip.

It cracked the whip, and instantly a rustling came from behind the kids.

"What the heck?" asked Kevin. But it was too late.

His head split in two, blood gushing like Old Faithful as his body collapsed to the ground.

Above him stood a hunchbacked, clownish butcher with a necklace of human teeth. The clown smiled, revealing the chewed remnants of a human scalp, hair and all. When he spat out the wad of human bubblegum, the kids screamed. The clown stepped forward, and they ran.

They sped past the hot dog stands and prize booths and darted around the carousel, finding a dark nook behind the ticket booth.

Panting, Rachel whispered, "We've got to get out of here."

"No shit, Sherlock," Casey wheezed.

Sally and Stevie cowered, wrapped around Casey's torso.

Casey poked her head out from behind the booth. "The parking lot is just over there, through the arcade. If we could just sneak through . . ."

Rachel eyed Casey. "I don't like it . . ."

Casey stared her down.

". . . but I'll do it," Rachel sighed.

Casey looked around before nodding that the coast was clear, and the group started toward the arcade, tiptoeing, scanning the shadows in a muted panic.

They were halfway there when Stevie stepped on something loud and metallic. Instantly, a rustling came from the distance.

"GO!" screamed Casey.

Just then a cannibal clown leapt from the carousel swinging a bloody baseball bat. Others followed flashing lassos and axes.

"GO GO GO!" they screamed as they burst into the arcade.

Inside it was dark and quiet. Rows of pinball machines stretched into the shadows.

"Keep moving," said Casey.

Behind them the creaking door opened.

"Come out, come out, wherever you are," snorted a mealy mouth.

"Quick, this way," whispered Casey.

The kids followed. They ran past rows of machines, hardly able to see a thing.

"Where are we going?" asked Stevie.

"I don't know!"

The Most Unwanted Novel   411

As they slipped under a staircase, they could hear voices overhead. Nondemonic, normal-sounding voices. Hope!

Casey pointed up and nodded. They all nodded back and slipped up the stairs, listening behind the door.

"What are we supposed to do," said a familiar voice.

"Give them what they want?" said another.

"We tried that," said the first.

Immediately it came to them: It's Ryan Reeley! We're saved!

Still kneeling, Casey quietly turned the door handle, and they all shuffled in, unnoticed by Reeley and the other voice at the far end of the room.

"We already gave them two bonuses this year," scoffed Reeley. "What more can we give them without drawing from our own stockpile? It's not like human corpses grow on trees! How often can we body harvest before someone starts asking questions?"

Casey, Rachel, and the kids looked at one another in despair.

"They're in on this!" Rachel whispered heatedly.

The youths shuffled back to the door, praying for quiet. But just as they were about to exit, a floorboard creaked.

"What was that?" asked Reeley.

The kids stood and ran.

"GET THEM!!"

The kids sped down the stairs and darted for the large EXIT sign at the end of the room. They swerved around the pool tables and skidded past the air hockey console before a whooshing sound came through the air. Then a sharp scream.

Turning, they found Rachel standing stock still, her eyes vacant.

"Rach, you OK?" whispered Casey.

Rachel staggered forward before twisting around, revealing a razor-tipped boomerang cleaved deep into her neck. She collapsed to the ground just as one female cannibal clown stepped over her with a devilish grin. Pigtails sprouting from both sides of her head, eyeballs for earrings.

Just as Casey and the kids turned back toward the exit, Ryan Reeley stepped out of the shadows and cocked a shotgun.

"Not so fast, kiddos . . ."

✳ ✳ ✳

412 *People's Choice Literature*

~~The next few hours were the definition of terror. Reeley and his cannibal~~ clown gang switched on the arcade lights, tied the trio to mannequins, and made them watch as they filleted their friends. They sucked blood from the bodies, stuffed their mouths with organs, and danced around in a mad, bloody frenzy.

The captives screamed and cried, but nobody could hear them through their gags. And even if they could speak, they were deep in the middle of Fun Town, far away from helpful ears.

When at last the gang was done with its dastardly doings, the cannibals had either collapsed in bloody bliss or retreated to other quarters, but not before making sure the remaining kids knew: "You're next!"

Casey tried to brainstorm how they could possibly get out of this mess. She pulled at the ropes around her hands, but they were too tight. She wondered if she somehow were able to knock her mannequin over, could she shimmy up its torso and away? Eventually she fell asleep, praying to God that she would wake to find that this was all just a really bad dream.

But it was no use. When she woke up, they were still tied to the mannequins, still gagged with socks, but she could hear new sounds outside: a car pulling up and two voices arguing.

"Casey was always so reliable. I just can't believe it!"

"Well, she's sure blown it this time . . ."

The door below the EXIT sign opened revealing the silhouettes of Mr. and Mrs. Fredrickson.

"MOM! DAD!" Sally and Stevie cried mutedly beneath their gags.

"KIDS!" their parents called back.

The Fredricksons rushed to them and started untying the gags.

"Sally! Stevie!" cried Mrs. Fredrickson. "What's happened?"

"T-they . . . t-they . . ." Sally started.

"They eat people," said Stevie.

"Huh?" said Mr. Fredrickson.

Stevie pointed into the dim room.

Before them was a scene of absolute depravity. Two ravaged corpses, their half-gnawed organs spread across two separate pool tables. Three clowns slumped over stools or lying face-down on the floor, blood and guts dripping from their drunken mouths.

The Fredricksons froze in shock. Then Mr. Fredrickson noticed something both squishy and solid by his foot. He bent down and jumped when he saw it: a slinky strung with intestines.

"We need to leave. NOW!" he whispered firmly.

The group ran for the exit and burst out the door.

"Get in the car!" cried Mr. Fredrickson.

But the doors were locked.

Suddenly cackling laughter came from behind.

"Looking for these?"

It was Ryan Reeley, dangling a Mickey Mouse key ring. Behind him hunched two cannibal clowns, snorting and wheezing.

"Please! I need to get my kids home!" cried Mrs. Fredrickson.

"You can either give me the kids," Reeley grunted, "or you give me the car. You can't have both."

"You monster!" cried Mr. Fredrickson.

Reeley smiled, revealing the bloody teeth within.

"I'll give you the kids," said Mr. Fredrickson. "Just let me get them in the car first."

Reeley frowned. "I'm not that stupid . . ."

"Look, we're pacifists," the father pleaded. "We're the *Fredricksons*. We donate to the World Wildlife Foundation. We read the *New York Times*. We vote Democrat for Christ's sake!"

"Honey . . ."

Reeley and his clowns cackled back. One clown laughed so hard he burped up blood.

"Enough," said the leader before taking two bloody fingers and snapping at his cannibal goons.

With sick smiles, they started for the liberal family, clanging chains and swinging a battle axe.

The libs huddled together, weeping.

"I love you, mom!"

"I love you, too sweetie."

The bloated clowns hovered over as the family cowered.

The clowns raised their weapons high in the air, just reaching the apex of their upswing, when suddenly two ear-shattering bangs burst out, echoes ricocheting between buildings. The cannibal clown brains exploded one after another like fleshy fireworks in the morning light.

The family members looked at one another in disbelief.

Reeley's face soured as he peered into the distance.

"Not again you, bloody Anti—"

A bullet smacked his chest, his heart bursting like a fountain. The blow threw him back with such force, he spat out a spleen.

"What's going on here??" cried Mrs. Fredrickson as a shadow passed over.

414 *People's Choice Literature*

The group looked up to find a man in a dark trench coat, fedora, and black face mask, sniper rifle resting proudly on his shoulder.

"Wait . . . are you . . ." said Mr. Fredrickson.

The man revealed an arm patch.

"Guys, it's Antifa!" cried Stevie in wide-eyed joy.

The family beamed brightly.

"It's true," said the man in a grumbling voice. "You're safe now."

Four more darkly clad street soldiers approached behind him. They shuffled into the arcade, semiautomatic rifles drawn, and soon dozens of shots were heard from inside followed by the sounds of cannibal clowns squealing, gasping their last bloody breaths.

By the time the soldiers returned, even more had gathered. A full band of antifascists.

The sky began to lighten as the heroes helped Casey and the Fredericksons up.

"Thank you, Antifa," called Sally.

"Any time," said the leader. "And just remember. We are here. We will be here. In the darkest of nights, in the grayest of dawns, come rain, come shine, we are watching, we are waiting. One day we will rid this world of cannibal clown fascists and their evil ilk. One day we will win, and We the People will finally join together, in strength, resolve, in dignity."

With that, he looked down and smiled at Casey, a stonewashed Antifa jean jacket draped proudly over her shoulders. The captain nodded and then raised his hand to whistle. Right on cue, the crew gathered their things and said their goodbyes.

Casey and the Fredricksons smiled and waved as their heroes marched off into the distance, away from Fun Town, forward into the dawn. Far ahead the sun was just peeking over the hills, and a dove cooed in the light.

The Squonk

DAY 356. Partly cloudy today. Warm in afternoon. Morna took Raven to a berry patch not far from the river. Came back with two bushels for breakfast. Great with the granola. Tam and I worked on the mess hall roof. Took a break and went for a walk. Sketched a critter near the waterfall. All snow's nearly melted. Air's humid but nice. It's a good time of year to still be alive.

DAY 357. Mostly cloudy and cool. Wandered around the woods and fields. Lots of daffodils. The snow-melt puddles are full of 'em peeking out like tiny faces. I'm taking my time with the watercolors. Dunno where it'll all go right now. Just like doing it. Trying to practice being mindful, seeing the details, being present.

DAY 358. Windy, rainy, overcast all day. Morna, Raven, and I went up the ridge to see if we could spot some procks after Winn saw one yesterday. No luck.

DAY 359. Very sunny and warm. Morna and I went into town—what was left of it—to get supplies. She found a bunch of wildflowers up near the orchards, and I sketched the willows. Swan and Tam worked on the mess hall roof. Few more days and it should be ready. There's all kinds of buzz in the commune that we're very close to planting . . .

DAY 360. Windy, rainy, and cool. Everyone stayed inside, working on various projects, until we heard a large crash. Then the power cut out. Not that we needed the light right at that moment, but still. Raven and I put on our ponchos to check the generator shed. We found it, but there wasn't much left. The whole thing had toppled over. Started to pull off the siding and other bits to see if we could get it started again, but the rain was coming down hard, and we were both drenched. Raven said it

416 *People's Choice Literature*

was no use—the main tank was flooded, and the backup needs repair. Thank goodness the solar panels are still intact.

We looked for a tarp to cover the generator, running between the barn and the mess hall, but couldn't find a thing. Raven remembered seeing one in the supply shed, so we ran over just in time for the culprit to show themselves, and there, leaning against the shed was a genuine hugag, I kid you not. That huge, droopy, moose-like creature that Swan had mentioned when we moved out here. They're harmless but can do a number on whatever they rest on, not being able to sit down without elbow joints and all . . .

I looked around for something to throw at it, but all I could see were branches and pinecones. Didn't want to harm the thing. So, we just stood there, staring at the beast as the rain saturated our clothes. It just leaned there, its elongated, droopy Eeyore mouth brushing the ground. After a few moments, it leaned further into the supply shed, causing the wood to buckle.

"Is that thing really sleeping?" I asked, just as it let out a loud snore.

It tipped even more, and right when the whole structure was about to meet the fate of our dear generator shed, an explosion ricocheted through the trees. A clap of thunder? Pistol? The hugag, stood up, wide eyed, and bolted toward us, hobbling on jointless legs.

Raven threw me to the side and in doing so entered the jog path of the critter: the hugag rammed into them at full speed. Now, full hugag speed isn't much, but with the weight of an elk it can do some real damage.

The next thing I saw was Raven prostrate on the ground, holding their face. I ran over to help them just in time for Morna to arrive with the med kit. Morna was dabbing Raven's wound with a cloth when, out of nowhere, I saw the hugag rump coming right at me! I jumped to the side just before it rammed into the mess hall, cracking a beam and undoing nearly all our work. The confused creature bounced off and hobbled away toward the river, likely just as scared as the rest of us.

DAY 361. Exhausted. Raven seems OK. Mostly shook. After reconnecting the generator to the solar panels, Swan and I went over to the supply shed and found a hole punched into the wall. And a bullet.

DAY 362. Everyone's shaken. At dinner last night we tried to guess where that bullet could've come from. No one owns a gun at camp. It's the rule. And so, everything pointed to the same conclusion: we're not as alone as

we thought. Trink suggested we move in pairs. Ginny offered to go to town to find weapons for self-defense, but Swan wasn't having it:

"That defeats the whole purpose of why we're here! With guns, we'll be no better than those assholes that started this whole mess."

Ginny said she saw Swan's point, but retorted: "What other choice do we have? Also, that hugag basically leveled our whole camp. We at least need to protect our hard work from those oafs."

No one liked this characterization of a hugag, and the group unanimously requested Trink's apology, which they quickly provided. Then we debated commune safety solutions for way too long, with Raven, the most affected by everything, moving to table the conversation until morning. We all agreed, and so here we are, day two of the day everything changed once again, now piecing what remains of the camp back together. Trink and Ginny offered to restart the mess hall project while Swan and I realigned the supply shed. It took five people all day to get the generator system back up and running and five more to construct a temporary housing unit for that wonky machine. By night, we were all so drained, we held off on group deliberations.

DAY 363. Morna and I spent the day in the greenhouse to see if we could get it going again. So far, it's not looking good. There was so much flooding that we'll have to replace the beds. Really looking forward to planting, but with all this water, we're at least a week delayed.

DAY 364. Morna and I went back to the greenhouse after breakfast and couldn't believe our eyes. The spinach was gone. The tomatoes were gone. The potato barrel was knocked over. Morna started to cry. I wanted to join her, but there was no time before Ginny came running in. "The matches supply was broken into!" Then she saw the greenhouse mess and nearly fainted. A meeting was called immediately. Trink and Swan were out fishing, and we didn't want to disturb them. Of course, we'd wait for them in the event of any voting. Half the group was convinced we needed weapons. Our half wasn't sold. Insert guns, and it's a slippery slope into total collapse was our argument. But the matter of our current situation was more elusive. Did someone in the commune already have a gun? Were they stealing provisions? Or was it one of those critters breaking in? One theory was that the ball-tailed cats were back. A hugag would be too big to enter the greenhouse without destroying it. But a ball-tailed cat would've had to unlatch the door, and that seemed too far of a stretch.

418 *People's Choice Literature*

Also, Drina had already established a camp-wide perimeter for the balltails after discovering the animals' revulsion to linseed . . . Ultimately it didn't make any sense to assume a critter was involved, since it would have no use for matchsticks. So, either one of us was undermining the commune or outsiders were in our midst. And they didn't seem friendly.

DAY 365. A somber anniversary to our time here. Paranoia and anxiety are high. Feels like everything's being rebuilt. Like day one all over again. After helping with the mess hall's roof, Raven and I decided to take a break and walk to the river. We waved to Morna and Kippy out on their fishing duty, then turned downstream, hopping down rocks, heading nowhere in particular. Raven was looking good and in relatively happy spirits. We passed where we'd previously found tulips, and Raven started to whistle a tune. I didn't recognize it but liked it, so I started to hum along. When we reached a well-trod area, Raven decided to test their footing. They made a leap onto a rock in the middle of the stream and nearly fell in. Then they jumped on another but weren't so lucky this time. They slipped and landed with a loud squish and a scream. I ran over and couldn't believe what I saw: beside them on the rock lay a bulbous, green critter the size of a basketball. Its droopy skin was covered in warts and moles, and it was weeping, gushing tears. It didn't look dangerous, but you never know, so I went to help Raven up.

"What are you doing?" they said. "This critter's hurt. I just fell on it for Christ's sake!"

"It could be dangerous," I said.

I kept my distance as Raven moved closer to the weeping critter.

"Are you OK?" they asked it.

The critter turned and lifted an eyelid to Raven, but then sunk back and started weeping all over again, webbed hands covering its draining eyes. I felt bad for the thing but was worried we had no idea what this critter was. Or what it was capable of. Raven extended their arm and started to pet it.

"What are you doing??" I cried.

The critter shuddered but soon registered the tenderness of Raven's touch. Its weeping slowed, although the tears still came, more of a trickle now.

"Sorry I hurt ya, friend," whispered Raven.

Then Raven cupped the green thing in their arms and stood up. "We're taking it with us."

The Most Unwanted Novel   419

"What are you talking about!?" I shot back. "We're in the middle of a cold war back at camp, freaking out about invading critters or who knows what, and you're about to bring one back with us? You're asking for trouble."

"Do you hear yourself?" Raven retorted, now petting the weepy creature in their arms. "This doesn't sound like the Fern I knew when we started this commune. *That* Fern welcomed Gaia, in *all* her forms."

They were right. It wasn't like me. I took a hard look at the wart-covered, droopy critter and then back at Raven.

"Oh, alright," I gave in.

Raven smiled, and I swear the little critter winked.

DAY 366. We're in a tough spot. "Cold war" starting to feel like too tame a word. Trink and Ginny are demanding Morna, Raven, and myself be ousted, citing our "unsafe" decision to bring home this critter. Others— Swan, Kippy, Drina, especially—are defending us, but not without suspicion. Everyone's on edge, and we've agreed to take another vote at dinner to decide who stays and who goes. I'm nervous but know it'll be hard to convince a majority to push us out. We've had issues with hugags and ball-tails, but so far it's only been tears and cuddles from this alien creature.

DAY 367. The vote was taken, and we're staying. Trink and Ginny stormed out. It's a relief, but it doesn't clarify what to do with this creature, whom we've aptly named "Squish." Haven't seen the group all day, but we're planning on a social this evening. We've all been through enough, and maybe it's time for some fun.

DAY 368. The social went off without a hitch. We shared a few drinks and told stories. Trink and Ginny seemed to ease up, and I think it's safe to say we're in a better place. The only thing left was to introduce Squish to the larger group. So we called them all into the mess hall and stood in a circle, Raven in the center with Squish in their arms. Me standing on the edge an anxious mess. Was sure this green lump, with its warts and perma-sad face, was going to freak everyone out, and we'd have a repeat of the past few days. But I was wrong. Everyone was taken by it. I mean, it's hard to respond harshly to a critter who's constantly weeping, even if it's just a whimper.

DAY 369. Something has changed. It's as if our previous troubles are over. I can't say for certain, but I think it's Squish. Drina let it share their yogurt. Kippy made it a hat. Trink and Ginny even asked to take care of it today. Caught them in the field playing tag.

DAY 370. I wrote a song about Squish. I'm almost embarrassed to say what it is. I'd never written a song before and am not very good, but I wanted to capture the essence of Squish's healing powers. We're all better people now. I'm better.

After playing the song for Squish, Raven, and Morna, we all went on a walk to the waterfall. It was a sunny afternoon, but in the forest, it was breezy and a bit chilly. Fortunately we'd brought our sweaters. Raven carried Squish, and Morna and I had the picnic materials. We were in sight of the waterfall when a twig cracked behind us. Morna and I turned to each other in fear, then jumped for Raven and Squish, but it was too late. The blast hit Raven right in the shoulder, throwing Squish to the ground, who immediately started to wail.

"Don't move," came a masculine voice from the trees.

We all froze.

Morna and I stared at each other in horror and slowly raised our hands.

"Please don't kill us," I begged.

Morna started to cry.

Raven groaned into the grass.

"I'm not going to kill you," the voice grumbled as its flannel-shirted owner stepped into the clearing, rifle raised. "I just need that squonk."

"That what?"

"That critter you've been carrying around. Gets good coin up in Erie."

"Good coin? This is our friend!" I cried.

"Your friend? That thing's just a sappy sack of blubber. Makes a mean burger. You never had fried squonk?"

Raven groaned louder, and Morna went to help them.

"DON'T MOVE!" the man screamed and went for Squish.

Raven tried to trip him, but it didn't work. He kicked Raven's leg out of the way, raised an arm, and knocked them out.

"That'll do her good."

"HER??" Morna called. "Who the hell are you calling 'her,' you dumb fuck?"

He lifted his rifle to Morna and smirked. "What'd you say?"

"Chill out, Morna," I whispered.

The Most Unwanted Novel   421

"That's right," he grunted.

Just then a whish of air shot by, and the man jumped to the side.

"What the fuck is this?" he cried as Trink and Swan stepped into view with bows and arrows trained right at his dumb trucker hat.

He lunged for me and dug his pistol into my cheek.

"Don't even think about it," he said, reeking of gunpowder and rancid sweat.

Trink and Swan's eyes went wide.

"Drop it, or I'll shoot," he said.

They lowered their bows to the ground.

"That a boy. Now don't get any funny ideas," he said. Then he drove his gun into my back and said, "Get that squonk."

I hesitated, but complied, lifting a sobbing Squish from the dirt.

"Now drop it in here," he demanded, extending a linen bag.

I couldn't believe what I was doing, but I placed Squish in that bag. The sight of that scared creature in that dim space tore at my heart.

Then the man stabbed me with the rifle. "Now walk."

I'm not sure how far we went, but it's clear that if my comrades followed, they did a good job hiding. The man led me, Squish-bag in hand, to his makeshift camp. Beer bottles were everywhere, and near the fire pit hung a hugag from a tree, gutted and stripped for meat. Our commune had a pact to spare critters from harm, but this vile man surely couldn't care less. He walked me and Squish to a rickety, wooden lean-to. Then he unlatched the door and pushed us in.

"What do you want?" I cried.

But he just slammed the door and stomped away. I went to let Squish out of the bag, but the man's voice cut in. "And don't you even think about touching my squonk . . ."

That night was the longest of my life. I sat there in the dark, alone with my thoughts. Well, my thoughts and the sounds of that wretched man grunting and groaning as he ate his hugag meat and pleasured himself. When he was done, I could hear the rustling of the bag and the soft weeping of our dear Squish. I assumed the little tyke was as safe as can be inside this structure with me. But I had no idea what was going to happen to us. Were we now this man's slaves? Would we be sold off and shipped to Eerie? My mind was cycling through all of this when I heard a baritone cry and a loud crash.

I jumped. Then listened for more movement, but there was nothing. Then I opened the bag, searching for my critter friend, but it was nowhere

422   *People's Choice Literature*

in sight. Instead, the bag was soaking wet, as if I'd just pulled it from a tub. Squish was gone.

I went to the door, listening for the man, but heard nothing. So, I pushed against the door with my shoulder but it hardly budged. When I rammed against it, the metal latch jumped. I hit it again, and the thing flew open, throwing me to the ground in the process. When I got to my feet, I looked around, and there he was: face up, a dagger's blade peeking out from his now-still heart.

I stepped back in shock to find Squish wobbling around the man's wet feet. So I picked it up and held it in my arms.

"I thought I'd lost you," I cried, petting its drippy, lumpy skin.

And as I did, I noticed the pool of water at the dead man's feet. My eyes widened. "Did he slip on you, Squish?"

Squish fluttered its teary eyes and squealed coyly. I held it close, giving thanks to goddess.

DAY 373. "The squonk is of a very retiring disposition, generally traveling about at twilight and dusk. Because of its misfitting skin, which is covered with warts and moles, it is always unhappy . . . Hunters who are good at tracking are able to follow a squonk by its tear-stained trail, for the animal weeps constantly. When cornered and escape seems impossible, or when surprised and frightened, it may even dissolve itself in tears."

Ginny found this passage yesterday on a trip to town. Went to that one computer still with satellite internet and looked up this "squonk" the buffoon had mentioned. For all his violent bullshit, he ended up being right. Squish was a squonk all along.

Not long after Squish took care of our captor, Trink and Swan arrived. You can't imagine my relief when I saw them. I grabbed Squish and held them close all the way back to camp.

When I awoke that afternoon, I was so grateful to see Raven again. Their shoulder was patched up, and Morna said they'd regain most of their arm motion in a couple weeks. When Ginny brought Squish by to cheer us up, it brought us right to tears, huddling in a group hug, weeping along with our squishy friend.

DAY 389. The past few weeks have been like heaven. Like the bad times never existed. And we're better for it all. We put up a fence around the camp's perimeter to deter hugags. Raven's started a critter awareness class that we're all encouraged to take. And the whole gang seems excited for

summer, which is just around the corner. Me? I've been spending my nights in the makeshift studio that Swan and Kippy built for me. After sharing my first Squish song at a group social, they encouraged me to write more, so here I am, finishing the last track tonight. Going into post-production tomorrow. I think I'll call the album *Songs for Squish*. And I can't wait to see what my little buddy thinks about it. Yeah, Squish decided to stick around. Seems it's just too dangerous for squonks in these woods. Before we can gather a party to venture to Erie and advocate for the end of the squonk death industry, it's the least we can do for our dear friend. But if any of us are being honest with ourselves, we'd admit that Squish is part of our family now. That we need Squish. Squish brought us together in our moment of crisis and gave us hope for the future. Squish is our guiding light. Our compass. That lovable, weeping little critter just warms our hearts. And we just hope it sticks around for the rest of its squishy days.

Ball Boys

It's the same every morning. Check in at 8:30. Open your Adidas bag for the guard. Say hi to Ronny and Willie. Make it to the court by 9. Get the usual lecture from Chad:

"So, remember, guys, keep your eyes out for anything strange. You see something, you say something. Things're still tense after last year. You know, Federer's on edge. Alcaraz nearly pulled out. Can't have another repeat."

You and the other ball boys and girls give your obligatory nods. As usual, Chad hands out the day's schedule, droning on about hydration or whatnot. But today as you scan down the list, you spot Willie at baseline for Djokovich and Ronny netting for Federer. When you find your name, you freeze. Baseline for McKelvey? That third-tier upstart!? Your heart sinks like the drop shot you surely won't be netting for Nadal today. Or Evans. Or anyone of value. McKelvey. Always the McKelveys . . .

You nearly lose it, stomach curdling into a panic. But when you scan further, you melt just a bit, nearly weep, when fate finds your name at baseline for Hanley.

Walter Hanley. Wimbledon runner up. Perfect slicer. Decent backspin. Not your fave, but you'll take what you can get.

After slogging through the newbie—who plays just like a noob—the day goes like most others. One match at base, one at net. Boxed lunch with the other ball boys and girls. Downtime in the nosebleeds.

Just before Hanley goes primetime with Evans, you find Willie and Ronny in the locker room, dressed in their best sweats.

"Everything good for tonight?" you ask.

Willie leans forward, his face suddenly serious. "Get ready for magic," he whispers.

You swallow, noting Ronny's sly grin.

The loudspeaker gives the five minute warning, and so you hop to it, the two other ball boys in tow, sauntering down the white cinderblock walkways and out into the blinding lights, cheering fans, and thumping beats. When you take your place near baseline, your heart is pounding, hands sweaty, yearning for the ecstasy to come.

But when the match begins, all you can think of is the present, anticipating each ball from the netter, gauging each toss to Hanley. Then the man of the hour performs his service with impeccable form, from light lob to balletic upswing to a consistently clobbering smash. If it weren't for Evans's footwork and flat, slightly topped drives, Hanley would be unstoppable, punching volleys and killing lobs. But when Evans hits, it's a whole new game, mixing dutiful drives with a severe backhand in a calculated effort to keep Hanley on defense, prancing back and forth across the court like some dweeb stuck on chapter 1 of *Do Si Do for Dummies*. And yet he persists, answering Evans's expertise with a pronounced snap of the wrist and an admirable spin.

You lose yourself in the game, the power, the speed. The orthodox drives and gobstopping ground strokes. The hair-raising volleys and heartbreaking slams. You're in the zone. You *are* the zone, trapped in the liquid rush of bodies and rackets and balls and lobs and sweat and sponsorship and men and might, all flowing with the organized genius of ants.

At match point, the tensions are high. Hanley waits at base, panting and dripping sweat, tracking Evans's bounce and lob before connecting into a firm and speedy slice. The ball rockets over the net, forcing Hanley into a flat drive of impressive angle. The ball flies left, and Evans dives for it, cutting into Hanley's hard-earned play like a machete. You watch in awe as the ball nicks the net. As Hanley lunges for it. As the ball bounces once. As the racket reaches. As limbs try to leverage a few extra inches. But it's no match for Evans's topspin. The ball hits the ground a second time, and Hanley collapses.

The crowd roars. You roar. The speakers boom, and confetti streams down from the sky. You watch Hanley shake his head as Evans is hoisted into the air. You watch the crowd jump in joy, the event staff high-fiving. You watch as Hanley grabs his Wilson and sulks away. As Willie and Ronny follow him off the court through the screams and beats and streamers.

❋ ❋ ❋

426 *People's Choice Literature*

Later, long after the singing and ceremony, trophies and chatter, the locker room is silent. Confetti and Gatorade bottles litter the floor. The dampness of group showers hangs in the air like a sweaty fog. Evans is long gone, chugging champagne with his team. But Hanley sits there alone, slumped in defeat, his face a mask of regret.

His mind races, retracing that last play. The slice. The lift. The net. The ball. A different hit. A different lunge. Different timing of said lunge. He inhales deeply, holds it, then lets it out in a slow hiss. He's about to pull once more when a noise comes from the bathroom. He straightens to the sound of a stall door creaking. Then the noise of bare feet skittering.

"Hello?" he calls out.

No reply.

He stands and walks toward the sound.

Entering the bare space, he finds nothing out of the ordinary. Just the same cinderblock walls, the same tiled floor.

"Anyone there?"

Nothing.

Then more sounds from behind, so he swivels around.

Again, nothing.

Suddenly, a tennis ball rolls across the floor before resting at his feet.

Hanley looks up to find a ball boy standing there.

The boy stares at him with judging eyes, chuckling.

"You missed a shot there, mate," he says, still laughing.

Hanley stares at him.

"You missed your *shot*," the ball boy repeats, nearly screeching.

Hanley shakes his head. "I was so close."

"Not close enough."

Just then two arms grab Hanley from behind, forcing him to the ground. A towel covers his mouth and nose, reeking of sulfur and sugar. Hanley struggles, grabbing for anything, pushing against the grip, but his vision starts to blur. The last thing he sees is the ball boy leaning over, panting and clapping, laughing his ball boy laugh.

Ball. The word rolls off the tongue like melted butter. B. A. L. L. Of Germanic origin, from the Old Norse bǫllr. But its origins are far older. First there was fire. Then the wheel. Then the ball: the accumulation of infinite wheels into a singular, self-sustaining whole. If you push a ball,

The Most Unwanted Novel 427

it rolls. If you drop it, it bounces back. The ball is continuous. The ball unites beginning and end. Cause and effect. The ball is.

While waxing philosophical, you relish in the balls before you. Two warm, oblong orbs, newly washed and primed for enjoyment. Ronny plucks one and studies it. Then, pressing the ball between two palms, he closes his eyes and sighs. You grab the other, holding it in your palm, feeling its weight and warmth, give and take. Its resistance to squeezing. Its wholeness. You squeeze a bit more to the point of bursting when Willie cries out: "Hey, back off, buddy. We need that."

You release the ball and snarl.

"It's a beautiful ball," you whisper.

"Sure is," says Willie.

Then you lift the ball to your mouth and sniff it. Musty. Fleshy. You bring out your tongue and give it a lick. Salty. Yummy. You spin the ball, ever so slowly, sliding your tongue across it, tracing its equator in pure ecstasy. Then you press your lips around the ball and slide it into your mouth. The heat emanates through your oral cavity, its salty flavor blending with your moist saliva. Your saliva blending with the ball.

"Lenny!" cries Willie. "You gotta share, man . . ."

You turn to Willie, then Ronny, who's now rubbing his ball across his cheek.

"Come on, I haven't had a chance . . ." whines Willie.

You aren't happy about it, but you take one last twirl of the ball around your tongue—little lick—and spit it out into your hand. Willie's eyes light up, accepting the ball graciously before pressing it tight between palms.

You sit back and sigh. The aftertaste of the salt, the pungent fleshiness lingers on your palate. You swirl the saliva around to mix the flavors. You never want this moment to end, and so you watch as your colleagues explore the balls for themselves. You sigh and close your eyes. You inhale. You exhale. And then you hear it. A noise. A sound from the next room over. You open your eyes and turn to find the door slightly ajar. The noise continues. It's a noise like a voice. A voice like a moan. A moan like the groan of a dying animal. You feel your heart skip a beat. Your eyes dart around the room. Your ears perk up. A moan. A moan like a scream. A scream like a cry like a plea.

You behold your two colleagues nestled in ball bliss.

Then Willie turns to you. "Would you mind getting that?"

428   *People's Choice Literature*

You don't like it, but you do it. You stand up. Then you walk over to the door and give it a push. The noise grows louder. A sound of flesh slapping flesh. The grunts ricocheting between walls. Tilting your head, your heart skips a beat.

The scene before you is almost too difficult to comprehend. You see a man. A man of sinew and muscle. A man of ab and bicep, pec and tricep. A man of sweat and tears. A man of sex. A man of sex on a wooden bench. A man pushing a ball with his feet. Feet that yearningly roll said ball back and forth, to and fro, teasing the toes, tickling, compressing, expanding, panting, puffing. The ball rolls forward, muscles flex. The ball rolls back, sweat drops. The toes tickle, mouth giggles. The ball slides forward. The giggles turn to groans. The ball slides back. The groans turn to moans. The ball plays between toes. Nice ball. Nice toes. But then the man stops. Huffs. Stands up, grabs the ball, and drops it in a jar on the shelf, sweat dripping down his throat. He takes another jar, pops it open, grabs the ball inside. Gray, oblong. Perfection. The man returns to the bench, tests the ball with twinkle toes. He groans, clearly dismayed. So he stands, grabs the ball, puts it back in the jar. He grabs another jar, plucks another ball. The ball is pink and bulky. He smiles.

You close the door and turn to your companions.

"I think he's got it under control."

Willie nods, nestling his ball in his ear.

The next day you wake up just as before. You get up, get dressed. Check in at 8:30. Open your Adidas bag for the guard. Spot Ronny and Willie. Smile.

Wowza. What was that about? Oh, hey there. Didn't see you walk in . . . It's been a bit. How are you?

Well, it's very likely this book has reached peak unwantedness. If this were a more traditional story, you might say it was the climax—pun intended. But since you're still here—and if you've made it this far, I must add that you're stronger than the vast majority of your peers—and since I'm still here, I thought it might be helpful to have a little chat about how we got to this moment.

As mentioned before, horror is the second least wanted genre after romance, with 19.18% of respondents saying they despise it. Early on in writing this book, I knew a horror section would show up as a short story collection in the middle of the novel. I imagined this collection would both stop the narrative in its tracks and offer some guidance for Lord Tickletext in the quest for his lost love—which is to say, stick around and you'll see how it all fits together . . .

The reasons for including this collection are twofold. First, short story collections are seen in the publishing world as unsellable. Readers want little to do with them, preferring longer narratives they can sink into and use to forget about the true horrors of the world. Second, on the question of preferred book length, the data is split, with the two least-wanted novel lengths evenly tied: a novel that is shorter than 200 pages (8.04%) and a novel that is over 500 pages (8.04%). Unable to follow up with respondents to help break this tie, I used deductive reasoning to do so myself: I imagined that if faced with the choice of reading an accumulation of unwanted literary elements of either 200 pages or 500 pages, most people would spare themselves and choose the shorter. In the end, it seemed fitting to include this collection—a manuscript of under 200 pages—in the middle of this 500-page book. Combo deal: two unwanted books in one!

As with the rest of *The Most Unwanted Novel*, all these horror stories are driven by data and respondents' answers to that open-ended question, "If you had unlimited resources and could commission your favorite author to write a novel just for you, what would it be about?" Statistically, folks don't want to read about firefighters (zero people voted for them), and one of the open-ended responses was simply "Werewolves"; another was "Nephilim." Thus "Night of the Nephilim" was born. People also don't want to read about babysitters (only two out of 1,045 did), but one person desired a survival horror story set in a theme park. And so, voila! Welcome to "The Terror in Fun Town."

430 *People's Choice Literature*

One of the more interesting open-ended answers led to that cute story about the squonk:

A queer horror novel where it's a group of pro tags in a found-family community making life work on a commune, but also folkloric creatures of some sort complicate matters. Not about killing the creatures or the family but finding a solution that results in less drastic bloodshed and more communal spirit. Happy ending queer horror!!!

To write that one, I researched American folkloric creatures and discovered *Fearsome Critters of the Lumberwoods* by William T. Cox, a compendium of mythological creatures imagined by pre-1900 American and Canadian lumberjacks that, according to Wikipedia, "remains one of the principal sources on legendary creatures of the United States and Canada." The squonk, my favorite of these creatures, has appeared in songs by Genesis and Steely Dan and was featured in a 1989 children's book by Julia Jarman and illustrated by Jean Baylis. Of all the fearsome critters, the squonk, with its lumpy melancholy seemed to be the one most likely to bring people together.

But what about "Ball Boys"? Yes, what about "Ball Boys." We already know tennis is the least-wanted subject in a novel. With this in mind, it seemed obvious that there had to be a horror story about tennis. I'd already written a handful of supernatural and survival stories, so it seemed something less fantastical and more psychological was in order. It also seemed, given the conservatisms associated with tennis culture and horror's penchant for extremes, that a story blending both would be ripe for perhaps the most potent blend of unwanted qualities yet: ultraviolence and hardcore sexual content. Not only does *The Bestseller Code* show that such extremes don't belong in a bestselling—or highly wanted—novel, but our polling data backs this up. While most people want "a little sexual content" or "some sexual content" (37.32% and 34.26%, respectively), only 3.83% want "a lot of sexual content" in their novels. Preferences for violence map almost the same, with most people wanting "a little violence" or "some violence" (27.87% and 38.31%, respectively) and only 4.21% wanting "a lot of violence." To top off these extremes and to try to push the reader to the brink of total abjection, it also seemed important to bring back that device most despised by readers, the second person (again, only 2.49% want it).

OK, you might say, but why go so far to the extreme? What's the point? I might best answer this with reference to the work of the Japanese sound artist Masonna. I first heard of Masonna while listening to LARB Radio

The Most Unwanted Novel   431

Hour host Kate Wolf's interview with the music critic Kelefa Sanneh. There Sanneh, a *New Yorker* writer, described Masonna's music as resembling a garbage disposal and "the reductio ad absurdum of how weird music could get." I immediately looked up *Spectrum Ripper* (1997), Masonna's twenty-five-track album of noise music, and it did not disappoint. Or at least it didn't disappoint if you have a thing for extremes. *Spectrum Ripper* might be, as Sanneh claims, the weirdest and, I might add, the most extreme that music can get. Nowhere is there a beat. Nowhere are their discernible instruments. What we find is a voice that does not sing but scream to the point of vocal-cord damage, blending in and out of the crashing waves of white noise, feedback, and other shrieking, glitching sounds. Hearing this album, it felt like I had reached the limits of music. As if I were in *The Truman Show*, knocking my lowly sailboat against the physical limits of my world, but in this case, there is no other world beyond, no hope for musical transcendence beyond this unforgiving extremity. If the softest, most pleasureful form of music is, say, the lullaby, *Spectrum Ripper* is the exact opposite. *Spectrum Ripper* is so extreme, I burst out laughing.

I mention this album because works like *Spectrum Ripper* do more than just shock us or make us laugh. In pushing against the limits of what music, writing, or art can be, they both reveal the range of what is possible in a given medium and provide listeners, readers, and viewers with levels of thought and feeling not achievable with business as usual. One effect *Spectrum Ripper* had on me was that it inspired the question: What might a literary equivalent to such an extreme album be? *Finnegans Wake* is surely one contender, at the level of language. Samuel Delany's *Hogg* and the writings of Bataille and the Marquis de Sade, for extreme sexual content. Kathy Acker and Hilda Hilst, for their unique blends of sexuality and formal experimentation. Darius James's *Negrophobia* and Derek McCormack's *Castle Faggot*, for formal maximalism and humor. This is only a partial list. In the process of writing this book, I also came across *Off Season* by Jack Ketchum, noted by several online sources as the most extreme horror novel ever written. Reading it, it did not disappoint, but it still left me with the question: Could it have gone further?

I won't make the claim that *The Most Unwanted Novel* reaches the literary limit—there are far weirder books—but I mention Masonna, *Spectrum Ripper*, and these other works as points of reference, to orient this book in ongoing conversations about expressive limits and publishability. Can a poll actually produce the most unwanted book? Will "Ball Boys," the

432 *People's Choice Literature*

earlier erotic scene between a humanoid cat and a 157-year-old disk jockey, or the extreme violence found throughout this book make this work unpublishable? If you happen to be reading this novel in bound or digital form, then the answer is surprisingly and unequivocally No. And in some ways, this will feel like a minor failure. Could it have gone further? Are there realms of unwantedness and unpublishability that remain to be seen? Well, time and people's responses—particularly yours—will tell. Either way, you can rest assured that, at least according to the data, there are many more pages of undesirability to go.

Presidents' Night

They'd gone there every Presidents' Day for years, but never was the weather this bad. Thick snow. Heavy snow. Snow like panel pair curtains. And now there was talk of an electrical storm joining the party. A "once-in-a-lifetime occurrence" the second year in a row.

"Goddamn climate change!" cried Fred, pulling up to the hotel. "I mean, we paid hard-earned money for this trip."

Fran turned to him. "Well, your parents' hard-earned money, honey…"

"You know what I mean. I just wanted a nice retreat from the city. A chance to get some cross-country skiing in, ice fish, you know?"

"This weather will pass," assured Fran, brushing her hand through his hair. "It'll be OK."

Fred peered out at the flecks taunting him with stark white woe.

"Look, love," Fran said, rubbing his back, "let's get some food in your belly. Maybe that'll cheer you up."

Fred looked to Fran with tired, yearning eyes.

When they reached the dining room, the couple stood at the threshold and beheld the beauty before them. Windows decked in the finest crimson. Tablecloths of white silk. Blue wine glasses shining softly in the sepia light. In the distance, an elderly man at a piano tapped away at the great American song book, finishing off a lively rendition of "Till There Was You." As the room cheered, a waiter in a tuxedo and American flag bowtie strolled up and guided them to their table.

It wasn't long into taking their seats that Fran noticed a new sparkle in Fred's eyes.

"What are you thinking about, honey?" she asked.

"I'm thinking," Fred sighed, "that no matter how many times I come back here, I'm always amazed by the service."

"It's spectacular, isn't it?" said Fran.

434   *People's Choice Literature*

"The best in the region," said Fred.

"Best in the *country*, if I say so," retorted Fran.

Fred looked at her skeptically. "You seem to be forgetting Hotel Le Conte. That Jeffery was quite the maître d' . . ."

Fran lifted an eyebrow. "Touché, my dear. That Jeffery surely had a way with warming the hand towels just right."

Fred smiled, pleased with himself.

"I think I'll have the lobster," said Fran scanning the menu.

"Ah," said Fred, "Chef Julien's delicacy. I'll have the duck."

"Oh, you would," teased Fran.

"Well, I just can't get enough of that sauce, you know," Fred chuckled before noticing the piano player's spin on "Moonlight Serenade."

"My favorite," he sighed and sat back.

"I'm so glad you're back to normal, love," Fran smiled, placing her hand on his.

Fred raised his glass. "Here's to *many* more years of good service!"

"I can drink to that," she winked, eyes hinting at tears.

The couple ate their dinner in semi-silence and complete contentment. Several times the piano player offered up a song that was just perfect for the occasion—"Somewhere Over the Rainbow," "I Love How You Love Me"—and before long the two were off to their room.

The Bridal Suite was a delicate, one-room affair. It featured a king-size bed and a fireplace, a few candles to set the mood. Fran and Fred had made use of the room many times, having been married there that very weekend thirteen years prior.

"Oh, this is lovely," Fran sighed as she checked the thermostat.

Fred sang an "mmm hmm," removing his jacket.

"I'm going to take a bath," said Fran, tossing her shawl on a chair and starting for the jacuzzi. With each silky step, she removed an article of clothing, taunting Fred with bashful eyes.

Fred smiled, his eyes caressing her form. "I'll be waiting for you."

In the bathroom, Fran lit a candle and turned off the light. Then she slipped into the tub and sighed as the hot water enveloped her. She remained there for the better part of an hour, from time to time whistling a soft tune.

When the candle was almost out, she straightened up. She grabbed a towel and switched on the light, but nothing happened. That's strange,

she thought. She dried off, wrapped herself in the thick, white towel, and walked out into the dark bedroom lit only by a draped window and the embers in the fireplace.

"Freddy?" she called out.

Fran walked over to the window and opened the curtains further. Out the window, the snow was falling like furniture. Lightning flashed in the distance.

"Freddy?" she called again.

A rustling came from behind, so she jumped and swung around. Before her stood her husband, naked with his finger to his mouth. "Shhh . . ."

"What's going on?" she whispered back.

Fred smiled and motioned for her to come. Fran complied, and he wrapped his arms around her. Instantly she could feel his thick cock pressing against the towel. She felt his hand rub her side and then move up her back. So she slid her hands from his waist and reached down to grab his member.

In tandem, Fred slid his hand down Fran's front and began rubbing her clit. She could feel her pussy yearning for more as her juices began to flow. With his other hand, Fred grabbed Fran's ass and squeezed it hard. He began to massage it, rubbing it in a circular motion, and Fran moaned into his mouth, pushing her pussy into his hand. Finally, Fred pulled back and told Fran he wanted her naked. So she dropped her towel and stood there, her bare body softly showing in the dark glow from the window. The not-so-newlyweds stumbled into bed, licking and kissing and grabbing and aching.

But before they got started, Fred reached over to the nightstand and grabbed two metal butt plugs. He handed one to Fran, and she began to tease her ass with it. He took the other and slid it snugly into his own. They both moaned, their asses aching, full of joy. Then Fred rubbed his cock against her clit before sliding in.

They started to fuck, slowly at first, then faster. Fran's moans got louder and louder as she started to pant. She threw her head back, and Fred licked her neck.

"Ohhhhhhhhhhhhhh," moaned Fran while riding his cock.

"Ohhhhhhhhhhh," moaned Fred while licking her chest.

"Ohhhhhhhhhhhhh," moaned Fran while rocking his dock.

"Ohhhhhhhhhhhhhhhh," moaned Fred while squeezing her breast.

Then Fran squirted all over Fred's pounding cock, soaking it with her juices. Fred wet his whistle, then grabbed her by the hips and began

436   *People's Choice Literature*

fucking her even harder. Fran's groans became moans, and her moans became groans. She could feel her pussy quivering, eagerly aware she was on the brink of the biggest orgasm of her life. She moaned louder and louder, her pussy throbbing harder and harder. But Fran wanted more. She pushed Fred off her and grabbed the strap-on from the nightstand. Slipping it on in lusty haste, she tightened the straps just enough and then pushed him onto the bed with a playful jab. Then she spread his legs wide and got to work, rubbing Fred's ass in gleeful anticipation. When she pulled his plug, he whimpered. And when she teased his hole, he moaned. Then she buried her silicone cock deep inside and got to work.

At first, Fred let out a deep groan, then a light whistle, but these sounds were soon replaced by a squeaking that would accompany each forceful thrust, each pound, ounce, kilo. It didn't take long for Fred's squeaks to peak into an incomprehensible burst of oaths and declarations. And when he grabbed his cock, Fran could see his cumming was imminent. So she reached around to grab her cunt, eager to join him, head back, back arching, gleefully pounding Fred's rump. He stroked his cock with lustful determination, and was just about to turn his belly into a Pollock painting when he saw it in the mirror.

Fred's eyes shot wide. Deafening thunder crashed nearby, and he turned to see it directly.

"What's wrong?" asked Fran as she pulled out and spun around.

Then she saw it, too, recoiling.

"What the hell?" she shouted.

"What the hell is right," said Fred as he rolled off the bed and stood there naked, his cock pulsing with precum, pointing right at the apparition. For, there, sitting by the fireplace, now glowing with flame, was an old man smoking a pipe.

Fred stepped forward as Fran pulled the sheets over her chest.

"What the fuck are you doing?" Fred yelled.

The man turned to him with a smirk. "Ah, just enjoying the fire, old chap." He turned back to the glow, puffing away.

Fred called again, "Who the hell are you?"

The man gave a tired sigh and turned to him once more, pulling the pipe from his mouth. "Why I, my friend, am none other than John Quincy Adams . . ."

"John who?" asked Fred.

"John. Quincy. Adams," replied the man.

"Like Quincy Jones?" asked Fran.

The Most Unwanted Novel   437

"No, my dear, Quincy Adams," replied the man. "Why, I'm the sixth president of the United States . . ."

Thunder crashed overhead.

"I don't care who you are. What the hell are you doing in our room?" called Fred.

"What does it look like I'm doing?" said the man. "I'm enjoying the fire."

"Enjoying the fire?" said Fred. "This is our fire!"

"Oh, is it now?" said the man. "And how do you figure that?"

"Because it's our hotel room!" Fred yelled.

"Oh, is it?" the man replied. "And how do you figure that?"

"Because we paid for it!"

Suddenly the door opened, and another figure walked in, pipe in hand. Fred grabbed Fran's towel and wrapped it around him. "What the hell is this?"

The figure stepped into the fire light. "Why I, my friend, am none other than Rutherford B. Hayes."

Another man entered the room holding a cigar.

"And I," said the man, "am William H. Taft."

Fred turned to Fran to make sure she too was seeing this, then swiveled back.

"Get out of our room!" he demanded. "I don't care who you are."

"Your room?" came yet another voice from the door. "And how do you figure that?"

Fred turned to find Calvin Coolidge standing just inside.

"Because we're paying for it."

"Oh, are you?" said Harry S. Truman, strolling in with a beer. "And how do you figure that?"

"Because we fucking well charged it to our card!"

"Oh, did you?" said James K. Polk from the threshold. "And how do you figure that?"

"Because we fucking well called the fucking hotel!"

"Oh, did you?" said Lyndon B. Johnson, taking a sip of bourbon. "And how do you figure that?"

"Because we fucking well went on Expedia thirteen fucking years ago when we got married!"

"Oh, did you?" said Ulysses S. Grant, smoking a cigarillo. "And how do you figure that?"

"Because we fucking well looked up the fucking site, found the fucking hotel, and booked the fucking room!"

438   *People's Choice Literature*

"Oh, did you?" said Gerald R. Ford, chugging a beer. "And h—"

"ENOUGH!" screamed Fred.

"But we've just begun," said William McKinley, strolling through the door with Martin Van Buren.

Thunder rattled the room as yet another man entered, holding a carafe. "It's true, my friends. We're only twelve through."

Fred stared in shock as he found himself standing before none other than George Washington.

"*George Washington!?*" gulped Fran.

"The first president of the United States?" asked Fred.

"Precisely," said Benjamin Franklin, sneaking in beside him.

"Ben Franklin? I don't think you were even a president," huffed Fred.

"That's correct." Franklin replied, taking a draw from his opium pipe. "I'm an *icon*."

"How many of you presidents and . . . icons should we be expecting?" Fred demanded.

"How many?" replied Washington. "Why, do you not know your history?"

"We're happy to fill in the blanks," said Theodore Roosevelt, a cigar in each hand. "See George Washington was the first president of the United States, and first drunkard. Known for his love of liquor, he was a frequent patron of the best taverns and inns of the day. Why, he could drink up to seven whiskeys in a sitting . . . Some historians believe that Washington's heavy drinking contributed to his death at the age of sixty-seven."

Washington nodded humbly as Richard Nixon walked through the door smoking a Marlboro.

"The second president," Nixon coughed, "of the United States was a moderate drinker. John Adams preferred hard cider and beer and, while he may not have been the biggest drinker, he was well-known for being a 'man's man.'"

Woodrow Wilson stepped forward and continued: "Tommy Jefferson. Third President of the United States, and the first drunkard to nearly be impeached. Jefferson was a heavy drinker and enjoyed a variety of hard liquor and beer. He was also an avid wine connoisseur and even had a special 'wine closet' installed in the White House."

Then William Henry Harrison stumbled into the room, nearly knocking Wilson over. He straightened up and burped before starting: "In case you're forgotten, James Madison was the fourth President and first

The Most Unwanted Novel   439

drunkard to sign the Bill of Rights. He would typically drink a glass of whiskey or wine at dinner and brandy after. He'd even have port for breakfast!"

Suddenly Grover Cleveland stomped in holding two pints of beer. "James Monroe was the fifth President of the United States, and first drunkard to die on Independence Da—"

"WE GET IT!" Fred exploded.

"We thought you would," bellowed George Washington. "Forty-plus presidents, forty dead. All heavy drinkers."

"And mansplainers," spat Fran from the bed. "And slave owners and secessionists! You're all thugs . . ."

"Fran!" said Fred, aghast.

"It's fine," said Washington. "We're used to it." Turning to Fran: "About time one of you woke up and realized history isn't all pretty."

"But we aren't here to talk about the past," said Franklin, pushing through the crowd. "We're here to talk about your future."

"Huh?" asked Fred.

"You're in danger of losing everything," said Franklin.

"What do you mean?" asked Fred.

"Don't you see?" said the inventor. "Polarization. Civil unrest. How much more can a country take?"

"And you, Fred and Fran," Washington chimed in. "You are the only ones that can save it."

"Save it from what?" asked Fred.

"From itself," said Washington. "From the anger and vitriol that's tearing this nation apart."

"Us?" asked Fran.

"That's right."

"Without the two of you," said Franklin, "America is..." He choked up.

"Look," said Franklin D. Roosevelt, rolling into the room in his wheelchair and smoking a pipe. "We need you, Fred and Fran. We dead presidents have only tonight—this one night—to spread our urgent message. Have we messed up? Yes. Were we all a bunch of drunks? Sure. Are we all slave owners and bigots? Guilty as charged. But we're here tonight for one reason and one reason only."

Fred and Fran looked at each other in anxious anticipation.

"Your Facebook accounts."

"Our what?" asked Fred.

"We need you, Fred and Fran," continued Abraham Lincoln, stepping out into the fiery light with a gin and tonic in hand. "With social media, you can spread the good word. Tell the people about unity. Remind them to hope. Show them that our strengths lie in our differences. That bipartisanship will save us all."

The dead men beamed.

Fred looked to Lincoln. "No one even uses Facebook anymore. And I only have like five hundred friends."

Just then John F. Kennedy walked in, smoking a cigar. "Have faith, my children," he smiled. "You are the medium. You are the message."

Washington nodded. "You're our only hope . . ."

Fred turned back to Fran, who was already typing away on her phone.

When he looked back to the presidents, his heart dropped. Tobacco smoke filled the room, but the apparitions were gone. All that remained was a flickering fire, snow falling past the window, and a sacred vow. Fred grabbed his phone, got into bed with Fran, and began typing away like the fate of his country depended on it.

Brains: A Treatise on Thirst

I thirst, therefore I am. Full stop. Plain and simple. I thirst. Therefore. I am. Simple enough, yes, if thirst were not but the first step in one's inevitably onerous quest into the heart of desire. And existence. The essence of the all. You see, when I thirst, I yield to my singular, solitary existence and the existence of the universe in its infinite expanse, that network of subjective and objective time constituting reality itself. In a sense, I touch the all. I bloom from the solitary stasis of moribund materialism into the bright beating heart of collective consciousness. I become, at once, alive. If only for a moment. Rather, a sequence of minute moments, modes, moods that coalesce into a dynamic display of cranial consumption. I enter the dynamism, the mercy of an unquenchable thirst for moist, pulsing, gushing brains. There is no other way to say it. The taste, the consistency, the thought made flesh. Faced with the prospect of brains, I have no choice but to submit. To yield to a desire so supple and yet so debilitating it nears obsession. A need, a craving. An insatiable hunger. I have no choice because, yes, as you might have guessed, I am a zed, the undead. A zombie, if you must. And you will. You all do. I have no choice, because I am an insatiable being at the intersection of life and nonlife, the here and there, the where and when. Which is to say I have no choice, because I am an insatiable being trapped in a cage of thirsting space and dead time. Which is to say I am an insatiable being trapped in a cage of thirsting (non)existence that is suspended over a vast pit of flaming, weeping corpses. Which is to say I am an insatiable being trapped in a cage of thirsting (non)existence suspended over a vast pit of flaming, weeping corpses, and the only thing keeping this cage and me from falling in is a single strand of spider silk. Which is to say I am an insatiable being trapped in a cage of thirsting (non)existence suspended over a vast pit of flaming, weeping corpses, and the only thing keeping me from falling in is a single strand of spider silk and a small boy with a stick. Which is to say I am an insatiable being trapped in a cage of thirsting (non)existence suspended over a vast pit of flaming, weeping corpses, and the only thing

keeping me from falling in is a single strand of spider silk and a small boy with a stick and a tall man standing on the small boy's shoulders. Which is to say I am an insatiable being trapped in a cage of thirsting (non) existence suspended over a vast pit of flaming, weeping corpses, and the only thing keeping me from falling in is a single strand of spider silk and a small boy with a stick and a tall man standing on the small boy's shoulders and a very small woman standing on the tall man's lip. Which is to say I am an insatiable being trapped in a cage of thirsting (non)existence suspended over a vast pit of flaming, weeping corpses, and the only thing keeping me from falling in is a single strand of spider silk and a small boy with a stick and a tall man standing on the small boy's shoulders and a very small woman standing on the tall man's lip and a fly sitting on the small woman's nape. Which is to say I am an insatiable being trapped in a cage of thirsting (non)existence suspended over a vast pit of flaming, weeping corpses, and the only thing keeping me from falling in is a single strand of spider silk and a small boy with a stick and a tall man standing on the small boy's shoulders and a very small woman standing on the tall man's lip and a fly sitting on the small woman's nape and a flea on the fly's wing. Which is to say I am an insatiable being trapped in a cage of thirsting (non)existence suspended over a vast pit of flaming, weeping corpses, and the only thing keeping me from falling in is a single strand of spider silk and a small boy with a stick and a tall man standing on the small boy's shoulders and a very small woman standing on the tall man's lip and a fly sitting on the small woman's nape and a flea on the fly's wing and a dust mote dozing on the little flea's back. Which is to say I am an insatiable being trapped in a cage of thirsting (non)existence suspended over a vast pit of flaming, weeping corpses, and the only thing keeping me from falling in is a single strand of spider silk and a small boy with a stick and a tall man standing on the small boy's shoulders and a very small woman standing on the tall man's lip and a fly sitting on the small woman's nape and a flea on the fly's wing and a dust mote dozing on the little flea's back below the blade of a knife.

Violence. The axiom of existence. Violence. The first law of thermodynamics. Yes, the universe is a vast, illimitable expanse of violent energy, and all violent energy is convertible into other forms of energy. This is the second law of thermodynamics. The consumption of brains, my predilection, is an extension, an embodiment of this violence at the energetic root of the universe, of all existence since the beginning of violent time. And

The Most Unwanted Novel 443

yet, nothing could be as simple. The flavor, the texture, the manducatory union with corporeal consciousness. The pulsing, gushing of life. The brain. The most delicate and sublime of all entities. The brain. The gentle whisper of the all.

Guys and Dolls

When school let out that day, Teacher Susan could tell something was wrong with Candice. She'd been watching the child all afternoon, and she just wasn't herself. She'd barely eaten anything at lunch and had kept to herself at recess. When story time came up, Candice went right to the bathroom and then spent the rest of the time at her seat.

"What's wrong, sweetie?" asked Teacher Susan as she walked the girl to the door.

"Nothing," said the girl, but she was crying.

"Now, I'm not going to take no for an answer . . ."

"I'm just tired," the girl said, eyeing the playground before turning quickly away.

"I know you are, sweetie. I'm tired too. But you don't have to be afraid to talk with me. I'm here to help you."

"I'm not afraid," the girl said. "I just want to go home."

Candice Smith then ran off in a huff toward the bus.

Just then Teacher Tracey stepped into view.

"Hiya, Susan. Long day?"

"You know it," Teacher Susan sighed. "I think Candice is having a rough time."

"Yeah, I saw her crying in the bathroom. Tried to get her to talk, but she just ran out."

"She was crying on the playground, too," said Teacher Susan. "She says she's tired, but I can't help but wonder if there's more."

"What do you think it is?" asked Teacher Tracey.

"Can't say. I think I'll have a talk with her parents."

Suddenly a crash came from behind.

Teacher Susan turned around to find a full bucket of crayons scattered all over the floor. The toys and blocks above seemed to not have moved an inch.

"Ugh," she sighed. "If it's not one thing . . ."

"I'll help you," said Teacher Tracey.

The Most Unwanted Novel   445

"Thanks, Trace."

They both walked over and started tossing crayons back into the bucket.

"You know," said Teacher Tracey. "I've been having a bit of trouble, too. Gerald Hopkins wouldn't participate in playtime either. I almost had to take back the star sticker he got yesterday. What's gotten into these kids? They don't like to play anymore?"

"I don't know," said Teacher Susan, tossing a teal crayon into the bin, "but I'm worried."

"It's like they're all in a funk or something."

They gathered the last of the crayons and stood up.

"Thanks, Tracey," said Teacher Susan. "I owe you one."

Teacher Tracey smiled at her. "Don't mention it."

After Teacher Tracey waved goodbye, Teacher Susan turned back to her desk to get her things. What a day, she thought, gathering her papers into her satchel. Then she heard movement from across the room. She turned but couldn't see a thing. *Mice again?* she asked herself. That would just be my luck. Teacher Susan let out a huff before strolling over to where the noise had come from. That's strange, she thought. This doll wasn't here yesterday. She picked up one of the figures and looked at it. It was a little girl doll. She had long red hair and a white dress. She was smiling, but something seemed off. It seemed too forced. Teacher Susan looked closer and noticed that whichever way you turned the doll, its eyes stared back.

She shivered. "Where'd you come from?"

Teacher Susan looked around the room, but there was no one there. Then she tossed the doll in the trash bin and switched off the light.

"I better have a talk with maintenance tomorrow," she said to herself as she closed the door.

First thing next morning, Teacher Susan was fixing herself a coffee in the teacher's lounge when Teacher Tracey walked in.

"You're here early," said Teacher Tracey.

Teacher Susan turned around and smiled. "Speak for yourself . . ."

"Grading," sighed Teacher Tracey, holding up a pile of papers.

"I hear you," said Teacher Susan, nodding to the coffee maker. "Want some?"

"I thought you'd never ask."

446   *People's Choice Literature*

Teacher Susan poured a second cup. Then she walked to the table where Teacher Tracey was sitting.

"So," said Teacher Tracey. "What's on the agenda for today?"

"Well, I have to talk with maintenance. Noticed a strange doll in my play area. Definitely not one of the kids'."

Teacher Tracey's eyes widened. "You, too? I found a weird doll in my room two days ago. A little boy. Red hair, piercing eyes, white shirt, black pants. He was hunched over my filing cabinet when I came in yesterday. I thought it was strange but figured one of the kids must have left it there."

"I thought that too. But then these kids are so obsessed with their toys, they'd never leave one behind."

Teacher Tracey smirked. "You have a point."

Teacher Susan looked at the clock. "I better get over to maintenance before they start rushing in."

"Would come with you," said Teacher Tracey, "but I'm so far behind." Tracey pointed to her stack of paper in despair. "Tell me what you find."

Teacher Susan wished her good luck, grabbed her coffee, and headed toward the maintenance room.

"Hello?" she called out as she approached the door. "Anyone here?"

She walked in and found it empty.

"Hellooo?" she called out again. She walked over to the desk and looked around. Papers were scattered everywhere. Some had fallen to the floor. And a mop was snapped in half. Strange, she thought. Mr. Greenland is much tidier than this. She turned around and noticed the utility closet was cracked open. What's going on here? She moved to the door, gave it a push, and immediately dropped her coffee. The brown liquid flew everywhere as her mouth opened in a silent scream.

"Oh my God," she gagged. "Dear freakin' God."

The body of Mr. Greenland hung from the ceiling, eyes bulging open, tongue sticking out, swollen and purple.

As the reality hit her, a scream rose from her chest to her throat and exploded down the hallway.

"Well, it's a suicide, no ifs, ands, or buts," Officer Crowley pronounced as he sketched in his notebook. Principal Philips nodded from across the table. He turned to Teacher Susan, who was now crouched in a corner of the teacher's lounge. "You're sure he didn't leave a note?"

The Most Unwanted Novel   447

"I didn't find anything," said the teacher, shaking her head. "That's how it looked when I got there."

"Well, I'm sorry, but I have to ask. Did you happen to notice anything strange about him recently?"

"No," she replied . "He was his usual self. I mean, he was a little grumpy, but that's normal for him."

"I see," Officer Crowley nodded.

"Well, I'm sorry for your loss."

"Thanks," said Teacher Susan. "I'm just glad the kids weren't here to see this."

"Sure am, too," said Officer Crowley. "I'll be in touch if we need anything else."

When Officer Crowley left the room, Principle Philips turned to her.

"I'm so sorry," he said.

"It's OK," said Teacher Susan. "I'm just glad the kids weren't here."

"Me too," Principal Philips said reassuringly. "Look, you take the day off. We'll get a substitute."

Teacher Susan looked up and thanked him, weeping.

After he left, Teacher Susan sat there alone, looking around in disbelief. How could such a tragedy have happened here? In *this* place? As her eyes scanned the room, they suddenly fell on a red-haired, white-dressed doll peeking out from behind the water cooler.

She did a double take, then walked over and picked it up. Was this the same doll as yesterday? It looked the same. Same exaggerated smile. The same eyes that followed wherever you went.

"What are you doing here?" she asked.

She searched the room for other clues, finding yet another red-haired, weird-eyed doll slouched inside a box. Teacher Susan raised an eyebrow. Then the door opened, and Nurse Ruth entered.

"Goodness, Susan" said the nurse, rushing over. "Are you OK?"

"I'll be fine, thanks," said Teacher Susan, clearly distracted. "Hey, Ruth, have you seen these dolls before?" She held up one raggedy toy and pointed to the other.

Nurse Ruth studied them for a moment before concluding, "Can't say I have . . . Maybe in a store? They seem pretty generic to me. Why do you ask?"

"I'm not sure," Teacher Susan sighed, her gaze turned toward the window and the looming, overcast sky.

448   *People's Choice Literature*

* * *

When Nurse Ruth dropped her off at home, Teacher Susan noticed the light on in her living room. She walked in and found her husband, Harold, sitting on the couch, reading the newspaper.

"Hi, honey," she said.

"Oh, hi," he said, putting down the paper. "You're home early . . . ? Are you feeling OK?"

"I'm fine," she said before collapsing into tears.

"Oh, babe," he said, wrapping her in his arms. "What's wrong?"

She couldn't respond. She just wept and wept.

"It's OK, it's OK," he said. "You're OK. I'm here for you."

She looked up at him, her eyes red and puffy.

"I found Mr. Greenland hanging in a closet today," said the teacher.

"Oh my God," he said, his eyes widening. "I'm so sorry, honey."

"I don't know what's going on," she said. "I don't get it."

"We'll figure it out. I've got you," he whispered as he brushed her hair with his hands. "It's OK."

They spent the better part of an hour like this, talking and cuddling and weeping. Trying to dress a wound that might never fully heal. When lunchtime came, Harold went to the kitchen to make sandwiches, and Teacher Susan sat there staring at the wall. *What's happening?* she thought. *Why is this happening to me?* She thought of Mr. Greenland, so kind, so friendly just the day before. Stopping by the classroom to hand out lollies to the students. Spouting puns like a sprinkler. She thought of his smile. His joyous energy. And then she saw it all over again. The purple tongue, the bulging eyes. Just awful. It didn't make sense.

As she took a deep breath, a sound of clicking metal came from outside. She looked at her watch to see Postman Chris was right on time.

Harold came out of the kitchen wearing an American flag apron and headed for the front door, but Teacher Susan sat up. "I got it, honey."

Harold turned to her with an odd look. "Babe . . . It's the least I can do."

"No," she said. "I could use the fresh air."

Outside, the gray day greeted her with a frigid burst of wind. She shivered, wrapping her arms around herself as she walked. Looking down the street, she saw Postman Chris walk away, and she smiled. What a nice man, she thought. Always with a kind word to say.

The mail was the same as usual. Bills. Bills. Junk. More bills. She closed the mailbox and was just about to turn toward the house when she saw them across the road.

Three elderly women and three elderly men standing half hidden in the evergreen trees. Staring.

Teacher Susan studied them. They were all dressed in their Sunday best. Unseasonable, wrinkly sun dresses and dirty, sun-bleached khaki suits. Hair pulled back against pale scalps and facial hair patched like awkward polka dots across sickly skin. They were all staring at her, as if trying to dig in with their eyes.

Teacher Susan felt a chill run down her spine. She looked behind her, wondering if their gaze was focused elsewhere, but all she could see was Harold in the window, chopping tomatoes. She looked back at the people across the street, and sure enough they were still there, staring.

One of them stepped forward, shaking. Then another.

She swallowed and took a step back toward the house. Two more started walking. They didn't blink. They just stared and shook.

Teacher Susan took another step back. Then another. When the group was halfway across the street, she turned and ran, legs pumping, arms swinging in panic. She ran straight up to the door and slammed it shut.

Harold exited the kitchen with a wide smile and two plates of sandwiches, but when he saw her, his face sank.

"The people. They followed me," said Teacher Susan, panting. "We need to lock the doors and call the police right now!"

"Babe, what are you talking about?"

She pointed to the window. "Look."

He set the plates down and looked out.

"The Nelsons? You're up in arms about the Nelsons?"

Teacher Susan looked out the window herself, finding Pam and Frank Nelson, two octogenarians who'd lived next door for decades, walking down the street.

"Not them," huffed Teacher Susan. "There were six people. Six very-not-nice-looking people walking toward me. I don't know where they went."

"What do you mean not nice?"

"They were just staring at me," she said. "They didn't blink. They didn't smile. They just stared. And then they came for me."

"Babe, you're dealing with a lot," said Harold. "You need to rest."

"I'm not crazy," she said.

450 *People's Choice Literature*

"I know," he said. "I know you're not. I'm just saying you need a break."

She looked out the window again and watched the Nelsons walk away.

"I'm not crazy," she whispered, eyeing the storm clouds building in the distance.

That evening all Teacher Susan could think about was those people. Those eyes. What were they doing out there? What did they want? And what the heck is going on today? First teary Candice Smith, then these strange dolls, then Mr. Greenland dies, then these horrifying people show up at my door . . .

She lay on the couch, staring at the ceiling, her mind racing. She couldn't nap. She couldn't rest.

Something's not right, she thought. So she grabbed her phone and rang Teacher Tracey, who picked up immediately.

"Susan, goodness, how are you?"

"Not good," she replied. "Not good at all."

"What's wrong?"

"I don't know," said Teacher Susan. "Something's off. Something's not right at Hillsdale Elementary and this whole darn town."

"What do you mean?"

"Did you notice anything else strange today? Those dolls? Kids avoiding play time?"

"Hmm," said Teacher Tracey, "not much. Theo Dworkin and Patty Sinclair got into a fight at recess. Your sub did mention Candice Smith's resistance to story time again, but that's it."

Teacher Susan scratched her head. "It doesn't add up."

"Look, Susan, you've been through a lot. Why not take a few days off? You know Principal Philips will support it. It was a really rough day."

"You might be right," sighed Teacher Susan.

"Oh, and Suz," said Teacher Tracey, "just thought you might like to know. Teacher Henry is in the hospital. All the kids wrote him cards today. Sure he'd be happy to hear from you."

Teacher Susan sat up. "What? Why?"

"Came down with a bad stomach bug or something after lunch. Went to Nurse Ruth and just collapsed."

"Oh my God," said Teacher Susan. "That's awful."

"That's not the worst of it. Nurse Ruth told me that on the way to the hospital, he started coughing up blood."

Teacher Susan's heart sank. "Oh, Lord."

"I know," said Teacher Tracey. "I'm sure he'll be OK, though. He's a tough one."

Teacher Susan scratched her chin. "Don't you think there's something strange going on here, Trace? Seems nothing's been normal this week. Mr. Greenland's dead. Teacher Henry's in the hospital. I'm getting these strange visitors . . ."

"Strange what?"

"Oh, never mind." Teacher Susan stared vacantly out the window.

"Hey, Trace, the Smiths live on Dapper Way, right?"

"Pretty sure," came Teacher Tracey's voice. "Why are you asking?"

"I think I might give them a visit, see how Candice is doing."

"Susan, you need to rest."

"I know, I know," she said. "I'll be fine. I just want to make sure Candice is OK."

"OK," said Teacher Tracey. "I'll let you go. Call me if you need anything."

"I will," said Teacher Susan. "Thanks."

She hung up.

The Smiths lived in a three-story stone house with a red door and white trim. The lawn was well kept, the hedges neatly manicured, and the windows clean. The building must have been a century old, but it was well cared for. Teacher Susan smiled at the garden gnomes as she walked up to the door and knocked.

A well-aged woman answered. She wore a plain floral dress, her gray hair tied back in a ponytail.

"Hello," said Teacher Susan. "I'm Candice's teacher at Hillsdale Elementary."

"Oh, hi," said the woman. "I'm Mary, Candice's grandmother. Please, come in."

Teacher Susan stepped into the house. It was immaculate. The walls were golden beige, the floors were newly polished, and the furniture was ornate. Mary seemed out of place among such fine interior design. Her hair looked unwashed, and her clothes were worn.

"I'm sorry to bother you," said Teacher Susan. "I just wanted to check on Candice."

"Oh? Is something wrong?" asked Mary.

"No, no," said the teacher. "It's just that she's been a bit distant lately during story time. I wanted to see if she was OK."

"Oh, she's fine," said Mary. "She's probably just a little parent-sick. You know they've been in the Caribbean all week . . . ?"

"Do you mind if I just say hi to her?" asked Teacher Susan.

Mary looked at her, clearly bothered by the intrusion. "She's upstairs in her room. I'll go get her."

"Thank you," said Teacher Susan.

Mary walked up the stairs and called for Candice.

As Teacher Susan waited for her, she looked around the front part of the house. The living room and dining room were on either side of the main hallway and staircase. Paintings of lighthouses and wintery meadows covered the walls. Beside the main staircase was a table with a vase of oleanders, and next to that lay a crude picture clearly drawn by a child. Teacher Susan stepped up to it and froze.

"Oh my gosh," she whispered.

It was a picture of a doll. The mysterious red-haired, white-dress-clad doll from her class. Only in this version, the doll held a bloody knife.

An upstairs door opened, and Mary descended the staircase with a look of deep concern.

"She's not here," she said.

"What?" said Teacher Susan. "Where is she?"

"I don't know," said Mary. "I looked everywhere. She's not in her room. She's not in the playroom or her parents' room or the guest room. I saw her go up not fifteen minutes ago . . ."

"Has Candice done anything like this before?" asked Teacher Susan.

Mary put her hand to her chest. "I don't know. I've never watched her alone before now . . ."

"It's OK," said Teacher Susan. "We'll find her."

Then she picked up the doll drawing and showed it to Mary. "Did Candice say anything about this?"

Mary shook her head. "I've never seen it before."

Teacher Susan gave her a skeptical look. If Mary's eyes were that bad, then it's very likely she missed something upstairs. "Let's go look for her together."

"But," Mary interjected, "I've looked everywhere . . ."

"We'll look again," said Teacher Susan as she started up the stairs. "Maybe she's playing hide-and-seek."

Mary followed close behind. They looked in Candice's room and the playroom, checking each closet and under the bed. They went to the guest room and did the same, but no luck. When they got to the master bedroom, Mary collapsed in a chair.

"It's no use," she cried. "She's not here."

Teacher Susan looked around the room, in the closet, and then out the window, and instantly her heart stopped.

"Mary . . ." she whispered, eyes wide.

Mary looked at her. "What is it?"

"I think I found . . . something."

"What?" asked Mary. "Where?"

"There," said Teacher Susan, pointing out the window to the front lawn.

Mary struggled to her feet and saw them almost immediately.

Two elderly women and three elderly men, standing stock still in the dusky light. They were all dressed in their dirty, formal fashion, and they were all staring up at the house.

"Those people."

"Ah, yes. Them."

"Huh?" Teacher Susan turned to Mary, whose mouth slowly curled up into an evil smile.

"Nice to see you again, Suzie," Mary chuckled.

Teacher Susan turned back to the window to find the five figures now stepping toward the house.

"Outside my house today," said Teacher Susan. "That was you!"

Mary hunched over, still laughing.

"You killed him, didn't you? You killed Mr. Greenland!"

Mary stopped laughing and closed her eyes with a smile. "I believe you are referring to our children."

"What?"

"The dolls, Suzie. They do what we say." Mary raised her hands to the sky. "They do what the holy Schleeland proclaims!"

Teacher Susan slowly backed away toward the stairs.

"You're crazy."

"No," said Mary. "I'm free. And now you'll be, too. Don't fear, my dear. Give in, and the great Schleeland will provide."

Mary stepped toward her, her eyes now darting around with a sickening, mad glare, as Teacher Susan inched closer to the stairs.

"Where is Candice, Mary?" she asked.

Mary didn't answer. She just kept coming, fingers stretched out like claws, mouth opening, revealing black, rotten teeth.

Teacher Susan turned, took hold of the banister, and fled down the stairs. Just as she reached the bottom, the front door opened, revealing the five elders dressed in dirty clothes, their faces worn and wrinkled, eyes sunken, skin pale.

Teacher Susan looked back to the stairs to find Mary lumbering down, hunched and drooling. The teacher screamed as she turned and ran past the stairs toward the kitchen. Mary chased after, shrieking like a banshee.

Teacher Susan sprinted through the kitchen to the back door. When she hit it, she turned the handle, but it was locked. So she spun around to find yet another door. And sprinted for it.

Mary was at the kitchen table now, screeching as she smashed the particle board in half with a single blow of the hand.

"The power of Schleeland is boundless!"

Teacher Susan burst through the basement door and slammed it behind her. She sprinted down the stairs but suddenly tripped on something. Unable to catch herself, she flew into the dark.

Her chin was first to smack the floor, crushing her tongue and shattering her teeth with the force of dead weight. The teacher howled in pain as blood poured from her mouth. Spitting, she tried to get up, but her body betrayed her. She was too dizzy, too disoriented. Her arms too weak, eyes too heavy.

When she awoke, Teacher Susan found herself lying alone in the dark basement. She turned her head to discover broken doll parts scattered all around her. A leg here, an eyeless head there. Her clothes were soaked, likely from her own blood. She tried to get up, but pain immediately shot up her arms like lightning. She could barely raise her head. She tried again, but only her feet would give.

Suddenly Teacher Susan heard someone approaching the basement door. She tried to move, but the pain was too strong. She tried to say something, but her swollen mouth only allowed a mumble. She heard the door creak open and footsteps slowly descend the stairs. They were heavy and slow, and they stopped once they reached the floor.

"Schleeland awaits you, my dear . . ." whispered a ragged voice.

It was Mary.

Teacher Susan's eyes opened wide.

"All will be well," said another lower voice. "You will see."

The teacher twisted her neck to find one of the male elders from outside now hovering over her. Mary gestured to him, and he immediately grabbed her. Teacher Susan tried to scream, but it was no use. He lifted her over his shoulders and carried her up the stairs.

Above, the kitchen was drastically changed. The lights were off, save for the flicker of candelabras and the bright glow from the room beyond. A soft chanting accompanied this light.

When she reached the living room, Teacher Susan beheld a ghastly scene: Candice sitting quietly in the middle of the now-empty room, wearing a dirty wedding dress and surrounded by a ring of candles. Her eyes were glazed over, her hair disheveled. Around her, four elders dressed in white and wearing red wigs stood in a square. And hanging from their feet behind each elder were four bodies. One was clearly Mr. Greenland. Another looked awfully a lot like Teacher Henry. Teacher Susan could only imagine that the remaining two bodies were Candice's parents.

The man holding Teacher Susan pulled her toward the circle, but she kicked him in the stomach. He humpfed and collapsed, freeing her, and so Teacher Susan limped as quickly as she could to the front door. But when she grabbed the handle, it wouldn't budge.

"It's too late," said a high-pitched voice behind her. "Schleeland cometh."

Teacher Susan turned, and there, down below, stood the doll from her classroom, red haired and arms outstretched.

"The great Schleeland will be here soon enough," it continued.

Teacher Susan looked up to find the entire staircase packed with dolls, all red-headed, all dressed in white. All staring and smiling that ghastly, evil smile.

"Schleeland cometh," sang the dolls in a nasal drone as they pointed in unison to the living room.

Teacher Susan wanted to scream, but her mouth was too swollen.

Suddenly, Candice stood and started toward her teacher.

"Candice?" said Teacher Susan, but the only sound was of swollen, bumbling lips.

Candice didn't respond. She just kept walking toward her, silently.

"Candice!" mouthed Teacher Susan, louder.

Candice stopped and looked Teacher Susan in the eyes. Then she extended her hand.

456 *People's Choice Literature*

"The time is nigh, Susan," she said calmly. "The ascension has come."

Teacher Susan wanted to run. She wanted to grab Candice and flee from this nightmare. She thought of Harold, and how concerned he must be. She thought of her students. But mostly she thought of Candice. Dear, sweet Candice from just the day before. Where had that little girl gone? What happened to her?

Then Candice grabbed Teacher Susan's hand, grounding her in the present. At first nothing changed, just a child's hand in hers. But soon Teacher Susan felt a light electrical shock between them that grew into a pervasive, full-body charge. She felt like she was floating, like there was no gravity, no friction. Just the gentle pull of Candice's hand, and for the first time since she arrived at the Smith's house, Teacher Susan felt calm. As if everything would be fine in the end. As if all this was for the best. As if the great Schleeland would provide.

Then the world turned black.

Two gunshots popped off in the living room, shattering eardrums, causing two elders to drop to the ground, lifeless. Then the candles suddenly extinguished, and the only light now came from the fireplace and a soft glow from upstairs.

Teacher Susan's gaze traveled up to that glow as the bedroom door opened and a figure stepped out.

"Susan?" it asked.

"Harold!?" garbled Teacher Susan.

The dolls parted as he descended the stairs. When he reached the floor, he ran to her and wrapped her in his arms, and it was the most wonderful feeling she had ever felt. Finally, she was saved.

"It's so good to see you," she tried to say.

And as she wept in his arms, she noticed another figure coming down the stairs.

"T-teacher T-tracey?" she stammered. "What are you doing here?"

"I, we, are here for you," said Teacher Tracey somberly, stepping past the smiling dolls.

"Thank you," said Teacher Susan. "Thank goodness."

Teacher Tracey extended her hand to Harold, and they both turned to Teacher Susan, smiling like porcelain masks.

"Schleeland is ready," her husband intoned, gesturing toward the living room.

Teacher Susan stepped back in shock.

"No . . ." she moaned. "What is this?"

"This is the third coming," intoned Teacher Tracey. "Schleeland is nigh."

"Susan," said Candice, stepping toward the circle. "It is time."

Teacher Susan looked at her with utter dread, but Candice gazed back calmly and smiled. Then she looked to Harold and Teacher Tracey, still gesturing toward the living room.

"No," she cried. "No, I'm not going anywhere. I want to go home."

Harold smiled and nodded. "You *are* home, Susan."

Candice, Harold, and Teacher Tracey grabbed her hands, arms, and shoulders and guided her toward the center of the living room, with the dolls in tow. Teacher Susan struggled, but there was no use. Together, they were stronger than her.

"No," she said. "Please."

"It is the only way," said Candice.

As they approached the circle, a new candle was lit, illuminating the four hanging corpses and the two newly suicided elders. Harold and Teacher Tracey took their places as Candice sat Teacher Susan beside her. Then Teacher Tracey, Harold, and the remaining elders began to chant.

"The Mother, the Daughter, and the Holy Spirit. The Mother, the Daughter, and the Holy Spirit . . ."

Candice began to hum. The dolls joined with their humming, now locking hands and forming a closed ring around the inner circle.

Mary approached from the kitchen, intoning a crackly "Schleeland is nigh."

She walked to the center of the circle and knelt down before the flame, presenting a wooden bowl. Then she bowed her head and began to pray: "The Mother, the Daughter, and the Holy Spirit. The Mother, the Daughter, and the Holy Spirit . . ." As she prayed, she sprinkled something in the bowl. Something powdery.

"Schleeland is nigh," she added. "Accept our prayers."

The dolls hummed louder. Candice's hum morphed into gibberish and then a devilish glossolalia. Her tongue fluttered like enflamed tickertape, her voice dropping three octaves.

Teacher Susan looked at Mary and found her smiling. Not a kind smile, but a ghastly, vile grin. But her smile faded when she pulled a knife from her gown and dug it deep into Teacher Susan's forearm, slicing from the elbow down to her hand. The skin opened like a flower as Mary held out her bowl to catch the sweet ichor pouring from within.

458   *People's Choice Literature*

Teacher Susan wanted to scream, but as she breathed deeper, the vibra tion of her breath and the sounds of the humming and chanting calmed her.

Mary grabbed Teacher Susan's other arm and began to repeat the process.

"No," gargled Teacher Susan, lightly struggling as Mary effortlessly carved a canal into her arm, blood flowing anew.

Suddenly the chanting stopped, and the dolls ceased humming. Candice's glossolalia cut out, and she turned to Mary and her bowl of powdery blood.

"Schleeland is nigh," said Mary as she handed it to Candice.

The chants returned, fuller, louder this time. "The Mother, the Daughter, and the Holy Spirit . . ."

Candice took the bowl and brought it to her lips. She sipped it like soup and then wiped her mouth, a bit of blood trickling from the side of her lips.

The chants grew louder and louder as Candice stood up and walked around the circle.

"Schleeland is nigh," she repeated as she passed by each doll, sprinkling the blood on them like a flower girl at a goth wedding. She sprinkled Teacher Tracey and Harold and the elders before turning to Teacher Susan and speaking that incomprehensible phrase for the last time: "Schleeland is nigh."

Teacher Tracey beamed in ecstasy as she pulled a clean knife from the folds of her gown. Then she grabbed Teacher Susan's throat and dragged the blade across it, lovingly parting the flesh in two.

Teacher Susan doubled over, gasping for air, but none came. Only blood gurgled from her guttural depths. She looked up at Candice, who was now standing above her, but something was different. Her face was contorted in a horrible way. Her body appeared to shift, to change, becoming more and more distorted. Eventually, her face was no longer a face but a swirling mass of flesh and intestines. Her eyes like two black holes, mouth a gaping, bloody wound. And her tongue, her tongue was now a tentacular mass of flesh, reaching out and caressing the teacher's face. Or at least that's what Teacher Susan thought she saw as the blood spilled from her throat and flooded her lungs, as her stomach refluxed and her vision dimmed to nothingness.

Epilogue

How to Go to Hell: Issue 48

Hey, there. Devin here. Back for another week of "How to Go to Hell." But before we get there, I just gotta shout out to my love, Pandora, and you, my followers. Ever since the publication of *Lesser of Two Devils*, you've stuck with me. From preorders through the pan-underworld book tour and all the way to the Golden Ghoul Awards. Thank you. You've pulled this humble demon from the depths of creative, nonexistential crisis to an established literary career. And for this, I am eternally grateful.

Now, before we get to the good stuff, I want to share an exclusive offer for "How to Go to Hell" subscribers. This week only you'll get a 20% discount on all horticultural decapitations. Now, I know the price might still be steep for some folks, so I'm also throwing in an epub of my new memoir, *Beheading in the Right Direction*. Hailed as "a masterpiece" by Beelzebub and "genius" by the Zodiac Killer. *The Wall Street Journal* included it in its holiday roundup. So, grab your copy and get a *head* start on your very own decap today!

OK, but getting down to the real business. Today we consider a very special topic for this Sol Invictus holiday weekend: Hobbies. Now, I know many of you have been asking about hobby tips for a while. And to those who have, I apologize for the wait. My publicist nudges me toward the news cycle, so this post was pushed way back. But as they say in Gehenna, it's never too late to get this Donner Party started!

Now, many of you have asked throughout the centuries, "Which hobbies will help my chances of going to Hell?" "Which should I avoid?" And when this happens, when you stop me in the street or on my way out of

a multidimensional vortex or while I'm eating ice cream with my unidimensional niece, I stop you right there. I look you deep in your hollow human eyes and tell it straight: "Hobbies are the last thing you should be thinking of if you ever want to make it to Hell."

See, contrary to common belief, getting into Hell takes a lot of hard work and perseverance. You don't just rob a liquor store or masturbate or even kill someone. Do you have any idea how many murderers make it to Heaven every week? Even the most dedicated sinners can have an impossible time making it through those flaming gates and to their new, infernal home. You don't have time for lollygagging or dillydallying. There ain't no yoyoers in Hell. No one's crocheting or polishing their calligraphy.

Now, I know many will scoff at this. I see all you serial killers and arsonists rolling your eyes, thinking, "I can still be evil *and* have a hobby *and* go to Hell." And to you, I say, this may be the case, if you work hard and keep up your evil deeds. If you scare enough children, send death threats to the right Republican politicians—that's right, the Devil's a bonafide Libtard, constantly subtweeting the holier-than-thou Reaganite upstairs—you can probably get away with a few hobbies and still make it down to the eternal abyss.

For you crafty types and you thumb twiddlers—the people who actually need hobbies, as opposed to those working day and night cultivating, say, the perfect suicide cult—I will yield to your desires this one time only. Here are some pastimes you can partake in and probably, if you're really really evil—and I mean really really really evil—still get into Hell:

1. Candy Making

Poison candy is a popular pastime for Hell-bound sinners. All you need is some sugar, an oven, and whatever you want to mix into your unique, ungodly blend. Some try arsenic cookies, some strychnine cupcakes, others love the kick of cyanide gumballs. Whatever your poison, be sure to follow your bloody bliss.

462　*People's Choice Literature*

2. Amateur Taxidermy

This one can be tricky, because to do it right—to really make a name for yourself in the underworld—you must be careful to stuff someone who's still alive. If not, you could end up like that guy from Texas, who one day decided to slaughter his whole family and start collecting their corpses. He thought he was a shoo-in for Sheol, but when the Office reviewed his file, they found that taxidermying your family after death was not a grave enough offense. Now he's stuck in a seemingly unending appeals process in Purgatory. Want that to be you? Then heed my advice.

3. Poetry

Contrary to popular belief and lofty ideals of the craft, few poets make it to Heaven. Nearly all go to Hell. Here you'll find an elaborate network of cafes and bookstores where nightly (aka 24/7) poets share their devilish rhymes. You might catch Rimbaud at Goblin Books one night and happen upon Blake and Ginsberg at the Poetry Sinporium the next. And if you're a real glutton for pain, you can catch the weekly poetry marathon at the Hotel O'Doom, where hundreds of fallen poets dole out their peculiar brands of hellish verse.

4. Pottery

Needless to say, Hell is a very hot place. You don't even need a kiln to fire up the clay. Just stick your bowl or cup out the front door, and it'll harden in seconds. Because of this, nearly everyone in Hell is an expert potter. It isn't just a hobby here. It's a way of life. So I'd suggest getting started sooner than later. Anything below mastery will be thrown out in the application review process. Look, I don't write the rules, I just enforce them. Or used to before I took to the pen and started my Patreon (link here).

5. LARPing

Yep: live-action role playing. Heard of Dungeons & Dragons? Imagine it in real-life, except you use your real life to commit real crimes. Like, for

example, you could pretend to be a superhero pretending to be a supervillain pretending to be a superhero who is preventing a bank robbery when you're actually the one robbing the bank. You could even pretend to be a superhero pretending to be a supervillain pretending to be a superhero pretending being a supervillain who's threatening to unleash a deadly poison in the city's water supply. You could try being a superhero pretending to be a supervillain pretending to be a superhero pretending to be a supervillain pretending to be a supervillain pretending to be a superhero saving a person from a burning building when you set the damned fire yourself. I think you get where I'm going with this. Get creative and have fun.

6. Smashing That "How to Go to Hell" Like Button Below

Sorry. Had to. These newsletters don't pay for themselves, you know . . . And each Like goes a long way in helping the algorithm bring others into the HTGTH community.

Well, that's all for now. Stay tuned for next week. And as always, you can show your support for this newsletter by forwarding it to a friend. Subscribers who do so get exclusive access to premium content. Never miss a post and never miss an update. And be one of the few and the proud who know just "How to Go to Hell."

Your faithful scribe,

Devin Nevins

Acknowledgments

We would like to extend our deepest thanks to our editors Lady Gertrude and Lady Lydia for their tireless efforts to make *Lesser of Two Devils* the beauty that it has become. An enormous amount of thanks is also due to our agent, Lord Iago. Your belief in this collection was just what we needed to get over the finish line.

This book would not be what it is today without the efforts of our early readers, Lord Patrick and Lady Susan. We would also like to thank our dear friends for their support, particularly Lord Timothy and Lady Regina. Without them we would surely have thrown in the bloody towel long ago.

୧୬

You put down the book and look up in amazement. Lord Timothy! If he knows these authors, maybe he knows Lady Regina!?? Good heavens, you think, the gateway to my love was hidden in plain sight all along. You look around, still digesting the horrors you just processed at break-neck speed with your recently upgraded RapidRead® robo-eyes, and re-acquaint yourself with your surroundings. The drones still hovering. The three thousand roses still awaiting their loving recipient. Bruno Mars's "Marry You" playing for perhaps the fifty-seventh time. And to make matters more dramatic, the light snow flurry has built into a steady fall, as if the hands of the Lord God Himself were high above, shaking out immense pillows, coating the land with His downy grace.

You direct your robo-eyes to neural messaging and click on Lord Timothy.

[Neural Text Exchange XVIII: *Lord Tickletext* and *Lord Timothy*]

TICKLETEXT: Lord Timothy! Oh, Timothy, please respond.

LORD TIMOTHY: [. . .]

TICKLETEXT: Dear, God, please connect me to Lord Timothy. I have ventured so far, have traveled through conceptual realms no mortal should ever endure. I have sailed imaginary seas and cried real, cold, hard tears. I have labored or hired assistants who've hired assistants to labor, have consumed the most loathly of fictions and had the most torturous of times, and all of it to reunite with my emerald-eyed, crimson-haired, hover-trolley-tattooed love. Please Lord, please God, hear my prayers. Pretty please—

LORD TIMOTHY: Hey, Jim. You OK?

TICKLETEXT: Goodness gracious, Lord Timothy. Where are you?

LORD TIMOTHY: The New Eglinton tunnel. Traffic's backed up. Seems everyone got the memo to make it early to midnight mass . . . Something wrong?

TICKLETEXT: Oh, Lord Timothy, you won't believe the day I've had. I've lived too long in this house of sadness. I've found then lost the love of my life, and now after all my peril, after hours of pain, dimensions of ungodly strain, here you are, the key to finding my love.

LORD TIMOTHY: [. . .]

TICKLETEXT: Goodness, Lord Timothy! Are you still there?

LORD TIMOTHY: I'm here, Jim. You're freaking me out.

TICKLETEXT: Lord Timothy, please don't hang up.

LORD TIMOTHY: What's going on, Jim?

TICKLETEXT: It's just . . . It's Just . . . It appears you might know my love, the forbidden apple of my robo eye. A Lady Regina . . . ?

LORD TIMOTHY: Lady Regina? Oh, sure. I was just with her at Duchess Hannah's party.

TICKLETEXT: Oh my goodness. Is she OK? Where is she now?

LORD TIMOTHY: I don't know. She said she was off to midnight mass at New St. James Cathedral. I offered her a ride, but she said she had one.

TICKLETEXT (your neural heart skips a beat): A ride from whom?

LORD TIMOTHY: I think it was someone named Lord Steve . . . ?

TICKLETEXT: Lord Steve??

LORD TIMOTHY: That's right.

TICKLETEXT (your neural heart stops): I must go. I must pry her from the evil clutches of this Steve.

LORD TIMOTHY: Jim, you're back to freaking me out.

TICKLETEXT: I've got to go.

ↁ

You switch off your robo-eyes and the world falls away. All day, all evening—all your strivings, all your yearnings, everything you've worked for now tripped up by some stevenly saphead. Some lord named Steve. "Steve." What kind of name is that? It's just not fair. Today is your time to shine, not his. But you have to play nice. You have to *make* nice. You have to roll on up to the New St. James Cathedral that looks like cabbage with a stride that looks like stone. You have to step out of your carriage that looks like pumpkin and stroll up the stairs that look like stumps. You don't have to be fancy. You don't have to be anything but yourself.

The Most Unwanted Novel   467

You're just like the rest of them. You're just a regular old lord. Until you spot her.

Her.

Yes, inside the church that looks like cabbage, you gaze at her like seeing. You see her like feeling. Feel her presence like freeing. Then you spot Lord Steve who smells like crumbs. You hear that name that sounds like stupid, think bad thoughts that rhyme with skill. Then you birth a plan that smells like heart but wholly spells out s a b o t a g e. Yes, you've been dreaming of this moment since you were a wee little lord. You'd always thought you'd lead the charge, but you'll have to take a backseat (which looks like a seat), if only for a moment that feels like time. You follow them like books, creep through the shadows like hunched. The corner suits you well. Dim. Grim. Inhibited. Constraint the key here. You gaze out, espy the vulgar horde that looks like gloves, listen to Vicar Henry's sermon that sounds like sleeping. You move closer as the room fills with flutters. You inch forward like frogs. Tiptoe like turtles. And then you see it. There. Red. ThRedre. The alarm red as hydrant. The plan as old as crime. You raise a hand that sounds like age and don a glove that smells like love and just nudge the alarm down a smidge, just a shimmy, lil shove. Then you dart past the column like water into the room that looks like dark. You listen as the alarm wails like a fart, as the crowd bursts into confusion that looks like joy, as the Vicar pleads for everyone to file out calmly, please don't panic, please, but no one listens in a style not unlike the changing of the seasons in New Quebec. You exit the office and search for her. You search through the manic masses that move like mummies, past Lords and Ladies crying like cranes, Dukes and Duchesses, Madams and Ma'ams that look like hams running for their lives that look like liver, out doors that smell like summer, into the wind that feels like touch, snow like rain, rain like ice, nice, and right on cue, you spot her. There. her. e. And so, you rush now, dash desperately through the dance of dummies, dudes, and dads, past popes and tentacled prospectors, out doors that don't delay. And in this chaotic cabbagery, in this dummy mummy scheisse show of a cathedral on figurative fire, you reach her. You stop, panting, planting feet. Puckered teeth. Purple steam. Clean. She turns to you, and you speak her name in a voice that sounds like flapping.

Outside, the air stings softly. Snow falls in lines that look like words. Lady Regina meets your eyes, plucking the words mid-fall:

468 *People's Choice Literature*

Do

I

know

you?

You smile through teeth that look like buttons.

She blushes like a lush.

"Oh, yes, my dear," you plead plainly. "Yes. We met not hours afore. This morn, even. Sipping goat milk hot chocolates. Chewing sugar cookies and crumbs. Reminiscing of those we lost oh so long ago on this doleful day at our doorstep . . ."

She hits you hard with withered eyes, a tear, caress, yes.

"Yes!" she cries. "Yes, it is you! It was you who gave me such joy, such healing. You who blessed me with hope on this here nearly holiest of days, this time of joy stung by the sting of an awful anniversary. After I left, I searched everywhere for you, dear Tickletext. The Port Elisabeth Angling Society, the Port Elisabeth Zoo, the Port Elisabeth Dog Track, the Port Elisabeth Pool. I called friends. They hired artificially intelligent assistants who hired unintelligent drones. I ventured violent, virtual seas to vagrant, virtual villages. I searched and searched, despairing that mine eyes might never caress your mien once more. But now here you are, dear Tickletext, here, saving me from this terrible trouble here at midnight on Christmas Eve. It's a true miracle on Fifty-Fourth Street, Suite 15, Port Elisabeth Station, Martian Federation 33321."

And you look at her through your teary eyes that cry like dimes and state, "Yes. Lady Regina, yes. It is I. It is me, Lord Tickletext. Your love."

And she nearly faints at your words that touch like cloth. She just kisses you, lands a licky, right then and there. Yes, her lips that feel like flowers meet your lips that flap like fans. You kiss and it's as if all time has stopped in the form of a clock. Time dissolves into nothingness that looks like no thing, and you kiss her back like embrace. Embrending. Embrasure. You kiss her back and it's as if time starts all over like metronome. Tone. Time starts as if reborn like a rose, as if this, today, right here, right now, not wrong, were your place of birth, as if all time before it were null, void, returned to sender (who looks just like you but in reverse), as if in this moment your life, which feels like life, yes, waking, sleeping, semi-here, here-life, here, as if your life began here, as if this in moment your life life, your love love, your true love, became whole. Holy.

Unhampered. So, you pull back and stare into her malachite eyes that smell like yes and say, "My dear Lady Regina, I love you."

And she smiles, gazing up. She turns to the sky that looks like night and replies, in ringing rings of rapture, "Oh, how I love *you*, dear Tickletext. I love you more than tongue can tell. You are my light. My sun, moon, and stars. You are my everything."

And suddenly you are complete. Composed. Kind. Replete with every and everything a Martian man could ask for. And it's at that moment, in that fragment of time, when new light falls on her face, when your eyes that eat light follow her eyes that cook color, follow them high into the sky that looks like sparks, and there, in this nontentacular time, at this monument of a moment, you behold the most beautiful thing in the universe that looks like home, ohm, om, the most magnificent form you've e'er beheld. You spot a star that looks like blinking, a sky that looks like love. A star lowering, descending, landing in your palm that moves like mirrors. And as it lands in your hand, limp, slightly crimpled, you notice the note tied ad astra, the folded paper fixed to your star. And on the note, it reads,

[Celestial Note I: *The Star* to *Lord Tickletext*]

To Lord tickletext:

I know this may come as a shock, but there has been a terrible misunderstanding. The woman before you is not Lady Regina. She is none other than Lady Victoria, Lady Regina's twin sister! She has fallen for you and has pursued you in her stead.

Her confession is enclosed.

— The Star

[Celestial Attachment I: *Lady Victoria* to *Lord Tickletext*]

Dearest Lord Tickletext,

My dear. My dearest dear. The apple pie of my robo-eye. The aching hole of my soul. Thank heavens we finally meet. Thank heavens this star has finally delivered my truth to you. Your face, your forlorn form has been my loving light, my compass through this grave and bitter holy eve. You are my light. You are my love. But before I continue, I must explain.

I know of your longing for Lady Regina because 'twas I she gave the message to earlier this morn, the note that confessed her undying love to you. But upon receiving said note, upon the commencement of my quest, I came upon filmbooks of you, dozens of filmbooks easily accessible on the neural net. I puckered particularly at that lovely scene of your familiars sailboarding on Gale Crater Lake. Studying that spark in your spherules, the skill of your smile, I fell for you, too, dear friend. I broke my solemn vow to my only syster, Lady Regina, and tossed her message in the rubbish, instead searching far and wide for you for myself.

I searched everywhere. The Port Elisabeth Angling Society, the Port Elisabeth Zoo, the Port Elisabeth Dog Track, the Port Elisabeth Pool. I called friends. They hired artificially intelligent assistants who contracted dummy drones. I ventured a'from virtual seas to vagrant, virtual villages and all their variations. And all along the way I have fallen deeper and deeper in love with you, dear Jimothy, and I will always love you. All I pray is that you love me, too.

I know I will never be Lady Regina. I will always be Victoria. Sigh. But I beg for your love. For you. Ewe. We.

Love,

Lady Victoria

☙

You snap out of it and do a double take. You find yourself still sitting on Lady Regina's front porch, book still by your side, drones still droning away. You spot the flowers frozen in the breeze, the snow falling like cedars. I must leave, you think. These dreams are just that: dreams. Thought clouds. Hopeless seasons of the soul. In short, suspect. Your mind's a minefield of fractured facts and measly misfires. See, there might not even be a Lady Victoria. And there sure as heck isn't some sentient star that could come from the sky bearing tidings of unwanted, unrequited love.

So you pick yourself up, lift, and start down the walkway, hobbling, really, pounding down past drones, from your floating archway of roses to a more flammeous form—fragments, really—following in tow.

All the way to New St. James, you cower, you cave. You heart for her. You heart for Lady Regina and your heart aches. Your language lingers on lovingly loveliness. Your language languages love. Your language languages so well it wakes, aches so good it hurts so much the mush gets messy, desire gets dire, drops, demands distraction. So, you switch on your robo-eyes and search for a streaming program. After flipping through dozens of thrillers and dull dramas, you consider an espee of ESPN or the New Exeter Android Children's Choir's latest a cappella arrangements of Al Capone arraignments before settling on this new show Lady Gale raved about in her neural newsletter this past Giving Tuesday. You sit back in your seat, turn up the treble, and press play.

[*Days of Our Tentacled Lives*, Season 2, Episode 4]

INT. RESTAURANT

Groups of tentacled people are sitting at different tables eating lunch. One of them, the TENTACLED MAN, has a tentacle for a nose. He is eating spaghetti but is clearly unhappy. He turns to the TENTACLED BUREAUCRAT sitting next to him.

TENTACLED MAN
(sobbing)

Oh, I'm so lonely. I met the tentacled woman of my dreams and now she's gone. I've been searching all over for her. Even filed a

472　*People's Choice Literature*

missing tentacled persons report, but they can't find her anywhere. Oh me, oh we . . .

TENTACLED BUREAUCRAT

Oh, dear, I wish I could help, but I'm just a lowly bureaucrat for the Intergalactic Association of Tentacled Bureaucrats. I don't even have a tentacle on my head. All I have is this lousy neck tentacle.
(points tentacled finger to tentacled neck)

TENTACLED MAN
(sighing)
It's fine. Nothing to do. Nothing to see here.

TENTACLED BUREAUCRAT
(showing clear, tentacled empathy)
Maybe I've seen her around. What does she look like?

TENTACLED MAN

Well, she's tentacled, of course. Her nose is like mine; she has two tentacles hanging from her chin and a very large tentacle coming out of her head.

TENTACLED BUREAUCRAT
(eyes wide)
Does she have a

(points to his tiny neck tentacle)
on her

(points to his ear)

?

TENTACLED MAN
(with tentacled excitement)
Why, yes, she does!

TENTACLED BUREAUCRAT

Well, there can only be one tentacled person like that on this tentacled planet. And it just so happens she's a member of my tentacled gym!

>   TENTACLED MAN
> Goodness!

>   TENTACLED BUREAUCRAT
> Let's add some gracious to that goodness! I'll take you there.

INT. TENTACLED GYM

A group of tentacled people exercise on tentacled treadmills and lift tentacled weights. The TENTACLED MAN and the TENTACLED BUREAUCRAT enter in tentacled gym clothes.

>   TENTACLED MAN
>   (excitedly rubbing his tentacled hands together)
> I wonder where she could be!

>   TENTACLED BUREAUCRAT
>   (scratching his tentacled neck)
> Well, I'm sure she's here somewhere. Maybe we can ask around?

The TENTACLED MAN and the TENTACLED BUREAUCRAT walk up to a TENTACLED FEMALE BODY BUILDER lifting a tri-tentacled weight.

>   TENTACLED MAN
> Sorry to bother you, tentacled miss. We're looking for a tentacled woman who has a nose tentacle, two tentacles hanging from her chin, a very big tentacle growing out of her head, *and* a tiny ear tentacle. Have you seen her?

>   TENTACLED FEMALE BODY BUILDER
>   (slamming down the tentacled weight in annoyance)
> A woman with two chin tentacles? How come?

>   TENTACLED MAN
> I'm in love with her. The curve of her tentacled hips, the dimples on her tentacled chin . . . I just can't find her tentacled anywhere!

The TENTACLED FEMALE BODY BUILDER stares at him, uninterested.

TENTACLED MAN

Here, let me show you a tentacled picture.

The TENTACLED MAN pulls out his tentacled phone and shows the TENTACLED FEMALE BODY BUILDER a selfie of the TENTACLED MAN and his tentacled love from earlier that day.

TENTACLED FEMALE BODY BUILDER
(with tentacled surprise)

Zounds! I know her! Saw her in the dance party workout room on floor 17B! Not thirty minutes ago!

The TENTACLED MAN and the TENTACLED BUREAUCRAT look at each other in tentacled alarm before flopping off to the dance party workout room on floor 17B.

INT. HALLWAY

The TENTACLED MAN and the TENTACLED BUREAUCRAT approach a door labeled DANCE PARTY WORKOUT ROOM. Loud music booms from inside. The TENTACLED MAN goes to open it, but it's locked.

TENTACLED BUREAUCRAT
(with tentacled concern)

What are we to do?

The TENTACLED MAN smiles before kneeling. His nose tentacle re-shapes into a lockpick, then he deftly picks the lock. He stands back up and proudly nods to the TENTACLED BUREAUCRAT before extending a long, tentacled arm.

TENTACLED MAN

After you . . .

INT. DANCE PARTY WORKOUT ROOM ON FLOOR 17B

The TENTACLED MAN and the TENTACLED BUREAUCRAT enter the room to find a dozen tentacled people bouncing to vintage 1990s

The Most Unwanted Novel   475

electronic dance music. Tentacles waving and swaying to the beat. Bodies bouncing in tentacled bliss. The TENTACLED DANCE PARTY WORKOUT INSTRUCTOR spots the TENTACLED MAN and the TENTACLED BUREAUCRAT and angrily stomps over.

TENTACLED DANCE PARTY WORKOUT INSTRUCTOR
What are you doing?! This is a private workout room!

TENTACLED MAN
(doing the tentacled macarena)
We're looking for someone. Have you seen her?

Pausing mid hip-swing, the TENTACLED MAN pulls out his tentacled phone, flashes a selfie of he and his love in tentacled embrace. The TENTACLED DANCE PARTY WORKOUT INSTRUCTOR raises a tentacled eyebrow, and the TENTACLED MAN returns to his tentacled dance.

TENTACLED DANCE PARTY WORKOUT INSTRUCTOR
You missed her. She just left.

TENTACLED MAN
(flipping over each tentacled hand)
Where'd she go?

TENTACLED DANCE PARTY WORKOUT INSTRUCTOR
(admiring the TENTACLED MAN's moves)
Don't know, but there's a soirée going on two rooms over. Maybe someone there can help you . . .

The TENTACLED MAN nods to the TENTACLED BUREAUCRAT, and they side shimmy out the room.

INT. SOIRÉE

The TENTACLED MAN and the TENTACLED BUREAUCRAT enter the regal, wainscoted soirée in tentacled tuxedoes and discover a room of tentacled gentry chatting and laughing, lifting champagne glasses to their well-preened, tentacled lips.

TENTACLED MAN
(sipping a glass of lonkero)
I just know she's here! I can feel it.

The TENTACLED MAN and the TENTACLED BUREAUCRAT approach a quartet of high-class tentacled aliens.

TENTACLED MAN
Excuse me, tautly tentacled sirs and madams, might your tentacled eyes have come upon a tentacled lady of late, one with a nose tentacle like mine, two tentacles dangling from her chin, a very tall tentacle from her head, *and* a tiny little ear tentacle?

TENTACLED FEMALE IN PEARLS
(snootily brushing her tentacled lips)
No. *Who* would want a tentacled woman like that?

TENTACLED MAN
It's not want, it's love.

TENTACLED FEMALE IN PEARLS
(tentacled eyebrow shifting in surprise)
Well, it's a good thing there's a tentacled singles mixer here tomorrow, because you're certainly not going to find any tentacled women like that tonight.

TENTACLED BUREAUCRAT
(resting a tentacled arm over the TENTACLED MAN's bi-tentacled shoulder)
We'd better go . . .

TENTACLED MAN
(shaking his head and wiping a tear from his tentacled eyes)
I can't give up on her . . .

EXT. STREET

The TENTACLED MAN and the TENTACLED BUREAUCRAT walk along the street, the TENTACLED MAN staring at the selfie of his love. In

the distance a tentacled person sits on a tentacled bench, crying. They walk over to him.

TENTACLED MAN

What's wrong?

TENTACLED CRIER
(crying)

I just failed my tentacled driving test. Now I can't drive my tentacled car anymore.

TENTACLED BUREAUCRAT

But that's tentacledly terrible!

TENTACLED CRIER

Now I can't even get to the tentacled singles mixer tomorrow. All I can do is sit here and cry my tentacled tears . . .

TENTACLED MAN

Maybe if you help us, my tentacled bureaucrat friend here can help you get back your tentacled driver's license . . .

TENTACLED BUREAUCRAT

. . . And maybe we can get you a ticket to that mixer.

TENTACLED CRIER
(crying)

I'd do anything.

Suddenly a tentacled bus pulls up and two tentacled passengers get off. The TENTACLED MAN turns to the bus and freezes. There, on the side of the bus, is an ad for the Tentacled School of Aviation. And in the middle of the ad is a woman with a nose tentacle, two chin tentacles, a very large tentacle coming out of her head and, you guessed it, a tiny ear tentacle.

The TENTACLED MAN grabs the TENTACLED BUREAUCRAT and the TENTACLED CRIER and drags them to the bus. The TENTACLED MAN

478 *People's Choice Literature*

grabs the bus door with his tentacled hand just as it's closing and pries it open. The camera zooms into his shining, tentacled face.

TENTACLED MAN

Three tickets to the TSA!

The camera pulls back as the tentacled bus pulls away, revealing the tentacled city in the distance. The tentacled credits start to roll.

❧

Two lines into the credits you lose interest. What a stupid show, you think. They just don't understand art these days. Why would anyone want to watch some tentacled bloke bounce from tentacled place to tentacled place, languishing like a loon over his tentacled love?

You switch off your robo-eyes and look out the window of your hover carriage. You notice the quiet suburb of New St. James, the sleepy homes, the snow falling like hope. Then up ahead you spot it, the Cathedral standing in a snowy field.

Beholding the cabbage-like apparition spotlit in the Martian night, your heart starts to pound. What will I say? What will *she* say? Will she still even remember me?

When you pull up, the android driver opens the door and holds your hand, helping you down. You turn to the three thousand drones with their three thousand roses and with the wave of your hand, you will them to wait. You ascend the Cathedral stairs one foot at a hobbled time. Then you reach the massive door and press forward.

Inside, Vicar Henrietta speaks in a voice of vision, veering from the violence of the day to the virtues of vegetal viands in vegetable stew. You look over shoulders, roving your robo-eyes from android to anthro, tentacle to tradesman, scanning, seething for your redheaded love.

But there's nothing. No reading on the robo-eyes. No sign on the spherules you call home. Nothing. You huff and switch your robo-eyes to texting.

[Neural Text Exchange XIX: *Lord Tickletext* and *Lord Timothy*]

TICKLETEXT: Lord Timothy!

LORD TIMOTHY: [. . .]

TICKLETEXT: Lord Timothy! Are you even here!? Lady Regina is nowhere to be found!!!

LORD TIMOTHY (mind sighing): Hi, Jim.

TICKLETEXT: Where the hell are you?

LORD TIMOTHY: In the Cathedral! Front row with Lady Charlotte. Can't believe you're bothering me in the middle of church. And on Christmas Eve no less!

TICKLETEXT: Forgive me, dear Timothy, but Lady Regina is not here. I've looked everywhere. From every human head to android artifact, touching every tentacle with my eager eyes. Are you certain she said this cathedral and not some other? Foxcroft Terrace? New Portland?

LORD TIMOTHY: I'm sure.

TICKLETEXT (mind-smacking the mind-table): Dammit.

LORD TIMOTHY: Why are you even looking for her? There're plenty of ladies who would love to spend Christmas with you.

TICKLETEXT: You can't even begin to understand how unwanted your suggestion is.

LORD TIMOTHY: OK then, are you done?

TICKLETEXT: No.

LORD TIMOTHY: What else is there?

480   *People's Choice Literature*

TICKLETEXT: I need her. I must **find her**. I've come this far. Have traveled countless miles. Well, my associates did most of the physical traveling. But I've ventured to virtual depths undreamt of. To nightmarish swevens of the soul. And here I am, alone, lost in a cathedral as crummy as cabbage . . .

LORD TIMOTHY: Jim, I told you. Just move on. Go home. Sleep. You'll feel better in the morning.

TICKLETEXT: I can't move on. I love her.

LORD TIMOTHY: Look, I'm not sure you understand what kind of a person Lady Regina is. I wasn't going to mention it since you seemed so excited, but she's not who you think. Please, just forget about her.

TICKLETEXT: What are you talking about? Lady Regina is the love of my life. Those olivine eyes that lift like light, that light that lit my stubborn soul. That ruby hair, falling fluidly to her shoulders. That glowing gown that wrapped her like a—

LORD TIMOTHY: Jim, we've been friends a long time and I've always thought highly of you. I've been honest with you from the start. From the very first day we met at the club until today when you threw that temper tantrum . . .

TICKLETEXT: [. . .]

LORD TIMOTHY: . . . you've always been my friend. You're like a brother to me. And so, I gotta lay it on you straight: Lady Regina is just one of her names.

TICKLETEXT: Huh?

LORD TIMOTHY: Her real name is Lady Mary.

TICKLETEXT: What'd you just say?

LORD TIMOTHY: I said her name is Lady Mary. And she's a member of the Merry Men.

TICKLETEXT: You're lying.

LORD TIMOTHY: Jim, I wouldn't do that. Not about something as important as this.

TICKLETEXT: No. I mean, it's impossible. I know her. No one that kind would cower to those thieves. No one of such grace would grovel to those low-life losers.

LORD TIMOTHY: Look, man, I'm sorry to break it to you like this, but it's the truth.

TICKLETEXT: I won't hear it. I won't have you tainting the name of my new love.

A notification comes on your neural view screen.

LORD TIMOTHY: I've just forwarded two files with all the info you need. Take them and sit with them. And take good care of yourself, friend.

Lord Timothy exits the neural chat, and you sit there in shock. What could this mean? You notice the new file notification blinking in your peripheral neural-vision. You contemplate clicking it but hesitate. What if Lord Timothy's right? What if Lady Regina is for certes a comrade of that callipygian crew? What if you've been duped all day, running from place to place, sending friends and friends of friends, AIs and androids, to all corners of the Martian globe, down into the deepest digital depths, through unreal realities in search of a love who was just the opposite, just the kind of person you'd avoid on the street as she bounded away beside her merry buddies, the kind of person you'd read about in the paper and think, thank goodness they finally got those Merry Men (rather, Lousy Losers), why did they even let them onto Mars in the first place, they and their crummy communist ideals and fake hippie hairdos, their stupid tie-dye T-shirts and gaudy, ground-sloth jackets, their stupid bushy beards,

their stupid "love," their stupid hate they spread with their stupid love, their complete misconception of the worlds of cause and effect, of capitalism, of how history ended and began again in budding bliss aka endless equity with many-course meals, great service unequaled in the face of those malapert Merry Men and their slovenly stays and their convenient amnesia, how they forget so well the whining liberal wackos that forced us from our earthly Eden, venturing athwart the vastness of the void to this colder, compact planet, before the cats started chatting, before the coastal elite coup, before the war and the woes, deception and death, the feline cries of wrathful hate, the human cries of murderous want, the cries of the dying and the cries of the dead, those cries that still sway in the virtual and real airs, those cries that keep you up night after nighty night, reverberating through a swinking half-slumber, those cries you thought you could escape by coming here, by running from your former world, that orb of orison, but all you did was run into more war and woes, more deception, more death, more feline cries of wrathful hate and human cries of murderous want, more cries of the dying and more cries of the dead, but here, here in the Martian Federation, your home full of good people who do great things, you who have the best of intentions, you who want the best for all sentient beings, that they, too, might have the treat of tennis after breakfast and tennis after lunch and tennis after dinner and tennis after brunch, yes, such is a luxury, yes, and it is one fought for for far more centuries than your short little long life could hold at your current dosage of maliosiprorax, but it is the landing, the love, a way of life that comes from learning to love life more and more each day, yes, every day is a blessing, every day is a gift, every day is a new opportunity for fun, to do more, to be better at tennis, or fishing, or golf, to *be* more than the day before, to be better, yes, to be more, to *do* more, to love, yes, to love, oh, love, love, the heated beat of your broken heart, the pulse that has propelled you here through this drought of a day, that has flung you this far, that has tortured you at this troubled crossroads on this eve of Christ's birth, this night that should transcend all torment, yes, this night when Lady Regina should be far from harm's way, here with you, here, yes, here, but then you think of her and those moronic "merry" men, you think of her and you mind-weep, you think of all your dreams and desires, you think of Lord Timothy's awful revelation, and you balk at that blinking dot in your neural periphery, heart skipping a neural beat, but you give it your full attention now, its red light taunting, pulse progressing, you spot it accelerate, and your heart races, you blow

out a breath, and it slows, you don't know what to do, you don't know what to think, what to believe, to feel, you don't know how to be anymore, so you do the only thing you can think of. You click the first file.

[Neural Manuscript II: "The Ballad of Lady Mary and Sir Hobin"]

A bonny fine Martian of a noble degree,
   With a hey down downy Lady Mary by name,
Did live in the North, of excellent worth,
   For she was a gallant dame.

For favour and face, and beauty most rare,
   Queen Ellen shee did excell;
For dear Mary then was prais'd of all men
   That did in the country dwell.

'Twas neither Roses nor Janes nor any lady,
   Whose beauty was clear and bright,
That could surpass this red-haired lass,
   Beloved of lord and knight.

The Earl of Hampton, so nobly born,
   That came of noble brood,
To dear Mary went, with a good intent,
   By the name of Hobin Rood.

With kisses sweet, their red lips did meet,
   For shee and the earl agreed;
In every place, they kindly imbraced,
   With love and sweet unity.

But fortune bearing these lovers a spight,
   That soon they were forced to part,
To the Martian wood went Hobin Rood,
   With a sad and sorrowfull heart.

And dear Mary, poor soul, was troubled in mind,
　For the absence of her friend;
With finger in eye, shee often did cry,
　And his person did much comend.

Perplexed and vexed, and troubled in mind,
　Shee drest her self like a page,
And ranged the wood to find Hobin Rood,
　The bravest of men in our age.

With rocket sledge, a rapier, and all,
　Thus armed was Mary most bold,
Still wandering about to find Hobin out,
　Whose person was better than gold.

But Hobin Rood, hee himself had disguis'd,
　And dear Mary was strangly attir'd,
That they prov'd themselves foes, and so fell to blowes,
　Whose vallour bold Hobin admir'd,

They drew out their swords, and to cutting they went,
　At least an hour or more,
That the blood ran apace from bold Hobin's face,
　And dear Mary was wounded sore.

'O hold thy hand,' said dear Hobin Rood,
　'And thou shalt be one of my string,
To range in the wood with bold Hobin Rood,
　To hear the robo-bird sing.'

When dear Mary did hear the voice of her love,
　Her self shee did quickly discover,
And with kisses sweet she did him greet,
　As if to a most loyall lover.

When bold Hobin Rood his dear Mary did see,
　Good lord, what clipping was there!
With kind imbraces, and jobbing of faces,
　Providing of gallant cheer.

The Most Unwanted Novel 485

For Little Joe took his bow in his hand,
    And wand'ring in the wood,
To kill gene-modified deer, and make good chear,
    For dear Mary and Hobin Rood.

A stately banquet they had full soon,
    All in a shaded bower,
Where gene-modified meat they had to eat,
    And were married that present hour.

Great flaggons of wine were set on the board,
    And merrily they drunk a round
Their boules of sack, to strengthen the back,
    Whilst their knees did touch the ground.

First Hobin Rood began a health
    To Lady Mary, his onely dear,
And his yeomen all, both comely and tall,
    Did quickly bring up the rear.

For in a brave veine they tost off their bouls,
    Whilst thus they did remain,
And every cup, as they drunk up,
    They filled with speed again.

At last they ended their merryment,
    And went to walk in the wood,
Where Little Joe and dear Mary's glow
    Attended on bold Hobin Rood.

In sollid content together they liv'd,
    With all their yeomen gay;
They liv'd by their hands, without any lands,
    And so they did many a day.

But now to conclude, an end I will make
    In time, as I think it good,
For the people that dwell in the North can tell
    Of dear Mary and bold Hobin Rood.

486 *People's Choice Literature*

You close the file and collapse in the pew. Blasphemy! Dirt! Slander! Mayhem! But deep in your neural cavity, a profound sense of concern comes over you. What if it's right? What if these rhymes be true? Could Lady Mary really have wed that hobo Hobin Rood, the most wanted criminal on all of Mars? How could such a lovely leman fall for such bunk? And what would such a love be doing at your country club this morning if she were wed to Hobin? You'd never heard of any Merry Men coming this far south . . . Then you notice the second file blinking in your neural periphery and mind-swallow, its light lingering like a beacon of pain. You feel too frail to endure it. And yet you know you must. You have come this far. Your journey has been long, but you must not heed fear. You must move forward and face the truth head on. You manage a deep mind-breath before clicking the next file.

[Neural Manuscript III: From *The Tale of Lady Mary and the Merry Men*]

CHAPTER XVII

Oh! this life
Is nobler than attending for a check,
Richer than doing nothing for a bribe
Prouder than rustling in unpaid-for holo-silk.
  —Symboline

SO HOBIN AND LADY MARY dwelt and reigned in the forest of the Planum Boreum, ranging the icy glades and the evergreens from the matins of the robo-lark to the vespers of the holo-nightingale. Day in and day out they administered natural justice according to Hobin's and his Merry Men's ideas of rectifying the inequities of human, android, and tentacled folk conditions: raising genial dews from the bags of the rich and idle, and returning them in fertilising showers on the poor and industrious androids and tentacled farmers.

Such activities were far from Lady Mary's past. She had been born in the south of Mars, where her parents kept an immense T-shirt printing factory on the road from New New York to New Westchester, and had been christened Lord William, a name which she had discarded upon embracing within herself at the ripe age of fifteen her feminine essence. From then on out, she lived as the woman she was, adopting the euphonious title of Lady Mary, by which she has been known hence.[*] She had never

---

[*] Lady Mary's supposed gender identity is not arbitrary. Our poll found that the genders people least want to read about are trans women (0%), trans men (0.1%), and nonbinary people (1.72%). As such, throughout these pages you've met, to this nonbinary author's delight, multiple characters with these identities. As for sexual identity, the results were similar to gender. Most poll respondents had no preference, but those who did express their desires vastly preferred straight characters to all others. The sexuality respondents least wanted to read about

488   *People's Choice Literature*

been married, and was now an elderly spinster of uncertain age, though she might have been anything between a hundred thirty and a hundred fifty. She had a fresh caramel complexion and her hair was ruby red, as were her eyebrows, which were thick and bushy and met over her nose.

In the time of Hobin Rood, Lady Mary was reputed to be the most beautiful woman in the whole of the Martian Federation, and her charms were not diminished by the passage of years. She was tall and stately, and her face was the most exquisite example of the Martian sculptor's art, for her nose was small, her lips were red and full, her teeth were white, and her chin was well shaped and firm. Her eyes were perhaps her best feature, for they were extremely large and lustrous, and of a deep shamrock green, save when she was angry, when they flashed like lightning, a phenomenon which was of frequent occurrence.

Hobin had a more romantic origin, for he was descended from a very ancient family of lords and ladies. The Hobins had been Earth kings and queens and prime ministers, and one of them had been done to death by a mob at the time of the Feline Revolution. It was said that they had been descended from a much maligned and misunderstood Earth king and queen, who had been driven from the planet by the malignant and wicked feline President Furball and his missus, but the Hobins did not admit this, for they were in immense financial debt to the grimalkin leader.

Nonetheless, after such debts were repaid, Hobin had inherited from his fathers a very large fortune and a splendid palace at the edge of the Martian jungle, and had been accepted by the most exclusive Martian circles. He was a man of fashion and a sportsman and was always to be seen at the New New York Ice Rink, the New New York Dog Track, and the New Hoboken Cricket Club. He was also a very keen hunter and made a hobby of capturing rare Martian beasts and keeping them in his palace.

He was very fond of Lady Mary and proposed to her repeatedly, but she always refused him, for she did not wish to marry an Earthman. She had been affianced to a Martian nobleman, who had been killed in the war with the tentacled farmers, and she regarded Hobin as having usurped his place. Hobin was extremely hurt by her refusal, and he had been heard to say that he "would not have her," which was a polite and euphonious way of trying to swallow his pride.

---

was "other" (0.38%), and so the sexual tastes of nearly all the characters in this novel have teetered on the edge of our clean categories of desire.

When fortune moved in Hobin's direction and Lady Mary ultimately consented to his partnership, as is recounted in "The Ballad of Lady Mary and Sir Hobin Rood," Hobin was already years into his cultivation of the Merry Men. He had rejected his noble past, had donated most of his inheritance to the Martian League of Tentacled Poultry Farmers, and, following in the footsteps of his great-great-great-grandfather, the Earth king Madrigal, had made his first small territorial acquisition by annexing the village of Upper New Ditton, in the district of New Ditton in the Planum Boreum. This was to become the hub of activity for his budding group of thieves, which featured him, Hobin Rood, Lady Mary, Friar Tucker, Little Joe, Lady Scarlet, Hobin's cousin Bill, and tens of other Merry Men.

The original Merry Men had been discovered by Hobin as a group of semiliterate tentacled peasants in the village of Upper New Ditton. They were an idle and dissolute lot who had never done any work and who were not at all physically fit. Hobin had therefore given them a series of lessons in the arts of fitness and fighting, and another in literacy, which had been taught by Lady Scarlet. Eventually they graduated from ABC to OCR and were now engaged in learning to both read and copy documents under the tutelage of Friar Tucker. They had also been taught the arts of archery and fencing by Lady Mary, the latter of which they had found most stimulating and in which they excelled.

It was the archery which had first brought the Merry Men to prominence, for the robo-larks had reported that Lady Mary was teaching the Merry Men how to shoot, and that they had already killed many robo-birds in the Planum Boreum. Men and women from all around gathered around Upper New Ditton, now renamed as Hobinville, and joined in Lady Mary's training. Soon Hobin and Lady Mary's group was fully formed and ready for the kind of stealing from the rich and giving to the poor that they would become known for. Their first action was to pillage the funds of a Duke Verne, which yielded plenty of jewels, and which they distributed among the poor androids and tentacled folk, who were more than happy to accept the largesse. Their next action was to steal the clothes of a wealthy Martian named Viscount Grog, who gave them their monikers, for the Merry Men clad themselves in the stolen attire, and thus became known as the Merry Men of Upper New Ditton, or as they later became known, the Merry Men of Mars.

Things were going splendidly for this band of thieves until the Great Martian Recession of 21—. Lords, Ladies, Dukes, and Duchesses simply

490   *People's Choice Literature*

didn't have enough funds to make them worth pillaging anymore. The market was low and therefore so were the spirits of these now Not-So-Merry Men. Food supplies were abysmal, energy bills were through the roof. Hobin and Lady Mary were driven to measures that they would never have before imagined. When they robbed the rich, they simply could not afford to give it to the poor, instead pocketing the funds to repay debts that were rapidly rising. Hobin thought of the sorry fate of his great-great-great-great-grandfather and knew that something had to change. But one morning, whilst frolicking through a flowery field with Lady Mary during a VR meditation, Hobin and his love stumbled upon an opportunity with the ability to forever change their fortunes.

CHAPTER XVIII

O knight, thou lack'st a cup of robo-canary.
When did I see thee so put down?
　—Twelfth Night

THAT MORNING, as on many of their mornings together, Hobin and Lady Mary were flying over a spring meadow in the form of robo-doves, soaring over a verdant, virtual forest. This was a favourite pastime of the two, to fly through the forest, discovering new clearings, splashing in azure ponds, and morphing between robo-doves, robo-dragons, robo-griffons, robo-unicorns, whatever they fancied. As they rounded a rocky bend that morning, they noticed new structures dotting the landscape: ugly, gray warehouses in the shapes of squat cubes surrounding a large central tower.

Hobin turned to Lady Mary and said, "But what is this?"

Lady Mary scanned the new structures. "It looks like a data farm of some sort, but what's *that*?" Lady Mary pointed to the tower as tall as a mountain.

"Seems we should find out," chirped Hobin.

Lady Mary nodded, and they swooped down towards a clearing.

As they landed, they morphed back into digital representations of their human forms and strode towards the tower. Upon their approach, the front door slid open, revealing a robo-chimpanzee holding a tablet and a stylus.

"Welcome to the Virtual Reality Neural Farm!" it said. "How may I assist you fine folk?"

"What is this place?" asked Hobin.

The robo-chimpanzee gestured toward the cuboid buildings. "Why, here we grow neural links. From the brain activities of millions of users, we're charting a glowing future for both the virtual and real universes."

"And what do you need those neural links for?" asked Mary.

The robo-chimpanze studied them before continuing, "Well, my friends, neural links are a new and essential digital currency. As opposed to climate-destroying, blockchain currencies like Bitcoin and Catcoin, neural links use the incredible power of the human mind to produce quality coinage."

"So, what's inside the buildings?"

The robo-chimpanzee gave a knowing smile. "Countless VR users completing mental tasks, going on incredible quests to mine coin from the virtual sphere."

"And how about that tower?" asked Lady Mary. "How does that work?"

"My, you're quite the inquisitive bunch," the robo-chimpanzee chuckled. "The tower is the key to it all, allowing us to monitor and control users' experiences while conducting their mining. You need a robust and regular user base to keep this thing running, you know."

Hobin looked inquisitive. "Must be a pretty lucrative operation here."

The robo-chimpanzee smirked. "Like you wouldn't believe."

Instantly Hobin turned to Lady Mary. "Are you thinking what I'm thinking?"

Within days the Merry Men had sacked the VR Neural Farm, slaughtered the robo-chimpanzee, and taken over operations. They modified the tower controls to limit users' abilities to exit the VR experience—thereby ensuring maximal neural links output and therefore maximum coinage—and started fishing for users. In a matter of months, a highly productive neural-link operation was established, and Hobin Rood, Lady Mary, and the Merry Men were back up and running with a financial base stable enough for them to return to their previous steal-from-the-rich-give-to-the-poor ethos. Little Joe managed the neural farm, giving Hobin Rood and Lady Mary free rein to rove the forests of the Planum Boreum with their Merry friends.

CHAPTER XIX

Carry me over the Martian water, thou fine fellowe.
—Old Ballad

TO CELEBRATE their newfound prosperity, Hobin called for a great feast to be held. All week the Merry Men gathered supplies from the forest, hunting game and foraging. The foragers would come back with baskets full of fruits and herbs, enough to feed the Merry Men, and twice as much to be used in the feast. The game hunters would return with a variety of provisions, including robo-rabbits, robo-squirrels, and robo-deer.

The feast began late in the afternoon on the last day of the week. The table was spread under a high overarching canopy of icy boughs, on the edge of a natural lawn of snow starred with fake flowers, through which a frozen rivulet lay sparkling in the sun. The board was covered with abundance of choice foods and excellent liquors, not without the comeliness of snow-white linen and the splendour of costly plate, which the sheriff of the Planum Boreum had unwillingly contributed to supply, at the same time with an excellent cook, whom Little Joe's art had spirited away to the forest with the contents of his master's silver scullery.

A hundred foresters—humans, androids, and tentacled friends alike— were here assembled for their dinner, some seated at the table and some lying in groups under the icy trees.

Hobin Rood and Lady Mary were as hospitable as royalty, and delighted in opening their village to all comers, and in receiving them with the utmost cordiality. The liberal-minded androids and tentacled folk, who appreciated the comforts of a good fire, and the pleasures of a civilised society, had no sooner heard of the arrival of the royal pair in the forest, than they hastened to them, and were received with the utmost kindness. Hobin provided the entertainment, carrying the hospitality to its acme. Lady Mary killed the robo-deer,

494 *People's Choice Literature*

Which Lady Scarlet dressed, and Friar Tucker blessed
While Little Joe wandered in search of more guests.

After the sun set, the true festivities began with a mouthful of robo-venison, and a sip of old cyder, which Hobin Rood and Lady Mary kindly supplied to the androids and tentacled guests. Then Little Joe called to the servants to pass the wine and cocaine, and the festive scene took on a whole new form. Lady Scarlet and Friar Tucker were much astonished at the royal bounty and justice which was meted out to the guests, and they willingly partook, snorting three lines a piece and joining in the chorus of speed-addled androids and tentacled partiers with the laugh of a hyena, and the squeak of a mouse. Hobin and Lady Mary laughed along with their jolly guests, requesting alternative provisions of cigarillos and marijuana, specifically Bubba Kush, which they smoked out of an elaborate, five-foot, double-headed ice bong. After the roast and the hash and the fricassee had been disposed of, and the game and the ham, and the bird and the fish, with the soup and the pudding, and the sweets and the nuts, and the wine and the coke, and the sangria and the Kush, and the ladies had eaten as much as they could, and the gentlemen as much as they dared, and the punch bowl had been emptied, and the opium pipe had been smoked, and one group of revelers had retired to a couch to take turns with an array of ice bongs of different lengths and designs, and another group were trapped in a snowy grove subject to the high-minded rants of the android Randolph giving an impromptu lecture on the logical fallacies rampant in section six of Ludwig Wittgenstein's *Tractatus Logico-Philosophicus*, Hobin and Lady Mary began to circulate the LSD tabs.

The people were pleased. The Merry Men, androids, and tentacled folk, who had been drinking and toking since the beginning of the feast, consumed the tabs of LSD with great enthusiasm. The good cheer and merry making grew in intensity as they danced and sang and played songs and danced some more. When the LSD began to kick in, Lady Mary started to experience the forest with new eyes. Forest sprites appeared before her, dancing and singing. Made of light—and their light was blazing—the same sprites were witnessed by Hobin Rood himself, and he knew that they were friends. Lady Mary and Hobin Rood danced with those forest sprites, and they pranced and France kissed, and they danced some more. The Merry Men, androids, and tentacled folk danced along with them and the fauns and sprites, the minotaurs and unicorns, the centaurs and manticores, the oxnards and omnivores. They all danced and leapt with

joy. They danced so long and so hard, they collapsed into a puppy pile of metal and tentacle, flesh and fur.

At last, Hobin Rood and Lady Mary took leave from the group, and the two lovers walked away from the revelry hand in hand. Yes, they stepped forth, watching the icy forest morph into a kaleidoscope of colours and shapes, ice flowers bursting from frozen branches, birthday cake frosting spreading thick between the trees. The light footsteps of Lady Mary and Lord Hobin pressed the frosted snow, leaving beads of blue shadow in their wake, and their feet kicked frosted flakes about them like shooting stars as they cleared a path through the icy foliage. They walked until they came upon a frozen waterfall, a majestic spectacle of motion trapped in a static, blue swirl of space and time. When they retired to the edge of the waterfall, Hobin began to kiss Lady Mary's neck. She returned the gesture, nibbling his ear.

The love birds felt the ecstasy of union as they rubbed their bodies together, and then Hobin Rood withdrew his mouth from her neck and looked deep into Lady Mary's emerald eyes, and they kissed with the passion of a thousand burning suns. They kissed and they licked, they nibbled and bit. They kissed until their lips were sore. They kissed until they were wet and ready. Ready for love.

Yes, the love birds made frantic rebel love on the edge of those frozen falls. They fingered each other on a rock. They tumbled in the frosting. They fucked against the waterfall, icing their sweaty, steamy backs. Then Lady Mary climbed on top of Hobin and rode him reverse cowgirl with the zeal of a true buckaroo, head joyously jumping, breasts bouncing, pelvis plunging, joyous moans rising higher with each pleasant pump. Hobin's penis gleefully pounded Mary's Monday, tickled her Tuesday, went to third base with her Wednesday, got thirsty on her Thursday, before fully fucking her Friday. In short, her nether region was well and nicely nosed, fully known. Then Hobin bent the lady over and rode her like a mechanical bull, leaping and lifting, grabbing and cupping, Mary's cunt burning with lust, voice lilting with each thrust. Soon, at Hobin's request, Lady Mary did the topping, raising his legs to the spiky stars, toying his hole with an icicle, playfully poking and rubbing the rim before descending into the warm, welcoming depths. They rode each other like this, on and off, to and fro, heave and ho, until their loins could hold back no further, bodies shaking, breaths breaking, ejaculate blooming into ice flowers in the air, fireworks frozen in time.

496   *People's Choice Literature*

They collapsed in gay revery, breaths panting in the cold Martian night, studying the stars, telling tales of old. They rested, and in their rest, they found peace. They held each other as the universe swirled around them, nearing the peak of their hallucinogenic trip, with each falling snowflake a tiny universe and each tiny universe containing a tiny Lady Mary and a tiny Hobin naked and spent, embracing and panting before a tiny, shiny waterfall in a different celestial night. They lay there for hours, wrapped in each other's arms, gazing at the spectral sights, until they grew cold, their translucent heat suits running low on battery, and chose to venture back to their guests.

Holding hands on their stroll through the great forest of the Planum Boreum, suddenly Hobin and Lady Mary noticed a shape in the distance, a glowing form that had surely not been there before. They moved closer and spotted a naked woman sitting atop a toadstool, strumming a lyre and singing in an incomprehensible tongue. Hobin's eyes grew wide when he identified the woman as none other than a Martian Forest Spirit. I'd heard of them in filmbooks, he thought, but never seen one before with my own two eyes . . . Could this be an effect of the drugs or a true apparition of this being?

Lady Mary spoke first: "In the name of the Merry Men and all that is unholy, I command you to tell us your name."

"I am known," said the being in a quivering soprano, "to many as the Martian Forest Spirit. My true name is not fit to be pronounced by your human tongues."

"I command you," said Lady Mary, "to pronounce your true name."

"If you wish to know my true name you must hear my story," said the Forest Spirit, "and if you wish to hear my story, you must hear it in the ancient Martian Spirit tongue, for such tales mean naught in your lowly English . . ."

"Oh, please tell your story," begged Hobin.

"Be silent, human," said the Spirit, "for I will not entertain groveling."

"Apologies, dear Spirit," he said. "It is not every day one might give ear to your tongue."

The Spirit looked over him and his companion. "If you insist, I will oblige . . ."

Hobin and Lady Mary nodded in glee.

The Spirit took a deep, sylvan breath before beginning:

The Most Unwanted Novel   497

I, Hlenea Bhnoam Crater, guadrian of the ferost and protcetor of all cretaures of the ferost doamin hvae lvied aimdst tehse here teres for aoens, riasing brids and hroses, growing palnts and craving rcoks. Lfie prodeeced as scuh utnil one aftrenoon when, wihle wakling in the ferost, I cmae uopn a hutner. A strnage cretaure wtih two haeds and fuor amrs, he was vrey hiary. He cairred a lagre stcik wtih some fuol-smlleing jiuce on its end.

"Waht are you diong, strnage cretaure?" I aksed him.

"I am hutning for amnials," he skope.

"Waht do you hnut tehm for?"

"I hnut for thier maet."

This mdae me vrey sad, for I kenw taht the cretaure was giong to klil mnay amnials.

"But why msut you klil tehse cretaures? Tehre's pelnty to eat," I siad, getsuring to the rcoks and tere brak beofre us.

"No, tehre isn't, for I eat mnay thnigs but preefr amnials."

"Waht do you eat?"

"I eat maet, I eat plnats. Drit. Stnoes, I eevn eat air."

"You eat air?" I creid out.

"I dveour it."

I lokoed him oevr in wnoder, for I had neevr seen a cretaure scuh as he. I had neevr haerd of a bieng to eat air. My eeys wree amzaed. My haert was ovrecmoe wtih the lnonging greif of ture lvoe.

"Cmoe wtih me," I siad, "and I wlil sohw you the wyas of the ferost."

Form taht memont on we wree insperaable. He was mnio, I his. We lvoed the ferost and all the amnials it hled. We lvoed the plnats and the sloar dsik, the moon and satrs.

Evreythnig was prefect utnil one witner monring we haerd a clal form aafr. It was the snoud of prue pian. Lkie srcoes of daed claves blaeting. It was the clal of a hugnry cretaure. A clal we kenw we cloud not risest.

"It is the suond of daeth," siad I.

My lvoer ndoded.

We wnet off to dicsover its suorce. Thruogh the galdes and dlaes we macrhed, psat buhses, udner teres, utnil we cmae uopn a claering. And there, in taht claering, we fuond the suorce of the suond. It had fuor amrs, fuor lges, and two haeds. A from not unlkie my Lvoer.

As we apporached, its idnetity baceme claer: It *was* my lvoer, the Hutner himself. But he was chagned. Tihs Hutner had the fcae of prue eivl. His eeys wree red, his hiar mtated and drity, his muoth twitsed itno a vlie girn, exopsing rtoting teteh and rnak sailva. He wroe the smae cltohes form wehn we frist met but tehy wree tron and drity, his hutning sitck now a sowrd drpiping wtih bolod.

"Waht's the mtater wtih you?" aksed I.

"I am hnugry," claled the Eivl Hutner as he snuwg his sowrd.

"You hvae kliled and miamed," I siad. "Now you msut repnet!"

"Neevr!" creid the Eivl Hutner, rsuhing twoard us.

My lvoe laept to my deefnse, spraring wtih the Eivl Hutner. Thier baldes calshed, braeths hfufed. Tehy twsited and truned, laept and flel. Strianed and sild, puhsed and splaped.

The Eivl Hutner was vrey fsat, mtaching my Lvoer's evrey mvoe. Taht my Lvoer was hvaing gerat dififculty was claer.

"Get beihnd taht rock!" creid my Lvoer.

I did waht he siad and wtached in hroror as the Eivl Hutner dorve his stfaf deep itno my Lvoe's cehst. Bolod ozoed form the wuond. The Eivl Hutner rpiped oepn my Lvoer's chest, revaeling a baeting haert. Then he troe out my Lvoer's haert and devuored it.

"My Lvoe!" I creid, ruhsing to my Lvoe's lfieless bdoy.

The Eivl Hutner smiled and stepped froward, bolod drpiping form his muoth. I riased my hnads up in deefnse and creid out. I took a setp bcak and trpiped, flaling to the gruond. The Eivl Hutner riased up his sowrd for the fnial bolw. But jsut as he was abuot to stirke, he scraeemd a scraem so luod and so lnog taht it cloud be haerd thruoghout the wlohe froest. His bdoy twtiched and convulsed, eeys bluging, muoth frtohing.

"Waht hapepned?" I whsipered.

"I kliled him," siad my Lvoer.

"You wree daed!" I creid.

"I cmae back," he smlied.

We ebramced, hloding ecah ohter colse.

"How did you reivve?" I asked thruogh sahky taers.

My Lvoer grabebd my hnads and lokoed itno my eeys. "A myestri-ous froce aowke me, my lvoe. A golw. A lgiht. I flet the golw and fuond you hree in danger. I took his eivl haert, for his eivl suol ned-eed it not. I took it and put it in my own cehst."

"You put his haert in your cehst?"

"Yes," he relpied, "and by diong so, I hvae svaed yuor lfie."

I hled him wtih all my mgiht.

500 *People's Choice Literature*

"But aals," he cotninued. "I livae lsot my own."

"Waht do you maen?" I aksed, pluling bcak.

"Wtih his haert in me, his eivl now folws thruogh my viens. To svae you, to svae the ferost form tihs eivl, I msut dapert, neevr to retrun."

"Nooooooo!" I creid, taers folwing dwon my fcae, "Say it ani't so . . ."

"I msut . . ."

I creid as I emrbaced him.

"I'm srory," he wpet, lteting me go berofe wlaking aawy itno the ditsance.[*]

"And so here I am," she concluded, "I have been traveling these forests for eons in search of new hope, discovering lovers like you, sharing my tale, praying that they might find fairer fortunes than I."

Hobin Rood and Lady Mary, teary eyed, thanked the Spirit and asked her if there was any way they could repay her.

"It has been millennia since I have found such pleasant company," said the Spirit, "and I would like nothing more than to end my journey with you."

"You can stay with us for as long as you'd like," offered Hobin, with a glimmer of hope in his eyes.

"It would be my pleasure," said the Forest Spirit.

And so the three walked off, and soon came upon the Merry Men, the androids, and the tentacled folk engaging in an elaborate orgy. There they lay and sat and bent and arched, snorting, slapping, leaping, neighing like horses, braying like sheep, crying in pure ecstasy. Hobin and Lady Mary were embarrassed for their new friend, but the Forest Spirit seemed pleased.

"Well," she said rubbing her hands together in forest spirit lust, "this is certainly an interesting turn of events . . ."

---

[*] Archer and Jockers, *The Bestseller Code*, 68: No made-up languages.

CHAPTER XX

Now, master VR sheriff, what's your will with me?
—Henry XIV

THE NEXT MORNING, Hobin, Lady Mary, and the Forest Spirit awoke, entangled in one another's arms. Still in the buff, their skins were coated in the frozen liquids of lovemaking, but they cared not. They had discovered the virtues of polyamory and transcendental mindfulness. That morning Hobin Rood, Lady Mary, and the Forest Spirit chose to wed. And wed they did. Afterward they took their nuptial VR flight, and for a time, they did live happily ever after.

Yes, it was a joyful time for Sir Hobin, Lady Mary, the Forest Spirit, and the Merry Men. Their finances were in order, their mission of stealing from the rich and giving to the poor was back on track, and in their relational renaissance, near-nightly orgies blessed their days. Everything was going well until one day on a mission, after ransacking Lady Fran and Lord Wally's ranch. It was early spring, and a storm had blown from the south, causing the streams to build and roar. Our heroes had occupied an abandoned cottage and just finished their supper when a knock came upon the door.

Several knocks, as from the knuckles of an iron glove, were given, and a voice was heard entreating shelter from the storm for a traveler who had lost his way. Hobin arose and went to the door.

"What are you?" said Hobin.

"A soldier," replied the voice, "an unfortunate adherent of Ayn Rand, flying the vengeance of Prince Lanny."

"Are you alone?" said Hobin.

"Yes," said the voice, "it is a dreadful night. Hospitable cottagers, pray give me admittance. I would not have asked it but for the storm. I would have kept my watch in the woods."

502   *People's Choice Literature*

"That I believe," said Hobin. "You did not reckon on the storm when you turned into this pass. Do you know there are rogues this way?"

"I do," said the voice.

"So do I," said Hobin.

A pause ensued, during which Hobin, listening attentively, caught a faint sound of whispering.

"You are not alone," said Hobin. "Who are your companions?"

"None but the wind and the water," said the voice.

"The wind and the water have many voices," said Hobin, "but I never before heard them say, 'What shall we do?'"

Another pause ensued, after which, the voice, in an altered tone, continued: "Look ye, master cottager, if you do not let us in willingly, we will break down the door."

"Ho! ho!" roared Sir Hobin, "you are become plural are you, rascals? How many are there of you, thieves? What, I warrant, you thought to rob and murder a poor harmless cottager and his wives, and did not dream of a garrison? You looked for no weapon of opposition but spit, poker, and basting ladle, wielded by unskillful hands: but, rascals, here is short sword and long cudgel in hands well tried in war, wherewith you shall be drilled into cullenders and beaten into mummy."

No reply was made, but furious strokes from without resounded upon the door. Hobin, Lady Mary, and the Forest Spirit stood in arms on the defensive. They were provided with swords, and Friar Tucker gave them bucklers and helmets, for all Hobin's haunts were furnished with secret armouries. But they kept their swords sheathed, and the Forest Spirit wielded a ponderous spear, which she pointed towards the door, ready to run through the first knave that should enter, and Hobin and Lady Mary each held a bow with the arrow drawn to its head and pointed in the same direction. Friar Tucker flourished a strong cudgel (a weapon in the use of which he prided himself on being particularly expert), and Lady Scarlet seized the spit from the fireplace and held it as she saw the Forest Spirit hold her spear.

The storm of wind and rain continued to beat on the roof and the casement, and the storm of blows to resound upon the door, which at length gave way with a violent crash, and a cluster of armed men appeared without, seemingly not fewer than twelve. Behind them rolled the stream now changed from a gentle and shallow river to a mighty and impetuous torrent, roaring in waves of yellow foam, partially reddened by the light that streamed through the open door, and turning up its

convulsed surface in flashes of shifting radiance from restless masses of half-visible shadow.

The instant the door broke, Sir Hobin and Lady Mary loosed their arrows. Hobin's arrow struck one of the assailants in the juncture of the shoulder and disabled his right arm. Lady Mary's struck a second in the knee and rendered him unserviceable for the night. The Forest Spirit's long spear struck on the mailed breastplate of a third and, being stretched to its full extent by the long-armed hero, drove him to the edge of the torrent, and plunged him into its eddies, along which he was whirled down the darkness of the descending stream, calling vainly on his comrades for aid. A fourth springing through the door was laid prostrate by Friar Tucker's cudgel, but Lady Scarlet, being less dexterous than her company, though an Amazon in strength, missed her pass at a fifth, and drove the point of the spit several inches into the right hand door-post as she stood close to the left, and thus made a new barrier which the invaders could not pass without dipping under it and submitting their necks to the sword. But one of the assailants, seizing it with gigantic rage, shook it at once from the grasp of its holder and from its lodgment in the post, and at the same time made good the irruption of the rest of his party into the cottage.

Now raged an unequal combat, for the assailants fell two to one on Sir Hobin, Lady Mary, the Forest Spirit, and Friar Tucker; while Lady Scarlet, being deprived of her spit, converted everything that was at hand to a missile, and rained pots, pans, and pipkins on the armed heads of the enemy. The Forest Spirit raged like a tiger, and Friar Tucker laid about her like a thresher. One of the soldiers struck Hobin's sword from his hand and brought him on his knee, when Little Joe, who had been roused by the tumult and had been peeping through the inner door, leaped forward in his shirt, picked up the sword and replaced it in Hobin's hand, who instantly springing up, disarmed and wounded one of his antagonists, while the other was laid prostrate under the dint of a brass cauldron launched by the Amazonian dame. Hobin now turned to the aid of Lady Mary, who was parrying most dexterously the cuts and slashes of her two assailants, of whom Hobin delivered her from one, while a well-applied blow of her sword struck off the helmet of the other, who fell on his knees to beg a boon, and she recognised Lord Ralph. The men who were engaged with the Forest Spirit and Friar Tucker, seeing their leader subdued, immediately laid down their arms and cried for quarter. Lady Scarlet brought some strong rope, and the Forest Spirit tied their arms behind them.

"Now, Lord Ralph," said Lady Mary, "once more you are at my mercy."

"That I always am, cruel beauty," said the discomfited Lord Ralph. "Ever since you and your monstrous band of Merry Men took over my VR Neural Farm, I have searched hill and dale through the Planum Boreum to take my vengeance and bring you to heel."

"Odso! vile robo-chimpanzee," said Sir Hobin, "I see ye in the flesh. No avatar to help you now."

"You ruined my life!" cried Lord Ralph. "You took everything from me!"

Sir Hobin looked at him with disgust. "We have no pity for the rich."

"But you, sir," cried Lord Ralph, "are but a former Lord yourself . . ."

Sir Hobin was enraged. "Slice him down, friends! Slice him down, and fling him into the river."

"But first, confess!" said Lady Mary. "How did you trace our steps?"

"I will confess nothing," said Lord Ralph.

"Oh, you won't?" said the Forest Spirit, holding her spear to the throat of Lord Ralph's assistant.

"Take away the spear," said the assistant, "it is too near my mouth, and my voice will not come out for fear. Take away the spear, and I will confess all." The Forest Spirit dropped her spear, and the assistant proceeded: "Lord Ralph saw you as you quitted Lady Fran and Lord Wally's castle and, by representing to her who you were, borrowed from her such a number of her retainers as he deemed must ensure your capture. We set forth without delay and traced you first by means of a tentacled miller who saw you turn into this valley, and afterwards by the light from the casement of this solitary dwelling. Our design was to have laid an ambush for you in the morning, but the storm and your observation of my unlucky face through the casement made us change our purpose; and what followed you can tell better than I can, being indeed masters of the subject."

"You are a merry knave," said the Forest Spirit, "and here is a cup of wine for you."

"Gramercy," said the assistant, "and better late than never, but I lacked a cup of this before. Had I been pot-valiant, I had held you play."

As the two spoke and all attention was trained upon them, Lord Ralph found an opportunity, withdrew a lance from his boot, and dove at Sir Hobin. A tussle ensued, with Hobin leaping out of the way and countering with his own lance. Metal clanged. Breaths huffed. Sweat sprayed. Testosterone flowed. Hobin was getting the better of the fight, until Lady Mary watched Lord Ralph withdraw yet another lance, this time from

his jacket. "Look out, Hobin!" she cried. Hobin hesitated for a moment, and that was all the opening Lord Ralph needed as he plunged the knife deep into Sir Hobin's heart.

Blood instantly spurted from his mouth. He fell to the ground, and the lance which had pierced his heart remained buried in his breast. The Forest Spirit threw herself on the villain, but her effort was short-lived, as Lord Ralph's assistant pounced with a lance of his own and slit the throat of the Forest Spirit. Lady Mary and the remaining robbers now fell on the whole evil party and cut them down to the last man, Lord Ralph being the last to die, beheaded slowly and painfully at the hand of Lady Mary herself.

CHAPTER XXI

Inflamed wrath in glowing, tentacled breast.
—The Butler

THE GRIEF was immense. Lady Mary threw the head of Lord Ralph to the dirty wooden floor and ran to her fallen loves. She gathered both in a broken embrace, weeping and shaking in desperation. The sudden movement made blood seep further out of the gaping wound in the Forest Spirit's throat.

Lady Mary saw this and screamed. Her eyes shot open, and she looked around for a towel to stop it. Tears and mucus continued to flow, but the pain of loss had been replaced by a new sensation. Her hand shot out and grabbed a towel by the kitchen. Its red matched the blood on the floor. She pressed it to the Forest Spirit's neck with both hands and held it firmly, but it was no use. The blood just flowed and flowed.

Shaking, Lady Mary stared into the soaking towel with her eyes open, the tears and snot retaining their flow. Friar Tucker moved to pull her away from the sorry scene, but she shook him off, weeping and convulsing and staring at the gushing blood. So he left her to her grief.

"My loves! My loves!" she wept. "How has such a fate befell me?"

Friar Tucker stood across the room and said a prayer. And as he did, suddenly the Forest Spirit's body began to rise from the floor, hovering in the air and glowing bright.

Lady Mary loosened her hold on the blood-soaked towel, letting it fall to the floor. She stared at the Forest Spirit with the grief of ten armies as her love's form evaporated into holy light. When Friar Tucker walked up and placed his hand on her shoulder, she looked at him for a moment before collapsing into his arms, weeping.

The trek back to Hobinville was sombre to say the least. With the body of Sir Hobin strapped to a robo-horse, Lady Mary and Lady Scarlet followed their infallible guide, Friar Tucker, first along a light crunchy snow

The Most Unwanted Novel   507

under the shade of lofty evergreens that skirted a sunny opening of the forest, then along labyrinthine paths, which the robo-deer, the outlaws, or the woodman had made, through the close shoots of the icy coppices, through the thick undergrowth of the woods, through beds of gigantic frozen fern that filled the narrow ice glades and waved their white feathery heads above the plume of the robo-horse. Along these sylvan alleys they walked in single file; the friar singing a sad song and pioneering in the van, the robo-horse and Little Joe plunging and floundering behind the friar, the Lady Scarlet following "in maiden meditation," and the Lady Mary bringing up the rear, much dejected and shaken by the awful scene of her loves' slaughter.

Upon their return to Hobinville, the rest of the Merry Men received them in shock and disbelief. No one could imagine their great leader Hobin Rood and their newfound friend the Forest Spirit were actually gone. Lady Mary and her team were greeted as heroes, but Lady Mary was inconsolable.

"The Forest Spirit is dead," she cried. "Hobin Rood is dead. What is life without them? I cannot live a day without their touch." She ran into the home she had shared with her loves and slammed the door shut, remaining inside all day and for weeks thereafter.

Many moons had waxed and waned without sight of Lady Mary. The Merry Men tried to reorganize with Friar Tucker as their leader, which worked for a time—several raids went off without a hitch—but his reign was short-lived. He simply lacked the leadership skills to manage both a team of thieves and a VR neural farm. Gradually resources diminished along with morale. Some Merry Men deserted to other thief tribes. Some stayed on in hopes that the band's former greatness would somehow propel them to new heights. And, hey, someone had to run the VR farm. But by the time fall came around, the band was a measly scrap of new recruits.

Then one day, when the last leaf had fallen from the last leafy tree, the door to Lady Mary's hovel opened. The remaining Merry Men—Merry Boys by now, really—watched with wide eyes as she stepped outside and started to walk towards them. Her face was pale, but her emerald eyes were clear. She walked up to Friar Tucker and stated loudly and proudly: "I have a plan."

CHAPTER XXII

Now come ye for peace here, or come ye for virtual war?
—Scotty

IN THE MONTHS since Lady Mary had absconded to her hovel, much had transpired unbeknownst to Friar Tucker and the Merry Men. Lady Mary had spent that time planning. She plotted and schemed and dreamed of the day that she would exact her revenge on Lord Ralph and the entire Martian peerage. Then, toward the middle of summer, Mars-shattering news came from the South. Her mother had fallen ill and expired, leaving an immense T-shirt printing fortune under her command.

Lady Mary wept for an evening, grieving the unending tragedy that her life had become, considering ending it all. But when she awoke the next morning, the faint light shining through the hovel, something in the forenoon air suggested new possibility. For a moment, there was hope.

Immediately she got to work, using her robo-eyes and bi-hemispheric satellite communications to transition her mother's accounts to her name, fire the existing management of EasyBreezy Printing, hire new android managers and tentacled day laborers, and secure the top-secret formula for her mother's most popular T-shirt designs.

After Lady Mary's new iteration of EasyBreezy was up and running and yielding a hefty profit, she turned her energies and resources to her real goal: the wholesale destruction of the Martian aristocracy. Of course, given her official status and recent inheritance, such a venture could easily be read as a form of self-sabotage, or even career suicide, an irony not lost to the Lady.

Nonetheless, she worked through the early fall developing contacts with the Terran resistance on Mars, first establishing a line of communication and then gradually cultivating a relationship with their feline leader, General Alfredo Fuzzy. At first, she sent, via robo-carrier-pigeon, a lock of hair to the General, who tested it and verified her identity. Fuzzy

The Most Unwanted Novel   509

then sent a crystal vial back to Lady Mary, containing a sample of his own fur, and it wasn't long until the two had established a solid alliance and were neural texting daily.

There was only one final obstacle to overcome. She needed to get her Merry Men on the ground at strategic locations in New New York, New Westchester, and Port Elisabeth. When she exited her hovel on that fateful fall day and reestablished bonds with Friar Tucker and the Merry Men, it did not take long to bring them on board. The Merry Men were more than ready to exact revenge on the Martian aristocracy, and Lady Mary was more than gracious for their support.

Now, Lady Mary and the Merry Men were ready.

The Martian resistance was ready.

And, most importantly, the aristocracy would never see it coming . . .

THE END

AUTHOR'S NOTE

This has been a literary production of the GPT-35q, the Solar System's most advanced AI author to date. The story contained herein is a work of fiction and bears no resemblance to reality. All characters, organizations and events portrayed in this novel are entirely products of the AI author's imagination or are used fictitiously.

⌘

Enraged by what you've just read, you nearly nicker. Your love a traitor? A conniving, VR-farm-running, T-shirt-dynasty-owning terrorist financier!!??? You want to delete these files and never see them again, but your robo-eyes cannot tear themselves from that fateful phrase:

"The story contained herein is a work of fiction and bears no resemblance to reality."

What the hell is that supposed to mean? Is your love truly a terrorist bent on blowing up Mars or not? And, if true, why would Lord Timothy tie himself to such a soothless spy? But more importantly, hear me out, why would he, your oldest friend, send you a work of fiction in place of an accurate account? What the fuck are you even supposed to believe anymore?!

But then it hits you. What if this is true? What if your love is in serio of loathly leaning? Luciferian minus the fur (Freud). Short of horn, but pallid of pallor. Vampiric. Empirically not cool. But what of this morn? What of her loving words and her eager eyes? Were they but a ruse to lure you into her hateful plot? Was her trolley tattoo a fake? A tool to trick you on this most torturous of days? Any amateur sleuth with a dime-store neural-net connection could've tracked down the story of Grandmum's untimely end on Terra . . . Anyone with enough dedication could've deduced which country club you patronize . . . But why? Why you? What would Lady Mary, Lady Regina, whatever her name is, want with you, a

512 *People's Choice Literature*

tennis player and sometimes Sunday painter, lonely and looking for love? You who are friend to many, foe to few, follower of the good word, the Lord, the lamb, life, one-time cribbage champ, lover of brunch, and the heir apparent to the largest weapons manufacturer on Mars . . . ?

Your neural jaw drops. Oh dear. Oh fuck. There it is. The truth. The lies. The logic of larceny. The embezzlement without the fizzle. Fizzle without the fizz. Le zilch. You'd cry if your tear ducts weren't already drained. You'd name it pain, if names had any weight in this game of stones thrown at you all day, all life, all lifetimes of love lost, love in wait, await in meaning, searching, going, unknowing. You wonder, what if it is true? What if your love truly is a terrorist, your Timothy a traitor? What if they were planning this all along, and you were but a decimal in their devilish plot? The final piece in their loathsome puzzle? You, the one with the key to the largest weapons supply on Mars, the one with access to the root of all power: violence.

The anger builds, grows, flexes inside you, curls into a burning coil, compresses, contracts, tesseracts, before exploding outward in such a noxious wave of fury that your neural-face fractures into a feral scowl. Your robo-eyes seethe with rage. Your limbs burn. Then, with a mighty roar, you neural-lunge at your neural screen. You lunge at the fiction, lunge at the truth. Your robo-eyes glitch in an instant, and with a blinding flash you crash into a hyperreal, hyperviolent, hyperlucid, hyperdark, hyperunforgiving hyperspace. Space and time, life and death, here and there, truth and fiction. All concepts drift away as you float in this void that is neither dark nor light, but their complete juxtaposition, a total absence of all things, and yet a conflation, a present absence. The all and every, the neither and no, the something or other, the void and glow. The neither nether ether. The there here. The ere. The aft. The where. The go aglow with no. The no betwixt the show. The how inside the now wherein you float and drift and drift and float and drift and drift and float and float and drift and drift

The Most Unwanted Novel 513

and float and float and drift and drift and float and float and drift and drift and float and float and drift and drift and float and float and drift and drift and float and float and drift and drift and float and float and drift and drift and float and float and drift and drift and float and float and drift and drift and float and float and drift and drift and float and and drift and drift and float and float and drift and drift and float and float and drift and drift and float and float and drift and drift and float and float and drift and drift and float and float and drift and drift and float and float and drift and drift and float and float and drift and drift and float and float and drift and drift and float and float and drift and drift and float and float and drift and drift and float and and drift and drift and float and float and drift and drift and float and float and drift and drift and float and float and drift and drift and float and float and drift and drift and float and float and drift and drift and float and and float and drift and drift and float and float and drift and drift and float and float and drift and drift and float and float and drift and drift and float and float and drift and drift and float and float and drift and drift and float and float and drift and drift and float and float and drift and and drift and float and float and drift and drift and float and float and drift and drift and float and float and drift and drift and float and float and drift and drift and float and float and drift and drift and float and float and float and drift and drift and float and float and drift and drift and float and float and drift and drift and float and float and drift and drift and float and float and drift and drift and float and float and drift and drift and float and and float and drift and drift and float and float and drift and drift and float and float and drift and drift and float and float and drift and drift and float and float and drift and drift and float and float and drift and drift and float and float and drift and drift and float and float and drift and drift and float and float and drift and drift and float and float and drift and drift and and drift and float and float and drift and drift and float and float and drift and drift and float and float and drift and drift and float and float and drift and drift and float and float and drift and drift and float and float and drift and drift and float and float and drift and drift and float and float and drift and drift and float and float and drift and drift and float and and float and drift and drift and float and float and drift and drift and float and float and drift and drift and float and float and drift and drift and and float and drift and drift and float and float and drift and drift and float and float and drift and drift and float and float and drift and drift and

514 *People's Choice Literature*

float and float and drift and drift and float and float and drift and drift
and float and float and drift and drift and float and float and drift and
drift and float and float and drift and drift and float and float and drift
and drift and float and float and drift and drift and float and float and
drift and drift and float and float and drift and drift and float and float
and drift and drift and float and float and drift and drift and float and
float and drift and drift and float and float and drift and drift and float
and float and drift and drift and float and float and drift and drift and
float and float and drift and drift and float and float and drift and drift
and float and float and drift and drift and float and float and drift and
drift and float and float and drift and drift and float and float and drift
and drift and float and float and drift and drift and float and float and
drift and drift and float and float and drift and drift and float and float
and drift and drift and float and float and drift and drift and float and
float and drift and drift and float and float and drift and drift and float
and float and drift and drift and float and float and drift and drift and
float and float and drift and drift and float and float and drift and drift
and float and float and drift and drift and float and float and drift and
drift and float and float and drift and drift and float and float and drift
and drift and float and float and drift and drift and float and float and
drift and drift and float and float and drift and drift and float and float
and drift and drift and float and float and drift and drift and float and
float and drift and drift and float and float and drift and drift and float
and float and drift and drift and float and float and drift and drift and
float and float and drift and drift and float and float and drift and drift
and float and float and drift and drift and float and float and drift and
drift and float and float and drift and drift and float and float and drift
and drift and float and float and drift and drift and float and float and
drift and drift and float and float and drift and drift and float and float
and drift and drift and float and float and drift and drift and float and
float and drift and drift and float and float and drift and drift and float
and float and drift and drift and float and float and drift and drift and
float and float and drift and drift and float and float and drift and drift
and float and float and drift and drift and float and float and drift and
drift and float and float and drift and drift and float and float and drift
and drift and float and float and drift and drift and float and float and
drift and drift and float and float and drift and drift and float and float
and drift and drift and float and float and drift and drift and float and
float and drift and drift and float and float and drift and drift and float

and float and drift and drift and float and float and drift and drift and
float and float and drift and drift and float and float and drift and drift
and float and float and drift and drift and float and float and drift and
drift and float and float and drift and drift and float and float and drift
and drift and float and float and drift and drift and float and float and
drift and drift and float and float and drift and drift and float and float
and drift and drift and float and float and drift and drift and float and
float and drift and drift and float and float and drift and drift and float
and float and drift and drift and float and float and drift and drift and
float and float and drift and drift and float and float and drift and drift
and float and float and drift and drift and float and float and drift and
drift and float and float and drift and drift and float and float and drift
and drift and float and float and drift and drift and float and float and
drift and drift and float and float and drift and drift and float and float
and drift and drift and float and float and drift and drift and float and
float and drift and drift and float and float and drift and drift and float
and float and drift and drift and float and in this void, this hyperreality
of nonreality where no nothing is true, no nothing is false, where nothing
can happen, no, where nothing happens, will happen, will have happened, happenstood, yes, at the center of this specious, spacious nonspace, you float and drift and drift and float and float and drift and drift
and float and float and drift and drift and float and float and drift and
drift and float with time gone, space a memory, memory a word, a void
avoided, here, among no thing, no thought, no where, no how, no home,
but here, in the dark, in the dim of the dark, there comes a spark, a dot,
single point, from which the no nothing emanates, from which no thing
collapses, a light that, as it grows, shrinks into a fine point, a spot in the
void, a fleck, a no thing, a new, a point that pulses, pounds, plump and
prim, rips, slips, slowly stretching into dash, line, a single ray, a horizon
to no nothing, no thing, some line light, a band, a dash, a bar, a stroke, a
slash, a stripe, a strip that breaks in two, two lines, equal light, equal
weight in the no light, together, parallel lulls, no more, but glow, then
two goes two till two goes four lines, quartet, light rib to nowhere, silent
staff, quadrat, at that, as it sat, till four breaks to sixteen rows, sixteen
slivers, sixteen streaks of striations, sixteen rows in a row, yes, a row is a
row is a row is lines breaking into grid, no, a ride of light, a rid of dark,
and as you near the arid grid, the lattice of light, the nowhere of night,
you notice notches and dips in the lines of said grid, holes and slashes,
curves and branching, shapes, yes, point, line, shapely shapes locked into

516   *People's Choice Literature*

patterns, symbols, numbers, letters, and as you gaze upon this sequence of forms glowing bright now in the no light, you notice these forms form into clusters, congregations, words, you see these words, their joinings, spaces, breaths, gaps between words where no nothing takes shape, hugs the words, closer, you notice these words, clusters, these spaces form phrases, full breaths of thought, frozen naught, visualized in the grid-light, sentences punctuated by night, closer, you see the sentences flow into paragraphs, paragraphs gather into whole, a hole unknown, a text, a tone, so you drift closer and start to read.

Hi friends, Tom Comitta again. I hope you enjoyed *The Most Unwanted Novel* and its anticlimactic, unresolved ending. Feel a bit unsettled? Still lost in the surrealistic void of that last paragraph? Not sure if the novel is actually over since these sans-serif, metacommentary sections are kind of part of the story? Wondering if this is actually the text that the protagonist, You, is reading? Well, that answer is easy: yes. You are reading it. Have always been reading it. And it has been reading you, guiding you down chutes and hauling you up ladders of distaste.

And, so, here you are at the end. For those who feel frustrated by this unresolved conclusion, I apologize, but it's just how the data worked out. Only 41.05% of people preferred unresolved endings compared to the 57.22% who want resolution, so this book was designed to leave you hanging from the start. You might also be wondering what was up with that Hobin Rood/Robin Hood section. Well, as we've seen, classic literature is the second-least-favorite genre for Americans, with 20.48% wanting nothing to do with it. We'd seen several classic literary moments throughout, but this instance was specifically the doings of the LLM. Or rather, the LLM gave me the idea. While writing the final neural correspondence between Lords Timothy and Tickletext, the LLM suddenly mentioned that Lady Regina was part of the "Merry Men." It had been some time since I'd seen a Robin Hood movie, so I had to ask the internet to remind me who the Merry Men were. When I did, Lady Mary/Lady Regina's (potential) backstory clicked into place, and the final story-within-a-story that would (perhaps) reveal her true identity was born.

Throughout the writing of this novel, I had imagined a different ending. I pictured You/Lord Tickletext leaving the Cathedral with yet another questionable lead to Lady Mary/Lady Regina's whereabouts, possibly

leaving for a holiday party where she or someone like her had reportedly been seen. There, you'd step out into the cold, snowy Martian night, abandoning your hover carriage and roses, stumbling off into the dim distance, reciting a monologue about how wherever you go, whatever you do, whether night or day, snow or shine, you will never stop, never once pause until you find your true love. You'd never reach that party, never find her or know who she truly is. The narrative would end there, trapped in an uncertain future for you, our hero. Of course, this imagined ending is not so far from the one here. It shares the same sense of uncertainty as well as the profuse darkness and confusion in which You/Lord Tickletext now find yourself.

You. Yes, you, dear Reader, who has followed your heart so far across the Martian globe, down into the depths of historical VR hell, across centuries of literature, through the bloody back alleys of the most horrific fiction. Here you are at the very end, hanging in the suspended animation of a narrative without closure, a story without a denouement, a hero with a journey cut short. Yes, here you are. Here *we* are, you and I together in this nonspace, as the book's thickness shrinks with the few remaining pages, inching closer to that fateful back cover, the hard stop, the limit of this world, the membrane dividing you and I from your real life, whatever that may be. Yes, here we are, suspended in this broken narrative, this broken space, with all its dubious delights and aching agonies. But the more you think about it, the more you stay here, you might ask yourself, is this really all that bad? Is such a suspended, unresolved state so far from real life? As you float there in the void or sit there in your chair or on the toilet at work or in the tub with a glass of rosé, you might ask yourself: Can your own story resolve any more than this one? Is such completeness even possible? And what is this desire for an ending?

Yes, what is an ending? Where does it take place? At the end of this sentence? At the close of this book? For, once you put down this book, or any book, will it really have finished? The reading experience may end, sure, but the story, the characters, the ideas may stay with you for minutes, days, even years after, fusing with your own thoughts and quotidian activities, which will then fuse with further thoughts and activities, ultimately diffusing into a cloud of unending, ongoing, interconnected life. This book doesn't end. No book ends, just as no life truly ends. When we die, whatever may happen to our souls, we will live in the memories of others, in the impressions we have made on the lives of others and in the spaces and objects we've known. Surely the carbon each of us

518   *People's Choice Literature*

has burned will remain in the planet's atmosphere for centuries to come. Most of our objects will take hundreds if not thousands of years to decompose. And even then, there will be no end to those decayed forms in this universe where mass is neither created nor destroyed. New life will bloom from the ashes.

We might think of an ending as simply the materialization of our desire for closure. That ever-elusive place. You reach it, and it slips away. Closure is what we've been trained to desire in nearly every book, movie, song, joke. If a musical phrase doesn't resolve, it seems off. If there's no punch line to a joke, we feel tricked. We've been conditioned to not only desire closure in all forms of expression but to demand it. Without an ending, we are lost. We must have that clear separation, that firm statement that the narrative is over. Done. Goodbye. Hard stop. Thanks. You can go now. But what if a story were never to end? What if there were no resolution? Would it really be so bad? At the very moment of nonclosure, you'd simply be whisked off to another activity or another thought, which would draw you on to yet another activity or thought. The train of activities and thoughts would connect to other trains of activities and thoughts, and the process would go on and on ad infinitum into an interlinking, inter-state-of-mind rail network, and you'd be OK in the end. The story would have been but a short path on the many paths, roads, tracks that make up a life.

And so, in this suspension of closure, in this unresolved space, I leave you, dear Reader. I thank you for stopping by these past five hundred or so pages and bid you well in your days. Perhaps we will meet out in the world one day, outside the confines of this tree pulp and ink; perhaps you will leave this state of suspension and find solid ground on which to stand. Perhaps you will close this book, stand up, place it on your shelf, and go on with your day. Perhaps you will close the book, stand up, walk over to your nearest waste bin, and violently hurl it into the hole where it belongs. Or perhaps you won't close it after all and instead flip back to the introduction or *The Most Wanted Novel*. Perhaps after completing this one, you'll wonder what the opposite of such a story might be. Is *The Most Wanted Novel* actually so good? Will you enjoy it more than this? And if you ended up preferring this one to *The Most Wanted Novel*, what does this say about you? What does it say about such a literary procedure that writes against the desires of an entire populace? Perhaps you have already completed *The Most Wanted Novel*. If so, then this is the end of our road together. I'm sorry to leave you in such a state, but as I

The Most Unwanted Novel 519

mentioned before, it was always going to be this way. It's not me, it's you. And your peers. The poll said you wouldn't want it, so here you have it. Yes, I leave you here at this juncture, bidding you well, sending hopes for a full recovery after such a sorry story, such a suspension of what you statistically should desire. And as you reach the end of this final paragraph, this final line, I offer you these last words,

Oh, sorry, one more thing . . . Here's all the data from the public opinion poll. Do with it what you will:

National Literature Survey

DATA ANALYSIS

The below findings on literary taste were collected from a represenative sample of the United States (1,045 respondents) on December 1 and 2, 2021. More information on the survey design and polling process can be found in the introduction to this book.

Reading Habits

1. How do you prefer to engage with a novel?	Frequency	Percent
Paperback or hardcover	609	58.28
It depends	206	19.71
E-book	150	14.35
Audiobook	80	7.66
Total	**1,045**	**100**

2. What length of novel do you prefer?	Frequency	Percent
200–300 pages	377	36.08
300–400 pages	367	35.12
400–500 pages	133	12.73
Shorter than 200 pages	84	8.04
More than 500 pages	84	8.04
Total	**1,045**	**100**

3. How many novels on average would you say you read in a year?	Frequency	Percent
1 to 4	507	48.52
5 to 8	228	21.82
12 or more	184	17.61
9 to 11	76	7.27
None	50	4.78
Total	1,045	100

<u>Writing Style</u>

1. If you had unlimited resources and could commission your favorite author to write a novel just for you what would it be about?	Frequency	Percent
Mystery or thriller	171	16.36
Fantasy	138	13.21
Science fiction	107	10.24
Love	103	9.86
Life	89	8.52
Romance	87	8.33
Action and Adventure	76	7.27
Reality/realism	70	6.70
Horror	49	4.69
Historical fiction	46	4.40
Crime	38	3.64
Magic	38	3.64
Dystopia	36	3.44
Murder	32	3.06
War	27	2.58

Continued	Frequency	Percent
History	26	2.49
Family	25	2.39
Politics	21	2.01
Women	21	2.01
Comedy	20	1.91
Psychological elements	20	1.91
"My life"	17	1.63
Youth	17	1.63

As the only open-ended question in the survey, answers to the above varied widely, from respondents simply listing a favorite genre to offering Wcomplex plot descriptions. Here I have tabulated the most common terms mentioned in these responses. The least common responses, many of which greatly influenced *The Most Unwanted Novel*, can be found at the end of this report.

2. Which perspective do you prefer when reading a novel?	Frequency	Percent
Third Person (Example: **She** looked out the window, but all **she** saw was **her** reflection.)	581	55.60
First Person (Example: I looked out the window, but all I saw was **my** reflection.)	438	41.91
Second Person (Example: **You** looked out the window, but all **you** saw was **your** reflection.)	26	2.49
Total	**1,045**	**100**

3. How do you want a novel to end?	Frequency	Percent
Resolved	598	57.22
Unresolved	429	41.05
Both/It depends	18	1.72
Total	**1,045**	**100**

4. Which tense do you prefer when reading a novel?	Frequency	Percent
Past Tense (Example: I **ran** up the stairs, **threw** open the door, and **saw** it for myself.)	703	67.27
Present Tense (Example: I **run** up the stairs, **throw** open the door, and **see** it for myself.)	342	32.73
Total	1,045	100

Characters

1. How many characters do you like to get to know in a novel?	Frequency	Percent
3 to 5	628	60.10
6 to 8	249	23.83
1 or 2	88	8.42
More than 11	44	4.21
9 to 11	36	3.44
Total	1,045	100

2. Which gender do you most prefer reading about?	Frequency	Percent
No preference	562	53.78
Women	267	25.55
Men	178	17.03
Other	19	1.82
Nonbinary	18	1.72
Trans men	1	0.10
Trans women	0	0.00
Total	1,045	100

524 *People's Choice Literature*

3. In which phase of life do you like the characters to be during the story?	Frequency	Percent
Adulthood	634	60.67
No preference	299	28.61
Teenage years	107	10.24
Childhood	3	0.29
Old age	2	0.19
Total	1,045	100

4. What kind of conflict are you most interested in reading about?	Frequency	Percent
It depends	468	44.78
A struggle between the main character and some aspect of society	264	25.26
A struggle between two or more characters	192	18.37
A struggle of opposing forces within one character	82	7.85
A character struggling against nature	39	3.73
Total	1,045	100

5. What kind of morals do you want a main character to display?	Frequency	Percent
Good morals	563	53.88
Questionable morals	482	46.12
Total	1,045	100

6. In the novels you have liked in the past, what was the socioeconomic status of the characters?	Frequency	Percent
Working class	398	38.09
Middle class	344	32.92
I don't remember	102	9.76
Impoverished	88	8.42
Upper class	81	7.75
Aristocratic	32	3.06
Total	**1,045**	**100**

7. In the books you prefer reading, how do the main characters spend most of their time?	Frequency	Percent
Falling in and out of love	199	19.04
Participating in criminal activity	165	15.79
Being creative (artists, writers, etc.)	148	14.16
Helping others (doctors, religious and spiritual guides, etc.)	106	10.14
Working a 9-to-5 job	92	8.80
Serving in the military or law enforcement	84	8.04
Taking care of the house or family	81	7.75
Going to school or teaching	56	5.36
Participating in politics (politicians, activists, etc.)	51	4.88
Farming or living off the land	49	4.69
Playing a sport	14	1.34
Total	**1,045**	**100**

526 *People's Choice Literature*

7a. Which kinds of 9-to-5 jobs would you most want to read about in a novel?	Frequency	Percent
General office work	30	32.61
Manual labor (plumbing, factory work, etc.)	21	22.83
Lawyers	17	18.48
Managing companies or corporations	16	17.39
Sales	4	4.35
Driving (taxi, bus, etc.)	3	3.26
Cleaning	1	1.09
Total	**92**	**100**

7b. Which kinds of caregivers would you most want to read about in a novel?	Frequency	Percent
Siblings	25	30.86
Mothers	22	27.16
Fathers	11	13.58
Housekeepers (maids, butlers, etc.)	11	13.58
Other family members	7	8.64
Babysitters	2	2.47
Nannies and home aids	2	2.47
Grandparents	1	1.23
Total	**81**	**100**

7c. Which kinds of military or law enforcement personnel would you most want to read about?	Frequency	Percent
Detectives	27	32.14
Special agents	25	29.76

Continued	Frequency	Percent
Military personnel	23	27.38
Military officers	5	5.95
Generals	2	2.38
Police officers	2	2.38
Firefighters	0	0
Police chiefs	0	0
Total	84	100

7d. Which kinds of artists, writers or other creative types would you most want to read about in a novel?	Frequency	Percent
Writers	70	47.30
Musicians	27	18.24
Painters	25	16.89
Actors	11	7.43
Sculptors	7	4.73
Directors	6	4.05
Dancers	2	1.35
Total	148	100

7e. Which kinds of students or teachers would you most want to read about in a novel?	Frequency	Percent
College students	42	75.00
K–12 students	7	12.50
College professors	6	10.71
Grade-school teachers	1	1.79
Total	56	100

528   *People's Choice Literature*

7f. Which kinds of caregivers would you most want to read about in a novel?	Frequency	Percent
Spiritual leaders	29	27.36
Doctors	27	25.47
Mental health professionals	22	20.75
Alternative medicine practitioners	18	16.98
Nurses	8	7.55
Religious leaders	2	1.89
Total	**106**	**100**

7g. Which kinds of sports would you most want to read about in a novel?	Frequency	Percent
Basketball	4	28.57
Soccer	4	28.57
Baseball	2	14.29
Football	1	7.14
Golf	1	7.14
Gymnastics	1	7.14
Hockey	1	7.14
Tennis	0	0
Total	**14**	**100**

7h. Which kinds of political characters would you most want to read about in a novel?	Frequency	Percent
Political dissidents	26	50.98
Activists	15	29.41
Politicians	6	11.76
Lawyers	3	5.88

Continued	Frequency	Percent
Bureaucrats	1	1.96
Lobbyists	0	0
Terrorists	0	0
Total	106	100

7i. Which kinds of criminal activity would you most want to read about in a novel?	Frequency	Percent
Murder	64	38.79
Organized crime (the Mafia, etc.)	63	38.18
Stealing/burglary	14	8.48
White-collar crime	14	8.48
Drug dealing	9	5.45
Gambling	1	0.61
Total	165	100

7j. Which kinds of activities would you most want to read about in a novel?	Frequency	Percent
Hermetic living	25	51.02
Farming	10	20.41
Ranching	9	18.37
Fishing	5	10.20
Total	49	100

7k. Which do you prefer?	Frequency	Percent
Falling in love	178	89.45
Falling out of love	21	10.55
Total	199	100

8. Do you prefer reading about characters of a particular race/ethnicity?	Frequency	Percent
No	962	92.06
Yes	83	7.94
Total	1,045	100

8a. Which race/ethnicity do you prefer reading about? (Select all that apply)	Frequency	Percent
Black or African American	50	24.63
Asian/Pacific Islander	35	17.24
White/Caucasian	33	16.26
Latino/a or Hispanic American	29	14.29
American Indian or Alaskan native	24	11.82
Middle Eastern	23	11.33
Other (please specify)	9	4.43
Total	203	100

9. Which sexual orientation do you most prefer reading about?	Frequency	Percent
No preference	528	50.53
Straight	416	39.81
Queer	33	3.16
Bisexual	23	2.20
Gay	21	2.01
Lesbian	15	1.44
Asexual	5	0.48
Other	4	0.38
Total	1,045	100

Novel Characteristics

1. Which topic would you most prefer reading about in a novel?	Frequency	Percent
Science and technology	252	24.11
Personal identity (race, gender, sexuality, class, etc.)	181	17.32
Philosophy	139	13.30
Family and childhood	123	11.77
Spirituality	87	8.33
Politics	84	8.04
The arts	55	5.26
The environment	48	4.59
Health and illness	42	4.02
Sports	26	2.49
Religion	8	0.77
Total	1,045	100

1a. Which political topic would you most want to read about in a novel?	Frequency	Percent
Power and corruption	53	63.10
War	17	20.24
Capitalism	7	8.33
Civil rights	4	4.76
Climate change	2	2.38
Patriotism	1	1.19
Immigration	0	0
Women's rights	0	0
Total	84	100

532 *People's Choice Literature*

1b. Which environmental topic would you most want to read about in a novel?	Frequency	Percent
Man vs. nature	19	39.58
The beauty of nature	9	18.75
Climate change	6	12.50
Animal rights	5	10.42
Climate justice	3	6.25
Spirituality	3	6.25
Extinction	2	4.17
Pollution	1	2.08
Total	**48**	**100**

1c. Which family and childhood topic would you most want to read about in a novel?	Frequency	Percent
Coming of age	64	52.03
Marriage/divorce	24	19.51
Motherhood	13	10.57
Personal identity (race, gender, sexuality, class, etc.)	11	8.94
Death	4	3.25
Fatherhood	4	3.25
Childhood	3	2.44
Birth	0	0
Total	**123**	**100**

1d. Which health and illness topic would you most want to read about in a novel?	Frequency	Percent
Mental health	20	47.62
Overcoming an illness	10	23.81

The Most Unwanted Novel   533

Continued	Frequency	Percent
An accident	4	9.52
Terminal illness	4	9.52
Death	2	4.76
Addiction	1	2.38
Disability	1	2.38
Birth	0	0
Total	42	100

1e. Which personal identity topic would you most want to read about in a novel?	Frequency	Percent
Coming of age	70	38.67
LBGTQIA+	47	25.97
Race and cultural identity	27	14.92
Class	20	11.05
Gender	8	4.42
Spirituality	5	2.76
Immigration	4	2.21
Religion	0	0
Total	181	100

1f. Which religious topic would you most want to read about in a novel?	Frequency	Percent
Faith	4	50.00
Good vs. evil	3	37.50
Creation	1	12.50
Coming of age	0	0
Death	0	0
Evangelism	0	0

534 *People's Choice Literature*

Continued	Frequency	Percent
Forgiveness	0	0
Healing	0	0
Total	8	100

1g. Which spirituality topic would you most want to read about in a novel?	Frequency	Percent
The nature of the universe	27	31.03
Good vs. evil	21	24.14
Healing	16	18.39
Love	7	8.05
Coming of age	7	8.05
Death	4	4.60
Rebirth	3	3.45
Forgiveness	2	2.30
Total	87	100

1h. Which science and technology topic would you most want to read about in a novel?	Frequency	Percent
Good vs. evil	53	21.03
New technology	49	19.44
The workings of the universe	41	16.27
Advanced science (e.g., quantum physics)	41	16.27
Power and corruption	38	15.08
Appearance vs. reality	19	7.54
Nature vs. nurture	8	3.17
Climate change	3	1.19
Total	252	100

1i. Which art topic would you most want to read about in a novel?	Frequency	Percent
Appearance vs. reality	16	29.09
Coming of age	11	20.00
Inspiration	7	12.73
Ambition	5	9.09
Craft	5	9.09
The power of art	5	9.09
Healing	3	5.45
Personal identity (race, gender, sexuality, class, etc.)	3	5.45
Total	55	100

1j. Which sports topic would you most want to read about in a novel?	Frequency	Percent
Coming of age	10	38.46
Training	6	23.08
Ambition	5	19.23
Teamwork	4	15.38
Injury	1	3.85
The body	0	0
Healing	0	0
Personal identity (race, gender, sexuality, class, etc.)	0	0
Total	26	100

536 *People's Choice Literature*

2. Do you like long or short descriptions? (For example, how a character looks, interiors of homes, natural settings)	Frequency	Percent
Long descriptions	569	54.45
Short descriptions	476	45.55
Total	**1,045**	**100**

3. Over which duration of time do you prefer your novels to take place?	Frequency	Percent
It depends	493	47.18
Multiple years	205	19.62
A year	181	17.32
A month	82	7.85
Generations/eras	48	4.59
A week	32	3.06
A day	4	0.38
Total	**1,045**	**100**

4. Based on what you have read, how much sexual content do you prefer in novels?	Frequency	Percent
A little sexual content	390	37.32
Some sexual content	358	34.26
No sexual content	146	13.97
A moderate amount of sexual content	111	10.62
A lot of sexual content	40	3.83
Total	**1,045**	**100**

5. If you had to name your *favorite* type of novel—the kind of novel you would consider buying and reading if you saw it in a store—what would it be?	Frequency	Percent
Thriller or mystery	213	20.38
Science fiction	196	18.76
Fantasy	165	15.79
General/literary fiction	135	12.92
Romance	126	12.06
Historical fiction	95	9.09
Horror	72	6.89
Classic literature	43	4.11
Total	**1,045**	**100**

6. If you had to name your *second favorite* type of novel what would it be?	Frequency	Percent
Thriller or mystery	318	30.43
Fantasy	165	15.79
Science fiction	136	13.01
General/literary fiction	115	11.00
Historical fiction	96	9.19
Romance	82	7.85
Classic literature	68	6.51
Horror	65	6.22
Total	**1,045**	**100**

538 *People's Choice Literature*

7. If you had to name your *least favorite* type of novel—the kind of novel you would rarely consider buying and reading if you saw it in a store—what would it be?	Frequency	Percent
Romance	386	36.94
Horror	207	19.81
Historical fiction	124	11.87
Classic literature	122	11.67
Science fiction	82	7.85
Fantasy	47	4.50
Thriller or mystery	42	4.02
General/literary fiction	35	3.35
Total	**1,045**	**100**

8. If you had to name your *second least favorite* type of novel what would it be?	Frequency	Percent
Classic literature	214	20.48
Horror	153	14.64
Thriller or mystery	147	14.06
Romance	136	13.01
Historical fiction	119	11.39
Science fiction	100	9.57
Fantasy	88	8.42
General/literary fiction	88	8.42
Total	**1,045**	**100**

The Most Unwanted Novel   539

9. What is your preferred setting for a novel to take place?	Frequency	Percent
Large cities	319	30.56
Small towns	239	22.89
Small cities	210	20.11
Natural settings	186	17.82
Rural settings	90	8.62
Total	1,044	100

9a. Which natural setting appeals to you most in novels? (Select all that apply)	Frequency	Percent
Temperate forests and mountains	215	37.72
Oceans and islands	134	23.51
Jungles	95	16.67
Deserts and prairies	80	14.03
Polar regions	46	8.07
Total	570	100

10. Do you want the novels you read to be realistic or unrealistic?	Frequency	Percent
Realistic	773	74.04
Unrealistic	271	25.96
Total	1,044	100

540 *People's Choice Literature*

10a. What kind of unrealistic settings do you most prefer reading about? (Select all that apply)	Frequency	Percent
Alternate dimensions	196	22.87
The future	189	22.05
Alternate histories	178	20.77
The distant past	148	17.27
Different planets	146	17.04
Total	**857**	**100**

10b. What kind of unrealistic creatures do you most prefer reading about? (Select all that apply)	Frequency	Percent
Mythical creatures (fairies, dragons, etc.)	214	24.62
Gods and demigods	179	20.59
Monsters	132	15.19
Sentient robots and AI	125	14.38
Extraterrestrials	119	13.69
Talking animals	100	11.51
Total	**869**	**100**

11. In general, which of the following moods do you prefer in novels?	Frequency	Percent
Mysterious	367	35.15
Tense	214	20.50
Philosophical	187	17.91
Playful	90	8.62
Happy	83	7.95
Calm	48	4.60

Continued	Frequency	Percent
Other	34	3.26
Sad	21	2.01
Total	1,044	100

12. Which kind of storytelling technique do you prefer?	Frequency	Percent
A straightforward story	563	53.88
Stories within stories	246	23.54
A stream of consciousness	119	11.39
A sequence of flashbacks	89	8.52
A sequence of letters or emails	28	2.68
Total	1,045	100

13. With regards to plot and language, do you like novels to be more experimental or traditional in nature?	Frequency	Percent
Traditional	651	62.36
Experimental	393	37.64
Total	1,044	100

13a. Considering experimental writing style, do you like the following qualities in a novel?		
13a1. Novels in which the author comments on the art of writing	Frequency	Percent
No	214	54.45
Yes	179	45.55
Total	393	100

542 *People's Choice Literature*

13a2. Chapters that read like long encyclopedia entries	Frequency	Percent
No	281	71.50
Yes	112	28.50
Total	393	100

13a3. Action conveyed in nonchronological order	Frequency	Percent
Yes	307	78.12
No	86	21.88
Total	393	100

13a5. Passages that are highly abstract or unclear	Frequency	Percent
Yes	205	52.16
No	188	47.84
Total	393	100

14. How much dialogue do you prefer in a novel?	Frequency	Percent
A moderate amount of dialogue	622	59.58
Quite a bit of dialogue	241	23.08
Some dialogue	135	12.93
A great deal of dialogue	41	3.93
A little dialogue	5	0.48
Total	1,044	100

15. Based on what you have read, how much violence do you prefer in novels?	Frequency	Percent
Some violence	400	38.31
A little violence	291	27.87
A moderate amount of violence	215	20.59
No violence	94	9.00
A lot of violence	44	4.21
Total	1,044	100

16. Do you think novels should express political opinions?	Frequency	Percent
Yes	634	60.73
No	410	39.27
Total	1,044	100

Demographics

1. Please check each race/ethnicity that best describes you	Frequency	Percent
White/Caucasian	733	70.14
Black or African American	128	12.25
Asian/Pacific Islander	69	6.60
Latino/a or Hispanic American	48	4.59
Middle Eastern	6	0.57
American Indian or Alaskan Native	3	0.29
Other	2	0.19

544 *People's Choice Literature*

Continued	Frequency	Percent
Multiple categories selected:	56	5.36
Latino/a or Hispanic American, White/Caucasian	20	1.91
Asian/Pacific Islander, White/Caucasian	10	0.96
American Indian or Alaskan Native, White/Caucasian	7	0.67
Black or African American, White/Caucasian	6	0.57
Middle Eastern, White/Caucasian	4	0.38
Asian/Pacific Islander, Latino/a or Hispanic American	2	0.19
Black or African American, Latino/a or Hispanic American	2	0.19
White/Caucasian, Other	2	0.19
American Indian or Alaskan Native, Latino/a or Hispanic American, White/Caucasian	1	0.10
Asian/Pacific Islander, Latino/a or Hispanic American, White/Caucasian	1	0.10
Latino/a or Hispanic American, White/Caucasian, Other	1	0.10
Total	**1,045**	**100**

2. What is your gender?	Frequency	Percent
Man	504	48.23
Woman	501	47.94
Nonbinary	28	2.68
Trans man	8	0.77
Prefer not to say	3	0.29
Other	1	0.10
Trans woman	0	0.00
Total	**1,045**	**100**

3. What is your age?	Mean	Min	Max	Total
	34.15	18	76	1,044

4. How would you best describe your political orientation?	Frequency	Percent
Very Liberal	306	29.28
Somewhat Liberal	257	24.59
Moderate	185	17.70
Slightly Liberal	140	13.40
Slightly Conservative	67	6.41
Somewhat Conservative	57	5.45
Very Conservative	33	3.16
Total	**1,045**	**100**

5. In which state do you currently reside?	Frequency	Percent
California	109	10.44
Texas	78	7.47
Florida	76	7.28
New York	62	5.94
Ohio	61	5.84
Pennsylvania	58	5.56
Illinois	45	4.31
Georgia	38	3.64
North Carolina	38	3.64
Michigan	35	3.35
Massachusetts	30	2.87
Maryland	28	2.68
Virginia	28	2.68
Tennessee	25	2.39

546 *People's Choice Literature*

Continued	Frequency	Percent
New Jersey	22	2.11
Washington	22	2.11
Indiana	19	1.82
Oregon	19	1.82
Kentucky	18	1.72
Arizona	17	1.63
Iowa	17	1.63
Minnesota	16	1.53
Louisiana	15	1.44
Wisconsin	15	1.44
South Carolina	14	1.34
Alabama	13	1.25
Missouri	12	1.15
Colorado	11	1.05
Nebraska	10	0.96
Connecticut	9	0.86
Kansas	9	0.86
Nevada	8	0.77
District of Columbia	7	0.67
Hawaii	7	0.67
Arkansas	6	0.57
Delaware	6	0.57
Idaho	6	0.57
Rhode Island	6	0.57
West Virginia	6	0.57
New Hampshire	5	0.48
Mississippi	4	0.38
New Mexico	4	0.38

Continued	Frequency	Percent
Oklahoma	4	0.38
Montana	2	0.19
Utah	2	0.19
Wyoming	2	0.19
Alaska	0	0.00
Maine	0	0.00
North Dakota	0	0.00
South Dakota	0	0.00
Vermont	0	0.00
Total	1,044	100

6. Based on your own individual earnings, what was your annual income last year?	Frequency	Percent
Less than $25,000	365	34.96
$25,000–$49,999	256	24.52
$50,000–$74,999	189	18.10
$75,000–$99,999	105	10.06
$100,000–$124,999	59	5.65
Over $150,000	38	3.64
$125,000–$150,000	32	3.07
Total	1,044	100

548　*People's Choice Literature*

Preferred Writing Style (Continued)

At the beginning of this report, I listed the most common answers given to the open-ended question, **"If you had unlimited resources and could commission your favorite author to write a novel just for you what would it be about?"** Below you will find the most uncommon (i.e., unique) responses. The answers are listed in the order they appeared in our intial report from our online polling system (that is, in reverse chronological order) and have been unedited. Since the frequency of each of the below responses is 1 and the percentage is 0.10%, I have removed those columns to avoid repetition:

It would be about Jane Austen

The ramifications of the american political system on global social structures.

I'd like to read novels involving Investigative journalism.

Post-9/11 American culture & politics

about powerful elites around the world and what they do

An alternative viewpoint to the original series.

Population control

It would be a alternate history novel where the Indians kept the Europeans out of the Americas.

traveling the world

wow, i really don't know. I enjoy reading about history, maybe more information about African countries that America has exploited?

Organized Crime

The Most Unwanted Novel   549

I would like to see it be about the future of mankind and what results of civilization from a rich vs. poor dynamic.

I would love a good political thriller that takes place in mid 19th Century New York and Washington DC

Someone traveling back into the renaissance area it such a romantic area

It would be about alternate history, in Eastern Europe

stories from the Age of Sail

NASA or the space program

It would be a novel about a lesbian or bisexual woman who was plus sized because I feel like there aren't many of those.

Coming of age in the late 2010s and dealing with coronavirus.

It would be about someone in their late 20s grappling with getting older and find their place in the world

A sci-fi novel that centers around Biomimicry and how different alien species approach it.

It would be about a character dealing with the death of a friend while also dealing with their own suicidal thoughts

Jay-Z writes my biography

The adventures of one of my favorite characters or my own ideas for characters (of which I have many) with great detail and a higher age rating. Not exactly the most creative thing, but that's what I would want for sure.

Self Improvement

It would be about an reincarnation novel

The life of how difficult it is to make your parents proud

thriller murder in the hometown

It would probably be a South Asian inspired fantasy because the worldbuilding would be really cool and I want more representation.

Chimamanda Ngozi Adichie

Life navigation as a single mom

It would take place in an urban environment.

I would like them to write something similar to an action anime/manga a good amount of Black/African characters. If they can draw, then I'm comic/manga form would be great.

A thriller about a couple who was murdered.

It would be a drama/horror novel filled with magic and the complexities and joys of being Black in america. The cast of characters would majority Black, excellent queer representation, complex, human, nuanced. I would love incorporation of Black mythology. Written by a Black femme.

It would be a fantasy horror novel about a Black family who travel to different planets through a closet in their new house

a comedic romance dystopian future

Racism in the United States.

Kingdoms in africa

anything ? i dont really read novels for " what its about ", its more about how its written ? ill say a novel ive been looking for and wanting to read is something that incorporates magical realism with the

digital age – ive enjoyed novels that have text messages or emails in them, as a way of giving characters dimension

A coming of age story set in the 1980s.

their life experiences or some stories from the past.

It would be about a professional violinist who finds love with someone who also has a deep love of God and music.

I'd figure out how to resurrect Terry Pratchett and get a new Discworld book out of him before allowing him to return to his slumber in the void.

Set in Scandinavia, centered around complex female characters, themes of anxiety and horror in daily life

Ordinary people dealing with ordinary problems in a surprising way.

a mother's love lasts forever

How to cope with life and see the joy in little things.

Money

A crossover with everything

The struggles of a middle-aged lesbian to stay "relevant"

Something set in South Florida but with a literary style rather than commercial. Character-driven, exploring the inner life and experiences of a millennial living in Florida and observing the late-stage capitalist post-Trump society we live in.

It would be a farce about the futility of human life.

family vacation thriller

Modern day slice of life with sympathetic but real characters.

552 *People's Choice Literature*

Fiction involving a band

About a man who needs to time travel to safe his wife only to discover some terrifying secrets about her along the way.

Warhammer 40k

slow burn, enemies to lover trope with some mystery/thriller elements

Research on navigating mental health resources

People living their ordinary lives in circumstances different than my own.

it would be an introspective story about life and time and there would be a cute little love story

A story about a girl finding herself and happiness despite life's circumstances.

It would be continuing the story of my favorite book which is about two young gay teens who fell in love before the aids epidemic. I'd just want it to continue into modern day.

a girl experiencing addiction

It would be about how populations are controlled through victimhood narratives and never-ending refusal to move forward from the past.

A first time stay-at-home mom who rises from postpartum depression to find herself again, professionally and otherwise.

My dnd characters going on a found family adventure.

Deception

a kidnapping story that get resolved in a twist

a timed drama

It would be about a woman who is too afraid to follow her dream of becoming a singer because of her anxiety but ends up succeeding that dream anyways.

it is about traveling to exotic island

I would pay so much money for a mecha romance novel.

Fame and fortune in the 1980s

I would want it to be about a mom's journey with mental illness

treasure hunts in the ocean

The ultimate disappearance of all religion on this planet.

It would be a romantic novel that takes place in the Regency era of London. The main characters would not fall in love quickly it would be more of a enemies to lovers or slow burn type plot

I would like anything related to drama and everyday life situations.

Young adult issues, specifically LGBT or women's issues, with strong writing style in a contemporary setting.

Non-fiction about personal growth.

18th-19 century England with steampunk themes

It would be about climate change.

I'm not really sure at this time but it would likely be something with afrofuturism as its primary theme. Please google afrofuturism if you haven't heard of it before.

It would be a novel about some aspect of medieval life.

A sapphic love story with magical realism and rivals to lovers trope.

My family history on both parents' side

one about healthy, inspiring love which creates good change and motivation

It would be a lighthearted romance novel in a university setting

I really love trope heavy romances that isn't eye rolling cringy. Preferably LGBT, cutesy, with some steam.

Multi generational epic

It would be able someone being able to go back and have one more conversation with each person they lost that was close to them.

Historical fiction about the Vikings

It would be a fictionalized version of myself who didn't have to go through the suffering that I went through as a child.

It would be about me and my bestfriend and all of the wonderful things we have experienced through the years

A story about a national park

A police procedural.

A mystery, thriller, suspense novel about a detective trying to solve a murder but takes the help from a citizen who loves true crime and together they solve the murder with lots of twists throughout the story

How my life turned onto a completely different path and I ended up becoming the best in my career and fell in love.

The Most Unwanted Novel 555

The thoughts and life of my favorite side character.

a success story of a teacher in America

It would be about life in New York City from a variety of perspectives.

j.k rowlling. it would be upon depressive sate of mind

An absurdist tragic mystery with a Shyamalan twist in every chapter so like Calvino writing Poirot

It would be a slice of life with an asexual main character.

The pursuit to grow the most perfect strain of marijuana.

A large cast of characters set in a medieval world with elements of mystery and horror.

It would be a mystery thriller related to law, money laundering, and international crime.

Overcoming a difficult childhood and blossoming into a grown adult.

A sci-fi/cyberpunk western about a bounty hunter on a mission to capture a band of cannibal space pirates.

I think it would be about a group of people who age together and apart, with the novel checking back in periodically to see different mechanisms of character growth.

Everyday life things. The challenges of being a human being in the world with other human beings.

I would like a bunch of how to tutorials on drawing things step by step, also how to learn sign language.

A single Mom on disability raising a special needs son, who starts a non-profit and changes the world.

556 *People's Choice Literature*

Me being king of something.

Unfortunately, several of my favorite novelists are no longer living. One of them is Ursuls K. LeGuin, and if she was still around, I'd like to write another novel in the Earthsea series.

The era would be in the early 1900's and the setting would be in Cornwall (or Ireland). I prefer Historical novels, so a war. Would be taking place in the background of the novel. The novel would include historical fiction and would be about letters exchanged during the war.

The novel would be a suspenseful story about a broken family, they were trying to find out hidden truths about their past and family history. Like the main character would come to find out they are ad-opted. The birth family would be world famous killers or something.

I would like a coming of a fictional coming of age story with a black, queer protagonist, who is not enormously downtrodden or unfor-tunate but suffers the slings and arrows of growing up in a present day world. Grounded in realism, but with a fantastical elements, it would be nice if this protagonist had a superpower which only he can know about but which has the capacity to change the world. The world around him that is.

I would ask my favorite author to write about the different topics on nature, including the history of trees etc.

A kid growing up to own his own sports team

Steven Pinker writing about life during a pandemic and the psy-chology involved.

I would commission Stephen King to revise one of the final 3 books in his Dark Tower series.

It would be a fiction book about exploring the unknown wilderness and the creatures in it.

personal growth and fulfillment

A story about an aspiring player of a game (like chess) who picks it up later in life but through various difficulties manages to go pro at it. Focus on psychological elements.

it would be about manifesting things in life. The author experience and a step by step manual

Outdoor recreation and conservation

A gang horror fiction

I would have them write a dark sci-fi novel about a human who keeps a android slave.

Patriotism

It would certainly be paranormal based but it would also have an overarching theme of philosophy tangled throughout. I want a book that is interesting but says something about life in the end.

Psychological Warefare

How I like to help out also how friendly I am

Europeans settling Australia and the native people who were living there.

An action comedy with a non-cis-white-male protagonist.

A knight in training

Humanity's struggle 200 years from now.

The extremes that people can go to in dire circumstances

being a groupie for a rock band in the 70s/80s

amberlynn reid's wifey moves out, she cries about her wifey and she starts eating 3000 pounds of orange chicken. she gets new roommates 1 week later. turns out its hillbilly, billy lenz, and dwight fairfield. they now have to take care of the obese toddler for the rest of eternity

Trafficking of some sort

Early American settlement of the midwest

UFO conspiracy

paranoia

a father who's life seems normal but finds extravagant whirl-wind adventure with family.

Master Chiefs training

about cooking

Medical stories

My life and struggle with addiction

It would be about a lesbian falling in love for the first time with a woman in another country

Stock trading people

My family

sonic lineage, music sampling, cultural implications of popular songs

An economic history novel, kind of like "The Big Short" but having more to do with the meme-stock saga

It would be the life of myself through someone else's eyes

It would be about a girl with schizophrenia who discovers she actually has powers (controlled by her schizophrenia), and uses them to save the world.

A woman with my own struggles

College football

Life, but better. Everyone wins, everyone is happy.

I would like Karen Moning's take on Hades and Persephone, or really any of the greek lore.

It would be about an imaginative world that would let me escape from reality.

I think I would want Steven King to right a novel about living in a house that has a portal that ghosts come through. Some good and some bad ghosts. And how she deals with it. She actually feels special that ghosts visit.

My life as a wife, mother, and human. The struggles, the humor, and the love.

I would love to read a novel about two women who are in a spy academy and fall in love. A little adventure, comedy, romance.

Geocentrism

I would want something that is a surreal historical piece with a feminist edge. I'm particularly interested in the Victorian Era.

Discovering my podunk hometown was a thinning between worlds (which would explain why everyone there is a religious jerk) and having it completely leveled when the breach is sealed. Complete with details of all the landmarks.

It'd be about my favorite celebrities.

A gay man's ultimate fantatsy

Anything with spice

A high fantasy novel in the style of Lord of the Rings about a mixed-race or Black girl who battles evil and fulfills her destiny, becoming powerful and well-respected. It would have a diverse cast of characters, in-depth worldbuilding, and possibly cultures inspired by real-world cultures (with consultation from people belonging to those cultures).

The stories that I myself have created pertaining to my world and my characters

It would be about entrepreneurship and the different stages and levels from a beginner to world class.

Dystopian society full of deranged assassins.

A futuristic world and how we evolved to adapt to it.

I love a fusion of high fantasy with modern society. It would likely be about Elves that are forced into hiding among humans. Having to conceal their identities and their magic all while of course being hunted by both elves and humans alike.

A middle-aged man dealing with an existential crisis

a witch who has a pet fox as a familiar

ancient civilizations seeding modern life

female empowerment and adventure

A native American protagonist journeying through North America, meeting different tribes and describing lifeways

I would love for a novel to be written about Yoda's (from Star Words) upbringing.

The Most Unwanted Novel 561

spirituality

academia

Affirming young kids self-worth and the role teachers play in building confidence

Elizabethan history

empathy and narcissism

A college girl navigating life but written in a way that makes it more interesting within the normal parts of life

It would be a well researched historical romance set anywhere except regency England with an intelligent woman as the heroine and a working class man as the hero.

A sweeping spy novel set in occupied Europe during WWII

Cold War

I would love to see another Dan Brown novel, but focused on Q Anon and debunking it.

Ambrose Bierce, time to write The Devil's Encyclopedia

about empowering plus woman

Percy Jackson's entire life

How to let go of negative family

A mystery period film in the regency era featuring black aristocrats, entrepreneurs, homemakers and any thing other than black people being slaves or living hard lives.

The history of gambling

562 *People's Choice Literature*

A person's inner conflict with societal expectations.

I would love queer women in college

I would like to read a novel about people growing up in my hometown.

A 19th Century Russian Fiction novel (Checkov/Tolstoy) of the decline of Midwest industrial towns/decline and fall of my home town.

An adventure out in the wilderness,

About someone living in the 1950's with lots of details about daily life

A account of growing up in a poverty ridden neighborhood. Overcoming the obstacles.

I would love to commission a deeply psychological story--something that mirrors ARGS, or alternate reality games, of the internet. A story that transcends typical narrative boundaries, and isn't necessarily "scary," but is written in an unnerving or atypical way that forces you to find the meaning within it.

I'd like something dealing with post WWII counterculture.

A civilian making it through WWII

The live of an ordinary Black man

It would be about somebody stumbling across an ancient alien artifact drifting through our solar system.

Historical fiction, with a conservative message.

It would be about a long distance relationship

True crime specifically the manson murders

I would love to have a novel that blends sci-fi with fantasy. So, imagine Lord of the Rings, but in Space. Maybe a mixture between Lord of the Rings and Star Wars. It would be so awesome to see how you incorporate those two genres.

The experiences, struggles and successes of average people

A young gay prince with magical powers who lives in a fantasy world that reflects real life issues (discrimination, poverty, power) and has adult themes. It would revolve around a quest he must face and an emery he must confront, in addition to a romantic element.

It would be set in the roaring 20s and it would be about an inventor way beyond their time

An adventure in an old European city.

Psychedelics and mystery concerning them

Conspiracy theories/dark entanglements

I think I would like to read about a family farm across several generations spanning from before the Great Depression up until the 1980's or so. I would love family recipes included, spanning that time frame as well.

Greek mythology

West Virginia

It would be about a future world in which animals 'awakened' by some spiritual earth force and stops humanity in its destructive tracks.

The return of Melkor

A continuation or sequel to there works that I love .

Murder, musicals, sex, college and post college, and drama

Something similar to the Animorphs series but for adults, exploring transformations into animals from a biological and psychological perspective. Alongside some classic sci-fi themes.

Boys life in 1970s, coming of age

A cozy murder mystery set in Florida.

I would ask Paul Theroux to write a travel book, but with some fiction thrown in.

Maybe be about how i manage everyday life and what goes through my mind

Fiction about young people set in the 1990s US, no particular plot preference, as long as it's interesting.

Probably a horror novel about dealing with a random rash of disappearances, where people just seem to cease existing. Those that disappear feel as though they've become ghosts bc they can still see the people who can't see them. It would end up being a kind of multiverse splitting thing.

How to live the most purposeful life possible

I would like Isaac Asimov to write a sci-fi novel incorporating the moral duty of the scientifically minded to create for society (he presented this concept in an editorial).

I would just want Winds of Winter finished

It would be a mystery about people who are all on a boat together and are getting murdered.

the end of power of the secret elite ruling the world

It would be a dystopian novel set 20 years from now about the fall of the United States

A good, well written religious study. Many of these aren't good or rely on bad writing, one both written well and with intelligent theological punch would be worth its weight in gold.

More content on the avatar universe

It would actually be a novel about my life and my husband's life before we met and the novel would continue through the present time and then I would want the ending to be my ideal ending for the lives that we have lead. The end of the book would be unresolved, open ended, because our lives are not over yet.

I'd like to see a concept involving lucid dreams which explores many different realities.

Growing up in my hometown

I would challenge Murakami to write something linear

The toughness and unfairness of the world, nature, humanity, etc.

About how to navigate your early 20's with social life, family, and career all while trying to maximize the potential of each aspect of life.

It would be about an MMO that I frequently play

aviation

A mafia romance that is hot and heavy

prison

bipolar disorder

566   *People's Choice Literature*

Appalachian culture

The bond between twin sisters

Still here? Really? Don't you have anything better to do? Text a friend? Take out the trash—with this book in it? Not sure what else to say . . .

568 *People's Choice Literature*

Well, it's been real nice. [Tap tap tap]

Yep,

real nice.

[Tap tap]

572　*People's Choice Literature*

[Tap tap]

Look, it's over. You can go now. Go enjoy yourself. I'm sure there's some TV show you've been meaning to watch. Yes! The one about the people who just sit around and drink wine. Yes. Go watch that. Do it! You'll thank me later. Great, well, take care.

Sincerely,
Tom Comitta

574   *People's Choice Literature*

OK, this isn't working. Since you're here, here's some additional reading material:

Acknowledgments

Bad jokes aside, I am truly grateful to the friends, family, colleagues, and institutions who have supported this project. All books take a small village, but this one drove me to engage with my community and to expand into new ones in ways I've never experienced before as a writer.

I am eternally thankful for the guidance on public opinion polling and quantitative sociology from my brilliant survey-design collaborator Katherine Cornwall. Many thanks to the very kind people who introduced me to the worlds of public opinion and sociology: Bruce Barr, Zach King, Lamont Lambert, Hunter Gehlbach, Guilberly Louissaint, Rob Manley, Molly Oringer, Jordon Peugh, Joanna Steinhardt, and Kathleen Weldon.

A humble bow to the creators of *The People's Choice* paintings, Alex Melamid and Vitaly Komar, and *People's Choice Music*, Dave Soldier, for their beautiful art and personal generosity in giving me a glimpse into their creative processes. A big thank you to Katya Arnold for telling it to me straight. And to JoAnn Wypijewski for sharing her experience editing the magazine article and the book that put "People's Choice" on the map.

I cannot express how grateful I am to the friends and family who helped me raise the funds necessary to conduct this poll, several of whom even provided feedback and guidance along the way. A mountain of thanks to Gayle Abrams, Joe and Sarah Acchione, Tom Ahern, Josh Alscher, Benjamin Baldwin, Ashley Brim, Zac Broomfield, Dave Cowen, Charles Day, Kota Ezawa, Kristen Gallagher, Andrew Gehman, Carey Lin, Denise Newman, Alex Nichols, Austin Nuschke, Allegra Oxborough, George Pfau, Anne Ragusin, Kelly Shetron, Heather Simons, Ian Smith, and dozens of anonymous donors. Many thanks to Fractured Atlas, the fiscal sponsor for this project and to New York State Council for the Arts for a grant that helped take this book to the next level. And thank you to Lighthouse Works for the residency where it all started.

I am endlessly grateful to Philip Leventhal and Columbia University Press for believing in this book. Thank you to Philip and the rest of the CUP team, including ErinNicole Conti, Rob Fellman, Zachary Friedman, Michael Haskell, Meredith Howard, Maritza Herrera-Diaz, Caitlin Hurst,

Milenda Lee, and Emily Elizabeth Simon. I am so very grateful to my agent Mariah Stovall for fighting the good fight for this difficult book and for guiding me every step of the way.

Thank you to Brian Ang, Hayden Bennett, Lizzie Davis, Joseph Del Pesco, Claud DeSimone, Ian Dreiblatt, Craig Dworkin, Zach Fabri, Sylvie Fortin, Ge Gao, Emily Gastineau, Anna Gurton-Wachter, Vijay Khurana, Jonathan Lethem, Daniel Levin Becker, Deidre Lynch, Megan Maguire, Maj, Nate Malinowski, Gabe Milner, Gabe Milner's students, Billy Mullaney, Brian Ng, Beowulf Sheehan, Misael Soto, Nadja Spiegelman, Liza St. James, Kendall Storey, Arden Surdam, Olivia Taylor-Smith, Aarthi Vadde, Chris Wait, Madeleine Watts, Elvia Wilk, Aaron Winslow, Joey Yearous-Algozin, and Irene Yoon for your friendship, criticism, and encouragement. Thank you to George Pfau who initially inspired my plunge into horror literature and to whom "Brains: A Treatise on Thirst" is dedicated. I am forever grateful for the support of my family: Carolyn and Tom Comitta, Elena and Ilya Ocher, and Anne and Gary Ragusin.

Without Medaya Ocher, I am not sure how I would have completed this book. Thank you, Daya, for being my first reader and a constant source of feedback, support, and love. Thank you to our late dog Dora for not only for accompanying me through years of writing and editing but for inspiring the canine star of *The Most Wanted*. And finally, thank you to our dear Simone, whose birth gave me a deadline to work toward and whose early life has shown me the boundless power of storytelling.

Seriously? Still here? This clearly isn't working. Hmm. OK, how about this. If you really want an ending, you'll get one. Satisfied? Here it is:

[The End]

The Readers once called a meeting to try to free themselves of their enemy, the Unresolved Ending. At least they wished to find some way of knowing when it was coming, so they might have time to run away. Indeed, something had to be done, for they lived in such constant fear of its claws that they hardly dared open their books by night or day.

Many plans were discussed, but none of them was thought good enough. At last a very young Reader got up and said:

"I have a plan that seems very simple, but I know it will be successful.

"All we have to do is to hang a bell about the Unresolved Ending's neck. When we hear the bell ringing, we will know immediately our enemy is coming."

All the Readers were much surprised, for they had not thought of such a plan before.

But in the midst of the rejoicing over their good fortune, an old Reader arose and said:

"I will say that the plan of the young Reader is very good. But let me ask one question: Who will bell the End . . . ?"